ENCOUNTERS

Revised Edition

Anne Azel

I

Copyright 2004 by Anne Azel

ISBN 0-9755739-3-4
First Printing 2004
Cover art and design by B. L. Magill

Published by:
Dare 2 Dream Publishing
A Division of Limitless Corporation
Lexington, South Carolina 29073

Find us on the World Wide Web
http://www.limitlessd2d.net

Printed in the United States of America and the UK by

Lightning Source

Special Notation

Please note that our authors are international. You may see spellings and some words that are unfamiliar to you. These words are not spelled incorrectly but, rather, represent the national spelling of the writer.

We at **D2D** encourage international authors to submit their manuscripts to us and have elected to leave them in their original format in the hope that you will enjoy the international flavour as much as we do.

My thanks to B. L. Magill for the wonderful
cover design.

To Donna, for her friendship.

Amazon

Encounters

> **Note:** All the flora and fauna described in this story are real, as are the Indian groups and natural topography. They are a collection of descriptions and experiences taken from my own field notes of the area. Cats Paw is being studied as a possible treatment for cancer.

Morgan Andrews peered out of the Cessna's window with eyes sparkling with excitement. Below, the undulating grasslands of the Grand Savanna spread out in all directions, cut here and there by wide muddy rivers and belts of trees. Grey, wispy clouds occasionally blocked the view outside and then Morgan's eyes would turn with interest to observe her traveling companions. At the very back, hedged into the tail section, was a retired couple from Florida. They had just sold their citrus orchards and were now traveling in their years of retirement. Morgan liked them. They would have been good parents, caring and full of fun. Morgan had met Betty and Joe Harris just this morning, in the tourist van that had picked them up at their hotel to bring them to the small airstrip.

She had also met Arthur Berkler, a businessman on his way to bid on rainforest timber lots. He sat beside her in the middle row of seats, his brief case open on his lap. Morgan had been reading over his shoulder periodically on the two-hour flight and now knew quite a bit about Berkler's offer. She smiled. It was lucky for Berkler that he worked for a company that developed wood products and not medicines. Morgan's mission to the area was far more secretive. Berkler was way overweight and was taking up far more than his share of space. Fortunately, at this altitude the air in the Cessna was cool and crisp. Morgan was glad because he'd been pretty hot and sweaty when they'd first been allotted their seats in the "flying tin can" as Betty called it. Berkler seemed content to ignore them all and this suited Morgan just fine as she had pretty strong feelings on companies that cut down the rainforest.

The little plane bounced over some rough air and Morgan swallowed. *Please don't let me embarrass myself by throwing up in here*, she prayed. The craft was old and stuffy and smelt of dusty leather seats and sweat. The plastic windows were scratched and the pilot's radio sat on his dashboard attached to the plane by thin, green and red wires. A gaping hole in the control panel indicated where the old radio had been removed. Normally, flying didn't bother Morgan, but she felt a little uneasy in a plane that was clearly held together by local creativity and luck.

The clouds now had surrounded them and they flew blindly through the grey. Moisture beaded on the windscreen and rolled along the side windows. The pilot, a big, burly Brazilian seemed bored. Now and again he would fiddle with the dials on the radio. His skin was copper and his five o'clock shadow heavy already, although it was not yet past noon. His face had that blotchy fleshiness of a heavy drinker, Morgan noted with some concern. At first she had thought he looked quite old, but maybe he wasn't. His hair was without grey and was thick and wavy, curling around the large, black earphones that he wore. Morgan wished she had a set. The six-seater's engine roared noisily making any conversation difficult except at a yell.

The person who really interested her, however, was the tall woman who sat by the pilot. She had sauntered out on to the airstrip at the last minute and had talked to the pilot in rapid Portuguese, then had turned and quickly covered the distance back to the main hanger with long, purposeful strides. The pilot had asked Morgan politely to move from the front seat that he had assigned her into the middle one where she had to wedge beside a hot, sticky Berkler. A few minutes later the tall woman had reappeared and swung into the copilot's seat where Morgan had been.

She was startlingly handsome, with lean, classic planes to her face and a tall, willowy body that managed as she moved to convey at once the grace of a leopard and the strength of an ox. Her eyes were pale blue in juxtaposition to her dark hair and complexion and there was something not quite mortal about them. They were ice cold and seemed to glow with their own inner light. For a second, they had met Morgan's and she had been held fast by them until the woman had released her by turning away. The brief eye contact had sent shudders up Morgan's spine.

The strange woman was dressed in tough khaki shorts and a cotton, sleeveless, button-down shirt. She wore ankle-high hiking boots of much polished brown leather and a wide, tooled, leather belt. She looked like she had fallen from the pages of a Ralf Lauren safari ad. *Yeah right*, snorted Morgan to herself. One look at the lady's tough confidence left no doubt that she was the real thing. Not that there could be any doubt of that when she turned around to reveal that the strap across her chest held in place on her back a brown leather sheath containing a machete.

The woman slipped this weapon off as she swung into her seat and closed the door, nodding to the pilot that he could now taxi for take-off. All conversation in the little six-seater stopped at her arrival, all eyes fixed on her. If the woman was aware of this, she gave no indication, she simply ignored everyone. Now all Morgan could see of the strange woman were her shoulders and the top of her dark head. She caught herself wishing she were in Berkler's seat so that she could observe the profile of the woman as they flew. Morgan noted that Berkler kept looking up and his eyes would travel hungrily up, down and over the woman in the co-pilot's seat. *Forget it, Berkler, she'd eat you alive,* Morgan thought with a mental giggle. *That is if she noticed you at all!*

Morgan snapped out of her musings. Their little plane was still surrounded by grey, wet clouds. *I guess this is why it's called a rainforest,* Morgan reasoned, trying hard not to give into panicky thoughts of running into a mountain or of the plane's single engine stalling with the rain!

She looked up and almost gasped to see those blue eyes staring back at her through a mirror attached to the back of the window visor that the strange woman had just flipped down. "You Andrews?" asked a deep and melodic voice rolling over the "r" in her name in a manner that Morgan found very pleasant.

"Yes," she responded just as tersely, more out of shock than design.

The eyes gave a single nod. "I'll be guiding you into the villages," stated the woman and the visor snapped up, effectively ending the conversation. Morgan found she was holding her breath and when she released it her heart pounded wildly. *This is my guide! Oh boy! Wait until my family finds out I'm lost in the jungles with an Amazon woman!*

The clouds started to break up, much to Morgan's relief, and when again she could get a good look at the ground from her window she saw the green canopy of the rainforest at the edge of the Grand Savanna. Morgan was surprised that there was no gradual change; rather the rainforest met the grasslands as a solid wall on the very edge of the huge Amazon basin. Within a few minutes the grasslands were left behind and now Morgan looked down on the solid canopy of the rainforest. Here and there its lush growth was cut by a wandering river, a dried up switch back that had not yet returned to the jungle or a still, round lake. The foliage was dotted now and again by the bright red leaf of some jungle vine or by the blue ghost trail of an Indian campfire five miles below. Morgan squirmed with delight. Her dreams of adventure

5

were finally coming true!

The pilot slowed the small plane's engines and banked. Now, over Berkler's body, Morgan could see through the opposite window a grassy compound and airstrip cut from the rainforest. The plane leveled and dropped slowly, kissing the ground with its back wheels first and then bouncing down on its nose wheel. The metal bird was once again a lumbering earth creature. Morgan's face was glued to her window as the plane bumped down the dirt airstrip and then turned ninety degrees and taxied along until it turned again and came to a halt in sight of the buildings of the compound.

The dark haired woman opened her door immediately, as if she had found the confined space of the aircraft too much to bear for a second longer. Before the pilot had shut down, the strange woman was already striding away. The pilot folded the co-pilot's seat back, allowing Morgan to squeeze out and jump down onto the compound's grass. Now the cool, crisp air trapped inside the small aircraft was replaced by the intense heat and humidity of the Amazon. The air at mid-day was stifling and soggy to breathe and seemed somehow to be strangely lacking in oxygen.

Betty squeezed out and Morgan offered her hand to the older woman as she slipped down from the plane. "Thanks." Betty smiled. "My God, if Joe had told me before we left that we'd be flying in this little bitty thing for three hours, we'd still be in Florida today! I was so scared!"

Morgan laughed and gave the woman a reassuring hug. "You had every reason to be scared. All that bouncing around, you were lucky you didn't end up with my lunch in your lap!"

Betty's husband Joe came around from the other side of the plane. "Honestly, you girls, I thought women were supposed to be the tougher sex these days. Hell, that wasn't so bad," he drawled slowly. Morgan liked the way Joe held on to words, giving them far more syllables than they should have.

Betty gave her husband an affectionate poke in the ribs then turned back to Morgan, who was retrieving her bag from the pilot. "He flew 'copters in Viet Nam so he's used to flying by the seat of his pants," she explained. Turning back to her husband she laughed, "And I'm plenty tough to have put up with you for thirty odd years!"

Morgan followed along behind the others, enjoying the gentle banter of the Harrises as her eyes wandered over Los Amazonos compound intently. She was truly interested in getting first impressions of her new surroundings but she had to admit that she was looking too for the tall, dark haired woman who was to be her guide.

6

From Carlos' hut, Kris watched the group, her face deadpan. Her eyes lingered on the petite woman with the strawberry blond hair. *She seems a little stiff from her plane ride but relatively fit anyway*, she concluded, letting her eyes trail up the newcomer's frame. *Nice. Seems too young to be a research doctor.* Of course, anyone with any ability or experience would want to stay back home and make a career for themselves not come out here to do field research. That sort of activity was for undergraduates. Kris sighed. *Shit, I hope she's not some tree lover or a fanatic out to save the world by devoting her life to the study of earthworms.*

Carlos wrapped a blanket around his shoulders and sauntered over to stand at Kris' side. "That little one, humm, she is nice," he leered playfully.

Kris snorted. She was well aware that the handsome and flirtatious Carlos was a happily married and loyal man. He just felt he was letting his Latin blood down if he didn't play the game. Kris decided to play along. With a movement as quick as lightening, her arm shot up and her hand grabbed his jaw in a vise-like grip. Turning his face so that his surprised eyes met hers, she gave him her most intimidating look. "She's mine," she whispered softly with an edge of anger. "Don't... touch." Carlos swallowed hard and Kris held him for a second longer before smiling with bright white teeth and patting him affectionately on the cheek.

"Mother of God! Kristinia Thanasis, don't do that! You scared me half to death!"

Kris shrugged and raised her hands as she backed away playfully. "Do what?" she asked innocently. She turned and let Carlos enjoy looking at her long lean body as she retrieved her machete and ducked her head under the strap. Over her shoulder she said, "Gotta go talk to Fernando." Then she was gone. Carlos shook his head, glad that Kris saw in him a friend. He'd hate to have her as an enemy, because he suspected that all the rumors about her were true.

* * * * *

Morgan saw the woman from her cabin as the dark-haired guide crossed over to the main building where the dining hall and kitchens were. She saw her hug the short, round owner whose name was Fernando and then settle herself alongside him at the open-air bar on the verandah. Surely, he wasn't her husband! Morgan turned away, annoyed by the woman's display of affection towards the man for reasons that she could not explain.

The heat was awful.   Her clothes stuck to her and rubbed uncomfortably.   She got out shorts and stripped her blue jeans off. Time to reveal her true self anyway, she thought, pulling her pant leg off the brace on her right lower leg.   It wasn't that she minded the brace, after seven years she had come to accept it, but she hated the part where people were too polite to ask.   She sighed, slipped her shorts up over her muscular legs and tucked her cotton T-shirt down over her flat, hard stomach.   The clothes were cool and yet conservative enough to cover most of her scars.

She heard the Harrises emerging from the bungalow beside hers. They had all been invited by Fernando to have an afternoon drink on the verandah.   Morgan looked around to make sure that everything was packed away, as Fernando had cautioned them to do when he had greeted them and allotted bungalows.   He had explained that the monkeys felt free to help themselves to loose articles.   What was it that Fernando had joked?   Something about the monkeys being here at five o'clock... Morgan smiled and made a metal note to take a picture of her bungalow for the folks back home.   It consisted of a grass hut on three-foot high posts.   There was a small covered verandah with a hammock while a room beyond that contained two single beds covered in mosquito nets and a wood sink.   Behind a grass partition, there was a crude shower offering cold, brown water and a toilet of dubious origins. By the sink were three old whiskey bottles filled with fresh water.   The walls of the bungalow only went up about five feet.   The rest was open to allow for air circulation, except for the posts that supported the grass roof.

Satisfied that everything was stowed properly, Morgan closed her door and stepped down the stairs of her porch.   She knew without looking up that those pale, cold eyes were fixed on her.   She could feel it like an icy tingle running up her spine.   She forced herself to look up and make eye contact as she headed over to join the others.

Berkler had cornered Fernando at the bar and was talking to him and Betty and Joe were ordering drinks from the local bartender-come-waiter.   The dark haired woman vaulted over the verandah rail and met her half way along the path.   This close, Morgan had to look up into those eyes.   The woman was at least a head taller than herself.   "We need to talk," stated the taller woman, looking down at Morgan with a scowl.

Now seeing the woman close up for the first time, Morgan realized that she was older than herself by a number of years.   "Okay," agreed Morgan, turning to follow an already retreating figure.   The woman strode over to a large, round grass building with a conical roof of thatch. She held open the door with one arm and waited for Morgan to go ahead. Inside was sort of a rough conference area of wood benches and a rustic lab. As in all the buildings the smell of moldy grass and damp cement floor was strong.

"The university uses this facility as a field lab. You are welcome to use its limited resources while you are here. Sit," demanded the woman.

"Am I a dog?" inquired Morgan, colour rising in her face as her green eyes flashed with sudden fire.

The woman's mouth rose slightly on one side in what may have been a smile and intense blue eyes slowly looked her up and down. Morgan held her ground. "No, you're not," said the older woman with a soft, dangerous voice. "Please be seated, Ms. Andrews. I am Thanasis, Kris Thanasis." The older woman folded onto a bench and placed one long, bent leg up on the next row. She raised a dark eyebrow and Morgan shelved her anger and sat.

Morgan met the woman's eyes and said very determinedly, "Don't even go there."

The older woman looked puzzled and then surprised. "Go where?"

"You are going to say that a cripple doesn't belong in the rainforest. And when you do I'm going to tell you to go to hell," stated Morgan, mounting anger colouring her face.

The eyebrow went up again. "No. No, actually I wasn't," responded Kris with quiet control. "If you want to try walking with that brace on, that's your decision and you live with any consequences. It just adds one more complication for me, that's all."

"I am not a complication, Ms. Thanasis," growled Morgan.

"That remains to be seen. What species of flora are you after, out there?" asked the dark-haired woman, her ice-blue eyes locking on Morgan's.

Morgan hesitated. "We'll discuss that when we get to the area."

The eyes narrowed. "I'm not interested in your petty little patient wars, Ms. Andrews. I just don't want to waste my time walking in the wrong direction. What do you think this plant can do for mankind?"

Morgan raised a hand and pushed back her hair. "I won't know for sure until I find and test it. Don't worry, Ms. Thanasis. All I need is a guide. I'll handle the rest."

The angular face hardened into stone and the eyes flashed with anger. "Let's test that theory, shall we?" she purred viciously, getting up in one smooth movement and making for the screen door. Kris

9

pushed it open and held it for the petite woman who still sat in surprise on the bench. Kris made a point of watching Morgan's leg as she pushed herself awkwardly to her feet and plowed past the taller woman with grim determination etched on her face. Kris smiled cruelly. *I'll soon wipe that look off your face, you stubborn little bitch,* she thought.

Kris set off down a narrow bush path through the jungle. The path ended up sloping down a rutted, muddy hill to the riverbank. She turned at the bottom to watch Morgan gingerly work her way down. *My luck,* thought Morgan, *steep, uneven hills: the one thing that's difficult for me.* She side-stepped across a wide rut and shifted her weight to her braced leg. Just as she did, her foot slipped on the muddy surface and she toppled forward.

Hard, warm arms snatched her out of the air and up into Kris' arms. The taller woman had in a split second covered the distance back up the embankment to break Morgan's fall. "Hang on tight," she instructed the surprised doctor and flipped with Morgan in her arms down to the pebble beach below. There she lowered the small woman's feet to the ground.

Morgan stood stiffly. She was angry with herself and a bit dizzy from the flip, one forgotten arm still clinging to the taller woman's muscular forearm for support. Silence. Then, Kris took the smaller woman by the shoulders and gently turned her around so that she leaned against the taller woman's body. Over Morgan's shoulder, she pointed with her long arm to the brackish water of the river. "There. Do you see them? Stingray. Spotted ones. You find plain ones in here too."

Morgan twisted her body and looked for a long time into Kris' eyes. Out here, only a few feet into the jungle, the eyes had softened into the palest sky blue. "I fell," she stated bitterly.

"I caught you," replied Kris matter-of-factly. "That's an added complication. But as you saw, I'm up to it. Are you? Can you let me help you or are you going to be pig-headed and fall some place when I'm not there to help?" she challenged.

Morgan turned and watched the mud-coloured bodies of the river stingrays drift gracefully in the shallow water. One suddenly darted forward leaving a cloud of mud behind. "They can move really quickly when they want to," she observed.

"Yes," answered Kris still standing behind her. Silence. Then a surprise decision. "Do you want to skip drinks and go for a paddle downstream in the dugout?"

Morgan turned with curious green eyes that searched the blue depths. "I'd like that a lot," she softly responded.

10

Kris nodded seriously and moved away to push the twenty-foot log dugout off the pebble beach and into the tea coloured water. She picked up a hand-made paddle of dark wood, the blade of which was shaped like one of the "spades" on a deck of cards. Turning, she met Morgan's eyes and reached out her hand to offer the little doctor help in stepping into and walking along the two foot wide hull to a cross plank that was used as a bench. For a second Morgan hesitated, then smiled and put her hand in the strong woman's and allowed her to provide balance as she moved back to the seat. "You back-flipped to the beach with me in your arms," stated Morgan, shaking her head in disbelief as she watched her guide push the canoe into deeper water and quickly run along the gunwale past Morgan to take her place in the stern.

"It's a skill that's not greatly in demand these days," responded the guide dryly. Morgan looked over her shoulder at the strong woman and saw the sparkle in her eyes and laughed. Then she turned back and let Kris propel them down the river with silent, powerful strokes.

Kris watched the shoreline as she paddled with slow, long strokes. Why the hell had she done that? She'd been angered by Morgan's attitude and had planned on humiliating her and then putting her on the first plane home. Instead, she'd saved both her hide and her face and had offered her the scenic tour of the river. *Shit! What's going on with you, Thanasis?* The truth was she kind of liked the little doctor's spirit. She wasn't going to let the brace hold her back and when it didn't work out, she'd admitted her mistake without any excuses. Kris had to admit that she was reluctantly starting to like Morgan. Maybe guiding her wouldn't be so bad.

"See the holes along the bank? The Green Kingfishers nest in them this time of year when the water is low. But when the rainy season comes, they'll be underwater and then the electric eels use them for nesting," explained Kris.

"Subletting, huh? They do that where I come from too," remarked Morgan happily and was rewarded with a snort from behind her.

"That bare tree with the dark fruit hanging in bunches is called a bat tree. The fruit looks like bats hanging from the branches of a dead tree so the birds leave the fruit alone," Kris explained. They moved on down the river, mostly in agreeable silence unless Morgan asked a question or Kris provided information in her laconic style of speech. It was nearly dusk when they nosed against the beach again and Kris slipped past Morgan once more, balanced on the thin side of the canoe. She pulled the heavy dugout farther up the beach and then reached out to offer Morgan a hand in moving along the narrow craft and stepping out. Then she let Morgan go and busied herself tying up the craft and stowing the paddle.

"Thanks, that was great! I learned so much!" enthused Morgan, her eyes wide with excitement at all the amazing things that she had seen in just a small span of time.

"Good," stated Kris in a business-like tone, "'cause the reason I wanted to talk to you is to tell you I can't guide you to the villages for a few days. Fernando's regular guide, Carlos, is recovering from malaria so I'm going to help him and take the tourists out," finished Kris with a scowl.

"The Harrises are in for a rare treat then," responded Morgan confidently and Kris looked up in surprise. "Ah... I mean... Would it be okay if I go along too? Just to fill in the time until you're free?"

Kris raised an eyebrow in surprise, then nodded as she turned and headed up towards the bank. She looked at Morgan and offered her hand again. This time there was no hesitation. Morgan walked over and allowed the powerful woman to pull her up the hill. Once at the top, Kris was quick to let go and allow Morgan to handle the path herself. Half way along the trail, Kris stopped and placed her long, slim fingers around Morgan's shoulders. Leaning close she whispered, "Look up slowly. See the big beak sticking out of the hole in the trunk? It's a toucan nest."

"Toucans!" whispered Morgan with a stifled giggle. "Like in Fruit Loops?"

Kris nodded with a ghost of a smile. "Yeah, except in real life they're not very nice birds. They steal the eggs of other birds. That's what the long beak is for, reaching into nests. It's not very practical in flight. They sort of undulate up and down as they fly," explained the tall woman, demonstrating with her hand. "The beak keeps pulling them down."

Morgan nodded and the two moved off along the trail. Kris was an incredible source of information, Morgan realized. She spoke English with no accent and yet she also seemed to be just as comfortable in Portuguese and Spanish. Who was she? She was incredibly strong too! Morgan knew from her training as a doctor that few athletes would have had the flexibility and strength to have done that back flip while holding someone.

They stepped out of the rainforest and into the cleared compound just as an incredible noise broke out. Instinctively, Morgan took a step towards the taller woman. "What's that?" she asked.

Kris shrugged, "The five o'clock monkeys," she stated matter-of-factly. "The spider monkeys have learned that the compound is a safe zone. So at dusk, which is around five o'clock, they come out of the nearby forest to sleep in the trees of the compound, safe from their natural night predators like the jaguar."

Morgan listened to Kris' explanation as she watched the small-bodied monkeys with their long arms, tails and legs swing and jump through the trees. They squawked loudly as they swung into tree trunks, missed branches or bumped into each other. "Good grief! In the Tarzan movies they never have these problems!" laughed Morgan.

Kris gave a short, bitter laugh. "Yeah, well in real life, things can be surprising, especially when you're swinging through the trees!"

"Another one of your rarely used talents, Ms. Thanasis?" teased Morgan.

"That's Kris," stated the tall woman as she walked off. Morgan watched the woman break into a run, eating the ground up until she disappeared down past the bend in the airstrip. She shook her head. They'd got off to a pretty rocky start thanks to Kris Thanasis' brusque manner and her own thin skinned reaction. And yet in just a short time, she found herself really drawn to this strong, mysterious woman. Strange. She sighed and headed over towards where the others still sat on the verandah.

As she stepped up onto the verandah she felt rather than saw those that were sitting there take quick looks at her leg. She gave a mental sigh. *Here we go again. Maybe I should just wear an explanation written on a cardboard sign around my neck!* "Morgan! Where have you been? Come and sit down here," Betty said, patting the seat beside her on the couch.

Joe, however, leaned forward from where he sat in the bamboo armchair and touched the brace on Morgan's right leg. "Hell, honey, what happened to you?" he inquired, with his long drawl conveying both curiosity and concern at once.

"Joe!" exclaimed Betty in shocked embarrassment. "Maybe Morgan would rather not..."

Morgan laughed and gave Joe a warm look of affection. *Thanks, Joe for just getting it over with*, she thought. "Actually, in my undergraduate year I had my leg flattened when I was run over by a car," explained Morgan. "There was so much damage that I need this plastic support up the back of my leg in order to stand or walk with any kind of reliable stability." Morgan turned her leg a little so Joe could see the plastic brace that molded to the back of her leg up to knee height. Velcro straps on leather wrapped around her leg to hold it firmly in place.

"Well, honey, I hope you got his license number!" barked Joe,

13

genuinely upset for Morgan.

"Oh yeah," responded Morgan simply as she thought bitterly, *Yeah; I had lots of time when they backed over us three times!* Perhaps her face revealed too much at that thought, for Betty reached over and gave her hand a squeeze and Joe sat back and quickly changed the subject. The rest of the time before dinner passed in pleasant conversation mostly involving Morgan prompting the Harrises to talk about the family orchard business that one of their sons now owned and their growing number of grandchildren. Morgan felt like she was part of a Humphrey Bogart movie as she sat on the bamboo and wicker couch and looked across the grassy compound to the darkening rainforest. The sky was inky black and dotted with a dazzling array of stars. With delight, Morgan saw, for the first time, the Southern Cross constellation that adorns the Australian flag. The night air was cool and carried on its fragrant, earthy scent the buzz of crickets and a thousand other insects that made the Amazon their home.

Julio, the waiter, called them into the dining hall that was a large room with screened walls and a wood roof. Inside, picnic benches in a row acted as the dining table. With careful concentration Julio served their meal of chicken, beans and mealy potatoes that were a pale purple in colour. Fire ant sauce was available as a garnish and the group laughed at Berkler's face when he took a big bite of chicken that he had covered in the bright red mixture saying that he liked hot Mexican food! Morgan tried a little bit and found it to be very hot but acidic too. She figured she could adjust to the taste but she wasn't sure that she could get used the crunchy little bits of thorax in the mix.

The room went quiet and Morgan looked up to see the dark-haired woman behind her. With a graceful movement she silently claimed a seat beside Morgan and Julio rushed to see to getting her a meal. "Fernando," she remarked as a greeting.

Fernando looked up from tearing his bread apart, a delighted smile on his face. "Ah, my beautiful warrior, you honor me!" Kris' eyebrow went up in mock annoyance and then she turned her attention to her meal.

Morgan liked the woman's scent. She'd clearly showered after her run and smelt of soap and sun-dried spice. The woman's body radiated a warmth as she sat only inches away from the petite doctor. "Morgan," Joe's voice interrupted her musings, "what kind of doctoring do you do?"

Morgan lowered her fork. "Well, after my car... accident, it was clear that I couldn't stand long enough to perform any lengthy surgery and that was the area I was interested in pursuing. So I ended up in research. I work for a drug company. I'm sort of the mad scientist you see in movies, sitting in a lab full of boiling test tubes! I don't normally do field work but well... this assignment came up and... well... I just needed to get away," she explained. A lump formed in her chest and she found it hard to keep the lightness in her voice. No one seemed to notice. Betty used the opportunity to launch into some tale about how a friend of hers had gotten into plastic surgery in a big way and was working her way through her dead husband's estate at an alarming rate. As Morgan sat there feeling the anger and fear building inside her again, a strong hand reached behind her and rubbed her back for a second. Morgan looked up at the silent woman beside her but there was no indication that she had touched her. Morgan gave the strong arm a small bump of thanks with her shoulder and was rewarded with a quick look and smile from Kris. At the end of the table, Fernando watched with sad, interested eyes.

* * * * *

After the meal, Kris said goodnight and disappeared. For a while the remaining five sat on the verandah with their coffee and talked. Berkler explained the need for lumber and how companies like his provided jobs and opportunities to underdeveloped nations. Morgan spent her time trying hard to mind her own business.

After eating in the kitchen, Carlos wearily returned to the building that acted as a central dorm to find Kris filling a backpack with clothes. "I thought you were staying and helping me out?" he asked in surprise.

"I am," muttered Kris in a preoccupied manner. "I decided to board in with Morgan."

Carlos' eyes got real big. "My god! Kris, I had no idea that you and her... I would never have..." he spluttered until Kris cut him off.

"I don't know her, Carlos, nor am I planning on jumping her bones. It just makes sense, with this unscheduled lay-over, to establish a working relationship with her while still living in relative comfort. It's always a piss-poor time to find out you can't work together out on the trail," Kris explained with disinterest from inside the bathroom as she gathered her personal articles from the shelf.

Carlos nodded in agreement. He'd been on a few excursions in his time where the combination of personalities had made for a very miserable trip. "I am sad. I hoped to spend the night with you sleeping in the hammock beside mine. Ahhh!" he finished in surprise as Kris pinched his bum in passing.

Kris looked at him over one shoulder as she hefted the backpack onto the other. "Just as I thought." She winked, looking him over slowly. "All talk and no action. Poor Maria!" she teased and she sauntered out the screen door.

Carlos laughed and shook his head. "That one, ees, so bad!"

When Morgan reached her bungalow, she found that a flickering oil lantern was sitting on a table just inside her door. She smiled at the thoughtful service and switched off her torch that she and the Harrises had shared on the walk back to their cabins. There was no electricity in this remote area and the generator that powered the main lodge was only run for four hours each night. Stepping inside she almost jumped out of her skin, her heart beating rapidly until she realized it was Kris sprawled on one of the cots under a thin mosquito net. She was in her underwear reading her flight journal. "You scared me half to death! I didn't know we were sharing a cabin."

Kris looked around her journal. "Yeah, I'm staying here. It'll give us a chance to work out a routine," she explained, going back to her book.

Morgan nodded and turned to her bags, hesitating. Then she sighed. Out on the trail, Kris was going to see the scars. She might as well get it over with, she concluded, slipping her T-shirt over her head and then turning to sit on the edge of her bed to remove her shorts more easily from over the brace. Looking up she met startling blue eyes looking at her. "Not very pretty, huh?" she said, looking down at the scars that crisscrossed her torso as she bent to remove the brace from her leg.

"You're in great shape," observed the guide. "That will make it easier on the trail. You got any internal injuries that I should know about?" Kris asked, keeping the situation on a professional level, sensing Morgan's discomfort.

Morgan shook her head. "No, all healed now, pretty much," she responded, glad of Kris' objectivity and forthrightness. She got up and moved over to the crude hollowed log that was used as a sink. Pouring water from the whiskey bottle she washed and brushed her teeth then, after using the facilities and washing her hands again, she headed for her cot.

Kris ducked under her net and walked over. "Get in and I'll tuck the mosquito net around you. The smallest opening and the buggers nail you." Morgan slipped under the white sheet and Kris lowered the net that hung from a central hook over the cot. Carefully, she tucked the edges under the mattress all the way around. Then she capped the oil lamp and padded over to her own cot. Morgan could hear the

16

springs of her cot creak as she got in and then heard her tucking the netting around her own bed.

Silence. "Those scars on your abdomen, are they bullet holes?" asked Morgan.

"Yeah." responded Kris openly.

"Was there damage?" she asked.

"I heal well. There's no problems," came the reply.

"Kris?"

"I've got a few enemies," came the startling response.

Morgan fell silent. This woman was becoming more and more of a mystery to her. Fernando had pulled her aside before she had left tonight. 'Little one', he had said, 'You can trust your life to the warrior but always remember that she is dangerous. Be careful.' Was this what he had meant? That Kris Thanasis had a dark history? Or was there more?

Breakfast was a merry affair with much teasing and bantering back and forth between a group of strangers who now, by the nature of their isolation, were becoming close friends. Even the business orientated Berkler had relaxed a bit and had told some tales of his experiences with custom agents. Today, Fernando would be arranging for Berkler to meet with local government representatives in the lumber town some hundred and fifty miles to the east. The roar of the Piper Cub could be heard warming up on the airstrip as they finished breakfast.

Kris had not had breakfast with them. When Morgan had woken sleepily from a hot, stuffy night under her mosquito net, she found that Kris had gone. Her backpack was neatly lying on the center of her made bed. Morgan had rubbed the sleep from her eyes and tried to shake off the dull headache and queasy stomach from jet lag and the oppressive heat. Had she only arrived in South America two days ago? She forced herself to swing up into a sitting position on the edge of her bed and automatically reached for her brace. Her hand stopped half way. The plastic brace had been lined with a layer of cotton. Anger rose quickly and then subsided. Kris was the expert. If she felt the brace needed a lining, then she'd better use it. Actually, it made sense. The material would absorb moisture. She had noticed yesterday that the normally comfortable brace was damp and rubbing against her skin by midday.

Then she noticed the folded piece of paper tucked behind the strap of her brace. Morgan picked it out and unfolded it.

Didn't want to wake you when you'd had such a restless

17

night. The cotton will help prevent chaffing that could lead to tropical ulcers. Bang out your shoes before putting them on. Ugly things like Black Widow spiders like warm shoes to sleep in.
I'll see you after breakfast. K.

Morgan followed Kris' instructions. First, because she realized that Kris was worth listening to and second, because she suspected that not to follow orders might not impress the mysterious woman that the local inhabitants called "Warrior." Before she left for breakfast, she made her bed and left her bags neatly in the centre. She wanted to send a message to her guide that she was a fast learner and could be trusted to fit into a routine. After all, wasn't that the reason Kris was bunking in here?

Kris finished her run and trotted through the kitchen to grab one of the flat cakes that Fernando's wife fried for breakfast. She munched on it contentedly as she headed back to the cabin. Morgan was gone of course; Kris had heard her laughter from inside the dining hall as she passed. Her eyes slid to Morgan's bed and she gave a satisfied nod. Morgan had left everything ship-shape and the cotton material had clearly been used. Turning to her own pack, she found a note written on the back of the one she had left Morgan.

I hope I didn't keep you awake tossing about. Thanks for worrying about my safety. I appreciate your attention to details and will try to live up to your standard when we are out on the trail. M. P.S. Banged out the shoes really well! No stowaways thank God!

Kris smiled and dug into her pack for her toilet bag and then headed for the shower. Behind the partition she turned on the water and stripped down. The small enclosure contained the lingering smell of Morgan's morning rites. There was a faint, fragrant scent of sweet grass and herbs that really appealed to the guide. So far things were working out okay. The next few days should indicate whether Morgan was going to be a hazard or a help on the trail. So far, except for the surprise of the brace, the kid seemed to be measuring up. But Kris was worried about the look of hurt and confusion that seemed to haunt the girl's eyes. Emotional troubles were the last thing she needed out in the rainforest and Morgan was clearly running from someone or something, from the way she had reacted in the dining hall and the nightmares that seemed to plague her dreams last night.

Kris toweled off, scowling. She hated dealing with unknowns.

And she hated emotion. *I'll just have to play it by ear*, she thought. At least she found herself liking Morgan. That was a good start anyway, she concluded, tucking her shirt into her shorts and zipping the fly. Then she sat on her cot and put on socks and her hiking boots. Checking to make sure everything was neat; she headed out to act as nursemaid to three inexperienced tourists! *Christ, how my life has changed!* she mused darkly.

The next few days proved to be surprisingly fun for Kris. The Harrises turned out to be a happy and willing pair and the foursome spent each day exploring under Kris' leadership. The first day, she took them down river in the dugout. Along the way, she would point out the many exotic birds of the area, or a lazy Cayman basking in the sun. They hung over the side of the dugout and watched stingrays gracefully fly underneath or looked up in delight to see flocks of parrots fly overhead. Kris found that she was seeing the land again through the delighted eyes of her charges.

Okay, she had to admit she'd shown off some too. She'd run along the gunwales to the delight of the Harrises and dived into the tannin stained water, coming up a few seconds later with a serving dish size Mata Mata in her hands. With care, she had placed it in the dugout and then used her arms to propel herself up and into the canoe once again. Then, to an enraptured little group, she explained that the coarse looking turtle was one of the oldest unchanged species on planet Earth. She showed them its leathery shell and cute little pointed nose and then gently lowered it back into the water. Morgan passed her a towel with complete adoration in her eyes that made Kris feel ten feet tall. Really it was ridiculous the way she was reacting to this little tourist group of hers.

Betty had called her a hero too! My God! If the woman only knew who she was being guided by! It had happened later on the first day, when they had stopped for a swim at a beach. After lunch, Joe had wanted to try his hand at fishing and Kris had given him a line from the canoe's supplies and caught a grasshopper to bait it with. Joe pulled a flipping fish to shore after only a few casts but as he reached for it, Kris dived from nowhere and just got her hand in the way. The flapping, orange piranha bit down on Kris' finger and she had to pry its jaws open to get its sharp teeth out of her flesh. Removing it from the hook, Kris killed it quickly. Blood dripped freely from her hand. Suddenly, Morgan was there with a first aid kit, gently holding Kris' hand and applying pressure. "Hey, it's okay. I'll just put a little gasoline on it to kill any infection," she'd shrugged.

Morgan looked up in disbelief. "Do I look like the kind of

doctor that allows my patients to disinfect their wounds by frying their skin with chemicals?" In the end, Kris had been forced to sit on the edge of the beached canoe while Morgan disinfected the wound properly and bandaged it. "If it's still bleeding when we get back, I'm going to put a stitch in," she warned and Kris raised an eyebrow in disbelief.

It was then that Betty declared their guide a hero even though the very embarrassed guide in question had tried to explain to her group that the perpetrator of the crime was the solitary, orange piranha that rarely attacked unless provoked and was not the dangerous grey piranha that swam in schools and could rip a large animal to its bones in minutes. She explained how, before they had swum, she had tested the water by throwing in a bit of sandwich meat to see if it would attract such a school. "I knew there were solitaries in the water we were swimming in but it wasn't dangerous until you caught one," she'd explained.

Before they had left the beach that day, she had carefully packed the fish away in the cooler that had held their lunch. That night, at dinner, the cook proudly served Joe his piranha as an appetizer, much to the delight of Kris' group. They each took a turn tasting the dark, oily flesh, very pleased with their adventure of having swum with the piranha and eaten one too.

"That was a really nice thing you did bringing back the piranha for Joe," Morgan had commented later that night after she had finally cornered the reluctant Kris to let her look at the bitten finger. Kris blushed at the praise. She wasn't used to being seen as "nice."

"My God! Look at this!" exclaimed Morgan, running her finger over the closed skin where the bite had occurred. "Boy, do you heal quickly!" Kris had smirked and pulled her hand away with an "I told you so" expression.

On the second day, Kris had taken them on a five-mile hike through the jungle. As they walked along she would stop and explain the use of various plants or point out birds high above in the canopy. She'd catch insects to show them, including a little elephant bug that got its name from the small trunk that it waved about. They stopped on top of a massive cutter ant colony and watched the line of workers carrying the leaves like sails on their backs to the huge nest. Kris explained that they would chew the leaves up to make a fertilizer on which a fungus would grow that was the ants' only food. Tired and bursting with knowledge, the little party had retired early. Kris had asked to see Morgan's leg and was pleased to see that the cotton seemed to be preventing any chaffing, at least on this easy walk. "Do I pass muster?" Morgan had asked, a little annoyed.

"Yes," Kris had responded bluntly.

"Would you have refused to take me if the brace was rubbing?" asked Morgan.

"Yes," responded Kris meeting Morgan's eyes. "What gives you nightmares?" asked Kris.

Morgan's face closed. She got up without a word and disappeared behind the partition. A second later Kris heard the shower running. *Guess I'm not going to find out the answer to that question any time soon,* she sighed.

On the last day of the Harrises' tour of the Amazon, Kris took them up river in the dugout. She showed them how the butterflies massed on the sandy spits to mate and how the cormorants spread their wings to warm in the sun after diving in the cool water for fish. Much to her party's delight, she took them to waterfalls that bounced down terraces of rock. There they had spent most of the afternoon sliding down the smooth rocks to the pools of deep water beneath each small falls.

At first Morgan had sat at the edge of the lower pool, content to watch the others. Now and again she would lower herself into the pool and cool off, her brace left safely on shore. Suddenly, the tall body of the warrior was beside her. "Do you want to go for a slide?" she had asked. Morgan had explained that without her brace she couldn't climb up the rocks and Kris had playfully whispered in her ear, "I know." Then she had picked a surprised Morgan up as if she was a rag doll and had gleefully run up the rocks to where the Harrises were waiting. As soon as she reached the top, she lowered Morgan to her feet but stood behind her, offering her quiet support. The Harrises pushed off down the layers of falls, splashing from one to the other with much laughter. Then Kris lowered herself into the stream and pointed to the space between her legs. "Sit here and I'll take you down in my arms," Kris had explained to the nervous Morgan and Morgan had lowered herself to the ground and slipped into place within the protective walls of the larger woman's body. With a strong push they were off down the falls until they broke over the last lip and fell with a splash into the bottom pond. The day had gone really well, Kris thought. She really couldn't remember when she had last...well...just played. It had felt good. It was a surprising revelation to Kris that she could have fun playing.

That night, after Kris had said good-bye to the Harrises after dinner, she found Joe had followed her out. "Ah, listen Kris," he said, reaching for her hand, "This is just a little something from Betty and me for the great tour. You really put yourself out for us and we appreciate it." Joe smiled and actually patted the stunned warrior's cheek. Blood roared through Kris' body and her hand clutched into a fist around the money.

Then Morgan was there, pushing against her chest. "Hey Kris, before you take off could you give me a hand?" she asked, smiling back and forth between Joe and Kris.

Kris gave a weak smile. "Sure Morgan," she choked out, raising her hand to punch the money back at Joe. To her surprise she found Morgan's hand wrapped around her shaking fist.

"That's great! Come on!" Morgan bubbled happily, pulling Kris back into the darkness. "I'll say good bye in the morning, Joe," she called over Kris' stiff shoulder as she continued to pull the woman away.

"Sure thing, sweetheart," called Joe, oblivious to how close he'd come to getting punched out by one insulted warrior.

Once they were a good distance from the dining hall and out of sight, Morgan turned around and took Kris gently by the forearms. "Kris, what is it? I could feel you in the dining hall. This awful anger... What happened?" she asked with worry.

Kris still bristled with anger. Through clinched teeth she hissed, "He tipped me," and opened her hand, dropping the bills on the ground. Morgan covered the laugh that came bubbling out with a hand. "It... is... not... funny!" emphasized Kris in a harsh whisper.

"Kris, it's okay. He didn't mean to insult you. He doesn't realize that you are not what you seem," explained Morgan, gently giving her a shake. "Look, take the money," she went on, bending to pick it up and handing it out to Kris, "and tell Fernando that Joe gave it to you to share amongst the others." Kris hesitated for a long moment and then slowly took the money. "You okay now?" Morgan asked. Kris nodded, looking pouty. "Come on, I really need you to show me what and how to pack," Morgan said and took Kris by the arm again, keeping up a one-way conversation with her guide back to their cabin.

With stiff, abrupt words Kris instructed Morgan in the proper gear necessary for such an expedition. And while Morgan packed and then repacked to fit everything in, Kris sat on her bed and dismantled and cleaned first a handgun and then a rifle. Morgan realized that Kris was just barely holding her anger. She tried to hold her tongue but just couldn't. "Kris, we're not taking those with us are we?" she asked, trying not to sound disapproving.

Blue eyes looked up sharply. They burned with an inner fire that caused Morgan to take a step back in surprise. Long, strong fingers rubbed the dark metal surface with hungry strokes. "Yes, we are," came the determined reply.

Morgan sank down on her cot and tried to control the beating of her heart before she continued. She swallowed, her eyes unwillingly sliding back to Kris' hands as they caressed the gunmetal. "I... I... don't like guns," she stated.

"I do," came the defiant response.

"Are they necessary? I mean, you didn't carry any weapons the last three days," argued Morgan, using a shaky hand to brush a piece of hair behind her ear.

Kris snorted and got up, her body bristling with violent energy. "We're not going on a tourist sightseeing hike here, kid. We're going into really dangerous territory. And we'll be out there alone a very long time. If you're afraid of guns then maybe you're not up to this field work," she snarled.

Morgan was in her face in a second but much to her surprise her forward movement accelerated and she found herself flipped onto her back on Kris' bed. Kris slammed a knee into her chest and held her down, "Don't... ever... come at me!" the warrior snarled, looming over the petite blond. Morgan's world scoped and tumbled into one dark night seven years ago. The pavement was wet with winter snow and blood. Her blood and Rick's. The heavy weight of his dead body pinned her to the cold ground. "Morgan! Morgan!" she heard someone calling but she couldn't escape. Her body was too broken and Rick lay dead on top of her.

Sometime later, Morgan became aware of warm, strong arms holding her. A beautiful deep voice sang softly in Spanish close to her ear. With effort she tried to open her eyes.

"Hey, you okay?" asked Kris softly, looking with worried eyes into Morgan's face. Morgan nodded and ran a shaky hand over her damp face. "I think you had a panic attack or something. You sure you're okay? I didn't mean to scare you that badly. I was just reacting. I wasn't going to hurt you," Kris tried to explain, awkwardly patting Morgan's shoulder.

Morgan nodded and then, realizing she was lying on top of her guide who was gingerly holding her in her arms, she pulled away and sat on the edge of the cot. "I'm okay, Kris. It wasn't really you. Not that you're not pretty scary when you're angry," she added with a nervous giggle. "It was just for a minute there I flashed back... I..." Morgan stumbled to a halt.

"It wasn't just a car accident, was it?" probed Kris bluntly, reaching to put her hand on Morgan's arm.

Absently, Morgan reached out and played with Kris' long

23

fingers, much to the dark-haired woman's surprise. "No. I knew this Hispanic man in meds. We were just good friends, you know?" Morgan explained looking at Kris for understanding. Kris nodded. "He'd been in a street gang but had straightened himself around and had gone back to school. Anyway, to make a long story short, another gang saw him out walking with me. They shot him in passing then circled back and ran over us... a few times. It had snowed and Rick was on top of me. That's why I survived," she finished, looking down and realizing that she had been playing with Kris' hand. She dropped it. "Sorry!" She got up quickly, moving across the room and back to her bags. "I'd better finish packing," she muttered. Kris nodded and got up and left.

* * * * *

Kris stood moodily in the early dawn light. A troop of Howling Monkeys were nearby, their cries echoing across the misty rainforest mountains like an eerie wind through a canyon. She was in a rotten mood. She was still mad about the tip and upset with what had happened between Morgan and her last night. It was sure to affect their working relationship. Morgan would be scared of her now. *She'd got a good taste of what a savage I can be,* she thought. *Maybe it was for the best.* And then there was all the other shit that Kris' pragmatic mind was having a hell of a time coping with, like how had Morgan felt her anger towards Joe? And what about her own rage at those who had tried to kill Morgan, as if it was anything to her! There was the nervous turmoil she was feeling about upsetting Morgan too. She shook her head to clear away the confusion and broke into a run.

Morgan waved good-bye to the plane that was taking the Harrises on to a tour of the Andes. Now there was only her and Kris. At least she hoped that was the case. She hadn't seen Kris since last night. She sighed softly and turned to walk smack against the chest of the warrior in question. In a black T-shirt and runner's shorts stretched tight over her muscular body, glistening from her run, she looked like a deadly black panther. Morgan squealed in surprise and Kris immediately stepped back, her blue eyes dark and wary. "You scared me half to death!" panted Morgan, one hand spread over her chest.

Kris' face was etched stone. "Which time?" she asked coldly.

Morgan looked up in shock, wondering if she should dodge the confrontation. *No. Tell her the truth.* "You scared me when you told me you have enemies. Ones who hate you so much that they would shoot you. It scared me when I was told to trust you with my life but to never forget that you are dangerous. It scared me when you flipped me and held me down like I was no more than a rag doll. And it scares the shit out of me that you are taking those guns." Blue eyes narrowed and blazed with cold fire. "But do you know what really scares me, Kris?" The blue eyes contacted hers with sharp interest. "What really scares me is that I might not measure up and you won't guide me." The blue eyes opened in startled confusion. For a second, they almost warmed as the silence hung between them.

"I'm the only guide who knows the area, so you're stuck with me. We leave in twenty minutes," came the response at last as the tall woman turned and strode off to change and grab her gear.

Morgan managed a weak smile. That... had been close.

Kris loaded the dugout carefully, covering the cargo with a sheet of plastic that she tied down. Satisfied, she silently helped Morgan into the bow, having arranged things so that she could lean her back against their supplies. With a strong push, she shoved the heavy log craft off the pebble beach and sprang onto the bow. With her arms extended for balance, she quickly moved along the gunwale to the stern and picked up the second paddle. Strong, experienced strokes brought the awkward boat around and headed them down the Alto Ventuari River that would take them eventually to the waters of the Orinoco. Morgan picked up her paddle and tried her best to match the long, steady stroke of her silent companion.

Within a short time, Morgan was soaked with sweat and dizzy with heat. The air was close and stale and the breeze that had made the last few days so pleasant had disappeared. They pushed on and on, Morgan silently keeping going with grim determination. It was well into the afternoon when the taciturn warrior finally called a halt, beaching their craft on a sand spit in a green lagoon. As Morgan edged out of the dugout on stiff legs, something large broke the still waters and disappeared, leaving only a ripple of water to convince her that she had actually seen anything. "Ah, Kris, I think there is something in there," she whispered nervously, breaking the silence that had been between them most of the day.

"Fresh water dolphin. There's a pod of six that fish here," explained her guide, busily pulling items from a pack under the plastic. Just then two dolphins broke the surface side-by-side and arched back under the water.

"Wow!" exclaimed Morgan, her eyes wide with delight, scanning the surface intently for another sighting.

Kris smiled slightly at the delight of her traveling companion. She wasn't sure why she had needed to give Morgan this experience; it wasn't like they were out sightseeing or anything. She'd been hired to take the client to the area that she wanted to go and that was it. Much to her surprise, she had liked the three days guiding the Harrises. She had especially liked Morgan's innocent delight with the rainforest. Hell, she just liked Morgan! It was stupid and the attraction made her both angry with herself and giddy with a hummy sort of happiness that she hadn't felt in a very, very long time. "I thought maybe we'd make an early camp here and swim with them," stated Kris a bit awkwardly. To her complete surprise Morgan walked over to her and gave her a quick hug. "Hey! Whatcha doing?" grumbled the taller woman suddenly very embarrassed, as if Morgan could read her thoughts.

"I'm expressing my thanks to the big, bad warrior who paddled like crazy most of the day so there would be time to spend here," smiled Morgan, turning to rummage through her own bag for her swimsuit.

"Just worked out that way," mumbled the embarrassed guide, scowling as she unloaded supplies.

Morgan watched the tall woman work out of the corner of her eye as she helped with the unloading and changed into the swimsuit. Kris was incredibly good-looking. Not cute or even pretty, her face was too angular for that, but she was classically beautiful, strong and noble, like a Greek sculpture. She was both fascinating to watch and scary at the same time, like being close to some beautiful but deadly wild animal. Morgan ran a tongue over dried lips. *Shit! Get a grip here, Morgan!* And the small doctor turned to sit on the edge of the dugout and remove her brace.

The dolphins were small, about six feet in length and light grey in colour. They had long, tube-like jaws and blocky little heads. As the two women swam about, the playful creatures would come up and push against them. Once completely waterlogged and cooled from a hard day's paddling, the two made for shore, Kris automatically scooping Morgan up as they neared shallow water and placing her on her feet near where she had left her brace. Then she threw a towel in Morgan's direction. "Thanks. That was just great. You know I'm supposed to be here working, but so far the Amazon has been just one amazing playground. I feel kind of guilty," confessed Morgan.

Kris stopped drying herself and looked with serious eyes at Morgan. She could still feel the warmth of the smaller woman's body against her chest. *I gotta put an end to this,* Kris thought, giving herself a metal shake. "It's not going to stay like this. The Alto Ventuari is a black river. That's one high in tannin. The acidic nature of the river gives it its clear, tea look. It also prevents the breeding of mosquitoes. When we get closer to the Orinoco, things will change. We'll be deep in the Amazon basin and it will really get buggy and hot.

"The Orinoco is a white river. The high silt content neutralizes the water and makes it look like tea with milk. You can't see what's in there. And believe me, there are some pretty dangerous things to watch out for in that water. In white water, mosquitoes breed and there is far more wild life. Don't ever go near the shore unless I'm with you. The Amazon Basin teems with life and some days it's in your face all the time. As well as flora and fauna, we'll be meeting some pretty unpredictable Indian groups too. So enjoy these days. It's going to get pretty rough, pretty quick."

Morgan nodded, a little taken back by Kris' sudden sharpness. Once they were changed and their swimsuits laid out to get drier, Kris explained that in high humidity nothing ever really dried once it was wet. The warrior showed Morgan how to set up camp, well back from the water, in case rain in the mountains caused a flash flood. Hammocks with mosquito net covers were tied between trees, to keep the ground insects out and to reduce the chances of catching malaria. And the foliage was cut way back, so the danger of snakes was reduced. Morgan followed the lesson seriously, eager to show Kris that she wasn't just a lightweight. The implied criticism in Kris' earlier lecture had really stung. Somehow this woman's opinion of her mattered. Kris built a fire and they shared a hot meal prepared by Morgan of tomato soup with rice. It appeared the one thing the capable guide did not do was cook!

After dinner, Kris cleaned and oiled her weapons while Morgan ignored her and wrote in her field diary. *Okay*, thought Kris, *so I was a bit sharp with her and she doesn't like the guns.* Kris squirmed inwardly, not liking the uncomfortable silence. She put the weapons away and got up to look through one of the packs. On impulse, she had stowed away a treat that she had spied back in the lodge kitchen before they had left. It seemed like a good time to get it out.

Sheepishly she brought a small bag of marshmallows over to Morgan as a peace offering. "Ah, these were in the food supplies. They'll mold pretty quick. Ah, maybe we could roast them or something," she suggested awkwardly.

Morgan looked up in surprise and then, a little unsure of the warrior's sudden mood swings, she smiled nervously. "That would be fun...okay?" she stammered. Kris nodded and hid her blush by disappearing into the darkness to cut a couple of sticks.

A full moon rose overhead as, like children, they tossed the marshmallows on the end of the sticks that Kris had cut from the forest behind them. "Kris, can I ask you a personal question?" asked Morgan as they sat quietly under the soft moon's rays.

Kris' gut tightened. The last four days had been so nice. She really wanted to keep that feeling going for a few more days. She just felt relaxed with Morgan. It wasn't merely that she found the woman attractive; it was more complex than that. The woman simply seemed to bring to their interactions something that Kris normally was missing. Hell! She'd played in the waterfalls with the Harrises like some kid, just to show off to Morgan. "You can ask. I don't know if I can answer," responded the dark-haired woman with a sigh, looking sadly into the fire.

"Why do you have enemies that would try to kill you?" Blue eyes snapped up and filled with anger and then sorrow in rapid succession. "I'm here to guide you, not entertain you," came the cutting reply. Morgan looked like she had been hit, then she nodded quickly and turned to stare into the fire, bewildered hurt filling her eyes.

The tall woman rose and turned to walk from the circle of firelight, then sighed and turned and sat again. "Sorry, why don't you ask me something else," muttered the mysterious woman, clearly making an awkward effort to be sociable.

Morgan hesitated. On the one hand she really wanted to know about this woman that she found so incredibly fascinating. On the other... "Your name sounds Greek," observed Morgan, trying to encourage the stoic woman to talk now that she had started. Kris flinched.

Oops! Hit another nerve. Damn.

"I... I changed my name. Took my mother's maiden name. My maternal grandfather, he was Greek. Immigrated after the war. My father's South American. He doesn't know I'm still alive..." For a while Kris stared into the fire. "You got family?"

"Yeah, parents. Mom's a family doctor and dad's a mechanic. My dad has Greek ancestry too, but I think it was farther back."

Kris looked up in interest and seemed to relax a bit, as Morgan had hoped. "That's a strange combination. How did they meet?"

"Mom had an old, beat-up car that dad kept on the road for her while she was doing her internship. He always says she had to marry him because she owed him too much money to pay him off!"

Kris smiled. A real smile. The first that Morgan had seen. A flash of white, even teeth and a sparkle that danced across her eyes making her look much younger. *On a roll now!* Morgan thought. "I have a younger brother too, Scott." The smile wavered and was forced to remain by stiff lips. *Now what?* "Do you have any brothers or sisters?"

Kris winced and swallowed, getting to her feet in one, smooth motion. She looked down at the green eyes that met hers with such compassion. "I had a younger brother, Neil. Two years ago, I injected him with an over-dose of cocaine. He died," confessed the warrior. In the shocked silence, Kris looked up at the stars blinking back the tears of pain.

"Is that when you changed your name?" Morgan asked.

Kris nodded and then turned away, disappearing silently into the trees. Morgan stayed by the fire, realizing that Kris had shown a remarkable amount of trust in sharing even a small part of the pain that was inside her and knowing instinctively that the warrior now needed time alone.

She could understand that. Wasn't that why she had requested this field study? To be alone. Away from the sympathetic looks. To try and make peace with her own inner anger. She hoped she was more successful at doing so than Kris. The woman was an enigma. Outside she seemed so incredibly strong and capable and yet inside her soul seemed fatally wounded. Morgan wanted to find her and hold her until the pain lessened, but she knew the strange dark-woman couldn't accept comfort for her guilt yet.

For another five days they pushed on down the river, gradually developing a routine that allowed the two of them to work well as a team. On the sixth day it rained. Not one of the frequent small, intense downpours that occur in the Amazon but a steady, cold rain that continued all day. To make matters worse a sharp wind was blowing down the mountainside, chilling their wet bodies to the bone. "How can I be so close to the equator and so cold?" muttered Morgan through chattering teeth.

"It's not really cold, you've just lost too much body heat," responded her guide, who didn't seem to be too bothered by the miserable weather. Morgan nodded. She wasn't going to become a whiner, that was for sure. Putting down her paddle, she picked up the plastic cup they were using as a bailer and set to work, scraping the thick plastic cup along the axe-hewed wood and tossing the water over the side. Suddenly, Kris yelled, "Paddle!" Morgan dropped the bailer and grabbed her paddle and dug in as the first of the rising water hit them. Within minutes, they were being shot downstream on the turbulent, muddy waters. Kris fought with all her considerable strength to keep their craft in safe waters.

Finally, recognizing a well-used shoreline, she shot the little vessel over to the eroded bank and beached it between some rocks.

Quickly, she grabbed Morgan and pulled her out, and then pulled the dugout as far out of the rushing stream as she could, carefully securing it by rope to a big tree some distance back from the water. Following Kris' instructions, Morgan helped her unload their cargo. She had just got their backpacks to safety when a wall of water rushed around the bend and hit the dugout, smashing it against the rocks. Morgan felt the sand beneath her feet turn to water as she awkwardly dove for an overhanging branch. Her body was now submerged in muddy water up to her hips, and the pull of the current was incredible. She could feel her hands slipping.

Then Kris was there, pulling her to safety from the bank above. "Thanks," panted Morgan, shivering with fright and cold.

The warrior nodded. "Come on, there's an Indian family around here," she explained, helping Morgan through the underbrush that grew thickly along the shore until they were on the path that led from the water to the Indian family's land.

It wasn't much to look at, just one wattle and daub house, round, with a conical shaped grass roof and a lean-to not far away that was the cooking area. The family greeted Kris warmly and she talked to them in their own tongue. She led Morgan into the hut, which was recessed into the ground. She stripped her down and wrapped her in a blanket, and then removed her own clothes and changed into dry ones. The fascinated Indian family crowded in and watched from the far side of the hut.

Morgan was past caring. She was past thinking. All she wanted to do was curl up and go to sleep but her teeth were chattering too much to let her. Kris sat down behind her and pulled her against her chest wrapping warm, strong arms around her. She talked softly to the Indians and the adult male and two children left. "Kris," Morgan mumbled, "how can you be so warm and dry?" but she was asleep before she heard the answer.

* * * * *

Morgan woke to the sound of Indian voices and the smell of wet earth. Forcing her sleepy eyes open, she found herself alone in a round mud hut, on a red earth floor. To her surprise, she found she was naked except for a scratchy, grey blanket that was wrapped around her. She sat up and rubbed the sleep from her eyes as memories of yesterday slowly worked their way back into her conscious mind. Where was Kris, she wondered? Her backpack lay against the wall and she quickly put on some clothes wishing that she could shower first. Her hair was dirty and scraggly and her body powdered with a thin layer of river mud. *This must be the place where it gets rough,* she thought, recalling Kris' words as she squared her shoulders and set a determined jaw.

Kris sat on her heels listening to the talk of the two men who sat with her around the fire under the lean-to. They talked in minute detail of the events of a day's hunt and bragged, as men do, of their own contributions or laughed at themselves for some moment of bad luck or judgment. Kris found their talk relaxing. These were hunters like herself. Occasionally, one of the men would poke at the thickening substance in the pot that sat on the hot coals. They were making the poison that they would need for the darts of their blowguns. Kris unconsciously mimicked the mannerisms of the men, becoming one of them even though the tall guide towered over the short men of the rainforest.

Her mind, which had been thinking about Morgan, focused now on their plans for today's hunt. She was pleased that they allowed her to lead and take the right of the first blood but her face remained deadpan. She nodded acceptance, without pride or conceit, as was expected of her. She took leadership not by issuing orders, which would have been rude by Indian custom, but through example, dipping the points of her borrowed darts in the mixture and carefully blowing on the tips to dry the drug.

She was aware of Morgan standing at the doorway of the hut watching her and was pleased that the small doctor had not taken her face by joining her as she sat with the men. Morgan just always seemed to understand. She must be a good doctor. She had a way with people. Carefully gathering her darts, she dropped them into a bark holder that she strung from a long strap from her shoulder. Then she picked up the long, tube-like blowgun as she stood. Some five feet long, the hard wood pipe was perfectly straight and balanced. It felt familiar and comfortable in the warrior's hand. She ducked under the lower edge of the lean-to and walked across the yard to where Morgan waited.

"Good morning, sleepyhead," growled Kris looking down at Morgan.

Morgan smiled with delight and shielded her eyes with her hand from the morning light. "Hi, yourself!" *My god!* The woman radiated power and control, Morgan acknowledged, looking at the muscular body leaning casually on a long stick

Kris looked down for a second, scuffing a boot in the dirt as she gathered her focus. Damn, the woman was incredibly beautiful even covered in river mud! Her hair flashed highlights of red in the sunlight and her eyes sparkled with life. Kris' wary and veiled eyes looked up to meet Morgan's. "Ah...I'm going to help with the hunt today. They need food and we've lost a lot of our supplies so we can't really afford to share," Kris explained, then asked as if an afterthought, "Are you okay?"

Morgan's face broke into a happy smile and she tilted her head and looked at Kris with dancing eyes, "Yes, I'm fine.... You be careful, okay?" she added earnestly.

Kris smirked, raising an eyebrow. "Afraid you'll be left in the middle of the Amazon?"

"No, just care about you," Morgan answered in friendly honesty. To her surprise, the casual remark caused a deep blush to rise up Kris' face and the mighty hunter of a few seconds ago seemed suddenly very vulnerable. Then the mask fell and Kris turned abruptly away, moving back to the group of men that now waited for her leadership.

She handed one her blowgun and ducked back under the lean-to. Bending she picked up a small gourd and brought it back over to Morgan. "Here, drink this," she instructed, holding the bowl out to her charge.

Morgan sniffed and pulled a face. "What is it?" she asked.

The taller woman shrugged. "A root, from the forest, cures stomach infections. You might have taken in some river water yesterday. I thought it best to be sure."

Morgan took the makeshift cup and drank down the bitter substance without question. How much did Kris know about jungle medicine? And did she know of Ellburn's plant? Morgan wondered as she swallowed with effort, pulling a face.

Kris smiled and touched Morgan's arm for a split second then she turned and yelled to the men who waited. One tossed her the blowgun, which she caught easily, and they trotted off through the tall trunks that supported the dense canopy of leaves high above.

Morgan spent the day cleaning and airing their gear. The contents of a mud-soaked bag, clearly rescued from the river, were partly salvageable but they had lost a lot of their dehydrated food. Fortunately, Morgan's field test kit and medical supplies were safe, as were their personal knapsacks. When Morgan acted out washing, the two Indian women and the children led her to a clear stream with much laughing. They all needed to touch and feel Morgan's long, strawberry blond hair, which she tolerated with easy grace as she did their laundry under the fascinated eyes of the Indian family. Morgan enjoyed the quiet day and the opportunity to get reorganized and recover from the previous day's misfortune. But as the day wore on she worried more and more about Kris and was relieved when, just before dusk, the two men returned with her guide, each carrying the body of a large monkey.

Kris dropped the burden from her shoulder and walked over to Morgan. "Everything all right?" she asked, her eyes inspecting Morgan for any signs of change.

Morgan gingerly took away the long stick Kris still held in her hand and leaned it against the hut. "I'm fine. What is that, anyway?" she asked, looking at the taller woman and then at the wood rod.

"Blow gun," explained the guide in her usual concise manner.

"Really!" exclaimed Morgan turning with interest to look at the weapon. She looked back at the older woman. "Another one of your many skills?" she teased and was rewarded with a crooked smile. "Show me," asked Morgan excitedly.

The warrior rooted around for a dart and held it out for the doctor to see. In her hand was a black needle about six inches long. Around one end was tied a bit of white fiber for balance. "It's a type of tree thorn," Kris explained. "The tip is soaked with a drug that is extracted from the skin of a miner frog. It doesn't kill the animal as most people think. It paralyzes it, allowing you time to kill it." Morgan nodded her understanding, realizing that Kris wanted to share this interest, even though Morgan was secretly cheering for the animal.

Kris reached behind Morgan to grab the blowgun, bringing their bodies close together. Morgan could smell the tangy spice that was the warrior and feel the dry heat that her body always seemed to radiate. "The tubes are long to keep the accelerating dart on course. The longer the tube the more accurate the shot." Kris dropped a dart in the end and then held the long blowgun close to her face. Taking a deep breath, she puffed into the tube with a sudden, fierce blast. An explosion of air jetted out of the far end and the lethal dart embedded itself into a tree trunk some distance away. Morgan looked at Kris in amazement and gave her a sudden, quick hug. This time Kris did not stiffen with the contact but smiled sheepishly down at the little doctor.

"You are something else, do you know that, Kristinia Thanasis!" Morgan laughed, looking up at Kris and shaking her head in disbelief.

Kris scowled playfully and leaned the blowgun back on the hut wall. "Come on, show me where I can clean up and then let's see what there is to eat. I'm starved," she stated and Morgan led her to the stream to bathe, waiting a short distance away until Kris returned scrubbed and in fresh clothes. Then she led the guide over to the lean-to where she surprised Kris with a good meal of vegetable stew made with a chicken broth base of dehydrated soup. For dessert, they ate a banana from the family's garden. They sat side by side leaning against a log upright, watching the men cut up the meat and the women spreading the thin layers of flesh on elevated racks to smoke over hot coals covered with damp leaves. As the grandfather and father worked, they told their women folk and children about the day's hunt, talking excitedly and often pointing in Kris' direction. Occasionally, Kris would laugh at something they said or blush deeply.

Morgan sat quietly eating her meal and watched the interaction with interest. She didn't have to understand the language to know that the men saw Kris as the hero of the day. She smiled with pride and found herself, to her surprise, leaning against Kris' arm. If Kris noticed or minded she gave no indication, so Morgan stayed where she was, enjoying her comfortable backrest. *This is silly*, she mused, watching the Indian family work. *I'm showing clear signs of possession. Taking pride in Kris' accomplishments and feeling a need to touch her when others are talking about her... get a hold of reality here, lady! Kris is your guide. You've known her now for just over a week. She just seems like a close friend. It's hard to remember that she is a stranger.*

Kris sighed, quietly pleased with the hunt and happy to see the family with a decent food supply. She didn't tell Morgan that it had been her who had found the group of monkeys and her who had managed to kill all three of the older males, leaving the troop still healthy and strong. Yet she kind of figured that Morgan realized. The little doctor just seemed to know things about people. She liked the way Morgan showed that she trusted her, leaning comfortably against her for a backrest. This woman was smart, well informed. She of all people had seen, through her training, what drugs do to people and yet she didn't judge Kris or fear her as so many others did. Kris realized that what she was feeling was happy. She hadn't felt really happy in a very long time. *I think that's because you're my friend*, she thought looking down at the younger woman who was half asleep beside her. Kris carefully wrapped a protective arm around Morgan, letting her lean into her side to keep her warm against the cooling night. A friend. That was a surprising but nice thought, Kris decided.

"Morgan?"

"Hmmm."

"Why do you have nightmares?" asked Kris softly. She felt the body so close to her own stiffen then force itself to relax.

"I think, dealing with my own injuries, I never really had time to deal with what had happened that night. I... I... don't know... Anyway after all these years, the police caught the three who had killed Ricky. They came to trial this year and got off on a legal technicality. I just couldn't deal with it. I guess I'd gotten by on being brave and carrying on and all of a sudden I had to face being victimized. I thought volunteering to come out here would help. You know, just getting away... But it hasn't."

For a while the two of them stared into the fire. Then Kris' voice came softly, like disembodied words from a confessional box. "I'm like them. I've done bad things and never really had to pay for it."

Morgan looked down at the arm that curved around her back and reached up and squeezed the long, strong hand that hung down past her shoulder. "I don't know what your past is, Kris, but I do know that you feel remorse. They didn't. You've faced your past. They never will." There was no answer. The two sat in silence once more. Gradually, Morgan's eyes closed.

The family had left the meat to smoke, returning occasionally to poke a hard wood stick under the glowing embers to feed the fire. They sat now in quiet talk around the cook oven as the sleepy children leaned moodily against an adult's leg or played quietly near by. Morgan woke to find herself safely secured to her human backrest by Kris' arm. The night was pleasant and the stars brilliant over head. She could hear Kris' breathing as she dozed beside her. Morgan smiled feeling for some reason remarkably content. She couldn't recall feeling that way in a long time.

Looking up she met the eyes of the little Indian girl. She watched Morgan and her dozing friend with shy fascination. Morgan beckoned with her hand but the welcoming smile on her face froze, suddenly twisting into horror as she looked past the infant and made contact with cold, yellow eyes half hooded as they stared back at her. Instinct reacted, before Morgan had time to think. In a split second, she'd rolled to her feet grabbing a blowgun as a weapon. As the spotted jaguar leapt on the child, Morgan used the blowgun as a fighting stick, cracking it on the back.

The growling animal sprang back with a cat's horrible screech and prepared to leap at the brave doctor who stood over the child, ready to defend her with the thin pole to the death. Suddenly, Kris was in front of her, taking the force of the jaguar's leap squarely against her chest. Down she went into the darkness, a mass of tumbling muscle and blood. Morgan scooped the wounded child up and herded the shocked family into the safety of the hut, gently handing the crying child to her mother. Then she turned to run back to her weapon, determined to rescue her friend from the predator.

There in the dim fire glow stood Kris, the corpse of the jaguar in her one hand and a bloodied knife in the other. Her face was distorted in a hideous expression of pure, vicious joy. Looking down, her cold eyes met Morgan's in a violent impact of challenge then faltered as they recognized the little doctor. Morgan gasped and took a step back and Kris mouth curled up slightly in a cruel smile. "Go help the child," she growled, radiating barely controlled power. Morgan nodded and backed away, then turned and ran awkwardly back to the hut, hearing a moan of rage from the darkness behind her.

The child had a deep claw mark down her back. Morgan worked carefully, very aware of the appalling sanitary conditions around her. She cleaned the wound and was relieved when the old grandmother brought a clay pot of hot water. She cleaned her hands with a disinfectant cream and sewed up the worst cuts after using most of her supply of freezing on the area. Then, she carefully bandaged the wound, talking softly to the child as she worked. The mother looked anxiously at the small doctor and Morgan smiled her reassurance as she gathered up her equipment and with a worried frown went to look for Kris.

She found her sitting, leaning against the post that supported the lean-to again. The dead body of the jaguar was nearby and Kris still held the bloody knife in her hand. Her eyes were far away and the look of despair on her face wrenched at Morgan's heart. Kneeling beside the woman, she carefully pulled the bloody knife from Kris' limp fingers and set it aside. Then she gently moved aside the shredded shirt to see better the damage. Kris' left arm and shoulder had been mauled and blood ran from a bite mark near her neck. A little closer and it could have been her jugular, Morgan realized, and that made her heart jump with fright. She wet a cloth in the hot water and cleaned away the excess blood and then went to work sewing the warrior's wounds, well aware that she had no freezing left to offer her.

Kris watched with tired, disinterested eyes. Occasionally, the eyes would tighten in pain or a quiet gasp would escape her lips but that was all. Morgan talked to her softy, telling her what she was doing and funny stories about things that had happened to her while she was doing her internship. She wrapped Kris' arm and shoulder in a deep layer of bandages and then gave her a shot against infection. Kris watched every move but said nothing. As Morgan leaned back from her work, her soft green eyes locked to confused, hurting blues. On a sudden impulse, Morgan leaned forward and kissed Kris lightly on her damp forehead. "Thank you. You saved my life again." She smiled into those blue depths and saw there for a split second a look of utter relief before the eyes dropped. "Can you help me? I need to get you into the hut," explained Morgan, wrapping an arm around Kris and trying to stand with the weight of the fallen warrior over her good leg.

Kris stood up and swayed a little. Then she took Morgan by the shoulders and looked down at the startled woman in the fading firelight. "You scared the hell out of me," she whispered.

Morgan smiled back at the confused and upset face. "Yeah, well you scared the hell out of me!" responded the shorter woman honestly. Kris smiled nervously and allowed Morgan to help her to the hut. Inside, Morgan fussed over getting her guide settled and then sat between the bodies of the warrior and the little child, caring for them during the night.

When Kris woke in the morning it was to pulsating pain. It took her a few minutes to be aware of anything else. When she was, she found to her surprise her friend sleeping soundly, her head gently resting against the guide's stomach. On impulse, she lifted a weak hand and picked up a lock of the blond hair, playing with it thoughtfully. A slight shifting and she looked up to see sleepy green eyes looking back at her. "Hi," she mumbled tentatively.

Morgan smiled and raised a tired fist to rub at her eyes. "It's nice having a friend that's such a good pillow," mumbled the doctor closing her eyes again. She felt her pillow shake with the soft laughter of the warrior underneath her.

"What if your friend needs to get up and get us ready for the trail?" challenged Kris gently, well aware that she was weak from the loss of blood and wouldn't be going anywhere for a while.

"Not going to happen," explained the little woman confidently, looking sideways at the startled face.

An eyebrow rose. "Says who?" the warrior asked incredulously.

"Said your doctor," smirked the smaller woman keeping her head firmly on the warrior's lap.

Blue eyes looked at her with a mixture of confusion and uncertainty. "I'll be okay, Morgan. I heal really quickly," the dark-haired woman explained.

"Yeah, I know. I've been watching the wound in amazement all night. It almost closed before my eyes. But both my patients are running low-grade fevers and I'm exhausted. So be a good little pillow and lie still, okay?" said Morgan, reaching over to touch Kris' cheek with the back of her fingers to see if the fever had risen any while she had slept. Kris shook her off with a scowl but lay quietly and closed her eyes. For some time Morgan just looked at her.

So Kris let me this close. Major risk and victory, Morgan mused. *I want her. I think I wish I had more experience. Hell! I wish I had any experience!* The truth was Morgan had excelled through school. The child prodigy who never had peers her own age with

37

whom to socialize. And then later, during her internship, when the age differences wouldn't have been as noticeable, there had been that fatal night and afterwards the long struggle to recovery. She was pretty sure she liked women. At least, when Ricky and she had opened up to each other she felt comfortable with that decision. And she was attracted to Kris. *My God! Who wouldn't be?* But this wasn't hypothetical now. She was lying here with her head cradled on the guide's body and Kris was allowing it. It was exciting and very, very scary.

* * * * *

The morning had been a success, Morgan thought. She'd kept Kris in the hut until the sun was well up. Then she had suggested that the guide might want to clean her guns and this kept the woman busy until the oppressive heat of the noon sun. But now she could see definite signs of restless irritability coming on. Morgan sighed, wrapping up the healing wound of the small child and patting her mom encouragingly. These last few weeks, as her tall patient had healed, were teaching her a real healthy respect for the nursing profession! She pasted on a bright smile and walked over to the guide, who was pacing back and forth across the yard like a caged animal. "You want to go for a walk?" asked Morgan looking up at her patient.

Kris looked sulky and murderous. "I've always hated doctors," she rumbled, "and now I remember why!"

Morgan smiled patiently and pulled on Kris' good arm. "Come on, let's put the time to good use. You can tell me what to watch out for now that our canoe is lost and we have to cut overland."

This argument anyway seemed to appeal to the guide's pragmatic mind and Morgan soon found herself trying to keep up with the long strides of the restless woman who was leading them deeper and deeper into the rainforest at a breakneck pace. "Whoa! Stop!" gasped Morgan, flopping down on the ground. Some distance ahead, the guide turned and realized she had lost her company and sheepishly sauntered back, rubbing her nose.

"Ah, sorry, I... ah." She shrugged then froze. "Morgan, don't move," whispered the worried older woman. Morgan froze and stifled a scream as she felt hairy legs crawling across her bare ankle. Looking down, she saw a large, glossy black spider moving up her leg. Kris slowly squatted beside the terrified doctor.

"Tell me it isn't what I think it is," Morgan whispered, feeling more secure now that the capable guide was so near.

"Yeah it is," sighed the warrior as her hand shot out with

incredible speed and knocked the Black Widow spider off Morgan's leg. With her other hand she pulled Morgan up and away, propelling the little woman against her chest. Instinctively, Kris' arms wrapped around the smaller woman, steadying her. She looked down just as Morgan looked up and they shared the warm, sweet air from each other's mouths. Morgan's arms slid up Kris' arms and Kris lowered her head. Then she stepped back suddenly swallowing. "Ah... er... lesson number one," Kris stuttered trying to get hold of herself, "always look before you sit down an..." Kris' lesson was cut short by Morgan turning her around and reaching up on tiptoes to gently brush her lips against the warrior's.

She lowered herself back down again and waited nervously for some sort of reaction from the stunned guide. Then long, strong arms wrapped around her pulling her in close, and a dark head dipped, capturing Morgan's lips in a long, passionate kiss. Morgan's lips parted and Kris entered her, demanding more. Their tongues caressed and Morgan moaned into her warrior's mouth as desire rocketed through her being. The kiss ended leaving them both shaken, Kris holding Morgan tightly to her, her head resting on top of her friend's.

"This can't happen," moaned the guide, rocking Morgan gently in her arms.

"It has," stated the smaller woman, burying her head in Kris' chest.

"You don't know me. I can't bring you into my world. You deserve better, Morgan," argued Kris, her voice filled with pain.

Morgan looked up, wrapping her arms around her warrior's neck. "I've got the best," she answered the argument simply.

Kris pulled her close again. "You ever..."

"No." Suddenly the little woman stiffened and turned away from the warrior. "I'm sorry. That wasn't fair of me. I... I... I mean I guess you know a lot of beautiful and interesting people and I'm... crippled and scarred and..."

Kris wrapped her arms around the shaking back. "You are so beautiful that looking at you makes my body ache with desire. When I'm with you your soul reaches out to me and... and I'm happy. Really, really happy," confessed Kris, hurting at her friend's insecurity. She walked around her small friend and looked into eyes wet with tears. Bending she kissed them away gently then captured Morgan's mouth again in a sweet, tender kiss. "I'm so scared that you'll get hurt because of my past."

Morgan buried her head against the rough, cotton shirt of her friend. "It's like I've always known you. Like I'm coming home."

Morgan realized that Kris couldn't be pushed, that she needed time and space to come to terms with what had just happened. She realized too that her accident and the demands of her training had robbed her of the years when she should have been dating and forming relationships. She was worried if she could please the worldly Kris, if she could handle such emotion with so little experience. "So what was lesson one?" Morgan asked, backing off.

Kris wrapped an arm over her shoulder and gave her a squeeze. Then she pulled away herself and walked over to where Morgan had been sitting. "See this hole in the ground about the width of a finger? That's a Black Widow nest. See the little bit of webbing at the mouth? You got to watch out for them because it's their habit to jump out and attack their prey." Kris demonstrated with the tip of a stick and the angry spider darted out and then scurried back into its hole.

"Hmm," observed Morgan, "from now on I'm circling around three times like a dog before I sit!"

Kris laughed and came over to stand in front of the little doctor. Their eyes met and the guide leaned over cautiously and kissed Morgan's forehead. "It wasn't a dream. Was it?" she murmured into Morgan's soft hair.

"God, I hope not," responded Morgan, hugging her friend to her as hard as she could. They parted and Kris smiled broadly, matching the silly grin on Morgan's face. Then the guide jerked her head towards the path and they set off again at a more moderate pace. The walk was pleasant and Morgan realized just how much the dark guide knew about the world in which she had lived for so many years. Kris talked in her abrupt, concise speech, naming and describing the flora and fauna around them.

At a waterfall they stopped to rest and talk. Kris pointed out to her the wild parasitic orchids that clustered to the tree trunks near by. Under a damp ledge, she showed her a small, black frog with gold spots, the skin of which produced the nerve drug used on the Indian darts. "They call it a miner frog because you find it amongst rocks and it has these gold spots," Kris explained. It was late afternoon when they returned to the Indian encampment hand in hand.

Kris went immediately to inspect the jaguar hide that the women were curing and Morgan sorted through the few remaining supplies to put together a special meal for her...what? Girlfriend? Lover? No, not yet. No. Soulmate. Kris was her soulmate. Somehow the scary, haunted woman made her feel complete. Did Kris feel the same way, she wondered?

They ate under the lean-to, as was their routine. Morgan served

Beef Stroganoff over rice from their dwindling dehydrated food supply. Then for dessert she showed her friend how to spear the pieces of pineapple she had cut up onto a stick and roll them in brown sugar. She held the stick close to the hot embers of the fire to caramelize the sugar before offering the sweet morsel to Kris. Kris opened her mouth and let Morgan feed her and Morgan shook at the intensity of emotion that passed between them. Kris pulled her eyes away and prepared a piece for Morgan. But when Morgan slipped the caramelized fruit into her mouth, Kris leaned forward and kissed her, the sweet fruit passing from Morgan's mouth to Kris'. For a very long time the world stood still for the two of them. Then Morgan blushed and looked away, finding the desire in Kris' eyes hard to bear. Kris made another piece and handed the stick to Morgan, allowing her some time to adjust to the intense love play that Kris had instigated with dessert. "This is excellent, Morgan," said Kris toasting a piece for herself.

"It's better when you roll it in whipped cream after you caramelize the sugar," stated Morgan, popping another into her mouth.

Kris looked up with an evil grin. "Whipped cream, huh? That would certainly have added to the... dessert," she suggested in a silky voice, raising an eyebrow.

Morgan laughed and gave her a push with her shoulder. "No, it just gets very messy!" The body beside hers stiffened and went very still. Morgan turned to look into hurt eyes.

"You've made this for someone before?" Kris tried to ask casually, fighting down horrible images of someone else licking whipped cream from Morgan's lips.

Morgan's eyes danced with laughter. *Kris is jealous! Of me, for God's sake!* "Uh huh, a really good-looking woman whom I lived with for ages," explained Morgan, watching Kris' face harden. She leaned over and whispered in Kris' ear, "My mother."

Relief washed through Kris' body and she laughed at her own insecurity. Morgan gave her a quick peck to the cheek and then started to clean up while the warrior watched her every move. The two of them carried their dishes to the stream and washed them, then stripped down and got into the water together.

Kris forced herself to give Morgan space even though every fiber of her being was demanding satisfaction. Only when they had finished washing did Kris move close and let her naked body touch Morgan's. They kissed, long and intense as their hands explored each other's lines. Then, pulling away with a groan, Kris helped Morgan to where her brace lay and left her to dry and dress while she did the same. With Morgan tucked under Kris' arm, they walked back towards the

41

homestead. Coming on an area of slash and burn agriculture, Kris paused, a strained look on her face as her jaw muscles tightened. She broke contact with Morgan and walked over to some straight green plants growing among the root crops and sat on her heels.

"This is cocaine, Morgan," explained Kris bitterly, pulling off one of the green leaves and idly playing with it between her fingers. "Most villagers have a small plot." The jaw worked and Morgan waited, silent and still, allowing Kris to say what she needed to say in her own way. "My family is very, very rich, Morgan. Billionaires." Kris turned to make eye contact with the doctor who had come to mean so much to her so quickly. "Because of this," she said, holding up the now mangled leaf. "Drug lords, my father... me," she admitted softly, "until I left." She looked away unable to deal with the shock in Morgan's face. "I... I've done some horrible things for my father." Silence. Kris stood, dropping the leaf to the ground through her long fingers. "I'm sorry, I should have told you before we started to... Look it's okay... we don't..." Kris turned away swallowing. This was so damn hard.

Suddenly, Morgan was there, holding her cold hands. "I... don't like this Kris. I... I'm going to have some trouble with it. That you've done... that you could... but I don't think you are that person now. I'm counting on it because I don't want to stop what is happening between us. I believe in you, Kris."

Kris inhaled with a choke and wrapped Morgan to her. "I don't deserve this to be happening," she groaned roughly, holding on tight.

"Shh, let's not deal with it all at once okay? Let's just see how everything works out. Come on," smiled Morgan bravely, patting Kris' arm. Kris smiled shakily and willingly allowed Morgan to lead her on.

"Does this family always live all alone?" asked Morgan, changing the subject to allow Kris to get over some of the deep emotion that had come to the surface when she had confessed to her.

Kris cleared her throat and looked everywhere but at Morgan, her pragmatic mind confused by her actions. *Christ! I've just told someone who I am! After being officially dead for two years! What the hell am I getting myself into? What am I getting Morgan into?* She tried to relax. "Pretty much. Black rivers don't support a large food supply, so the area has a pretty low population density. Here you only find single-family dwelling sites. When we get into Yanamamo territory you'll see palisade villages. It's a pretty dense population there and there is a lot of warfare."

Morgan nodded, wanting to take in as much information as she could, wanting to understand Kris' world.

That night, Morgan rolled out her blanket in the hut to sleep while the eyes of the Indian family watched her. Kris ducked into the hut last and barricaded the doorway before she dropped down beside Morgan. Rolling over on her side, she placed a long arm over the little doctor's body and kissed her on the cheek. Morgan rolled towards her and Kris pulled her into her side, touched when the small woman placed her head on Kris' shoulder and wrapped a possessive arm around her body.

The villagers giggled and one of the men said something to Kris in their language. Kris answered back good-naturedly and the little family laughed wholeheartedly and then settled down to sleep. "What was that about?" muttered Morgan, feeling a little embarrassed.

"Ah, well, it was a little barroom humour, I'm afraid. Guess I'll have to tolerate a bit of that under the circumstance," replied Kris.

Morgan looked up into Kris' eyes. "Explain," she ordered.

Kris blushed. "Ah well, he asked if I was a man now and I told him there was enough of the hunter in me to satisfy you."

For a moment their eyes remained locked, Morgan trying to read Kris' complex and ever shifting mind. Then she snuggled down again. "You'd better be able to live up to that boast, hunter," she warned. She felt Kris' body relax and a gentle, strong hand rubbed her back until she fell asleep.

The next day they left, Kris shouldering a much larger, heavier pack against the wishes of her doctor. They followed the Indian path for some distance into the rainforest and then were forced to cut a path of their own. In the rainforest there was very little underbrush, Morgan noted. The dense canopy a hundred feet above their heads blocked out so much of the light that young plants found it difficult to grow. Only where a mighty tree had fallen did a multitude of plants compete for the exposed sunlight. Even then the fallen tree would often send out its own suckers to reclaim the spot. But the ground was uneven with roots, muddy and covered with dead matter and branches and Kris, in the lead, sometimes had to cut with her machete or toss branches aside to clear a path. If a large log lay in their way or a steep embankment had to be negotiated, Kris would take the packs over first and then help Morgan across. Several times they came to streams in deep ravines and Kris would cut a branch to act as a bridge. The first time, she ran across the log tightrope as if it were flat ground and continued on her way until she heard Morgan's protest.

"Kris, I can't," she had called, unable to make herself walk across the narrow log. She was hot and tired and irritable that Kris was not, but mostly she was angry with herself for giving into her fear. She had stepped out onto the bridge confidently enough, but then she had looked down. The inky water ran in rills, black like the draining blood that night. It was the sound that had triggered the flashback. She had lain waiting to die for a very long time, listening to the icy-black water rushing below. Finally, the siren had drowned the sound, the flashing light washing them with another shade of red.

Kris looked at her friend frozen with fear and frowned. Quietly, she took off her knapsack and laid it on the ground, then walked back over the log. She helped Morgan ease her pack over her stiff shoulders and carried it across to lean against her own. Then she returned for her friend.

"Come on, you can do it," Kris had encouraged, holding her hand out and walking backwards along the log.

Something snapped in Morgan's mind. "No I can't! You God damn show-off!" she screamed and was horrified at the look on Kris' face. It was as if she had taken a knife and stabbed her.

Kris came over and stood a few feet away from Morgan. "Ah, is it okay if I carry you?" she asked awkwardly, nervous in her confusion.

"I... I... It's the bridge," Morgan managed to stammer out. "It happened on a bridge." Morgan turned away, unable to look at the guide.

Bridge? Shit, when she was run over, realized Kris, stepping forward to wrap Morgan in her arms. "Shh, it's okay," she said to the sobbing woman. "I'm with you now. And you're safe." It was a stupid statement, Kris knew, but she couldn't think of anything else to say and she couldn't stand seeing Morgan so upset. *Yeah, safe with you, Thanasis. Not likely, when your life is already forfeited! And then there is the devil in your soul...* Morgan quieted in her arms.

"I can do this," Morgan said softly. "You help me, Kris." Slowly, Kris edged the terrified Morgan along the branch. This wasn't working, Kris thought, and there were going to be lots of these crossings.

Kris led Morgan on until she was in the centre of the make-shift bridge. Then Kris moved close, standing right in front of her with Morgan clinging to her in panic. "Look at me, Morgan," she whispered, placing her hands on either side of Morgan's face. Morgan looked up in fear. "Trust me?" The small woman nodded. "I have only known you for a few short weeks and yet I feel so close to you. I love you, Morgan," confessed the warrior, bending down and capturing Morgan's lips, then kissing her neck until she reached a particularly tasty ear into which she whispered the softest words of love. Slowly, the hands clinging to her body relaxed and explored her arms and back.

Kris kissed her again and again, and then held her tightly.

"Kris?"

"Hmmm?"

"Am I still on a bridge?" mumbled Morgan.

"Ah huh," affirmed Kris.

"Love bridges," sighed Morgan. "Love you." The words shot through Kris like a thunderbolt. *Does she mean it? Can she love me?*

Kris pulled back and carefully helped Morgan the rest of the way off the bridge. But the fear was gone now and she knew Morgan had got past another barrier on the way to recovery. "Thanks," said Morgan, giving Kris a hug. "Sorry, I was rough on you. You're wonderful you know."

Kris hugged her back. "Come on, not too many miles ahead we'll camp." They walked on for a few more hours, the going slow due to the tangled, muddy footing and the intense heat. After a while, Kris stopped by a brown mass the size of a soccer ball that was wedged between two branches. She knew the inquisitive mind of her friend would enjoy knowing about the nest but mostly she was looking for an excuse to let the young doctor rest without embarrassing her. "See this, Morgan? It's a termite nest. They're pretty common in the rainforest. You can eat termites. They're high in protein. It's a good food source if you are running short of supplies on the trail."

"Ugh! You first," said Morgan, sarcastically pulling a face.

"Okay," grinned Kris, enjoying the look of complete shock on her friend's face as she scraped away some of the powdery layers from the nest. Worker termites immediately appeared to repair the damage and Kris allowed them to crawl onto her finger. She then popped the finger into her mouth and pulled it out clean. She chewed and swallowed, smiling happily at Morgan.

"Arrgh, that's gross! I'm never kissing you again, Thanasis! God knows what you've been putting in your mouth!"

Kris raised her eyebrows up and down mischievously. Then she put her finger back up to the nest and let a few termites climb on. She held the finger up to Morgan's mouth. Morgan sighed heavily and rolled her eyes. Then she leaned forward and took Kris' finger into her mouth. Kris pulled her finger out over the warm, soft lips and tried hard to control her baser instincts. "Quick, chew and swallow," she instructed. Morgan did so, pulling the funniest faces as she did. "Well?" asked Kris.

"Sort of herby, leafy... I can safely say that even dipped in fire ant sauce these guys are not going to catch on as a fast food favorite in my neighborhood," groaned Morgan, holding her stomach, rolling her tongue around her mouth and spitting out bits of termite. Kris snorted and passed her friend her water bottle. Morgan took a long, grateful drink and returned it to Kris, who bent her head back and let the warm water drain down her dry throat. When she brought her head back, her eyes met the deep, soft green of Morgan's. Morgan stood on her tiptoes and licked the drops of water from Kris' lips. As she lowered back down, Kris' head followed, capturing Morgan's lips in a long, hungry kiss. "Just as I thought," whispered Morgan mischievously, "termites are one of those meals that needs to be shared."

Kris laughed and resettled her backpack and rifle strap more squarely on her shoulders and then headed off again with Morgan following close behind. "So is it bigger than a bread box?" Kris asked with a grin over her shoulder.

"Is what?" asked Morgan, carefully stepping over some tangled, muddy roots.

"The mysterious plant you are after. Is it bigger than a bread box?" clarified Kris, holding a thorny branch back with her machete so Morgan could get by.

"Nope, not that I have any idea just how big a bread box is. I keep my loaves in the freezer," responded the doctor, getting into the silly game.

"Is it green, yellow, or brown?" asked Kris playfully.

"That's three questions and the answer is yes...to one of them..." And so they went on.

Some time later, Kris suddenly stopped and looked down. Morgan followed her gaze and gasped to see the ground for as far as she could see a seething carpet of ants. "Run!" cried Kris, grabbing the woman by the arm and pulling her forward. Morgan ran as best she could with her damaged leg. But after a short distance Kris realized that Morgan couldn't run far or fast enough. She changed direction, plowing through the bush, pulling the stumbling doctor painfully behind her. Kris didn't stop when she reached the bog but plowed right into the water, dragging Morgan with her.

"Kris!" exclaimed Morgan as her feet sank into the mucky bottom and the green slime of the bog closed in around her shoulders. Kris wrapped an arm around her and waded quickly across, pulling the exhausted woman up the bank on the other side. For a few minutes they sat in the mud and panted. "What happened?" Morgan finally gasped.

"Army ants. They don't stop for anything. We could have got swarmed. Couldn't out-run them, so I had to take us through the bog. They won't cross water. You okay?" asked Kris, reaching out to touch

Morgan.

Morgan looked down at her sweaty, filthy, wet body and sniffed. There was a strong reek of body odor and bog rot. Her leg hurt painfully too, having been twisted and overworked with the run. "Yeah, I'm okay. Do you want to kiss me?" she asked impishly. Kris grinned through her own mud and leaned forward and kissed Morgan gently. "It must be love," Morgan sighed happily and Kris laughed, pulling her friend to her feet.

Some time later, they came to a round clearing in the centre of which was a nicely shaped shade tree. "This is a nice spot, Kris, can we camp here?" asked the hopeful doctor. Her leg was very sore now and she was limping. To make matters worse the heat had become oppressive, the humidity even higher, and mosquitoes were starting to swarm around.

Kris snorted. "No, not here. You see that little tree? It's called a punishment tree. It has a symbiotic relationship with a type of ant. The ant lives in the pith of the tree and in return for the nice house it runs along the roots of the tree and spits acid on any intruding roots. That keeps the competing trees back. This tree doesn't have to grow tall; the ants make sure it gets enough sunlight. The Indians used to take their prisoners to these trees and tie them to it. Then they'd bang on the trunk and the poor bastard would die a horrible, painful death. Watch." Kris walked forward and hit the trunk with the side of her machete. Immediately the trunk was covered with small red ants.

Kris walked back to Morgan who looked up at her in horror. Better get it over with, she thought. She had to know before things went too far. "I've done that to my father's competition to make them talk," Kris admitted quietly, then turned away and walked on, leaving the stunned doctor to follow.

* * * * *

They arrived at a black river that flowed to the Orinoco. Here Kris turned downstream and shortly they came to a lovely spot of open out-cropping. Out of the dense canopy, the air was fresher and a breeze helped dissipate some of the overpowering humidity. Under the sun, the mosquitoes had retreated to some extent too. Morgan cocked her head, aware that something was different. Kris smiled. "Bugs. Once you move out of the rainforest that buzz saw noise that is the billions of insects is less obvious." Morgan nodded. "We'll make camp here," explained the warrior, taking off her pack then helping the tired doctor with hers. "Ah, you can swim here, it's safe," stated the warrior awkwardly, not sure how Morgan was now feeling about her.

Morgan raised a muddy hand and placed it against Kris' chest. "I wish you hadn't been that person. It must be an awful thing to live with, but that's not the person I love. The one I love steps in front of leaping jaguars to protect me and holds me tight when I'm afraid. She's bright and caring and so very capable." Kris hung her head in confusion. She wanted very much to develop a relationship with Morgan but she felt she owed it to her to warn her that she was falling in love with a very evil person. "Hey, want to try something?" coaxed Morgan, pushing back Kris' dark hair affectionately.

"What?" mumbled the warrior.

"Maybe if I washed some of that mud off you, some of the black mood will be washed off too. Want to try?" Kris looked into intensely green eyes welling with compassion and she nodded, getting a smile from her friend. Hand in hand they walked to the water's edge and Kris found an easy place for Morgan to remove her brace and clothes and slip into the water. Kris followed once she was sure Morgan was safe. They sat on the water-smoothed rocks and enjoyed the sensuous feeling of washing each other's sensitized bodies. Washing turned to caressing, caressing to kissing, kissing to passion. Kris hadn't planned it. Hadn't even wanted to move this quick this soon, but her need to be one with Morgan was over-powering when the smaller woman begged into her ear, "Make me yours, hunter. I want to be yours."

With a deep growl of need she picked the smaller woman up and laid her on the hot, smooth rocks. Then slowly, she lowered her cool, wet body down over Morgan. Their mouths moved together in a passionate dance and Kris' hips rocked against Morgan's wet warmth. Kris slowed, fighting for control, willing her needs to wait while she used her hands and mouth over Morgan's curves to bring her to climax. They lay together after, Kris' head nestled close to Morgan's hot centre. After a while, Kris felt Morgan caressing her hair and she slipped her hand up to touch where only a short time ago she had feasted. Morgan arched to her touch, moaning softly. "Morgan, we don't have to go any farther, not if you don't want," stated Kris, fighting the raw desire that was building once again.

Morgan pulled Kris up alongside her until they were eye to eye. "I've waited a long time," said Morgan quietly, "and no matter what happens between us, I want it to be you who takes me first." A hot, aching ball of raw need pooled in Kris' loins and she lifted herself over Morgan and kissed her with all the love and joy with which her heart was brimming. She made love to Morgan. She loved her gently and passionately and in the end she joined with her, feeling her inner warmth and the pulsing of her being as an extension of herself. God it was wonderful! After, she held Morgan in her arms and gently stroked her hair. Kris could not remember when she had felt so at peace, so... whole.

"You okay?" she whispered to her quiet friend.

"Hummm," came the contented answer from between her breasts. "You okay?" asked Morgan with a suddenly worried voice, leaning up to look into Kris' blue eyes. *They darken when she makes love*, Morgan thought. "I didn't... I mean ... you must need..."

"No. Not now. I'm fine. I needed to love you. You deserved my full attention. Thank you, Morgan, that was...the most wonderful gift," Kris whispered, kissing Morgan's lips softly.

Much later they quietly set up camp, Morgan insisting that she was sharing a hammock with Kris. Morgan prepared a meal of rice and smoked meat and Kris returned with some monkey fruit that had fallen from the canopy above. The fruit was so called because it was a favorite food of monkey troops. It was plum size and yellow in colour and the taste was like a cross between carrot and lime. Kris explained that the rainforest provided a wide variety of food but that much of it ripened in the canopy of the towering trees and wasn't easily accessible. Nor was it wise to wander off too far in search of food when trekking from one destination to another.

Once the sun set, the mosquitoes descended with a vengeance. The women retreated under Kris' mosquito net, Kris on her back in the small hammock and a comfortable Morgan draped contentedly over top of her.

The next morning was cloudy and thunder rumbled off in the distance. Kris woke with a pain in her lower back and the beautiful warmth of Morgan's breath against her chest. *Christ! I'm in love!* she thought and a silly grin spread across her face. She softly caressed Morgan's hair, amazed that this gentle, caring soul could love her. "Morgan, love, it's time to get up," she said softly. No answer. She gave the hammock a little bounce. "Sweetheart, come on, it's morning." One sleepy eye opened and looked up at Kris.

"Morning?" came a grumpy question from the still limp form.

"Ah huh," affirmed Kris. She put one arm around Morgan's shoulders and another under her legs, then sat up and lowered her own long legs to the ground, spinning the little doctor so that she now lay in Kris' lap. Gentle arms wrapped around Kris' neck and pulled her down for a kiss.

"Kris, I love you so very much," Morgan stated sincerely.

Kris swallowed a lump in her throat and looked over Morgan's head to the darkness of the forest beyond. "You don't know me yet," she got out painfully, her body stiffening with the fear of losing Morgan.

"Yes, I do. I've been waiting for you all my life. You just don't know yourself yet, my hunter," argued Morgan, hugging the insecure and sad woman closer. Kris held on to her so hard she almost cried out in pain. Then the older woman stood up, carefully lowering Morgan to the ground and bending to strap on her brace while she leaned on Kris' shoulders for support. It was funny. She'd never let anyone do that before. She would have been furious that anyone would think she couldn't take care of herself. She rarely let anyone know she even had a problem if she could avoid it. Yet when Kris absentmindedly just bent to put it on, it wasn't insulting. It was like two married people, relaxed and comfortable with each other.

Kris looked up and their eyes met. For a minute Morgan fell through sky-blue, her heart feeling the hope and pain that dwelled there. Then Kris stood and looked at her, a blush slowly rising in her face. She looked down and from her little finger she removed a ring. Taking Morgan's hand she slipped it on like a wedding band. "This was my mother's. I want you to have it. Yesterday, you gave me a precious gift and... and... I want you to be able to look down at your hand and know that moment will always be the most special time of my life. I... I... I love you, Morgan." Morgan was too moved to utter a word. She threw herself into her lover's arms and held her tight. After a long while, Kris pushed her gently away. "Got to get going. You break camp. I'm going to run down river a bit and see how close we are to the Orinoco."

Morgan nodded, still speechless at Kris' sudden gesture of love. She watched as Kris' trot broke into a run as she disappeared between the trees. Thunder rolled closer and the wind gusted around her causing the forest around to swirl in a green tide of motion. Morgan smiled. *So this is love. Wow!* Then she sighed and turned to neatly breaking camp.

* * * * *

Kris watched from the darkness of the rainforest, a solid lump in her chest, as the three men busied themselves loading the long dugout along the shore of the Orinoco. She knew the canoe. It was one of Fernando's. She couldn't believe that either Fernando or Carlos would have betrayed her. That meant they were dead or worse. The anger that she carefully kept locked in her soul rose, a blind rage that seemed to tap into strengths that were frightening in their power. She would have liked to deal with them here and now but she didn't want to leave Morgan very long.

Where was Rodreque? She knew him well enough to know that he was too proud to let anyone brag that they had killed the warrior. No, he had made her and only he would be allowed to destroy her. That was his way. These were only his stooges. Suddenly, a pit of fear opened in her gut. He'd be doing what she was, scouting around. He'd know by now that they had left the river. He'd have got it out of the Indian family one way or another. Morgan! Turning, Kris disappeared silently back into the forest and as soon as it was safe she broke into a run.

She heard Morgan's voice first, crying out her name in fear. The sound burnt into her heart as she plunged through the forest and rounded the river bend to break into the clearing where they had camped. Morgan was on her back, the powerful man kneeing over her holding on to her fighting arms as he laughed at her. Blood dripped down the side of Morgan's mouth and the nightmare horror in her eyes tore Kris apart. She charged across the clearing with a primeval scream and dived at Rodregue with all her force. They tumbled over each other and separated as they hit the edge of the water.

"Kristinia! I thought I'd left you dead. Daughter of the Beast! You have more lives than a cat!" He smiled proudly, but the smile was cold and calculating.

Kris' face was white and tense with rage. "Kris?" came a frightened question from a small voice beyond the red haze that outlined her vision.

"Meet my father, Morgan. They call him the Beast because he is, and his army of followers are the servants of Satan."

The handsome, coarse man growled a laugh. "Very poetic, my darling. Might I remind you that you are the devil vomited from the belly of the Beast," he hissed. "Ah, but I forgot, they call you warrior now don't they? The poor, pathetic souls who turn to you for help. Do you really think you can wash all that blood off your hands, Kristinia?" he mocked, shaking his head in disbelief.

"No, I don't," stated Kris through tight lips.

"You should have had the sense to disappear, my special one. As soon as I started to hear of the warrior, I knew you were alive. Come back to me. You know you love the power, the blood. I know about the rage you control," he whispered, tapping his own chest, "in here. I have it too. It is what makes the Rodreques great! Come, my Kristinia, admit your hunger."

"I can live with it," growled Kris, shaking with the effort of control. "You want to use me and when I'm no longer of use you will kill me like you had me kill Neil."

The tall, handsome man smiled evilly. "You killed Neil, my beauty. He trusted you to care for him and you shot enough crap into him to explode his heart."

Tears rained down Kris' face and she shook her head slowly. Suddenly, Morgan was there in front of her. "Leave her alone, you bastard!" screamed Morgan reaching back to touch the woman whom she loved. Kris' shaking hands fell to Morgan's shoulders holding on to her for support. The same blue eyes of her lover trapped in a hard, chiseled face widened in surprise and then glowed with an inner delight.

"So, Kristinia, I see you have maintained at least one of your perverted ways," he laughed softly. The eyes ran up the little doctor, so like the ones she loved but without the passion and warmth. "I will enjoy her. Often."

Morgan felt the power of the rage that energized her lover's body instantaneously. It radiated from Kris and burned into Morgan's back. "You touch her and I will destroy you," came a choked voice.

The eyes of the Beast lit up. "But I've already had a nice feel, haven't I, blond one? I was just teaching her some obedience when you arrived."

The air was shattered by a piecing scream and Morgan felt herself pushed clear as Kris hurled herself at her father. A knife appeared in Rodregue's hand just as Kris smashed into him, sending the two of them crashing over the layers of rock. A bloody trail marked their passage as they rolled then parted to stagger to their feet panting. Blood ran down from Kris' thigh.

"You're going down this time, my baby," Rodregue snarled, swinging at Kris' belly with the blade. Kris jerked back. "I thought for sure I'd killed you. I should have known the daughter of the Beast could not be killed by mere bullets!" He swung at her again, this time leaving beads of blood oozing from a scratch on her forearm. Kris shifted her weight and side-kicked the drug dealer in the gut. He roared in rage and dived at her, the two of them splashing back into the water. Kris used the deeper water to her advantage spinning her flexible body behind Rodregue before they broke the surface. She pulled her knife from her belt...

Morgan watched in panic as the two disappeared under the water. Then they torpedoed up and the look on Kris' face was the same as the night she had killed the jaguar. "No! Kris, don't!" screamed

Morgan in horror as the blade in Kris' hand moved across her father's throat in a clean sweep. Blood poured over Kris' arm that held the jerking man and rained into the water. Then she let the now limp body go. It fell face down in the river and slid over the rocks past Morgan and down into the pool below.

Kris quickly washed Rodregue's blood from her body and knife, then limped over to where Morgan crouched crying. *God! Don't let her be hurt, please!* she prayed, her stomach churning in fear. She dropped to Morgan's side. "Sweetheart? You okay?" she asked, earnestly reaching out to place a hand on her lover's shoulder. Morgan cringed back and looked at Kris as if she were a hideous monster.

"Get away! You killed him because of me. You killed him! My God!" sobbed Morgan. Kris reached out again, opening her mouth to explain, but Morgan screamed and curled into a little ball sobbing. Shock washed through Kris' being, ending in a vice-like grip around her chest. All the castles she had been building crashed down into the sand. She swallowed. Then swallowed again. Her eyes turned cold and the mask she so often wore in the past shut her emotions deep inside.

She got up painfully and moved over to their bags. Faint with exhaustion and loss of blood she pushed back the shock and concentrated on finding the medical supplies. Suddenly small, dainty hands were pushing hers away and she lay down and let the doctor see to her wounds. Neither spoke. Neither tried to make eye contact. Kris stared at the corner of Morgan's mouth, bruised and stained with blood. She couldn't take her eyes off it even though the sight ate through her guts.

Morgan sobbed as she worked, her hands trembling and clumsy with the nightmarish horror of the violence that once again had become part of her life. Kris never moaned or moved. Her body was cold and stiff like a corpse. Once done, Morgan staggered to her feet and hobbled to the edge of the forest were she retched out her guts. Then she collapsed into a heap and cried.

For a time Kris lay on the rocks painted with her own blood listening to Morgan's sobbing. Her eyes stared blankly at the grey sky. Then her jaw clamped and with a sneer she forced herself to her feet and walked over to where Morgan huddled.

The warrior grabbed Morgan by the shirt and heaved her to her feet and gave her a hard shake. "Stop it! Stop it!" she demanded and the terrified doctor choked and gasped back her tears. She looked up into the coldest, most murderous eyes she had ever seen and her heart stopped. Kris gave her one more shake. "Shut up! I mean it! Now get your god-damn backpack. We're out of here!"

The rain started shortly after they left. Short, hard downpours intermittent with periods of stifling heat and humidity. The bugs swarmed around, the buzzing driving Morgan almost as crazy as the bites. The bug repellent she put on regularly seemed to attract them more than discourage them. And then there was the silence, like a huge void between them. Kris moved on ahead with an uneven gait, staying barely in sight of the emotionally exhausted Morgan as she struggled to keep up. She didn't really remember leaving camp. Didn't really remember clearly all that had happened after that man came out of the forest. It was all jumbled up with the night of the accident. Ricky had been killed because she had insisted on a walk along the river in the falling snow. They'd decided to cross the bridge and walk up the hill for coffee... they shot him just because of his jacket, just because they'd been driving by... he died in her arms as the car rolled over them... Kris had killed her own father... another death... just because of her.

What had happened between her and Kris? What had she said? Kris had tried to talk to her. Tried to help her. 'You god-damn show-off!' No, that was back on the first bridge. Why was she always attacking Kris? Tears rolled down her face and the stifled sobs jerked painfully in her chest. *Oh God! What have I done?*

They made camp in the jungle. Everything was too wet for a fire. They ate separately in their hammocks, under their nets away from the bugs and each other, chewing on dry, smoky pieces of monkey meat. Morgan choked it down and then lay silently looking at the other hammock some distance away. There was no sound, no movement. It was a very long night.

Morgan was relieved when the sun rose and she could roll out of the uncomfortable hammock. She cleaned up as best she could then looked through the bags to see what she could put together for breakfast. A sound drew her attention and she looked up to see a large, ugly animal the size of a pony advancing on the hammock where Kris still slept. Morgan grabbed a stick from the ground and ran, placing her back to the hammock and facing the monstrous, wild creature, her weapon raised. The grey creature's long snout sniffed the air and it raised a hoof to move closer. Morgan raised her weapon to defend the sleeping woman. Suddenly, the stick was snatched from her hand and the tall guide was at her side. "It's a tapir, for god's sakes. Leave it alone," she muttered angrily. "It's harmless. They eat leaves," snapped the exhausted warrior as she shooed the gentle creature back out of their camp.

"I was only trying to protect you!" snapped the overwrought

doctor.

Kris spun awkwardly and limped back slowly to Morgan, her face cold and hard. "I don't need protecting. I don't need you. I don't need anyone," she snarled. "Get ready. A half day's walk we'll be at the village. Then you can go look for your stupid, mysterious plant," spat Kris, pushing past Morgan and working to take her hammock down. Morgan silently went to pack up, her heart as heavy as lead.

The Yanamamo lived in palisade villages. They were a small people and unlike the last Indians they had stayed with did not wear old European clothes. They barely wore anything in fact. They greeted Kris with an awkward mixture of excitement and fear. She towered over them and scowled, making no attempt to hide her black mood. To Morgan, she barely talked at all, just instructing her where she should put her bag and then hobbling off to talk to the men.

Inside the palisade, the walls were lined with platformed lean-tos, each section seeming to belong to a nuclear family. The women and children did not seem to mix with the adult males unless the male came to them. Morgan sat quietly, surrounded by interested children. She smiled at them and played string games to amuse them but all the while she watched Kris. She was acting strangely, recklessly. Where normally she was quiet, watchful and in control, today, she was loud and aggressive. At dinnertime she came over with food for Morgan after she had eaten with the men. "Kris, what's going on?"

"Nothing."

Morgan ate silently, forcing the ashy yams down that Kris had delivered on a banana leaf. "Please be careful. I can feel... something is not right here," said Morgan softly.

Kris snorted. "Oh yeah, when did you become such an expert on Amazon cultures? There's nothing wrong. Just the usual. The men are going to get high tonight and tomorrow they're going to raid the village up stream. Neat, huh, Morgan? I'll get to kill even more people." She grinned cruelly, looking down at Morgan from where she stood at the edge of the lean-to.

Morgan licked her lips. "Kris, don't do this," she begged, getting up and walking over to touch the taller woman's arm. "For God's sake, Kris."

Kris shook her off in contempt. "I'll do what the hell I want. In fact, I think I'll accept the invitation to join the men in a little hallucinatory drug snorting tonight," stated the warrior, looking over to where the men were preparing the powdered plant and getting out the short blowpipes. "It'll beat reality all to hell," she concluded, pushing forward and heading over the square to where the men sat.

Suddenly, the little doctor was there in front of her. "Like hell you will. Stop feeling sorry for yourself, damn it!" screamed Morgan, punching at Kris. The warrior grabbed the fist and for a second Morgan thought she was dead. Anger vibrated from Kris like radiation. Then her face softened and she pulled the small woman to her, leaning down and kissing her with gentle, hungry caresses. She pulled away and looked back over at the men. "Stay with the women. You'll be safe."

"Kris, please," pleaded the younger woman, holding on to the guide's arm.

Kris' face was emotionless. "Do as I say," she growled softly and pulled away, walking over to where the men sat.

The wood pipe was passed to Kris. She held the end up against her nostril and the man facing her shot a short forceful blast of breath up the pipe. Kris grimaced as the powdered drug smashed against her sinus cavity sending an acute pain into her head. She waited. Soon the world distorted slightly and colours flashed across her eyes. She was slipping into another world. Her brother's world, one she swore she would never visit. She didn't like the way it made her feel. Why was she here? *Oh, yeah, Morgan, who said she loved you and then discovered who you really were. Heart rate up, maybe it will kill me. Why'd she try to stop me? Why'd she let me kiss her? Meant it to be insulting. Hard. Kissed her like a lover instead. Is my nose running? She let me kiss her like a lover? Stupid can't get up so good. Go ask her why.* "Morrrrrr…"

Morgan watched in fear and nervous disgust as Kris allowed the Indians to blow the drug into her system. *Kris, Shit! Don't do this! I didn't mean to hurt you. You're not a monster, but I made you feel like one, didn't I? I never gave you the chance, did I?* She saw Kris stagger to her feet, her unfocused eyes trying to seek her out. "Morrrr…"

"I'm here. Come on, lean on me. Over here, no this way. Okay, just lie down here on the platform. Let me get a blood pressure reading. Damn it, Kris, what have you taken! Here, let me listen to your heart." Warm fingers slipped under her shirt.

"I love you, you know," muttered the high warrior, drifting in and out of consciousness.

"I love you too, Kris. Very much so," whispered the doctor, wishing she had something to give the woman she loved that would help get the stuff out of her system quicker. She took out a handkerchief and cleaned the mucus from Kris' face. Then she did another reading.

56

"Well, well, if it isn't Kris Rodregue, flat on her back and vulnerable! Never thought any man would have seen that!" laughed the coarse, dirty man who had stepped up on the platform to look down at Kris. He laughed and signaled one of the two men with him to pass one of the villagers a sack of goods. The Indian smiled and trotted off.

"It's a trap," whispered Morgan softly as realization smashed in. "Kris, it's a trap!" she yelled, shaking the semiconscious woman's shoulder. The man gave a hard laugh that turned into a growl. Then he stepped forward and started to kick at Kris' body with all his considerable strength. She rolled in a ball groaning in pain. "Your father thought he'd get you but you killed him instead, didn't you? You bitch!"

Morgan leaped up and pushed the man. "You leave her alone, you bastard!" she screamed. The man grabbed her and tossed her aside. With a crack her head hit against a rock forming a fire pit and blackness tunneled her vision. "Kris!" she screamed as loud as she could before vomiting into the cold ashes. Through her semi-conscious state she heard a scream of rage. *Get them Kris*, she thought and blanked out.

Rough, uncoordinated hands were holding her and wiping her face with a damp cloth. She opened her eyes to look into blurry blues overflowing with tears. "Don't die, Morgan," sobbed a slurred voice. Morgan closed her eyes against the pain that shot through her head as she giggled. Some hero of hers. High as a kite and barely able to focus her mind. She sighed and sat up, leaning against her hallucinating friend.

"I'm okay, Kris," she soothed as her lover held her painfully tight in her arms. "Hey, not so tight!" she giggled softly, pulling back a little to see the silly smile on Kris' face. "Did you kick butt, warrior of mine?" she asked, looking to see if Kris was hurt.

"Yup," muttered Kris looking down, her body suddenly tense.

Morgan fought her immediate reaction. "Good," she said instead with as much confidence as she could muster. Kris looked up with a puzzled, disoriented look on her face.

"You're not mad?" she asked.

Morgan looked off somewhere over Kris' shoulder. "I don't like violence, Kris. It really upsets me," she stated, looking back into the eyes of her friend. "And I don't think you do either or you wouldn't have given up the life you led. So I guess if you resorted to violence there must have been a desperate reason to do so," stated Morgan, cupping Kris' cheek in her hand. "When you are feeling better we'll talk about it." Kris smiled and leaned drunkenly back against the

57

palisade wall and Morgan curled into her, her head on Kris' shoulder and her arm wrapped possessively around her waist. Kris smiled and let the colours flash across her eyes and her body relaxed into her lover.

* * * * *

The sun rose into Kris' open eyes. She had awoken a few hours ago and had been content to hold the sleeping doctor in her arms. She'd acted like a fool yesterday and it had endangered Morgan's life and her own. Funny, a month ago, that wouldn't have upset her much. She'd gotten pretty tired of living on the run. But now, now there was Morgan, and everything had changed. She sighed and looked down to see worried green eyes looking up at her. "You okay, hon?" her lover asked.

Kris nodded and smiled weakly, "Yeah, thanks to you. I acted pretty stupid yesterday, Morgan. I'm sorry."

"I acted pretty stupid yesterday too. I'm sorry," echoed the smaller woman. "Can we talk?"

Kris nodded but for a long time neither of them said anything. Then Kris started softly, "My brother had made a deal to turn my father over to the authorities. I didn't know but dad found out. Neil had been getting really bad and I'd been supplying him with stuff so he wouldn't get shit or overdose or anything. I thought I had him convinced to come with me to a clinic for treatment. Anyway, my father, without my knowledge, replaced my supply with a deadly mixture and then let me kill my own brother with a lethal injection."

"Kris, that's awful! It's inhuman!" whispered Morgan in shock, holding on to her hunter tightly.

Kris laughed cruelly. "He was a drug lord. Kindness for him was skin deep and the price of his love was blind loyalty. He never loved Neil and he could see that I was changing. He needed a hold on me, so he got rid of Neil and set me up. Gotta give it to him, the man was smart."

"What did you do, Kris?" asked Morgan, her head in Kris' lap while her soulmate absently played with her hair.

The hand stopped. "After the funeral, I drove him up into the mountains and told him I was going to spend the rest of my life trying to put him behind bars for Neil's death."

Morgan looked up. "That was brave."

"No, that was stupid. He pulled a gun out and shot me twice then left me for dead in a ravine."

"Oh God, Kris! How awful!" moaned Morgan, holding on to her

partner tightly. The hand started stroking her hair again.

"Nothing more than you've gone through. Anyway, a herder found me and took me to a mission clinic. It took a long time but I recovered. I changed my name and disappeared. Mostly, I've worked as a guide when I wasn't trying to find proof that it was my father who killed Neil... Morgan?"

"Hmmm?" came the quiet response.

"About the other day..."

"I know. It didn't matter that Rodregue was your father. You had to kill him because if you hadn't he'd have killed you and then me." Morgan looked up into pained eyes and smiled. "You'd have taken a chance maybe with your own life but never with mine. I'm sorry you had to do it, Kris, but I understand. The other day... it was all tied up with my own nightmares and I couldn't see past that. Please forgive me, Kris. Please," whispered Morgan earnestly.

Kris bent over and planted a kiss on Morgan's head. "Only if you forgive me for reacting to what happened like such a jerk," sighed Kris softly.

Morgan turned her head and caught Kris' lips with her own. "I love you."

Kris smiled down at the woman who was using her lap as a pillow. "I love you, too."

For a long while they sat together watching the village slowly come to life. The Yanamamo stayed well away from them, having witnessed the warrior's rage yesterday and fearing that she might take revenge on them for turning her over to Rodreque's men.

"What happened to those three guys?" asked Morgan, looking up at Kris.

"Took their weapons and I let them run off. I've been under a death sentence for two years now and I'm hoping it's over and I can get on with my life." Kris pulled Morgan closer holding her tightly. "I can't count on that, Morgan. That guy who pushed you, his name is Bogara, Juan Bogara. He was real loyal to my father... I don't know," she trailed off, swallowing hard and pulling Morgan even tighter into her embrace. "If he'd really hurt you. I don't know how I could handle it. Morgan, I can't... I love... I wouldn't have you in d..."

Morgan covered Kris' lips gently with her fingers. "Kris, if my life was in danger, where would you want to be?" she asked, searching the pained blue eyes for the answer she already knew.

"That's different," protested Kris seriously.

"Why?" asked Morgan in surprise, sitting up to look at Kris intently.

"Because you're a doctor and your research helps people and you're just a really nice person. You deserve to have a good life, happiness, and security. Me, I've done horrible things and I deserve what I got and a lot more. I don't want you punished for my crimes," explained the dark-haired woman looking down at a piece of grass that she was worrying between her fingers.

To her surprise, she felt the front of her shirt grabbed by the smaller woman who was brisling with rage. "You watch it, Thanasis. You're trashing the woman I love! And I'm not going to let you get away with it. Kris is gentle, intelligent and caring. And the things she did before were caused by her father's evil influence and went against her kind soul. I believe that, Kris. I really do! Don't you ever pull this stunt on me again! You hear!"

Kris looked into Morgan's forest green eyes in surprise and wonder. "Morgan, I don't know if I am that person you love," she protested.

Morgan wrapped her arms around her insecure lover. "I'm willing to take the chance. I believe in you, Kris. If you tell me honestly that you don't love me anymore, I'll go away, but otherwise I'm sticking to you like glue!"

Kris wrapped her own long arms around Morgan and buried her head into her lover's soft hair. "I'm never going to fall out of love with you, sweetheart. You are more than just my lover and friend. I feel... bonded to you." She pulled back to see how Morgan was going to take that revelation.

Morgan smiled and nodded. "My soulmate." And Kris smiled too.

Morgan settled at Kris' side under her strong, protective arm. For a few minutes they sat in comfortable silence. "Kris, you're not going to take drugs again, are you?"

Kris stiffened. *Well, I guess I had that coming.* "I never have before and God knows I had every opportunity to do so. Yesterday, I thought I'd lost your love," explained Kris fidgeting with embarrassment. "I just couldn't deal with knowing that the person I loved couldn't love me because... I thought, when you saw the devil that's part of my soul that... I just wanted to die."

"Oh Kris! I'm sorry I hurt you so badly. I know what you've done and... and I'm not comfortable with it. But that was your past and I want so very much to be part of your future, if you'll let me."

Kris looked down at Morgan, ice-blue eyes filled with pain and worry> "All I can really offer, Morgan, is one day at a time. My deeds, who I am, what I was, I'm going to have to deal with all those things

60

sooner or later. I can't offer you anything permanent." Kris felt the little body beside her tremble.

Morgan swallowed and blinked back the tears, "Okay, it's not what I want but if it's all you've got to offer then I'll accept it for now." She sat up with a deep breath and looked around. "Do we have to stay here, Kris? After yesterday, I'd just rather be somewhere else."

Kris looked at her wounded lover and felt her heart contract in sorrow. *It's better this way... to be honest with her. Right?* "Sure we can move on, I know a place. You going to tell me about this mysterious plant now?"

Morgan turned around and looked at Kris in surprise. "Kris, I'm so sorry! I forgot that I hadn't told you! What with everything that's happened..." She reached into her knapsack and pulled out a folded piece of paper. "This was in an old journal by a man called Ellburn that I researched," Morgan explained, handing it over to the hunter.

Kris unfolded a Victorian water colour print of a vine. It was identified only by the date it was found and a longitude and latitude reading that were certainly close to this area. She studied the plant more closely. "Cat's Paw," she concluded and handed it back to Morgan.

"You know this plant?" exclaimed Morgan.

"Yeah, you see it around, why?" asked Kris in a disinterested tone.

"It might lead to the cure for cancer," Morgan explained.

Kris looked up to see if her friend was serious. The eyes leveled at her were intense and concerned. "Really?"

"Last year, a group of Indians in North-West Peru were studied by a medical team. They were surprised to discover that there were virtually no signs of cancer in the tribe. The local Shaman said it was because they used a plant similar to this one in their food preparation. Before any follow-up research could be done a fire started by a lumber company wiped out the area where the plant grew. This species," said Morgan tapping the paper, "is very close in likeness. We want to take a look at it."

Kris sighed and looked off into the distance. It seemed to be her day for disappointing Morgan. "Look at these people, Morgan. They cling to life in a world that is just about as hostile an environment as it is humanly possible to live in. They just don't live long enough to die of cancer. They eat healthy, basic food and their world is simply not as polluted as ours. I'm not sure the team in Peru found anything out of the ordinary." She looked up to see Morgan sitting with her head down, playing with the corners of the folded paper. "But you never know I guess. I've never heard of this plant being used by the Indians for anything in particular."

Kris got to her feet stiffly. "Come on, let's get something to eat and then see if we can get a canoe off these people. I think they owe me." Kris smiled, raising an eyebrow and looking mean.

Morgan shook her head and got up with an answering smile. "That's my hunter. Go and kick some butt while I see about trading with the women for some food." Kris moved off happily and for a second Morgan followed her with sad eyes. She knew she loved Kris, but the violence that was part of her life, part of her... that was really difficult for her.

An hour later they were shoving off into the waters of the Orinoco.

* * * * *

After some time of paddling silently down the river, Morgan gave in to her natural instinct to fill in silence with good-natured chatter. "So what kind of a spot do you have in mind for us to set up our field camp in?"

"How about a bamboo lodge with real camp cots and a hot shower?" suggested Kris.

Morgan snorted. "Don't tease the girl here, Kris. I've learned to be happy when nothing living falls out of the tree I'm sleeping under into my hammock! And the simple joy of not finding anything disgusting in the toe of my boots? It makes my day."

Kris' giggle drifted from the stern of the dugout. "Do I detect a degree of sarcasm here, O love of mine? No. I was serious. I know this guy. We go way back. He lives a couple of days' canoe from here. I think from there we will still be in the area where Cat's Paw can be found. What do you think?"

A moment's silence. Then a worried little voice asked, "You go way back?"

Kris grinned delightedly. The woman was jealous! Wow! She really did love her! "In friendship, Morgan. Nothing else. When I first knew him, he was a priest, actually."

"And then he met you, right?" asked Morgan knowingly.

"Nah, He just decided to get away from it all. You know, like Saint Francis."

"He lives with the animals?"

"No, more the animals live with him," responded the dark-haired woman happily.

62

"Great," the petite blond responded, "I knew there had to be a catch."

* * * * *

The day was intensely hot and close. Swarms of mosquitoes buzzed around them, making their journey down river hellish. Morgan placed her paddle across her lap and stuck a hand back into the pocket of her knapsack to pull out her repellent. She saw Kris in the stern raise an eyebrow in amusement as she liberally spread the liquid over her arms, legs and neck in a desperate attempt to defeat the insect air force with chemical warfare. "Okay, I give up! How come you are not being terrorized!" Morgan sighed in frustration.

Kris grinned. "Oh, I'm taking some bites, but they prefer you. Some people's skin odor is more appealing to the insect community than others. I've noted they prefer blondes and don't like muscle. I've never been a popular target. Just not tasty I guess!" the hunter chuckled.

Morgan looked over her shoulder and let her eyes slowly work their way up Kris' body. "I find you incredibly tasty," she whispered, her tongue licking her lower lip. Her teasing was rewarded with a slow, deep blush that rose up Kris' neck.

"Paddle," came the embarrassed response as Kris looked back sternly. Morgan laughed and returned to her job. They continued on all day, snacking on the last of the smoked meat as they went. To stop and let the insects at them would be worse than keeping out in the water. It was a very tired pair who finally pulled into an old clearing late in the day.

"Used to be a village here. Burnt in an attack," explained the warrior in her economical way. Kris gracefully ran along the gunwales and bent to pull the dugout higher on the sand beach. Then she reached to help Morgan out.

"Tribal wars?" asked Morgan, looking around the weedy area.

"No, My men, my orders," stated Kris bluntly, looking down to see how Morgan was going to react. She needed to know. Was Morgan really ready to deal with who she was or should she cut her losses now and end this relationship.

"I'm sorry, for them and for you," said Morgan after a moment's hesitation. Blue eyes met green and then Morgan walked into Kris' embrace. Kris wrapped her tightly to her and buried her head in Morgan's hair. Her heart was beating wildly and she knew Morgan could feel her shaking. *I can't give her up! I can't!* a voice inside Kris screamed and Kris sighed in relief that maybe Morgan was now willing to deal with her violent soul.

"Kris, what is it? What's the matter?" asked Morgan, drawing back and searching the complex emotions in her lover's eyes.

"I... I don't want to lose you," came the awkward confession from the insecure older woman who blinked back tears.

Morgan's heart contracted in pain for her warrior. She reached up and kissed the smooth, hard jaw with a soft, tender kiss. "I don't know how we are going to work out what has happened between us, Kris. Our worlds, our lives, are so different. But I do know that from the moment I saw you on the airstrip, I was drawn to you. I know I love you. And I know I want us to be together."

Kris pulled away and bent to snap off a strand of grass. She looked intently at it as she nervously played with it between her fingers. "Ah, I... I... I don't know if you can handle who I am. You know you've got this fear... I understand... I mean..." She swallowed, trying not to let her chin quiver.

"Yes, I do. I was victimized and I've got a lot of baggage from that night. And I know that if I stay with you I'm going to have to deal with your past," responded Morgan honestly.

Kris sighed. "It's more than that, Morgan," she said, turning to face her soulmate. "I am the daughter of the Beast. There is in my soul an ugly darkness. I was a violent person." Kris searched Morgan's soft, caring eyes and then looked away again. She took a deep, ragged breath and just said it. "I still am. That's why they call me the warrior," she confessed. Silence. Kris' heart contracted in pain and she closed her eyes against the terrifying reality that now faced her. Morgan was going to leave her, just as she had done when she had seen her kill, only this time she wasn't going to come back.

She sensed Morgan shift away and the tears that had been held back by closed eyes rolled down her face. "Kris," said a soft voice and the hunter opened her eyes and looked down to see Morgan standing in front of her. "Hold me," the smaller woman begged. Kris reached out with trembling hands and pulled her lover to her. Sobs racked her tall frame as she leaned her face against Morgan's head.

Morgan held her tight. "Shhh, babe, it's okay. I am in love with a warrior. A brave, caring one. That makes me proud. You know what?" asked Morgan, leaning back in Kris' arms and forcing the upset woman to look at her.

"What?" asked Kris, trying to wipe her face and clearing her throat awkwardly.

"I was so proud of you back in the Indian village. They were bragging about how you had killed the monkeys weren't they?" Kris nodded, unsure where Morgan was going with this because she kinda figured that Morgan would not support the killing of animals. "I suddenly realized I was leaning against you. I was being possessive. Letting the villagers know with my body language that you might have helped them but you were my hero." Morgan looked down and laughed nervously, then looked up to meet the surprised eyes of the woman that she adored. "I can't promise you, Kris, that I'm not going to have some difficulty with the violence. I can promise you that you will always have my love if you are using that soul of yours to fight for the greater good."

For a minute the two opposites searched each other's eyes for acceptance, then Kris smiled and picked Morgan up in her arms. Morgan laughed and wrapped her arms around her hunter's neck and drew her lover's lips down to meet her own.

"So you ever done anything illegal, Doctor?" asked the relieved warrior, cradling her lover in her arms.

"No!" responded Morgan indignantly.

"About time then," smiled the tall woman, lowering her partner with regret. "We need food. We're going to get it by fishing in that stream over there," explained the warrior, pointing over her shoulder as she headed for the forest in the opposite direction. Morgan looked at the stream, then at the warrior going the other way and trotted to catch up with a worried, puzzled frown on her face. Kris was looking at the various trees until she came to one massive grey trunk with old knife scars running diagonally across it.

Kris picked a wide leaf and then looked over her shoulder at Morgan. "Stay back," she ordered and Morgan nodded. Kris used her machete to cut a deep slice across the tree bark. A milky sap immediately ran out and Kris very carefully collected it in the hollow of the leaf. "This sap is really dangerous, so the government has made it illegal to use. But deep in the jungle, many villagers still use it. The sap's chemistry is a deadly muscle paralyzer. You're going to put it in up stream and choke the fish's gills. I'll wait down stream and pick up the larger fish and cut their heads off before the drug can taint the fish's flesh. Okay?"

Morgan nodded. "This is safe, huh?"

"No. That's why it's illegal," pointed out Kris with laughing eyes as she carefully carried her supply of sap over to the stream. "It's going to kill everything in a small stretch of the river and if I don't cut the heads off quick enough it could kill us. I don't ordinarily use this technique but we need food and our fishing gear is probably in the

Atlantic Ocean by now. Wade out," ordered the hunter.

Morgan took off her boots, socks and brace and limped awkwardly out into the stream. Kris carefully passed her the leaf. "Don't let any of it get on you," she warned as she ran off down steam. A voice floated back, "Okay, bend forward and just let the stuff drip into the water." Morgan gingerly followed the instructions and watched the thick, milky substance dissolve into the stream. Within a short time the bodies of fish started to float to the surface. They drifted like tug boats around the bend and Morgan could hear Kris splashing about. She made her way to shore and carefully dropped the leaf upside down on the ground. Once she had her brace and boots back on she buried the leaf under some dirt. Then she headed down to the beach where she could hear Kris working away. Seven nice sized fillets lay on a rock and Kris was busy building a smoky fire. Morgan flopped down beside her lover and their eyes met. "Fortunately for you, hunter, my hunger is far greater than my conscience about the stream community at the moment."

Kris smiled as she looked back at the fire. "I picked that spot because it was close to where the stream runs into the river. The river will quickly dilute the substance so that it is harmless. We really didn't do that much damage to Mother Nature. I'm making the fire smoky to keep the bugs away. You can take your pick, stay up wind with the bugs or down wind in the smoke." Morgan got up and moved over closer to the smoke and Kris laughed.

That night they again shared a hammock. "Kris? You can explain now," remarked Morgan, getting comfy on top of her long suffering warrior whose back was taking quite a beating in the name of love.

"Spl'an what?" mumbled the tired hunter.

"Explain why you needed to have that talk with me today and not wait until we were at your friend's place."

"Oh," responded Kris guiltily. "Am I that transparent?"

Morgan snorted. "Only to me, my love. Now the truth, please."

"It was Peter who kinda headed me off on the right track. I'd been wounded pretty badly in the attack and my men left me for dead. Glad to get rid of me," sighed Kris sadly. Morgan kissed her cheek softly and the warrior went on, "I tried to paddle down stream but I must have passed out. Anyway, I drifted down near Pete's. He recognized me but took care of me in spite of that. He tried to convince me I could be a different person. He sowed some seeds that took a while to germinate. Since then, well, I've helped him out a few times with villages that were having problems with drug dealers and terrorists. You know."

Morgan hugged Kris tightly. "Yeah, I know. You're risking your life to help the underdog. I am so proud of you and so terrified for you, Kris," confessed Morgan.

"I've got a lot to pay off, Morgan," Kris explained.

"I know," mumbled Morgan, burying her head into Kris' shoulder and wrapping her arm possessively around her lover as she drifted off to sleep.

By noon the next day they had arrived at Pete's compound. It was an area of about an acre of land cut from the rainforest and consisting of a number of huts on stilts similar to the ones back at Los Amazonos. Morgan smiled. Was it only a few weeks ago? It seemed like years and several life times ago. She remembered how primitive that lodge had seemed and now one nowhere near as big or well equipped looked positively civilized! A month ago she couldn't have imagined having a sexual relationship with someone she barely knew. Now, her heart and soul belonged to the tall, dark and incredibly complex woman who steered their dugout to shore.

Kris ran forward on the thick, wood sides of the hollowed log and jumped to shore. She pulled the craft higher on the beach as if its heavy, cumbersome weight was nothing. Morgan moved forward, bent over so that she could use her hands for balance on the wet, slippery wood. At the bow she straightened and reached out to Kris who swung her out of the canoe and into her arms. She looked up into Kris' serious face and smiled.

"What are you thinking about?" inquired her lover, raising an eyebrow as she looked down at the sparkling green eyes and strawberry blond hair that always delighted her.

"I was thinking about a moody warrior and prickly doctor arguing about whether I was going to be a complication or not," Morgan laughed, reaching up to stroke the strong planes of Kris' cheek.

The corner of Kris' mouth rose in her mini-smile that Morgan had come to find very adorable. "Guess I was right, huh?" teased her hunter.

They both broke into wide grins and Morgan slapped Kris' stomach playfully. Then she looked down and away from the suddenly intense, hungry look that appeared on Kris' face. *Oh God! I want her*, she thought and then gasped in horror as she pulled Kris up off the beach to the safety of the grass embankment above.

Kris laughed and put her arm around Morgan, looking down at the immense Cayman that lay sunning on the beach. "It's okay, Morgan. Meet Katie Cayman. She's one of Pete's "friends"."

"Oh boy," Morgan muttered, her hand over her heart.

Kris jumped down to the beach and began tossing bags up to her. "Pete found her caught in a trap as a baby. You know it's her because she is missing part of her right, front foot. He swears that she is as passive as the family dog. But my advice is keep a safe distance. I think she is just well fed and so doesn't bother attacking visitors. One of these days some poor sucker is going to show up when Katie feels like a snack and then I'm afraid it's going to be ugly," explained Kris as she carried the last of their bags up the bank.

Morgan gave a weak smile and turned to look around. "Where is your friend?" she asked.

"Over behind the power shed with his gun trained on us," stated Kris' matter-of-factly. "He's as blind as a bat without his glasses on, so he doesn't know it's me."

Morgan closed her eyes and shook her head. "You know, Kris, my world is kinda dull compared to yours. Most of my friends just look through the security eye or use an intercom system. In fact, a lot of them just open the door and say hi!"

Kris grinned and put her arm around the petite woman. "Yeah? Wait till you meet Walrus," commented Kris as they headed towards the power shed.

"Walrus?" asked the surprised doctor, looking up at the handsome profile.

"Ah huh, he and I go way back. He's been known to greet me with a lit stick of dynamite. Of course, I did cut his ear off in a bar room brawl and he's still a little sensitive about that."

"Kris, I don't want to know," stated Morgan, sighing and shaking her head at her lover. Kris looked down and smiled warmly, giving her soulmate a reassuring squeeze.

"Stop right there," came a gruff voice from the shadows of the power shed. The barrel of a rife peeped out around the grass hut.

"Pete, it's Kris Thanasis," announced the hunter with a sigh.

"No, it isn't," came the grumpy answer.

Kris looked suddenly worried and pushed Morgan behind her. "Pete, it's me. What's the problem?"

"Thanasis don't touch no one," came the knowing response. There was an awkward silence into which Kris cleared her throat. She blushed deeply and rubbed her ear in embarrassment. "Yeah, well remember when you said that some day I was going to fall hopelessly in love and make a fool of myself acting like a love-sick puppy?"

Silence. "Yeah," at last came the response.

"Well, it's happened," stated Kris, reaching back to make contact with the smaller woman who was giggling behind her.

Out stepped an old man with a two-day growth of bristly white hair dressed in only baggy, dirty shorts. His head was bald and his eyes a milky brown but the most amazing thing about him was that he was blue! From head to foot his entire body was stained a brilliant royal blue!

He came closer until he could see through squinted eyes that it was indeed Kris. Then he gave a big, toothless grin and engulfed her in a bear hug, the barrel of the rifle pressed right under Kris' chin. Kris grimaced and pulled the rifle away from her friend, "Give me that before you put a hole in our friendship," she muttered, stepping back. "Pete, I want you to meet my soulmate, Doctor Morgan Andrews. Morgan, this is my old friend Father Peter Cummings."

Pete hopped over and gave the surprised Morgan a big hug. "Well, the Lord works in mysterious ways! Imagine an ugly savage like you getting hitched up with a pretty little thing like this. Honey, has she been honest with you? Do you know about Adam?"

Kris stepped between the two of them and gave Pete a dirty look. "Don't even go there!" she warned and Pete shrugged good-naturedly. "Is it okay if we have the cabin?" asked Kris.

A look of sheer devilment came into Pete's eyes. "That depends. Did you make her an honest woman or are you two livin' in sin?" he asked with righteous dignity.

Red rose up into Kris' face and her hands curled into fists. Pete just stared back with a comical look of stubbornness on his face.

"In case you hadn't noticed, Peter," the hunter said between clutched teeth, "we are two women and the fucking church establishment frowns on what we are." Morgan moved forward and wrapped her arm around Kris, rubbing her back reassuringly.

Peter smiled. "You using that as an excuse not to do the right thing?" he asked accusingly.

"No!" snapped Kris.

"Good. Stow your gear. We'll get you hitched directly after we eat," ordered Pete as he walked away.

Two completely shocked women stood and watched him go. As he walked he raised his arm and a green parrot flew out of a nearby tree and landed on his hand. He gently lowered the bird to his shoulder where it perched happily as he climbed the stairs and disappeared into the cookhouse.

Kris turned and looked down at Morgan, a look of shocked wonder on her face. Morgan on the other hand looked up in annoyance. "Who is Adam?" she inquired, poking Kris in the chest.

A bright red blush crept up Kris' face. "Ah, well... let's go get our gear," mumbled the shaken warrior.

Morgan grabbed her arm and for the first time looked at Kris with real concern and insecurity. "Kris, are you married or something?" she asked in a soft, hurt voice.

Kris looked down at her feet and fidgeted in embarrassment as fear gripped Morgan's heart. "No, nothing like that, Morgan. Adam is a... friend of Pete's. He thinks he's... well in love with me," stammered Kris awkwardly.

"Are you in love with him?" asked Morgan in a shaky whisper. Kris went even redder. "Well?" asked Morgan desperately needing to know.

Kris looked up in shock. "Oh course not! Damn it! Adam is a monkey!"

There was silence and then Morgan broke out into gales of laughter as Kris stood there in embarrassed silence. It finally ended with Morgan draped in Kris' arms for support, wiping her eyes on Kris' shirttail. "It isn't funny," remarked Kris with some dignity. "The damn thing keeps attacking me." The laughter started again and Kris was forced to hold the collapsing Morgan in her arms. "I repeat, it is not funny," muttered Kris with a sigh. Morgan nodded her head in agreement, the tears of laughter still streaming down her face.

Between bouts of laughter, the two managed to get their cargo transferred to a small hut. To Morgan's delight there was an old, rusty, double bed with a saggy, musty mattress. Outside, close to the edge of the rainforest, was an outhouse. Back behind Pete's house there was a bathhouse where water could be heated in an old boiler so that a hot shower or bath became an added blessing. The place was heaven.

While Morgan got their bags reorganized and pulled out the items that were going to need washing, Kris went and fired up the boiler. Then the two of them stripped down and stood under the hose that gravity-fed the warm water down on them. It was, Morgan concluded, the nicest shower she had ever had. Back at their hut they changed and lay together in the hammock on the small porch.

Kris' mind was a mass of conflicting views and emotions. Only two days ago, she had made it clear to Morgan that her life could still be in danger and she could offer her lover only the moment. Shit! They came from worlds miles apart both physically and in experiences. There was no common ground for them to build a life. And yet Pete's mad insistence on marrying them had been like an explosion that blew her pragmatic mind apart. However crazy the concept, Kris wanted this! She wanted Morgan in her bed, and in her life forever. She wanted commitment. She wanted a house, curtains, a damn pet and she wanted it with Morgan.

"Morgan?"

"Hmmm?" responded the little doctor, turning to kiss Kris' throat.

"Will you marry me?" she asked nervously, looking down at the woman in her arms for some sign of hope.

"Marry you?" asked Morgan in surprise, sitting up and looking into Kris' eyes.

Kris nodded seriously. "I love you, Morgan. I want to make a life somehow with you. Will you marry me?" Kris asked again, her heart in a vise-like grip of anxiety.

Kris listened to the far away chirping of the tropical birds as the seconds passed. Morgan looked deep into her eyes, searching their blue depths. What was going on here? Was this some kind of cruel joke? No, Kris wasn't like that. But she had said...

"Yes," came the simple answer. And two silly grins spread across their faces as Kris pulled Morgan into her arms for a tight hug.

They lay there for awhile, Kris' arm wrapped around Morgan who drew figure eights gently on the v of tanned skin between the collars of Kris' shirt. Morgan gave a soft giggle. "What's so funny now?" asked Kris dreamily. She was in a state somewhere between shock and bewilderment at the course of events that had brought her to this moment.

"How am I going to explain to my middle class family that I married a gay ex-drug lord, whom I barely know, in the middle of the Amazon Basin and that the priest was blue and the witnesses were a green parrot and a Cayman called Katie."

Kris giggled softly. "Well, at the moment, it's one of the few places in the world where it could happen at all! And the parrot's name is Pecker. You worried about telling your parents about us?"

"Only the part where I tell my United Church family that I was married by a Catholic priest," giggled Morgan.

Kris' eyes got big, "Do you mean to tell me I'm marrying a heathen?" she asked in mock horror. Morgan nodded, her eyes sparkling with merriment. Kris considered. "Well, okay, but our kids have to be raised Catholic," mused Kris and Morgan punched her.

"Ah Kris, I know I'll probably regret asking, but just why is our priest blue?"

Kris looked down at the golden top of Morgan's head as she snuggled into Kris' chest. "He couldn't find a tux on short notice?" she offered and Morgan gave her a dirty look. Kris smiled. "Actually it's a sap from another tree. When you first take it out it's clear but if you rub it on your skin, after about ten minutes it turns blue. The local Indians say that it keeps the mosquitoes away."

Morgan sat up. "Keeps the mosquitoes away! Why didn't you tell me? Where do I get this stuff?" asked Morgan excitedly.

Kris rolled her eyes and sighed. "It doesn't wash off, Morgan. Once it's on it is days before it eventually wears off."

"Don't care!" stated Morgan stubbornly.

Kris raised an eyebrow and looked at Morgan in mock anger, "Well I do! I'm not spending my wedding night with the bride's something blue being her entire body!" growled Kris and Morgan laughed delightedly.

* * * * *

Dinner was a merry affair. Pete turned out to be a basic but competent cook. They could choose from platters of fish, meat, fruit and yams and wash it all down with the local suds called Polar Beer. Pete kept them in stitches with stories about his animals, with which he appeared to have a love/hate relationship. He finished by telling a few tales about Adam's courtship of Kris that had the doctor in tears and Kris red with embarrassment.

"Lucky for you, Kris, old Adam has finally found a troop to join or I wouldn't know who to marry you off too!" laughed the outrageous priest. Then he turned and looked at Morgan. "Now, doctor, you go get yourself pretty while I have a word here with Kris," ordered Peter, suddenly serious. Morgan looked combative but Kris reached out and placed a reassuring hand on her knee and she nodded and got up. She gave Kris a quick kiss before heading back to their hut.

The priest sat for a while in silence, playing with the moisture on his beer can. Kris waited. "She's a bright young thing, that's for sure," he commented.

"Yes, she is," responded Kris seriously.

"I got a radio message from Los Amazonos Compound a few days ago," revealed Peter, looking at Kris. He saw her jaw set in anticipation of bad news. The only sign of emotion in her still features was the movement of neck muscles as she swallowed. *So she knows,* he concluded. "The Beast roughed up Carlos pretty bad. Fernando said he'd be all right though." Kris' head dropped, hiding her features. "Carlos didn't talk but it didn't take much guess work for them to figure out you'd gone down river. He knows you're alive, Kris and he'll take you and Morgan out when he comes. You know that, don't you?"

Kris looked up. "He's not coming, Pete, ever," she explained.

Pete's eyes grew large in surprise. He reached over and covered Kris' hand. "If you need to talk..."

Kris shook her head. "He attacked Morgan. We fought. I won. It's over, I hope, although we've had a run in with Juan and his two pet goons since," explained Kris.

Peter nodded. "You'd do just about anything for that little one, wouldn't you, warrior?"

The woman looked up, her blue eyes brilliant with their unearthly blue glow. "No limits, Pete, I would do anything for her," she replied honestly.

The old priest nodded. "Marriage, isn't about a legal document or the politics of faith, it is about making a commitment to someone else's life. You can't go into a marriage thinking about what it's going to give you. You gotta be thinking how you can change to accommodate that different being in order to give her happiness. Marriage is about giving, not taking. You've been a loner all your life, Kris, can you be a good partner?"

Kris watched a moth battle to get closer to the flame within a glass hood. "I know that I can't live without her. I know when she hurts I hurt. I... I... I've got to control my... violence. It scares her. She was involved in a gang attack against her boyfriend. He was killed and she was badly hurt." Kris' eyes moved to Pete's. "You saw the brace?" He nodded. Kris swallowed and looked at the table, flicking bits of crumbs to the floor. "I don't know if I can be what she needs. I hadn't planned on this, it just happened. I just need her, Pete."

"Need? That's taking, Kris. What are you willing to give?"

Kris looked up sharply and answered with fire, "Everything. Whatever it takes. I want this more than life itself, Father. I want to have a life with Morgan."

Peter smiled and nodded, patting Kris' long, powerful hand. "Good girl. She's a damn lucky woman to have caught you." He chuckled at Kris' blush. "I'm going to have a talk with the other half now. Why don't you wait for us in the chapel?" He got up, leaving the emotionally drained warrior sitting at the table.

Morgan brushed her hair absentmindedly, worried about what Peter wanted with Kris. Did he understand how fragile a person the warrior was? How emotionally insecure?

"Hey, anyone home?" came a familiar voice.

"Come in Pete," responded Morgan, putting down her brush and going to meet the grizzly old priest.

"So you sit down now and we'll have a little talk," said Peter, pointing to the bed. Morgan sat on the edge, suddenly nervous. Had Kris got cold feet? After all, only two days ago she hadn't wanted to commit to anything more than one day at a time in their relationship. Peter pulled up an old wood chair and sat down. "You love her?"

Morgan looked him straight in the eye with a clear gaze, honesty written all over her face, "Yes, I love her. I'd do anything for her. She is everything I want," stated the doctor.

Peter's eyes narrowed. "What if she doesn't want you?" he asked shrewdly.

The little body hunched as if she had been hit. For a moment there was silence, then a very shaky voice responded, "Then I'd let her go. But life without her... I... I..." Tears welled in the blond woman's eyes.

Peter looked alarmed and moved over to wrap an arm around Morgan. "Sweetheart, it's okay. That woman loves you near to distraction. I just want to know how you feel about her."

Morgan sniffled and looked up at the priest with renewed hope. "I love her. I can't explain it. It's not rational. I just know that without Kris, I'm not whole."

Pete looked at the floor for a bit and then sighed. "She's got an awful sinful past, Morgan. If you commit to her, you have to accept some of the responsibility for the consequences of her life. That's not very fair to you."

"Kris won't ask anymore of me than I'm willing to give. But I can tell you, Pete; there is nothing I wouldn't do for that woman. She's gone through hell and she deserves some love and happiness in her life," responded the petite doctor determinedly.

Peter looked deep into those passionate eyes. "What about what she is? You can't change that, Morgan. She is a very dangerous individual. I think sometimes she is not quite human."

"Then you don't know her like I do because she is the most loving and loyal human I have ever met. She is so vulnerable and she needs such tender care. I know she is violent. I know I can't change her nature, but I can help her follow the path of good that she has started down. And I can make sure she is emotionally safe while she is out there facing the world alone."

Peter wrapped an arm around the remarkable young woman. "Honey, I gotta tell you if I wasn't afraid of being pummeled by a certain warrior and then hit by lightning from the Almighty, I'd marry you myself! Come on, let's get the two of you hitched."

Kris paced back and forth in front of the table that was the altar in the small bush hut. She noted that fresh orchids were sitting in a bowl. At another time she would have appreciated their beauty but now, now all she could think of was whether Morgan loved her enough to make a commitment to her. Would Pete make her realize that her violent soul would make it too painful for Morgan to have a life with her? For the third time, she headed for the door to go find Morgan. Then she turned back again and stormed back to the altar to wait.

Suddenly, there was the gentle scent of sweet grass and sun baked herbs and she turned to see Morgan entering the small hut with Peter behind her. To her surprise, Peter was wearing a black robe and his collar. Pete led Morgan across the room and placed her hand in Kris'. Then he stepped behind the altar and bent his head in prayer.

After a few minutes, he looked up to see the two women still standing transfixed in front of each other. "Kris Thanasis, before me and in this house of God, express your commitment to this woman."

Kris smiled softly, looking at the woman she loved. She stepped closer and took both Morgan's hands. A woman of action not words, she bent her head to brush her lips gently over her soulmate's. "I love you. Please marry me, Morgan. I want to spend the rest of my life making you happy," whispered the warrior.

"Morgan Andrews, what is your commitment?" asked the priest.

Morgan's eyes opened dreamily. "I love you, Kris Thanasis. Your passion, your gentleness and your warrior nature. I want nothing more than to be your partner."

"Kris, do you take this woman to be you partner and care for her and support her through the joy and the trials of life?"

"I do."

"Morgan, do you take this woman to be your partner and care for her and support her through the joy and the trials of life?"

"I do."

"Then I bear witness that before God you have expressed your love and have joined as one. Please share a kiss to seal your everlasting commitment of love."

Morgan slid her hands slowly up Kris' chest and Kris lowered her head until their lips touched and then the warrior pulled her partner to her as they let their lips express the emotion that each was feeling.

"Well congratulations, Morgan," beamed Peter, leaning forward to peck the beaming doctor on the cheek. Then he turned and shared a look with the warrior.

They wrapped their arms around each other and Kris whispered into his ear, "Thank you, for giving me my soul back." Pete patted her on the back and pulled away.

"Come on, you two. I think this calls for a bit of a celebration!"

* * * * *

Kris had woken early and now lay staring up at the thatched ceiling of the hut, her arm wrapped around the small doctor whom she had taken as a life-long partner. Her mind was in such a state of shock that she had not been able to gather any coherent thought for a very long time. It was all so wonderful and absolutely bloody terrible at the same time. What had she been thinking of? What had she done? Christ! Morgan moved slightly in her sleep, snuggling closer, and the warrior automatically wrapped her tighter in her embrace. She smiled at the ceiling. *I'm in love and the one I love has made a commitment to stay with me through life!* The smile broadened into a particularly silly looking grin as she turned to wake Morgan with kisses moving from tender to passionate.

Later, Morgan lay beside her lover, absently, running her fingers over the layers of muscle in Kris' forearm. *Wow! I married this person. How am I going to explain this back home? Can I go home? It's not a legal marriage or anything and yet for me it binds me to this woman closer than any blood link could. Does she feel the same? I hope so because I don't think I could live without her.* Morgan looked up to meet deep-sated blue eyes. "Afternoon, my warrior," Morgan whispered, leaning forward to plant a gentle kiss on Kris' lips.

The dark-haired hunter smiled back, wrapping an arm around Morgan and pulling her in for a long kiss. "Mm, good afternoon, my special one," murmured Kris in a deep, husky voice that sent shivers to the core of Morgan's being.

"I was lying here trying to come to grips with what I've done," Morgan said, idly tracing patterns across the contours of Kris' shoulder. The body beneath her touch went still.

"Y... y... you don't have regrets this morning, do you, Morgan? Did I hurt you? I... I'm stronger than most people... I might have... did I scare..." stammered the insecure being that lay within the warrior.

"Shhh, my hunter, shhh," reassured Morgan, feathering kisses on Kris' tense lips. "You would never hurt me. You were strong, and passionate, and demanding and ever so caring."

The tall body beneath her relaxed a bit but worried blue eyes still watched her intently. "You do want to be married to me, don't you, Morgan?" came the shaky question.

Morgan buried her head deep into the soft curls that cascaded over Kris' neck. "Very much so, my love. I am just... I guess starting

76

to realize what it all means in terms of a life with you. We never discussed it. We just sort of moved on impulse."

Kris sat up and swung her legs over the bed, continuing the smooth motion until she was on her feet. She walked over to the small table and poured herself some warm water from the flask there, drinking it like she was tossing down a strong shot. Then she turned and looked at Morgan, who was watching her with worry. "Impulse! Impulse! What, like getting drunk and ending up in some sleazy motel somewhere?" The glass in Kris' hand shattered and blood and shards dropped like rain.

Morgan leaped from the bed and grabbed a towel to wrap Kris' hand. "Leave it, damn it!" growled Kris, pulling her hand away.

"No!" snapped Morgan, grabbing the arm and looking Kris in the eye, "That is not what I mean at all! Now give me your hand." Stiffly, Kris moved her hand back and Morgan gently wiped it clean, checking for any glass and then wrapping it in the towel. "Come over here," she coaxed, pulling on Kris' arm. Morgan sat on the edge of the bed and patted the spot beside her. After a moment's hesitation Kris joined her.

Morgan turned and looked Kris in the eye, holding her chin with her hand. "Now you listen to me, warrior. I love you. And that is forever. You got that! I am not insecure about my love or my decision to take a vow of loyalty to you. I just need to talk to you about where we go from here. You understand?" she demanded.

Kris swallowed and looked down. "You scared me. I... I... want this to work. Yeah, I woke up this morning thinking, oh shit, now what?" Morgan chuckled and Kris gave a nervous smile. "I guess we need to find your Cats Paw samples first. That'll mean we'll have to go back to the States. There are things here... I might have to come back..."

"We might have to come back," corrected Morgan firmly.

"No. I'm not pulling you into the shit of my past life. You are a new beginning. I don't want you to be part of the... violence again," stated Kris, plucking at the bloody threads of the towel moodily.

"Too bad, Thanasis," stated Morgan with determination. "I married a warrior. My choice. And that means I have to find a way to live with what you are, not try to change you."

Kris' jaw tightened in anger. "Yeah, and what I am won't let me expose the one I love to danger."

Morgan smiled and rubbed a knuckle over Kris' tight jaw. "Yeah, well what I am won't let me leave your side if you are in danger! So I guess we'll just have to compromise and let me have my way," responded Morgan with a confident smile.

Blue eyes snapped up and bore into green. Then Kris laughed. "This is going to be one fiery marriage! So am I going to just sit here and bleed to death or are you going to stitch this hand?" asked Kris.

Morgan sighed. "Seems like I'm always patching you up, hunter!"

* * * * *

For a few weeks, they hiked around the nearby rainforest looking for the Cats Paw vine without success. If possible, they returned to Pete's place each night, otherwise they would camp out. Kris was delighted at how quickly Morgan had learned to understand and respect the world around her. She would only have to be told something once and she would remember. Now, a few months after her arrival in the Amazon Basin, she could identify many plants and animals and was learning the uses of the vegetation that grew in the area.

Kris smiled softly, remembering the day that they had found the Cats Paw vine growing around the trunk of a fallen tree. They had collected samples of roots, leaves and stems and carefully packed them in Morgan's field kit. Kris realized pretty quickly that they had a problem as they turned to head back, but she didn't see any reason in worrying Morgan until they were safely back at Pete's. There she revealed to the disgusted doctor that they had picked up wood ticks from the fallen log.

They stripped down and sure enough the once barely visible boring creatures were now quite evident as tiny black spots, their bodies now engorged on the blood of the victims they were burrowing into. "Gross!" exclaimed Morgan but Kris just shrugged and smiled, knowing there were far worse fates in the Amazon. She got a pair of tweezers and carefully pulled the ticks one by one out of her friend, being careful to get the heads that were embedded under the skin so that tropical ulcers did not form. Then she spread on an antibiotic cream. Once finished, Morgan had seen to Kris' treatment and the medical exploration of Kris' body had led to far more pleasurable pursuits.

"You're staring at me," remarked Morgan, giving her soulmate a smile as she looked up from writing in her field journal. Although they had located plenty of Cats Paw now, Kris was continuing to provide Morgan with many different types of plants that were used by the Indian people. Morgan had carefully pressed, identified and recorded every example in her journals for future study.

Kris smiled back. "My prerogative," stated the warrior possessively. "I was thinking that you are really starting to know your way around this part of the Amazon Basin," Kris clarified.

"Are the other areas so different?" asked Morgan, leaning forward and paying close attention. She had learned quickly that Kris was a storehouse of information on the rainforest. And she also knew to take advantage of the rare opportunities when the hunter relaxed and felt talkative. They were few and far between.

Kris considered. "Well, rainforest is rainforest. On the surface it's much the same wherever you go. But there are specialized life forms that create distinct regional differences in the flora and fauna. The Amazon is sort of ridged like an old washboard. Those elevations divide the basin into very different areas. That's why clear cutting is such a tragedy because once an area's gone, it's gone forever."

"Like the mystery plant in Peru." observed Morgan.

"Yeah, like that," agreed Kris, putting away the rifle she had been cleaning as she sat on their saggy, old bed. She knew Morgan would not come close until the weapon was gone and she had got so that she needed Morgan's touch like her brother needed his drugs. Love. Love was a wonderful form of vice, Kris thought.

Morgan got up and came over to sit beside Kris, allowing the warrior to pull her close into her arms. Kris was like that. She never asked. She rarely showed weakness. But she got this look in her eye, like a lost, hurt child and then Morgan knew that she needed her love to keep her memories at bay. They sat quietly now, the smaller woman enjoying the play of candle light across Kris' tanned muscles as she allowed her insecure lover to reestablish the warmth she found only with her.

"Eh? You two decent?" came Pete's grumpy voice from out in the darkness.

Kris sighed. "Come in, Peter," she called, holding on tightly to Morgan to let her know that she had no intention of releasing her little lover no matter who walked in. Morgan leaned back again into Kris' embrace, letting her know with her body language that she was comfortable with their love.

Pete hopped in out of the darkness with his funny, bouncy step and plunked himself down in the chair that Morgan had not long ago vacated. "Gotta tag the Cayman tonight, Kris. Could do with some help. I'm gettin' a might old for hoppin' in and outta dugouts."

"Sure, Pete. Glad to help out. You can handle the canoe and Morgan can hold the light while I go overboard and catch the 'gators," organized Kris, swinging both Morgan and herself up onto their feet.

"Hang on here!" interrupted Morgan, holding out her arms to stop the two crazy people whom she loved very much. "Your better half needs more information. Am I to understand that you want Kris to get into the river in the middle of the night and catch alligators with her bare hands?"

Pete and Kris looked at each other and shrugged. "Yes," they said together.

"No!" responded Morgan, taking Kris' arm. "If you don't mind, I'd rather my marriage last at least until next month!"

Peter snickered. "Henpecked," he muttered behind his hand.

Kris blushed red and stiffened. "Ah Morgan, it's okay, I've done this before. We are only after little ones. You'll see, it's relatively safe."

Morgan looked up at her partner. "Relatively. Great. I'm a doctor so I know these things. If there are little ones then there is a mom and dad nearby." Kris raised an eyebrow and looked at Pete. Pete looked at Morgan. Morgan sighed. "Okay, but I'm not patching you up if some alligator bites you, Thanasis!"

Pete and Kris beamed like little children who had been allowed to go to the amusement park. "It's fun, Morgan," she said. "You'll see," she reassured as the three headed towards the beach.

Neither woman was surprised to see that Pete had already packed the necessary cargo into the dugout. "Okay, we are going to catch alligators in the middle of the night, why?" asked Morgan as she settled on the slat of wood that acted as a bench in the dugout.

"The Cayman are becoming endangered, Morgan. Pete and others are tagging the populations so that they can be studied and a better plan can be developed to protect them," explained the hunter, using her powerful shoulders to propel them through the darkness. Morgan looked around, unable to see anything but the stars overhead. How the two veterans knew their way through the darkness was beyond her. The river and rainforest were one black veil to her, in fact she could barely make out Kris paddling the canoe steadily down river only a few feet in front of her.

After a time, they quietly drifted towards shore and Kris signaled to Morgan to turn on the powerful light. Red, beady eyes stared back at them from the tangle of branches edging the water. Kris balanced on her toes ready as Peter silently headed their craft closer. With barely a ripple, Kris was over the side and reaching through chest deep water for the two-foot long body that was trying to slip through the branches. With considerable splashing the young Cayman fought its captor but Kris held on to the jaws and tail of the reptile and passed it up to Pete.

Then she hoisted herself up into the dugout and prepared a tag. Using a pair of pliers she clipped the plastic tag on to the 'gator and then Pete lowered the creature back over the side.

Morgan watched with fascination. The spotlight highlighted her lover in sharp relief, golden muscles flexing, glistening with moisture as she fought the power of the primitive creature in her strong hands. It was like a flashback to some ancient time. The savage beauty of the scene hit some cord deep inside Morgan that she could not comprehend other than to know that some trace memory within her had experienced something like this before.

Kris sensed Morgan's eyes on her and squatted down in front of her partner. Morgan looked up into a strong, angular face outlined with wet, dark hair. A wave of desire washed down her body and settled in her loins. Kris gave a lazy, sexy smile and leaned over and captured Morgan's lips. *Oh God! Right here. Right now!* Morgan's mind cried.

"Would you two knock it off!" growled Pete and Kris leaned back and winked a promise at her lover. "Hell, have you two damn women forgotten you're in the company of a man of the cloth!"

Morgan and Kris looked at the scruffy, swearing old man and broke out laughing.

Pete scowled good-naturedly. "That's what I get for marrying ya. Now the two of you are ganging up on me!" They paddled on and tagged a half dozen Caymans before heading back. Morgan helped the two 'gator hunters carry the gear back to Pete's storage hut. Then she walked hand in hand with Kris back to their quarters. She knew her warrior was tired. Even small alligators are very powerful and the water had chilled her lover's body.

"I'm just going to shower the 'gator smell off me," yawned Kris, "Why don't you go ahead and warm the bed for me."

Morgan reached up and gently kissed her lover's lips. "Don't be long, my hunter. You need some rest." Kris nodded and walked away into the darkness. She did not come back.

Kris' return to consciousness was both painful and nauseating. Her head spun and the disorientation made her stomach retch its contents up into her mouth. Realizing she was choking, Kris gagged and let the vomit escape onto her chest. She was now aware that she was being dragged through the bush by her arms, the heels of her feet bouncing over the ground. She feebly tried to struggle but the effort sent agonizing arrows of pain through her head. *Cracked skull,* Kris concluded through her semi-conscious haze. *I'm in trouble.*

She tried to support her head on her out stretched arm, aware that her nose was running and that her eyes wouldn't focus. She tried hard to think but other than a vague impression that this sort of experience was not unusual in her life, she had no real memory of anything before regaining consciousness. *Shit, I'm in big trouble.* She was dragged along a bush path and then dropped to the ground. The impact caused the blackness to once again wipe out the pain.

Morgan got up and got dressed. Something was wrong! Kris should have been back by now. She grabbed a flashlight and headed over to the bath hut. The hut was in darkness and Morgan's heart raced in fear. She broke into a trot and covered the remaining distance with her uneven lope. Entering, she swung the light beam around. No Kris, but a thick streak of blood left a clear trail out the back entrance. Morgan whirled and made for Pete's hut yelling his name.

"Pete! Pete!" she cried, stumbling up the steps, "Bogara and his men have Kris! Pete, for God's sake wake up!" cried Morgan, banging on the door. The door opened and Morgan fell against the wiry old man. "She didn't come back from her shower. There's blood. I think they must have dragged her out the back way," explained the shaken woman in a rush as Pete held her by the shoulders.

Pete growled and disappeared into his hut, returning with his rifle, a skinning knife and his first aid kit. He tossed Morgan the canvas bag that held the first aid kit. Without a word he headed for the bathhouse, Morgan on his heels. Once there, he took Morgan's torch and looked at the bloody evidence. Three sets of footprints could be seen in the red stains. Then he slapped the torch off and handed it back to Morgan. "We gotta hurry," he said and headed off through the darkness with a frightened Morgan close behind.

They moved quickly and quietly. It was clear that Pete knew where they must be headed. He only stopped once to check with Morgan's torch at a fork in the path, then cursed softly and moved off at an even faster pace. Soon, up ahead, they could see a light from an oil lamp. Rough male voices floated back to them. Pete stopped and flicked the safety off his rifle. He took out the knife and handed it to Morgan. For a second she hesitated, then her jaw set and she reached for the knife. This was Kris. She was prepared for whatever it took to keep her safe from her father's men.

They crept forward until the air was suddenly shattered by a bang, then Kris' screams. The two of them charged forward, breaking into a clearing. Kris was tied to a punishment tree, blood covering her face. Thousands of ants were crawling over her as she twisted in agony. Morgan ran forward as a shot cracked through the night. She slipped behind Kris and used the knife to cut the rope that held the tall woman to the tree of torture. She was vaguely aware that there was gunfire going on but all her attention was focused on the woman who screamed in agony on the ground. In cutting the rope, Morgan had herself received some of the sharp, painful stings. She couldn't imagine what Kris was going through.

She grabbed her friend by the feet and dragged her over to a small stream that trickled nearby, dropping her in and then tearing her clothes off. The ants bit at her painfully but as she washed Kris' body, they retreated until fewer and fewer remained to torture her wounded partner. Now Morgan stopped long enough to use her torch. Kris' skin was blotted and blotched in ugly red spots. She was gasping for breath and turning blue.

Anaphylactic shock, Morgan realized, and dug madly into Pete's first aid kit, knowing she had only minutes to save her partner's life.

At the scream, Pete had charged forward, knowing what was happening to his friend. He entered the clearing and aimed his rifle at the three men who stood laughing at Kris' cruel execution. Morgan ran from behind him and struggled to cut Kris free. Then all hell broke loose. One of the men dived for a rifle that leaned against a tree and Pete fired. Another pulled a gun but was hit by Pete's second shot before he could aim his weapon. The third man raised his hands and begged Pete to show mercy. It was a test of his faith not to blow the bastard's head off.

"Lay down on your stomach and put your hands on the back of your neck and cross your ankles," Pete commanded. The scared man willingly complied and Pete looked about for something with which to tie his prisoner up. In the darkness, he could hear Morgan sobbing Kris' name and the running of water.

He tied the criminal up tightly and then went to find Morgan. Kris' naked body lay still in the water, a ghostly white in the rising moon light. Her face was completely obscured by blood. Her body, swollen and covered in bites, was now turning blue. Morgan sat in the mud, Kris' hand wrapped in her own, a look of anguish in her features. "Morgan?" Pete whispered.

Morgan looked up. "Pete, help me. I've got to get her to the hut. We'll need a back board."

Pete looked at the woman lying in the water. "Is it bad?"

Morgan swallowed and whispered, "Very. I used your snake bite kit. That helped a little but her skull... I don't know." Pete nodded and went to get a wide plank from his workshop. They carefully pushed it under the unconscious woman and then tied her gently to it. Slowly and painstakingly, they carried her back to their hut and laid her down on the table. Pete grabbed the sheets off the bed and covered her while Morgan got her own medical supplies and took Kris' signs.

Pete used the sheets covering Kris to dry her body and the surrounding area as best he could. Then he got a fresh sheet and blanket and covered Kris carefully. Meanwhile, Morgan cleaned and dressed Kris' head wound, then mixed up a solution with which to wash her body to decrease the chance of infection. She also gave Kris a shot.

"Well?" asked Pete.

Morgan sat down heavily and held on to the cold hand of her soulmate. "She is just barely hanging on, Pete," she whispered painfully. "S... she... I think she would want to have the last rites," Morgan added, tears now rolling down her face. Peter nodded and left to get prepared.

After Peter's prayers, Morgan sat beside her lover, her head leaning against the damp wood table. She listened to her lover's shallow breathing, her heart contracting in fear at every ragged breath. Pete slipped quietly away to see to his prisoner and to bury the dead. Then he got on his ham radio and arranged for the authorities to send out a patrol unit.

Twenty-three hours later Morgan still sat by her soulmate. She had left her side only when it was necessary and then Peter had sat by the fallen warrior. She had slept in her chair, her head next to Kris' cold hand, willing her to live with every ounce of her being.

"Morgan," came a soft whisper that gripped the small doctor's heart.

She sat up and leaned close to Kris' bruised and swollen face. "How are you doing, my hunter?" asked Morgan in a shaky voice.

"Not feeling too good. You okay?" came the weak reply after a moment's hesitation.

"I'm fine. Look, I need you to follow my finger. That's it. Okay can you squeeze my hand?" Morgan slowly worked through some basic response tests and was delighted to realize that Kris could move, talk and recognize things around her. Her reflexes were slow but she was, unbelievably, showing signs of recovery. Tears rolled down her face.

"Why are you crying?" asked the tall patient.

"Here, I need you to take in some water. It's important. Come on." Kris sucked dutifully on a straw.

"I've been sick, huh?" reasoned Kris.

Morgan laughed. "Yes, you've been a little sick," Morgan responded, using a shaky hand to brush Kris' bangs back from her eyes.

"But I think you are going to be just fine now."

Kris smiled. "Good. I love you, Morgan."

"I love you too, Kris."

Morgan sat in a wicker chair on the porch of Los Amazonos Compound. After four months in the rainforest it seemed strange to be leaving to return to the States. This strange and wonderful place seemed like home. She watched a lean and pale warrior walk with her friend Carlos across the tough grass. Her soulmate hugged the loyal guide in her arms and kissed his cheek, then turned and walked over to where Morgan sat. "The plane is ready."

Morgan nodded and got up to follow her lover. Then she stopped and looked around once more. "Promise me, Kris, that we will always come back," Morgan requested, turning to look into those remarkable blue eyes.

"I promise," Kris smiled. Then she pulled the small woman close so that her head tucked comfortably under her chin. "But my home is you."

"And you mine, my warrior."

Turkish

Encounter

Gunnul Dedemann unlocked the old wrought iron gate to the small grove that contained their grave. She pushed through the tangle of underbrush and stood by the dark tomb. Here, close to her, she always found some peace and comfort. Her long, strong fingers stroked the ancient, rough surface of stone. It must have been a beautiful grave at one time. Even now, the low relief carving of ancient Greek symbols covered the lid in a blurry image of a time long ago. Yet the eroded names carved 3,000 years ago in ancient Greece were not in the ancient language. Nor were the names from some ancient time. It made no sense. No sense at all.

Maybe she should stop coming here. The images that hovered at the edge of her awareness had gotten stronger over the years. This was the earliest memory she had of her childhood, pushing through the underbrush, looking up at a wall of ancient dark stone and knowing even then in her child's mind that she was standing at "her" grave. And strangely enough her own. Knowing, when she had crawled up on top to see the names that were engraved there, that something was wrong. Something had not been done properly. Once again Gunnul's hand reached out as it had that day so many years ago and traced her name: Morgan Andrews. *That is not your name is it, my darling? Why can't I remember?* Then her fingers slid to the name that she knew marked her own remains: Kristinia Thanasis. When she touched the letters she could feel their love. Tears welled in her eyes. Love was not an experience she had ever had. *Allah protect your souls until I can solve this riddle*, she prayed, then retraced her steps and locked again her special secret behind the iron gate.

* * * * *

Gunnul straightened her shoulders and walked through the beautiful gardens that surrounded her country estate. She employed an army of gardeners to maintain a paradise for her and Chrissy, but to her secret garden, no one was allowed to go. Her grave and that of her lover remained always private behind a green wall of wild growth. Servants respectfully stepped aside as she passed, leaving the General to her thoughts, knowing always to respect the powerful woman's privacy. Gunnul ran up the steps onto the marble patio that capped the cliff overlooking the Mediterranean Sea. The view was breathtaking, with the sea below and the towering Taurus Mountains behind. Today, Gunnul didn't notice.

She entered her den through open terrace doors and sat behind the ornate cherry wood desk, sinking into the calf leather of her office chair. Before her on the desk was a report on the harvesting of her opium fields. She set it aside and stared at the folder that waited her attention underneath. It was labeled, "Jamie Dedemann". Anger washed over Gunnul. It should be labeled "the whore", she thought cruelly. She opened up the red leather folder into which her private secretary slipped each item before placing it on her desk. Inside were two letters. The first was a copy of the one she had sent to the whore. It read:

Dear Ms. Dedemann,

My daughter, Christine, has expressed an interest in meeting her birth mother. Her father, my brother, Mohammed died two years ago of an apparent heart attack. I feel that it is advisable that she be allowed to satisfy her curiosity about her background in order that she come to terms with her father's death and her birth mother's desertion. For this reason, I reluctantly have arranged for you to visit Turkey.

I wish first to meet and get to know you. If I feel that your actions and attitudes will not hurt my daughter beyond the pain that she already carries in her heart then I will allow a meeting. Attached to this letter you will find all the necessary arrangements, and tickets for your trip.

Yours Sincerely,

Gunnul Dedemann

Gunnul nodded her satisfaction with the letter. Then with distaste she took up the letter that had arrived that day. She slit open the envelope and pulled out the response. She read:

Dear Gunnul Dedemann,

I am not only Chrissy's birth mother, I am her mother! And you are not! For ten years I have tried to trace the whereabouts of Moe and my daughter. You're damn right my daughter has a right to have contact with me! I've returned your tickets. I don't want your money; I know how it was earned. I'll pay my own way and will be on the next flight to Istanbul to get my daughter back!

Yours Sincerely,

Jamie Miller

Gunnul's eyebrows rose in consternation. Her brother was right about one thing. This woman was coarse and ambitious. Clearly, she planned to sue for custody so that she could get her hands on some of Chrissy's wealth. Gunnul sneered; that was never, ever going to happen. She might not have given birth to Chrissy but she had raised her from a baby and Chrissy was her daughter far closer than blood could have ever made her. She'd kill this woman before she would let her take her daughter away!

She leaned back and closed her eyes and felt the blood pounding through her temple. In her mind she could feel warm hands slip around her shoulders. It was the blond woman of her dreams, the secret lover of her fantasies who always came to comfort her. She leaned back farther into the leather and tried to catch the warm scent of herbs that she associated with her imaginary friend. *The whore wants to take Chrissy away from me*, she confided to her daydream. Green eyes looked at her with compassion. *Don't worry*, came the response from deep in her soul. Gunnul sighed and shook herself free from a world that she knew she had no right to. Her world was here and now, ugly and real. She pulled over the file on the opium harvest and started to read.

* * * * *

Don't worry, came the message from deep in her soul and Jamie sighed, and looked out the plane window to the Aegean Sea below. *Almost there, my friend*, she thought, as she reached out to the soulmate that she had never met. The dark shadow that always seemed to be nearby reached out and wrapped her close, easing her pain. When she was younger, she had been guilty and concerned about this presence that had gradually become part of her. It wasn't normal and she considered taking therapy. Somehow she had never got around to it.

The truth was she loved her secret phantom, loved her with all her heart and soul. That was what had attracted her to Moe. He had looked so much like her. She had deluded herself in to believing he was her soulmate. Instead, he had turned out to be her worst nightmare.

She had tried to make their marriage work, had tried to help her emotionally weak husband stand on his own two feet. But the only strength Moe seemed to possess was a love for violence. After their child was born a girl, and not the boy that he so desperately wanted, that violence was often directed towards her. Then there was that fatal night when he had come home drunk and high yet again and had beaten her near to death, then left her, disappearing with her child.

Chrissy had been barely six months old then. She would be almost ten now. Would she recognize her? They shared the same forest green eyes but where Jamie's hair was blond, Chrissy's had been dark like her father. She had his bone structure too, high cheekbones and classic lines. Yes, she would know her daughter. Except for the blue eyes she would look so much like the soulmate of her dreams.

She saw the blue of the sea turn to the brown of land far below. Soon she would face her greatest enemy, Gunnul Dedemann. Even Moe had been afraid of her. He always talked nervously about her ruthless actions. She was an anomaly, a woman accepted into a male dominated world. According to Moe, she made her living selling illegal drugs and it was she who had gotten Moe hooked in order to take control of the vast family empire. He had told her that his sister was beautiful outside but wicked inside and that she had killed hundreds of people. This was the person who had raised her daughter. A cold, icy lump formed in her chest; *Don't worry, Chrissy. Your Mommy's coming and she's going to get you back!*

Jamie stepped through customs into a mad house of noise and shifting bodies. Turks crowded the baggage terminal waiting for the aircraft to be unloaded. Jamie looked around in confusion. She couldn't manage her luggage by herself and she didn't know how to ask for a porter. Her hand tightened nervously on the aluminum crutch that encircled her upper arm and provided a handhold for her to lean against, taking the weight off her badly damaged leg. Maybe she could ask one of the passengers to help her.

"Excuse please. You are Jamie Dedemann?" Jamie turned to see a soldier looking down at her with a worried expression. He was dressed in a black uniform with much gold braid and a red sash. The formal appearance was undermined by the machine gun slung casually over his shoulder.

"Yes. Yes, I am," she responded nervously.

"I am Ohmir. I have been ordered to take you to the residence of General Dedemann. You come, please."

"Wait, what about my luggage and who is General Dedemann?" asked Jamie, stubbornly holding her ground.

The soldier looked surprised. "Gunnul Dedemann, the savior of our people. She has killed many people. She is famous soldier and hero. I show you. You come now."

"What about my luggage?" asked Jamie again.

"You give me baggage paper. I see to," explained the soldier, holding out his hand. Jamie sighed and reached into her purse to pull out her ticket, on which were stapled her luggage tags. Carefully, she removed them and gave them to the young soldier, then put her tickets back into her purse. There was a return ticket for herself and one for Chrissy.

"You come," said the soldier again, and walked ahead. Jamie followed, having a hard time maneuvering in the crowds with her crutch.

The soldier handed the tickets over to another who had come to attention at the sight of them. In rapid Turkish, the soldier was given instructions and Jamie's baggage tags, then Ohmir led her outside to where a limousine bearing the nation's flag was parked. He opened the back door and Jamie slid in, placing her crutch beside her. *A nice show of power, Gunnul Dedemann, but it won't work, I will defeat you and get my daughter back.*

* * * * *

Gunnul stared out of the hotel's window down to the busy streets of Istanbul twenty stories below. In her memory, Gunnul could hear her brother's mocking voice. "You think you are so good, Gunnul! The hero of the people! But I've got something here that you'll never have. An heir, Gunnul. I've got the Dedemann heir. I had her by the sleaziest American whore I could find. I even married her so that the slut's spawn will forever taint your precious family line. Here she is, Gunnul, the heir you deserve to inherit your legacy!"

But Mohammed's cruel actions didn't succeed in hurting his sister. Gunnul felt again the rush of love and protectiveness she had experienced when that little bundle had been thrust into her hands. She knew that child was hers and she didn't care what problems or background the little girl might have, she was always going to be there for her daughter.

She had adopted Chrissy legally, buying off her brother, who spent yet another inheritance wildly until the drink, drugs and wild life killed him. She had shielded her daughter from her brother as much as possible, just as she would shield her from her tart of a mother. Chrissy had grown into a beautiful, intelligent, caring child. She looked like Gunnul except for her eyes. Her eyes were forest green like those of Gunnul's imaginary lover. That's why Gunnul knew from the moment she made eye contact with the little baby that they were family.

Behind her the intercom clicked on. "Gunnul, Ms. Dedemann is here," came the voice of her secretary, Teefo.

"Thank you, Teefo. Please send her in," came the cold response. Gunnul turned, her face a mask cut from stone, and waited. Teefo opened the door and stepped aside. In hobbled a woman dressed demurely in a business suit of a good quality cut. She leaned heavily on a crutch and dragged forward a misshapen leg. When she looked up, Gunnul's heart stopped. It was the woman who had been the focus of her dreams for as long as she could remember!

* * * * *

Jamie was tired and felt grimy from her long flight. Her head pounded terribly but she gathered her resolve and followed the tall, serious looking secretary into the private office of Gunnul Dedemann, prepared to take on any challenge to get her daughter back. Looking up, she stopped breathing. The blue eyes of her secret protector looked straight at her, the dark form of her dreams now suddenly real. She took two wobbly steps forward and heard the secretary close the door behind her. Then the world spun and darkness closed in around her.

When she woke she knew she was where she belonged. The dark form of her protector embraced her and held a cool cloth to her aching head. Her head rested beneath her phantom's chin, up against her wide shoulder, and her arm was wrapped securely around the dark form's waist. Her eyes fluttered then remained closed. Whatever waited for her in the real world could wait a few minutes longer while she held onto the phantom that was the anchor of her life.

* * * * *

Gunnul lunged forward and swept the small woman up into her arms before she could fall. Suddenly, she was on a riverbank deep in a jungle, the familiar body of her lover in her arms. She shook her head to clear it and carried the limp form over to the sofa. She lowered the still body onto the cushions, then went to the bar fridge and wrapped some crushed ice into a towel. Returning, she slipped behind the small form and pulled her close, feeling with delight the woman take her place against her side, one arm wrapped protectively around her as she had done in her daydreams a million times over. She held the cold compress to Jamie's forehead and tried unsuccessfully to come to terms with the fact that her worst enemy was also the woman of her dreams.

Awareness hit Jamie a half minute later. She was snuggled up to Gunnul Dedemann, the woman who had stolen her child! She sat up with a gasp, and pulled herself away from the tall, dark woman. Madly, she looked around for her crutch so that she could get up.

Gunnul followed the frightened look as it searched the room until it settled on the crutch that lay on the floor by the door. The Turkish woman got up, went over and picked up the cane, then brought it back to the beautiful blond woman who was her mortal enemy. Holding it out she said, "I am Gunnul Dedemann. Because you are the birth mother of my child, you are welcome to my country and my home." She turned and removed a bottle from the side table, returning to where Jamie sat. On the way past her desk, she pressed a button. "This is lemon cologne. It is the tradition in my country that when a guest comes to our home, we greet them with this to refresh them from their travels. Please cup your hands."

Jamie did as she was told, placing the crutch nearby and holding out her hands. The beautiful, dark-haired woman poured a little of the lemon and alcohol based mixture into her hands and Jamie rubbed them together and then over her face. The lemon cologne did feel cool and refreshing. A quiet knock came at the door and the secretary walked in. He placed a large silver tray on the coffee table before the couch and retreated.

Gunnul sat down at the farthest side of the couch away from Jamie. "It is also our way to show hospitality to any guest who arrives by offering them Turkish Delights and coffee," explained the Turkish woman, offering Jamie a tray of beautiful squares of candy.

Jamie hesitated for a moment, then took a jelly square covered in icing sugar. If Gunnul was going to make an effort to get along, then she would too. "Thank you. I find your tradition most welcoming," she said formally and was rewarded by a dazzling smile from the powerful woman who looked up from a small brass propane stove she was lighting. "I am sorry about fainting. I... I don't usually. You took me by surprise. You look just like Mohammed."

Gunnul stirred the thick coffee grinds that boiled in a long-handled brass cup over the small stove. To the mix she added a good amount of sugar. "We were twins," explained Gunnul. She poured some of the thick mixture into a very small cup and handed the cup and saucer to Jamie. Then she poured one for herself and explained, "The grinds settle as a thick layer at the bottom. In the country, you can get old women to read the grinds and tell you your future. When you finish your coffee, you turn the cup upside down on the saucer. The fortune-teller will then lift the cup off. If there is a lot of suction then the fortune-telling, they believe, will be very accurate."

I know my future, Jamie thought. *It's to take my daughter home.* But out loud she said, "Thank you for making me welcome and explaining your ways. I will need to learn as much as I can about Turkish culture because my daughter has been raised in it."

Gunnul smiled. "I am glad you feel that way. But I have endeavored to raise Chrissy to be well aware of her European ancestry too. She speaks English fluently and has traveled through Europe. I think you will not find it too hard to communicate with her if you two should meet," explained Gunnul.

"I will meet my daughter, Miss Dedemann. You cannot stop me from being part of her life," stated Jamie.

Gunnul put down her cup and got up, walking to look out the window. "I have stopped you for ten years. And I would have continued to do so if Chrissy had not requested a meeting. She came to me as a baby. I legally adopted her from her father. In this country, Chrissy is my child. I love her. I do not wish to hurt you, but I will not let my daughter be hurt. She has grown up in a very privileged and refined world. She is a good Moslem girl. She doesn't understand your kind."

"My daughter is a Moslem?" exclaimed Jamie in surprise.

"Of course. Although the Turks' ancestry is Mongolian and Greek, we are Shiite Moslems. My brother was also," explained Gunnul patiently, even though she was having great difficulty keeping her boiling emotions under control.

"Moe never practiced any religion except a worship of substance abuse," snarled Jamie bitterly, and then realized that this was his twin sister. "Ah, sorry, that wasn't called for, I'm sure you loved your brother very much," she apologized, in a fluster.

Gunnul turned to look at Jamie. "No, actually I hated him. I tried to help him, he was family, but Mohammed was born with a fatal flaw to his character. I did not respect him. I tried as much as possible not to let him influence Christine," responded Gunnul seriously.

"Thank you. I... I've lived in fear all these years that he might hurt her. He could be... violent," confessed Jamie, wiping away a tear that threatened to fall from her eye.

"No. He never hurt her. I would have killed him if he had tried. Chrissy, she is beautiful, intelligent and caring. She is not like her father," revealed Gunnul, feeling suddenly sorry for the pain and worry this woman appeared to have felt. *Even a whore has the right to love her children*, she thought. She had not been treated fairly, realized Gunnul.

Jamie nodded, not sure if she should be relieved that this remarkable woman had protected her child or upset that she could talk so casually about killing her own brother. What had happened to Moe anyway? Things were not going as she imagined they would. She was completely unnerved by the fact that Gunnul was, physically anyway, the person who had haunted her subconscious all her life. And she was taken aback to find that Gunnul cared about her Chrissy very much and had clearly tried to be fair and open in her upbringing. And then there was the fact that her daughter was a Moslem. Gunnul had reassured her that they would find a common ground, but Jamie was just starting to realize that she couldn't walk into the life of a ten year old, foreign child and say, "I'm your mother, come home."

"I will show you to your room. You must be tired. It is a very long flight. Tomorrow we will start touring. For a few days, I will teach you about Turkey," explained Gunnul, as she moved away from the window and waited for Jamie to struggle to her feet and get her crutch settled around her arm.

"You mean I am to be observed for a few days and then you will decide whether I can have access to my own child," challenged Jamie, anger lacing her voice.

"Yes, I mean that," came the cold response, from the woman who towered over her. "Would you not do the same in my position? But also, it will be good for you to know something of our nation before you meet my daughter," explained Gunnul and then added as she caught the scent of sun dried herbs and sweet grass that was the fragrance of her dreams, "Our daughter."

Jamie, ready to take the offensive, suddenly choked back her cutting response and looked into the ice blue eyes of the woman who had raised her daughter. For a long time neither woman spoke. An energy seemed to pass between them. Slowly, Jamie's hand came out and grasped the hand of the woman who looked down at her. She nodded her agreement. "Our daughter," she repeated, and the tall woman smiled, lifted Jamie's hand and kissed her fingers. A jolt of passion shot through Jamie's small frame. She looked up into eyes that now glowed with an inner energy that was not quite human. *Be careful, Jamie! This woman is very dangerous*, her mind warned her, but her heart pasted a silly grin on her face that matched the one looking back at her.

"Come, I will show you to your room." They walked out through the outer office where her assistant worked. He stood as they walked by. Gunnul led her down a hall and opened a door to a suite. Jamie's luggage waited within. Jamie entered and to her surprise Gunnul followed. "Would you have dinner with me tonight?" the woman asked formally, as if making a date.

"Yes," responded Jamie without thinking, "I would like that."

The tall Turk relaxed noticeably and smiled. "I will call on you at eight. You are tired. We will make it a casual meal," she stated, and then left.

Jamie collapsed into the nearest chair. *Holy God! What is going on here!* Her emotions were on a roller-coaster ride. Part of her hated this woman who had taken her child from her, part of her was grateful for the apparent love and care that she had given Chrissy. Another part resented greatly this trial that Gunnul was insisting on before she would allow her to see her own daughter and yet one more part of her wanted to be back in this woman's arms making her fantasies all real. "Oh God," she whispered, "what do I do now?"

Gunnul felt numb. The shock of meeting the woman who had been an obsession for her all her life had been like a physical blow. That the woman should turn out to be Chrissy's birth mother had created an unbelievable complication in Gunnul's life. Worse still, she wanted this woman with a hunger that was taking all her self-discipline to control. How could she fall in love with a whore? She buried her head in her hands. How could she not?

* * * * *

At eight o'clock, Gunnul was knocking on Jamie's door. She wore blue jeans and a braided sweater that she had bought in Scotland. She had tied her hair back in a ponytail and hoped that she looked casually American. Jamie opened the door, her eyes opening in surprise to see the change from smart business suit to casual elegance. Ralf Lauren blue jeans and a hand knit Scottish sweater, noted Jamie, feeling a little intimidated in her Levi Strauss jeans and dark green T-shirt that she had gotten at the local mall back home. Peeking out of the pocket were the Winnie the Pooh characters. "You come," stated Gunnul, forgetting her perfect English grammar as she took in the lines of Jamie's petite body.

"O.K.," agreed Jamie, falling in beside her tall companion. They went down the hall of the hotel and took a short elevator ride to a private terrace on the rooftop. All of Istanbul and the Bosphorus stretched out before them. The view was magnificent! To Jamie's surprise and amusement, quiet servants served them a meal of hamburgers and French fries.

"So how often do you have hamburgers when you dine up here?" asked Jamie, wiping her mouth with her silk napkin.

Gunnul's hamburger stopped half way to her mouth and then returned to her plate, "Never. Was the food not right? How did you know?" asked the upset hostess.

Jamie laughed. "The food is excellent. You just don't look like the hamburger type. This is very sweet Gunnul. I... I... I mean, can I call you that?"

Gunnul blushed then looked up into deep green eyes. "What, Gunnul or that I am sweet?" she responded, with a tease.

Jamie laughed again. Gunnul decided that she liked the way Jamie laughed. "Is it O.K. that I call you by your first name?" Jamie asked again.

"Yes, if I may call you Jamie," came the answer.

"Okay, sweet," Jamie teased back and Gunnul laughed. They finished their burgers as Gunnul talked about Chrissy's education and how well she was doing at her studies. Jamie was impressed by Chrissy's apparent ability and also by the fine education she had been given and how seriously Gunnul took it. She found herself warming very quickly to this woman and was finding it hard to remember that she had made her fortune by selling drugs.

"Downstairs in my bedroom, I have pictures of Chrissy. Would you like to see?" asked Gunnul, now feeling very mellow, buoyed up by how well the evening had gone. She had also shared a bottle of wine with Jamie, something that she rarely did as the consumption of alcohol was against her religion. It had made her light hearted and light headed.

"Please, yes," answered Jamie, carefully standing up from where she had been relaxing in a lounge chair after their meal.

Gunnul stood too and the room swayed a bit. She smiled and took Jamie's hand. "This way," she said, leading the petite woman carefully down to her bedroom a floor below. Beside her bed were two pictures of Chrissy, one of her on her horse and the other a school picture of her wearing her school tie and blazer. Jamie felt her knees give out and she sank onto Gunnul's bed. She held the pictures in her hand and tears rolled down her face. Her daughter was a beautiful stranger smiling happily back at her from a world that was completely foreign to Jamie.

Suddenly, her dark protector was beside her. The pictures were taken from trembling fingers and placed back on the bedside table. Then warm arms pulled her close and Jamie wrapped her own arm around her phantom friend and cried her eyes out.

Gunnul held Jamie close and stroked her hair. She leaned forward and inhaled the sweet fragrance of the golden locks. They smelt of fresh air and shampoo and that unique blend of herbs that was her dream-mate. Her head lowered to place her cheek against Jamie's and the upset woman responded by wrapping her arms tightly around Gunnul's neck. Gunnul swallowed. She hadn't really had much experience at this sort of thing. In her world, to date and to be with boys was not seen as proper. To be with a woman was something that was known of but not discussed.

She allowed her lips to kiss the soft hair that her face was now buried in and let her hands drift lower to stroke Jamie's back. The feel of Jamie's warm skin beneath her shirt sent a hot rush of emotion down into Gunnul's groin. Head light with wine, she forgot her need for self control and pulled the little woman down onto her bed, rolling on top of her and kissing her with passion on the lips as she had seen in the American movies.

At first, Jamie was too shocked to react. Then she swung a hand free and clobbered Gunnul with her fist to the side of her head. "Get off me, damn it!" she growled, and Gunnul was off her and backing across the room in an instant. "What the hell do you think you were doing!"

"I was making love to you," stated the confused woman, "Did I not do it right?" she asked.

Jamie struggled to her feet and adjusted her crutch to her arm. "What made you think that I'd just turn tricks for you?" demanded the furious American.

Gunnul was even more confused and her head was starting to pound. "What tricks? You are a whore and I wished to make use of your services," Gunnul tried to explain, becoming now rather annoyed at Jamie's reaction.

"Whore! Who are you calling a whore, you goddamn, randy infidel!" yelled Jamie, hobbling to the door and slamming it closed behind her as she left.

Gunnul looked at the door in amazement. No one had spoken to her in that tone since she had been a child. No one would dare. Her face set in stone, she strode across the room and headed down the hall towards Jamie's rooms. The hall started to spin and Gunnul was only able to stay on her feet by leaning an arm against the wall. She turned and retraced her steps. *I am drunk*, she realized in amazement.

Jamie stuffed her things back into her suitcase, angry and humiliated by Gunnul's advances. *That will teach me to try and see the good in people. Everything that Mohammed said about this woman was true. She is beautiful but under that well manicured facade there is a real low life.* Jamie's hands were shaking so hard that she couldn't get the lock in place. She took a deep breath and sat down on the bed, trying to come to terms with what had just happened. She had kind of led Gunnul on. It had just felt so good to be in her arms. All her life there had been this barrier between her and the presence that was so much a part of her private life. Gunnul broke that barrier. Gunnul in so many ways was her secret friend.

When Gunnul had taken her in her arms she had snuggled close and wrapped her arms around the woman. She had enjoyed the feel of her lips against her hair and the softness of her cheek against her own. She had allowed and sighed encouragement when Gunnul had stroked her back. She had sort of told Gunnul with her body language that she was willing. Maybe in Gunnul's culture that made her a whore. *Goddamn it, all I want to do is get my daughter back but now everything was becoming so complicated!* Chrissy was a stranger to her and her culture. Gunnul was a stranger who felt like a lover. *Shit!*

Jamie reached for her crutch and limped to the door. She had to talk to Gunnul and find some way to get her daughter back. She opened the door to see a soldier standing there.

"Excuse me," mumbled Jamie, trying to slip past. The soldier turned to look at her.

"No. You are to stay to your room by order of General Dedemann," stated the soldier.

"What! Am I under house arrest?" asked Jamie in frustration, trying once again to get past the guard.

The guard used his rifle to push Jamie back into the room gently. "You must stay," he stated firmly, and closed the door.

For a few seconds, Jamie stood in shocked silence. Then fear slowly crept into her heart. Just how much trouble was she in? She had seen "Midnight Express" and hadn't taken it very seriously. It was just a movie, she had told her friends, the country really wasn't like that. But now she was under guard for turning down the advances of a very powerful, evil individual. She limped over to a chair and sat down, tears of fear and frustration trailed down her cheeks. *Oh Chrissy honey, your Mom has really messed up.*

* * * * *

Gunnul watched the sun rise in the east as she knelt on her prayer rug. Her hands slipped the prayer beads along their cord as she repeated the Shahada, "There is but one God and Muhammad is his prophet." God is great; God is merciful. She had prayed all night trying to find atonement but still her soul ached. Once again she picked up her Quran and read the words of the prophet Muhammad:

In the Name of God, the Merciful, the Compassionate.
Praise belongs to God, the Lord of all Being,
the All-merciful, the All-compassionate,
the Master of the Day of Doom.

Thee only we serve; to Thee alone we pray for succor.
Guide us in the straight path,
the path of those whom Thou has blessed,
not those against whom Thou is wrathful,
nor of those who are astray Quran 1:1-7

Three times she bowed to the east, to Mecca, to the center of the Islamic universe, and then she stood and made her way back to her chambers. She considered changing back into European clothes but chose instead to remain in her robes, finding security and comfort in wearing them. She moved silently as always down the halls and with a wave of her hand dismissed the guard who stood at Jamie's door. Lightly she tapped. "Come in," came the quick response.

Gunnul opened the door and entered. Jamie stood by the window, the morning light dancing on her golden hair. Gunnul tightened her resolve. "I wish to talk to you if I may," she stated quietly.

Jamie nervously wiped the sleep and tears from her eyes. "Yes," she responded, as neutrally as she could manage, turning, her eyes widening in surprise.

"I drank last night, when I knew it was a sin to do so. The consequence of that action was that I conducted myself in an unseemly manner and shamed my country and myself. I have prayed for forgiveness and strength and I have come to ask for your pardon," stated Gunnul.

Jamie looked at the stranger before her. Robed and hooded, her face covered by a lace veil from the nose down, all that remained of the Europeanized woman of yesterday were the remarkable eyes. "Does my daughter dress like this?" she asked.

"On Fridays. Our holy day. Yes," responded Gunnul, puzzled by Jamie's response.

Jamie nodded. "Part of what happened was my fault. My culture is different from yours. Perhaps I gave you the wrong signals. I didn't know that you didn't drink." A moment's hesitation. "Am I a prisoner?" Jamie asked seriously.

Gunnul's eyes widened. "No, of course not! I just did not wish that you leave until I had time to resolve the issue. I do not know what you wish. You have my word that I will not repeat my error. I wish that we continue with the program that I had laid out to you."

Jamie stared into the foreign eyes that had softened from ice to sky blue. "O.K. You are the way to my daughter so I haven't much choice. But I need to warn you; I made the mistake of forgiving your brother's violent behavior. The result was he beat me half to death and left me with a shattered leg. I will not let anyone put me in that position again. Do you understand?"

The eyes grew wide with horror. "You are telling me that it was my brother who did this to your leg?" the taller woman asked, in disbelief.

"Yes, and I'm never going to let myself be victimized again. Or my daughter," growled Jamie.

Hurt flashed across the blue eyes. "I would never hurt Chrissy," came the angry response.

"You better not have," came the challenge.

The eastern woman turned and was gone, leaving Jamie shaken and confused as to what was going to happen next.

* * * * *

A short time later, Teefo arrived at Jamie's door. "Please, the General, she has asked me to request of you that you join her today on touring Istanbul. She wishes to know if you will go with her alone or if you wish also a chaperone."

Jamie shook her head in disbelief. Gunnul wavered back and forth between being a strong, cold enigma and an insecure, warm, caring human. She was the most familiar and yet complex person that she had ever met. "Please tell Gunnul that I would like to tour Istanbul with her as my guide, and I see no need to take anyone else along."

Teefo nodded and retreated. Within a few minutes, Gunnul was at the door dressed again in European clothes. Today, she wore blue jeans with a button down shirt of natural cotton. She looked casually magnificent and Jamie wondered what it would have been like had she let Gunnul make love to her. Quickly, she buried that thought as deep as she could. All that mattered was convincing Gunnul that she should let her have access to Chrissy.

"You are ready to go, Jamie?" asked Gunnul.

Jamie nodded, taking a firmer grip on her metal crutch. "Let's go."

A Mercedes coupe in British racing green sat at the kerb waiting and the footman opened the doors for them. The now very European Gunnul slipped on her sunglasses and pulled out into the busy streets of Istanbul. Within a short time they pulled into a parking lot near the citadel.

"These are our two largest Mosques, the Blue Mosque that you see here and Santa Sophia that is behind it. Turks are mainly Shiite Moslem, not Sunnis. The Shiites in the Middle East are more fundamentalist. Shiites believe that the descendants of Muhammad are the true imam. The Sunni believe that the successors of the Prophet were correctly picked by the agreement of the people, not by kinship to the Prophet. It is a small difference that many have died defending. But not here in Turkey. We are Moslem, but I am afraid we are not always good Moslems," explained Gunnul with a smile. "We are, for Moslems, very liberal in our views. Come."

Jamie followed Gunnul through the crowds of worshipers and tourists to the entrance of the Blue Mosque. Here, Gunnul removed two headscarves from her shoulder purse and wrapped one around Jamie's head and then one around her own. They removed their shoes and entered the Blue Mosque. High above them a dome of intricate blue dominated the massive space. Geometric patterns of incredible complexity decorated the dome and the walls. Dusty light filtered through massive stained glass windows and fell to the royal blue prayer rugs below. Words failed to describe both the size and beauty of the building. Jamie stood, mouth open, looking up in awe while Gunnul waited patiently.

"Gunnul, it is so beautiful!" whispered Jamie. "Do you come here to worship?"

"It is an outstanding example of Byzantine Art. No, we do not come here. Although it is still used as a Mosque, tourism has made it too public a place of prayer for me. Come, you have not seen yet Santa Sophia."

They retrieved their shoes and walked across the courtyard to one of the most famous buildings in the world. "The Blue Mosque has six minarets, some say because the man who built it had six sons. But

Santa Sophia has four, which is the proper number. It was built first as a church by Justinian, the man who established the Byzantine Empire. Later it was converted to a Mosque. It was for a thousand years the largest dome in the world."

Once again they removed their shoes and went in. If the Blue Mosque was awe inspiring, Santa Sophia was almost a mystical experience. The dome seemed twice the size of the Blue Mosque and created within its walls a universe of faith. Gunnul showed Jamie the golden mosaics of Justinian and his famous wife Theodora. "Justinian, they say, was very polite and soft spoken whether greeting an ambassador or ordering the blinding of 20,000 of the enemy's army. He was the founder of the Byzantine Empire. It was his foundation that held the Holy Roman Empire together through the years of the European Dark Ages and with it all the remaining knowledge of Greece and Rome. What the Europeans are today is because of this soft man with the iron will. He was married happily for twenty years and after the death of Theodora he continued to visit her grave every day for the remainder of his life," explained Gunnul.

"It is a touching love story built on the blood of the vanquished. The people rebelled against the heavy taxes levied to build such buildings and Justinian was advised to escape but Theodora would not let him leave. She told him that it was better to die wearing the purple of leadership than to live in the poverty of defeat. They stayed and won," finished the Turkish woman.

Jamie looked up at her proud guide. "I think you are a lot like Justinian," she observed. "I think you could love that deep and be that violent."

Gunnul looked down at Jamie, searching the depths of her forest green eyes. "I have never loved but I have killed many," she responded, and turned to show Jamie the way out. Jamie followed, a cold shiver raising goose bumps on her skin.

Outside, Gunnul knelt and helped Jamie on with her shoes. Then she removed their scarves and tucked them away. "Santa Sophia was known as the Eye of the World," Gunnul commented, as she led the way back to the car. Jamie thought it still could be.

The day was packed with a kaleidoscope of amazing experiences and images. They walked through the busy streets of the city where the Roman chariot races took place in the Hippodrome. An Egyptian obelisk on a Byzantine base still marked the turning point for the chariots. Gunnul took Jamie to the Topkapi Palace and showed her the crown jewels that made the British crown jewels look like nothing. Jamie saw a diamond weighing eighty-four carats surrounded by other diamonds and set in gold, a silver serving tray filled to overflowing with emeralds, jewel and gold encrusted furniture and weaponry, egg cups of gold filigree and diamonds and dishes of the finest china. They wandered through room after room of incredible wealth, beyond most people's imagination.

They ate lunch near the Grand Bazaar, the central market since the time when the legendary Silk Road ended there. It was a barrel-vaulted medieval building with a main hall and side halls leading off it. Each area belonged to a different guild. The main hall was the gold smiths' and for two city blocks the windows were ablaze with dazzling gold jewelry. There were halls for leather, rugs, spices, copper and a thousand other goods for sale. Jamie would have liked to barter and buy, but her budget had barely stretched to getting the plane tickets.

Gunnul took Jamie to a rug weaver. There she saw silk rugs and gasped at their beauty. She would have loved to own one but the prices were in the thousands of dollars. Jamie found herself on overload by the time they were walking through the famous spice market, looking at the barrels and barrels of exotic spices and herbs being bartered for by dealers from all over the world.

They ate dinner at one of the open-air cafes along the shores of the Bosphorus and then took a boat ride along the shore to see the grandeur of the Ottoman palaces, mansions and fortresses. The wealth of the homes and richness of the city's heritage were truly amazing. Istanbul, the legendary Constantinople, was a spicy name filled with the romance and adventure of merchants, warriors and emperors for a thousand years. Jamie thought the city still lived up to its heritage in every way!

Gunnul leaned on the rail beside Jamie, a respectable distance away. All day, Gunnul had been polite and formal, the perfect guide and hostess and it was driving Jamie to distraction. The night air was cool after the heat of the day. "Gunnul," whispered Jamie.

"Hmmm?" responded the General, standing up and looking questioningly at Jamie.

"Why did you want to kiss me?" Jamie asked.

Gunnul turned and looked out across the darkening water. "I am attracted to you, Jamie. It is hard to explain."

"Do you still want to kiss me?" Jamie probed, sliding her hand along the rail as she moved closer.

Gunnul swallowed and stared out across the water. "Yes."

"Now would be a good time," whispered Jamie, looking down shyly as she placed her hand over Gunnul's.

Gunnul turned in surprise and looked at the smaller woman in confusion. "You now wish me to make love to you?" she asked.

Jamie laughed. "No. I don't know if I want that, but I would like you to hold me and kiss me."

Gunnul moved closer and placed her long, strong hands on Jamie's shoulders. "I do not know much of this," she said, her English failing as she became nervous.

Jamie moved into Gunnul's arms and reached up to capture the Turk's lips. "Relax, let me show you," she whispered against Gunnul's mouth, then nibbled gently at her bottom lip. When Gunnul gave a soft gasp, Jamie used the opportunity to slip her tongue into Gunnul's mouth. The taller woman froze in surprise and then pulled Jamie tightly into her arms, allowing her tongue to curl and stroke around Jamie's. Jamie pulled her tongue back and Gunnul followed, entering into Jamie's being for the first time. Jamie gasped and Gunnul immediately pulled back looking worried. "No. It's okay. What you are doing excites me that's all," explained Jamie.

"It excites me very much too," revealed Gunnul seriously and Jamie leaned her head against Gunnul's chest and let the powerful woman embrace her in her warmth.

Gunnul sat in her bedroom staring at the wall. Not long ago she had politely left Jamie at her suite door, kissing her softly on the cheek. Part of her had longed for Jamie to invite her into her bed and was bitterly disappointed when she did not. The other part of her was greatly relieved. Although her need was great, she was traveling on uncharted waters and it scared her. Jamie was a prostitute and must know so much about sex. Gunnul had never lain with anyone. First, because she had been raised traditionally and second, because the only person she had ever really desired was her imaginary lover whose soul dwelled in her secret garden.

Also, beyond the need for sex there were so many other complications. Chrissy had to be protected at all costs. And becoming involved with her birth mother was a really bad idea. The woman was much nicer than she had imagined she would be and yet she was not respectable company for either her or her daughter. She was, too, an infidel. Gunnul buried her face in her hands. She was like a moth burning itself alive with its desire. She knew she should fly away but she couldn't. This need was like a drug dependency. All she wanted was to be taught the art of love making in Jamie's arms, letting her soul burn with the desire that was overpowering her.

Jamie lay in bed. Her leg hurt terribly. The day had been very long and she had not wanted to complain, as everything that Gunnul had planned was both fascinating and exciting. She liked being with

Gunnul. It scared her that she might be making the same mistake that she had with Moe, getting involved with a very dangerous person because she looked and felt so much like her dark, imaginary protector. Then there was Chrissy. If she didn't go along with Gunnul, would that mean that she would not get to see her daughter? She didn't think so; Gunnul seemed an honorable person. But was she? She talked casually about killing and her money did come from being a drug lord. *Why, Jamie, are you even thinking about getting involved with a woman this dangerous? Her brother half killed you!* And it was obvious that Gunnul had none of her brother's weaknesses. She was quick, decisive and in incredible shape.

She was far away in a distant land that she knew nothing about. She could just disappear never to be heard about again. Those things happened. A shiver of fear ran down her back. That would be one way to prevent her from getting Chrissy back. Why had she agreed to travel with Gunnul? To do so had made her incredibly vulnerable! *Because Gunnul would never hurt you*, came the answer from inside her soul. *Please don't let me be deluding myself again,* she thought.

Then there was the worry about the amazing chemistry that existed between the two of them. For all Gunnul's power and authority, it was clear that she was a babe in the woods when it came to sex. *I don't think she had even kissed before! That's amazing! She must be close to thirty.* Was it fair to encourage her? Could she stop herself from doing so? *Oh Hell! What am I getting into?*

* * * * *

Gunnul was having a pleasant dream that involved her lying in a hammock with Jamie wrapped around her. Suddenly, an ice-cold arrow of an idea sliced through her heart. She woke with a start, her heart pounding and a cold sweat on her skin. Had not Jamie violently turned her advances down only yesterday? Then today, she agreed to be kissed and held. The woman was used to using her body as a tool. Jamie must be using her need to control her, to get at Chrissy! The bottom fell out of Gunnul's stomach and she rolled out of bed and ran to the bathroom to throw up.

Jamie dreamed as she had a thousand times before of standing under a tropical sky in Gunnul's strong embrace. She could smell the hot spicy scent that was so much her lover and feel the silk covered steel of her lover's body. Suddenly, a hideous realization exploded her dream into a shredded reality. Gunnul called her a whore! She didn't care about her! She was using the service! Wasn't that what she had said? And Jamie had been stupid enough to get sucked right in by a few words of apology. Gunnul had probably been smirking behind that veil! *Jamie, you are being manipulated so that she can say you are not good enough to have contact with your daughter! Oh shit!* Jamie rolled into a little ball, the pain too much to bear.

Teefo had arrived shortly after Jamie's breakfast tray. "The General wishes to leave today to tour the coast on your way to Antalya," he informed her.

"Is that where my daughter is?" Jamie asked earnestly.

Teefo looked surprised. "It is where Miss Christine is currently staying. General Dedemann's home is near Antalya and it is to there that she means to drive you. This is all I know," stated Teefo openly.

Jamie nodded. "How long will it take to get there?"

"Two to three days I should think," responded Teefo. "The General is anxious to show you some of the historical sites of Turkey."

Jamie gritted her teeth in frustration and forced a smile. "Then I had better pack," she stated, and Teefo nodded and left.

A stiff and formal Gunnul stood by the car as Teefo led Jamie out of the hotel. "Good morning, Jamie," she greeted her politely, waiting for Teefo to help the American into the car before getting into the driver's seat.

"Good morning, Gunnul," replied Jamie, equally as formally, and after Gunnul had exchanged a few words with Teefo in Turkish, they were off. They headed southwest along the European side of Turkey. The land was dry rolling hills dotted with small towns and irrigated farmlands.

Jamie was surprised at the number of houses under construction but when she made her observation to Gunnul the woman laughed, relaxing for the first time that morning. "We are not having a housing boom in Turkey. There are two aspects to our unusual building patterns. Our Prophet, Mohammed, made it illegal to charge or pay interest for a loan. We cannot, as good Moslems, hold a mortgage. But not many can save enough money to buy a house in these modern days. So people pay into building trust funds. The builders use the fund to build condominiums. As each floor is completed those who have paid in full for their apartment move in. Then the next story is built. People who build individual houses start with a small home and add on to it as they get the money. It is common for married children to build a second story over their parent's house to live there. Families are close in Turkey. But also there is another factor. You pay fewer taxes if your house is not finished, so most people leave a part of their house under construction to save money. We Turks are very practical people!"

"Is the home that you and Chrissy live in unfinished?" asked Jamie, observing the handsome woman as she drove.

There was a moment's hesitation. "I am quite wealthy and own several homes. They are all finished."

"How do you make your living, Gunnul?" Jamie asked, to see how the woman would respond.

"My business interests are quite diversified. But the foundation of my family's wealth has been the production of opium," stated Gunnul openly.

Jamie's mouth fell open and before she could think better of it she spluttered out, "You really sell illegal drugs! Moe said you did but I guess I couldn't believe anyone could be a drug lord and..."

The car bounced to the shoulder of the road and came to a screeching stop. "Drug lord!" Gunnul snapped, white with rage. "How dare you call me that! I am not some jungle criminal!"

Jamie too felt her temper snap. "Look, don't get cute with me! Moe told me how you got him hooked on drugs and stole his inheritance. And you can call it whatever you want, but producing opium for sale makes you a disgusting drug lord who feeds off the suffering of others!" Silence filled the car for a long minute as the two women stared into each other's eyes. Then Gunnul slammed out of the car and stood by the roadside, visibly upset.

Jamie waited, not sure what to do. On reflection, she realized that she might have just signed her own death warrant and her anger was very quickly being replaced by fear. After a few minutes, Gunnul got back into the car. She gripped the steering wheel and looked straight ahead. "I wish to ask you a question. Please be honest with me because I intend to check your response. Are you or have you ever been a prostitute?"

"What?" snapped Jamie. "Look, I realize that we see things pretty differently because of our cultures but I have never taken money for sex. Nor have I slept around. I work as a drug councilor at a rehab center. That is how I met your brother. He was volunteering there, supposedly one of our success stories having kicked the habit."

Gunnul's jaw tightened. "My brother told me that he deliberately had an heir by a prostitute to shame our family," the General explained.

"If you have mistreated my daughter or made her feel that she wasn't worthy, I'll kill you," snarled Jamie, barely keeping herself from grabbing the cold, still form beside her.

A hand shot out so quickly that Jamie didn't even see it until fingers hard as iron clamped around her jaw and pulled her close to a face devoid of expression. "Don't... ever... threaten... me," the dark-haired woman hissed and Jamie's heart pounded in her chest with fear as she felt the awesome power of the Turkish woman radiate out from her body. Gunnul fought for control and then let Jamie go, returning her hands to the steering wheel. "Chrissy's background has never mattered to me. It wouldn't have mattered what problems she might have had... I love her," she confessed awkwardly.

Jamie reached out and touched Gunnul's arm. "I'm sorry. I knew that. I was just reacting. I love her too, you see," choked Jamie, fighting back the tears. Gunnul nodded and put the car back into gear, easing back on to the tarmac.

After a few minutes, Gunnul said, "I am not a drug lord. Turkey is the biggest producer of opium for the medical trade and my farms produce most of that export. I do not trade in illegal drugs. Nor did I encourage or expose my brother to drug use. It is against our religion and against my personal belief. I have never taken an illegal drug," explained Gunnul. "If what you say is true, then my brother has lied to both of us for his own ends."

"You don't believe me?" asked Jamie, suddenly too weary of the intense emotion to take offense.

"I wish to, but I must protect Chrissy. I must not let... my feelings for you put me in a position that would result in my... our daughter being hurt," explained Gunnul quietly, her head aching from tension.

"You regret kissing me yesterday?" asked Jamie, staring out the windscreen afraid to look at Gunnul.

"Yes. It was not wise," answered Gunnul honestly, grimly holding on to the steering wheel.

"I regret it too," stated Jamie flatly. There was no more talk after that.

Having followed the coastal road along the Sea of Marmora in silence, Gunnul finally turned into a park region of lonely, bare hills. "This was once beautiful pine forests but a fire started by lightning some years ago destroyed most of the trees. This area seems doomed to tragedy. This park is the site of the heaviest trench warfare in World War I. This is Anzac Cove on the Gallipoli Peninsula," explained Gunnul. She pulled the car into a small parking area overlooking the cove below. Jamie was glad to get out and stretch her leg. It was still causing her some discomfort after yesterday's walk. The view from the top was magnificent. It was hard to imagine the sacrifice and suffering of the Australian and New Zealand troops who had valiantly fought to try to take this hill from an equally brave force of Turks. They had come, over the months of trench warfare, to respect each other and develop friendships that all too often ended in death as they were ordered to charge each other's lines. The trenches were still here. Sections of barbwire still coiled around wood supports. Wild flowers in bright yellow now grew between the strands.

A towering stature of a Turkish officer dominated the hillside. "Who is he?" asked Jamie.

"That is Attaturk, the founder of modern Turkey. He is, to my people, The Liberator," explained Gunnul. "As a young officer, he fought here."

After visiting Chanuk Bair, they went on to visit the Lone Pine Cemetery. The Turks still maintained the graves of the enemy they had come to respect with care and pride even after eighty years and the sight of all those graves of young men lost sent a shiver through Jamie. She turned to see Gunnul looking over the gravesite with eyes filled with pain. "You've been in war, haven't you?" she asked softly.

Gunnul forced her thoughts back from the past. "Yes, once. But it was not on this scale. Come, I will show you the monument to the Turks who fell." Gunnul drove the car back down the hill and stopped at a tall monument. Here they walked again through graves each marked by a small headstone and flowers. Jamie wandered over to a life size bronze statue of an old man holding the hand of a young girl.

"Gunnul, who is he?" she asked.

"He was the last Turk alive to have fought here. He died at the age of 101. He is holding the hand of his great grandchild," explained Gunnul. "When he died a grateful government made this statue. It is closure to a heroic but tragic part of my country's history," she explained, bending to place some wild flowers she had picked at the base of the statue.

Jamie looked at the face of the child and started in surprise. She turned to look at Gunnul. "That child is you, isn't it? And he was your great grandfather!" Gunnul nodded and walked away to wait at the car for Jamie. Jamie reached out and touched the two hands of bronze that were clasped through generations of time forever. Gunnul's great grandfather. Chrissy's great, great grandfather. Suddenly, Jamie began to realize why Gunnul had brought her here. Getting Chrissy back had seemed so easy when she had got on the plane at home. Now she was beginning to realize just how complex the issue of custody was going to be. She looked at their three hands together and quickly pulled her own back. Turning, she joined Gunnul at the car. Once again they drove in silence.

They lunched in the nearby coastal town on curried rice and chicken, eating huge, sweet oranges for desert. The conversation was polite and meaningless. Then Gunnul drove the car onto the ferry to take them across the Dardanelles Straits to Canakkale on the Asian side of Turkey. Late in the afternoon, they turned off the main road and bumped down between tall pines to a small, beautiful villa that sat on a bluff over looking the Aegean Sea. To Jamie's surprise, Teefo waited for them there. "Teefo will show you to your accommodations," stated Gunnul formally, after having talked to her secretary in Turkish for some minutes. The tall woman then turned and left.

"Please, you will come this way, Ms. Dedemann. Did you have a pleasant journey?" asked Teefo, leading the way to a simple but luxurious suite with French doors that opened onto a stone patio with an incredible view through the towering pines of the Aegean Sea below.

"Yes, Gunnul is a thoughtful and hospitable hostess," agreed Jamie formally, and as an afterthought she asked, "Teefo, can you tell me about the war that Gunnul was in?"

Teefo smiled, all too willing to brag about the hero for whom he had the honour to work. "It happened over ten years ago, when General Dedemann first inherited the family estates after the death of her father."

"Mohammed did not inherit as the only son?" questioned Jamie.

Teefo shook his head. "No, he wanted only money. It was Gunnul who wanted the land. She was with five others on the very eastern borders of Turkey, checking on some mining projects the family had out there, when they discovered an army preparing to invade Turkey through a narrow gorge. General Dedemann took control, even though she had no military training and was only a young woman of twenty. She caused a landslide so that the pass was very narrow. Then the six of them held off the enemy for three days until the Turkish Army could arrive. By then, only two were left alive. One died several weeks later but Gunnul, although critically wounded, survived. The last man had kept a diary. And that is how the Turkish people learned about General Dedemann's leadership and bravery. We do not have women in our armed forces although every man must do national service. But the Turkish Army was so impressed by her impossible deed that they made her a General. It is a very great honour!"

"Yes, it is," agreed Jamie, worrying about how badly Gunnul had been hurt. "Has General Dedemann not married?" she asked, surprised that her question had a tone of jealousy about it.

"No, her betrothed died at her side in battle. She was, you understand, badly hurt and can not bear children," Teefo explained, like an old village woman gossiping over the fence.

Suddenly, a blast of angry Turkish exploded into the room and Teefo went white. The two gossips turned to see Gunnul standing in the doorway, anger radiating from her. Jamie swallowed and Teefo hurried from the room. "I'm sorry. It wasn't Teefo's fault. I asked him, and he was just showing loyalty and pride in talking about your bravery and sacrifice."

Gunnul walked in and looked down at Jamie with eyes as cold as a glacier. Jamie held her ground even though she was shaking inside with fear. "You have a right to know about the person who is the mother of your daughter. I am reluctantly prepared to answer any questions you have. Please do not ask those who work for me," stated Gunnul through gritted teeth.

"Would you have told me what a hero you were?" challenged Jamie, "or what it cost you personally?"

"I would have told you the facts of the event," responded Gunnul honestly.

Jamie nodded, realizing that the General had been pushed to her limit. "This room is lovely," stated Jamie. "Do you own this house?"

"Yes," responded the dark-haired woman, still fighting for control of her emotions.

Jamie limped over to a chair and sat down awkwardly, pain knifing across her face before she could hide it.

Gunnul started forward. "You are not well, Jamie?" she asked nervously.

"I am fine. My leg hurts a little that is all," answered Jamie.

"I am sorry. I do not think. I have walked you too much for two days," exclaimed Gunnul, worry etched on her face.

Jamie laughed softly, finding the way Gunnul's English deteriorated when she was upset very endearing. "I am finding it hard to wait to see my daughter, Gunnul. But I understand why you are going to all this trouble and I do appreciate what you are doing to protect our daughter. I am sure you are a very busy woman."

Gunnul smiled and shrugged. "At night, I use the computer to handle my business. Also I have Teefo, who is as good a businessman as he is a gossip," explained Gunnul. "I came to ask if you would like to swim with me."

Jamie loved swimming but she looked down at the steep slope and sandy beach and wasn't sure if she could maneuver easily with her crutch.

Gunnul's intelligent eyes followed Jamie's. "Do not worry. It will be easy for me to get you to the beach and the warm salt water will help your leg," reassured the older woman.

Jamie smiled. "O.K."

Jamie quickly changed into a swimsuit and matching jacket. Throwing her towel over her shoulder she leaned on her crutch while she slipped one foot then the other into sandals. Now the scars that were usually covered by slacks or dark nylons showed clearly, running down her left leg from thigh to ankle. The reconstructed knee did not sit quite straight and her foot turned in slightly when she walked.

She met Gunnul out on the main patio and saw the look of horror and sympathy flash across Gunnul's face before she hid it behind a wall of studied politeness. "You are ready, Jamie?" Gunnul asked.

"Yes," replied Jamie, and was totally taken by surprise when Gunnul swept her up into her arms, skipped down the patio stairs and then headed down the path with long, easy strides. "Ah, I could walk Gunnul. I must be heavy."

"Your leg hurts and no you are not heavy. You are very light. I do not think that you eat enough," observed the older woman seriously, as was her way when she made an observation. Jamie liked the smell of Gunnul's warm skin. She found it spicy and exotic.

At the beach, Gunnul set Jamie down and let her remove her robe and place her towel and cane on a lounge. Then she once again picked the smaller woman up and carried her effortlessly out into the water. "You can swim, Jamie?" asked Gunnul when she was waist deep.

"Yes, I am a strong swimmer," Jamie stated, and Gunnul nodded and carried the woman farther out before lowering her into the warm seawater. The water came up to Jamie's shoulders as if Gunnul knew instinctively how tall she was. Once she was sure that Jamie had her footing, she released her and fell back into the water, backstroking away.

Jamie let her body relax and become buoyant. From a child, she had always been a good swimmer, but since her injury she had relished the opportunity to leave her awkwardness behind and move effortlessly again. Gunnul saw the delight cross the woman's face and when she was sure that Jamie could indeed take care of herself in the water, she turned over and did a steady, strong Australian crawl out to sea.

She had gone farther than she should, trying to use up some of the nervous energy that seemed to consume her these days. Sleep just wouldn't come as she tossed each night, her mind obsessing about the small woman who was here to steal her daughter away and had managed also to steal her heart. *I have to get over this attraction! I must put Chrissy first*, she thought for the thousandth time that week.

Preoccupied with her thoughts she didn't react at first when Jamie yelled a warning. The jet ski roared by, its owner unaware as he headed back to the resort located around the point that his hull had struck against a swimmer. Gunnul felt a searing pain and then knew nothing more.

Jamie dived for the third time. Her hands groped around in the sandy bottom. Just as her lungs were ready to burst her left hand touched a cold bathing suit. Desperately, she grabbed on and fought her way to the surface, dragging the heavy body with her. *Thank God this is salt water and buoyancy is better*, she thought. She got her breath as best she could while fighting to keep them both above water and clamped her mouth over Gunnul's as she used her legs to propel them towards shore. Once she got her footing, she worked again to keep air in Gunnul's water filled lungs as she pulled the larger woman towards shore.

It became harder to help Gunnul as they got into more shallow water. Jamie needed the buoyancy of the water to help support herself without her cane. She wrapped her arms around Gunnul and fell back, using her feet to push along the bottom as she partly floated. Closer to shore, she allowed the waves to carry them to the beach while she worked on Gunnul. How long had she been under water exactly? It seemed like hours but it had probably only been a few minutes. Jamie had already been swimming towards the unsuspecting Gunnul before the jet ski had hit her.

Gunnul's eyes fluttered and Jamie breathed into her mouth once again. Then the taller woman took a ragged breath and Jamie pulled her onto her side as she vomited up seawater and sand. "Teefo! Help! Teefo!" screamed Jamie, holding onto the barely conscious woman, trying to protect her from the wave action. Jamie was weakening fast, exhausted from the monumental effort to pull the much bigger woman to shore. Finally, she became aware of excited voices and gentle arms lifting her away from Gunnul.

* * * * *

Gunnul rested quietly. The doctor and the various servants had left but Jamie still sat at her side. Both the doctor and a shaky Gunnul had reassured her that the General was all right and that she should rest, but Jamie could not bring herself to leave the older woman's side. "You look so tired," muttered a sleepy Gunnul.

"A little," admitted Jamie. "It is important that you stay awake a bit longer. You have an awful bump on your head."

Blue eyes met green, blocking out the rest of the world. Slowly, Jamie leaned forward and brushed her lips against Gunnul's. When she tried to pull away Gunnul's hand came to the back of her neck and gently pulled her down again. Their mouths opened to each other's demands and desire built to passion. Jamie moaned as large, strong fingers slipped under her terry towel bath robe and pushed the material back from her shoulders while Gunnul nibbled and kissed gently at her throat. Jamie's hands tugged on Gunnul's robe and she felt the powerful woman surrender to her passion as Jamie's hand traced across her breast.

The tall woman visibly jerked when Jamie lowered her head and took Gunnul's hard nipple into her mouth. "I... I want to make love to you," moaned Gunnul, trying hard not to lose control as her hands roamed over the bare skin of Jamie's back.

Jamie crawled up onto the bed so that she now lay on Gunnul, the fresh cotton sheets the only barrier between them. "I think we are doing just that," whispered Jamie, and Gunnul gave a primitive growl deep in her throat as she rolled Jamie over and covered her with her body, their mouths hungrily seeking each other.

Foreplay lead to climax and release to exhausted sleep in each other's arms.

* * * * *

Gunnul woke with a pounding headache and a satisfied grin. She propped herself up on one elbow and looked down at the petite woman who nestled close to her side. *All my life I have loved you, little one. How do I tell you that? How can I make you understand how our grave in the secret garden affects me? You will think I am crazy.* Unconsciously, she reached out a hand and ran fingertips along the silken skin of her lover. Green eyes fluttered open and sparkled with recognition. Gunnul leaned in and captured Jamie's lips. Arms wrapped around her neck and Gunnul rolled back, effortlessly pulling the woman she kissed over on top of her.

The long kiss broke and Jamie, now draped over Gunnul's form, looked down at her with worried eyes. "Gunnul, this is not right. We shouldn't have done this. We still haven't... I mean we could still... we didn't really... there's Chrissy," she ended, a deep blush creeping up her face.

Gunnul's guts twisted in disappointment and fear. "I disappoint

117

you? I did not give you pleasure? I do not have experience, Jamie, but you could teach me," fretted Gunnul.

"No! No, you were wonderful. I've never... never had anyone draw so much passion and need from me. I can't believe how good it was," reassured Jamie, running a finger over Gunnul's lips and then, unable to stop herself, leaning forward to capture those lips again.

She gave up the General's lips reluctantly and buried her head under the taller woman's chin. It felt so right being here. It was her daydreams come true. At last, she was in the arms of her secret protector, but how did she explain that to Gunnul without sounding completely crazy! "My soul, my body wants this so much, Gunnul, but it is a really bad idea. What about Chrissy?"

Gunnul sighed. "I don't know. But I do know that I do not think I can give you up, Jamie," admitted Gunnul, rubbing her head against Jamie's.

"Gunnul, have you ever been with anyone before? I mean are you a virgin?" Jamie asked hesitantly, looking up at the Turkish woman with worried eyes.

"The damage from my wounds... No, no I'm not but nor have I ever slept with anyone before," explained Gunnul, colour rising up her neck.

Jamie stretched up and kissed the warm neck, remembering the horrible scars on Gunnul's side and abdomen. "You were engaged to be married. Are you sure you really want to be involved in a gay relationship?"

Gunnul nodded. "I am sure I want you, Jamie. My betrothal was arranged."

Jamie sat up in shock. "That's awful! How sexist and primitive!"

Gunnul smiled. "No, just different. I had the right to refuse his courtship. He was picked very carefully for me. Our lives, education, backgrounds, families all suited very much. I liked him. It would have been a satisfactory marriage. Your way does not seem to produce many happy marriages."

Jamie considered. "Well, it is left to random chance, and many do pick poorly. But when someone does meet their soulmate, that love is so profound that it's worth all the risks you take to get there," countered Jamie.

"You have slept with many people, Jamie?" asked Gunnul innocently.

Jamie shook her head. "I always thought I was gay. I lived with a woman at university. We were happy enough but always knew that we would go our separate ways. Then, once I started working I met Moe. I... I thought I could make it work but well, what I thought I saw in him wasn't really there. It was just an illusion."

Silence. "Is it there with me?" asked Gunnul softly.

Jamie snuggled down beside Gunnul again. "Yes," she confessed.

"It is for me too," whispered Gunnul. Silence as Gunnul's hand gently brushed over the warm hairs of Jamie's sex. "I wish to do things to you, Jamie. I do not know if it is proper," confessed a confused woman, trying to control her baser desires.

Jamie took the long, strong hand and placed it between her legs, gasping at the marvelous sensation that ran through her at Gunnul's touch. "Fuck me, Gunnul. Take me," she begged earnestly, and felt herself pinned to the bed by her lover.

Gunnul lay on her back, her lover snuggled on her shoulder fast asleep. Wow! She was having trouble dealing with the depth of emotion that had come out when the two of them had taken each other. Wow, was about as coherent as she could get at the moment.

She could smell the heavy scent of their combined sex and it excited her to the core of her being. She did not think that she could live without Jamie. She rubbed a hand soothingly over her lover's naked back. *Please, let it be the same for you, Jamie. Please don't leave me!*

Jamie woke to the steady heartbeat of her lover. For someone who had never made love before, Gunnul was incredible. Their two souls had danced to a love song close in each other's arms, bonding on a level that transcended time and space. She looked up at the dozing woman. *I love you, Gunnul. I've loved you all my life. How do I tell you that? How do I make what is happening to us work?*

* * * * *

They spent the rest of the day on the patio and the beach. Gunnul, although she professed to be fine, still looked pale and Jamie was worn out with the roller coaster ride of emotion over the last few weeks and with the massive effort it had taken to rescue Gunnul. Jamie read a book that Gunnul had given her on the history of Turkey. It appeared that just about anything of importance over the last two million years had happened in Turkey, from the incredible Neolithic site of Catal Hoyuk to the air support during Desert Storm! Gunnul used her laptop and cellular phone to deal with various business issues that could not be put off.

After dinner they sat together wrapped in each other's arms in a lounge chair. Gunnul took out her phone and looked at Jamie. "I am going to phone Chrissy now," she told Jamie and felt the little body beside her tense. "I phone her every night when I am away, if at all possible. I will speak to her in Turkish but I will tell her that you are here and that I am bring you home to meet her," stated Gunnul. Jamie was too emotional to speak. Tears trailed slowly down her face and her heart pounded in her chest. Gunnul could feel it. She pulled Jamie close and kissed her head as she used her other hand to punch her home number.

She talked rapidly to someone and then looked down at Jamie to explain. "Housekeeper. Chrissy is playing with her dog in the garden." Jamie nodded, her hands balled tightly in Gunnul's shirt. Gunnul turned back to the phone a wide grin of love on her face and talked away happily in Turkish.

"Mommy?"

"Hello, my sweet one! Are you being good for Shantu?" asked Gunnul.

"Yes. Today we went for a picnic over on the hill by the vineyards. I miss you!" replied Chrissy happily.

"A few more days and I will be home," explained Gunnul. "I am bringing home someone that I like very much, Chrissy. I think you will like her too," said the General.

"Who, Mommy?" questioned the little girl.

"Your birth mother," revealed Gunnul.

There was a moment's stunned silence. "Really! She is here! She is nice?"

"Very. She saved my life yesterday," confessed Gunnul and went on to explain the story to her daughter.

"Are you all right, Mommy?" asked the worried child.

"I am fine. Would you like to say hello to your birth mother?" asked Gunnul tentatively.

A moment's hesitation. "What should I call her, Mom?" the girl asked awkwardly.

A lump formed in Gunnul's throat and she swallowed it with difficulty. "I think you should call her mother too. She is your mother just as I am. Most children have two grandmothers, you seem to have two mothers!" joked Gunnul, trying to make a tense situation lighter.

Jamie could feel the tension in Gunnul's body and see the strain in her face. What were they talking about? Would Chrissy want to see her now that she was really here?

"Yes, I would like to welcome her to Turkey, Mommy," agreed

the polite child.

"Good," responded Gunnul with approval. "You must speak in English. She does not understand Turkish," explained Gunnul.

Gunnul looked down at Jamie. "Our daughter wishes to welcome you," explained Gunnul, holding the phone to Jamie's ear.

"Hello, Mommy?!" came a child's clear voice.

"Hello, Chrissy? Oh Chrissy, honey, it is so wonderful to hear your voice. I... I've missed you!" sobbed Jamie.

"I am so excited to meet you. Welcome to my country, Mom! Is it okay if I call you Mom too? My Mommy said it was okay?" questioned Chrissy.

Jamie looked up into Gunnul's tense face as she gave Jamie emotional privacy by looking fixedly out to sea. "Yes, we are both proud to have you as our daughter," she responded, reaching up and gently stroking Gunnul's cheek. Gunnul turned and looked down at her, a nervous smile hovering at her lips. This was really hard for Gunnul, she realized. "I can't wait to see you, Chrissy. I love you very much," Jamie choked. "Here, I'll give you back to your other Mom, so she can tell you our plans," explained Jamie, now barely holding it together.

Gunnul took the phone and talked briefly to Chrissy in Turkish while Jamie sobbed into her side. Then she held the woman that she loved, the mother of her child, close to her and let her cry all the bottled-up emotion out.

* * * * *

Gunnul had offered to take Jamie directly to Antalya but Jamie had agreed with Gunnul that, although it would be hard to wait, it was good to give her time to learn about Turkey and Chrissy time to get used to the idea of seeing her birth mother. She also realized that Gunnul needed some time to deal with her own emotions. It must be, Jamie reasoned, very hard to allow someone else that close to the daughter you love.

They sat over a breakfast of pita bread, rolls, fresh fruit, yogurt and of course white cheese and olives, which were a Turkish breakfast must. Jamie was making an effort to adjust to this breakfast variation. She wanted to be part of Chrissy and Gunnul's world as much as she could. "Jamie, why did you save my life?" Gunnul had asked in bed last night.

Jamie had looked up in surprise, "I couldn't stand by and let anyone die if I could help them," Jamie replied, reaching up to push

Gunnul's hair back, "and for you, there would never be any restriction. I would give my life for you."

Gunnul looked at Jamie in wonder. "It would have solved your problem of custody if you had not tried," she pointed out practically, looking deeply into Jamie's beautiful eyes.

"Gunnul! Would you have done that if it had been me?" she asked in shock.

Gunnul looked equally shocked. "Of course not!" The General looked pensive for a few seconds, playing idly with Jamie's hair. "It is hard for me to accept that anyone would be willing to sacrifice themselves for me. All my life people have wanted things from me or needed my support. I am strong and rich. It makes me feel very loved that you would risk your life for me. But do not do so again, Jamie. I... I couldn't... If anything happened to you..."

Jamie had reached up and kissed Gunnul to silence. "Hush, don't think about it. No one can predict the future. We are here together now and that is wonderful," Jamie said soothingly. Gunnul had pulled her close and they had made love way into the night.

Finishing breakfast, they walked out to the car and started once more on their way. Once they were on the main road again, Gunnul took Jamie's hand in her own. Jamie smiled softly; her lover was so strong and brave in so many ways and so child-like and fragile in others. She had noticed very quickly that Gunnul needed to have physical contact with her as much as possible, as if afraid that Jamie would disappear out of her life. Not that Jamie minded at all! Gunnul couldn't get close enough to suit her.

They drove only a short way and pulled into a parking lot beside a huge wooden horse. Gunnul looked up and sneered at it. "A reproduction of Homer's Trojan Horse," explained Gunnul with disgust. "The tourist would be disappointed if it wasn't here. This is Troy," she explained.

Jamie laughed at Gunnul's obvious chagrin and with sparkling eyes insisted that Gunnul climb the stairs into the massive wooden horse and look out of the windows at the ruins of Troy. Within the cool darkness of the body, Jamie wrapped herself around the Turkish woman and kissed her. "I find it hard to believe that Helen of Troy was as beautiful as you," she teased and Gunnul blushed and rewarded her with a kiss.

They walked around the crumbling ruins that where actually nine separate cities built on top of each other. "The treasures that were found here were secretly sent to Germany during the colonial days. During World War II, they were taken to Russia. For many years, no one knew what had happened to the treasures of Troy but recently Russia put them on display. Germany immediately said that they had been stolen from them and they must be returned!"

Jamie laughed, appreciating the irony of the situation. "I suppose that when Germany gets them back, they will return them to Turkey, the rightful owner," Jamie observed sarcastically.

Gunnul laughed too. "As you say, when piggies fly."

Gunnul let Jamie wander around observing everything. She wondered if Jamie would react to this place as she had many years ago as a teenager coming to Troy for the first time. *You are far more beautiful, Jamie, than Helen ever was*, she thought knowingly.

They walked together along a rocky path to stand on the foundations of the temple of Athena. "More than two thousand years ago, Alexander the Great stood here and looked out over the lowlands as we do now, Jamie. He ordered that this temple be rebuilt to the glory of Greece," explained Gunnul to Jamie's back as she stood on the edge and looked over the panoramic view of the lowlands.

Suddenly, Jamie turned and looked at Gunnul in shock. "I feel like I've been here before! Do you feel that way?" she exclaimed.

"Yes," Gunnul responded, shaken with the confirmation that Jamie was aware of the same trace memories as herself.

Jamie reached up and placed her hand on her brow. "Oh boy, this is going to get some getting used to." She looked up at Gunnul. "Do you have other memories. I mean of me and other places?"

"Yes, I have known you all my life. You come to me. It is difficult to explain. We lived in an ancient world, I think, but also we have lived in other times and places," revealed Gunnul.

"The Amazon," stated Jamie. "You have always come to me too. I call you my protector. This is very weird. I think we need to sit down and talk about this."

Gunnul nodded, and they returned to the car hand in hand, Gunnul explaining that this would not attract comment in Turkey, where girls often linked arms or held hands. Men too, she explained. And then laughed and said that traditionally, however, a man and woman would not hold hands in public.

Gunnul drove on while they tried to bring some sort of sense and order to their jumbled impressions. It was clear that they each had been aware of the other all their lives and that they were aware of living in an ancient world and in other times too. Gunnul finally called for a halt. "We are dealing with too much here, Jamie. Our feelings for Chrissy, our love, and the mystery of our past."

Jamie sighed. "You're right, Gunnul. Let's just see how things go for a bit. I feel like I am on overload!"

Gunnul nodded. "We are meant to be together, Jamie," stated Gunnul, partly as a fact and partly for reinforcement. She was still having trouble believing that Jamie loved her unconditionally. In Gunnul's life there had always been conditions. Except for Chrissy. Chrissy was the bright spot in Gunnul's life and now maybe there was Jamie.

"Yes. We are soulmates and I think always have been," agreed Jamie, readily wrapping her arm around Gunnul and leaning her head on the taller woman's arm. "It just took us some time to find each other again."

Gunnul drove on to Bergama, which sits under the mountain where the ruins of ancient Pergamon lie. Gunnul dodged tour buses around the steep, winding road to the archeological site while Jamie held on to her in fear. "Damn it, Gunnul, you could have slowed down!" grumbled Jamie, breathing a sigh of relief as they pulled into the parking lot at the top and got out.

Gunnul raised an eyebrow and looked at her soulmate with amusement. "But then there would be no excitement, Jamie," she explained innocently.

Jamie stopped, placing her free hand on her hip, and gave Gunnul a bemused look. "You get hit by a boat and nearly drown, your daughter's birth mother shows up to lay claim, you fall in love for the first time, and discover that your relationship is joined through space and time and you have to go looking for excitement because life is dull?"

Gunnul smiled sheepishly and shrugged. "I think we have lived more dangerous lives," she responded.

"Yeah," agreed Jamie, taking Gunnul's arm so that she would know that she wasn't really angry. "But for every life we've had, somewhere along the line we end up dead. Please keep that firmly in mind. It took a long time to find you this time and I'd like this relationship to last!"

Gunnul stopped abruptly and looked down at Jamie in wonder. "Would you, Jamie?"

Jamie realized that she had made some assumptions about their relationship that perhaps were not shared. "Well, I mean... yeah... if you were comfortable with it... I mean, I don't just sleep with anyone you know!"

"I have never slept with anyone. I wait for you, Jamie. It would please me very much if you were a part of my life," confessed Gunnul nervously.

Jamie looked at the rocky, dry ground, then up into Gunnul's eyes. "We've only known each other a few days. We didn't have a very high opinion of each other at the beginning. There is still the issue of Chrissy. Maybe we are moving too quickly."

Gunnul stiffened and looked like she had been hit. "Come, I will show you the site. It is very beautiful," she said, swallowing hard.

"Gunnul, no. Listen to me," begged Jamie, grabbing her lover's arm and almost being pulled off her feet. Gunnul reached out and steadied her. "Listen, I love you. I have loved you, I think, since the dawn of time. I want to be your partner for the rest of my life. But I'm trying to be realistic here. We are strangers. We come from two very different cultures... damn it, Gunnul don't look like that!"

Gunnul hung her head and then looked up at Jamie with hurt, worried eyes. "I love you too, Jamie. I don't want you to leave me. But I understand what you are trying to say. I will not push you into something you are not comfortable with."

Jamie smiled gently. "You are wonderful, my sweet one," she murmured.

Gunnul looked up sharply. "W... What did you call me?"

"My sweet one," repeated Jamie in surprise.

Gunnul grinned happily. "I have always liked it when you called me this," she stated and took Jamie's elbow to help balance her on the uneven stone ramp leading to the Greek acropolis.

White Corinthian columns, the skeletons of a long gone age, rose against a deep blue sky. The orderly beauty of the temple complexes transfixed Jamie. The broken sculpture, still stately in elaborate armor, amazed her with its beauty and fine workmanship. "Oh Gunnul, it is so wonderful here," Jamie gasped, taking in the miles of countryside bathed in bluish light and framed by the grace of the classic temple columns.

"Yes, it is very beautiful but I help you down here. It is more interesting underneath," replied Gunnul. A whole subterranean structure of layers of barrel vaulting lay underneath the acropolis. It had been constructed to level the steep mountainside to build the acropolis on. Jamie delighted in Gunnul's serious lecture on the structure of barrel vaults and Greek engineering feats. She couldn't help but smile. Her lover always missed the beauty and went straight for the practical.

Gunnul saw the bemused grin. "I bore you, Jamie?" she asked in worry, as they stood inside a dark barreled hall.

Jamie looked around to make sure no one was near and stood on tiptoes and kissed Gunnul. "I think, my pragmatic lover, that you have not changed one bit in thousands of years and I love you for it." Gunnul blushed and pulled Jamie close for another kiss.

Back on the surface, Gunnul showed Jamie where the famous library of Pergamon was located. Jamie stared through the security bars at the stone shelving within. "I was here, Gunnul, I can feel it!" she exclaimed, finding relief in being able at last to freely talk about her trace memories.

"This library was the second biggest in the ancient world. Only the famous library of Alexandria in Egypt was bigger. After Alexandria was burnt, Cleopatra asked that the books from Pergamon be sent to replace them. There is no record as to what happened to them," explained Gunnul.

"Oh Gunnul, could you imagine finding them! You would have all the knowledge of the ancient world at your fingertips! It would be amazing!"

Eventually, Gunnul pulled Jamie away from the beauty of the acropolis and from the row of merchants selling local curios to the tourists. "But I need to buy gifts for all my friends to take back!" Jamie had wailed and did not see Gunnul stiffen and the worried and hurt look that crossed her face.

They drove on to Asclepion, one of the very first hospitals in the known world. Jamie looked tired and when she thought Gunnul was not looking she would rub her knee. "We do not need to do this site, Jamie, if your leg is hurting you," Gunnul commented once they were parked. "It is a large site and as always the ground is uneven."

"Don't baby me, Gunnul," Jamie snapped unfairly.

Gunnul's face went still, a mask devoid of emotion. "Sorry," she stated quietly. "I feel guilt for what has happened to you. Knowing my family has hurt you."

"Gunnul, no." Jamie sighed, taking the woman's hand. "I made the decisions in my life. This one and all the others. If those decisions brought me some pain, they also brought me you. You are always trying to protect me. I love you for that but don't take on the guilt of my fate, okay? Your brother beat me with a baseball bat. I tried to protect myself with my leg. That is not your fault. I survived."

Gunnul had gone white with rage and Jamie could feel the anger radiating from her. "If my brother was alive, I would kill him for what he has done to you," she hissed through tight lips.

Jamie leaned forward and kissed those lips. "I wouldn't let you," she stated and smiled. Gunnul smiled too and they got out of the car and headed over to the shed that sold the entrance tickets. Jamie noted that Gunnul never paid. When she appeared, the military guards would come to attention and wave her through. This seemed to embarrass the Turk but she never mentioned it, simply smiling her thanks and whispering "Teashakequwe" which Gunnul had told her meant thank you.

"The archeological sites are always guarded by the army, Gunnul. Are you afraid of terrorist attacks?" asked Jamie.

"No," replied Gunnul. "So far Turkey has been spared the effects of the fundamentalists' movement in the Middle East, although their political party is developing a foothold among the poor. Turkey walks a thin line between the west and the east. Our country is partly in Europe and partly in Asia. In the west, people think that the wars in the Middle East have to do with religion and politics but that is not really the case. They have to do with water. Who has it and who doesn't and how much you are willing to sacrifice to get it. In the Middle East for the past five thousand years it has always been about water.

"Turkey is lucky. We have enough water. Our country is self sufficient in its ability to supply its people with food. So every man in Turkey must do national service. Always we must be on guard against those countries who envy us. That is a lot of soldiers. It saves the government money to use them to protect our nation's heritage instead of hiring security guards," explained Gunnul.

Jamie nodded as Gunnul helped her down the long marble street flanked on either side with Greek columns. "This is a test, Jamie. Here at Asclepion, you had to be well enough to walk down this avenue unsupported or the hospital would not treat you."

"Well, that lets me out!" grinned Jamie, giving Gunnul an affectionate poke so that she knew Jamie was joking. Gunnul smiled, proud of Jamie's courage and positive attitude. She wasn't sure she could be so brave. When she had been wounded in battle, she had been a terrible patient.

They entered the main court and stood before the amphitheater that was cut into the hillside. "The doctors here treated people through their senses. They thought illness was caused by your soul being out of step with its natural rhythms. There was drama, music, a library, dance, and steam and hot mud baths to help you get back in touch with yourself."

Jamie laughed. "Boy, this place would make a fortune in my neighborhood!"

Gunnul took Jamie down a long, dark, barrel vaulted tunnel that led to a round room with arches containing sleeping platforms. "When a patient first arrived here, the priests would make them come through this tunnel. Water ran through a drain along the edge because the sound was considered soothing and the tunnel was filled with mist to make it mystical. Once in the room, you would sleep and your dreams would be interpreted by the priests the next day so that they knew how to treat you," explained Gunnul, leading the way out with Jamie gamely following in the rear, making her way slowly over the uneven surface.

"Hell, I'd be dreaming of steam baths and a good scotch then," observed Jamie, and Gunnul came to a sudden stop and looked down at her in concern.

"You must not swear or drink, Jamie," observed Gunnul. "It is a bad example for Chrissy. We Moslems do not swear or drink. I would wish Chrissy to think the best of you."

Indignant anger roared through Jamie's being and then she choked back her angry words, realizing that Gunnul was not being judgmental, just protective of their daughter and wanting Jamie to be accepted.

"Okay, no swearing or drinking," she promised. "Why did you drink that first night?" asked Jamie.

"I was trying to be American and make you feel welcome. I shouldn't have. I made a fool of myself and insulted you," confessed Gunnul.

"Yeah, your true colours come out when you are drunk," teased Jamie, poking the serious Gunnul in the stomach. It made Gunnul smile and they went on in a happier mood. Gunnul stopped to show Jamie a broken column where for the first time the snake curled around a staff had been used to represent the medical profession. "The spring here is naturally radioactive, so maybe some people were really cured," finished Gunnul, holding the car door for the exhausted smaller woman to get in. They drove on to the city of Izmir where Teefo waited for them at the Hilton Hotel. Gunnul wrapped Jamie in her arms as the elevator took them up to the suite that waited for them.

Jamie felt incredibly warm and secure wrapped around her lover. Her damaged knee was cushioned on Gunnul's thigh; her head rested on the older woman's shoulder and one arm was draped over her chest. Gunnul tried to ease out from under her soulmate but green eyes looked at her through sleepy lids and the arm around her tightened. "Where do you think you are going at this disgusting time of the morning?" she grumbled.

Gunnul kissed her on the head. "Do you hear the Muezzin, the one who calls us to prayer from the minarets?" Jamie became aware of a wailing above the early morning traffic. "I go to pray."

"Can I come?" asked Jamie, leaning up on an elbow and looking at Gunnul.

Gunnul looked surprised and then pleased. "We can pray and I will instruct you. Come," encouraged Gunnul.

Jamie slipped out of bed determined to bridge the gap between her world and her daughter's. Gunnul rolled out a prayer rug and then started to explain, "We face east when we pray because that is the direction of Mecca, the spiritual center of the Islamic world. Your churches are also orientated so that the altar is in the east. My God is your God. I do not think that most people in the west realize this. Allah is not a strange eastern god. Allah is just the Arabic word for God. Our Quran teaches us the stories of the Old Testament and the New. We know the stories of Moses and all the other prophets and believe in Mary and Jesus. We do not believe that Jesus was the Son of God, nor do we believe that Muhammad was. In our religion, they were both great prophets of God."

Jamie nodded seriously, taking in all Gunnul had to say.

"There are five requirements for all Moslems. First, we must declare the shahada, that is to say that we recognize that there is only one God and that Muhammad was his prophet. Second, we must pray five times a day. Usually, that is at dawn, noon, mid afternoon, nightfall and evening but it does not really matter. We pray when we can and we do not need to gather in a church to do so because we know all over the world Moslems are united in prayer. It is called the salat. On Fridays, we have community prayer in the mosque like your Sunday. The third requirement is the zaqat; one tenth of your earnings should go to the poor. Fourth, we must fast from sun up to sun down during the month of Ramadan."

"Does Chrissy fast?" asked Jamie.

"Children, the sick, old and expecting mothers are not to fast, nor are you required to do so if you are traveling. Chrissy learned to fast for one hour a day when she was young. This was easy. Now she fasts all day except for a small snack at lunch time," answered Gunnul. "When she is fourteen, then I will expect her to fast properly," stated Gunnul, and then looked uncertainly at Jamie. Jamie nodded; this was not the time to pick a fight.

"The last requirement is to visit Mecca. Chrissy went with me to Mecca last year," finished Gunnul, indicating that Jamie should follow her. They went into the bathroom and Gunnul washed her hands, face and feet and then had Jamie do the same. "It is important always to wash before prayers. One should come before one's God clean of mind and body. Some westerners think that women in Islam are treated poorly because they do not pray with the men but must sit at the back.

This is not so. It is because we might have thoughts that were not clean to have before God if we were together.

"Islam improved the conditions of women greatly. In our faith infanticide or the abuse of women is not permitted. Wives must be treated properly and their wishes respected. Women may inherit and own property. Their roles are not separate from men, although traditionally the men lead, rather they support each other. Come, we pray."

Gunnul lead Jamie to the prayer rug. Three times they bowed to the east as Gunnul recited the opening surah of the Quran, "In the Name of God, the Merciful, the Compassionate..." Then they knelt and bowed three times, placing their foreheads to the ground. With each action prayers were repeated. The praying time took only about five minutes, then Gunnul rolled up her prayer mat and put it away.

"Do you pray five times a day, Gunnul?" asked Jamie, aware that this was the first time that she had seen her lover pray.

"I try to. I must live both in a western and eastern world. It is not always easy in business. If I can't stop to pray then I at least offer a prayer in silence where ever I am," revealed Gunnul. "Do you go to church, Jamie?"

"No. I was raised in the Greek Orthodox faith but I have never practised my faith seriously," replied Jamie honestly.

Gunnul nodded. "When all you have in life is desert, faith becomes perhaps more important. It gives you hope and strength. Are you hungry?"

"Always," laughed Jamie and they rang for a Turkish breakfast to be sent up.

* * * * *

"My God." whispered Jamie in awe.

"You are swearing again, Jamie." observed Gunnul seriously.

"No, I'm not," laughed Jamie. "I'm expressing my thanks for all things bright and beautiful!"

Gunnul looked confused. "This is a hymn. Why do you..." Then she saw the mischief in Jamie's eyes and laughed.

"My exclamation meant that this is the most beautiful facade I have ever seen," explained Jamie.

Gunnul nodded. They had driven up early to Ephesus to beat the crowds and they now stood above the sunken main square looking across the court at the three-story, curved facade of the library of ancient Ephesus. In soft, pink marble, the facade's illusory proportions, classic tiers of columns and statues in niches could not be fairly described. "Do you see the female statues in the niches, Jamie? They represent knowledge, friendship, understanding and wisdom. In order to honour his father, Celsus built this library. Celsus' crypt can still be seen inside. It was the third biggest library in the known world with some 40,000 scrolls. It is said that Aristotle taught here," bragged Gunnul.

Jamie beamed. "Help me down the stairs, Gunnul. I want to see inside!" Gunnul obliged the petite woman, delighted by Jamie's enthusiasm about everything she saw and experienced. Inside, the American limped around seeming to draw from the roofless walls, the memories of fresh parchment and ink, and the mumbling of scholars. Gunnul could almost hear the argumentative Aristotle conversing with the crowds on the steps outside. She had come here many times and been moved by the ruins but never had she felt so close to the ghosts of the ancient city as she was now, watching Jamie's delight.

Later, they sat in the perfectly preserved amphitheater that could hold 25,000 spectators and ate a box lunch that Teefo had arranged for them. "St. Paul came to this amphitheater, Jamie. He wanted to convince the people of Ephesus to become Christian. But the silversmiths in town were afraid that if the people became Christian they would lose business making silver idols. They organized a mob that chanted, 'Great is Artemis of the Ephesians!' for two hours so that St. Paul couldn't talk. St. Paul had to run from town so he wouldn't be stoned," recounted Gunnul. "That is why he had to write the letters to the Ephesians that are in the holy books!"

"Wow, that's amazing. I had no idea that so much history happened in Turkey," admitted Jamie. "St. Paul should have sold the silversmiths on the idea of crucifixes and indulgence tokens. They'd have welcomed him with open arms!" mused Jamie, making Gunnul laugh.

"This amphitheater is still used. Last year, Chrissy and her friends conned me into bringing them here to hear a rock concert by Sting. My ears are yet to recover! The sound vibrations damaged the stone structure so now only folk and classical music is allowed to be played here."

"Gunnul! Chrissy is far too young to be going to a rock concert!" exclaimed Jamie.

"Jamie, I am far too young to be going to a rock concert!" mimicked Gunnul. "I had no experience of such things and Chrissy, who can talk the leg off a donkey, convinced me that it was part of European culture and something she should experience because she was half American. The girls enjoyed themselves very much. I have not yet got over the experience."

Jamie laughed at the look of pain on Gunnul's face and hugged her affectionately. "I think you are something quite special to have gone to such lengths to make sure our daughter appreciated both sides of her heritage. It is one of the many reasons I love you," confessed Jamie, and Gunnul blushed deeply.

It was a long morning as Jamie insisted on going back again to see the mosaic sidewalks of intricate designs along Curetes Street, the main road through ancient Ephesus. She also wanted to take photos of the Trojan Fountain before returning again to the library. Gunnul showed Jamie the ancient public W.C. with its row of forty-eight stone seats and the footprint carved into the stone of the causeway indicating which way the brothel was! The site was very crowded when they left and Jamie was glad that Gunnul had insisted on an early start. They stayed that night near Kusadasi, at a resort on the Aegean Sea.

Gunnul lay propped up in bed with Jamie sitting between her legs and leaning against her chest. She picked up the phone and connected to her home while Jamie watched nervously. This time, Gunnul spoke in English. "Hello, Chrissy? Did you have a good day? Ah good. We toured Ephesus. Here, I'll let your American Mom tell you all about it." Gunnul passed the phone to Jamie and leaned back. *Family. Could we be a family? Why did Jamie take pictures? Does she mean to take them back to America with her curios? Would she leave Chrissy and me? Would she try to kidnap Chrissy?! No, no, Jamie would never try to take Chrissy back to the States, she is not like that,* reasoned Gunnul. She leaned back and relaxed and enjoyed the banter between her lover and her daughter. At first, it had been polite and stilted but now they were laughing and chatting away. *They could both talk the leg off a donkey,* thought Gunnul. *I am in big trouble!*

Next morning found a blurry-eyed Jamie rooting through her shoulder bag for her lip-gloss. She had cut down considerably on the makeup she wore, noting that Gunnul rarely wore any: wallet, passport, keys, tickets... lip-gloss. Jamie disappeared again into the bathroom. If Gunnul wanted to have early starts then she was going to have to stop making love for most of the night! Jamie smirked at herself in the mirror - forget that! They could just get up later!

Gunnul came into their room and raised an eyebrow at the contents of Jamie's purse all over the bed. Gunnul was meticulously neat and she found Jamie's randomness cute but frustrating. Sighing, she went over and started stuffing articles back into the purse. Not able to resist, she flipped open Jamie's passport and snorted at the wide-eyed, silly expression on the face of the woman she loved. Why were passport photos so awful? The wide grin faded as Gunnul's blue eyes scanned the page. The passport also covered Chrissy as a dependent. Gunnul looked at the airline tickets. One was for Jamie and the other was made out for Chrissy, one way to New York.

Jamie dropped her lip-gloss into her makeup bag just as the bathroom door slammed open. Gunnul stood in the doorway white with rage, her body quivering with violent energy that radiated out. Jamie gasped and took a step back. The blue eyes that bored into her blazed with a fire that was not human. "You have played me for a fool," Gunnul hissed. "You led me along and all the time you planned to kidnap Chrissy from me." Jamie shook her head in disbelief but no words would come out of her terrified mouth. Gunnul held up the plane tickets, now scrunched in her shaking fist. "Never will I let you close to her!" the woman growled, and spun on her heel and was gone.

Jamie sank down on the toilet seat and leaned her head on the counter. Never had she been so scared in her life! She had thought for a minute that Gunnul was going to hit her! Now she understood why Gunnul was accepted in a man's world and was respected as a great General. She was, when angry, a violent power unleashed. *My God! She found the tickets and thought I was using her to get to Chrissy to steal her away!*

Jamie sat up and took a deep breath. *And that was exactly what I had planned to do when I came. But not now, not now that I see what a wonderful life Chrissy has had and what a loving mother Gunnul is. I want Chrissy in my life but not at the cost of destroying Gunnul! I have to find her! She thinks someone is trying to use her again, to take from her again. She is too insecure to trust my love and she is not going to be able to handle this!* Jamie staggered from the bathroom and headed out to find Gunnul.

She limped down the road looking for any sign of the Turk. "Gunnul!" she called but no response came. Turning back, she went as quickly as she dared down the walkways to the shore. Trying to stay on the hard packed sand, she headed down the beach to where she could see two fishermen pulling a boat ashore.

"Did you see a woman, tall, dark, really good looking?" she asked them but they grinned back at her and shrugged. Jamie turned away in frustration and went to walk on but one of the men grabbed her arm, almost knocking her over.

"Hey! Let go!"

The man laughed and said something to her that could have been understood in any tongue by his body language. Jamie angrily pulled away just as the other coarse sailor came up behind her. He grabbed her cane out from under her arm and Jamie lost her balance and fell to the sand. The two men laughed and one bent down to grab at her shirt. Jamie tried to fight him off, panic rising quickly as she realized that she was in big trouble. Several quick punches to her head dazed her and she felt her defenses dropping.

Suddenly, a yell ripped the air and the standing man went flying into the sea. The one that kneeled over Jamie sneered and pulled a gutting knife from his belt as he stood to face Gunnul. He took a swing and Gunnul caught his wrist and bent it back with one hand as the elbow of the other arm came up and smashed him in the throat. Wrist bones snapped as the man gave a strangled choke and collapsed into the open dory.

The first man, blind with rage, was now splashing to shore to face the General. He faked a left jab and then came at her with his right. She let it pass her head and then brought her foot up, dropping him to his knees. The palm of her hand shot out and smashed the cartilage of his nose through the thin sinuous bones. Blood exploded out of his face as he dropped.

Gunnul looked down at Jamie, who was pale with fear and shock. The blue eyes were ice, still and cold. She looked around and found Jamie's cane washing along the water's edge. Picking it up, she handed it to the fallen woman without a word. Jamie crawled clumsily to her feet, then staggered forward on her cane, wrapping her arms around Gunnul.

"Let go," snapped the angry woman, standing stiffly.

"No, not until you listen to me," cried Jamie desperately, her arms tightening around Gunnul. For a minute there was only the sound of seagulls and surf, then Gunnul reached down and picked Jamie up effortlessly and carried her back to the hotel. In their room, she got ice and, wrapping it in a towel, placed it on Jamie's head as she nervously waited on the bed where Gunnul had left her. Jamie put her hand over Gunnul's and held on tight when Gunnul tried to pull back.

"No, please sit here," whispered Jamie, softly patting the edge of the bed. "Please let me explain."

Gunnul swallowed and looked at the wall as if she could find the answer written there. Then she swallowed again and sat on the very edge of the mattress, looking sadly at the floor. "I have lived with the horror of not knowing if my daughter was alive or dead and with the fear that she might have been beaten as I was. I knew nothing of you except what Moe had told me and that was a pretty ugly picture. I came here to rescue my daughter and I'd have done anything to do that, even sleeping with my worst enemy." Gunnul flinched and her shoulders slumped in pain.

"But I discovered instead that my daughter had been loved, supported and protected by the most beautiful and remarkable woman I have ever met. Gunnul, I love you. I wouldn't hurt you by trying to take Chrissy away from you. Nor would I hurt Chrissy by taking you out of her life. Whatever happens between us, I hope we can work something out where we can both share in Chrissy's life."

Slowly, Gunnul's pained and worried face came up and looked into Jamie's. Jamie sat up and wrapped her arms around Gunnul's neck, burying her head under Gunnul's chin. Hesitantly, strong arms curled Jamie into an embrace. "Love me," begged Jamie and Gunnul lowered the two of them to the bed. Their love was desperate, demanding and passionate, each trying to heal the emotional pain of the other.

They started their day much later than they had planned. Gunnul drove effortlessly with one hand while the other was wrapped tightly around Jamie's smaller one. Jamie looked at Gunnul's face. It was tense and drawn. *She is still really shaken by this morning. I know she wants to believe me but there are still doubts,* Jamie realized and raised their joined hands to kiss Gunnul's fingers. "Why don't you take the passport and tickets, Gunnul?" Jamie offered.

"Why would I do that?" asked Gunnul, with forced surprise.

"Because you are not sure you can trust me and I want you to," countered Jamie.

"It would not be much of a love if I have to hold you prisoner to keep you," responded Gunnul, her voice gravelly with emotion.

"No, it wouldn't," agreed Jamie, "but in time I'll earn that trust of yours." She leaned her head on Gunnul's shoulder. Gunnul squeezed her hand, unable to tell Jamie she trusted her but wanting her to know that she was trying to because she loved her almost to distraction.

They drove to the ruins of Aphrodisias, a Roman site where it was fairly easy for Jamie to maneuver. Jamie never complained and if the ground were too uneven for her to walk safely, then she would shyly take Gunnul's arm. When she did, Gunnul always smiled down at her to let her know that she liked to walk with their arms linked. On the rough hill overlooking the stone stairs of the amphitheater, Gunnul swung Jamie up into her arms and carried her. They sat for a while at the perfectly preserved stadium so Jamie could rest. "It is hard to believe it is so old. All you need is a crowd and it would be Rome all over again."

"Let us not wish that on my homeland," snapped Gunnul and then, realizing what she had said, they both broke out laughing.

"You do so hate the Romans," giggled Jamie, giving Gunnul a playful bump with her shoulder.

"Not me!" protested Gunnul.

They finished their walk inside a small but remarkable museum lined with Roman sculpture from the site. Then they drove on to Pamukkale, the "Cotton Castle". Here an underground river, heavy with dissolved lime, broke to the surface over a long ridge. Over the years, the hillside had become a fairyland of white, snowy stalagmites and stalactites, dotted here and there with large pools of warm aqua-coloured water. From this marvel of Mother Nature, you could look over the entire lowlands below. Teefo, of course, had booked them into the health spa on the top of the ridge. They could step out off the patio of their room down into a natural grotto of snowy limestone filled with the same aqua-coloured water, which was floodlit from below.

They sat together in the water under the stars, Jamie cushioned against Gunnul's strong arm. "Tomorrow we will be at my home," Gunnul observed. She felt the woman in her arms tense.

"What if Chrissy doesn't like me? I don't know if I could handle that," admitted Jamie, instinctively placing her head on Gunnul's shoulder and sliding an arm around her.

Gunnul pulled the nervous woman closer. "She will like you," murmured Gunnul.

"Does she know about my leg?" asked Jamie quietly.

"Yes, I have talked to her twice when you have not been around. I do not tell her anything you could not hear Jamie, but I thought it would be uncomfortable for..."

"It's okay, Gunnul. I understand. What did you tell her?" asked Jamie, with some anxiety.

"As much as I could tell a ten year old without overburdening her with adult concerns," responded Gunnul. "She knows about your leg and what I feel you can do without straining yourself. She knows you do not complain so she must be sensitive to this..."

"Gunnul!" protested Jamie, turning to look up at her lover with concern. Her soulmate raised an eyebrow and used the opportunity to place a kiss on Jamie's nose.

"I must tell her what I think! You will tell her what you think. Then she will make up her own mind," explained Gunnul. "She knows your injury was caused by her father when he was sick. I did not tell her how, just that you were hurt when you tried to help him," she continued, and when Jamie tried to protest, added, "No, she must deal with truth." Jamie sadly nodded, feeling Gunnul pull her closer and relaxing.

Gunnul kissed Jamie's temple and bent to look into Jamie's eyes. "I have told her that I love you, that I feel as if you are part of our family a... a... and that I hope you... you would stay."

"Oh, Gunnul," whispered Jamie, shaking her head and wrapping her arms around the older woman's neck. "You are so wonderful. I... I... wish I could..."

The pain shot through Gunnul, squeezing her heart until it forgot to beat. The expressionless mask that was Gunnul's defense against the world dropped into place as she pulled Jamie close and looked over her head at the Big Dipper in the black velvet sky. "I can't live without her!" a voice cried from her soul and she blinked back tears, burying her head in Jamie's fresh-smelling hair.

* * * * *

Gunnul lay in bed, eyes staring up at the ceiling. She felt totally empty inside. With a sigh, she untangled herself from Jamie and padded to the patio door. She looked out again at the stars, finding comfort in their familiarity.

From behind Gunnul, a voice came softly...

"We lie together
a blanket of stars
over us.
You tell me that
the stars
form the shape
of a Big Dipper.
I tell you
they look like
a silly bear.
You laugh
because I
never see
the practical.
I kiss you
because I want you
to see
the wonder."

137

Gunnul turned and Jamie fitted into her arms and her soul. "Don't leave us, Jamie," Gunnul begged.

"I don't want to, Gunnul. But I've a job. A lease on an apartment. I just can't disappear! How would I support myself? What if Chrissy doesn't like me or resents having to share you with me?"

"Chrissy will love you as I do," stated Gunnul firmly, not willing to consider any other possible turn of events. "I could have Teefo close your apartment. He has always wanted to go to America. You do not need to support yourself, Jamie, I am wealthy."

Jamie stiffened and pulled away, looking at Gunnul with flashing green eyes. Then she sighed and shook her head. Gunnul could be so innocent at times and so worldly and in control at others. "I'm not going to be a kept woman, Gunnul," she stated firmly but gently, and when her lover went to protest she put her fingertips over her lips. "No, we can't talk about this now. Wait." Then she placed her arm on Gunnul's and her soulmate helped her back to bed.

They made love, slowly and tenderly. Sensitive fingertips whispered over warm flesh repeating the age-old poetry of love. Soft lips played with the heartstrings of the other and sang out their climax to the starry night. Then, after, loving arms made a tender nest for sleep.

Jamie loved being in Gunnul's arms listening to her soft, even breathing. She felt complete at moments like this. Whole. Then the darkness would spread from that wound that she tried to keep hidden inside her soul. Gunnul was Moe's fraternal twin. They were both violent, only Gunnul's violence was far more terrifying in its intensity and focus. Moe's had only been like a little boy striking out in rage. To encourage Gunnul past this step would be to make a commitment to someone who would have far more power and control over her than Moe. Could she really trust this woman? She hadn't threatened her or touched her today, but the rage emanating from her had been like physical blows. Jamie kissed the arm that was wrapped around her and instinctively, even in her sleep, Gunnul pulled her closer. Jamie snuggled in, pushing the darkness back again. *I love you, Gunnul. There is just a part of me that hasn't healed very well.*

The next morning, a strangely quiet and nervous couple headed off for the outskirts of Antalya. They crossed over the Taurus Mountains which were covered still in thick pine stands, and came out on a ridge that looked down on the Mediterranean and off in the distance the port city of Antalya. Here Gunnul turned through a large stone gate and waved to a guard by its entrance. They followed a long winding driveway, first through pine forest and then beautifully manicured gardens and lawns to a fabulous villa with a panoramic view of the Mediterranean on one side and the Taurus mountains on the other.

Gunnul glided to a halt and a servant hurried out to open the car doors. Teefo, of course, waited on the steps. Jamie looked around her with her mouth open in shock. "Jamie, is there something wrong?" asked Gunnul, in worry. Jamie shook her head. Gunnul had said she was wealthy but damn it, this wasn't wealthy, this was filthy rich! Suddenly, the sound of small feet running could be heard and a beautiful child with dark chestnut hair came dashing out of the garden and threw herself at Gunnul. The Turk caught her with a laugh and tossed her in the air, catching her again in a big bear hug and kissing her cheek as they greeted each other in Turkish.

Then Gunnul took the little girl's hand and brought her over to where Jamie stood, weak in the knees and leaning heavily on her crutch. "Chrissy, this is your other mother, Jamie Dedemann."

Gunnul didn't know for sure which of them was going to need support the most. They were all pretty shook up by this meeting. In the end, the three of them wound up holding onto one another for a very long time. Then Gunnul put an arm around both of them and led them into the garden. They sat together, with Chrissy between them, on a Victorian wood swing beside a lily pond and talked. Chrissy held on to Gunnul for dear life with one hand and kept touching and stroking Jamie with the other. Jamie was all smiles but the tears rolled slowly down her face. Gunnul was silent, waging her own battle with the joy of seeing her soulmate with her child and with the fear that she might lose Chrissy. The other two, never at a loss for words, filled in the silence, two pairs of identical green eyes shining with wonder and tears.

Quiet servants set up afternoon tea there and Gunnul took pride in the way Chrissy, as the Turkish hostess, offered them lemon cologne and Turkish delights. Jamie said and did all the proper things using her few Turkish words and phrases, to Chrissy's delight. Then Chrissy made Turkish coffee and they drank it while the child told them what she had been up to while Gunnul had been away.

"I will leave the two of you to get to know each other better," said Gunnul, getting up after a while. "I will go to get things organized for your stay, Jamie, and see to some business matters." Two pairs of green eyes looked up at her in alarm. She squeezed Chrissy's hand gently and bent forward and kissed her head. A moment's hesitation, then she patted Jamie's knee and lightly brushed a kiss over her forehead. "You are my two favourite people," Gunnul reassured them, and then walked back to the house, leaving the mother and daughter to talk. It was the hardest and most painful thing that Gunnul had ever done in her life.

Teefo waited in the shadow of the house. "Teefo, Mrs. Dedemann's rooms..."

"I thought it more convenient to put Mrs. Dedemann in the adjoining chambers to yours, General Dedemann." Gunnul raised an eyebrow in surprise. "It will be easier for Chrissy if she can visit you both and not have to choose." The eyebrow went up farther. Teefo, however, showed his mettle by carrying on calmly, "The quarters are for the head of the house's partner and I presume I am right in assuming that is to be Mrs. Dedemann."

There was a moment's silence. Slowly Gunnul's lips curled on one side in a small grin. Teefo's face remained expressionless. "I hope to convince Mrs. Dedemann to accept such an arrangement," confirmed Gunnul.

This time Teefo's calm exterior failed him and he looked quite huffy. "And very lucky she would be too!" he exclaimed, and then blushed at his outburst.

Gunnul smiled and raised her eyebrow once more. "Thank you, Teefo," she responded.

Teefo cleared this throat in embarrassment. "You're welcome."

"And do you not think I am lucky?" Gunnul teased.

Teefo's face broke out in a big wolfish grin. "Most definitely!" he said wholeheartedly and then realized that he was appraising the woman whom his boss loved. "That is, if she suits you."

Gunnul burst out laughing. "You Turkish men and your love of blondes!" she grinned, her eyes sparkling, pleased that others found Jamie beautiful too. Gunnul changed the subject now. Enough had been said, even to one as close as Teefo. "Please bring me the folders to my office. I need to E-mail some companies," she instructed, and Teefo nodded and quietly left to carry out the order. Gunnul turned and looked back into the garden. Jamie was telling a story and Chrissy was sitting at her feet listening intently. They were both smiling. Pain shot through Gunnul's heart and she swallowed hard, then turned and walked quickly to her office.

"Chrissy, honey, will you do me a favour?" asked Jamie, after a long time of getting to know her daughter.

"Of course, Mom," Chrissy replied, with a soft accent that Jamie found delightful.

"Go find someone to take me to my room and then go see your other Mom. I don't want her feeling left out," instructed Jamie.

Chrissy smiled and nodded as she leapt to her feet and ran off.

Jamie looked around at the acres of gardens, the massive house and the spectacular view. *My God! What have I got myself into?* "Mrs. Dedemann?" came a soft voice.

"Yes?" Jamie replied, looking around to see an older woman shyly waiting near by.

"I am Shantu, the housekeeper. I will take you to your room, please," the gentle woman explained.

Jamie nodded and followed the woman through the most exquisite rooms she had ever seen. Shantu walked slowly and at the stairs she hesitated, too polite to ask if Jamie needed help.

"I'm okay, I can manage if I go slowly," Jamie explained, but she noted the worried woman followed directly behind to catch her if she should stumble.

They walked down a hall and the housekeeper opened a door into a large salon. French doors led onto a large balcony. The woman led the way to the right, which turned out to lead to the bedroom. It was almost as large as Jamie's entire apartment back home. Off the bedroom was a bathroom complete with whirlpool bath and sauna and a walk-in closet with an area of floor to ceiling mirrors. "Where does that door lead?" Jamie asked, after she had been shown how to find the entertainment centre and computer that were discretely hidden behind a false wall in the bedroom.

Shantu blushed. "Please, that door leads to General Dedemann's chambers."

Jamie smiled and wiggled her eyebrows and the older woman giggled as she left.

Chrissy happily trotted across Gunnul's office, around her massive cherry wood desk and crawled up into Gunnul's lap as she talked on the phone to an associate in Saudi Arabia. Gunnul wrapped an arm around her and kissed her daughter's temple as she wound up her conversation with the business associate. Hanging up the phone, she looked at her daughter, waiting for a verdict.

"She's nice isn't she, Mom?" Chrissy said proudly.

"I think so," responded Gunnul honestly.

"She tells funny stories. She's been to lots of rock concerts and she likes jazz and blues like you do! Once she had a dog called "Shadow". I told her your horse was called that too. Isn't that weird, Mommy? Her eyes are the same colour as mine but she thinks I look like you. Isn't her hair wonderful? It is just like gold but it is soft. She let me touch it. Have you touched her hair, Mom? It feels just like silk." Gunnul nodded, used to Chrissy's rapid-fire speech patterns.

Chrissy suddenly became very serious. "Her leg isn't shaped

right. Her knee has a funny bump and her foot goes in. Does it hurt her, Mom?"

Gunnul gave Chrissy a reassuring squeeze. "I think sometimes, yes, if she over-uses the leg," answered her mother.

"Does she need that metal arm thing to walk?" asked the curious child.

"I have seen her walk and stand without it when she is inside on a flat surface. But she really needs it to walk with any balance," responded Gunnul, feeling the pain of guilt clawing at her heart.

"My father, he was a very bad man. Will she hate us because of what he did?" asked Chrissy in a worried voice.

"No! Of course not Chrissy," protested Gunnul. "She knows that you and I are not sick like your father was and she understands that your father did bad things not because he was a bad person but because he became a very sick person mentally from drinking and taking drugs."

Chrissy nodded sadly. Then, "She likes you a lot!" revealed her daughter happily.

Gunnul reacted in surprise and asked nervously, "How do you know?"

"She told me the story about how two men tried to rob her on the beach and you beat them up and saved her! She thought you were wonderful," revealed Chrissy proudly. "And she likes your blue eyes!"

Gunnul grinned, pleased by the praise from her lover. "I told her you have the evil eye and she looked really surprised. So I had to explain to her that in Turkey people believe that the blue eye can be used to bring much bad luck on others. She said she hoped I didn't believe that! I told her no, but many did."

"Well, you two seem to have learned a lot about each other in a short time," observed Gunnul. "I am going upstairs now to make sure that your Mom has settled in. Why don't you go off and play and then join us for prayers and lunch?" suggested Gunnul.

"She is Moslem, Mom?" asked Chrissy excitedly.

Gunnul laughed. "No, but she is comfortable in praying to Allah in our way when she is with us. Scoot now," Gunnul commanded and Chrissy gave her mother a hug and then skipped out the French doors that led to the garden.

Gunnul found Jamie standing by the window in her bedroom looking out over the sea. Gunnul silently came up behind her and placed her hands around Jamie's shoulders. Jamie started in surprise and then, realizing it was Gunnul, leaned back and let the Turkish woman wrap her in her arms.

"You are okay?" asked Gunnul anxiously.

"Yeah, just on emotional overload," explained Jamie. "She is wonderful, Gunnul. Thank you!" Then she began to sob and Gunnul moved around so that the overwrought woman could bury her head under Gunnul's chin and sob out her emotions safely in her strong arms.

They all prayed together, Jamie now being able to recite the opening prayers in Turkish. *She has a real ear for language*, Gunnul thought proudly and was warmed with the knowledge that Jamie was willing to accept and appreciate Chrissy's Turkish upbringing.

After lunch, Chrissy and Gunnul showed Jamie around the estate. They had a late dinner on the patio overlooking the Mediterranean and then retired to the media room to watch soccer on the T.V. Gunnul explained that football was almost a religion in Turkey and that people took it very seriously. Jamie had to have the fundamentals explained to her but was soon into the game. Gunnul and Chrissy were cheering for one side, so Jamie cheered for the other. The game ended in a one-one draw and in a pillow fight on the couch.

Both Jamie and Gunnul tucked Chrissy in bed and Jamie told Chrissy the story of Paul Bunyon, which Gunnul seemed to enjoy as much as their daughter. Later, Gunnul and Jamie walked hand in hand back to Jamie's room. "You tell wonderful stories," praised Gunnul.

"Thank you," smiled Jamie.

"Ah," began the tall woman awkwardly, "I've always had this, this presence. A woman, who would come to me. I... I imagined she looked like you."

Jamie stopped dead and stared at her lover open mouthed. "It was like that for me too! I saw you. I felt you. I talked to you and you answered," she revealed. "I called you my protector," she smiled.

Gunnul walked over to the window and looked out into the night. "I have killed many, Jamie. There is darkness in me. I am very strong. I must always be very careful not to hurt people by accident." She turned and looked at Jamie. "Is that why you do not wish to stay with me, because of the violence within me?" she asked, her lip quivering with emotion.

Jamie sighed. "No, it is more complex than that. I thought when I met Moe that I had finally bridged the space between my special world and the real one. I was terribly wrong. I don't want to make that mistake again. I can't."

Gunnul nodded and swallowed. "You would like, Jamie, that I no touch you?"

Jamie shook her head and walked over to her confused lover.

"Come here, you," she whispered, her lips next to Gunnul's. "What I want is for you to pick me up and carry me to bed and make love to me all night."

Gunnul for once in her life carried out someone else's orders happily!

After prayers at dawn and a light breakfast, Gunnul and Chrissy went to wake Jamie. Chrissy ran across the room and leapt into bed with Jamie and gave her a big hug and a kiss. "Good morning, Mommy! Did you sleep well?" she asked, crawling under the sheets and snuggling close to the warmth of her American mother.

Jamie made eye contact with Gunnul, who was the picture of innocence. "I was exhausted and slept very well, thank you, Chrissy."

Gunnul snorted.

"Get into bed, Mom!" beckoned Chrissy and Gunnul smiled and came to lie on top of the covers by Jamie's other side, her back propped up against the backboard. Jamie smiled up at her. Only a few hours before, Gunnul had been in the same spot, only under the covers with Jamie curled around her.

"So Chrissy, how should we entertain your other Mom today?" asked Gunnul, reaching out to play with her love's hair and then fluffing up the pillow instead. Jamie giggled.

"I think we should go to Antalya and shop!" exclaimed Chrissy excitedly.

"Shop!" repeated Jamie, sitting up with her eyes sparkling.

"Yes! The stores in Antalya are wonderful! You will see. I love to shop for bargains."

Gunnul moaned. "So this is where she gets this disgusting trait," she growled.

Jamie pulled her tongue out at Gunnul. "You don't have to shop. You can just come along to help carry the bargains back to the car," suggested Jamie, and Chrissy laughed.

"I am not shopping at all! But I will take you to town and let you to loose while I see to some business," agreed Gunnul, slipping off the bed reluctantly. "Come, Chrissy, and get ready."

* * * * *

Gunnul dropped the two shoppers off beside the tall Ottoman tower that guards the picturesque harbor of Antalya. They agreed to meet at two o'clock. Promptly at two, Gunnul pulled the Rolls she was driving that morning up to the kerb. No shoppers. Gunnul sighed and pulled back out into the traffic to find a parking spot. Clearly, Chrissy and Jamie were planning on shopping to the last possible moment!

Gunnul looked at her watch as she stood by the tower. They were now fifteen minutes late and she was getting worried. At half past, she was past worry and into panic. What had she done? She'd handed over her daughter to a woman whom she had known only a week! A woman who had a passport and tickets to steal her daughter away from her. There was an airport in Antalya. Her daughter could be kidnapped and on her way to the U.S. by now! Would she be able to legally get Chrissy back from her birth mother once they were in the States? Probably not. Gunnul's heart tightened as fear washed through her system and her anger mounted.

At a quarter to the hour, she saw the two missing persons heading down the street each wearing identical T-shirts in green with Disney characters on the shoulder. Chrissy's was Pluto and Jamie's was Donald Duck. The two of them stopped short when they saw the murderous look on Gunnul's face. "Where... have... you... been!" she snarled out, her hands on her hips.

Tears welled in Chrissy's eyes and Jamie put an arm around her. "It's my fault, Gunnul. I'm sorry..."

"Sorry... I thought you'd taken... I was worried... Come. The car is over here," spluttered Gunnul, trying very hard to regain control. Jamie and Chrissy exchanged worried looks and obediently followed the upset woman. In the car everything was quiet for a minute. Then Gunnul sighed and ruffled Chrissy's hair. "Sorry, Sweetheart, you two scared me, that's all," confessed the Turkish woman.

"We're sorry we were late, Mom and made you worried. We would have been on time but something happened but I can't tell you because I promised," explained Chrissy honestly.

Blue eyes snapped up and met Jamie's. "What happened?" she asked calmly, but in a tone that indicated she was not going to stay calm if she did not get a reasonable answer quickly.

Jamie sighed and looked out the window. "You tell her, Chrissy," she muttered.

Chrissy was delighted to do so. "Mom tripped on an uneven part of the sidewalk and fell into a booth where they were selling trinkets and it fell over and then the man on the bicycle had to swerve and that scared the horse that was drawing the cart full of tourists and it started acting up and so the cars that were held up started hooking and the tourists were crying and the owners of the horse and booth were yelling and Mom was trying to explain while I translated and then the police came," explained Chrissy, on one long breath.

Silence. Then, "Are you all right, Jamie?" asked Gunnul

seriously.

"Yes."

"Is there anything else I should know?" questioned Gunnul quietly.

Chrissy responded, "The man on the bicycle didn't even stop and the police officer asked to see Mom's passport and took our names. But when I gave him mine he asked if I was your daughter and I said yes and he said we could go."

Gunnul nodded, looking out the windscreen her face devoid of emotion except for one eyebrow that was almost up to her hairline. She put the car in gear and they made a fast and silent trip back to the estate.

Once they arrived and had entered the main foyer, Gunnul said, "Chrissy, you take the shopping upstairs and sort it out while your Mom and I talk. Okay?"

Chrissy nodded and headed off, giving a worried look in Jamie's direction. Once she was out of sight, Gunnul opened the door to her office and indicated Jamie should go in. Her limp more obvious than usual, Jamie obediently went where she was directed, too worried to notice the beauty and richness of the room. She sat, a small figure in a huge, leather wingchair, in front of Gunnul's massive cherry wood desk.

Gunnul walked over and looked down at Jamie, then dropped to one knee and took Jamie's cold hands. "I am sorry. I panicked. Can you forgive me for my doubts?" she asked quietly, with an edge of real worry in her voice.

Jamie nodded, tears overflowing, and Gunnul pulled her into her arms. "Do not ask Chrissy to withhold the truth from me, okay? She has been raised to be always honest."

Jamie nodded. "It was really stupid of me, Gunnul. I don't want her or I to have secrets that you are not privy to. It's just that it was my first time taking care of Chrissy and I made a real mess of it. I was embarrassed."

Gunnul nodded her understanding and smiled, leaning forward to kiss Jamie's forehead. "Sorry I missed it. It seems to have been a very good riot you created!" joked Gunnul.

Jamie buried her red face in Gunnul's neck. "Yeah it was," she agreed.

"Now you will tell me where you are hurt," Gunnul ordered firmly, rubbing Jamie's back.

"A few bumps and scrapes, Gunnul, that's all, and I twisted my knee so now it is sore," she replied honestly.

"Do you need to see a doctor, Jamie?" asked Gunnul, trying not to sound too overly protective.

"No, I'm all right. I just need to rest it for a bit," responded Jamie.

Gunnul scooped Jamie into her arms and carried her up to her room. She got the whirlpool ready for her while Jamie undressed. When she came back into the bedroom she found her lover sitting on the couch wrapped in her housecoat with a parcel in her lap. "I bought this for you," she explained. Gunnul opened the parcel to find a green T-shirt with Mickey Mouse dancing on the shoulder and laughed. "I didn't want you to feel left out." Jamie smiled softly, a blush climbing up her neck.

Gunnul stripped off her two hundred dollar silk shirt and pulled the cotton T-shirt over her head. "Thank you, Jamie. I will enjoy wearing it!" Jamie smiled happily as Gunnul lifted her up and carried her into the bathroom.

Later, all three of them curled up on Jamie's bed, eating off trays as they watched a Disney video that belonged to Chrissy. Each of them wore their T-shirts. Chrissy explained seriously to Gunnul that she had Mickey Mouse on her shirt because Jamie had said she was the leader of their pack! Gunnul blushed and gave Chrissy a hug and Jamie a raised eyebrow.

That night, Jamie lay wrapped in Gunnul's arms. "Tomorrow, Jamie, I wish that you stay in bed in the morning." Jamie went to protest but Gunnul cut her off. "The leg needs to rest. This weekend, we will go to a wedding in Cappadocia. My second cousin is to marry. You must be rested."

"Gunnul, maybe your cousin might not wish a foreigner and stranger at her wedding," protested Jamie and Gunnul laughed.

"She will thank me many times! You will keep the evil eye away!" laughed Gunnul.

"I'll what?" exclaimed Jamie, laughing too at Gunnul's delight.

"It is a superstition. Blond, blue-eyed people are very lucky at a wedding. You will ward off my evil eye! You neutralize me!" giggled Gunnul.

Jamie poked Gunnul in the ribs. "I have green eyes! As you very well know! And I think your eyes are beautiful and if I hear anyone say otherwise, they will have bad luck!" argued Jamie, her green eyes flashing.

Gunnul went still and looked deep into those emerald depths. "Tomorrow, I will take you to see a very secret place, Jamie." Then she turned off the light and pulled her lover closer.

147

Before lunch, Jamie was dressed and easing her way down the stairs. Her knee still throbbed painfully but she did not want to waste what time she had with Chrissy. There had been no conscious decision on her part, just a slow realization that at the end of her leave time, she would be returning to America without Chrissy. A conscious decision would mean she'd have to face the reality that Chrissy and Gunnul were not going to be a permanent part of her life and she just wasn't brave enough to face that reality yet.

She stepped out onto the patio and saw coming up the sand trail from the pine forest below a peasant woman robed in simple, dusty blue, leading a grey donkey on which two Turkish children rode. The three chatted away and laughed happily as they made their way up the steep trail.

Jamie wished she had a camera. It was a real Kodak moment. Then she realized with a shock that the taller child riding on the back was her daughter and the peasant woman was Gunnul! *My God! I couldn't recognize them! I am so foreign to them. I don't belong in my own daughter's life!*

Gunnul felt her, as a pain in her heart, then looked up to see the distress on her lover's face. "Girls, take the donkey to the stables and groom and feed her. When your chores are done then the two of you may return to Fabina's tent with Shantu. I must see to something," ordered Gunnul, walking off swiftly.

Jamie had limped back into Gunnul's beautiful study. She looked around at the quiet, understated wealth and realized that even the European side of her lover was way beyond her frame of reality. There was no common ground.

"Jamie?" questioned Gunnul, coming up behind Jamie and placing her hands on the petite woman's shoulders.

Jamie started and then reached up to place a hand over her lover's. "It's okay, Gunnul. I just realized I must be leaving soon."

"Leaving?" came the startled response.

"Yes, next week," replied Jamie. "My leave is almost up." Then, not being able to stop herself, she turned and clung tightly to her lover. "I love you both so much! You take care of Chrissy, you hear! Please! Oh God!" she sobbed. Gunnul, too upset to respond, wrapped Jamie in a strong, deep embrace, wishing that she never had to let go.

"Shh, you no cry Jamie. I must take you somewhere so secret. You come, please," whispered Gunnul after a while into Jamie's hair. Her voice sounded stressed and tight.

Jamie nodded, wiping her eyes with her hand. Gunnul let go of her and got her a tissue from behind the desk. "Thanks," snuffled

Jamie, remembering not to blow her nose, which in Turkey was considered a very rude thing to do in public. "I'm okay. I'm sorry, I always seem to be crying on your shoulder," rasped the little American.

"I understand so I no mind," reassured Gunnul, with an intensely worried look.

Jamie laughed and looked up at Gunnul with loving eyes, "Yes, you do! I can always tell when you are upset because your English deteriorates."

Gunnul blushed and pouted. "It does not, I think," and then laughed with Jamie when she realized that she had proven herself wrong. "Come, there is something very important I must show you."

Gunnul took Jamie's crutch and left it by the desk. She offered Jamie her arm instead. For a second Jamie hesitated and then she realized that it would be nice to walk without it, especially with Gunnul to lean on. "I could get to like this," she giggled nervously, limping at Gunnul's side.

"I already do," observed the serious Turkish woman, reaching over to squeeze Jamie's small hand where it rested on her arm. They walked silently through the gardens, Gunnul automatically now adjusting her pace to that of her crippled soulmate. At the locked gate, Gunnul placed Jamie's hand on the wrought-iron railing while she removed the heavy lock. Then she picked Jamie up and carried her through the overgrowth until they got to the tomb. There she lowered Jamie's feet to the ground but maintained support by standing behind her with her arms wrapped loosely around Jamie's waist.

Jamie reached out and touched the ancient stone. "It's her!" she exclaimed, then looked up at Gunnul. "It's us!"

"Yes, I feel that too, but look at the names. They can't be the right ones."

Jamie hobbled a step forward and traced her fingers over the lettering. "Kristinia Thanasis. Gunnul, that was the name you had when we met in the Amazon! I can recall it from my dreams. But that makes no sense. That's now! And we aren't there, we're here. And these aren't our original names! Gunnul what is going on?"

Gunnul shook her head. "I don't know. Do you feel the energy when you touch the stone?" Jamie nodded. "It's like we are to understand some message but I don't! Do you, Jamie?"

"No, at least not yet," sighed Jamie, running her fingers through her hair. "I think we are still these people though," revealed the American. "It's like there is a link...a subtle awareness... that joins many of us as one. Do you feel it?"

Gunnul shook her head in frustration and wrinkled her brow. "I think so but I'm not sure if what I feel is real. Are we living in different dimensions and somehow are aware of each other? I don't understand."

Jamie nodded. It was some time before they left the tangled garden and relocked the gate.

* * * * *

Gunnul had yet another surprise waiting for Jamie when they returned. She led her towards the back of the villa to the private Turkish steam bath that she had ordered prepared for them. They stripped down and wrapped in fluffy, white towels to sit in the cedar lined steam bath. When they became too warm, they would step out and drop into a cool pool finished in Greek mosaics, then return to the hot room. When they were quite relaxed, Gunnul helped Jamie into a side room where a woman waited to massage them. Their naked bodies were covered in clouds of suds and they were washed with a coarse sponge to remove the dirt and dried skin. Then scented warm water was poured over them and more suds piled on so that they could be washed again with sweet scented herbs and spices with a soft sponge. Once rinsed with hot water, they were massaged with warm oils until every bone and muscle in their bodies was relaxed and rested.

Wrapping again in fluffy towels, they went into yet another room to lie on cushioned benches and eat dates, cheese, bread, nuts and fruit and to drink coffee. Gunnul explained that the baths were the traditional day out for women. It was, in the old times, one of the few places a woman could go without being escorted by a man. Women would take picnics and musical instruments and spend the day talking and doing business in the baths.

Much to Jamie's delight, after they had eaten Gunnul pulled out an instrument similar to a guitar and sang Turkish folk songs for her in a beautiful, melodic voice. And once the silent servants had cleaned up and left, they made love and slept the afternoon away in each other's arms.

Jamie woke to see those remarkable blue eyes looking down at her. Gunnul had kissed her awake gently. "Hmmm, that is the only way to wake up," Jamie murmured, and Gunnul captured her lips again, tasting on them their passion still. "Chrissy is going to wonder where we are," protested the petite woman weakly.

"Chrissy knows where we are," responded Gunnul. "Today and tonight she will spend at her friend's home. Fabina has been with the family goatherds in the hills but now they have returned. This morning, they set up their goat-hair tents in the lower pasture. Shantu will chaperone them," explained Gunnul.

"They're camping out, what fun! I used to do that when I was a kid," smiled Jamie, happy for Chrissy.

Gunnul laughed, "No, they do not camp. That is the way Fabina's family lives. They are nomadic farmers. Tomorrow, when we pick up Chrissy, you will get a chance to see how they live," explained Gunnul.

Jamie looked at Gunnul for a long time. "You are worth millions aren't you?" she asked bluntly. Gunnul frowned but nodded. "And Chrissy is your only heir?" Gunnul felt a dread creep into her heart. Had she been wrong about Jamie after all? But once again she nodded. "And yet, you let her play with the daughter of a nomadic herder!" Jamie smiled, shaking her head in disbelief.

Gunnul bristled. "I am not a poor mother, Jamie. They are a good Moslem family and Shantu or I always go to chaperone Chrissy, as is proper." Jamie burst into laughter. "What is funny?" asked Gunnul, still annoyed.

"You. You are so wonderfully sweet! I do love you, Gunnul," she said, wrapping herself around the prone body of her lover. "I think it is wonderful, the way you are so unaffected by your wealth and the way you have taught our daughter to be the same."

"Fabina's family are good people. They can not help that Allah chose to make them landless," observed Gunnul seriously, as was her way.

Jamie nodded. "In your den this morning, I was upset because, after seeing you in traditional dress, I felt so different from you and Chrissy. A stranger who didn't belong in the world of my child or my lover. I... I... went into your den and saw all the richness of the room and thought that I didn't even fit into your European reality. Gunnul, I live on a middle class income in an apartment smaller than the bedroom I am using now! It just makes me feel a little better that Chrissy sees that those differences don't matter," confessed Jamie.

Gunnul frowned. "Is it my wealth, Jamie, that keeps us apart?" she asked.

Jamie stiffened and rolled over on her back. "No, Gunnul, it is my fears. The problem is in me. A part of my emotions that just didn't heal very well," explained Jamie, turning her head to meet Gunnul's sad eyes.

Gunnul swallowed and looked at a piece of thread that she was worrying from the towel. "I too have insecurities about your intentions sometimes that stem from bad experiences in my past," confessed

Gunnul.

"It wouldn't work, Gunnul. A relationship is hard enough to hold together without starting off lacking trust. I don't want to make another mistake."

Gunnul nodded sadly and swallowed. "Would you like to go out for dinner tonight, Jamie?" she asked.

Jamie accepted the change in subject. "I would like that a lot," she whispered, snuggling into her lover again.

They went to a lavish hotel overlooking the Mediterranean and had a wonderful dinner under the stars surrounded by gardens of bougainvillea all in bloom back-dropped by the sea. After, they hired a local boat-taxi to take them for a moonlight cruise down to where the Antalya River poured over the limestone escarpment and fell in a white veil to the moonlit sea below. It was a wonderful, magical evening that Jamie knew she would hold in her heart forever.

* * * * *

The next morning, Jamie woke to find Gunnul already awake. "Morning, my sweet one," she murmured, and was rewarded with a kiss.

Gunnul looked serious and apprehensive. "Jamie, I have bought you a gallabeeya, a robe. You don't have to wear..."

"Where is it?" cut in the excited American, looking around eagerly.

Gunnul got up, looking relieved but still nervous, and Jamie tilted her head as she sat on the edge of the bed watching her lover expectantly.

"We go today to Konya, which is a very religious city. Chrissy and I will wear traditional dress, so if you feel comfortable you could too. But it is not necessary that you do so. You know that Chrissy and I are comfortable with your European ways," explained Gunnul in her serious way, making Jamie laugh.

Gunnul looked surprised and then confused. "Gunnul," laughed Jamie softly, "you are so cute when you are trying to be diplomatic. This is your country and I want to fit into your ways. When you and Chrissy come to visit America, then I will expect you to fit into my culture, okay?"

Gunnul's answer was a flying leap that knocked a surprised Jamie flat on her back on the bed with an ecstatic Turk alongside of her. Jamie looked up to see blue eyes sparkling like diamonds. "Yes Jamie! We can come visit you!? Yes?"

Jamie's heart overflowed with love for this remarkable woman. "As many times as you want, my love. You and Chrissy, will always be welcome in my home," reassured Jamie, wrapping her arms around the tall woman and giving her a quick hug. "Now show me my new outfit or we will never get out of here!"

Gunnul kissed Jamie's forehead, then pulled her up to a sitting position and trotted off happily, to return with a parcel. From it she took a dark green robe with delicate embroidery around the collar and sleeve. The colour was the same as Jamie's eyes. "Oh Gunnul! I love it!" enthused Jamie, and got off the bed and held on to her lover for support as she slipped it on. Gunnul stood staring down at her with a look of wonder on her face. "Well?" asked Jamie, becoming a little uncomfortable by the silence.

Gunnul shook herself from her trance and smiled. "You are so beautiful, Jamie! You take my breath away!"

Jamie wrapped her arms around Gunnul's neck and kissed her. "Thank you, for everything," she said, from her heart.

A short time later, two very traditionally dressed women were bumping across the pasture in Gunnul's Land Rover. They pulled up in front of three black tents to see two excited children run out. Chrissy hugged Jamie and then ran to hug Gunnul as she came around the front of the jeep. Then she ran back to take Jamie's hand and led her over to the shy girl who stood waiting a short distance away. "Mom, this is my best friend in the whole world, Fabina." Then to the pretty girl, she talked in rapid Turkish. Fabina smiled broadly and indicated by a generous sweep of her arm that they should enter the tent.

"You look nice, Mom," Chrissy whispered quietly, as they went in. "I helped Mommy pick it out for you," she added proudly.

Jamie gave her a hug and smiled lovingly at Gunnul, who had her public, emotionless face in place. Inside the tent, Shantu and Fabina's mother welcomed them with cologne and made morning tea. The men, they explained, had already taken the goats to pasture. The women served sliced cucumbers, white cheese, olives and pita bread. To Jamie's surprise, Fabina curled up under Gunnul's arm as soon as the quiet woman was seated. Gunnul hugged her close and kissed her dark hair. Chrissy sat beside Jamie and held her hand proudly. They talked quietly over breakfast about the summer grazing in the high hills. Chrissy translated quietly, explaining that Fabina was Shantu's niece.

Jamie was fascinated by the interior of the tent. Outside, they were heavy, black structures held up by several poles and tied down with coarse hemp rope. Inside, low platforms edged the tent, providing sleeping berths and storage underneath. The benches and floor were covered in overlapping layers of thick, hand-made carpets in beautiful, colourful patterns. Jamie realized that they would be worth a fortune in America. A brass oil burner provided heat and a cooking surface and an intricate water pipe stood in the corner. It was a simple but elegant life style.

Chrissy explained that the platforms that lined the walls in a traditional Turkish dwelling were called sofas. The Europeans had taken the Turkish custom and developed the idea into the long, freestanding seats to which they gave the same name. She also showed her the various patterns that were used on the rugs such as 'the Tree of Life'. In Gunnul's serious manner, Chrissy showed Jamie how the rugs were double knotted in Turkey and explained that a rug would have fifty to eighty knots to the square inch depending on its quality. She showed Jamie how the pattern on a good rug was just as clear on the reverse side as it was on the front. Then she took the silk on silk throw rug that was the centre piece of the lovely tent room and spun it around to show Jamie how the shade of the rug changed completely depending which direction you were looking at it. From one end, the rug was pale pastels and from the other a dark, rich colour. Jamie was fascinated when Fabina's mother shyly took her outside to the small lean-to that housed her large rug loom and showed her a rug she was weaving. Her hands moved so fast that Jamie could not even see the motions!

"It is amazing!" Jamie exclaimed to Gunnul, who had come up quietly beside her and now held her hand. It had taken Jamie a little time to get used to being free to hold hands in public but she really liked being able to touch Gunnul. She knew her emotionally insecure lover needed the reassurance of contact.

"There are three types of material in Persian rugs," explained Gunnul. "The lowest grade is wool knotted on cotton stringers. There is then wool on wool and silk on silk. Only the master weavers like Fabina's mother work in silk on silk. It is very difficult. It will take about nine months for her to finish a four by six foot rug. If a mistake is made, it can not be fixed. In order that the weaver and her family are not shamed by the terrible mistake, the rug is burnt and all that time and effort is wasted. That is why only the best weavers work in silk. Both Fabina and Chrissy have learned to work rugs in wool. They work from simple patterns. But the silk masters need no pattern even to do the most complex work."

A short time later, the three Dedemanns were seated in their Land Rover and were waving good-bye. "Fabina and her family are very nice, Chrissy. I am glad I got to meet them."

"They liked you too, Mom. Fabina said you didn't act a bit like a tourist," she said proudly, and Jamie laughed. "And she said your hair was gold and would bring very good luck to the family. Not like my other Mom, who they think is wonderful but they still must hang extra charms when she comes to ward off the evil eye." Jamie was about to object but Chrissy and Gunnul broke into gales of laughter. Clearly, they found the situation of Gunnul's remarkable eyes very funny.

Gunnul said something to Chrissy in Turkish and Chrissy leaned over and got an object out of the glove compartment. It was a thin, blue-braided silk cord with a blue glass medallion attached to it. The centre of the medallion was black to make a stylized eye. Tied to the bottom of the cord was a small brass bell. Chrissy leaned over and attached it to Jamie's cord belt. "This is one of the kind of tokens that you see all over Turkey to ward off the evil eye. Mom said you should wear it to protect you from her dangerous stares."

Jamie looked up and caught Gunnul's eyes in the mirror. Gunnul wiggled an eyebrow sexily and Jamie blushed. "I think that is a good idea!" she agreed as they turned on to the fine highway system of Turkey and headed on their way.

* * * * *

Mid-morning, they made a stop at the historical site of Perge. Here Jamie found the varying colour and patterns of the marble columns truly beautiful. A pool of water once had run the length of the main street overhung with trees and flowers to cool the weary traveler, and there had been a covered sidewalk of mosaic tiles in front of the shops.

Gunnul showed Jamie the impressive public steam baths, with rooms of varying temperature all controlled by underground steam ducts. Chrissy showed her the ruts worn into the marble street by ancient wagons and chariots and the small tortoise that she had found between the rocks. It took a raised eyebrow from Gunnul to convince the two animal lovers that they had not found a pet! With reluctance, the petite Mom and her daughter put the tortoise safely back under some bushes.

Chrissy ran ahead with the car keys to unlock the doors while her Moms followed along behind, holding hands. "You could close your eyes and be part of the ancient world once again," sighed Jamie. "These cities were so much more user friendly than ours today. Comfort and beauty went hand in hand with functionalism." She hesitated, and then went on, "We have been here before."

Gunnul frowned. "Yes, but there was fighting. You were wounded trying to protect a child. I was very worried," stated Gunnul, instinctively holding tighter to Jamie's hand.

Jamie saw the worry in her lover's eyes and lightened the situation. "Yes, and I'm going to be hurt again if you don't let go of my hand!" she yelped dramatically.

Gunnul let go immediately, smiling and looking adorably sheepish as Jamie laughed.

They also stopped at Aspedos to see the free-standing Roman Theater. Gunnul explained that it was the best-preserved Roman theater in the world. There were still numbers on the seats and some of the clay tickets still existed!

At noon, they stopped to eat and pray and visited the Caravanserai of Sultanhani. It was one of many medieval walled forts built every twenty miles along the Silk Road. The traders would stay in barrel-vaulted chambers off a main court. At night, the huge doors of the fort would be locked and wouldn't be opened again until everyone had packed and checked their cargo in the morning to make sure nothing had been stolen. The distance between the forts was the distance a camel could travel in one day.

As they drove on to Konya the land became flat, rocky desert. The dusty city sat in the centre of a vast desert plain. Here Mevlana established the Islamic sect of the Whirling Dervish. While they watched a white clad dervish perform, Gunnul explained that the process was designed to cause the worshiper to fall into a trance-like state in order to block out the world so that all thoughts were for Allah. Chrissy helped Jamie tie her white silk scarf correctly around her head and the three went to visit the mosque of Karatay Medrese and the Ince mosque with its famous turquoise dome.

As always, they removed their shoes to enter. Gunnul explained that the slanted sarcophagus did not contain the remains of the founder. His body was buried underneath. In Islamic belief, the dead must return to the earth within twenty-four hours. The large ceramic turban at the head of the sarcophagus indicated it was the grave of an important person. The size of the turban showed greater importance compared to other burials with smaller turbans.

It was late when they finally arrived in the area of Cappadocia. Jamie's leg was very sore and she limped heavily on her walking cane. Chrissy quietly came up beside her and placed an arm around her so that she could lean some of her weight on her daughter's shoulders while Gunnul booked them into the hotel. "I am sorry my father hurt you," she whispered earnestly.

Jamie leaned down and kissed her daughter's head. "He was a very fine man in many ways, Chrissy. He just lost control of his life because of his substance abuse. It happened a long time ago and as you see, having a crippled leg does not slow me down," Jamie soothed.

Gunnul joined them and they rode the elevator up to the third floor. To Jamie's surprise, Gunnul had got just one room with two double beds. Once everyone was ready for bed, Gunnul tucked Chrissy in with her new Mom and then lay across the foot of the bed while Jamie told a story. Chrissy was asleep shortly after and Gunnul picked up her slumbering daughter and tucked her in the other bed. Then she slipped in beside Jamie. "I'll slip back over to the other bed before Chrissy wakes," she explained, pulling Jamie to her side. Jamie sighed contentedly and wrapped herself around the woman whom she had come to love.

The next day, Jamie woke to find Gunnul and Chrissy talking happily in Turkish to relatives on the phone. Once plans were made and all morning rites seen to, they headed out to the Goreme area. Here amazing volcanic chimneys formed a fairyland landscape. Hundreds of years ago, persecuted Christians carved homes and churches into the soft rock. Gunnul insisted that Jamie leave her cane in the Land Rover and lean on her instead. When stairs or steep ramps were encountered, Gunnul would effortlessly pick her up and carry her. The ancient frescoes inside these early Christian churches were breathtaking in their colour and portrayal of the stories of the Bible. Later, they went to the Zelve valleys and Uchisar where the space-scape scenery was riddled with the man-made caves of the troglodyte dwellings. Some of these caves were whole cities underground where the people would hide out for months at a time when invaders arrived. The rounded tunnels went down stories into the ground. The most important people lived the farthest down, well away from trouble, and the livestock were kept in carved-out stables on the first level. Carefully placed air vents allowed for good ventilation and the removal of smoke. Some of the underground cities were joined to others sometimes miles away by passages, Gunnul had explained as she helped a struggling Jamie down the narrow, steep stairs that led from one level to another. The rooms were surprisingly roomy on each level and the light, sand-coloured volcanic stone kept the caves bright and dry.

They sat in an open plaza after and sipped Turkish coffee while Chrissy, drinking fruit juice, chatted away to Jamie. As they sat, an old woman came along and offered to read the grinds of their coffee. Gunnul let Chrissy have a sip from her cup and then turn the cup upside down so that she could have her fortune read first. "You are going on a long trip, little one, and you will be scared." Gunnul wrapped protective arms around her daughter and whispered in her ear not to worry, that it was just make believe.

The old woman sneered, and then lifted Jamie's cup and looked at the grinds. "There will be great anger towards you soon and then I see only darkness." Gunnul stood and snapped at the woman in Turkish. Her face white with anger, she waved the old fortuneteller away. They left to return to the hotel shortly after, the happiness of the day now marred by the fortuneteller's predictions and the sullen silence of Gunnul.

With Chrissy safely asleep in bed, Gunnul wandered out onto their balcony and watched the stars. That cluster, she always felt, looked like a fish. "Hey, you want to talk about it?" came a voice from behind her. Gunnul turned and leaned against the rail, pulling Jamie into her arms.

"No. I am not superstitious. I shouldn't have reacted as I did. It upset Chrissy. It just hit on a big pile of insecurity inside me that's all," confessed Gunnul.

"We've never talked about what this is doing to you, my sweet one. It must be very hard to suddenly have to share your daughter. You have been wonderful about it, you know. Chrissy was so lucky that you were there to come into her life. I'm lucky that this whole situation hasn't been really ugly. It wasn't, because of you. Thank you," said Jamie earnestly.

Gunnul pulled her close and snuggled her face into Jamie's sweet scented hair. "I get jealous sometimes," she confessed. "And not knowing how this is all going to work out is really eating at me. I love the two of you very much and I... I've got a lot to lose."

"Next week, I'll fly back to the States. I hope you and Chrissy will visit me often and if you'll let me, I'd like to come back to Turkey again when I can afford to," stated Jamie, finally expressing out loud what she knew she must do. "We both have pain from our pasts that we need to get over. Maybe some day there could be a future for us. I don't know; there is Chrissy to worry about. I do love you, Gunnul," finished Jamie, her voice breaking with emotion.

Gunnul's voice was tight with emotion too. "I will set up a fund so that there is always money for you to come visit us. No, don't object! I do it for Chrissy, who has a right to see her birth mother often. I... I... do it for me also. I... I don't think I can be happy now if you are not so near," confessed Gunnul. They stood under the stars for a long time and just held each other.

Finally, Jamie said, "I think that cluster of stars looks like a horse."

Gunnul pulled back in surprise. "I do too!"

Jamie frowned. "Another trace memory. I've been thinking about the mystery of our past and the grave, Gunnul. I think we are supposed to understand something really important but I don't know what. I've been trying to establish patterns. You seem always to be a leader of some sort. In the Amazon, you were involved with drugs and you are in this existence too. I'm not sure there aren't other realities too, that we are not aware of yet. Do you see any patterns?"

Gunnul thought about it for a moment. "In my memories, when I first knew you in an ancient world, you were healer. The thing that sticks out the strongest in my trace memory is you being hurt very badly in a battle and being terribly worried about you. In the Amazon, I think you are a doctor and you wore a brace on your lower leg. You didn't use a cane or anything though," revealed Gunnul.

Jamie frowned and walked over to the railing, looking out into the night. "So what do we have? A leader with remarkable strength and courage, who seems always to have a side kick. Drugs may be a constant or a symbol for something and I'm lame and so is my counter part in the jungle. Are we making any headway here? Wait, you always have those strange blue eyes that seem to glow from within."

"Yes," nodded Gunnul and sighed. "And the violence within," she added. Soon after that, they went to bed, curling close, two hearts with one soul.

* * * * *

Next morning, Jamie met at least ten thousand relatives, or at least it seemed so. Everyone was happy and excited about the upcoming wedding and Jamie was made very welcome. It seemed like everyone had to touch her hair and try out their few English phrases, to Jamie's delight. She had worn her gallabeeya that morning and did her best to speak Turkish whenever she could. Chrissy held on to her hand and introduced her around proudly. Gunnul had quickly been separated from her. She stood with the men rather than the women and it was clear that she headed the family.

Jamie was talking in broken phrases to the bride and her mother, Chrissy offering translation when necessary. Suddenly, Gunnul was there and the Turkish women lowered their eyes in respect. "You have met Jamie, I see," she smiled, ignoring the submissive attitude of the women. Immediately, they relaxed and smiled broadly.

"She ride with husband and I?" asked the bride.

Gunnul laughed. "Yes, of course. She will bring you much good luck! Jamie is a Dedemann. When she is in Turkey, she will head my households." The reaction of those around Gunnul was mixed. The two Turkish women looked shocked and then lowered their eyes in respect to Jamie. Chrissy beamed with delight and took Gunnul's hand. Gunnul looked down at her daughter and returned the smile, her blue eyes dancing with pride. Jamie looked from one to the other in confusion. It was clear that something important had happened but she wasn't sure just what it was.

Chrissy ran off to join some cousins in a game and this gave Jamie the opportunity to pull Gunnul aside. She placed her walking stick on a table and wrapped her arm around her lover's. "Walk with me for a bit?" she asked, and Gunnul smiled and patted her hand as they walked off down a garden path. Many noticed and turned away in politeness but one pair of eyes burned after them.

"Okay, everyone has started to treat me like they do you. What's going on, Gunnul?" Jamie asked.

Gunnul blushed and looked uneasy. "I have told people that you are a Dedemann. It is of course our surname but it is more than that. You see, Jamie, before the republic, people in Turkey did not have surnames. Attaturk insisted that we must take one. So everyone made up a surname and registered it with the government. My family took Dedemann. It roughly translates as chief or leader of the people. I head this family and really have a great influence on the district in which we live. The people come to me to solve their problems rather than the government. When I told people you are Dedemann and head of the household, I told them that you were second in command, m... my partner."

Silence filled the garden as Jamie looked unbelievingly at Gunnul. "Your partner," she finally managed to get out.

"I... I... know you don't want to be such, Jamie. And I will respect that and not force you to stay with me, but it is important that people understand for Chrissy's sake that you are one of the family and that I have recognized you as my partner, if only in the raising of our daughter. Chrissy is very rich and will be very powerful as she grows older. It is important that no one feels her right to the Dedemann estate should be questioned."

Jamie ran an unsteady hand through her hair and lowered herself to a garden bench. "You planned to do this and you didn't tell me?" questioned Jamie, in frustration.

Gunnul hung her head and looked worried. "I guess I should

have, Jamie. I am not used to having to share my ideas and decisions with another."

"Just what does partner mean?" Jamie asked.

Gunnul blushed and sat down at the other end of the bench. She did not look at Jamie but stared at a bush along the path. "I became a General. It is not the role of a woman. Neither is leading a family and yet I was the only heir. It would have been different if I had married, but my chosen one died in battle. I was so badly hurt... I can't have children. A man when he marries wants family, so I am not marriageable unless for my wealth and I would not marry someone for that reason. There is no role for me in traditional Turkish society. I am treated as a man, not a woman. It is... difficult to explain. Now I have fallen in love with a woman and I have declared you my partner," explained Gunnul. Jamie waited.

Gunnul sighed and went on, "That is not acceptable in Turkey either. But I have arranged with my lawyers that you do have custody over Chrissy and power of attorney over my estate until she is of age if anything should happen to me," finished Gunnul, sitting stiff and quiet, as far away from Jamie as she could.

"This is going to take some getting used to," mumbled Jamie, half to herself. "I see why you needed to do it. People could question her claim because her mother is foreign and she is your adopted child. I am speechless that you would trust me so completely, Gunnul. I wish I could..."

"Don't say it! I don't want to discuss it further at this time. Please, we go back to the wedding," begged an upset Gunnul, getting to her feet.

Jamie nodded. She knew that Gunnul had opened up some really raw spots in talking to her and now needed some time to heal. She stood and took Gunnul's offered arm, then reached up and kissed her cheek. "Will your family be okay with this, Gunnul?" she asked.

"Most yes, although shocked. They are used to having an oddity as head of the family," she answered sadly. "Some, who thought they had a chance at the Dedemann wealth and power if anything happened to me, will be upset. That is only a few. Do not worry. They are loyal to me."

That afternoon, Gunnul's cousin was married. This involved a civil service at the government office and then a religious service at the mosque. The trip in between, and later that day to a nightclub for the reception, was made by horse and buggy. It was accompanied by exuberant cheering and horn honking. The married couple insisted on Jamie riding in their cart and the people in the streets would stop and point at her and clap their hands with delight for the young couple's good luck.

The club had been booked for the wedding party only. It was carved out of the rock as were many homes in the Cappadocia area. Dishes of vegetables and nuts were piled on the tables by smiling waiters, as was chicken and beef shish kebabs, cheese and breads. Dishes of hot pepper beets, yogurt, pickles, salads and bean dishes were next. Lastly, came baklava and fruit. Folk dancers performed to traditional Turkish music as they ate, and with dessert the lights were lowered and a beautiful belly dancer performed a sensuous and exciting dance.

"There is always a belly dancer at a wedding," Gunnul whispered to Jamie. "At one time such women were not considered of good character but now, with the growing tourist trade, it is a more acceptable occupation."

Twice the belly dancer performed in front of Gunnul, once brushing her silk scarf around Gunnul's neck. She had worked around the round room stopping at each table but Gunnul was the only woman she had singled out and her attention and efforts seemed to Jamie to be far more sexual. She found herself wanting to trip the bitch up and was surprised at her jealousy. Gunnul watched the performance with her public non-emotional face. Was she enjoying the show? Jamie was suddenly stricken with the realization that she could never dance for Gunnul.

The music had changed while Jamie had sat looking at her plate. "Come, we dance," Gunnul said, putting an arm around Jamie.

Jamie swallowed. "Gunnul, I... I... can't."

"Yes, I help. Come," coaxed Gunnul, and Jamie, trusting her, let her pull her from her seat. Everyone was up dancing in one big long line that circled around and around and in and out of each other. Gunnul wrapped one strong arm around Jamie to support her weak leg and joined in the line, taking the hand of the man beside her. Jamie had one arm wrapped around Gunnul and the other was claimed by Chrissy, who had suddenly appeared from another section of the line. Soon Jamie was laughing and singing along with the others.

When Gunnul thought Jamie had put enough strain on her leg, she moved to the edge of the intertwining dancers and pulled Jamie into a quiet corner. "Chrissy has asked to stay in the room of her girl cousins. I have checked and they will be well supervised by an elderly great aunt. Is that okay with you, Jamie?" asked Gunnul.

"A sleep-over! Sure, Gunnul. They are wonderful fun when you are a kid," replied Jamie.

Gunnul nodded and left. Jamie saw her talk first to Chrissy and then to an elderly woman in the corner. She saw Gunnul bend over so the old woman could kiss her on the cheek. There were so many sides to Gunnul. She was so complex; scary, powerful, gentle, loving, and insecure all at once. It was like holding a grenade with the pin not quite out. As long as you held it you could feel the potential power, but if you let it slip...

"Hi Mom! Thank you for letting me stay over with my cousins tonight," bubbled Chrissy, giving her Mom a hug and kiss. "I come to say good night!"

"Good night, Chrissy! You have a good time and don't be any trouble for your great aunt," said Jamie, hugging her daughter back. Then Gunnul was there to get her good night hug and kiss too. When Chrissy left, Gunnul ordered a taxi and took Jamie back to the hotel. She needed Jamie. The last two nights had driven her crazy with desire. And she had to admit she'd been jealous all day. Everyone, particularly the men, had been swarming around Jamie like flies to honey. Jamie for her part had been friendly and attentive to them all. Gunnul had barely seen her, never mind got close to her. And that slimy Kaymaki had pushed it to the very limit. If it hadn't been her cousin's wedding she'd have punched his lights out!

They were barely inside the door when Gunnul grabbed Jamie and pushed her against the wall, kissing her with pent-up up passion. For a second, Jamie froze and Gunnul, sensing her fear, pulled back immediately. Then Jamie relaxed, realizing that Gunnul would not cross the line from excitement to violence. She leaned back against the wall and ran a fingertip down the planes of Gunnul's face and neck. "Do you know what I want?" she asked in a husky voice.

Gunnul raised an eyebrow. "What?" she growled.

"I want you to take me until I scream with delight," whispered Jamie, looking intently into Gunnul's eyes. Gunnul moved closer and slowly and deliberately peeled the clothes off Jamie until she was standing naked in front of her bold stares. Their eyes met. Gunnul's hand lifted her chin and she bent to claim Jamie's lips in a hungry, deep kiss. Jamie was lifted from her feet and tossed on the bed only to be covered instantly with Gunnul's long, hard body. Her General claimed all territory and Jamie, her willing prisoner, allowed her to take anything she wished. Their love was passionate and demanding. And each time Jamie came, she cried out her delight on her lover's name.

Much later, they lay together talking over the day. "I really like your family, Gunnul. Everyone was so nice to me. Boy, do you Turks know how to party!" she laughed.

"Turks like a good time," Gunnul agreed. "I was jealous. I did not like the way the men crowded around you," she confessed.

"Well, if it was jealousy that turned you into a raging lover, I'll have to use that trick more often," smiled Jamie, kissing her lover's lips.

Jamie felt the violent energy and suddenly she was on her back and Gunnul was leaning over her. "You will not go near Kaymaki. I did not like the way he was coming on to you. I should kill him if he touches you!"

Jamie pushed Gunnul away in anger. Shock at Gunnul's sudden aggression had hit on an old nerve. "You don't own me, Gunnul. I'll see and do whatever I want!" she snapped.

Gunnul went quiet and got out of bed. She slipped on a pair of blue jeans, pulled a sweatshirt on and went to stand by the window. A few silent moments went by. Then, in a strangled voice, Gunnul managed to get out, "I am sorry. I know you are not mine. I have a lot of power. Sometimes I forget I can't always have my way.

"Today, was a good wedding, no?" said Gunnul struggling to change the subject. "It was a good arrangement. The families will both prosper by this union."

"It was an arranged marriage! In this day and age?" gasped Jamie, in disbelief.

"Yes, of course. It is usually so. A girl meets a young man that she thinks she likes, or vice versa. She tells her mother or perhaps the mother hears of a good choice and approaches her daughter. Then the mothers, they will meet and talk at the baths many times and feel things out. If all goes well, then the young man and his family will be invited to the girl's house. She must make Turkish coffee for her future in-laws. She makes each cup separately, serving her future husband last. If she puts lots of sugar in the cups, this indicates she wishes to marry this man. If there is no sugar, then she is not interested. Also she will bring in a box of Turkish Delights but will not open them if she is not happy with the arrangement. Sometimes as a tease, the girl will not put sugar in the boy's coffee. He then will worry if there is sugar in the other cups of his relatives all evening!

"The young man must provide a dowry, which is usually a house or apartment and gold jewelry. The girl must provide a rug. Traditionally, it is one that she has made herself. The family comes then to an agreement and the wedding takes place. I have arranged a good marriage for Chrissy I think..."

"What!" snapped Jamie, struggling to her feet, awkwardly getting into her robe and grabbing her cane. "You've done what?"

"I start to make arrangements for Chrissy to marry. It is early but I need to feel out..."

"No!" yelled Jamie, facing Gunnul.

The two of them looked at each other as if for the first time. Then Gunnul spoke quietly, fighting for control. "Chrissy must marry well. It is her duty. She is a Dedemann. I will not leave such a marriage to chance," stated Gunnul firmly.

"Chrissy will marry for love," snarled Jamie. "Don't you dare sell my daughter to the highest bidder."

Gunnul's jaw tightened in rage. "You did so well in picking a husband?" she spit contemptuously.

The words hit home. A cold rage consumed the smaller woman. No one, not even Gunnul, was going to ruin her daughter's chance at happiness. "At least I had a daughter. I didn't have to steal one," she shot back. Then she realized what she had said.

Gunnul went completely white. She took a step towards Jamie, her fists clenched in rage. Then she was gone, the door slamming behind her. Jamie crumpled to the floor in horror and cried.

The next morning was hideous. Chrissy, of course, wanted to know where her mother was and Jamie had no idea. Gunnul had never returned. Jamie had gone through the rest of the night alternating from self-abuse for what she had said to Gunnul, to worry that she'd had an accident, to jealousy that she might have sought comfort in that belly dancer's arms! She realized that she liked knowing that Gunnul had only had her for a lover, that there was a part of Gunnul's life that was uniquely hers. The thought of losing that really upset her.

Chrissy and she ate breakfast in the hotel restaurant and then packed up to leave. Still, no Gunnul. Jamie was groggy and disorientated by lack of sleep. She had told Chrissy that Gunnul had left to see to some things and this seemed to satisfy her daughter, who was used to a mother who had many responsibilities that took her away at times. She suggested that they take the bags to the car so that they would be ready when Gunnul returned. Chrissy called a porter and they followed him to the car and watched while he put their bags in the trunk.

"Good morning, ladies," called Kaymaki walking up to the two after the porter had left. *Oh boy, this is just what I need,* thought Jamie, recognizing the man from the previous evening, *for Gunnul to show up now with Kaymaki here.*

But she said, "Good morning, Kaymaki. We were just on our way back to our room."

"We have to wait for Mom. She got called away on business,"

explained the innocent child.

"Really!" smiled Kaymaki. This was going to be so much easier than he had thought. From his pocket he pulled out a handgun. "I think you two ladies will come for a ride with me instead," he said.

Jamie hobbled in front of Chrissy. "You don't need the child. Just take me," she said.

"No. I need both Dedemanns, I think." He smiled, as four other men closed in around them.

"Mommy?" cried Chrissy in fear, holding on to Jamie.

"It's okay, Chrissy. Everything will be okay," Jamie assured the little girl, as they were pushed into a van that had pulled up. Kaymaki took the car keys from Jamie and threw them at one of the men, who got into their car and followed the van.

Some miles out, they turned down a rough dirt road and bounced along to a cave carved into a large pinnacle of rock. They were ushered through the interconnecting tunnels, down several stories, Chrissy helping Jamie as best she could. Several times, Jamie fell and her hands and knees were scraped and bleeding. The cave was crumbling and dirty, not like the ones they had explored before, and the air was still and dusty.

"Stop," ordered Kaymaki, and Jamie leaned against the wall with Chrissy tucked protectively at her side. "This is as far as we need go."

"What do you want? Ransom? Gunnul will never let you get away with it, Kaymaki," argued Jamie.

Kaymaki laughed. "No. I think much bigger than petty crimes, Mrs. Dedemann," he sneered. "No, the apparent heir is about to meet an untimely death and then there will only be Gunnul between me and taking over the Dedemann Empire." He raised his gun and pointed it at Chrissy.

"No!" screamed Jamie as the gun went off.

* * * * *

Gunnul trudged down the trail that led into the gardens of the hotel. She hadn't meant to be gone all night but once she had started moving she had covered miles before her temper had finally cooled. She had been just as responsible for the fight as Jamie. There were sure to be these cultural differences and they were just going to have to work things out, not insult each other. She hurried along, realizing that Chrissy would be back and wondering where she was. She came through the hedge gate and dropped down the bank to the parking lot. The car was gone.

Blood drained from her face and she broke into a run, pushing a porter out of the way and slamming into the elevator. She bounced nervously about waiting for the doors to open, then ran to the room and slipped in her card. Everything had been packed and their bags were gone. *My God! She's taken Chrissy.* Gunnul's eyes blazed with anger and she wheeled and headed down to the lobby. She was going to get Chrissy back no matter what she had to do.

* * * * *

Jamie had wrapped herself around Chrissy and felt the bullet tear through her side. Then the floor seemed to give out under them. Behind her, she thought she heard Kaymaki scream as rock and dust rained around them as they fell. When they hit bottom, pain shot through Jamie and she knew no more.

"Mommy! Mommy!" called a frightened voice, as small hands stroked her hair. Jamie opened her eyes and saw nothing. Pain lanced her side. She reached down and felt blood oozing freely from a gunshot wound.

"I'm okay, Chrissy," she reassured her daughter, lifting a hand to touch her. "Are you all right?"

"Yes, I am fine. Just scrapes and bruises. But you are bleeding! Kaymaki shot you!" sobbed Chrissy.

"Shhh, Chrissy. We just have to be brave and wait for your Mom to find us. You know she will," soothed Jamie, not at all sure that was going to be the case. Gunnul would tear the world apart looking for them, that she was sure of, but she would be looking in the wrong places. She'd think that Jamie had decided to kidnap Chrissy so that she couldn't be married off. God! What a stupid argument they'd had! "Look, Chrissy, I need you to tear my shirt in half and pack the cloth into the wounds. We have to slow the bleeding until your Mom gets here."

Chrissy did what she was asked, and Jamie bit through her lip trying not to cry out in pain. Wet with perspiration she lay back down. "Hey, why don't you snuggle into my side and I'll tell you some really good stories about the wild west," suggested Jamie.

A frightened little child curled up at her Mom's side and let her Mom's warmth and soft voice take the fear away. Jamie told story after story. She knew she was no longer really making sense. Death was near. *Please Allah, save Chrissy,* she prayed as she held the sleeping child close.

167

* * * * *

They'd looked for most of the day. The police, the army, and Gunnul's family. In the late afternoon, the car was found, but no sign of either Jamie or Chrissy. The area was riddled with caves, to the point where the ground was unstable. An officer came over to Gunnul.

"General Dedemann, there has been another vehicle here today. We think maybe a van. There are footprints in the soft sand over there. A child and a woman and perhaps as many as six men," he reported.

Gunnul turned and looked at him with eyes grey and stormy. "Tear this mountain apart if you have to. Find them!" she ordered. The officer saluted and turned, yelling orders that sent men running in all directions. Gunnul stood where she was. For the first time in her life she felt completely helpless. She'd failed to protect her family. They had been kidnapped and God knew what had been done to them! Gunnul swallowed. *Don't think like that,* she warned herself.

She looked up and blinked back tears and then she saw the cave entrance. She knew immediately, deep in her soul, that her lover was in there. She ran up the hill, calling to the soldiers nearby to follow her.

* * * * *

Jamie woke feeling clean and very sleepy. Opening her eyes, she realized that she was in a hospital bed. Oxygen was being fed to her and an I.V. was in her arm. Her side throbbed. She turned her head. Sleeping in the bed next to her was Chrissy. She looked peaceful and well. Then she became aware of a weight on her legs. Looking down she saw Gunnul. She was sitting in a chair and had gone to sleep with her head on Jamie's bed and her arm wrapped protectively around Jamie's legs. Her eyes were dark from lack of sleep and her cheeks hollow with strain. Jamie reached out with her fingers and touched Gunnul. Instantly, her lover was awake and at her side.

Gunnul took her hand and kissed her fingers and tears rolled down her face. "Hey, it's okay, Gunnul. I'm all right. Is Chrissy okay?" Jamie asked through dry lips.

Gunnul tried to smile bravely. "Yes, Chrissy's fine. And you are not okay. You gave Chrissy and I an awful scare. They've had to take your spleen out. It was...pretty close," Gunnul managed to say, her chin quivering with emotion.

"What happened?" Jamie asked.

Gunnul blushed. "At first, I was frantic and angry. Then I realized you wouldn't have taken Chrissy without talking to me. I trust you. I knew something terrible must have happened to you. I called out the police and the army and we searched all day. Finally, we found the car. We would never have found you in time, Jamie, but I saw the cave entrance and I felt you there. We headed down to where we could see a cave-in had taken place. There was all this blood in a pool by the rock and I thought..."

Jamie squeezed Gunnul's hand and the woman took a deep breath and went on. "We dug and it was Kaymaki. Dead. Then we saw the shaft and I dropped down and found you. The air was bad and you were both unconscious. It was only when we got you out that I realized you'd been shot and had lost a lot of blood. We took you by helicopter to Istanbul. That was three days ago. Chrissy told me what you did. Jamie, we have been so scared! I love you so much!"

"I'm tired but I'm fine now. Gunnul?"

"Yes," asked the woman, eagerly leaning close to hear Jamie's weak voice.

"I love you too," whispered Jamie, falling back into sleep. Gunnul leaned forward and brushed Jamie's lips with a kiss.

* * * * *

Some weeks later, Gunnul and Jamie were driving out of Istanbul to the town of Iznik. Gunnul had been nervous all morning and Jamie wondered what she was up to. Her recovery had been slow but steady and last week she had been released from the hospital. Teefo had been dispatched to America, much to his delight, to explain what had happened and to see to her bills and other items of concern until Jamie could return.

Jamie didn't want to return, at least not without her family. She had realized that night that Gunnul would never be like Moe. She had buried her ghosts and wanted nothing more than to be a part of Gunnul and Chrissy's life. But the subject had never come up. Clearly, Gunnul had made some decisions that fatal night too and they didn't include Jamie.

"We never solved the mystery of the grave site," she said, looking out the window and watching the rolling country go by.

Gunnul gave her a quick look before turning back to her driving. "I am not sure that we are meant to find an answer. Maybe we are just a part of the process. I don't know. I feel this calm, as if our part is done."

"Yes," said Jamie sadly, "maybe you are right."

They arrived at the town of Iznik and drove to a small, ruined church in the centre of a shopping area in the old town. Here they got out and Gunnul helped Jamie down the stone stairs and into the church grounds. Only the walls of the old building were left. A section of the mosaic flooring could still be seen and the aging altar nook still stood.

Gunnul took Jamie's hand and they walked over to the altar. "This is St Sophia. The Church of Holy Wisdom. It was here, many years ago, that the ecumenical council wrote the Nicene Creed that the Christians recite. It is the holiest place that I could think to bring you, Jamie," she said, taking Jamie's other hand too and looking down at her.

"I believe that we were meant to be together. I believe that our souls were joined by a greater power and that our love is eternal. I believe that our God is the same, Jamie, and that we can live together and love each other no matter what our cultural differences. I believe we can raise our daughter to love and understand all peoples. I love you. Please, Jamie, before our God, will you stay with me and be my partner."

Jamie looked deeply into those remarkable blue eyes that had captivated her all her life. "I believe in our love. There is no place I would rather be than with you and Chrissy. Yes, Gunnul, I want to be your partner. I love you."

From her pocket, Gunnul took two bands of gold. She slipped one onto Jamie's finger and then gave the other to her to slip on hers. Gunnul looked down into the rich green eyes that she had known in her dreams all her life and knew that she was home.

P. N. G.

Encounters

Anne Azel

Chapter One

Mary Giovani looked out the small rear window of the four-seater aircraft as it labored over the towering limestone peaks of the Southern Highlands of Papua New Guinea. Below was a country left behind in the Stone Age. Now, it was struggling in a single generation to enter the space age. Only flowing rivers of mist in the deep valleys broke the canopy of the dense green jungle. Here and there fire smoke escaped in ribbons into the sky, the telltale evidence of the Stone Age peoples, some of them once cannibals, who lived below.

Mary's strawberry blond hair caught the sunlight as with a sigh she sat back. She allowed her petite body to relax into the worn leather seat and closed her eyes. She was tired. For three weeks, she had been working as a freelance journalist at a new copper mine deep in the wild heartland of Papua New Guinea. It had been tough, living in a tent and putting up with the constant rain and mud and the occasional offensive remarks of male workers who had been away from their loved ones too long. But it had been worth it! She had witnessed first hand the wealth and the destruction that invades an isolated area when a multinational corporation moves in a full-scale operation. She would write a series of articles on subjects ranging from the destruction of the rainforest to the impact of modern technology on the aboriginal people...

"Misses! Misses! Em I gut bik-pella truble!" called the pilot, slipping into Pidgin, the trading language of the South Pacific area. Mary opened her eyes just as the plane lurched violently. She saw a thin line of red stream along the side window. A few downy feathers clung on against the force of the wind outside. The engine spluttered again and the plane dipped, wobbled and leveled off. The pilot was fighting to lower his altitude without causing a stall. Mary didn't have to be told how serious the situation was. The single engine plane had hit a bird in flight and the engine, clogged with debris, was failing. They would have to find a place to land or crash! The journalist pressed her face to the window, searching the terrain below for a possible clearing large enough to land.

"Over there!" she called, tapping the pilot on the shoulder and pointing to a tiny airstrip to their right. The pilot nodded and banked the plane sharply, curving around and straightening on a course for the small strip of flat grass that clung to the edge of a mountainside. The engine coughed and stopped. The silence was suddenly deafening. The small craft maintained its course but was now dropping much quicker than it was gliding forward. Mary tightened her safety belt, put her large, soft purse in her lap and leaned over it, covering her head with her hands. She'd read the safety instructions on large planes hundreds of times with only passing interest. Now it was for real and the little she could do made her feel hopeless.

The little red plane hit the grass runway with a terrific smash, then bounced up in the air again only to smash down once more. From the corner of her eye, Mary could see the plane's wheel fly past just as the little craft flipped upside down in the air and hit the ground for the third time. The thin aluminum roof crashed down on her. She felt her foot catch under the seat as her body launched in another direction. Pain shot up Mary's leg and through her temple. *So this is death*, she thought as blackness washed over her.

* * * * *

Doctor Jessica Vizirakis dated her journal: February 14th, Valentine's Day. She smiled ruefully. Some Valentine's Day! All day, she had been plagued by trace memories, daydreams maybe, of the Host pair and the Others. She suspected her awareness was greater than some of the Others but that did not make it any easier. On the contrary, she knew that all their loves were pointless if the Hosts had failed to hold their bond together and from what she could recall, their relationship had been doomed. Some years ago, she had seen two of the Others. It was like being able to see through a wormhole in space and time. The Turk had felt her presence and had hurried her beloved away. After they had gone, she had crept out of the tangled undergrowth and looked down on the Hosts' grave. The names were wrong of course. She'd run her long, strong fingers over the ancient stone: Jamie and Gunnul Dedemann, it read.

She'd smiled, feeling the peace that being close to the Host brought her. "I just came to tell you that it didn't work out for us. I wanted to tell you personally," she'd whispered to the grave. It felt cold to her touch. There was no answer.

Jess shook her head to clear it of the vivid memory. That was past history! This was real, here and now, she reminded herself. She forced herself to finish her journal and then neatly put everything away before ducking out of the pit pit grass hut that she called home. She stretched her arms up as far as she could reach to get the kinks out of her long, lean form. Her arms framed a face chiseled into beautiful, classic planes. Her hair was dark and the eyes which scanned the spectacular view of the long, narrow valley below were an intense blue.

Jess had loved her experience in this isolated community but there were days when she missed her own world. She looked down into the tropical valley. Here was a beauty beyond imagination, untouched by pollution and noise, a world where the legendary Birds of Paradise still nested high in the treetops. Yet there was another side to paradise. Tribal war, witchcraft, disease, and most deadly of all, a native custom called "pay-back". Payback called for revenge for the slightest offense to an individual in order to save face. Often a chain of paybacks led to violence. Jess had battled all of these deadly elements in the two years that she had been doing her field research.

The tall woman sighed deeply and looked up at the robin-egg blue sky of the South Pacific. "Send me a valentine," she whispered with a wistful smile and then frowned at her whimsical mood. *Won't I ever learn?* she thought bitterly. She shook her head in disgust. Maybe she should take a holiday. She smiled. For some time now, she had wanted to explore a cave near by that she thought might be huge. Several times, she had ventured in on small explorations and the limestone cave promised to be endless. Jess had taken up spelunking while at university. She enjoyed the adventure and the solitude of exploring caves. She liked too the solid, dependable adventurers who seemed to be as attracted to spelunking as she was. Maybe she would take a few weeks off and use up some of her pent up energy in exploring the cave. *After all*, Jessica mused, *a cave is far safer than a lover*. No one knew that better than she did!

Some minutes later, as she sat outside and worked at repairing a knapsack strap, she heard the drone of a passing plane's engine splutter and cough. She stood up and scanned the wide expanse of blue until she saw a dot of red swoop towards the earth. A second later, she had darted into her hut and grabbed her medical kit. Running back out, she was met by her Papuan assistant, Mone. Together they darted towards the clearing up the mountainside.

They heard a squeal of tires and a loud crash, emerging from the jungle just in time to see a little red plane flip into the air and come down heavily on its back. The plane skidded forward in a cloud of dust and debris, finally coming to rest in the underbrush at the end of the runway. By the time Mone and Jess had run the length of the airstrip, a small group of curious tribal people had gathered. Short and dark, they wore nothing but a wide, bark belt from which hand woven netting hung down between their legs. Their backsides were covered by only a few long leaves that had also been jammed under their bark belts. Their eyes were round and white with concern and they spoke quickly in loud, guttural spurts. Jess knew that they wanted to help but were afraid to interfere in a European problem. Too often they had been yelled at or chased off by Europeans who feared or were ignorant of their ways.

Jess spoke quietly to them as she reached in to get the vitals of the pilot. She explained that the plane was drenched in fuel and that a spark could trigger an explosion. They nodded their understanding. Jess sighed, the pilot was dead. The villagers, however, pointed towards the back of the plane and told Jess to take a look. She got up and came around the side and by looking through a narrow space left between the fuselage and the crushed roof; she could just see the arm of a woman. Jess moved back to the nose and, with Mone's help, pulled the dead pilot out through the window. There was a piece of metal through his chest. Jess wiped the blood from her hands and reached in to flip the passenger's seat forward. At the far back of the plane, Jess could just see long blond hair. Slowly, she crawled through the window and wiggled through the wreckage towards the woman. There was very little room. Jess' face ran up a long pair of graceful legs. She slithered forward once more. Now her head rested in the warm hollow between the woman's legs. At another time this could be a very enjoyable rescue, thought Jess, but not today with the overpowering smell of fuel and a dead pilot lying in the grass. There was now, too, the growing smell, sharp and metallic, of blood.

Once again Jess slid forward. Now her face was next to the woman's as Jess lay the full length of her. Her hair smelt nice, like sunlight and fresh, dried herbs. It reminded Jess of a time long ago. Carefully, Jess wedged herself between the woman and the tail compartment and eased the golden hair from her face. Mary Giovani! Jess' heart jolted. In high school, Jess had loved this woman to distraction. An old hurt built in Jess' gut and she swallowed it back down. *This woman is still way out of your league, warrior*, she thought. What strange twist of fate had brought the two of them together here, at the ends of the earth?

Jess shook her head to clear away the memories. She couldn't reminisce about a girl she'd loved long ago. There was a very real woman to save. A very real, beautiful woman, Jess thought as she started her examination. The tearing of her clothes had exposed one of Mary's breasts. Jess reached to cover her and a small, delicate hand tried to push her away. Huge, dark green eyes blinked at her in confusion and fear. "It's okay," Jess softly reassured her. "You're safe and we'll get you out as soon as we can."

"My eyes and skin burn," she whispered through dry lips.

"It's the fuel. Hang on. Everything will be fine," Jess responded gently even though her own stomach was in a tight knot.

Chapter Two

Mary became aware of a mixture of contradictory sensations. There was pain, dull and far away. Close and real was the feel of gentle fingers against her breast. She was warm and ever so relaxed and yet she could sense her nipples hardening in excitement. The next moment reality washed over her with the force of a tidal wave, sending gripping chills through her senses. She pulled away from the violating hands and sat up with a gasp of fear. Pain and nausea shot through her and strong, confident arms were immediately there again, gently lowering her back on the bed. When the pain and blackness subsided she opened blurry eyes and tried to make contact with a steady pair of ice blue eyes that revealed nothing in the way of emotion.

Mary fumbled, trying to pull the rough, gray blanket up to her neck as she realized that she was naked. "Get away from me," she slurred out in terror, aware of the sluggishness of her thoughts and the slow response of her body.

Bitter amusement sprung into the eyes and a deep, mellow voice snorted mockingly, "Hello Giovani. Still the Ice Queen, I see. Some valentine I get sent!"

Mary looked with surprise at the tall figure that sat half in shadow on the edge of her cot. She blinked her eyes, trying to focus them, but the world still tended to drift in and out in blurry patterns. The dark figure waited as unfocused eyes slid over her, taking in the dark brown t-shirt and matching shorts that enhanced her golden tan and then returning to her face. Mary's heartbeat slowed a little from its rapid beat. Did she know this woman? She looked very familiar. How did she know her name?

"You scared me. Don't touch me! My name is MARY Giovani and I'm a journalist and I am definitely not your valentine! Who are you?" demanded Mary angrily, trying to make sense of the distorted world she had returned to. Her head had started to ache awfully and she thought she might be sick.

"Slowly, Giovani," the dark form responded annoyingly. "You're firing words at me like a machine gun. I wasn't trying to scare you. I'm a doctor." Mary went pale and involuntarily raised her hand to her breast. A twinkle came into the blue eyes. "Don't worry, those parts are all present and accounted for and there won't be any lasting scars. You were lucky to survive. We had a hell of a job getting you out safely. Try to rest. You are under heavy medication and now is not a good time to try and think. How do you feel?"

"Vision is blurry and it's hard to think," mumbled Mary.

The woman nodded. "Anything else?"

"Pain... far away. My lips... it's hard to form the words," Mary tried to explain.

Again a nod followed by a hesitation, then, "I've had to amputate the toes from your right foot. There was no saving them with the limited facilities that we have here. Still, you survived. The pilot didn't," came the rest of the story in an emotionless voice.

Silence. Then, "Oh," Mary whispered in shock. She had liked the pilot and felt responsible for his death in so far as she had chartered the plane.

"You okay? You're not going to pass out are you?" the doctor demanded.

"No, no," responded Mary as memories of the crash started to seep back into her awareness. *I feel really sick*, she thought. Mary's head reeled and her stomach was turning over. She was confused and disoriented. Where was she? Who was this woman who said she was a doctor and who had touched her body so intimately? This wasn't a hospital; she seemed to be in some sort of local hut. Mary closed her eyes and tried to make sense of it all. She had been asleep in the plane when the pilot had called a warning to her. The next thing she remembered was the earth rising up to meet her. A shudder ran through Mary's body. Big tears rolled down her face and she started to shake with shock.

The tall woman wrapped her in the blanket and held her in her arms. She talked soft, soothing words to Mary as the big, jerky sobs subsided into sniffles. The larger woman's body was hard, warm and secure and Mary involuntarily snuggled deeper into her embrace, trying to block out the horror of the crash. Memories came crashing back. She could remember waking in terrible pain, pinned under the wreckage with the taste of blood and dirt in her mouth. The air was heavy with the small of fuel and her first fear was that she would be burnt alive!

180

She remembered calling for help and then the voices of local people yelling and murmuring around her. She had a sensation of a warm body crawling in beside her and talking to her, telling her it would be all right and wiping the blood from her face. Had it been this woman who held her tightly now? Yes, she thought so. The tall woman must have risked her life to help her while the local people tried to free her from the dangerous wreck. Yes, she could remember her now, looking down on her and telling her some funny story about wishing for a valentine and how a little red plane had fallen out of the sky to her. She remembered it had made her smile despite the pain. Her panic had left her as the strong woman had lain next to her in the fuel soaked wreckage talking.

Mary could recall now being lifted from the wreckage and screaming in pain. Sometime later, she had felt someone stripping off her clothes and washing the fuel from her skin. Cool lotion was spread over her body and the fuel burns lost their sting. The pain that had shot up her leg like jagged knives was then only a dull throb.

A deep blush swept through her body as she realized the woman who held her must have been the one who had cared for her. Here she was, clinging desperately to a complete stranger who must know her body intimately! Embarrassed, Mary buried her head in the broad shoulder. How was she going to thank her without acute embarrassment? Why was she clinging to her now?! Who was this woman? Mary pulled herself together with an effort. She mentally chastised herself and by exerting great emotional strength pulled herself away from the mysterious woman. She pulled the rough, wool blanket around her and tried to focus again on the face looking down at her.

Again a wave of nausea passed over Mary. She fought it down. Now was not the time to be sick. She needed to get back into control of the situation. "I... I... I'm feeling better... Thank you. I... I sort of remember. I... I mean I... you saved my life," she said as she blushed deeply. "I'm okay," she repeated again, aware that her lips were not really forming the words very clearly.

Jess looked closely at the colour returning to smaller woman's face. She sat back and said, "Good. Your plane has crashed in a remote area of the Southern Highlands. I'll do all I can for you, Giovani, until help gets here. I just wish that I'd been able to save your toes..."

Shock hit Mary like a thunderbolt as the words finally hit home to her. She gasped, a scream stifled by her own fear. "Oh God! No!" she heard herself groan as she leaned over and threw up on the taller woman's lap before passing out.

The tall woman got up with a curse and went to clean herself up in a bowl of warm water that sat on a roughly made table. Once relatively clean, Jess wrung out a cloth and went back to her patient, wiping her face and hands like a little child. She checked to make sure Mary's breathing passage was clear, then pulled the soiled blanket off and replaced it with a fresh one before she left the hut.

* * * * *

From distorted dreams, Mary woke with a start in far more pain but less confusion. *Jess! My God, it's Jess*, she thought. Blinking, she looked around, searching for visual clues that would help her get orientated. Vague impressions nagged at her consciousness. With dread, she accepted the horrid realization that the woman with the incredible blue eyes she had talked to earlier could only be a grown up Jessica Vizirakis.

She'd changed. She had been long limbed and gawky as a teen. Thin and wiry, she'd been a loner who prowled on the edges of the school community like a wild wolf. The high school was small and made up of the children from the upper middle class suburbs or the estates of the wealthy. Only a handful of kids outside this privileged economic bracket attended Winston.

Jess had been one of them; gaunt, quick tempered and silent. The teachers shook their heads in wonder at her intelligence. The kids laughed at her. Everyone called her Warrior because she was a cadet. She kept her uniform hanging in her locker like other girls kept their pictures of their boyfriends.

She lived with her grandfather, Old Bart, in two rooms off the stables. The stables had belonged to Mary's father, a rich businessman whose hobby was race horses. Mary's father used to say he only kept the old drunk on because Bart had an uncanny way with horses and because Warrior wouldn't have any place to sleep otherwise. As a child, Mary had followed the older girl whenever she could, envious of her dirty clothes and freedom and afraid of her fists. Jess had been her hero.

As she had gotten older, they hadn't spent as much time together although there was still a deep, unstated loyalty between them. The kids at school knew not to make fun of Warrior in front of her. And twice, Mary had got into shouting matches with kids when she had come to the defense of the stoic girl. Neither time had Jess thanked her for standing up for her. Jess was proud and Mary knew it bothered the older girl that she had heard the nasty things the other kids said.

When Mary had gone on her first date, she had caught a glimpse of Jess in the shadows. She suspected that Jess had been her invisible protector more than once. She knew Jess wouldn't violate her privacy and it gave her a sense of quiet comfort that Jess would always be there to protect her.

They had only fought once. It was when a female classmate of Mary's had invited her to go to the movies with her. Suddenly, Jess had been beside her in the show. Jess had insisted on driving Mary home after the movie and they had a terrible fight that had hurt them both very much. After that, they had rarely spoken.

It had been late in Jess' final year when they had become lovers. It was a Friday and Warrior had not shown up at school. The rumor circulated that Joel McGallin and some others on the football team had tried to rape her and got their asses kicked. Mary had signed out and driven the Range Rover her dad had bought her out to the stables.

She'd found Jess curled in a ball in the back stall, a cornered, hurt animal. "Jess, it's okay, it's just Mary. Mary Giovani. Are you alright?" she'd whispered softly.

The dark figure had rolled back into the shadows. "Go away."

But Mary hadn't, instead she had slowly moved closer until she could have reached out and touched the stiff form. "Jess?" coaxed Mary softly, kneeling down.

Jess turned and looked at her and Mary gasped in shock. Jess' face was swollen and bruised and she had a deep cut over her left eyebrow. "Oh no!" moaned Mary and without thinking she had wrapped her arms around the taller woman and was hugging her close to her.

"Let go!" the loner ordered.

"No!" Mary had snapped back. "Where is Bart?"

Jess shrugged and pulled away, sliding farther back, "Gone with your parents. He's riding in the trailer to keep the horses calm."

"Come on," Mary had said, trying to help the larger woman to her feet.

"Where?" asked the injured woman, pulling away and getting up to back into the corner.

"Up to the house," explained Mary.

The taller woman rolled her eyes. "Oh right," she snarled sarcastically.

Mary was careful not to block Jess into the corner although every ounce of her being was demanding that she go to her. "You've got a choice here, Warrior, you can have me spend the night here in the barn with you or you can come up to the house. You do realize, though, that if my parents phone tonight and I don't answer they'll probably call out the army?"

There was a long hesitation, and then Jess sighed and limped forward, wrapping her long arm around Mary's petite shoulders and allowing her to take the weight of Jess' injured knee. Together, they had stumbled up to the house.

Mary had taken Jess to her bedroom and started the whirlpool bath for her while she'd gone to get one of her father's sweat shirts and pants for the older girl to put on. She'd passed them in through the door of the steamy bathroom shyly and then had gone to get the first aid kit and make a snack for Jess. Jess was lounging on her bed flipping through the TV channels when she got back. She placed the tray on the bedside table, then sat on the edge of the bed and opened up the first aid kit. "We've got to clean those scrapes. Barns can be really dangerous you know!"

Jess snorted and raised an eyebrow. "Your daddy pays for our shots. He'd hate to be sued if one of us died of tetanus."

Mary ignored the sarcasm aimed at her father, who was a very nice man. Instead, she got even by dabbing an antibiotic cream on Jess' scraped knuckles. She'd smiled cruelly when Jess had pulled away and was rewarded with a surprised look and a raised eyebrow from the other girl. "So daddy's kitten has claws," Jess drawled.

"You bet," Mary had agreed happily, searching out other scrapes and cuts and treating them accordingly.

"I see you around a lot," admitted Jess guardedly.

Mary looked up into beautiful blue eyes that took her breath away. "I see you too," she responded softly, reaching out carefully to dab at the deep, split at the corner of Jess' eye. Warm breath tickled across her arm as she worked. "I've always been jealous of the freedom you've had," Mary admitted honestly.

Jess laughed then grabbed her nose as fresh blood spurted out. "Here," said Mary, replacing Jess' hand with her cloth and adding pressure. "Don't laugh."

"Don't say really stupid things!" mumbled a nasal Jess from under Mary's hand.

"I wasn't! I'd never be allowed to just act like I want or wear what I want or get dirty... I don't suppose you can understand that," sighed Mary.

"No, I can't. You ever tried to study in a horse trailer, or have to muck out stalls before you can go to school. You ever had to steal paper and pens and stuff from the drugstore so you can keep good notes, or rip somebody's textbook out of their locker 'cause you can't afford to buy your own. Shit! If not being able to wear ripped, stinking jeans is the worst thing that's happened to you, Ice Queen, you're doing all right!" snarled Jess, pulling the cloth away from Mary and getting up like a spring uncoiling. Her knee buckled immediately and she stumbled, Mary catching her in her arms half way to the floor. The two of them went down together.

The pain in Mary's foot brought her back from the past. She gritted her teeth. The last thing she was going to do in front of Jess was show any weakness.

* * * * *

Jess listened to Mone explaining in Pidgin to the new patient how to check every day for cuts or bruises. It was a ritual that all leprosy victims had to go through each day, stripping down and visually checking their bodies for signs of damage. It was the only way that they could keep in touch with themselves. Their eyes became their nerve ends sensing pain and danger. The loss of feeling often resulted in the loss of fingers and toes or worse, as small, unnoticed abrasions became deadly infected areas.

Jess handed over the medication to the silent highlander. He was dark skinned and stocky, as the highland people tended to be. He was probably five foot six inches, maybe five foot seven inches, Jess observed, tall really for a highland male. Beside Jess' six-foot frame, however, he looked short. He had a beard as was the custom. The tight, curly hairs were sparse however and his face lean and hungry. For a second, their eyes met. He saw the intense blue of the heavens. She saw hate burnt into eyes the colour of mahogany. The man turned and left without a word.

Mone watched Jess' eyes follow the highlander along the trail until he was out of sight. "That is Touy. He is a shaman. He is from Mendara," Mone explained.

"He involved in the land dispute?" asked Jess, filling in Touy's file while Mone cleaned up.

"Yes, he is a Mendara not an Eravey. Also, he will help Quen kill the Timp when the time is right," observed Mone. Like most Papua New Guineans he was not usually comfortable or open in sharing information about his traditional culture. He had learned, however, that he could trust Jess. She understood their ways and didn't judge.

Jess looked up in surprise. "He's a powerful man."

Mone nodded unhappily and moved off to do other chores. Jess busied herself checking stock and trying not to let her eyes stray over to the hut across the grass compound. Her mind wondered back to the weekend when Giovani had taken her in. Jess' knee had given out and the smaller woman had tried to catch her, the two of them ending up in a tangled heap on the floor.

They had made love right there on the damn rug, each of them unsure and tentative in their first attempts at a sexual relationship. In the end, instinct and desire had carried them into a paradise of sensual pleasure.

They had spent the weekend together, Jess in a state of bitter wonder at the luxuries and love that Mary took for granted, Mary fascinated by Warrior's dark roughness. They had shared not only their bodies but also a guarded secret. They both had the same repeating dreams, the same misty memories. It had been Mary who had called them the "Hosts", those two far off women who had lived, fought and loved in an ancient time. And at some time in their talk the rest, like them, had become the "Others." Mary had talked a lot, bubbling on an emotional high. Jess talked little, already aware of the outcome.

Mary believed that all the descendants of these remarkable two were fated to find each other and the same intense love. Jess didn't disillusion her. She couldn't. But she knew her awareness was far greater. She knew that Mary's ancestor had betrayed hers in a far off land. If history did repeat, she wasn't sticking around to let this kid betray and hurt her. They made love one more time on Sunday night. While Mary was still sleeping, Jess left, getting out of Mary's life and out of the world in which she had struggled to survive. Now Mary Giovani had fallen on her once again.

Chapter Three

Of the next few days, Mary remembered very little. Jess or Mone would arrive periodically with a needle and she would drift off into a blurry, half awake world. Occasionally, sensations of gentle, capable hands caring for her needs penetrated her dreams. She was glad to rest. Emotionally, she was not ready to deal with the plane crash, her maiming, or Jess Vizirakis.

One morning, she finally fought through the fog and woke with a dull headache. The hut was oppressively hot and stuffy. With difficulty, she got herself to a sitting position and then, steeling herself, she flipped back the blanket to look at her foot. There was nothing to see, just a white bandage carefully wrapped around a stub of a foot. The realization that her toes were really gone made her retch. She could still feel them throbbing, as if they were there.

She sat for a long time coming to terms with it. Then she forced herself to reach down and touch the amputated area. *It's just you, Mary. Don't let this scare you. You can deal with this.* Looking around she noticed that someone had fashioned a crude, hand cut cane and placed it by her bed. She nodded. Time to get up. With the help of the cane she got to her feet, surprised that her balance was not good. Slowly, she hobbled painfully over to where a basin of water was beckoning her. The water was warm and clearly recently placed there. The deliverer's movements must have been what had waked her. She lowered the blanket that she had wrapped around her form and started to wash away her sleep.

"Feeling better?" Jess asked as she leaned in the doorway. Mary started and covered herself up.

"Get out!" she ordered, "I'm getting washed. Have you no manners? You should have knocked!"

Jess raised her eyebrow, her face a mask cut from stone. "This is my hut, and I come and go as I please. I am your doctor, at least temporarily, and you are washing in the water that was brought here by my assistant Mone, so I could cleanse your wounds," responded the warrior. Jess pushed off the doorpost and half turned. "Mone?" she called.

"Yes, Doctor Jess?" came a distant response.

"Bring another basin of water, please," Jess requested before she turned back to Mary. "As for getting out, that would be a dangerous decision on your part. You must have been warned that even the smallest wound can infect and become a tropical ulcer that eats away at your flesh if it is not treated." Mary did know this. She was smart enough to realize that she would have to endure Jess close to her, even though to do so made her react with very strong and contradictory emotions. She set her chin firmly and taking her cane limped over and sat on the edge of the bed, trying very hard not to let the pain show.

A stocky, dark Papuan came in silently and placed another basin of water down on the table. "Giovani, this is my colleague, Mone. Mone, this is an old... friend... Mary Giovani, who dropped in to visit me on Valentine's Day!" Mone laughed and poked Jess in the ribs, saying something to her in the trade language of Pidgin that was too quick for Mary to understand. She gritted her teeth in frustration and smiled a hello to Mone.

He left grinning broadly and Jess turned to Mary. "Lie down and let's not have any of your false modesty. I've a job to do and there is nothing I haven't seen of you during the last few days." Mary complied, closing her eyes and looking away. So it had been Jess who had cared for all her personal needs! This whole thing was just one awful nightmare!

Jess worked quickly and gently, checking every abrasion for signs of inflection and spreading on a fresh layer of antibiotic cream before covering the wounds with fresh dressings. Mary was very aware of her body responding to Jess' touch as she cleansed the bad scraping on her left breast. Her body was stiff with tension and her face hot with embarrassment and anger.

As Jess worked she told her in a soft, confident voice what she was doing and how and what Mary should do in the days ahead to care for herself. When Jess was finished Mary was surprised to find her body yearning for Warrior's touch. *Get hold of yourself, Mary!* she warned herself. *You must have brain fever! This is Warrior! The bitch who took your virginity and disappeared into the night without so much as a good bye!*

"You can relax now. I'm finished. I washed my hands so I don't think any of my common touch got on you," Jess finished sarcastically.

"You've got a really lousy bedside manner, Vizirakis!" she snapped, pulling up the blanket and glaring at the doctor. Jess was gorgeous. Over the years, her body had filled out and the gauntness that had once been there had been replaced by smooth toned muscle under a deep golden tan. She moved with a grace and power that was mesmerizing to watch. And those eyes, not quite human, that glowed with an inner energy... Mary gave herself a mental slap, suddenly aware that Jess was waiting and letting her ogle her body.

Jess raised an eyebrow and drawled slowly, "I've never had any complaints about my bedside style before." Mary was just about to come back with a sharp retort when Jess placed her fingers on her lips to silence her. The warm silk of the journalist's lips sent a hot ball of desire dropping to Jess' loins. She pulled her fingers away, curling the warm breath inside them unconsciously.

"Before that machine gun mouth goes off again, a few facts. Part of our compound was lost in a mudslide last week and we lost our communications hut. We have no radio, so we can't get word out that you are here. If a search plane comes our way, we'll send up a flare, but otherwise you'll have to wait to get out when the supply plane comes in about eight weeks. You can fill in your time by helping around the clinic. I'm sure it will be the poor, little, rich kid's first taste of real work. That will teach you to go joy riding over remote areas!" Jess smiled bitterly and got up from where she sat on the edge of Mary's bed. The attraction she felt as a girl was still there, she realized. The best way to handle this situation was to keep the air as frosty as possible.

Mary went white with anger at the injustice of Jess' words. She felt cheated. Here was the woman that her body and soul had responded to completely as a teen judging her based on her social and economic level as a child! She was having trouble blending the contradictory messages that were being given. On the one hand, Jess had risked her life to save her and had given her tender care, and yet there was this cynical other side that took cheap shots at her.

Jess had known her for years! She had never looked down on Jess! How dare she find fault! Jess had been several grades ahead of her, always on the school's honour roll and always the school outcast. She remembered a weedy, wild looking girl, whose clothes always seemed too short to cover her long limbs, working around her father's stables. Sometimes she would see her in her uniform, hitchhiking into town. Then she was immaculately dressed, stern and aloof. Jess never said much but she used to let Mary tag along on wonderful childhood adventures that usually involved getting very dirty and scraping your elbows. Mary's mother had not liked her playing with Jess but her father always let her.

She did not see much of Jess at school. They were never in the same class. Winston had been a small high school in a rural area that had been developed into estates for the up and coming in nearby Marlbourgh. Most of the students were from fairly wealthy families. Warrior stood out as different. She always wore the same farm clothes that smelt of hay and she never talked about things that the other kids did. School was a war zone to Jess. At school, Jess hardly ever acknowledged her. It was only around the stables or out in the pastures that Jess relaxed and became her friend.

After Christmas holidays one year, Mary had met Jess in the school library and to be polite had asked her what she had got for Christmas. Jess had looked at her with an angry expression and had shook her head and walked away. Mary had gone after her. Somehow she had sensed behind Warrior's bad manners that she was really hurting. Had Old Bart not done anything for Jess for Christmas?!

When she had caught up to Jess, she had grabbed her by the shoulder and turned her around. Jess had looked surprised and confused and so very vulnerable. Mary had wrapped her arms around her and had whispered in her ear, "I care." For a split second, she felt their souls touch and she had known she was home. She felt Jess relax into her arms. Then some boys in Jess' class had come past and made some crude remarks about Mary not being able to find anything better and Jess had pulled away. She'd snarled at Mary before walking off, "Never come near me again! You hear?"

And she hadn't, although she was always keenly aware of Jess whenever she was around. And the next Christmas, she had asked her dad to decorate the stable and had slipped a present in the back stall where she knew Jess would find it. It was just a simple gold chain but she noted after that Jess always wore it. She had been wearing it that last weekend.

Jess had no idea of how quickly her life had changed. And yet here she was, spitting out cynical remarks based on old childhood hurts! It wasn't fair!

"I think you are despicable!" she snapped at Jess' back as the doctor busied herself at the table, tidying up her medical equipment. She had thought she had been Warrior's friend as a youth. She had taken her as a lover. It wasn't her fault how the other students treated her. Nor was she the spoilt, rich child out for adventures that Jess had implied. But if that was the game Jess wanted to play, Mary was just angry enough to be everything Jess expected and then some!

One thing she knew was that she would never tell Jess how her life had changed! Never! She didn't understand completely the strange bond that drew her to this rough cut woman but she did know she could get along just fine without Jess in her life. She felt nothing for Warrior but disgust. The woman was a reverse snob. Clearly, Jess felt all rich people were hollow and self indulgent and poor people were noble and good. What an idiot!

Jess fumbled putting away her ointments. *Damn*, she thought, *this woman is having an awful effect on me.* She had only to look at Mary and she could feel herself pulsating with need. *You have to take a holiday, Visirakis*, she thought in frustration. She knew it was important to keep a wall up between them and so far she thought she had been doing a pretty good job. The air around them crackled with hostility. *Good*, thought Jess, *let her hate me. That's an emotion I've had lots of practice handling with her kind.*

"And don't think a loser like you can order me around! I'll do what I want while I'm stuck here. And believe me, working with you is bottom of the list, Hayseed!" snapped Mary offensively. The second the words were out of her mouth she knew she had gone too far! Jess spun around and in two steps she was over to her cot and had lifted her into a sitting position by her shoulders. Her face was inches from Mary's. Mary could feel Jess' rasping breath hot on her face as glacial-blue eyes bore into her. Then the eyes dropped. The blanket that had been her only cover had slipped, revealing one soft, white breast.

A growl erupted low and deep from Warrior's throat. Mary tried to cover herself up but Jess held her too tightly. "No," she whispered shakily and Jess' eyes came up to meet and challenge hers. Mary licked her lips nervously, feeling her body coursing with excitement and anticipation even as her logical mind bristled with anger and fear. "No," she whispered again, her eyes fixed now on Jess' lips.

Slowly, Jess' mouth lowered to hers. Anger flashed in her eyes and in one quick movement she was pinning Mary's body to the cot with hers as her mouth joined Mary's. A deep throbbing need rose up in her. She struggled against Jess' strength and her own physical excitement, but her struggles just heightened the desire. The pressure of Jess' determined kiss forced her mouth open and Jess' tongue explored her depths.

Against her will she responded, the heat rising in her. All the stress and shock of the crash let go in a primitive need to rejoice in life. Her arms slipped under Jess' shirt and clawed at her back. Jess' lips traced a line down her throat as she moaned softly and then gasped as shudders of delight surged through her system as Jess' tongue played

191

with her hardened nipples. She would have let Jess take her. She could feel that Warrior's need was as great as hers but with a moan Jess pulled away and stood up. Without a word, she was gone.

* * * * *

The small, thin hands fumbled with the wood disc as the seer painted it in pie sections of red and white. It would hang today in the peak of the Hous Tambaran. The red symbolized the sun and the white the moon. The disc represented the passing of time. Twenty years for this cycle and so many more years since the brothers had been parted. The Seer grinned. The followers had decided last night that they must please the gods as instructed. It was easy to pick the sacrifice. Now all that remained was the opportunity. This would be the last cycle! Soon now, the cargo would return to their land and they too would be rich and powerful like the Europeans.

Chapter Four

Jess crawled out of the low doorway of the ceremonial longhouse into the blackness of the predawn day. It was cold and she pulled her jacket around her and zippered it up. At six thousand feet, the air was thin and the nights cold. It was hard to believe that only eight hundred miles away the hot, ionized air of the South Pacific blew gently against the foothills of the jungle. Here in the highlands, a very different world remained isolated and shrouded in the mists of time.

The terrified squeal of a pig and a dull thud that rose above the murmur of local voices brought Jess out of her thoughts. A tingle of excitement ran through her lean, muscular form as she caught the musky smell of fresh blood. With confident strides, she covered the distance that separated her from the orange fires that glowed in the dark distance.

The pig kill was part of the ceremony for the removal of one village guardian spirit in favour of a more powerful one. The village needed to have greater protection from the spirit world for soon they would attempt to capture the Timp. Jess set off just after they started the killing. The squeal of terrified pigs and another thud of the club echoed along the dark path as she drew closer.

Around the fire stood the men of the tribe. Their faces were painted black and some carried Stone Age weapons, including large stone axes, the wood handles tucked through their thick, bark belts. It was still quite dark and all this was seen by Jess by the highlights of the campfires.

A grey, coarse looking pig would be brought and held up by one warrior in the firelight. Another warrior would take a heavy length of wood and club the pig between the eyes. The animal's stocky body would slump in the warrior's arms. Blood ran from its snout as it was lowered to the ground. Quickly, the Shaman would drag the sacrificed pig over so that the blood from its snout dripped into a ceremonial hole. Jess knew that this hole contained the ancestral artifacts or spirit rocks of each clan. They would be brought from the stone houses and placed in the hole so that the pig's blood could flow over them. This sacrificial blood was a tribute to the spirits of the dead males of the tribe.

Jess watched from the edge of the darkness, her face etched in expressionless lines. After a while, her towering figure disappeared into the grey of the early morning mist. In the gathering light, she walked along the red mud trail and stood looking from the ridge across the mist filled valley to the rising grasslands pierced by the limestone peaks. Within her soul she felt the old darkness, the blood lust that dwelled on the edge of lost memories. Moments like this, when the old feelings resurfaced, unnerved her. Who was she? And what was her bond with Mary and the Hosts? Whatever it was, she didn't want to think about it because it seemed to involve waking the demon within her. She sighed and turned back. The villagers expected her to be there to add her white man's powerful magic to help trick and capture the Timp.

By the time all the pigs had been slaughtered, the red of the early morning light was burning through the mist. The dead pigs were now being singed and blackened on the fires to remove their coarse hair. Then they were dragged off and butchered with razor sharp bamboo knives. Carefully, the blood was drained off into bamboo cylinders filled with vegetable greens and the raw sides of meat were laid out on display on banana leaves. The head of the unfortunate animal with its backbone and rib cage, all carefully kept in one piece, was hung up on wood stakes around the ceremonial ground. Each village man took pride in the number of bloody carcasses that he claimed as his own.

Jess walked down the row of grisly remains, fighting back an ugly trace memory of humans spread-eagled on stakes. Her jaw tightened and she moved back to where the shaman, Quen, chanted the magic words to capture the Timp spirit. She stopped, her toes next to a miniature, curved, pit pit grass fence set in the ground a few feet away from where the medicine man worked. This structure was a warning to women to stay back, for they were considered unclean and would spoil the magic.

Quen looked up into challenging blue eyes. He shuddered at their coldness. He grunted and nodded his head and Jess' mouth curved on one side into a cruel smile as she stepped over the barrier into the world of men and magic. She squatted down by the hole and reached in with her long, strong fingers and lifted out the sacred stone artifacts still warm and dripping with the blood sacrifice. These she wrapped carefully in banana leaves and tucked into a waiting net bag called a belem. The shaman ignored her. He wanted to use the power that radiated from this strange white woman but he was not prepared to risk the health of his soul by talking to or acknowledging a woman.

The shaman covered the hole with wood and then buried it with dirt. If all the magic had been done right, then the old Timp was now trapped within the hole. If the signs were right, then in about the month's time a singsing would take place. This was a time of feasting and dancing.

Jess stood, swinging the belem over her shoulder. She turned without a word and walked off, cutting back through the ceremonial grounds. The villagers now moved back in fear, knowing that she carried the power of their ancestral spirits in the bag. Jess noted that the women had now taken the meat and bamboo cylinders of greens and blood and had wrapped them individually in banana leaf bundles. These, Jess knew, would be cooked in underground pits on hot stones. This ceremonial way of cooking was called mumu. Jess turned her back and strode off moodily down the winding, narrow trail that would lead back to her clinic.

* * * * *

Mary had not seen Jess since she had walked out on her the morning before. Mone, although friendly and helpful, was very secretive as to where Jess had gone. Mary had spent the two days learning to hobble along on her painful and crippled foot and familiarizing herself with her temporary base.

The compound consisted of a clearing of grass with bush buildings around the sides. To the north, the land sloped up and was bordered by two rough buildings, one, the hospital ward and surgery and the other, Jess' office and storage for hospital and camp supplies. A path between these two buildings led through the bush to the small runway where Mary's plane had crashed a few days before.

To the west was a lean-to where the local women cooked meals for any sick relative who had to stay at the compound. There was also a roofed patio that was the kitchen and eating area for Jess and Mone. Within was a propane stove and fridge of dubious origins, a few shelves made from planks and log up-rights and six folding garden chairs around two tin card tables. The washing up was done in a tin tub and the hot water had to be heated on a wood cook stove. Fresh water was at least handy, as it bubbled from a spring a hundred feet behind the kitchen. On this side, too, was a building for washing with a tin tub for washing clothes, a bucket used as a sink and a makeshift shower that amounted to a bucket on a hook with a few holes in the bottom. There was also a locked shed used to store their food supplies.

To the east was Jess' sleeping hut and beside it was Mone's hut. Some distance behind these were several outhouses. There was also a long, low building that Mone called a longhouse. It was only about five feet high and ten feet wide and it ran about thirty feet in length. There were a series of low doorways that could only be entered by crawling through on your hands and knees. Inside, the longhouse was divided into sections each with its own stone ringed fire pit. There was no escape for the smoke that quickly filled the longhouse and gradually seeped through the grass roof, making it look from the outside as if it was on fire. Mone explained that the smoke helped keep the roof warm and dry and slowed rot and that there were fewer fleas in a smoke filled hut. The longhouse was used as guest quarters for any relatives who had to stay over while a clan member was being treated in the clinic.

The compound sloped down to the south and should have been bordered by the communications hut. This, however, had been lost when heavy rains had caused the ground to give and slide a hundred yards down the mountainside. The loss of the communications hut was a serious set back to the little clinic but the toppling of a few trees did open the area up so that there was now a spectacular view of the length of the valley below.

Mone explained to Mary that the walls of the huts were made with the thick, round tubes of the pit pit plant that belonged to the grass family. First, a wood frame was put up and then the sections between were filled in with pit pit. These grass walls were held together by weaving long, thin strips of bark through them. The roof was a different type of grass called locally kunie. It was tied in bunches and was overlapped on the roof in a way similar to European thatch. Mary found Jess' hut to be warm at night but rather hot and stuffy during the day.

It was clear to Mary that she could earn her keep by cooking and reorganizing the clinic's supply hut. From what she could see, Mone and Jess lived on such basic stables as pork and beans, canned corned beef, and rice! When questioned, Mone did admit sheepishly that the village women sometimes gave them some of their food.

Jess' small office was neat and well organized. However, the supply room was a jumble of boxes and a mixture of several stockroom systems that had been employed by any number of workers at the clinic.

"What kind of medical problems do you get at the clinic?" Mary had asked Mone, as they shared an afternoon cup of tea under the roofed kitchen while rain poured down on all sides of them.

"Wounds, broken bones, skin diseases," explained Mone. "Any major problem we send on to Mendi by plane. This is a leprosy clinic mainly."

Mary's mug had stopped half way to her mouth and her face registered horrified shock. "I'm staying at a leprosy colony?" she asked incredulously.

Mone laughed, enjoying the shocked look on the small white woman's face. "You no worry," he explained. "A leper does not wear a bell for the rest of life and call out unclean when he enters a room. The fear that Europeans have of the disease is unfounded. Dry leprosy is not contagious at all and wet leprosy only has a very low contagion rate. The disease actually is in the same family of illnesses as arthritis."

"You're sure?" asked Mary with a worried frown.

"Yes, Miss Mary," responded Mone with a twinkle in his eye.

After tea, the rain let up a bit and Mone, looking worried, said that he had things to do. Mary cleaned up the kitchen and promised herself that she would do a decent job of cleaning and organizing when she could stay on her feet longer. She noticed that the few village women who had been huddled under the lean-to had also disappeared.

Taking her cane, she stepped out into the compound and suddenly became aware of how still and quiet everything was. There were usually always a few people around the compound but now there was no one.

Shrugging off her growing uneasiness, she went in search of Mone, who rarely seemed to leave the area. He was not in any of his usual haunts. Mary was becoming increasingly worried. Things just didn't feel right. The only place she hadn't looked was in the ward where she knew at least one patient was confined. Carefully hobbling across the wet compound, she entered the ward. What she saw there made her heart lurch in terror!

Her scream of horror echoed off the rocky walls of the long, narrow valley. It hit Jess as she came up the path like an arrow to her heart. She was running full out before she had even consciously registered that Mary was in trouble.

Jess met a terrified Mary on the path just at the edge of the compound. "Ah," Mary got out of her lips, stiff with shock. Her face was white and she shook violently. Jess wrapped her in her arms and held her close. Her own gut tied in a knot of anger and worry over what might have happened to Mary.

"Shh, easy. Okay, I've got you," murmured Jess, holding the smaller woman and trying to reassure her. Suddenly, Mary pulled away and stumbled back awkwardly.

"Keep away from me, you god-damn bitch!" Mary screamed hysterically, pounding at Jess' chest and face with her shaking fists. "I'm sick of your fucking mind games, you hear! Don't ever touch me again!"

Jess let the blows rain for a minute. She'd had it coming, she figured. Then she stepped closer and grabbed Mary's shoulders firmly, giving her a good shake. "Shut up, damn it! Come on, get a hold of yourself here! What the hell is going on?" she snapped.

Mary took a deep breath and pointed with an unsteady hand towards the hospital. "In there," she choked out between gasps.

Jess looked at the hospital and then down at Mary. "You okay?" she asked gently, stopping her hand before it had touched Mary's cheek. Tears rolled down Mary's white face but she nodded yes.

Jess gave her a hard, long look and then, satisfied that Mary was not physically hurt, she turned and jogged over to the hospital, entering cautiously. She saw that the young man, Kalla, who had been her patient, now lay on a blood soaked cot. A wood stake had been hammered through one ear and out the other. Jess' jaw tightened and her mouth narrowed into an angry line. Moving forward, she looked more closely. There was a crudely cut wound to his side. Jess went over to the supply cabinet and got out a pair of plastic gloves and pulled them on. Walking back over, she examined the areas of trauma. The boy's liver had been removed. Covering the grisly sight with a sheet and tossing the gloves into the trash, she walked purposefully back to where Mary waited at the edge of the compound.

"He's dead, isn't he?" Mary asked in a shaky, weak voice.

"Murdered." Jess frowned, placing her hands on her hips and looking very frustrated and angry. "You see anyone or hear anything?" she asked.

Mary shook her head. "It rained pretty hard. It was even difficult to make out what Mone was saying." Mary suddenly looked horrified. "Jess, Mone is missing! Everyone has gone!"

"Yeah, yeah, I know. The spirits are loose," Jess responded, looking around with a worried frown. There was nothing she could do for the murdered man right now. And the community was in peril as long as the sacrificial artifacts she carried were not returned to their stone houses.

She couldn't leave Mary here with a murderer about and Mary couldn't walk far.

"Look, I've got to see to something. It might not be safe to leave you here so you're going to have to come with me."

"I can't walk far," protested Mary.

"I'm going to carry you piggy-back," stated Jess as her blue eyes scanned the compound.

"Oh no, you're not!" snapped Mary, shaking her head. Her strawberry blond hair whipped around her face like ribbons of gold.

Jess' eyes snapped down and held hers with an icy stare. "You either let me carry you or you stay back here with the corpse and a possible murderer," she growled cruelly.

Mary swallowed in fear and nodded her understanding. Jess removed a net bag from her shoulder and handed it to Mary to carry. Then she turned and bent her knees, allowing the petite woman to wrap her arms around her neck. Jess captured Mary's legs with her elbow joints and headed off across the compound and up the trail that led past the airstrip and on up the mountain.

"Where are we going?" asked Mary, her face buried in Jess' soft, spicy smelling hair.

"To the home of the ghosts," responded Jess and said no more.

Chapter Five

They climbed steadily higher up a narrow, eroded path of red clay. Jess moved at an easy pace, seemingly unaware of the burden she carried on her back. Mary placed the side of her face against the firm shoulder and tried not to move. A feeling deep inside of leaning sleepily on the back of her warrior surfaced. *This is a part of who we were, Jess,* she thought.

Jess curved around a rocky outcropping and lowered Mary onto the ground. They were on a high ridge well above the clinic compound. Above them a near vertical column of limestone rose in a ragged pinnacle, eroded into weird greyish shapes by the afternoon monsoon rains. Then Mary's heart jumped and her eyes widened in shock. Not far above them and some twenty feet farther on, was a dark horizontal crack in the rock that formed a deep natural shelf. Sitting in neat rows on this shelf were hundreds of skulls bleached white and brittle by the sun. Amongst these guardians of the afterworld were stone bowls and club-heads.

Jess slipped the belem off Mary's shoulder and knelt down. Tearing open the leaves, she exposed two round, bloody forms. Mary jumped back with a cry of alarm and almost toppled over, needing to put out a hand to balance herself against the limestone cliff. With trembling hands, she lifted her cane and held it in attack position. It felt strangely familiar and gave her a strong sense of confidence. "Everyone was gone from the compound but you and me. My God! You sacrificed that poor boy and ripped his organs out! What is this place? Some sort of trophy room?" she snapped in anger.

Jess face went from surprise to violent anger in an instant. She shot to her feet and grabbed at the cane. Much to her surprise her hand met thin air and the hard, wood stick cracked down on her forearm painfully. "Shit! What the hell are you doing, Giovani?!" yelled Jess, ducking as the weapon came arching over her head and cracked into the limestone.

Jess saw her opening and grabbed Mary, slamming her up against the rock. Face to face, blue eyes of rage burned into green eyes

201

of terror. "What... the... hell... are... you... doing?" repeated Jess slowly, lifting Mary up by her bunched shirt and pinning her over her head to the rough rock. Mary choked and gasped for breath but said nothing. "Tell me!" roared Jess, slamming the small, limp figure against the rock.

Mary's hand came up to grab at Jess' wrist. The hand felt small and the grasp weak, observed Jess through her blind rage. Mary's hand dropped and she made a gurgling sound. Jess' eyes focused on the small face again. It was turning blue. "Shit!" she exclaimed and let go. Mary drew in an uneven breath as she slipped down the rock wall.

The next thing she was aware of was Jess wiping her face with a damp cloth. "You okay?" the warrior asked nervously. Mary nodded weakly, her eyes weary. "You shouldn't have attacked me. I... I... I kind of lose it when I'm hurt physically. Why do you always think the worst of me?"

Mary swallowed painfully and rubbed her sore throat, "There was a time when I didn't but now I know better, Jess," she observed bitterly, using the rock face to pull herself up onto her feet.

"That's ancient history!" growled Jess, getting up too so that she maintained the height advantage.

Mary looked at the red organs nestled in the banana leaves. "So what is going on here? How are you involved in Kalla's murder?"

"What! What the hell gave you that idea?" exclaimed the doctor, trying hard to keep her anger in check.

"The body parts," grimaced Mary, her eyes going in horror to the two red lumps still sitting on the ripped banana leaves.

Jess snorted in cold disgust. "It's two pieces of a stone age bowl. The people dig them up in their gardens and believe that the spirits leave them there for the village to put offerings in. They're covered in pig's blood. I've got to put them back. Stay here. You're unclean," snarled Jess in explanation and left the exhausted journalist to watch. She picked up the two bloody pieces of stone and edged along the narrow ridge to place the sacred artifacts back in their stone house. Now they would call the ancestral spirits back to rest and the people would be safe once again.

Jess carefully edged back along the ledge, then walked past Mary without a backwards look as she wiped her hands clean with the damp rag and threw it carelessly into the net bag. "Hey! You can't leave me here!" Mary croaked out.

"Watch me," snarled Jess, heading down the path.

Mary felt the anger explode in her gut. She scooped up her cane and sent it flying like a javelin. It embedded in the muddy bank between Jess' legs and tripped her mid stride. With a curse, the tall woman went face first into the red clay. With as much dignity as Mary could muster, she limped over to where Jess lay wiping the clay from her face and said calmly, "I said, you are not leaving me here, Vizirakis. You brought me and you can damn well get me back!"

For a long moment there was a deathly silence. Mary reached out without taking her eyes off Jess and pulled her new weapon out of the soft clay bank. Jess' eyebrow went up and a corner of her mouth turned up. "So daddy's little kitten has claws," she quoted.

"You bet!" responded Mary with a cheerful nastiness.

Jess nodded thoughtfully. Then she bent her head to the side and gave Mary a weary grin. "So if I get up slowly and go and retrieve the belem, are you going to beat me with your little stick?"

"That all depends. Are you giving me a lift home or are we both going to struggle down this mountainside as two cripples?" asked Mary, her hands tightening on the hard wood of the cane.

Jess sighed and got to her feet. As she passed Mary on her way back to pick up the belem, she snatched the cane from the smaller woman's hands. "Don't push your luck," she remarked to the startled journalist and then slammed the stick back at the smaller woman before she went back to get the belem.

Mary watched Jess clean out the leaves and shoulder the net bag. The doctor came back down the path with her eyes locked on Mary's. For a minute, they stood and looked at each other. Then Jess sighed and turned around. "Well, come on, Giovani," she said gruffly, stooping down, "I gotta see to a body." Mary wrapped her arms around Jess' neck and the powerful woman lifted her in place on her back. They headed down the path in a silent, cold truce.

* * * * *

That afternoon, Jess and Mone, who had turned up back at camp as soon as they had returned without the stones, placed the murdered man's corpse in a body bag and carried it on a stretcher back to his village. Mary stood silently as they went by. She didn't know if the villager would want it, but she sent a little prayer to God anyway, asking that his young soul be cared for.

The next day, Mary saw Jess only from a distance. She was impressed by how hard Jess worked at the small medical outpost to help the sick. Gingerly, walking on her damaged foot, Mary explored the small compound further. Each day, shy, laughing women from the nearby villages would take turns bringing food and preparing it for patients. Mone and Jess seemed to eat whenever they felt like it. Mary was told to help herself to anything she wanted.

When she had a free moment from helping Mone around the compound, Mary would stand and look out over the valley below where the Lia River roared through dense jungle. Wild, exotic birds called to each other high up in the trees and sometimes far off the distant drums and rhythmic singing of tribal peoples could be heard. It was very different from the noise of heavy machinery and loud entertainment that had been part of the mining community that Mary had investigated. The near naked villagers, herding their pigs or attending their gardens with Stone Age tools, fascinated Mary.

She had quickly made friends with Mone, whose job seemed to be to make sure that life ran smoothly both at the clinic and on the compound. When Mary offered to prepare the meals for the three of them, he beamed with delight and Mary knew she had made a fast friend. The larder was not overly exciting. Canned corn beef, fish and ham seemed to be the basic protein intake, supported by the vegetables that Mary could barter from the local women. The main food staple was the sweet potato.

Mary was determined that the propane cook stove and limited food choices were not going to prevent her from showing Jess that she was no hothouse flower. For dinner that night, she prepared a sweet potato pie that she felt was quite good. She set the table carefully, picking wild orchids and setting them in an empty peanut butter jar on the table. At six, Mone arrived and eyed the pie suspiciously. He refused to eat until Dr. Jess arrived from doing rounds.

When Jess arrived and saw Mone's suspicious face and Mary's frown, she laughed. "What's so funny?" demanded Mary, her hands on her hips.

"He's afraid you're trying to kill him. You know, witchcraft. He can't tell what's in that thing!" laughed Jess, pointing to Mary's beautiful pie.

"Mone! How could you think such thing?" cried Mary, in shock and distress. Mone said nothing but smiled sheepishly and hung his head.

Jess answered for him. "Because why else would you disguise his food?"

Mary turned to Mone. "Mone, I'm sorry. I didn't mean to upset you. Would it help if Jess and I ate first? I know you don't know me well enough to trust me yet."

"Mone hasn't time to eat. Eat without us and we'll make some sandwiches later. We've got a case of appendicitis that can't wait. Come on, Mone," ordered Jess.

"But Mone told me earlier that you were not going to operate tonight," argued Mary, limping close behind Jess' retreating back. Suddenly, the doctor whirled and Mary, caught unawares, ran right into her. Jess grabbed her by the shoulders and leaned her face close. Mary could taste Jess' breath and see the soft texture of her skin tight over iron muscles. Jess' hands dug into her shoulders painfully and she gave a gasp of surprise.

"Understand this, Ice Queen, my job comes first and I make the final decisions here. The highlands of P.N.G. are no place for a damn tea party," and with that she whirled around and was gone. Released from Jess' grip, Mary felt like her knees would buckle from the emotional stress. She was shaken by the power that had radiated from the tall doctor.

Banging pans about, Mary cleaned up and put the sweet potato pie untouched into the propane fridge. Her foot had swollen and she was tired and near tears. The days were warm in the highlands but at night it went quite chilly. Mary shivered and headed for her hut. Yellow light streamed from the surgery building. She hoped that the little girl would be all right and that Jess' sudden change in plans had not been the result of some complication. Quickly, she changed into her sleepwear and got under the covers.

Much later, she woke to the sound of Mone and Jess' voices, then silence. Now unable to sleep, she pulled a sweater on and headed over to the ward to see if the child was all right. There in a chair, beside the bed of the peacefully sleeping child, was a very tired looking Jess.

"What are you doing here?" she asked in a startled whisper.

"I work here," Jess responded sarcastically, raising an eyebrow. "What are you doing here?"

"I came to see if she was all right," responded Mary defensively.

"Do you think there is such a great danger in having me as a doctor?" Jess asked, stretching out her long legs and folding her arms smugly.

Mary felt her temper rising. It was clear that Jess intended to make her life as difficult as possible. "Well, the pilot's dead isn't he?" she snapped.

Jess was on her feet in a split second and towering over Mary. "Look, the pilot... he look..." stumbled Jess in rage. She reached out and grabbed Mary's arm, dragged her painfully into the next room and lifted her up onto the gurney.

"Don't! Don't!" cried Mary, struggling free, fearing that Jess was going to try to make love to her again.

But Jess had already backed off. "Don't flatter yourself, Ice Queen! What happened before in your hut was just a reaction to isolation. Any naked woman with her hands up my shirt could have gotten the same reaction from me.

Mary blushed red at Jess' cruel words but fought back with equal nastiness. "I'm sure you've never been fussy. You're an alley cat, love them and leave them."

"For Christ's sake! Get over it, Giovani! We were kids!" growled Jess in frustration throwing her arms up in the air and turning away.

"Where did you go?" asked Mary quietly.

"Military. I stuck it all through cadets because I knew that the only way I was going to get an education was to have the army pay. I finished my service a few years ago," revealed Jess awkwardly. She squatted down and rummaged through a box. Pulling out a piece of metal, she turned and walked back over to where Mary sat.

"You see this?" Jess said, holding up the fragment. "I kept it for evidence. I pulled it out of the pilot's chest."

The blood drained from Mary's face and the room blurred. Mary heard Jess curse from far away. Then strong arms grabbed her. Mary clung to Jess sobbing sadly. Jess whispered soothing words into her ear until she calmed. They stayed that way for some time, Mary's head against Jess' shoulder and Jess' chin resting in Mary's soft, fragrant hair. Then Jess pulled back with a start. "Listen, Giovani, I don't want any complications. Okay, so we have a childhood history and maybe there is still some need there. But I'm not interested. I know your kind, Giovani and I've fought too long and too hard to let you mess up my life now!"

Mary slipped off the gurney and stood tall, her body quivering with rage. "My kind? My kind? Just what is my kind, Jess? Rich, Italian, immigrant, Catholic, gay, female, journalist? Just what is it about me that offends you? Maybe it's just that you know you couldn't live up to the Hosts and their love. I remember, Jess. It was hot, real hot," tormented Mary spitefully.

The metal went slamming against the wall and clattered to the floor. "Don't you fuck with my mind, you damn bitch!" she roared.

Mary gave Jess the finger and limped to the door. "I hate you!" she yelled as she slammed out into the night.

Back in her hut, she was able to see that she had antagonized Jess, but she was still shaken by the violence of the woman's response. She was going to have to be careful. She washed her hands and face and changed her crumpled clothes.

Peeking out across the compound, she could see Jess' silhouette pacing back and forth in the hospital ward. She could hear her mother's voice from the past in her mind. 'My dear, what do you expect? The poor girl grew up in our barn!' and her father's practical response, 'so do all thoroughbreds!' Was Jess a thoroughbred, or was she just plain rude and violent? Mary found her emotions to be a swirling mass of contradictions.

Mary crawled into bed and was soon asleep from exhaustion. She was unaware of the strong, gentle hands that put an extra blanket on her that night and softly kissed her tear-stained cheek.

Chapter Six

Three days after the murder at the compound, Mary found Jess still over her coffee in the kitchen.

"Morning," Mary said stiffly and went about preparing her breakfast.

"Morning started three hours ago," responded Jess dryly.

"Get fucked, Vizirakis," replied Mary cheerfully as she spread peanut butter on wheat crackers and then peeled a banana.

Jess shrugged. "I got to go to the boy's funeral today. It is in the village just over the next ridge."

Mary looked up. "I want to go too."

"I'm not carrying you," stated Jess, tossing the last of her morning coffee break out onto the grass.

"I can walk that distance, if I go slowly. You just tell me the way," Mary said between mouthfuls of her breakfast. She sat at one of the small tables her back deliberately to Jess.

"You are not to walk around the highlands by yourself," ordered Jess. "If it is so important to you, I'll walk slow."

Mary kept her back to Jess although a smile did sparkle in her eye. It was an apology! A strange one perhaps, but Jess in her own way was trying to make up for their fight. She could meet her half way. "Thank you, that would be fine. When do you wish to leave?" she responded formally, still not turning around.

Jess walked over to the basin on the cook stove and dropped her mug in the hot water. Now Mary had to look at her back! "One hour," said Jess, turning to look at Mary. This was the first time they had been in the same room together since their fight at the hospital.

"Okay," responded Mary, meeting Jess' blue eyes with unflinching greens. "I have a question about my foot, doctor," Mary continued.

"Yes?" Jess' language changed unconsciously from stiff formality to concerned, intense professionalism.

"I want to know what exercises I could do to strengthen the foot so I can stop limping," stated Mary, starting to clean up her breakfast dishes and moving deliberately over to where Jess stood by the stove. She dropped her dishes in the pan and then realized that Jess had not answered her. She looked sideways and made contact with a pair of worried blue eyes. "Okay," she said calmly, even though she could feel her guts twisting into a knot, "what haven't you told me?" She turned and faced Jess and waited.

The muscles in Jess' throat moved as she swallowed. "You use your toes to propel yourself forward. Without toes you can't do this. That means having to switch the weight to your other leg and swing the damaged leg forward. You will always walk with a heavy limp," explained Jess honestly. For a moment, the two women looked at each other. Mary was trying to come to terms with the news without showing Jess any emotion and Jess was waiting for the explosion.

"I see," stated Mary quietly. "I'll meet you here in one hour then, doctor," replied Mary at last. She brushed by Jess and limped back to her hut. Once inside she hurled her cane against the wall, her jaw white with rage. That Goddamn bitch from hell was always hurting her!

They headed out an hour later at a snail's pace, following the ridge of the mountain to the east. Mary's face was unusually controlled and expressionless as she walked along with her uneven gait. Usually talkative and curious, today she was silent.

Jess cleared her throat and made an effort. "There is a lot going on in this area at the moment. It is a very unstable and dangerous time because the people are in the process of capturing the Timp. Timp is the spirit world, the united force of all the ghosts of the dead. The villagers are terrified of them. The Timp cults go in about twenty year cycles and we are coming to the end of one now. There is also a serious land dispute going on at Mendara. The villagers are trying to end it by having a Cassowary Race."

"They race Cassowary? You mean those big birds that look like an ostrich?!" interrupted Mary, getting caught up in what Jess was telling her and forgetting the awkwardness of her gait that she was going to have to deal with for the rest of her life.

"Yeah, those birds but it's not a race of the birds. It's a race to see which side can gather the most cargo before the day they will show their cassowarys, pigs and other wealth off and butcher them. It's a type of potlatch. The side that gains the most power by the killings and exchange wins the argument," clarified Jess.

Mary's brow wrinkled in thought. "This Race should end the dispute then?"

For a minute Jess was quiet. "Maybe, but there is going to be payback now because of the murder at the compound. That could lead to a tribal war."

"Payback, I've heard of that. It's revenge killing isn't it?" prompted Mary.

Jess turned and offered Mary her hand to help her down a steep and eroded embankment of slippery, red clay. Mary moved cautiously, side stepping like a crab. The pressure hurt her foot but she gritted her teeth and said nothing. Once at the bottom, Jess let go of Mary's hand as soon as she was balanced. "Yeah, it is revenge killing," Jess continued their interrupted conversation as she walked on slowly. "It is necessary to save face. If Kalla is not revenged then his relatives will seem to be weak. Weakness is a sign of a 'rubbish man', a useless individual. There is no worse label," Jess explained with feeling. "Also, Kalla's Timp will not be at rest until he is buried properly and his murder is revenged. All ghosts are dangerous. They can bring sickness to a village or drought to the area. Kalla's angry Timp could make them lose the Cassowary Race or release all the Timp that the villagers have been carefully imprisoning for the last twenty years. Then there would be chaos."

They walked on after that in silence, Mary having to concentrate on the uneven ground so that she would not lose her balance and Jess in moody thought. Now they could hear the mourning wail of the women. It was a ghostly sound that seemed to haunt the grassy hills they walked across. As they got closer still, they could hear angry male voices above the wail.

They came on the village quickly as they rounded a spur in the hillside and entered a wooded area of tall evergreens called Yar. The village was typical of the highlands. There was a large, open, rectangular field that was the village singsing ground. This was where all their major social and political gatherings would take place. Around the edge there were a few grass huts and a man's house. Jess explained that traditionally the men did not live with their women. Women were seen as unclean because of their menstrual cycle. If a man spent too much time with women, he became weak and his skin dried out. His knees became wobbly and he could no longer shoot his arrows straight. The two women exchanged a knowing look and broke out laughing. Some of the undercurrents of hostility that had made their conversation so stiff dissolved.

"Where do the women live?" asked Mary, realizing that she had learned more in the past hour about the traditional ways of the people than she had in all the time she had been at the mining camp.

Jess changed direction and led Mary to the side of the village. She pointed down a slope to where a field was arranged in neat mounds. In the center of the field, stood a grass hut surrounded by banana trees. "Each man has his own house in his fields. His wife, children and pigs all live together. When a boy has gone through his initiation rites at around twelve, he will move to the man's house," explained Jess.

"What do they grow in the mounds?" asked Mary, pointing to the fields.

"Sweet potato, it is the main food staple in the highlands," the taller woman answered, looking out over the fields. "Mounding stops root rot from setting in, and the water from the afternoon monsoon rains run off."

"If the women, children and pigs all share the same space and the men all share one house, ah, I mean where do they... you know?" asked Mary as red crept up her neck.

Jess turned and looked down at Mary, a ghost of a grin on her face. "Usually out in the tall grass somewhere. But they do have a custom that is kind of cute. When a man is courting a girl, he goes to visit her and they 'turn-em-head,'" explained Jess.

"What!" asked Mary laughing and turning to look up at Jess.

"Turn-em-head. They rub their heads, necks and faces together slowly. Kissing is not part of their traditional culture. Turn-em-head can be very intimate on a psychological level. You are very aware of the other person, you talk, you try to express your love, you don't get caught up in your own physical pleasure like we do when we neck. Turn-em-head is a giving experience, not a taking," Jess explained, looking softly into Mary's deep green eyes.

Mary licked her lips and looked away to lessen the tension. "It sounds like you've had lots of experience at love making," laughed Mary lightly, although she was aware of an unreasonable jealousy deep inside.

"We'd better go to the funeral," replied Jess abruptly and headed off at a quick pace towards the far end of the village where the plaintive sound of wailing could be heard rising and falling behind the yells of angry male voices.

Mary followed Jess' retreating figure. The air now had an unpleasant stench of rot. At the end of the singsing ground the land once again sloped down. From the top, Mary could see the funeral proceedings.

At one end of a small clearing, the women stood around two posts between which the decaying body of the murdered young man hung from a horizontal pole. The body was wrapped in dried fronds and only the feet and the top of the head could be seen. Body fluids dripped out and the women would move forward and capture the liquid in their hands and rub their hands together as they wailed in anguish. Some raised their arms above their head as they moaned. The women were covered in grey clay and around each of their necks was a thick and heavy layer of grey bead necklaces. Some of the women had hundreds of them on while others had fewer.

At the other end of the clearing, the men sat on the ground listening to one man as he stood and talked. In a row on the ground lay the half-moon shells called 'kina' that formed part of the traditional money system of the highland people, along with pigs.

Jess loped back up the path to Mary. To Mary's surprise, Jess now wore several grey necklaces and had grey clay smeared on her cheeks. "Women show mourning by wearing these necklaces made from the seeds of the Job's Tears plant. They also wear the grey clay just as we would wear black. Normally, I wouldn't wear this stuff, but Kalla died at our compound, so it is politically wise that we indicate that we are upset by that." She stepped closer as she explained and spread mud on Mary's cheeks and then dropped a few necklaces around her neck.

"When in Rome..." Mary shrugged and Jess smiled her thanks.

She offered Mary a hand and helped her down the slope as she explained, "Only men are mourned and only by the women. If the woman was close to the man, she will stay in mourning dress for sometimes over a year." Jess carefully led Mary to stand upwind of the corpse as they watched the women wail.

After a few minutes, the older woman touched Mary's arm and they moved off to where the men sat arguing. "It is important that Kalla's debts be paid off, otherwise his Timp will play evil tricks on the village. The men are arguing about who owes what," explained Jess.

"These are kina shells aren't they?" asked Mary, pointing to the long row of half-moon shells that sat on leaves on the ground.

Jess nodded. "They used to be traded up from the coast and by the time they got here, they were only little pieces. The men would make wood shells and place the precious bits in the centre. Those antique kina are called 'chop'. Now the kina is easier to get. These are not good ones. They don't have much "light". That's the pearl colours. Each of these shells is worth about twenty Australian dollars, so Kalla's worth is about four hundred dollars to these people. You never look at the backside of the shell because the people believe that will draw the colour away from the surface. The woven straps are so they can be worn on special occasions."

Mary nodded her understanding, appreciating Jess' knowledge and respect for the traditional ways of the tribe. As they stood there, a villager got up and came over to Jess, shaking her hand solemnly. Like all the others, the man wore only the bark belt and basic coverings. He did however wear a necklace that was a string from which hung small, wood tubes in a vertical row down his chest. On his arms above the elbow he wore woven armbands. He talked to Jess in Pidgin while Jess listened in respectful silence. In the end, she nodded and they shook hands again.

"Time to go," she said to Mary, taking her arm and leading her off.

"What did that man want?" asked Mary, looking over her shoulder. The men were back arguing again, ignoring their retreating forms.

"He is the headman of this village. You could tell that by his chest plate and armbands. He told me that the village wants payback and that I'm to do it," explained Jess as she stooped and lifted the stunned Mary into her arms and carried her up the steep embankment, placing her back down at the edge of the singsing ground.

"Thanks, Jess," mumbled Mary quietly. "What does that entail, getting payback?" she asked in a worried tone.

Jess shrugged and headed off with Mary close behind her. "It means I've got to kill the murderer," she revealed casually as she walked.

A second later, she was brought to a halt by a firm grip around her elbow. "You are not going to kill anyone!" Mary told her, looking up into Jess' startled eyes with determination.

"Yes, I am as a matter of fact. I need to be able to trust you with this," stated Jess, sending Mary a challenging look.

Mary scowled and pulled her hand away. "Jess, you can't do this!" she pleaded.

Jess placed a strong hand on Mary's shoulder and looked at her with searching eyes. "It's a matter of face, Mary. It happened in our compound. If I don't do this we'll be rubbish to the people and that means no end of trouble for us. I have to send a message that I am a warrior not to be messed with. Do you understand that?" she asked gently.

Mary nodded miserably, "Yes, but murder, Jess! Isn't there another way?"

"I need you to trust me on this one, okay, Mary. I can handle this," said the older woman, rubbing Mary's shoulder unconsciously.

Mary looked into those incredible blue eyes. "Okay," she agreed reluctantly. Jess smiled and they walked slowly back to the compound together. Along the way Jess explained that once Kalla's debts were paid today, his body would be taken to the cliffs and buried under bamboo stalks on a limestone ledge.

Mary was happy knowing the young man was finally going to rest in peace, but then Jess went on to explain that after the flesh had decomposed, the skull would be removed and placed in a little roofed stand in the family garden. That way his spirit would chase away anyone who tried to steal from their garden. Jess pointed out one of the small skull houses as they passed a village garden. She seemed to feel that this was a very practical use for the dead, but Mary was saddened to think that this was going to be Kalla's fate.

Chapter Seven

For the next few days, Mary worked around the compound. Her relationship with Jess, although not friendly, was at least not as antagonistic as it had been. The afternoon after they had returned from the funeral, Mary had made tea for Mone and they had sat and talked at the table as the rain beat down. Mone seemed to enjoy his afternoon tea break with Mary. It had quickly become a routine, though one that Jess had not shared in. Mone delivered her tea to her office where she worked on her reports. It was from Mone that Mary learned the next day that Jess had been sleeping in a chair in the hospital ward or on the operating table since Mary had arrived!

After the afternoon rains, Mary sloshed over to Jess' office and knocked on the doorframe. Jess was bent over a report. When she looked up, her eyes looked tired and sore. "We need to talk," Mary said gently. "Can I come in?"

Jess stood up and nodded, pulling over a chair for Mary to sit in. Mary sat and then a nervous looking doctor sat down too. "Are we talking as patient and doctor here?" Jess asked.

"No. We're talking... as friends. You can't sleep in a chair for eight weeks, Jess," Mary said and Jess rolled her eyes, looking annoyed.

"I've got a camp cot I sometimes set up," argued Jess in embarrassment, intently watching her own finger drawing patterns on the desktop.

"Yes, I know," stated Mary, "and I've asked Mone to put it in your hut." Mary met the blue eyes that flashed up with a strong, even stare. "There is no reason why we can't share the accommodations. I think we have come to a good understanding about what the limits are in our... friendship," continued Mary in a businesslike manner.

For a few minutes, blue met green in an internal struggle. Then Jess nodded. "Okay. Do you still snore?" she asked, tilting her head to one side as she looked at Mary.

"I do not snore!" denied Mary hotly. Jess raised an eyebrow but said nothing.

Mary did not see Jess again, except at a distance, until after she had retired to her hut. There was Jess' bed, only a foot away from hers in the small hut. She could hear Jess saying good night to Mone and she quickly kicked off her shoes and jumped into the bed, turning her back to the room.

She heard Jess come in and move about the room. Then the candle that was her only source of light was blown out.

"Do you usually sleep with your clothes on," asked Jess lazily as she stripped down in the dark and got into her cot next to Mary's. Every fiber of Mary's being was acutely aware of Jess beside her. She didn't dare answer her and kept her face firmly facing the pit pit grass wall. This was going to be much harder than she had realized. She could smell the spicy scent that was uniquely Jess and hear the rustle of the sheets against Jess' naked body. Sleep came very late for Mary and her sleep was filled with strange dreams of the two ancient lovers.

When she woke the next morning, Jess had already left for her morning rounds. Mary got up with effort and groggily went about her morning rituals. Then she headed over to the kitchen to have the coffee that was the final part of the process of her waking and facing a new day. Jess was there waiting.

"Good morning, what do you need to see me about?" asked Mary, sleepily heading for the metal coffee pot that was a permanent fixture on top of the cook stove.

Jess looked surprised. "What made you think I need to talk to you?" she asked, turning and leaning against one of the log supports that held up the thatched room.

Mary smiled, poured herself a cup of coffee and came over and sat at the table. "You never have your morning coffee in here unless you are waiting for me. What's up?"

Jess frowned and turned to look out over the compound. "I've arranged things. The killing's going to be today," she said quietly.

Mary put down her mug and got up and came over to Jess, placing her hand on the taller woman's arm. "Jess, I don't want you to kill anyone," she pleaded.

She smiled sadly down at her. "Mary, I was in the army for a dozen years. I was with special services. If you are trying to save my soul, it's too late," she sighed.

Mary moved closer and before either of them knew it, her head was tucked under Jess' chin and they had their arms around each other.

"You've got to trust me, Mary. Please." Mary nodded her head, but she knew in her heart that she couldn't let Jess attack and kill anyone.

They left sometime later, moving along ridges that led them farther into the isolated district. At last, they came to a narrow trail that led them through high pit pit grass that towered over their heads. In a few places, Jess widened the path using her machete. Mary struggled along, finding it hard not to entangle her lame foot in the roots and bent stalks. At last, they came out into a low meadow. There they found a man standing by a tall Yar tree.

"Apinun," Jess greeted the ferret-faced man. The eyes of the man slipped over to Mary. The look was cold and filled with hate. "Dispela misses, wontok bilong mi," Jess explained.

Mary understood enough Pidgin to know that Jess had said 'afternoon' and had explained that Mary was a wontok or tribal relative of hers. The man nodded.

Jess turned to Mary. "This is Touy. He comes to the clinic for treatment. He is not too happy about that. Touy is a very powerful medicine man. He will help us identify the killer and then murder him with witchcraft."

Mary's eyes widened in surprise but she managed with a great deal of effort not to say anything. Jess noted her struggle and smiled knowingly. After much loud bartering, a price was reached to both Jess' and Touy's satisfaction. Jess reached into her pocket and pulled out some dirty looking bills. The government issued paper money in Papua New Guinea was also called Kina, Mary knew.

Touy pulled the stone axe from his belt and handed it to Jess. Jess took it and commented politely on its quality. Then she walked over and used it to deeply notch the Yar tree. Mary was surprised at how well the primitive stone axe sent the chips of wood flying. Of course, it was Jess on the end of it. Mary could see her muscles rippling under her cotton shirt. Jess walked around to the other side, checked that everybody was clear and then with a series of powerful strokes she felled the tree.

Turning, she walked back to where Touy and Mary stood and handed him back his axe. She wasn't even breathing hard! Touy grunted and moved over to the trunk. Carefully, he slit the bark and pulled off a section a foot wide and about twenty feet long. This freshly cut bark he laid out on the ground with the inner surface up. It was wet and slippery with tree sap.

Touy came back over to where the two women stood. From a leather bag around his neck, he tipped out a dozen shiny, black stones. Jess nodded and Touy closed his hand and walked back to where the bark lay on the ground. "They are 'hotam'. Only certain men have the power to hold such magical stones. The people believe they have great power," Jess explained in a whisper.

The two women watched as Touy placed the killing stones at one end of the bark. He walked to the other end and then very carefully walked along the slippery bark and picked up a stone. Then he turned and carefully walked back again. He repeated this process until all the stones were collected. Touy's voice rose and fell in a primitive chant as he worked. "When he doesn't slip on the bark, that stone will be very powerful, Mary. It could kill maybe four or five people. The ones he picks up when he slips are less powerful. He is being very careful. This batch of stones will contain a very deadly magic," Jess explained.

When Touy once again had all the small stones in his hand, he moved over to where the tree lay on the ground. He sat on the ground some distance away and closed his eyes. Then he threw a stone towards the scar that ran the length of the trunk. As he did so, he called out a name. The stone missed. "What is he doing?" asked Mary, fascinated by this performance.

"He's trying to establish the murderer. He is calling out names and when the stone hits the tree that will be the guilty person," muttered Jess.

Mary looked up in shock. "Jess! You can't find someone guilty of such a serious crime like this!"

"Shh!" warned Jess, giving Mary a dark look.

Mary fell silent but she was not the least bit happy about the situation.

The fifth stone hit. The name was Rimrapasi. Touy turned and looked at Jess, a grin on his face. Jess nodded back and Touy collected the stones and disappeared down a trail. He came back a few minutes later leading a pig on a rope. "You might not want to look," Jess cautioned, just before Touy pulled out a bamboo knife as sharp as a razor blade and slit the throat of the pig.

"Oh God," whispered Mary, swallowing in revulsion, but she held her ground. Touy had turned the heavy carcass onto its back and was cutting the chest open. He reached into the warm guts and pulled out the liver. He took the bloody organ over to the far side of the clearing. Jess took Mary by the arm and led her over to where Touy now stood chanting the magical words. As he did, he rubbed the killing stones over the sacrificial flesh. On the ground in front of Touy was a small model of a man's house. A pole was stuck into the ground beside this model, looking like a huge flagpole.

Touy stepped forward and stuck the liver on the pole. Then he placed the bloodied killing stones inside the small house. The medicine man reached back into the house and pulled out a bow and arrow and held them out to Jess. Jess shook her head. Touy smiled cruelly and shrugged. He stepped back and placed the arrow against the bowstring, raising the bow and taking aim at the dripping liver. Mary noted that Jess stepped in front of her, instinctively protecting her if the arrow should go astray.

The arrow, however, found its mark, piercing the liver and disappearing into the bush. Touy turned and looked at Jess. She nodded. "Tenkyu," she said and took Mary's arm and led her off.

"Okay, what happened?" asked Mary, once they were far enough away not to be heard as they pushed their way back through the tall grass.

"The arrow released the blood of the sacrifice to the spirit world. In thanks, they placed the power of the killing stones on the arrow and made it disappear. The arrow will now fly to the coastal house of the murderer, Rimrapasi. It will hover unseen outside until she falls asleep. Then it will fly down her mouth and the killing stones will spread their poison," explained Jess.

"You don't believe that, do you?" she asked, turning to face Jess.

Jess looked down at her with serious, sad eyes. "I believe that if Rimrapasi is the murderer, she will die of witchcraft," she stated, "But that is not why we did it," she added, heading off again.

"Well, why did we?" asked Mary in frustration, limping along behind.

"Because we wanted a list of names of suspects and now we've got it," explained Jess.

Mary stopped in surprise and Jess turned to see what the problem was. "Warrior, you are one smart lady," Mary stated with a happy smile, hobbling to catch up to Jess.

"I always liked it when you called me that," commented the older woman, walking off again at a slow, easy pace.

When they got back to the compound they found a harassed looking Mone trying to keep an older woman from beating one of their leprosy patients, who had come to the clinic to pick up his meds. The scene was comical to say the least and Jess and Mary stood at the edge of the compound and laughed.

There was Mone is his habitual white shorts and T-shirt trying to herd a tiny woman half his size away from their angry patient. The patient was yelling insults at the woman over Mone's shoulder. The little village woman was old but feisty. Her brown breasts hung down almost to her waist and they swung as she used her fighting stick to try and poke at the Eravey that stood behind Mone. Her hair was grey, tight curls and her body sagged with age but she was still putting up a hell of a fight. She would swing with her paddle shaped fighting stick every chance she got and was yelling insults back at the man in a continuous barrage!

"Doctor Jess!" yelled Mone in frustration and Jess sauntered forward to finally come to Mone's aid. At the sight of Jess, the argument stopped. A silence fell over the compound as Jess, radiating authority, stood looking at the troublemakers. With a few sharp words, she dismissed the old woman, who walked off glaring occasionally over her shoulder. Then she instructed Mone to take their outpatient to the clinic and keep him there until the old woman was well on her way back to her village.

"What was that about?" questioned Mary, hobbling forward to stand at Jess' side.

"You just met one of the suspects. The old woman was Heorn. The man is an Eravey and uncle to the boy who was murdered. She doesn't seem to like him," explained Jess, with a white flash of a smile.

Mary snorted. "Well, she's number one on my list! Talk about your small stick of dynamite!" *Jess has a beautiful smile*, Mary thought, smiling back. She wished she would smile more often.

"Perhaps, but she couldn't have murdered Kalla without help," observed Jess with a frown. "Well, I'd better get to the clinic. I'll see you later," she continued, giving Mary's shoulder a brief squeeze and walking off. Mary stood and watched Jess go, appreciating the long legs and tight, round bottom. Then she sighed and turned to her own growing responsibilities around the compound.

* * * * *

Late that night, Jess woke to the tossing and mumbles of Mary as she experienced some terrible nightmare. Jess slipped out of bed and stroked Mary's hair, whispering to her softly until she settled again. Then she crawled gratefully back into her cot. The night air was cold and damp. A few minutes later, Mary was again moaning in her sleep. Jess sighed and got up, slipping a T-shirt over her long, lean form. She slipped in beside Mary and took her in her arms. Immediately, the nightmare subsided and Mary wrapped herself contentedly around Warrior's body and slept.

Jess nestled her head into Mary's hair and let the sensation of Mary's warmth seep into her being. By the Gods, she loved this little woman so much! But she knew it couldn't be. Their love was doomed by a pattern set thousands of years ago. She didn't understand why or how, but it had something to do with that tomb. It was actively calling the 'Others'. It called Jess all the time. But Jess had already lived up to the prophecy; she had removed the one she loved from her life, before the smaller woman betrayed her. Tonight, however, for just a brief time, she could allow herself a moment of loving, of being whole again.

The next day Mary busied herself in establishing a new coding system for the stock room, removing all the old identification labels and carefully gluing on new ones. Then she went over and made lunch for the three of them. Now that Mary had established herself at the compound, Jess and Mone had taken to showing up like vultures around meal times instead of eating just when they felt like it. Meals had become a companionable time. Mary was careful, after the sweet potato pie incident, to keep the food plain and recognizable. She soon discovered that Jess had very conservative tastes in food too. She was your basic meat and potatoes sort of girl.

Mone had even taken to showing up at the kitchen for brunch when he saw Mary arrive in the kitchen in the mornings. By then, although it was still early, Jess and Mone had been up for hours. It was Jess' way to get up well before dawn and run. Then she and Mone would start rounds in the dawn light. At eight, Mone would come over to the kitchen area and make coffee, taking a cup to Jess while she worked in the lab. Then he would come back and enjoy a late breakfast with Mary. He seemed to delight in stories about Jess' childhood and Mary did her best to recall any incident that highlighted the doctor's many talents while growing up.

One day, as the three of them ate lunch, a village man showed up and stood outside the kitchen waiting. "That's Samalli," Jess explained, getting up and going to greet the villager. They shook hands formally and Jess stood, legs apart, arms folded across her chest, listening seriously to Samalli's talk. She nodded when he was finished and responded in Pidgin, talking quickly and with confidence. The worried man seemed to relax a bit. He smiled and nodded and then walked off. Jess turned and came back to join the others.

"What you going to do, Doctor Jess?" asked Mone, who had been able to understand the rapid exchange of Pidgin where Mary hadn't.

"I'll go over there and sort them out after lunch," observed Jess. "They don't really want to fight or they would have started already.

They're probably afraid to get into a battle before the Timp is caught. It is too risky a time."

"Would someone tell me what is going on!" exclaimed Mary in frustration.

Mone and Jess looked at Mary in surprise. "Oh, sorry, Mary. We forgot that your Pidgin is still basic," apologized Jess. "That was Samalli. The Eravey have put up a fence around the land they are claiming from him. He told them to take it down and they refused. Samalli is a Mendari so they are backing him. Now the Mendari and Eravey are eyeing each other from opposite ends of the singsing ground and getting ready for war."

"Oh no, Jess! What are you going to do?" asked an alarmed Mary, reaching over and placing her hand over Jess'. Jess looked down at the small, white fingers resting on her large, tanned hand. Mary's touch sent shivers down her back and for a second she forgot her train of thought.

"Jess?" questioned Mary, patting the hand and then pulling her own back.

"What? Oh! I'll go over there and knock the fence down. Then neither side will have lost face," explained Jess, getting up.

"You be careful!" ordered Mary and was pleased to see Jess smile.

"It's okay. They are looking for a way out of this without losing face or they wouldn't have sent for me. There won't be any tribal wars until after the Timp ceremony," explained Jess. "I'll see you two later," she finished, heading off at an easy stride.

"Does she often solve the village problems?" asked Mary, watching the retreating figure of the doctor.

"Doctor Jess, big warrior. Plenty big magic too! Doctor Jess will solve the problem. The people listen to her. You see," explained Mone, getting up and helping to clear the dishes before he went back to the clinic. "When first she came here, some warriors tried to raid the compound. This had happened many times before. But Doctor Jess say no. When they attacked, she grab an axe and beat them all! One woman against many warriors! Em i-no save pret!"

"Huh?"

"She is brave," Mone translated.

Mary smiled. "Yes, she is," she agreed.

So that was Samalli, thought Mary after Mone left. He looked really upset and frustrated with the Eravey. Kalla had been an Eravey, Mone had said. Could Samalli have killed Kalla to get revenge for the Eravey stealing his land? Mary wondered about this as she added detergent to the basin of hot water on the cook stove. He seemed angry enough.

Jess returned about an hour later and reported the fence was down and that the two warring fractions had calmed down without any fighting taking place. Then she headed off to work in her office again.

While Mary was writing in her journal in the kitchen that afternoon, she was distracted by a flash of brilliant blue and orange as a bird swooped passed. *A Bird of Paradise*, Mary realized, and putting down her pen she limped outside to see if she could spot the elusive bird. There it was! It had flown to the far end of the compound and was sitting high in the branches of a tree near the landslide area. Carefully, Mary moved forward. She was pretty close when the crow sized, orange bird with the long, graceful blue tail flew in a low arc from the tree down to the bushes on the other side of the slide.

I bet it has a nest over there, reasoned Mary, and very cautiously she started to pick her way across the open scar of the slide. She moved slowly, being careful not to fall as she traversed the steep, loose soil. Half way across, the trickle of loose dirt that had rolled and bounced down the hillside with each step increased into a stream. The ground under Mary's feet moved down hill, taking her with it. She fell to her side and tobogganed forward on a river of red dirt. Pain shot up her leg and she gasped as she suddenly found herself rolling head over heels in an avalanche of red death.

Mary fought to keep her head clear of the mud but each time she forced her way clear, she would be hit by another wave of debris and buried. Finally, her forward movement stopped and she found herself buried beneath the earth. Her world was dark and damp, her arms pinned by the weight of the mud. Miraculously, her shoulders and head had wedged in a small hollow formed by tree roots and she had, for the time being, some sour, musty air to breath. Water dripped through the layers of mud and ran down her face and into the pocket of air below her. If help didn't come soon, she was going to either suffocate or drown.

Chapter Eight

Jess looked at the chemical breakdown of the drug again and sighed. She was missing something, she knew, but couldn't figure out what it could be. Not long after Jess had arrived in the highlands, a drought had ended with a few weeks of heavy rain. Papua New Guinea sat in the path of two monsoon belts and it rained everyday for a few hours, except for about a two-week span when the monsoon winds changed directions. But once every ten years or so the winds shifted farther south and there was a drought. Jess had hiked high into the hills and had camped in the protection of a small copse.

During the night, she had awoken to an amazing fairyland. Huge toadstools had sprouted up in the moist, forest decay and they glowed in the dark in pastel shades of pink, green and blue. Jess sat in wonder and stared at the remarkable beauty around her. She had seen fluorescent seaweed dredged up from the depths of the sea by a storm and she had witnessed the phenomenon in lichen deep in caves but this, under the rising moonlight, was just breathtaking!

The next day, she had gathered some samples and taken them back to camp. From the local people, she learned that the toadstools only appeared after a drought and that dried and ground, they put people in a painless, half awake state that the shaman used to contact the spirit world. When Jess had run out of painkillers, Mone had told her to try the mushrooms. They had worked very well. But she was having trouble isolating the chemical structure of the compounds. Part of the problem was that she didn't have the equipment for this sort of research, but she was beginning to suspect that the strange glowing mushroom was just an oddity in Mother Nature's world.

Jess had been experimenting with doses and found that the drug seemed to have very few side effects. It was this drug that she had given Mary to keep her pain free and calm until her mutilated foot could start to heal. Mary had seemed to have trouble focusing her eyes and thoughts while under the drug's influence but she had recovered very quickly when Jess had stopped the injections. Jess felt that the strange plant had real possibilities for medicine.

"Doctor Jess?" interrupted Mone into Jess' thoughts. "That hillside gave a little more, I think. I hear the rumble."

Jess sat back and looked at her colleague, "We'd better find some way of stabilizing the hillside then, before we lose any more of the compound," she commented and Mone nodded his agreement.

"We could terrace the hillside with logs," suggested Mone, "if we can afford to get the local men to work for a few days."

It was Jess' turn to nod, "That sounds like a plan. You want to talk to some of the locals?"

Mone smiled, "I see to it, Doctor Jess! You no worry." The small Papuan laughed and left.

Jess smiled. If she knew Mone, the work crews were probably already organized. Mone ran the compound and Jess was simply the figurehead and she knew it. Behind Mone's calm exterior was a rather large ego! The request had just been a gesture of politeness. Jess turned back to her research but found it hard to settle back to work. It was one of those nice, late afternoons, when the sky was a fresh blue and the air lacked the heavy humidity. She wondered if Mary would like to go fishing. Maybe they could catch something for dinner. As kids, they used to often go down to the river and catch fish. Well, Jess would catch them, by wading out and grabbing a fish as it swam by. Mary could never get the hang of it.

She got up and looked out the window. Mary was not in sight. *I wonder if she still likes to fish or if she is too much of a lady to get wet now?* Jess made a decision and headed to the door. Loping across the compound, she entered their hut; Mary wasn't there. Frowning, Jess did a circle of the compound and still could not find Mary. Surely she wouldn't wander off without telling Jess. She was stubborn but not stupid. Then a dread exploded in her heart and she ran over to the slide and anxiously searched the tumbled earth for any sign of the little woman. Near the base of a leaning tree, she made out muddy strands of blond hair. "Mone!" Jess screamed as she dived down the bank in three jumps and started to dig frantically with her hands.

Mary's neck ached as she tried to keep her head above the rising muddy water. Panic was her worst enemy and she did her best to stay calm. Her head felt wooly, her eyes heavy and she knew she did not have much longer. She reached out with her senses in one last effort and called out with her soul, *Jess, I need you!* Then darkness came.

Mone arrived shortly after and helped Jess dig. He had never seen the warrior in a panic before but she clearly was in one now.

Right from the beginning, it had seemed that Mary had a hold on the doctor's Timp. Mone thought this was a good thing. He liked to talk to Mary. He hoped she had not died.

Jess reached into the pocket of muddy water and supported Mary's head. She held the woman tenderly in her arms and with shaky hands checked her vitals. Mary was breathing shallowly and her pulse was steady but weak. Jess wiped some of the mud from Mary's face and green eyes trembled and opened. "Knew you'd come if I called," the journalist mumbled and Jess held her close as tears slowly ran down her face.

* * * * *

The Seer looked out over the darkening valley, aware of the eyes of the followers watching every movement. They sat around the fire, waiting. The magic hadn't worked. They had eaten the boy's liver days ago. Not cooking it, but biting into it and slicing off a mouthful using a ritual knife. They'd each eaten their share but the cannibalism had not fulfilled the prophecy. The Seer sighed and turned. "We need the liver of the older brother. We know where his soul now lives. We must set his Timp free and then capture him by eating the liver of the one that now possesses his spirit."

"That would be very dangerous!" one of the followers argued. "What if there was menstrual blood? We could be killed and our souls lost forever!"

The Seer nodded in understanding. "We have tried a blood sacrifice and it didn't work. We will try to get others to do the killing for us. I have a plan." The Seer threw dry cinnamon on the fire, remembering to keep well back when doing so. The cinnamon burnt off in sparkles, filling the air with a sweet spiciness. "I have a plan."

* * * * *

She was in the leprosy clinic when she woke, with a plastic oxygen mask over her nose and mouth. Irritated, she reached to remove if from her face. A strong hand covered her own. "Just for a bit longer, okay," came a deep melodic voice.

Mary turned her head to the left, feeling the stiff white sheets against her cheek, and met sky-blue eyes. Her own eyes were blurry again and she had that dazed, not quite real feeling. She thought Jess looked tired and rumpled. She must have washed and changed but she expected that the tall woman had slept in the chair beside her bed. "Thanks," she mumbled and the blue eyes looked away hurriedly.

229

"That was a really stupid stunt, Giovani! You're lucky you didn't break your neck or back! Don't you dare step off this compound without my permission!" snarled Jess, wrapping a blood pressure cuff around Mary's arm and pumping it up until Mary thought her hand would explode.

"I didn't mean to scare you," she said softly. She could remember the rescue. She knew that Jess had been shaking and crying as she and Mone placed her on a backboard. She realized that Jess' gruffness was her way of showing that she cared.

"You didn't," snapped Jess and then looked at Mary when the blonde reached over and covered her hand. Jess sighed. "You terrified me," she admitted. Mary smiled softly and pulled Jess' hand close to her cheek, cuddling the big, warm hand like a Teddy bear. She closed her eyes. "Hey, I need that hand!" Jess protested but did not pull it away until long after Mary had gone to sleep.

For a long time Jess just sat there looking at the blond woman that she knew that she loved. Could you defy fate and come out a winner? How many of the Others had been betrayed by their soulmate by now? Or had any of them? Maybe they could achieve what the Hosts had not.

Maybe. *Or maybe you'll get your heart broken, Jess. No one ever loved the orphan that grew up in a barn. Why should that change? Take care of yourself, Jess. Don't let anyone or anything stop you from having the life you've worked so hard to get.*

Last night, as Jess had slept in the chair, she had been wakened again by Mary's dreams. She'd called out her father's name over and over again. What was that about?

Jess sighed. She had liked Mary's parents even if they had been rich. They had always treated her fairly. Mary's dad never talked down to her and sometimes he would ask her about the horses if Bart was not around. Mary's mom, too, used to send baking out with one of the maids to give to Bart and her sometimes. *Get real, Jess! You think that good Catholic, immigrant Italian family is going to accept you as a daughter-in-law?*

She gently pulled her hand away and felt the warmth turn to cold. Her jaw set in a straight, firm line and her face hardened into an unreadable mask. There was no point in thinking in circles or in second guessing the consequences. The bottom line was, she knew the moment she realized Mary was buried in the slide, that the little blonde had to be part of her life. *I won this woman's heart once before and I can do it again*, Jess thought. *I hope*, whispered an insecure voice from deep inside.

Chapter Nine

Mary woke late in the night and saw Jess preparing a syringe. "Hi," she whispered. Jess turned, smiled at her and came back to sit by the bed.

"Hi, I got something here to take the soreness away," she said, lifting the needle in her hand.

"Is that the stuff you have given me before?" asked Mary pulling a face.

"Yeah, why? Does it make you feel sick or cause joint pain or anything?" asked Jess with interest.

"No, it makes my vision funny, my speech slurred and my thoughts slow," listed Mary, "and I don't want it. I've only got some minor aches and pains."

Jess frowned. "I was hoping that the patient would find this drug a much better pain reliever than some we have been using. There is no indication of addiction," reasoned the doctor.

Mary's eyes widened. "Are you telling me that this is some experimental drug that you have extracted from some hocus pocus tree?"

"Not a tree, a mushroom," clarified Jess seriously, not seeing the warning signs of a major storm brewing as she looked down at the clear liquid in the plastic tubing.

Mary shook her head angrily. "You have been using me as a guinea pig?" she snapped.

Jess looked up from the syringe in surprise. "No! I mean we don't call it that. You were a test patient..."

A pillow came sailing at Jess' head. "You are the most calculating, opportunistic, self-involved bitch from hell that I have ever met! Don't you dare give me anymore of that mushroom juice! Christ, Jess, how could you?"

"Mary, I've done a lot of testing and I've also had work done on it back in Australia. I know it is not approved yet, but up here, we don't have much in the way of...."

"Not approved! Get out! Get out!" yelled Mary, pointing to the door with a hand shaking with emotion.

"But..."

"Out!" Jess took the hint this time and, tossing the needle into a stainless steel kidney dish, she walked out.

Honest to god! Mary thought, *that woman is impossible!*

Jess stormed across the compound. *Nice play, Warrior*, she thought, *you're really winning her over with your bedside manner!*

* * * * *

Mary had served Mone his dinner and had done the cleaning up. Then she had taught him to play poker for matchsticks. This, he had thought, was great fun! Jess had "gone bush" to visit a few villages and provide medical care for a few days. If she had been speaking to Jess, Mary would have liked to go with her; her foot was rarely sore now.

The couple of days had given her time to calm down some and she realized now that without Jess' mushroom juice she would have suffered greatly those first few days after the crash. There really wasn't much in the way of drug supplies on the compound and Jess had tried to apologize the next day for not getting her permission to use the drug. Still, Jess had to learn not to be so damn focused on her goals, especially when it affected other people's lives. Dealing with Jess was hard enough. She didn't need the issues clouded anymore than they already were.

Mone said goodnight and Mary packed up the cards and made sure that everything in the kitchen was neatly put away or locked up.

Suddenly, a huge bunch of orchids was thrust in front of her face. She gasped, stepped back and then saw Jess peeking sheepishly over them. "Ah, I picked these on the way back. They're for you," the powerful woman explained, awkwardly pushing the flowers at Mary again.

Mary was taken completely off guard; nervously she pushed her hair back. Smiling insecurely, she responded, "Thanks, Jess, they are really lovely. I'll put them in water. Have you had dinner? No, of course you haven't. Sit down and I'll get you something." *I'm rambling*, she thought.

The silent doctor sat down on the wood bench by the potbelly stove and leaned forward to open the gate and stir up the embers with a dry stick. Then she threw on some more wood and left the door open to watch the flames. After a while, Mary slipped onto the bench beside her and handed her a Cassowary egg omelet and a few slices of freshly baked bread. One huge, green Cassowary egg easily fed three people.

Jess tucked right in hungrily, using a chunk of bread as a spoon. Mouth full, she stopped and deliberately chewed slowly. Putting down the bread that she had been using as a shovel, Jess picked up the fork that Mary had given her. She swallowed hard, feeling the egg and bread scrape down her throat. *Put less in your mouth and eat properly,* she chastised herself. *Mary's a lady not some ignorant hayseed!* She wished like hell, not for the first time, that Bart had taught her some social graces. She was painfully aware of the fact that Mary was watching her eat. "So," she quickly swallowed her food and almost choked, "anything happen while I was gone?"

Mary smiled. Flowers, table manners, polite conversation, Jess was trying to impress her! It was so cute! Still, she was not going to make this easy for Miss Kiss and Run! "Just the usual routine. Touy has been around a lot. I think we should put him on our list," Mary answered.

"What list?" asked Jess, fighting to get egg onto the damn fork.

"The list I made of the names of the people who might have killed Kalla," responded Mary, stealing a piece of Jess' bread and chewing on it absent-mindedly.

"Hey, that's mine!" said Jess, looking up from the difficult process of trying to eat gracefully with a tray in her lap. Mary smiled and broke off a piece of bread and held it up to Jess' lips. Jess' heartbeat accelerated into warp speed. She took the bread between her lips, but Mary looked away as if the gesture was of no importance. Jess swallowed the offering with a good deal of disappointment. Did Mary not see how hard she was trying here? Was she still mad?

Mary got up and took Jess' plate. She came back from the kitchen area with large mugs of tea and banana muffins for the two of them. "Muffins! This is great, Mary! I haven't had a muffin since I got here!"

"They're Mone's favorite," Mary explained, trying hard not to smile as she looked innocently at the fire.

"Mone," came the disappointed response. "You baked these for Mone?"

"Hmmm," murmured Mary feigning disinterest. "We've become close friends while you were away. He'll eat anything I'm willing to offer him now!"

"What!" exploded Jess, "I was only gone two days!" The tea in her mug sloshed over onto the dirt floor and she cursed under her breath. All this courtship stuff was hard enough without having Mone as a rival!

"Well, they are long evenings. We've been spending them together," remarked Mary playfully.

"Oh," sighed Jess with such sadness that Mary looked at her in surprise. The usually confident woman was biting her lip and staring forlornly at the fire.

"He is a really nice man. He knew I was missing you so he kept me company. I've been teaching him how to play cards," explained Mary, reaching over to touch her warrior's hand reassuringly.

Jess looked up, her eyes dancing like sapphires in the firelight. "The government does not approve of gambling, Mary," she said. *Damn! What a stupid thing to say, Jess. You're a real romantic*, she chastised herself.

"Some things are worth taking a chance on," responded Mary, looking into those remarkable blue eyes. The expression in them changed to desire. Jess put down her mug and moved closer to Mary. Mary gave her a friendly smile and got up to put another log on the fire. She reached into her shorts' pocket and pulled out a folded piece of paper.

"Okay, here is the list. Mone has been helping me fill out some of their backgrounds. You know, he is a very bright man," observed Mary sitting down again. "I've really learned a lot from him!"

"About what?" asked a startled voice beside her. Mary flattened out the piece of paper on her lap and then reached over to rub Jess' arm gently. Maybe she shouldn't have teased Jess. She was so confident and in control that it was easy to forget that Jess had a lot of pain inside that made her suspicious and insecure on an emotional level.

"Well, lots about you for one thing. Mone, I think, is very much in love with you," smiled Mary, looking up into Jess' worried eyes. "He's always asking questions about you." The worry was replaced by surprise.

"He is not!" she snarled, pulling her arm away and hoping that in the dim light of the fire Mary couldn't see the red creeping up her neck.

Mary hid her smile. *Don't tease the warrior*, she reminded herself. If she did, Jess was likely to go off all huffy or they'd end up fighting when Jess went on the defensive. "He knows all about your service record. Did you tell him?"

Jess looked at the fire uncomfortably. "I guess. You know, just in talking at night. Guys like to hear about that sort of stuff," justified

234

the doctor. She felt out of her depth in this conversation and she had a funny feeling that Mary was pulling her strings. Jess had never found it hard to find company or get what she wanted from them, but this was different. This courtship stuff was proving to be real hard!

"Would you tell me?" asked Mary softly, tilting her head so that her golden hair cascaded off her shoulder.

Jess leaned forward and poked at the fire with a stick. "Thought Mone had told you," she mumbled jealously.

"I want to hear it from you," Mary stated simply, smoothing out the creased paper on her lap with a gentle hand. Jess watched the graceful fingertips following the lines of the paper and imagined them tracing her lines. A deep need throbbed down low inside her.

I'm in trouble, she thought. A squeak came out of her tight throat when she tried to speak. She cleared her throat and tried again. "Why?" she managed finally to articulate. *You're acting like a goddamn school kid, Jess*, she thought!

"Because then I'll know you trust me," Mary explained, suddenly turning her head to met Jess' eyes.

"I trust you!" protested the warrior in frustration.

"Not the way I want you to," the petite woman responded. "Let's look at this list," she went on, changing the subject. Jess had been shaken up enough for one evening, she thought. "These are the names Touy called out when he was throwing the killing stones," she explained.

"Heorn is the mother of Rimrapasi who was raped by Turka, the brother of Kalla, the boy who was murdered here. Heorn is a Mendari but she married into the Eravey tribe, so Rimrapasi is an Eravey. Turka and Kalla are Eravey too, but from the Kutubu region. So, even though Rimrapasi and Turka were not related by blood, they were related by tribal links, so it wasn't only rape, it was incest! Turka is working in the copper mines in Rabaul, so the only way to get payback would be to kill Kalla!"

"This is what you and Mone talked about?!" asked Jess in jest. Well, at least partly in jest. She was still harboring some doubts and jealousy towards her assistant since Mary's earlier comments.

"Hey, you told him about being behind enemy lines in the Gulf War!" protested Mary.

"So!" snapped Jess.

"So, don't interrupt," responded Mary and went back to her paper. "Rimrapasi was next on the list. But I think she's a long shot. Not that she hasn't got good reason for revenge, I mean no highland male would have her, even with a bride price, after that, but Mone said she was really good looking and had a high school education. She ended up marrying an Australian anthropologist and is now living on the coast. They have a little boy and another on the way. I think she's too busy to worry about revenge. But you never know. I mean face IS face," explained Mary, getting caught up again in her story.

Jess put a booted foot on the bench and wrapped her hands around her knee. One eyebrow went up as she listened in amazement to the amount of information Mary had weaseled out of Mone.

"Next is Samalli. Now he's got motive. He's a Mendari. The Mendari were just a small clan and at the time they were at war with the tribe up the valley. So Samalli asked the Eravey to join them. He said they could use some of his land if they would help fight. The Eravey jumped at the chance because they'd been kicked off their land during another tribal war, so they really needed a place to go! Now, Samalli says the Mendari need all their land and the Eravey have to go. Only they won't. They say that they own the land Samalli lent them because they have farmed it for many years," explained Mary excitedly.

"I've heard about the Mendari land dispute," Jess drawled dryly.

"Yes, but don't you see? Kalla was an Eravey, so this could be Samalli's way of getting even!" Mary clarified earnestly to a skeptical looking warrior.

"Okay, go on," Jess said, smiling. She really liked the way Mary's face animated when she was telling a story.

"Okay, number four is Archa. He is an Eravey but word has it that he and Kalla were interested in the same girl. Archa is much older and so he thought he had the inside track because he could afford the bride price and there was no way Kalla could for a couple of more years. But Archa had to give the tribe all his mature pigs for the Cassowary Race to end the land dispute between the Mendari and the Eravey. He might have bumped Kalla off just in spite. Word has it he is pretty annoyed about having to give up his bride price!" Mary revealed with relish.

Jess laughed. "Sherlock Holmes had nothing on you, kid! So who is number five?"

"Quen. He's the shaman in the village we visited the other day," Mary stated.

"I know Quen," interrupted Jess. She liked Quen and felt Touy had only put him on the list out of professional jealousy. It was well known that there was rivalry between the two medicine men.

"Quen is a Mendari and he is also a traditionalist and Kalla was a Christian and..." Mary was interrupted again.

"Kalla was Christian?" exclaimed Jess, her body becoming suddenly alert.

"You think it was Quen?" asked Mary, leaning forward.

"No!" scoffed Jess in disgust, then realized she was trying to be nice. She went on more gently, "No, I don't. Quen's a good guy and a friend," she explained.

But the damage had been done. Mary was annoyed. "So a friend of YOURS wouldn't kill?" she asked incredulously, "The woman who single handedly garroted six..."

"Shut up!" snapped Jess, her body radiating anger.

The wind rustled the leaves in the darkness and the fire cracked in a splutter of sparks. Jess' breathing was harsh, like that of a violent animal. Mary swallowed. This was Jess' dark side. The one that had won her the reputation of a lone wolf and kept everyone at bay. It probably also won her that medal for bravery that Mone mentioned.

"I'm sorry, Jess, that was a really cruel thing for me to say. I don't like to have my ideas belittled and I over-reacted," stated Mary, meeting Jess' inhuman eyes with a steady stare.

Jess shrugged. "S'okay," she muttered, turning to look at the fire. Silence. "I shouldn't have yelled. I didn't mean to sound condescending. You did a great job collecting all this information."

Mary brightened immediately and moved closer in her delight. Jess looked up and smiled, her body relaxing again. She reached out her long arm and scooped Mary in close, giving her a hug and a peck to the temple. "Yeah, I think you're something else," she confessed. Mary sighed contentedly and to Jess' delight she didn't pull away but tucked up to the warrior's side.

"So who do you think did the murder?" asked Mary after a bit.

"I'm not sure yet, but you gave me some ideas to chew on," muttered Jess sleepily.

Mary untangled herself from Jess and stood up to close the stove and turn the damper. She wasn't sure how to handle this. The perimeters of their relationship were shifting and she didn't know just where the boundaries were going to be. "Well, I guess I'll see you in the morning," Mary said awkwardly as she gave a little wave and turned to head over to the hut.

Strong arms grabbed her and turned her back around by her shoulders. Eyes now dark and dangerous challenged her own. The tips of Jess' fingers slowly traveled along the edge of her jaw and raised her head as the taller woman leaned down. Warm, soft lips feathered across Mary's, sending chills down her back. Then strong arms wrapped her close in a blanket of warmth. A voice whispered in her ear, "I'm not leaving this time. I'm here forever or until you tell me to go." The message was sealed with a kiss as Jess buried her face in Mary's soft hair. It was a long time before they parted and walked back to their hut, hand in hand.

They changed in the dark and Mary slipped into her bed. Jess stood there undecided, torn between where she wanted to sleep and where she was supposed to sleep. "Jess," came a quiet voice through the darkness.

"Hmm."

"I don't get the nightmares when you are close," stated Mary. Jess didn't need any more encouragement. She slipped in beside Mary and felt the woman wrap her body around her. "Jess, I need time. I..."

"It's okay Mary. I understand," Jess cut in. She wasn't sure she wanted to hear why Mary didn't want to make love. It would be a reflection of herself she'd rather not see any more of tonight. She needed to build Mary's trust in her again. "Ah, in Kuwait, a patrol got taken prisoner. No one knew where they were. I ah, I let myself get caught. They... they..." Mary snuggled in closer and held her warrior tight. *Oh Jess, no*, she thought. "They made it pretty hard, but eventually I ended up in the same lock-up as the patrol. Then I got us out. That's when I had to kill those people," Jess explained painfully.

Mary kissed Jess softly on her neck, feeling the hard, rapid pulse of the tense woman. "You have always been my hero, Jess. Now even more so," she said sincerely and felt the strong woman relax a little.

For a long while they held each other, just enjoying the warmth and peace of being together. Jess thought Mary had drifted off to sleep when she felt a tear drop on her shoulder. "After you left, they found out mom had cancer. She suffered terribly, Jess! And dad, he just couldn't take it. He loved her so much! He forgot all about his business and just stayed with mom. They tried every possible treatment there was but she just got sicker.

"I came home from school one day and he... he had shot her and then turned the gun on himself." Jess wrapped her arms tightly around Mary and held her close, unable to think of anything to say. "He had mortgaged everything to pay for treatments. By selling everything left, I was just able to cover his debts. University was out. I got a job as a waitress and put myself through college in journalism. I worked my way up from a local paper to a big city daily and now I do mostly freelance work," Mary explained.

"I'm sorry," was all Jess could think to say as she held on to the sobbing woman. It seemed to be enough, because after a while Mary wiped her eyes and fell to sleep on Jess' shoulder. Jess took a deep breath and exhaled slowly, letting the tension go. That had been pretty hard on both of them but it was a good start, she hoped, in trying to build a relationship. That thought sent her heart pounding with new fear. That was what she was embarking on here. Not just an affair like those in the past, but a lasting relationship. She was too much in love to be scared off by her trace memories anymore. No matter what the hurt in the end, she had to try to make this work for them.

She turned her head and kissed Mary's forehead, then closed her eyes and let her breathing even out until it matched Mary's slow, rhythmic sleep.

Chapter Ten

Mary woke to find Jess long gone. She knew Jess liked to start her day with a run in the predawn. Then, after showering and changing, she headed over to the clinic. Around nine, she would finish her rounds and go to her office to write up her reports. Mone would bring her in a morning coffee there that seemed to tide her over until lunch.

By 8:30, Mary was in the kitchen feeding Mone toast and coffee. Much to her surprise, she saw Jess striding over from the clinic. She entered the open kitchen, ignored Mone and came over to Mary, leaning down to drop a kiss on her lips before wrapping a protective arm around her shoulder. "Iiiieeee," laughed Mone, waving his hand up and down as if it was on fire. It was a highland exclamation for amused surprise that Mary had seen used by various villagers.

"Get lost," growled Jess with a grin and Mone finished the rest of his coffee in a single gulp and left laughing and shaking his head. Jess looked down at Mary with one eyebrow raised.

Mary put her head to one side and met the look and considered. On the one hand, she was not about to let Jess treat her like spoils of war. On the other, she realized that the insecure woman beneath the hero needed to reassure herself that Mone was not a threat. About some things, anyway, it was not wise to tease Jess. *Let it go*, Mary decided. "Morning, Jess," she said, giving the smug warrior a hug. "Do you want some coffee?"

"Okay. You want to go see the ending of a Timp ceremony?" the doctor asked, following behind Mary and putting her arms around the smaller woman as she reached for a mug off the counter.

Hmmm, major insecurity here. Mary turned around in Jess' arms and reached up on tiptoes to claim Jess' mouth in a long, deep kiss. When it finally ended, they were leaning against the counter for support. "Where you go, I go, warrior," she said and felt a deep familiarity and comfort to the words.

241

Jess seemed to as well. Her body language shifted from over-protective and insecure to relaxed and happy. She reached behind Mary and grabbed the mug and after placing one more light kiss on the blonde's cheek, she went over and poured coffee from the pot that was sitting on the potbelly stove. "The day of the murder, I had been at the first part of the ceremony. Today is the second part. The village is some distance off, but it will take all morning for the men to put on their war paint and wigs. If you think you are up to it, we have time to walk slowly over there before the action begins."

"That would be super, Jess!" exclaimed Mary and hurried to put things away and change while Jess threw together a picnic lunch for them. They were soon on their way, following the narrow footpaths that wound up and down through the grass foothills of the mountains or dropped down into the tall grasses or dense jungle of the valley.

"Timp cults go in about twenty year cycles. The ceremonies start on the outer edges of the tribal territory. Gradually, the Timp spirits are captured or herded towards the centre of the tribe's lands. This process takes about twenty years. Finally, the Timp is killed and buried in a ritual funeral and then the process will start all over again. Each cult that moves through the valley has different magic and symbols. The cults start in the Gulf of Papua and the secrets are sold from tribe to tribe as each clan finishes off their Timp cycle. Gradually, the cult ends up in the Sepik River area and dies out," explained Jess as she carefully helped Mary along.

"Today, the last of the Timp spirits will be captured. There will be a ritual bride and then funeral. The day will finish off with a singsing and feast. Most of the people on your list will be there today. This is the most important ceremony to take place in the last twenty years," Jess continued. Mary smiled softly and squeezed Jess' arm. Warrior was trying so hard to be charming. Jess stopped at the gentle caress and leaned down to brush her lips against Mary's. Mary looked deeply into the clear blue eyes. "Want to stop for an early lunch?" Jess asked, anticipating the answer.

"You bet!" came the immediate reply and Jess laughed. They found a bit of shade under a lone tree with a pleasant view of the grassy highlands and ate quietly.

Mary watched Jess serving out the fruit, crackers and cheese carefully and self consciously eating her lunch with her best manners. *You have no idea, my warrior, how much I love you.* "This isn't easy for you is it, Jess?" she asked gently.

A smirk lifted the corner of Jess' mouth as she leaned forward to steal yet another kiss. "Oh yeah! It's really easy!"

Mary pulled back and Jess' eyes snapped up. Mary read startlement, then annoyance. "That's not what I meant," she stated.

Jess leaned back, looking uneasy as she rested on her side propped up on one elbow. Her eyes looked down the path. *She's going to kiss and run again*, thought Mary in fear. Jess licked her lips, hesitated, and made up her mind. "Yeah, it's real hard. I'm better at seducing, not courting. I don't have too many social graces," she admitted, feeling very uncomfortable. Her eyes flickered about, looking for some possible means of escape, even though she knew she couldn't take it. She looked anywhere but at Mary.

"Why are you afraid to make a commitment to me?" Mary asked, cupping Jess' profile in her small hand and turning the strong face to look at her own.

Jess swallowed hard. *Oh boy!* "This probably isn't a good place to have this discussion," she hedged.

"It's not a discussion. It's a question," stated Mary, her eyes serious and firm.

Jess looked down at the tough grass. "I don't trust easily. Anyone. It didn't work out for the Hosts, Mary," she revealed suddenly. "The one betrayed the other, somehow. If it happened to them, then why won't it happen to the Others? To us?"

"That's it!? You walked out on me because of some shared memories we had as kids?" exclaimed Mary in astonishment.

The temper flared. "Come on, Giovani! Get real here!" snapped Jess, rolling away and getting to her feet. Mary got up too, not wanting Jess towering over her if they were going to argue. "It was a great weekend, okay! But what was going to happen when Bart and your parents came home and found us in bed? Did you ever stop to think about that? Your parents would have gone mad. Bart would have got drunk and beaten me half to death again! It wasn't fairy princess stuff, Giovani. It was going to be ugly!"

Mary became aware of the wind rustling through the grass and realized that she had been staring at Jess, who was standing miserably a few feet away. Slowly, Mary walked towards her and wrapped herself in Jess' arms. "Oh Jess, I had no idea that Bart abused you," she whispered into the tall woman's chest. The body her head rested on felt rigid and quivered with energy.

"I don't want to talk about it now," Jess muttered. "Later... tonight."

Mary nodded against her chest and then gave her a tight hug before she pulled back. "Tell me about the wigs the highland men wear," Mary said and watched Jess sigh in relief as she turned to gather up the remains of their lunch before they headed off once more down the trail.

"The men wear human hair wigs. The women make them from the hair collected in cuttings, or when they remove the hair from the sick to let the evil spirits out. The shape of the tightly woven wig is unique to each tribe. Eraveys are the exception. They don't wear human hair but headdresses made of Cassowary feathers. The Mendi wig is rounded and they'll put a flat tower on top decorated in coloured bands made from bird of Paradise feathers. The Kutubu wig is like Napoleon's hat in shape. They often decorate theirs with yellow ever-lasting daisies. There are hundreds of wig styles but those are the three you are most likely to see today," instructed Jess, the slight quiver in her voice revealing the boiling emotions that were only just below the surface.

I handled this all wrong, Mary chastised herself. She had for so many years held a childish hurt towards Jess' actions that she had reduced the cause of Warrior's disappearance down to Jess acting like a jerk. She had never, as an adult, taken the time to consider the fact that there might have been more to Jess' decision than that she had gotten what she wanted and was leaving for greener pastures. What a hell of a place to open up a really sore wound! "Jess." The warrior stopped and turned around, looking tense and worried. "I'm sorry." Jess nodded and relaxed a bit.

"S'okay," the tall woman murmured. They walked off again in a comfortable silence until they came to the outskirts of the village.

Below the tall Yar trees, the captured smoke of wood fires formed a blue mist. Dark bodies stood pensively waiting within. The men's faces were painted in bright reds, yellows and blues. They wore their ceremonial wigs of human hair that Jess had described. Mary noted, based on the wig shape, that most of the villagers there were Mendari. Pushed into their wigs, two sticks supported a flat, narrow tower decorated in geometric bands of brilliant Bird of Paradise feathers. The women stayed in the background, unadorned and murmuring softly to each other. The men stood in front listening to the Shaman chanting, tensely holding stone axes or spears with human bone tips.

Jess took Mary's hand and they moved silently forward, Mary jerking sideways a little with each step. Mary could now see the shaman through the crowd. It was Touy. He squatted on the ground before a hole. In his hands, he held the carcass of a rat. He was pulling out its intestines and examining them as he chanted the magical words that would give him insight. The light palms of his hands were covered in blood. Finishing his observations, he buried the rodent quickly in the hole and then got up to talk quietly to the headmen who stood near by.

"What's going on?" Mary whispered.

Jess raised an eyebrow and looked cynical. "Touy was reading the future by examining the entrails of the rat. He's now telling the chiefs what was revealed. You can bet that whatever it is, it is to Touy's political advantage. Just like the name of our murderer just happened to be Rimrapasi, who was conveniently out of town," sneered Jess.

Mary looked at Jess in surprise and then got the worried little frown that she developed when she was thinking something important over.

The village consisted of a singsing ground with a few men's houses off to the sides. The ceremonial Haus Tambaran stood at the end. As usual two trees marked either side of the singsing ground. Mary became aware that two little girls had been dressed to be brides. When she asked why, Jess explained that these girls were the brides of the Timp. They were under the age of puberty and therefore were still clean. Yet because they were female, they still had all the built up creative power in them. It was not possible, Mary now understood, to use older women for this role. Menstrual blood could kill a man. Mature females would be very dangerous for the men, who were very vulnerable with the Timp so close. Jess explained that women were never allowed near the Haus Tambaran until the last day of the ceremony. The little girls represented the bride of the Timp or spirit. They wore the black net bag called a belem on their heads and their bodies were covered with oil and soot so that they shone black.

"Why are their faces painted half red and half black?" asked Mary.

"The black signifies the gaining of pigs and wealth. The red represents prosperity and health," Jess commented.

"That's why the flag of Papua New Guinea is black and red with a yellow Bird of Paradise on it!" exclaimed Mary. "It's cult magic!"

Jess nodded with a smile and continued, "The girls have to be very careful not to touch their faces. If either side is smudged that part will fail to come true. That is why the girls sit so still." Mary looked back at the little girls. They sat on a bench in front of the main pole that supported the Haus Tambaran. She felt sorry for them. What an awful responsibility for a young person, to have the well being of the whole tribe on her shoulders.

Hearing a noise, Mary turned. Across the clearing from them was a platform. Onto this wood frame, climbed two young warriors. They pretended to fight with axes and then the crowd shouted out for them to stop. Jess explained in a whisper that this symbolized the tribe seeking peace and harmony. As Mary watched, the two young warriors put down their stone axes and picked up a rattle each. These were woven from pit pit grass and contained stones. Now the two warriors stood shoulder to shoulder, going up on their toes and down on their heels to the beat of their rattles. This action symbolized the unity of the Warriors against the Timp, Jess explained.

As they watched, the men of the clan started to form rows. Each row was six warriors across. Armed with bows and arrows, stone axes and shields, they marched around the singsing ground in silence to the beat of the two rattles. Mary watched in deep fascination. It was like stepping back through time. A shiver ran down her back and she felt Jess move closer and place her big, comforting hands on her shoulders. Mary could feel the warmth of the warrior she loved seeping into her back. "It's Touy," Jess whispered into her ear. "He's heading this way."

Mary turned and instinctively put herself between Touy and Jess. She didn't know why but whenever Touy was near, she felt worried for Jess. It was silly she knew. Touy was a leper, smaller, and middle aged. He was no threat to the warrior who towered over him. And yet he looked at the doctor with such obvious hate that it brought out all of Mary's protective instinct.

She listened to Touy's fast, aggressive speech and then Jess' labored response in place talk. Touy sneered and moved off. "What did he say?" Mary asked.

Jess' eyes followed the Shaman. "He said he read in the intestines that the two bothers would soon be united and that the people of the highlands then could take what was rightfully theirs."

"Huh?"

"It is the origin myth. It takes many forms from tribe to tribe but the basic story is the same. In the beginning of time, there are two brothers. The older brother learns the secret for pleasing the spirits but he doesn't tell his younger brother like he should. The spirits become angry at the younger brother who doesn't do the magic right like he is supposed to, so they tear the island apart. The older brother floats off on his big island with all the cargo that the spirits have given him. The poor younger brother is left on a small island with nothing but disease and war.

"All the cults that come through the highlands have methods to try and find the secret that the other brother did not share. That is the reason behind the cargo cults. The highlanders now believe that the other brother sired the Europeans. They seem to have everything. These cults exist to try to get back from the Europeans the cargo that they feel rightfully belongs to them."

"Jess, that's kind of scary," interjected Mary.

"Yeah, it can be. But usually it is harmless enough. Still, I'd better report it to the local authorities in Mendi once we get a new radio. Just in case," reassured Jess, giving Mary a hug around the shoulder as they stood watching the events from the sidelines.

The lines of warriors disappeared into the Haus Tambaran. Suddenly, a warning was yelled and the warriors charged out, brandishing their weapons and screaming war cries. Mary unconsciously slid behind Jess, who was bristling with excitement. "What's going on?!"

Jess kept her eyes on the warriors as they now returned to the Haus Tambaran, yelling warnings over their shoulders and waving their stone axes menacingly. "There was an alarm that the Timp had escaped. The warriors ran out to protect their women. It is just the men strutting their stuff!"

Mary giggled and bumped Jess with her body just as another warning was given and the men charged out once more in mock rage. The two women shared a quiet chuckle. "Bet they wouldn't be so bold if there really was a ghost out here," laughed Mary.

"You got that right!" drawled Jess.

The men once again retreated to the ceremonial house. A few minutes later, a third warning was yelled. The men came pouring out ready for battle. This time two boys covered in grey clay and wearing bell shaped wicker frames over their upper bodies charged at the warriors. They represented the Timps' last battle to defeat the magic of the villagers. The warriors bravely held their ground, placing their shields of wood in front of them and chasing the last of the Timp spirits into the Haus Tambaran where the shaman could trap them.

Outside the women waited nervously in silence. Jess whispered to Mary that inside, Quen would now be performing the magic not Touy. Quen was strong and could spiritually fight off the Timp. Touy, as a leper, was too weak for such a dangerous job. Quen would pour palm oil into a hole through a piece of intestine from a sacrificed pig. Then he would breathe the magic words into the intestine to call the Timp. Weakened from its battle with the warriors, the Timp would travel down the intestine to feed on the oil in the hole. Quickly then,

Quen would seal the hole and the district would be rid of all harmful spirits until more people died and released their Timps.

Mary looked up at Jess' serious face. She delighted in her old friend's knowledge of the culture and her respect for it. Jess looked down and blue pools of sky touched green forest depths. The doctor turned and gently brushed her lips against Mary's. "You are something else, Jessica Vizirakis," commented Mary, once again caught by those intense blue eyes.

A cry from the Haus Tambaran made them both start. From its depths ran out four warriors. Each pair carried a pole between them from which hung the ritual body of the dead Timp. A man dressed as a woman in mourning ran between the two bodies mourning their death. Mary realized that a woman could not do this in case the ceremony was contaminated.

The five highlanders with the two Timp bodies ran around the singsing ground with the remaining warriors following, screaming their war cries. As they once again passed the ceremonial house, one of the warriors used his axe to hack down the main support beam and the Haus Tambaran collapsed in a crackling rush of snapping branches and bark. The wind sent the fire smoke spinning in wild waves around the dancing warriors. Their war paint and feathers were the only splashes of colour in a monotone world of evening blue and fire smoke.

Mary looked back at the shattered remains of the ceremonial house. A man wearing the armbands of a shaman stood looking about proudly; he turned and walked away into the crowd of men and women. *That must be Quen*, Mary realized. Mary's eyes drifted over the crowd of warriors now milling with their women folk and relating their heroics. After twenty years the Timp was dead.

"Come on. Let's see if we can beg some roasted sweet potato to eat on the walk back," suggested Jess. They had eaten lunch early. Now, late in the day, Jess was feeling very hungry.

Mary laughed. "Wow! Dinner out too. Boy, you really know how to show a girl a good time on a first date, Warrior!" she teased.

Jess' reply was lost in the sudden scream of war cries from all sides as warriors attacked. Mary was pushed down as three warriors charged at Jess. She grabbed the spear that was aiming for her gut and spun its owner off his feet. The second warrior got the wood shaft across his jaw in a baseball swing that knocked him out cold. The third warrior had used the extra time to come around to Jess' side, chopping at her with his stone axe. Jess ducked and spun. The sharp stone missed but her shoulder took the blow of the hard wood shaft.

Her temper snapped and she uncoiled from a crouched position with an incredible force, smashing her right fist into her attacker's face. He crumpled. Turning around, she saw Mary crouched at the base of a tree, covering her head from the human bone tipped arrows that shot through the air in all directions. Blood and mud mixed with dark bodies on the ground and Eravey's and Mendari fought in vicious hand-to-hand combat. Jess scooped Mary up and broke into a run with Mary over her shoulders. She dodged through the fighting in the singsing ground and ran off the embankment, doing a graceful flip as she dropped to the garden below. Here she lowered a rather startled journalist to the ground.

Mary clung to Jess for support until the world stopped spinning. "Don't think much of the dinner entertainment," she commented shakily.

"We gotta get out of here," responded Jess, looking around. "Come on." She grabbed Mary's arm and led her off at as quick a pace as she dared. Mary hobbled along awkwardly, trying her best to keep up with the warrior. She was soon gasping for breath from the exertion and the thin air of the high altitude. Jess stopped and Mary bent over panting and holding her side, where a stitch was knifing into her.

"Can you go on?" asked Jess, worry in her eyes. Mary straightened up and nodded. Jess led the way, moving only at a quick walk now. She turned right and followed a well-used trail into the gathering darkness. In a few minutes, they came to a wide, deep ravine with a vine bridge across it.

"The bridge is pretty old but I think it will hold us," commented Jess. "I'll go first."

"Jess, I'm not too good at heights," confessed Mary, looking at the swinging vine bridge that was held in place by some old, rotten looking stems wrapped around some dead trees.

"We don't have a choice," stated Jess. "You'd better go first, then. I'll follow."

Mary saw by the set of Jess' face that there was not going to be any arguing. She squared her shoulders, brushed by Jess, and making the sign of the cross when Jess couldn't see, she edged out on to the bridge. She held on tightly to the sides and side-stepped along the single pole that acted as a footpath at the bottom of the looped vines. The bridge swung and bounced and the pole tended to roll. Where one pole ended and another over lapped, it was particularly tricky not to trip. "Hurry!" ordered Jess' worried voice.

Mary could hear fighting behind her. *Jess must be holding the warriors back*, she realized. Mary moved as quickly as she dared to the other side, trying her best to look at where she was putting her feet but not beyond to the water so far below. With a gasp of relief, she reached the other side. "Jess! I'm across," she called, turning to see two Eravey's on the ground and a third clinging to Jess' back with his arm around her neck. Jess cried out with rage and her voice echoed like the wail of a banshee down the jungle valley and mixed with the pathetic scream of the last warrior as he was toppled over Jess' head and hit the ground heavily.

Jess ran across the vine bridge and then slashed out with her knife at the supporting vines. The bridge collapsed down on to the rock face of the opposite side. Angry warriors came to a stop at the edge and readied bows to fire arrows across. Jess grabbed Mary and they ran as fast as Mary could manage up the steep, mud path, Jess pulling Mary up when she would have slipped back. Only when they were over the lip of the ridge did Jess stop. Mary's lips were turning blue from the effort and she felt light headed as she gasped for breath. Jess too, was breathing hard.

Neither spoke, saving the oxygen for their burning muscles. Finally, Jess turned and squatted down and Mary wrapped herself around the tall, strong body. Wrapping her long arms around Mary's legs, Jess piggybacked Mary back to the compound through the moon lit night.

Chapter Eleven

The moon was full and high as they entered the compound. Crickets sang songs to the rhythm of the gentle night wind as it rustled through the needles of the Yar trees. Mone had left a fresh pot of coffee on the stove. Jess snatched it up and then tucked the container of banana muffins under her arm. "You get some cups, Mary, and some towels from the shower hut," instructed Jess.

Mary nodded numbly, too tired physically and emotionally to ask why. Obediently, she gathered the items and then followed Jess off the compound to the east. After only a few minutes, they came to a breathtaking sight. A crystal clear stream tumbled over a small falls into a rocky pool which overflowed slowly in a white veil that dropped to the Lai Valley far below. Under the full moon, the two falls glistened with fairy brightness and the hanging pool reflected the lunar light.

Mary placed her cargo beside Jess' on the edge of the pool and then stood to drink in the beauty around her. "Oh, Jess, it is beautiful here!" exclaimed Mary.

Jess smiled and took Mary by her shoulders, looking into eyes sparkling with moonlight, "You are beautiful," she whispered and sealed her compliment with a long, hungry kiss, wrapping Mary deep into her arms. A warm, exciting rush of need swept the sleepiness from Mary's being. She parted her lips and moved closer into Jess' embrace, meeting her demands with her own. She slipped her hands under Jess' T-shirt and the doctor's hard stomach muscles contracted with her touch. *Oh yes!* she thought and that was her last coherent thought.

Jess peeled Mary's shirt off slowly, intently watching the smaller woman's body being revealed to her once again. She lowered her head and kissed a white throat. The flesh was sweet and smelt of warm herbs and honey. A soft growl warned of her rising need. Leaving Mary's bra on, her hands flowed over a silken back and curved into Mary's waist as they slipped under her shorts and spread over a firm,

251

round bottom. She gasped as Mary's hand boldly slipped under her bra and ran across her breast. The shorts went, along with Mary's panties, and then the bra.

Jess stepped back, reluctantly breaking contact with the petite woman as she removed the rest of her own clothes. When flesh contacted flesh, hands roved freely over each other's bodies.

Mary felt her knees giving out. Raw need was overriding reason, as an age-old instinct demanded satisfaction. She moaned and Jess swept her up in her arms and stepped into the small pool hanging between two waterfalls. Slowly, she lowered the two of them in and Mary floated around to the front, gently pushing Jess against the bank until she lay on top of her lover. Her body tingled, reveling in the contrast between cold water and hot body heat. Their mouths played across each other as they whispered words of love and need. Jess lifted the smaller woman by her hips and lowered Mary's breast on to her mouth, teasing and loving Mary's warm, hard nipple with her lips. Mary arched and ground her sex into Jess' hips. Jess rolled over, pinning Mary below her. "I want to love you, Mary. I want to join with you under the stars and fly you to the heavens," murmured Jess as she floated feathery kisses down on Mary's swollen lips.

"Hmmm," Mary moaned. "Show me how high and far you can make us fly, my warrior," she challenged softly then groaned as lips trailed down her body.

Much later, Mary sat wrapped in a fluffy towel in Jess' arms. They shared a muffin and a cup of coffee together and listened to the night sounds sweetening the air with their rhythmic music. The moon was lower now and Mary was satiated, sleepy and so very happy. Jess stirred and lifted the smaller woman to her feet. "Come on, my love, it is time for bed." They gathered up their clothes and other cargo and headed back to the compound. Hand in hand, they walked to their hut and curled into bed together, Mary wrapping herself around her lover and falling to sleep in her strong, gentle arms.

Her eyes opened to darkness. Sight wasn't really necessary. Jess' keen hearing had already identified all sounds and registered that everything was safe and normal outside. She sniffed the air. It was that hour before dawn when the world was its coldest. She didn't have to get up yet, but soon. The casualties of yesterday's melee would be pouring into the clinic early.

The problem was how to handle this. If she got up and left, having made love to Mary last night, it would be sending just the message that she was trying so hard to live down. On the other hand, she couldn't lie here and wait for sleepy head to wake up! Jess gnawed on her lip. That left only one solution.

Mary woke to warm nibbles on her neck and a gentle hand stroking her back. "Hmmm, that's nice," she murmured. "I had this dream last night," she observed, stretching and reaching to kiss her strong, quiet lover. "I dreamt that the most incredible woman lit rockets in me and sent me shooting to the stars."

"Good, because the feel of you, the sight of you fills my universe with love," whispered Jess between kisses.

The body beneath her stilled and Jess pulled back and made eye contact with serious, intensely green eyes. "Do you love me, Jess?" Mary asked earnestly.

"I've always loved you, Mary. I've loved you from grade school. I... I... just..." the warrior stammered.

"Shh, we'll talk later. Let me just delight in the knowledge that I have the heart of the only person I've ever really wanted," soothed Mary and they made love slowly, intensely aware of every touch, breath and need of the other.

* * * * *

The day wore on endlessly. Jess arched her shoulder. It was aching painfully. Mary had massaged a heating rub into it before they had walked to the clinic but now, hours later, she hurt from having stooped over patients all day. With a sigh, she carefully supported the new cast in a sling and sent the last patient on his way. Then she crossed to her cubbyhole office and slumped down in the chair, placing her head on her desk.

She didn't open her eyes when she heard the footsteps, she didn't need to, knowing Mary's quiet, uneven tread. The sound of water and then a warm, soapy cloth wiped her face. She sighed with pleasure, keeping her eyes closed and enjoying being babied. Mary said nothing, letting her warrior concentrate on her actions. She caressed Jess' neck with the sweet smelling warmth. Then she lifted the doctor's shirt and let the cloth trace over the tired, stiff muscles of her back.

Mary rubbed oil into her hands to warm it. Then she continued to work on the knotted back muscles, now warm and fresh under her touch. She could feel the tension and weariness draining from her lover, being replaced with sleepy contentment. Leaning forward, she placed a kiss on the cheek of her warrior. "Mone is warming up a stew. How about we go over and sit by the fire and have some? You haven't eaten since breakfast and it's past seven now. Come on, my warrior," Mary coaxed.

Jess sighed and opened her eyes as she sat up and pulled Mary into her lap. "I don't know how I lived without you," she moaned, hugging Mary tightly. Then she stood with Mary still in her arms.

"Hey!" Mary protested and Jess raised an eyebrow as she claimed Mary's mouth once more while she lowered the silenced blonde to her feet. Together they walked across the darkening compound to where Mone sat by the fire of the potbelly stove.

"No good day, Doctor Jess," commented Mone as Mary ladled out a cup of stew for Jess.

"Yeah, pretty rough," agreed Jess. "Thanks," she smiled, taking the cup and spoon from Mary.

For a few minutes they sat and looked at the fire while Jess recharged her batteries with some hot chicken stew. *Mary is one excellent cook*, she thought. "This is good," she said, remembering to watch her manners as she ate.

"Thanks." Mary smiled, looking up at Jess from where she sat on an overturned bucket by the stove. "You need a hair cut, you know," she observed, gazing at her lover with a smile.

"NO!" protested Mone in fear. "Doctor must not cut her hair. Very dangerous now to do so."

"Why?" asked Mary in surprise.

"Mone!" protested Jess with a sigh.

"People try to murder her yesterday! Maybe now they try to kill her with witchcraft."

"Mone!" snapped Jess, but her friend and colleague was not to be quiet.

"You must not cut your nails or hair. If they were to get a piece of your body, then they could make very strong magic," argued Mone, his eyes wide with fear.

A shadow blocked out the light from the fire. Jess looked up to see Mary standing in front of her. "The truth. Now," ordered the little woman.

Jess sighed. "There was no reason to attack us yesterday, Mary. The raid was over the land dispute. It was Eravey against Mendari. It had nothing to do with us. The three who came at us had a completely different mission. They used the tribal war as a cover. In fact, they just knocked you out of the way to get at me. Someone wants me dead," explained Jess.

Mary sank to her knees and placed her head in Jess' lap. "Oh shit," she whispered in shock. Jess stroked her hair comfortingly as the three of them sat and watched the fire die.

Chapter Twelve

Jess slipped into bed beside Mary and sighed with contentment when the small blonde immediately snuggled into her tall frame. She felt very tired tonight and yet she knew that there were issues that Mary was not going to let lie forever. She tried to relax. *Let Mary decide to get into this or not*, she thought

"Jess?"

Oh boy! That was quick! You'd better get this right, Jess, this is important, she warned herself. Out loud she responded, "Hmmm?"

"I've taken a real emotional chance letting you get close to me again. Do you understand that?" Mary asked softly, in a voice laced with sadness and concern. Jess rubbed her back reassuringly and tried to think how to respond to that.

"Jess?!"

"I know what I am and why you shouldn't get involved with me!" Jess responded with a little more edge to her voice than she intended. She felt Mary stiffen then pull back slightly. *Oh shit!* "I... I want to be... involved with you. I always wanted that but..." Jess floundered for words, feeling herself getting sweaty and tense.

"Hey, I'm here," Mary responded, stretching up to place a kiss behind Jess' ear. "I need to understand, Jess, that's all. You just tell me in your own way, okay, my warrior?"

Jess had an uncontrollable urge to bolt for the door. Instead, she took a ragged breath and tried. "My old man, he liked fast cars and women. My parents, they were killed in a car crash 'cause he was driving too fast. Bart, he did his duty by me but he didn't want to be saddled with a grandchild at his age. He was okay, you know. He taught me a lot about horses and he made me read and stuff. But when he'd been drinking, he could turn nasty. I could have killed him, Mary. Even when I was little, I was strong and a good fighter, but it wouldn't have been right to hit an old man who had given me shelter and food. So I used to just let him hit me. I promised myself that as soon as I was old enough I'd enlist, and I did."

Mary didn't say anything. She just gently rubbed her hand in a slow figure eight over Jess' stomach, and felt her relax a bit. "It's hard for me to believe in love. I never knew it," she confessed awkwardly and Mary kissed her shoulder.

"I love you Jess," she said simply.

"I know that now. I... It meant a lot to me that you trusted me to handle the payback. I am not sure why it was so important to me, that you trusted me to do what had to be done, but it was. I just want to be able to live up to your loyalty and love. It's something new for me, commitment."

Jess pulled Mary tightly into her arms and kissed the top of her hair, breathing in the sweetness of a hot summer day that seemed to be part of Mary's being. *Sweetness and light, that is what she is like*, Jess thought. "You smell nice," she said and smiled when Mary giggled happily.

The sound encouraged Jess to go on. "The Hosts, I know where they are," she revealed and Mary propped herself up and looked at Jess with growing interest in the dim light of the moon. "Their tomb is in Turkey. I can sense them. Feel the tomb calling. I saw some Others too."

"What!" exclaimed Mary in surprise, forgetting not to interrupt.

"They look kind of like us," Jess went on. "Not identical or anything, but side by side you'd know we were closely related. They seemed happy together but I know the Hosts' love... Well, it didn't work out. I think it ended real bad for them. I don't know..." stammered Jess uneasily. She wished Mary would snuggle back into her side again. It was easier to talk when Mary was close.

There was silence in the darkness for a few minutes. *Maybe that will be enough*, Jess hoped, her heart beating a little too quickly. "Go on," Mary urged softly, amazed at what she was learning from the woman she loved.

Jess couldn't stand it anymore. She reached up a hand and stroked Mary's temple. Mary seemed to understand. She turned her head and kissed the hand that shook just a tiny bit. Then, she laid back down, her head comfortably resting under Jess' chin. Jess sighed in relief and hugged her close. "I'm... I'm afraid. The Other, in Turkey, she's lame and I think they all are. I think. I just get feelings, bits of memories and dreams. You know?" she questioned worriedly.

"A little," confessed Mary. "I think my Host had a child and your Host hated it. I get this repeating dream... It scares me."

"I scare you?" asked Jess in a voice shaky with pent up emotion.

"No. Even my Host wasn't afraid of you, just of what you might do. I don't think my trace memories are as strong as yours. Except for that one sort of confused nightmare, I only get sort of vague feelings about the Others and our past," explained Mary, stroking Jess' belly again.

She felt more than saw Jess nod. "The tomb... it well... it's kind of alive. You know, it radiates energy but it's icy cold to touch. It doesn't have the real names on it. The Others, they must have had it changed or something, because it is their names, Jamie and Gunnul Dedemann.

"I think I know the name of another one of your Others too. I saw her picture in a paper when I was stationed in the Middle East. She's a big shot archeologist. Her name's Malone. I thought it was you at first, that you'd married, but it wasn't."

There was silence for a long time as Jess tried to figure out how to confess the worst of it while Mary digested all the information that Jess had revealed. "Mary, I don't think you would have been lamed if you hadn't run into me again," the doctor stated bluntly.

Mary's hand stilled, then continued its comforting movement. "Why do you think that?" she asked.

Jess licked her lips. "It was one of the reasons I left. I suspected that the Others like you were all lame but you weren't. I thought maybe it wouldn't happen if I wasn't around. I think there is a pattern we all gotta follow. You know, we're fated," Jess tried to explain painfully.

Mary shifted onto her back but made sure she held on to Jess' hand. She realized that this was an awful tough thing for Jess to do and she was only doing it to show her love. Mary squeezed the hand affectionately. "Why do you think that is happening?" she asked.

Longer silence this time. "There is a darkness in me. I have to control it. I could... I have done some really... I think, I've always hurt you. I didn't mean to, Mary! Honest!" Jess pleaded, sitting up and looking worriedly through the darkness at the blonde.

Mary reached up and pulled her warrior down so that Jess' head rested between her breasts. "It might mean you have hurt me. It might mean our relationship was undermined. It might mean that at some time our relationship was crippled. It might mean nothing," whispered

Mary, stroking Jess' soft hair. "I'd like to understand better what it all means, Jess, but I'm far more concerned with us in the here and now. You know what I think?" she asked, ruffling Jess' hair playfully.

Jess leaned back and shook her hair back out of her face, "What?"

"I think that we can do the past more good than they can do us harm," she stated firmly.

"If we travel through life together, there could be trouble," Jess warned.

"That's what friends and lovers are for, Jess. To help each other," stated Mary confidently.

Jess smiled. Mary sensed it in her heart more than she could see it in the darkness, "Okay, friend." They settled down together again, their friendly embrace turning slowly into the caresses of lovers.

It was very late at night and Mary was warming water on the propane stove to mix with powdered milk and chocolate to make a hot chocolate for the two of them while Jess was getting a fire going in the potbelly stove. Try as she might, Mary had no success at building fires in the stove. She usually got Mone to do it if Jess was not around. They had made love, slept a bit in each other's arms and then hunger and a need to be close, now that the barriers were falling, had driven them out into the quiet night in search of a midnight snack.

Mary carried the hot chocolate over and slipped in beside Jess, who immediately wrapped a long arm around her lover. "Jess, about what Mone said tonight, are you in danger?"

Jess sighed and considered, stretching out her long legs and crossing her ankles. "Some danger, I guess. I know who killed Kalla and who is now trying to kill me. I think I know the motive for the killing. What I don't understand is, why me? Maybe I read it all wrong," muttered Jess, leaning forward to pick up a branch to throw on the fire.

"You know who killed Kalla?" Mary exclaimed in surprise turning to look at Jess in irritation.

"And you didn't tell Mone and me! Jess!"

"Hey! Wait! I just sort of figured it out yesterday. But then, when I was attacked... I don't know, it just doesn't make sense!" clarified Jess.

"What doesn't?! Tell me!" demanded the impatient blond.

"Nope," smiled Jess, looking into the flames.

"Why?" demanded Mary, pulling back to look at the classic profile of her strong lover. *Lover. I like that.* The sound of that name sent shivers of excitement through her.

"Because I think it would be really fun for you to try and make me!" laughed Jess, leaping to her feet and heading off. Mary was only a few paces behind her as the two women played like children, dodging around the buildings of the compound in the night, their laughter echoing eerily down the valley.

Jess dodged once more away from Mary's grasp, making sure that she did not make the game difficult for the crippled woman. She slowed and turned when she got to just the right spot. With a giggle of delight, Mary tackled Jess and the two of them rolled to a stop in soft moss. They lay, catching their breath, on a small outcropping under an old gum tree. The moon washed the valley below them with silver and a warm breeze rustled the leaves above them, covering them in a kaleidoscope of patterns.

"I mean to make you sing, warrior," murmured Mary softly as she slowly stripped Jess of her nightshirt. *Easy here, Mary*, she thought. Playing out this love fantasy was like stroking a wild black panther. It caused a heady rush of excitement mixed with the fear of the explosiveness of the situation.

Jess allowed her shirt to be undone and peeled back and off her shoulders. It fell and pooled around her naked hips as she sat waiting, watching Mary. *I started this*, she thought. *I've never put myself in this role with a lover before. Normally, I'd have found it threatening and a real turn off, but this game with Mary, this is different, physically exciting and yet a little scary too.*

Mary gently pushed her back, following Jess down so that she lay alongside her, leaving her lover room always to escape. "I am going to do things to your body, my love, that will make you want to share everything in your soul with me," Mary whispered as she picked up Jess' hand and nipped and kissed the soft underside of her thumb. Jess watched in fascination as the velvet tip of Mary's tongue tickled the sensitive flesh between her first two fingers.

Oh boy, I'm in trouble, Jess thought, feeling the heat of passion starting to pulsate through her body.

Mary felt the shiver of desire pass through Jess' frame and smiled as she sucked one of Jess' long fingers into her mouth and caressed it with her tongue. Slowly, she pulled back, letting the digit run gently over her tongue and lips. Her eyes met her lover's and Jess saw the sexy challenge in the half hooded eyes. Mary slipped up onto Jess' body, pushing the taller woman's legs wide as she settled her own hips over Jess' sex. The older woman arched in need and Mary leaned down and kissed the sensitive, pale flesh under the captive warrior's jaw.

259

"I love you, Jess. I am going to show that to you now. I'm going to hold you, not by force, but just by the will of my love. Surrender, my warrior, surrender to my love as I surrendered to yours," whispered Mary, feeling the throbbing of Jess' pulse on her lips as she dropped caresses on the soft skin. Her one hand now let go of a wrist and slowly curved down the underside on Jess' arm, then across her shoulder and down the lean hardness of her lover's side. The body under her jerked with a rush of excitement.

"Shh, slowly, my love," cautioned Mary, sliding forward to look down at Jess. Like a feather drifting down, she lowered her lips until they touched Jess' and the world exploded in a hot ball of desire. Their lips tasted each other hungrily and they entered each other's mouths and tasted the promise of sweeter fruits to come. Jess' head followed Mary's as the petite woman leaned back, their lips still eagerly seeking contact. But Mary had other plans for her lover.

She now moved lower and nibbled playfully along the underside of Jess' breast as her hand slipped down, floating over the curve of a hip and feeling the muscles bunching in a strong thigh. Her hand glided over a knee and then moved up, caressing the sensitive inside of Jess' thigh. Her lips whispered onto a hard nipple, "I am the keeper of your realm, my warrior. I am the one who holds your heart. All I will ever claim from you is this sweet surrender of your heart." It was in the pink glow of sunrise that they finally moved sleepily back to their hut, entwined in each other's embrace and forever one.

* * * * *

"Touy! You think it is Touy!" smiled the smaller woman as she lay the next morning in Jess' embrace. "Wow! I was right!"

For an answer, the silent warrior kissed the golden head. Jess was blissfully happy. Last night, she had entered into a world that she thought she could never have. She wasn't a lone warrior anymore. Now she was a couple, part of a household. Household, she liked that. Maybe they could buy a small horse farm back in Australia. Would Mary like that?

"Jess?"

"Ah," came the startled response as Jess realized she had been far away in her daydream.

"I asked you why you think it is Touy," Mary repeated, kissing Jess' still swollen lips. "Where were you?"

"Would you like to have a horse farm, Mary? We could buy a little spread and build it up over time. I could look around for a community practice," asked Jess earnestly.

Mary sat up and looked at Jess in wonder. "Are you offering me a commitment, Jess?" she asked in a voice which trembled with emotion.

An ice ball formed instantly in Jess' gut. "I... I thought... I mean, I guess I should have... will you stay with me, Mary? Be my partner?" stammered the insecure warrior, searching Mary's eyes for an answer.

The eyes danced with joy. "Oh Jess, yes!"

Jess pulled Mary into a tight embrace, feeling her heart start to beat again. "Did I just propose?" she asked with a shaky laugh.

"Hmm, and you need to know, warrior, I'm a forever sort of girl," giggled Mary.

"Good," whispered Jess, swallowing a lump that had just formed in her throat and rubbing her cheek in the fresh summer heat of Mary's hair.

* * * * *

The Seer watched the two women making love and then walking naked back to their hut. Europeans looked like ghosts, the colour drained from them. He suspected they were like this because they knew the magic that let them communicate with the spirit world. It was this bond that allowed them to get the cargo. The whiteness was, to the Seer, a mark of the older brother's betrayal at the beginning of time.

He knew that there were women who liked other women. This was because their mothers had slept with another warrior and not just her husband! There were men too who liked men, not women. They had sucked too long at their mother's breast. But this tall woman, it was because the Timp of the older brother lived within her. He had often felt the Timp. The energy of it radiated from the doctor like the heat of a fire when she was angry.

Capturing her Timp would not be easy. The three warriors he had sent had failed miserably. Touy's magic was not strong enough now that the doctor had sent the sickness to numb and eat at his body. But the Seer had a new plan. One that would deliver the doctor to his doorstep. The followers of the true fire would not fail again!

* * * * *

The two women dressed, the process made slow by the need to caress and hold each other close. "Mone is going to wonder where I am! I'm surprised he hasn't been over here yet to see what is going on," sighed Jess, reluctantly pulling herself out of Mary's embrace.

Mary giggled and placed a quick peck on her warrior's cheek. "Mone is not stupid, Jess! He knows exactly what is going on!" She bit her lip in amusement as red crept up the warrior's neck.

"Great! Just what I need is that big, grinning Papuan teasing me all day," groaned Jess as the two of them headed over to the kitchen area. Mone had left a pot of coffee on the stove and Jess poured while Mary sliced bananas to put on the oatmeal she had simmering. They ate in companionable silence, enjoying their first breakfast together as a couple. Then Jess leaned across the table and kissed Mary gently. "See you later, sweet one," she murmured.

"Hmm," sighed Mary. "I'll clean up and be over later to help in the clinic."

Jess nodded and Mary watched her lover lope over to the hospital. Mone met her at the door, a big grin on his face, and slapped her on the shoulder. *Careful, Mone!* Mary thought. Even softened with love, the warrior was still not someone to push too far.

Chapter Thirteen

Days went by in a pleasant routine. Jess still got up early and ran but then she would have a quick shower and return to her lover's bed. She left the morning rounds to Mone and had her breakfasts with Mary. They talked a lot about future plans and dreams or whispered words of love, each delighting in romancing the other. The days at the clinic were busy. Jess and Mone had their regular leper patients and general treatment clinic for the villagers, plus the casualties of the tribal war returning for check-ups. Mary had finished her coding system and was now involved in the complex process of organizing the medical stocks and lab.

In the late afternoon, after her coffee with Mone, Mary would leave Jess working in her office or lab and Mone cleaning the clinic and walk down the ridge to where the village women met to barter their garden produce. Mary had now learned enough Pidgin to bargain for a good price. She had learned to be careful as well. She knew never to step over the small piles of food that the women piled on the ground in front of them. To do so would contaminate the produce and it would have to be thrown away. Worse still would be for a woman to step over a baby or the legs of a child playing on the ground. That would be seen as murder by the highlanders. She would have been instantly attacked and killed as payback.

Mary would wander through the small and crowded market carrying the belem that she had bought. These village-made net bags were tough and durable and never seemed to completely fill up no matter how much you stuffed into them. The village women always carried one, the long net straps knotted over their foreheads and the bag hanging down their backs. This too was how they would carry the heavy loads from their gardens, often bent over with the weight of sweet potato.

In the traditional highland society, the women did all the daily work. The men would clear a new garden for their shifting agricultural practices every five years or so and they handled the political and religious ceremonies of the village and made war. Although a matrilineal society, the highland cultures were male dominated in the extreme. Jess had explained that in worth, men were at the top, followed by male children, then pigs and then the women and female children. Mary followed the taboos because it was their country and their customs but she hoped that with improved government education, such beliefs would change over time.

One night, Mary did cut Jess' hair, making sure that she dropped every strand into the fire so that no magic could be used against her lover. Jess had teased her about this but Mary had burnt the hair anyway, explaining that Mone would worry otherwise. In her heart, though, Mary knew that she just didn't want to take any chances when it came to the woman she loved. It was the first time that she had felt truly happy and whole in a very long time and she planned on keeping that feeling all her life.

Returning to the compound one day, she was distressed to hear screams of pain coming from the clinic. She dropped her belem on the table in the kitchen area and then limped hurriedly over to the hospital to see if she could do anything to help. Mone was leaning over a village man who was writhing about in agony on a gurney. The man had a strange mad grin on his face and drool foamed at the corners of his mouth.

While Mone held the man down, Jess was in her lab looking at a slide under her microscope. "Damn, it's Kurukuru alright, Mone!" she called, straightening up and coming back into the clinic area. "Mary, help me get restrainers on him. Mone, once we've got him secure, you'd better go talk to his family. We are going to have to report this and find out what the hell is going on around here," the doctor ordered as she got out the restraining straps.

She and Mary slipped them over the man's chest and legs and fastened them down tightly while the villagers watched from the doorway or looked with concern and interest through the windows. "What's wrong with him, Jess?" Mary asked as Mone got up with a sigh and moved off to talk to the family outside.

"He's in the last stages of a disease known locally as Kurukuru or laughing sickness," she explained as she tried to get a blood pressure reading. "The weird smile is caused by lock jaw. His spastic muscles are so tight that they can actually break the bones."

"Oh Jess, is there anything you can do for him? He must be in agony!"

"Yeah, it is a hell of a way to die. No, I can't help him other than to ease the pain." The tall doctor was now busily filling a needle. "Hold him steady," she ordered and Mary had to use her body to pin the arm long enough for Jess to administer the shot.

In a few minutes, the man calmed and developed a far away look in his eyes. With the locked, hideous grin on his face, he seemed quite mad. Jess sighed and leaned against the counter looking at the man. "Laughing sickness is caused by a virus that attacks the brain cells," Jess explained. "The only way to get the disease is to eat the brains of someone that already has the disease."

"Cannibalism!?" asked Mary in shock.

Jess nodded. "There hasn't been a case around here in years. I've got a really bad feeling about this, Mary."

"Why, Jess?" the smaller woman asked as she wiped the sick man's forehead with a damp cloth.

"Kalla's liver was missing. Originally, I thought that it had been taken for some sort of Timp ritual. I've heard rumors of other villagers disappearing over the last year or so too. And Touy talked about the 'older brother' returning soon. I think we've got a dangerous cargo cult forming. One based on ritual cannibalism."

Mary shivered in disgust and then her face tightened in fear as she walked over to Jess. "My god, Jess, they tried to kill you! You don't think that they planned to..."

Jess pulled Mary into her embrace. "Yeah, I think I'm next on the menu. I just don't understand why!"

"Jess, we have got to get out of here!" exclaimed a frightened journalist, clinging tightly to her lover. "I just got you back. I'm not going to lose you again! I can't!"

Jess held her partner close and swayed gently back and forth as she dropped kisses on Mary's head, "Hey, it's okay! Don't worry. Everything will be fine. You'll see! Come on now. We've got to care for this guy. Let's make his last hours as comfortable as possible."

Mary nodded and after another tight hug she went back to trying to keep the man's fever down. Jess took some blood and made a few more slides for her records, returning every now and again to monitor the man's vitals or to give him a shot.

* * * * *

The Seer smiled. They had lost a number of the followers of the true light with this strange disease. When they had first shown signs of sickness last year, after they had cannibalized several of the enemy killed in a tribal war, the Seer had refused to let them go to the doctor's clinic. The Seer had explained to them that the Europeans had used witchcraft, to cause the disease to prevent them from following the true way. One by one, recently, those afflicted had died. Now this was the last one. The family had only been allowed to bring him to the clinic when he was beyond talking. That was important. Even the most loyal might talk of secrets when the pain got too great.

They were so close now to understanding the secrets that would make them able to please the gods and get the white man's cargo. It had been the Seer that had realized the answer when he had gone to the mission station and had stood and watched the faithful take what the missionary called communion. They had pretended to eat the blood and flesh of their god, Jesus.

Then the Seer understood. The white people used cannibalism to please their god! That was why they passed laws that said cannibalism was bad. They didn't want the highlanders to discover the secrets that would let them get their cargo back from the descendants of the older brother. But knowing the secret did not mean that you knew the magic to go with it. The Seer and the followers had tried many methods over the last few years but all had failed.

They had tried the Timps of warriors, but that had not worked. Then they had tried a Christian warrior, but his life force had not given them the answer either. No, the answer was only known by the older brother. And the Timp of the older brother was caught in the heart of the tall doctor who could defeat an army of warriors by herself! Only by eating her brain, heart and liver could they gain the knowledge they needed to get the cargo back!

Soon, very soon now. The plan was going to work this time. It had become so easy now that the Timp of the older brother had been badly weakened by being too much with the little woman with the hair like fire.

* * * * *

The Kurukuru patient did not last long. He died several hours later and Jess and Mone had slipped the body into a body bag and returned it to the mourning family. Now the three of them sat around the stove fire and ate the soup that Mary had prepared. None of them had felt much like eating. It had been a grisly death. "Did you find out anything from the family, Mone?" asked Jess, at last forcing herself to deal with the issues and put the hatred of losing a patient behind her.

"Some, Doctor Jess. The family was afraid to talk. They said that Torgamonga had been sick for a long time. They said that he got the sickness from the caves. He went there often, they said, and knew how to go deeply inside. The spirits that lived there made him sick. They said others used to go with him to make magic but most of them are dead now too, of the same illness."

A fire flamed in those ice blue eyes. "The cave, huh? I've always wanted to explore that cave."

Mone looked shocked. "No! No, you must not go there! A very bad and strong Timp lives there, Doctor Jess! You no go!"

Now Jess smiled and laughed bitterly. "Believe me, Mone, there is no spirit as bad or powerful as mine. I have within me a Timp that has lived on through the darkness of time."

Mary reached out and rubbed Jess' arm. She didn't like to see Jess like this. It was like she was giving in reluctantly to some monster that lived deep within her. It scared Mary and fascinated her at the same time. But she knew that whatever was going on in Jess' mind and soul, it was upsetting her soulmate deeply. It seemed to upset Mone too. He said no more and shortly after he said goodnight and disappeared.

Mary snuggled into her warrior's side and felt the strong arm wrap around and pull her close. The crickets chirped in the night and occasionally the fire would flare up and snap. The smell of wood smoke and wet earth permeated the air. "I'm going to have to go and check out that cave," Jess finally admitted.

"Not without me," Mary stated firmly.

"You're staying behind with Mone to take care of the clinic while I'm gone," responded the doctor with determination.

"No, I'm going with you," explained the petite woman, looking Jess in the eyes and not blinking at the coldness she saw there.

"It might be dangerous, Mary. Last week, when we were attacked at the village, I realized how vulnerable you are with a lame leg. It really scared me. I'm not going to put you in that sort of danger again!" confessed the warrior awkwardly, looking down at the fire.

Mary leaned forward to look at Jess. She took her hand and turned the tense face towards her so that their eyes once more locked. "Jess, I'm crippled. I can't say that doesn't bother me. It does. But I also know that if you hadn't been there to help me I would probably have died of infection or at least have lost the leg. I am going to be lame for the rest of our lives. I've come to terms with that, why can't you? You have to treat me as an equal, Jess. I'm not going to be over-protected by you. That would not be fair to either of us! Where you go, I go, warrior!"

Tears rolled down Jess' face and she pulled Mary close to her. "Okay," she muttered in a voice choked with conflicting emotions. Mary held her lover tightly and stroked her back, calming the violent soul that she knew was a part of the complex person she loved.

Later, they made love in bed. It had been slow and gentle, each giving more than they were taking. Now they lay in each other's arms waiting for sleep to claim them. "Jess, when are we going to go?" asked Mary.

"Soon. We'd better not wait too long. Whoever is behind this is very powerful or I would have known long ago that something was going on. Whoever is leading this cult doesn't just have control of one tribe but many. Touy shouldn't have that sort of power. Maybe he is just a middleman for the real power, but I haven't got the slightest idea who that could be.

"With the Timp cult going on and the Mendari land dispute, tensions have been running pretty high between the various tribes in the valley. I don't know of any villager who could move easily from one tribe to another spreading his or her doctrine. Whoever it is has access to all the tribes or at least most of them. That is really unusual. I might have badly underestimated Touy."

"If we find them in the cave, what are we going to try and do?" asked Mary.

Jess squirmed uncomfortably. Could she trust Mary to understand? This time, if there was killing, it wouldn't be ritualism. Mary seemed to sense Jess' reluctance. "I know that if it turns violent, then so will you, Jess. I am not comfortable with physical force but I think I'm a big enough girl to understand that sometimes violence can only be defeated by violence. What I'm asking is, what we can do to try and avoid getting to that point," Mary clarified, slowly stroking Jess' belly, trying to keep the building energy in check.

Jess was amazing when she got like this. A power just seemed to radiate from her. Her eyes seemed to become inhuman, reflecting light from within. Her skin was hot to touch, not with fever but with a raw energy that seemed to pulsate from every pore. Mary wondered what the Host must have been like if this was the power her descendant possessed. *Who were the Hosts?* she wondered. *And what did they need from the Others?*

Chapter Fourteen

Two days later, they were ready. They each carried a knapsack. In Mary's were clothes, a small camp stove and dehydrated food and in Jess' were sleeping bags, fuel packs, water flasks and miner's lights. Into her deep pocket, Jess tucked another item, after much thought, that she hoped she would not have to use. They left a worried Mone in charge and headed off down the main trail in the early morning light. "You ever spelunked before, Mary?" asked Jess as they walked.

"No. I've been in a few caves that have been opened to tourists though, and they don't really bother me. And I've done a bit of mountain climbing," responded Mary honestly.

Jess nodded her approval and lifted her head to catch the early morning light on her face. The more time she spent with Mary, the more she realized how well they suited each other. She couldn't remember being so happy. *Please don't take this away from me*, she thought, fear gripping at her heart. Her hand wrapped around Mary's as they walked and she held on tight to the smaller woman, who bounced up and down with her uneven gait.

Mary saw Jess' face change from joy to insecurity and reached for her lover's hand just as Jess groped for hers. Mary let her small hand be wrapped inside the big, capable fist. Jess was like that, fearless and powerful on the outside and insecure and, yes, sometimes even defenseless on the inside. Her tall lover was a complex individual who carried some real issues from her past on her shoulders.

Mary was short of breath and very tired when they finally reached the cave entrance in the early afternoon. Jess called for a stop and Mary gratefully sank to the ground in the shade of a gum tree while Jess pulled out some fruit, cheese and crackers for them to eat. "They have tried to cover the trail but this path has been used recently," Jess observed.

269

Mary nodded. Now that they were here the tension and fear was mounting in her gut. "Jess, you be careful, okay?" she let slip in an anxious voice.

Jess got up from re-packing her pack and wrapped her arms around Mary. "I've never had anyone to love me before. I'm not going to throw that away by doing anything stupid. I promise. But you gotta promise me too, that you'll stay out of trouble!"

"I promise. I'll just be there right behind you all the time. Okay?" soothed Mary, feeling so much safer now that she was in Jess' arms.

"Okay," smiled Jess, softly brushing a truant lock back into place in Mary's bang. Then she bent and picked up her backpack, slinging the heavy bag effortlessly over her shoulder. She took the two oil burning miner's lamps that she had removed from her pack and showed Mary how to wear the headgear and attach the fuel pack to her waist. Jess then showed her how to light it and tucked a flint striker into a button down pocket in Mary's jacket. "Let's go," she said when she was finished.

The cave was the result of the slow erosion of limestone by the daily monsoon rains. It twisted and turned on itself in a strange world of distorted rock formations that suddenly loomed out of the darkness as their lights passed over them and then faded away. Jess pointed out that the low ceiling showed clear markings of torch smoke and Mary could detect, too, the damp, burnt smell of old wood fires in the closed spaces. After groping through a narrow, low passage using their hands as much as their feet, they came out into a fairly large cavern, half of which was filled with a subterranean lake. Here dim light illuminated the rock cavern from a few small, eroded holes above.

Jess helped Mary through and then they stood and slowly surveyed the space. Stalagmites and stalactites produced weird shadows. Over the lake, roots from trees on the surface choked the holes, looking like long, crippled fingers made white by the glare of the torchlight. Water trickled down into the black waters. The other half of the cave floor rose sharply in a high slope to the cavern roof. Only a narrow area where they stood was truly flat.

"Stay behind me," Jess cautioned, pushing Mary back with her hand. Her head turned. Standing at the other end of the narrow flat stretch were Mone and two warriors. More warriors appeared from out of the shadows high up the slope, their bows and spears ready. "I thought I left you taking care of the clinic," stated Jess, trying not to show her shock at seeing her trusted assistant there. To give herself time, she casually removed her backpack. *Can't trust anyone,* she thought in disgust and then felt Mary rubbing her back gently. *Except for Mary*, Jess' thoughts modified. "I suppose if we went back down the tunnel we'd meet some more of your friends," Jess smiled.

"Yes, I make no mistake this time," Mone said, returning the smile.

"Why, Mone? Why are you doing this?" asked Mary, emotion making her voice shake. Jess reached back and took her hand.

"All my life I have seen the wealth of the European. I must put up with their orders and arrogance in my own country. I think: 'Mone, you get a good education then you learn the magic to getting cargo.' But instead, I do not learn my own ways. I am an outcast of my village and the European society does not want me either. So I learn my own magic. I see you fight off a whole tribe and then I understand. The Timp of the older brother lives on in you!"

Mary moved to Jess' side. "Mone..."

"Shut up, slut!" the Papuan snapped.

Mary grabbed Jess before she could charge her assistant. "No, Jess!" she cautioned, feeling her warrior fighting to control the violence within her.

Through gritted teeth Jess managed to growl, "Surrender, Mone. You have seen me in action. I don't want anyone getting hurt."

Mone laughed and signaled to some of the warriors who waited on the rock slope to come down. In the next instant, all eyes were wide with shock, as Jess stood with a lit stick of dynamite in her hand. She had pulled it from her leg pocket and lit it by the flame of Mary's miner's lamp. "So let's play for keeps, shall we?" she said and then hurled it up the bank. Grabbing Mary, she tumbled into the water just as a terrific explosion filled the cavern with a fireball. Shock waves bounced off the walls and rock fell like depth charges around Mary and Jess as they surfaced. Jess grabbed Mary and pulled her under again.

Water poured into Mary's mouth and she fought against Jess' iron grip. She felt herself pulled deeper and she fought to keep her mouth shut and not gag in more water. Her head pounded and her chest felt like it would explode. Against her will, she gasped for breath and felt herself drop into darkness.

Jess pushed Mary through the tunnel and let the current take her as she followed close behind. Breaking out into the open, she grabbed at the limp and sinking body of her lover and pulled her to the surface. "Mary! Christ!" Jess swore, treading water as she closed her mouth over Mary's and forced air into the water-filled lungs. Jess wrapped an arm around her unconscious partner and stroked for where she hoped the shore was. As soon as she could stand in the water, she started mouth to mouth again. "Come on, come on," Jess whispered in near panic between breaths.

Mary choked and coughed and Jess pulled her over on her side and let her cough up the water. It was some minutes of retching and coughing before Mary was able to function. Then she hauled off and belted Jess on the arm, hurting herself more than the warrior. "Ouch! You almost drowned me, you big, dumb warrior!" she gasped.

Jess stroked back her hair. "Hi, I can't see you but you sure sound like the woman I love," she responded, her lip still quivering with stress and fear.

Mary took the large hand in her own and kissed the palm. "You want to tell me what happened between the explosion and me almost drowning?" she asked.

"It wasn't safe in the cavern. We could have been hit or buried by falling rock, so I pulled us under and through an underwater passage to another cave. I've explored the lake before so I knew generally where it was," explained Jess, pulling Mary into her arms.

"Next time, Jess, would you mind saying, please take a deep breath, Mary!" the petite woman sighed, cuddling deeper into Jess in the darkness.

"You wouldn't have heard me," reminded the warrior practically.

"Do they know where we are?" asked Mary.

"I don't know. But they can't follow. The tunnel filled in behind me," responded Jess calmly.

"Oh good," said Mary more confidently as she caressed the large hand she was still holding.

"Nope, bad. I don't know the way out yet," revealed the older woman.

Silence.

"Jess?"

"Hmmm?"

"There is one, right?" asked Mary tentatively.

"Has to be," stated the warrior confidently and then continued, "It just might not be off this passage."

"You had to tell me that, didn't you?" groaned Mary.

Jess stiffened indignantly. "You said we had to have honesty in our relationship!" she pointed out.

Mary laughed.

"What?!"

"Here we are, trapped in a cave surrounded by cannibals, and we are having a tiff about honesty!"

"You started it!"

Mary ended it too, by covering Jess' lips with a heart felt kiss. Jess sighed good-naturedly, "Okay, you win! Here, I'm going to pull us up to higher ground slowly. I'm not too sure of the terrain, although I seem to remember a fairly flat floor in this chamber." Jess felt ahead with her foot and finding secure ground, gently pulled Mary completely clear of the water. "Okay, now I'm going to let go and search to see if either of us still has a light," Jess explained.

"Mine slipped down. I can feel it around the back of my neck," stated Mary, "and I think I still have my fuel pack."

"I've got a fuel pack but my light feels smashed. I'm going to take yours and see if I can feel to attach it to my pack. Then I'll have to try and dry it out enough to get it lit."

"Okay, but I'm going to hold on to you, alright? This dark is really spooky," stated Mary nervously as she felt about and then grabbed on to Jess' arm.

"Here," said Jess softly and transferred the small hand to her ankle. "I need that hand." Jess worked for some time trying to attach and dry the system in the dark. Then, satisfied, she took Mary's striker and after many tries finally got a spark. It flared brightly for a split second and then went out, leaving red spots in front of their eyes. Finally, Jess managed to get a weak, flickering light in the lamp. As the wick dried, the flame became stronger. Mary sighed in relief and Jess smiled smugly.

"Better, Giovani?" she asked.

Mary smiled up at Jess. "You're my hero. Just one suggestion. Next time we are facing down angry cannibals, do you think you could think of a more appropriate weapon? I don't know, maybe a small cannon or flame thrower!"

"It was the only thing back at the clinic that was remotely useful as a weapon," grinned Jess, "but I'll keep the flame thrower in mind for the next time!" Mary rewarded her with a wry look and then a broad smile.

"Nice to see that smile again," observed Jess, reaching down to cover the hand that was still clutching her ankle for dear life.

Mary let go and took the hand, "You're a sight for sore eyes too, Vizirakis!" Jess leaned over and they kissed softly, each painfully relieved to see the other safe.

They worked together to wring out and sort what was still usable in Mary's small knapsack. Jess had slipped out of the big knapsack as soon as she had realized they were in trouble. If they were careful they had enough food for a number of days, but they had no water except what was available in the cavern. "Won't matter," observed Jess. "Our best option is to follow the river anyway, if we can. We might be able to get out the same way the river does."

"What if we can't?" asked Mary, wringing out the canvas knapsack.

"Then we come back here and I dive back down that tunnel and try to clear a passage in the dark," muttered Jess, playing with the pieces of the cook stove to get them back together again. Mary frowned but said nothing. She noticed that Jess had checked their fuel supply carefully and she wondered how long it would be before they were without light.

They headed off a short time later, moving slowly and staying close together to share the illumination from the miner's light on Jess' head. It was late evening by Jess' watch when they stopped to camp. Mary used the small, single flame stove to heat soup in the tin pan that the stove was stored in. They had lost any other utensils and had to take turns sipping out of the pan. Too tired to talk, they ate in silence and with few words cleaned up and settled down to sleep. The darkness was absolute and the slow movement of the river sounded loud in the deep cavern, once Jess blew out the light. Mary snuggled as close as she could to Jess' warm body and Jess wrapped her taller body around her lover. It was a long night, as they slept fitfully, each concerned more for the other's safety.

Two days later, they came to a dead end. The passage now was very narrow and low and they had to travel bent over, wading through the water. The underground river was only three feet wide at this point and about the same in depth. The river disappeared under a low lip and there was no indication how far it traveled beyond that point.

"We'll go back," said Jess grimly, "and I'll try to clear the tunnel back into the main chamber." She looked at Mary, who was shaking with cold and soaked to the skin. She was pale and had lost weight. "I think we'll have enough fuel for the miner's lamp to get us back if we are careful. We'll find a way, Mary," she tried to reassure her partner.

The petite woman moved forward and wrapped her arms around Jess, holding her tight. She could feel her lover's ribs more sharply now and feel the slight shiver from the cold that had even chilled Jess' warm body. "I love you," she said, having nothing else to say to raise their hopes.

"I love you too," responded the taller woman, hugging her close. Slowly, they slogged back through the water, their backs brushing against the rough rock ceiling in places. For Mary, almost a foot shorter, it was easier going, but she worried about Jess.

Finally, exhausted and cold, they drank some lukewarm tea and ate the last of the biscuits before curling together in sleep. It was some time later when the sound of bats startled Jess awake. She carefully untangled herself from Mary and lit the miner's lamp. Thousands of bats flew past in a steady stream. "Mary! Mary! Come on, wake up!" yelled Jess, the bats now reacting to their movements with high pitched squeals.

"Wha... Oh God!" Mary yelled, burying her head into Jess' chest.

"Come on, we're going to follow these bats to the way out!" Jess explained, pulling on Mary to get her to her feet. Quivering with fear and loathing, Mary followed Jess as she edged along the cave beside the shadowy swirl of bats. Occasionally, one bumped into them and Mary bit her lip to stop from screaming. Jess tried as much as possible to protect Mary from the leathery wings. She gritted her teeth, hating the close proximity to the bats as much as Mary did. The bats disappeared through a narrow crevice in the rocks that appeared to be little more than a shadow.

The two women followed, wedging through the rocks as bats collided against them. Once through, they found themselves in a chimney of rock. High above was the night sky. Exhausted, emotionally drained and suddenly relieved after being trapped underground for days, they sat on the muddy ground and Mary sobbed in Jess' arms. "Hey, it's all right. I gotcha," Jess whispered, gently rubbing Mary's back.

Chapter Fifteen

The sun was well up when Jess woke to the smell of fresh, earthy air. She blinked in the intense light even though they sat in the shade cast by the massive rocks around them. Looking down at the light bundle wrapped in her arms, she realized how much Mary had been put through.

Green eyes blinked open and for a split second, blue sky was reflected in them. Then they scrunched closed. "Hey, we made it, didn't we, Jess!" Mary giggled weakly.

"Yup," agreed the taller woman, giving her lover a hug. "All we gotta do is get to the top."

Mary sighed and sat up, looking around her, shielding her eyes with her hand. They were in a deep, narrow chasm that rose about thirty feet above them. They sat on a muddy floor some four feet in diameter. "Any ideas?" she asked.

"I'll climb up and go and get help to get you out," said Jess.

Mary looked up at her exhausted partner. She was beautiful even with dirty, ragged hair and a muddy face. "You got any better ideas?" she asked, looking stern and raising her eyebrows.

Jess smiled and kissed her head. "Sorry love, I think it is the only way."

Mary nodded and smiled bravely back. "How is your back?" she asked.

"S'okay," the warrior responded, looking away.

Mary laughed and got up awkwardly, offering her hand to the older woman and watching her get up stiffly with the assistance. "Vizirakis, you lie like a rug!" she stated, shaking her head.

Jess blushed through the mud, "Well, it's going to hurt anyway by the time I get to the top," muttered the embarrassed warrior.

Mary gave her a final hug. "Be careful!" she ordered and Jess nodded as she put her back to one rocky wall and braced her feet against the other. Slowly, she worked her way upwards. Mary watched her go and marveled at Jess' fortitude and strength. At the top, Jess placed her hands on the surface, gave a mighty push and shoved with her feet. Mary saw her friend disappear over the top, only her feet now hanging over the edge. The feet disappeared and a head reappeared.

"Mary, I think I can get you up with a vine. Stay there!" The head disappeared.

Hands on her hips, Mary shook her head as she looked up at the inviting blue sky, "So where do you think I'm going to go, Vizirakis?" she sighed. Long minutes later, a stiff vine started to wiggle its way down the side of the rock chimney. The head popped up again. "Tie it really tight around you, Mary, and I'll pull you up," instructed the warrior.

Mary didn't argue. She made a loop and tied it off twice then slipped it over her head and around her shoulders. "Okay," she yelled to her invisible friend and slowly she was yanked to the surface.

Jess sat in the coarse grass, her feet braced firmly in the dirt. Her biceps bulged as she pulled up the vine hand over hand until Mary's golden head appeared at the rim. Then she leaned forward and with one arm pulled her friend up to safety. Mary collapsed beside Jess in the grass and let the warm tropical sun, now almost directly overhead, beat down on her. "This feels wonderful!" she exclaimed and Jess, sitting quietly beside her, smiled.

This must be love. The petite woman lying beside her was streaked in mud and bat dirt and yet she was the most desirable being that Jess had ever seen. She stretched out, propping herself up on one elbow, and leaned forward to kiss Mary softly on the lips.

"Hmm," responded the blond, teasing Jess' lower lip with her teeth. "My hero. My warrior. My love," the journalist whispered and Jess became aware only of the sensation of hot sun on her back, a fresh breeze and the intoxicating scent of the woman under her. It took all her self control to eventually pull away and sit up to survey their situation.

"We've traveled north. The clinic is on the other side of that ridge," she observed, pointing down the valley. We're about ten-twelve miles away."

Mary groaned. "That's a long walk back."

"We're not going back. I probably killed a few of them with the dynamite and you can be sure that if I wasn't before, I'm sure top of the list for payback now. We gotta get out of here."

Mary sat up, alert now. "Where should we go?" she asked, looking at the tall, dark woman beside her with worry.

278

"The mission station. It's about fifty miles west of here. Four day walk, if the terrain isn't too rough. First, let's get cleaned up and steal some food. Then we'll head out. We want to avoid human contact as much as possible."

Sometime later, they sat naked in a clear, cold stream, rubbing the filth off their bodies while their clothes dried a bit in the afternoon sun. "Jess?"

"Mmm?"

"If I wasn't with you, would you be going to the mission?"

"Why did you ask that?" asked the older woman, getting up and offering her hand to her lover. Mary accepted the lift up and the quiet support to get over the slippery rocks to the shore.

"Why haven't you answered me?" countered Mary as the two of them shook as much water as they could off their bodies and then put the uncomfortably damp clothes on over their still wet skin.

"If you weren't with me, I'd go after Mone," Jess answered with aggression roughing her voice.

Mary looked at the warrior she loved, searching the ice blue eyes that could turn so viciously cold when she focused on strategy and yet could soften to the colour of a blue summer sky when she reached out to touch her. She nodded. "Then we forget the mission and go after Mone."

"No!" snapped Jess angrily, the eyes flashing white fire.

"Yes!" responded the fiery strawberry blond.

"No," stated Jess, sitting down to lace a boot on.

Mary looked down at Jess, who was pretending not to notice her. "Are we partners?" The hands lacing the boot froze and then finished their task slowly while Jess thought.

"Yes, we're partners. But this isn't everyday stuff, Mary. This is combat," the warrior explained, getting to her feet and looking down into the serious green eyes.

"All the more reason for me to be there," concluded Mary. "You think he is alive then?"

"Maybe. It's hard to say," responded Jess, realizing that a decision had somehow been made without her knowledge. *Damn. I'm henpecked*, she thought in amazement!

"Can we capture him?" asked Mary, moving closer to reassure her warrior. She could see the look of uneasy bewilderment in Jess' eyes.

"That would be best. Listen, Mary..." A delicate finger touched her lips and Mary moved closer, wrapping her other arm around Jess' waist.

"I will do everything you say. I just need to be with you," Mary pleaded, even though she knew she had already won. Mary understood there were boundaries in Jess' ego that could not be crossed, at least not openly! She felt the stiff body relax and Jess wrapped her close in her arms. *Gotcha, warrior*, she thought.

Jess sighed. The woman played her like a trout on a line and somehow, she didn't care a bit! *This has got to be love!* She sighed and kissed the wet, sweet hair. "I'll hold you to that promise, Giovani, so you had better be good!" she growled. Then, sizing up the distances and her options, she went on, "We need to get a few things before we head off." Mary nodded. There was a time to stand up and have your way and there was a time to go along meekly.

* * * * *

"Pardon me! Excuse me."

The village woman looked up from tending her garden to see the small blond standing between the mounds of sweet potatoes. She leaned on her digging stick and scratched a spot under her drooping left breast, smiling broadly at the European with the hair like sun. Then an unbelievably strong arm wrapped around her throat, a sudden pain and she knew no more.

Jess caught the slumping body and dragged the village woman into the tall grasses. "She'll be okay, won't she?" asked Mary.

Jess nodded, focused completely on the mission now. "The choke cut off the jugular vein, stopping the blood from reaching the brain. She'll have a headache when she comes around but that's about it. Come on, we haven't got long."

Jess picked up the woman's belem of sweet potatoes and Mary her paddle shaped digging stick that was also used for fighting and they headed over to the hut. Jess had already ascertained, from an earlier scouting, that no one else was near. She took out the wood slats that barricaded the low door and disappeared inside while Mary stood waiting, scanning the area for any sign of people. In a few minutes, Jess returned with a stonework axe and a coil of rope. "Let's go," she muttered and Mary lumbered along behind, trying not to slow Jess down.

Jess didn't go far. She stopped by some banana trees that grew near the hut and snapped off a ripening bunch. Then she moved on a little farther and used the axe to cut some lengths of sugar cane. "Here, this will have to hold you until later, I'm afraid," she said. They hadn't had anything but water since the tea and biscuits the night before.

Mary used her teeth to strip off the hard outer bark and then bit off a piece of the fibrous pith. The warm, sweet sap trickled down her throat as she chewed. When she could get no more from the pulp, she spat it out and then bit off another chunk. Jess did the same as they walked along, keeping to the ravines, high grasses and shadows as much as possible.

That night, Jess caught fish in the river, much to Mary's delight. The fish would make a super meal but more than that, the activity brought back happy memories of when they were young. They shared some of those memories as they ate bass and roasted sweet potato and then chewed the remainder of their sugar cane. Then, exhausted, they curled up in a small hollow and went to sleep. When the moon rose, Jess eased away from her lover and stood. In the moonlight, she cast a dark shadow and her eyes were the colour of ice-cold steel. Once away from their camp, she broke into an easy run.

Mary woke to the sunlight and the wonderful feel of her lover still wrapped behind her. She blinked, trying to clear the fog from her thoughts. It wasn't like Jess to sleep late. She hoped that she wasn't sick! Then her eyes fell on a large belem filled with items including fresh clothes. She spun around and met serious blue eyes. "Jess!" she sighed.

The eyes filled with laughter. "We needed a few more things, so I just ran back to the clinic and got them."

"Was Mone there?" asked Mary, her voice filled with apprehension.

Jess shook her head, "No, the place is deserted. I was actually surprised that none of the stores have been rifled yet. It's an awful tempting target."

Jess built up the fire and made instant coffee from the stores she had brought. They ate bananas for breakfast, then headed off again. "Do you know where we are going?" asked Mary as she limped along uncomplaining.

"I've a pretty good idea," stated Jess, offering her hand to help Mary over a log bridge. "I think they are probably up on that peak," she said, stopping to point out a high, craggy outcropping. "There is a dream house up there. It is very old and very sacred."

"Why there? Because of its religious value?" asked Mary, resettling her load of the supplies in a more comfortable position on her back.

"That and there are caves associated with the site where a secret society could meet. Also there is a legend that it was on that peak that the older brother discovered the secret of the magic," explained Jess.

It took them two days to walk to the peak and another to slowly climb to the top. This had to be done at night to avoid detection. The moon was waning, making the night dark and hazardous. Mary, struggling over the rough ground with her uneven gait, fell a number of times, adding to the number of cuts and bruises she already had. Jess had brought back some basic medicines and had carefully cleaned every cut and given Mary a shot against infection. Mary found Jess' grumpy attention adorable in the extreme.

Jess was very over-protective and caring and tried her best to cover her soft heart with a protective layer of indifference. Mary was never offended by Jess' ways. She knew how hard the woman was struggling to make their relationship work, even though she had little experience in making an emotional commitment. When Jess growled "Giovani!" her eyes lit up with love and Mary's heart melted. *God! My warrior has a sexy growl!*

"Giovani," Jess whispered. "Are we sneaking up on the enemy here or are we just going to announce our arrival by knocking boulders down the mountain side? You all right?"

"It was a pebble. I slipped and yes, I'm okay," responded Mary, allowing Jess to take her hand and pull her up on a rocky ledge.

"You stay here while I scout ahead. I'll be back in a minute," instructed Jess.

Mary opened her mouth to protest but stopped when she saw Jess raise an eyebrow. "Okay," she said meekly. The eyebrow rose a bit higher and Mary smiled innocently. Jess snorted softly and leaned forward to drop a kiss on Mary's cheek before heading off.

Mary looked around for a place to sit and found none. For a while she stood and looked out into the night. Then she started to explore about a bit. Hearing a noise, she moved along the ledge and looked around an outcropping of rock. Silhouetted against the star lit sky was a warrior moving slowly over the uneven terrain towards where she stood. She gasped, pulled back and turned to see Mone now standing on the path. "Mone!" she said nervously, trying to regroup. "Jess just stepped around the corner," she lied, pointing behind her.

Mone smiled and raised his ceremonial axe over his head, ready to strike. Instead, an arm wrapped around his neck and with a gasp, he dropped to the ground.

"Am I glad... ugh!" grunted Mary as Jess pushed her aside and met the warrior who had come running around the corner. Jess was off balance from pushing Mary out of the way and the warrior used the opportunity to slam Jess against the rock face. Blood dripped down

Jess' face from a gash over her eye as she groggily tried to fend off the attacker.

The next instant, there was a dull thud and the man who had held her in an iron grip slumped forward onto her. Jess pushed him off in disgust and he slid to the ground. Looking up, she saw Mary standing there, shaking with rage and brandishing her fighting stick.

Jess smiled and tilted her head in question and Mary looked suddenly embarrassed. "No one, picks on my woman!" she protested and Jess laughed as Mary flew into her arms. They tied the prisoners up and Jess explained that she had met one guard and then returned to take out Mone and the other guard. They seemed to have caught them unawares. No doubt they had felt safe, believing that Jess and Mary had drowned in the underground lake.

"What about the other followers?" asked Mary as she dabbed at Jess' eyebrow, trying to stop the bleeding and disinfect the area.

"I think they'll be no problem, if we can convince Quen to take a stand against this cargo cult movement."

"Can we do that?" asked Mary, stopping her ministrations to meet Jess' eyes.

Jess shrugged, "If we can't, we're probably looking forward to a shallow grave. Maybe you should walk out to the mission while I handle this."

"Vizirakis, don't even go there!" responded Mary determinedly. Jess sighed in defeat.

* * * * *

They walked down the mountain the next morning, their three prisoners tied in a line on the rope.

Drums soon started echoing along the valley with the cry of voices. "What's going on?" asked Mary nervously.

"The long, narrow valleys have great acoustics. The village headmen are calling out messages that bounce down the valley from one village to the next and then are passed on again. They are saying that we have captured Mone and that we are heading to Quen's village."

"Did they happen to say how they feel about that?" asked Mary, instinctively moving closer to the woman she loved and keeping her new weapon at the ready.

Jess shrugged. "Well, we are still alive!"

A large crowd of angry villagers met them in the singsing ground, brandishing axes and spears. Quen stood quietly waiting. Jess walked forward and handed him the rope. For a long while, they talked to one another in Pidgin. At one point, Quen yelled at Jess and the crowd responded by raising their weapons at her and giving war whoops. Mary moved forward, fighting stick up.

"Will you keep that temper of yours in check, Giovani!" muttered Jess, grabbing the fighting stick and wrapping a protective arm around her champion.

"Hey, they were threatening you!" grumbled Mary, pulling free and giving the crowd a dirty look.

"How would you know!" grumbled Jess, refusing to let go of Mary's weapon. Suddenly, Quen snarled something and laughed. The crowd, after a moment's hesitation, followed suit. Jess went beet red and stiffened.

Uh oh, thought Mary, Jess was mad! Quen yelled some orders and several warriors stepped out of the crowd and led the prisoners away. Then Quen deliberately turned his back on Jess and walked away, while the crowd laughed and pointed at the two women.

Jess glared down at Mary with a positively murderous look. Then, her mouth tight with rage, she turned on her heel and walked off. Mary followed in an awkward hop-run. "What did I do?" she asked in frustration.

Jess spun on her. "You... took... my... face!" she spit out, hands on hips.

"Oh boy," whispered Mary in a small voice and, biting her lip, she asked nervously, "Are you really mad?"

"Yes!" snapped Jess and then, seeing the look of worry on her lover's face, relented a bit with a sigh. "Giovani, come here," she ordered. Mary moved closer and Jess grabbed her up and threw her over her shoulder.

"Hey!" yelled Mary and then "Ouch!" as Jess' hand came down firmly on her backside three times. An iiiiiieeeee rose from the crowd as they laughed and pointed at the two women and shook their hands back and forth. Jess moved off with long strides, Mary still firmly over her shoulder.

"Hey, what was that for!?" grumbled Mary. "Let me down!"

"You probably saved our hides, Giovani, you know that?" revealed Jess, as she walked along with her human cargo still over her shoulder.

"I did?" exclaimed Mary in surprise, bouncing along upside down.

"Yeah, Quen had just threatened to kill me as the evil spirit of the older brother when you stepped in and started henpecking me," Jess grumbled.

"I wasn't...."

"Shut up, Giovani. Then Quen laughed and said he'd made a mistake, that anyone as weak as I was from a love charm couldn't have the spirit of a great warrior inside them! He said Mone must have been wrong."

"Oh boy." Silence. "You'd probably have preferred to die, right?" Mary asked nervously.

"Just about," responded Jess, walking on steadily.

"Jess?"

"Hmm?"

"I'm sorry."

"I know," Jess responded softly, stopping and lowering Mary to the ground. She looked into those soft green eyes framed by a blowing curtain of golden hair. "Tell me, is my whole life with you going to be like this?"

Mary smiled challengingly. "Most of the time, I'll let you be the warrior, I promise." Jess laughed and bent to kiss the woman that she loved.

* * * * *

Jess lay in the sun looking up at the blue sky and listening to the two waterfalls. Mary lay asleep beside her, naked and contented. Jess smiled. She had a friend, Jo, back in Australia that she used to go spelunking with when she was in medical school. Jo, she knew, had a large ranch in New South Wales. Maybe, if she contacted her, she would know of a place that might be for sale...

Egyptian

Encounter

Warning: The introduction to this story is based on the events of November 1997 at Deir el-Bahari, Egypt where fifty-eight Egyptians and tourists were murdered in a violent terrorist attack. Some readers might find the introduction disturbing and might wish to skip over it.

Introduction:

They had fought that morning. Their first real fight. There had been tiffs before but not a real fight. This had been a fight. In the end, Cheops Malone had taken the day off from her Dig and taken the two children, against Wilhelminia Kyrtsakis's wishes, to visit Queen Hatshepsut's cliff temple. Major Kyrtsakis had stormed off to see to her duties.

It was barely eight o'clock when they started out from the Valley of the Kings where Cheops was working and headed up the famous Agatha Christie trail that would take them over the ridge that separated the Valley of the Kings from the Valley of the Queens. It was warm already, the winter months of cool now giving way to the coming summer heat. Cheops took her sunglasses out of her pocket and slipped them on.

As they walked up the barren ridge, Cheops told the two children about how Agatha Christie had written many well-known murder mysteries. Her husband had been an important archaeologist and so Christie had used the setting of the Valley of the Kings for one of her novels. In the novel, Hercule Poirot had walked over this path with some other characters to visit the Valley of the Queens. Since the publishing of the book, the path had always been called after the author who had made it famous.

Cheops' daughter laughed and asked a million questions along the way about the author and the novel, her strawberry blond hair golden in the sunlight. Quietly, Willy's son walked on ahead. He never said much but Cheops knew that he took everything in. He was handsome and dark like his mom and like her too, he moved with a graceful assurance and controlled strength.

From the top of the ridge, they could look down on the famous cliff temple. Its three long stories were perfectly balanced and orderly and joined by a wide ramp of stairs. As they carefully walked down the steep, winding trail, Cheops told them how King Thutmose the Third had probably been responsible for the Queen's death. He had hated her because she had stolen his leadership from him when he was too young to rule and had refused to give it back.

On her death or murder, he had ordered that every name, statue and painting with her likeness as a pharaoh be destroyed. Not satisfied with killing her in the real world, he was determined to destroy her eternal life too. Cheops' daughter shuddered and took her mother's hand. Willy's son nodded, appreciating the need to demoralize the supporters of an enemy.

That was why they had argued that morning. Cheops had suggested that Willy reconsider sending her son back to boarding school in Britain where he was being carefully schooled for entry into Sandhurst when he was old enough. She felt the boy would be happier if he could have a normal childhood. It was the word 'normal' that had set Willy off. She had taken it as an attack against her profession, which in a way it was.

"I might not be 'normal' in your snobby little academic world but it's my kind that are going to be on the front line protecting this world not yours. You want to talk about meaningless existence, what about digging in the dirt for bodies dead a thousand years!"

"Four thousand, and would you stop yelling insults! Damn it, Willy, can't we have a disagreement without you having to win at all costs?"

Cheops shook her head to get rid of the echoes of the morning fight as she led the children up the stairs and into the temple to show them the amazing frescoes that still remained so clearly on the walls. She chewed on her lip in thought as they went. As soon as they got back, she was going to phone Willy and apologize. She had no right to tell her how to raise her son, no matter how close they had become over the winter.

Willy pulled to the side of the tarmac road. The black strip of highway wound its way across the rock desert to the ferry that would carry her jeep across the Nile to the city of Luxor. She had a busy day today. Plans for the security of an up coming visit by high British government officials were almost in place. At a time when terrorism was on the rise, nothing could be taken for granted. As a security officer with special services, it was her job to make sure the visit was a safe one.

She sighed and turned the jeep around. Fortunately, Egyptians understood the concept of time over the ages and not according to daily planners. She would take the next ferry and be late and still, no doubt, show up too early for the meeting with the Minister of Security. She needed to go back and apologize to Cheops. She had said some really stupid things.

* * * * *

They were in the inner rooms of the temple surrounded by a group of German tourists and a handful of Egyptians when the attack came. Cheops remembered that at the first shots and screams, she had looked back and been relieved to see several tourist police at the entrance. Then they had lifted guns and opened fire again. There was no escape.

The bullet shattered a rib as it went through her and another shattered her wrist bone as she went down. Instinctively, she rolled to put the children under her, unaware as yet that both were already dead. The gunfire stopped but the screams grew more frantic. She looked up to see that the killers were now walking among the bodies using machetes to slash at faces and disembowel the living. She curled around the children and prayed that they would survive.

* * * * *

Inge met Major Kyrtsakis at the entrance to tomb KV-5, pleased that Cheops had left her in charge of the Dig while she took the morning off to be with the children. "I'm sorry Major, Cheops has already left. They took the Christie trail about... That's gunfire! Quick!" Inge yelled to the workers that were out in the open. "Get inside the tomb!" Concerned with the protection of her crew, she was only vaguely aware of the Major taking off up the dry valley, her powerful, long legs eating up the distance as she ran along the trail.

Inge stood at the entrance watching in worry. Tourist buses continued to arrive but now the guides were getting messages on their phones that terrorists dressed as police were killing people at Deir el-Bahari. She wished her Egyptian were as fluent as Cheops', who had spent her childhood summers in Egypt with parents who had been archaeologists themselves.

From the little she could understand, she realized that the situation on the other side of the ridge must be bad. For a while, the firing had stopped but screams could still be heard. Then the firing started again and rumors spread that the terrorists were heading to the Valley of the Kings. No one came. After awhile, the gunshots and screams stopped and silence filled the gulf. The tourist buses unloaded.

An extra squad of police showed up and Inge ordered the crew to return to their work.

Ishmael, Cheops' Egyptian foreman, came to stand by Inge. "Those bloody terrorists," he moaned, tears rolling down his face, "they have cut the legs out from under my children. How will they feed their families if the tourists go away?"

"Cheops was over there with the children. I can't leave the Dig. Cheops would be furious if anything was taken and she has the key, so I couldn't lock the gate. I don't want to put you in danger, Ishmael, but we have to know if Cheops is safe. Will you go find her?" Inge asked, her voice cracking with worry.

Ishmael wiped his face immediately. "I go," he said, already heading off.

"Be careful!" warned Inge, wishing that she could leave her responsibilities and go and search for Cheops too.

Willy met one of the last of the terrorists on the trail as she came over the ridge. An Egyptian worker had held him by his leg and that had slowed his escape until he had shot the man in the hip. Willy slowed him too, with a right hook that sent him tumbling down the hill towards a group of Egyptian workers who kicked at him in their fury until he was dead. Willy charged through, across the open courts and up the stairs, calling Cheops' name.

A tourist guard tried to stop her but she pushed him aside and ran into the temple, slipping on the gore and blood that coated the floor like a blanket. She looked around in a panic. *Please no, don't let them be here*, she prayed and then felt her heart stop as she saw Cheops' body lying in a growing pool of blood. Her lower right leg had been hacked nearly off and the shattered end of white bone hung out of the bloody stump. Willy groaned in dismay and whipped off her military belt as she hop scotched over the dead to get to the woman she loved.

Quickly, she wrapped the belt tightly around the leg below the knee. Then she stripped off her shirt to bandage the severed foot tightly to the stump. She fought to keep her stomach down and her hands from shaking in fear. It was then that she saw her son's arm sticking out.

Gently, she lifted Cheops clear. The two children were curled together. Her son had wrapped himself around the little girl to protect her. Their innocent beauty was marred by the look of horror frozen on their faces. Willy sat in the blood and held her son to her as her world closed in around.

Two Years Later: Turkey

Gunnul stretched out her long legs, deliberately capturing Jamie's small feet between her own. Her soulmate looked up from her side of their large partner's desk and smiled. "I love you, Jamie," Gunnul said in the serious way that she had when she felt something very deeply and was having trouble finding the words to express her emotions.

Jamie smiled. "I love you too," she responded. Once she had replied, I love you more, much to Gunnul's confusion. Gunnul's English was excellent but sometimes meaning was lost in translation or in the interpretation by the Turk's very linear mind. Believing that Jamie did not think that she loved her enough, poor Gunnul had been devastated! It took some explaining and an evening of love making to reassure Gunnul that all was well in their relationship!

"Next week, you will have made your home with me for one year, Jamie," Gunnul observed, rubbing her leg along Jamie's. "I think that it would be good if we took a second honeymoon."

Jamie reached over in delight and captured Gunnul's long, strong hand, "That would be wonderful! But Gunnul, we can't go to Disney World without Chrissy, she would never speak to us again!" Gunnul's eyes widened in surprise and Jamie laughed delightedly. "I saw the travel guides in your briefcase when I was looking for the monthly reports," she explained.

Gunnul's eyebrow went up in mock annoyance. "Then we will..."

"Mommies! Mommies!" called a frantic voice as a pretty young girl ran into the den through the open French doors that led to the terrace.

Gunnul was on her knees beside their daughter in a split second with Jamie only a few steps behind. "What is it?" Gunnul asked worriedly.

"You must come quick!" explained Chrissy, looking back and forth between her two mothers. "The secret tomb in the garden is falling apart!"

"Jamie, bring Chrissy!" ordered Gunnul as she sprinted away. Chrissy and her mother followed as quickly as they could with Jamie's crippled leg. Gunnul's long legs and powerful stride got her to the tomb several minutes ahead of them.

She stood in shock, looking down at the tomb that sat in a tangle of wild garden behind a tall, wrought-iron fence. Jamie and Chrissy came up to stand at her side. The stone lid of the tomb snapped softly as they watched and another hairline crack formed. The once beautiful lid of ancient Greek patterns could barely be seen now through the crumbling stone.

"What does it mean?" asked Jamie, reaching out to touch the tomb. Gunnul stopped her hand.

"I don't know," murmured the taller woman.

"They are unhappy. They no longer speak to each other," Chrissy said, tears rolling down her face.

Jamie wrapped her arms around her daughter. "Is it the ancient ones you sense, Chrissy?" she asked.

The miserable child nodded. "Yes, the ancient ones and the ones that live close to us," explained the serious child. Gunnul and Jamie exchanged looks.

"Where do they live, Chrissy? Do you know?" asked Jamie, gently stroking her daughter's hair.

Chrissy shook her head. "No, but somewhere hot and dry like Turkey. You won't leave us, will you, mom?" Chrissy wailed, grabbing Jamie tightly. Gunnul's eyes darkened with the fear that was still fed by her insecurity.

Jamie wrapped one arm around their daughter and reached out with the other to take Gunnul's hand. "No, no matter what happens the three of us will always be a family," she stated confidently. "And we'll send all the love that is inside us, shall we, to help the ancient ones find their way too?"

Egypt

It was late when the plane from London touched down in Cairo. Willy hung back until most of the five hundred passengers had left in a swarm to wait in an equally large swarm to get their luggage. Willy had only a carry on. Years in the military had taught her to travel light. She walked down the dusty green hallway and stood on the yellow line painted on the floor, waiting for the guard in the ill-fitting wool uniform to indicate that she could move forward. The passport stamping was little more than a formality. Egypt was eager to welcome any tourist these days. Since the "incident", tourism had dropped from three million visitors a year to one. Willy knew this. Willy had researched very carefully over the last few months in hospital.

She picked up her passport and walked across the airport lobby. At this hour, the few tourist shops were closed. "Taxi, lady?" came the bleat of the drivers, who stood in a knot near the entrance. "You speak American? German? Taxi, lady?" Willy moved past them and stepped out into the warm night. The airport sat in sand, built beyond the boundaries of the fertile, green strip that hugged the banks of the Nile River.

Willy crossed the road and looked down into the parking lot situated in a depression. She pointed to the old limo that she thought looked the most roadworthy and a driver kicked off from the side of another vehicle where he had been smoking with a few others. Willy walked down the cement stairs to the lot and over to the limo where the driver waited. "Giza, the Mena House," she commanded. The driver nodded and opened the door for the strange, tall woman. She looked like she had been sick for a very long time.

It had been a long trip, across Cairo, over one of the many bridges that cross the Nile and on to Giza. Willy leaned back into the worn leather seat that smelled of heat and dust and tried to control the shaking in her hands. She felt strangely detached and she knew that her speech was slightly slurred. The effects of the drugs still came out when she was over tired. She would have to be careful at the hotel. The taxi turned left, passed the guard at the gate, and entered the hotel grounds. The Mena House was a sprawling hotel, extended year after year as the tourist trade mushroomed. The oldest section had been built in the 1800s for the Victorians who had come to steal the local heritage.

She had learned that from Cheops, she remembered, as she paid the driver and allowed the footman to take her overnight bag. She followed, a little unsteady on her feet. Booking in took some time as the Egyptians seemed to love paperwork and Willy needed to write slowly and carefully. With relief, she finally walked out of the main building and crossed through the garden oasis to the west wing. One flight up, turn right, third door, then double check the number before slipping in the room card and opening the door. There could be no mistakes.

Out of habit, she smelt for body odor, listened for breathing, checked for movement or shadows. Then she turned and locked the door before she went to the window and balcony door and made sure they were secure. Her bag was already sitting on the luggage rack, her bed was turned down and on the T.V. the in-house computer service had left a message of welcome. Willy flicked the T.V. off, stripped down, and fell into bed. The drugs were playing hell with her over-tired system tonight and every joint ached.

Cheops woke slowly, her alarm set to ring at intervals, raising her step by sleepy step to consciousness. This was always the worst time - when she lay alone in her bed in the morning and the house was still and quiet. She sighed, pushed herself to a sitting position and swung her legs over the side of the bed. The one leg had no foot or ankle, just a stump.

She covered it quickly with her prosthesis and went about the morning rituals of facing another day. The next two weeks were going to be difficult. She was leading a tour. "The Archaeological Tour of the Nile #2", to be precise. She had done so now for a good many years. It helped to pay the bills. Shortage of funds was a way of life for field archaeologists. It was the problem of adequate funding that was on Cheops' mind as she dressed and prepared a traditional Middle East breakfast of pita bread, goat cheese, and black olives. Popping a sweet date into her mouth to finish off her breakfast, she picked up her Tilley hat and sunglasses and stepped out of her mud brick house to face another day. The house was in Giza and had originally belonged to her parents. It was a humble village home, but it had a number of wonderful advantages. First, it was less than an hour's drive from downtown Cairo and second, from her backyard she could see the great pyramid of Cheops, also called Khufu, towering over the desert.

Her parents had done their field research at the gravesites of lower officials that rest in the shadow of the great pyramid. The great pyramid towered 482 feet into the sky and was the largest single human structure ever built. Cheops had been named after it. After her parents had died, she had kept the small mud house. When she wasn't living in her apartment in Luxor or lecturing at Leeds University back in England, she would stay here.

With a sigh, she popped her Tilley hat on and stepped outside to face another day. She picked up the dusty path that cut behind the main streets and headed across the stony desert towards the Mena House. She knew that the tour bus would already be waiting there. It was early yet, the sun barely over the horizon. She thought she might walk around the hotel's green, tropical gardens before she went to the main lobby to gather up her bewildered tourists for their two-week glimpse of five thousand years of history.

Willy saw her first and bent over with the force of emotions that washed through her, settling as a gut eating mass in her stomach. She stepped back into the shadows and watched as Cheops came down the stairs with a pronounced limp and walked slowly around the pale blue pool and tropical gardens. *She is just as beautiful as I remember*, Willy thought. *Her leg must not have healed properly.* It didn't matter; she would be dead soon.

Chapter One

Cheops was enjoying the lush green of the oasis garden when suddenly a tall shadow loomed in front of her. With a gasp she stepped back, then felt the blood drain from her face as she saw Willy standing in front of her.

"Hello, Cheops," Willy said quietly.

Cheops recognized the dangerous tone and checked her movement forward to touch the taller woman. Willy looked terrible. Gaunt and pale. Cheops looked around quickly for a way to escape. A footman and gardener were on the terrace above them. If she had to, she could call to them. No. She would be dead before she could get a word from her lips. She could see the look of hate in the ice-cold eyes and she knew she was facing death.

"Hello, Willy," Cheops forced out between tight lips. "I never thought I'd see you again."

The tall woman nodded and Cheops waited for what would happen next.

"I'm on the tour," Willy revealed.

Cheops head shot up. "What? What sort of crap are you up to, Kyrtsakis? You and I both know you don't give a damn about archaeology! What kind of game is this?"

Willy's face was cut stone. "I'm going to kill you, Cheops, like you killed my son by taking him with you, when I had told you not to. But not right away, no. No, I want you to feel it coming. I want you to die with the same look of horror frozen on your face as my son."

"So, I'm to be afraid? Of what? I watched OUR children murdered. Was left to die by the woman I loved. It was weeks before I even knew where my daughter was buried. And you want me to fear a little thing like death? Well, I don't. Kill me whenever you feel like it, Kyrtsakis. I don't give a damn." Cheops turned and walked back down the path. She could feel those cold eyes following as she took the stairs again in an uneven gait.

Willy waited until she was out of sight and then followed the same path. In the lobby of the hotel, she stood in a far corner watching Cheops greet her group. A slight tremor in the hand but the face was smiling and the voice clear, warm and pleasant. *You're good, Cheops, really good. But then I fell in love with you because of your bravery that first day.*

It had been the end of summer and the heat had beat down in sweltering waves. Dust hazed the air and streaked faces as sweat trickled down from saturated hat rims. Major Kyrtsakis had walked down the market street to pick up some fruit to take back to the hotel. She had lingered, enjoying the banter, smells and exotic culture. She hated shopping but somehow these open area markets always gave her a sense of peace.

The commotion ahead had exploded in loud voices onto the market scene. Instinctively, Kyrtsakis had moved forward. There an angry woman with short, strawberry blond hair was screaming, in Egyptian, at a man whom she had pinned to the ground with a broom handle.

As she stood with a grin, her arms crossed, watching, Kyrtsakis could make out that the man in question had tried to steal the lady's satchel with disastrous results. The market people seemed to know the woman and were supporting her side with much laughter. Then out the corner of her eye, Willy saw the knife. She hurled herself at the woman, sending them both flying. The knife caught the skin of Willy's arm before it buried itself in a wood door.

The crowd surged forward in concern, yelling for the police and offering help. In the confusion, the thief slipped away, no doubt to meet his accomplice, the knife thrower, at some planned location.

"Wow! That was close! Thanks!" smiled the petite woman, getting up on her knees. "I'm Cheops Malone."

Willy smiled back. "Major Wilhelminia Kyrtsakis," she responded, holding out her own hand. The small hand she grasped was surprisingly strong.

"Hey! You've been hurt!" Cheops exclaimed, seeing for the first time the blood running down Willy's arm.

Willy got to her feet, pulling Cheops up as she did. "It's okay. I'll see to it back at the hotel," she murmured, smiling as she turned to walk off.

"No! My house is not far from here. Let me clean it properly and give you a tetanus shot," Cheops had argued. And perhaps because of the heat, and her loneliness for her son, who was still back in school in England, she had agreed.

They had walked a few blocks to the outskirts of Giza and entered a small mud brick home. Inside, the walls were plastered and painted with scenes from ancient Egypt. The furniture was wood, plain and practical. Along the walls were sofas piled with cushions and rugs in the eastern style. Willy sat at the table and Cheops had cleaned her arm, disinfected and bandaged it and had then given her a shot. She had stayed for dinner, met Cheops' daughter and never really left, at least not until the 'incident'.

Willy let the memories fade and checked out with professional interest the people who would be on the tour. There were only a few. There was a New York couple with the loud, flat accent that stereotyped them, and a new-age couple carrying their reference book and looking intense. They were from Salt Lake. Lastly, there was an older man traveling with a rather bored looking son. Cheops was handing out information packages and nametags. With one left, she came over and handed it to Willy.

"I need to talk to you," she said, a worried frown on her face. "I'll see you later."

Willy's face did not show the surprise she was feeling. She merely nodded and watched as Cheops sighed and turned to walk back to the others. "Okay, ladies and gentlemen, let's board our minibus to go to the Cairo museum." Cheops smiled happily and led the group forward. Willy followed a few steps behind.

On the drive from Giza back to Cairo, Cheops talked about the history of Egypt, explaining that there had been three major empires in its ancient history: the Early, Middle and Late Kingdoms. She then went on and talked about the Greek invasion under Alexander the Great, the Roman influence by Caesar and Anthony and in modern times the colonization by Britain and eventually the road to freedom under Nasser.

At the museum, she got the tickets and led everyone through the tight security, then let them go to see the exhibits on their own. As always, to Cheops' amusement, they made a beeline to the area where King Tut's artifacts were kept. As an archaeologist, she knew that there were far more significant pieces of ancient history stuck in the dusty corners of this famous museum than were found in Tut's tomb, but people loved gold and mystery, and Carter's dig had lots of both!

She turned to see Willy waiting. "I just wanted to say that I'm not going to be a willing victim. I don't want to die. But I'm not afraid to either, and I'm not afraid of you. But I am worried that you might hurt the tourist trade of Egypt when it can least afford any more bad publicity. All I'm asking is that if you should succeed in this mad revenge, do it in a way that won't reflect badly on Egypt."

"Agreed," Willy responded and Cheops nodded and, after a second, walked off. Willy's eyes followed her, admiration reflected in the cold blue.

Cheops walked past the book and souvenir counter then turned down a hall that she knew would take her to a small, open-air courtyard. It was a quiet oasis inside the famous museum, away from the crowds of tourists, where a person could think.

She could notify the police that she had been threatened, but with the extreme steps the government of Egypt was taking to protect tourists from more 'incidents' it would be unlikely that they would have the manpower to protect her from a trained killer such as Willy. That's if they believed her at all!

She could notify the R.A.F. that one of their officers had gone over the edge, but she wasn't sure that Willy was still attached to the military. It appeared, anyway, that she was here as a civilian. The military would not see it as their responsibility even if they took the claim of a threat seriously.

She did have a colleague at Leeds, Roger, whom she knew had worked with soldiers who had experienced war trauma. It might be a good idea to contact him for some advice.

But right now, there were only two ways out of this situation: either Willy was going to make good on her threat or Cheops was going to have to talk her out of it. The second scenario seemed the more appealing, Cheops concluded with a bitter smile. But how did you reason with a person as passionate and focused as Willy? And was she mentally stable? She looked and acted as if there was something very wrong. She'd noticed the other tourists looking at her in apprehension. There was a slight slur to her speech and a tremor to her hands and a stiffness in her movements that was unlike the woman she had fallen helplessly in love with.

She had put her exhausted daughter to bed that night with promises that Willy would be invited back soon. The stiff soldier had mellowed with the arrival of her daughter and the three of them had played soccer together in the desert behind the house. When she returned to the living room, she had offered Willy a Turkish coffee and they had talked late into the night, each enjoying the other's company and the heady sexual tension that lay beneath the subtle teasing and flattery.

She had been surprised to find Willy had a son, the product of a long and turbulent affair with a fellow officer that had ended with the soldier's death in the Gulf War. Cheops told Willy about her unhappy marriage to a college professor that had ended shortly after the birth of her daughter. He had not been interested in raising a family. Cheops had returned to her maiden name and was happily raising her child as a single mom.

When Willy was leaving, with a promise to return the next night, they had stood awkwardly for a moment. Willy had leaned down, hesitated for a second in case Cheops had wanted to step away, and captured the archaeologist's lips with her own. Cheops surrendered without a fight and welcomed the warrior into her heart.

She had thought that their love would endure forever. Soon after that first evening, Willy's son had arrived and the four of them had bonded into an apparently inseparable unit. Until the 'incident'. Then life had changed forever.

Cheops sat in thought in the small courtyard, enjoying the morning sun that was heating the desert air, forcing her mind away from Willy's threat and onto the itinerary for today. After the museum, they would return to Giza to see the pyramids there. Then there would be dinner that included a folk dancing show. She sighed; it was going to be a long day.

"I brought you some Turkish coffee," said a voice from beside her and Cheops jumped in surprise. She looked up to see Willy standing quietly, a small cup in each hand. The classically beautiful face was still, emotionless, revealing nothing.

Cheops reached up, taking hold of the small cup filled with the thick, syrupy coffee. Her fingers brushed against the warrior's and both women's eyes came up in surprise at the intensity of the touch. Eyes locked, then both looked away.

"I hated you, you know, for leaving me to die and for taking my daughter's body," Cheops' confessed.

"I didn't leave you to die," Willy snarled.

"It was Ishmael who found me and took care of me until medical aid arrived," stated Cheops, staring moodily into the dark depths of the coffee. "He said when he arrived you were carrying the children out."

"I know what I was doing! It is etched on my mind forever!" snapped Willy. "I put a tourniquet on and wrapped your leg. Didn't it heal right? You limp."

Cheops ignored the question, "Why did you leave?"

"I found my son," stated Willy, looking blankly out at the garden.

"And my daughter," reminded Cheops angrily.

303

"I sent a message to the hospital that I'd buried them together," explained Willy, looking at Cheops suddenly. The blue eyes were burning with an intense light that seemed to come from within. They were, when she was angry, inhuman eyes.

"I didn't get it," responded Cheops, meeting the stare with green eyes flashing with emotion.

"Not my fault. I did my duty."

"Duty! For Christ's sakes, Willy! They were our children!" Cheops exploded, tears welling in her eyes.

Willy said nothing. The words were too hard to utter. She raised the cup to her lips and allowed the thick, bitter coffee to push down the rising lump in her throat. Her hand shook.

Cheops face turned from tense anger to confusion. "What's wrong with you, Willy? Are you sick?" Cheops looked up with pleading eyes.

"No," came the cold response.

Cheops nodded and looked away. "Thank you for the coffee. Is this some sort of Special Services ritual, providing coffee and conversation before the kill?"

"It is important that you understand that I did not fail you," came the cold response.

Cheops hurled her cup across the lawn as she leapt to her feet. "Damn you!" she yelled, brushing past Willy, tears streaming down her face. "Damn you to hell!"

After she had left, Willy stood for a long time, staring at nothing. *I am already damned, Cheops*, she thought. Then she went and retrieved the cup from the flowerbed and carried the two of them back to the refreshment counter. Revenge at a personal level, she was finding, was not sweet.

"I'm tellin' ya, Abe, any guy who has all his gold buried with 'im ain't civilized. As soon as we get back to New York, we're going to the lawyer's. Ya hear! You're not taking it with ya!" said Betty, slapping the arm of her long-suffering husband playfully.

"Yes, Betty," Abe responded, rolling his eyes and smiling. Behind all the toughness, his wife had a heart of gold and he knew it.

"Hey you, come here," Betty suddenly demanded over Abe's shoulder, as she beckoned with her hand. Abe felt a tall presence behind him that sent icy shivers down his back. He moved aside and saw the strange woman who had been lurking at the edge of their group all morning. *Betty! What are ya doing now?* he thought.

"Look, Honey, I seen you on the bus rubbin' your head. You gotta headache? I said to Abe, she's one of those half-starved models that die young from taking diet pills, didn't I, Abe?" rambled Betty as she dug deeply in her enormous purse.

"Ahh, Betty I don't think..." started Abe.

"Here! I picked up a banana off the breakfast table this morning," explained Betty, proudly thrusting the item in question at the bemused warrior. "Ya eat that, okay? It's got stuff in it women need."

"Betty! Ya don't know if she's a model! Ya outta be mindin' your own business!" grumbled Abe.

Betty rolled her eyes in annoyance. "Tell him," she demanded of Willy.

Willy's amused eyes flickered from Betty to Abe. "I was just medically discharged from the R.A.F. Special Services Unit. I was captured by a terrorist group... it wasn't too pleasant," explained Willy although she was not sure why. Betty had sort of appealed to her with her rough kindness to a stranger. She held up the banana. "Thanks, I'll take it out and eat it on the bus," she promised and walked on.

"Model!" scoffed Abe, giving his wife an affectionate poke.

"Well! She could have been! She's gorgeous!" Betty said in defense.

Cheops got herself under control and then went in search of her group. She found the couple from Salt Lake City and the father and son waiting dutifully in the allotted spot. "Hi, just the Laytons to wait for and we can be off!" she remarked.

"What about Wilhelminia Kyrtsakis?" grumbled the older gentleman. "You going to leave her behind?"

Cheops' insides jumped hearing the name of her ex-lover. "You know Willy?" she asked in confusion.

"Nope, read her name tag," responded the wiry old man smugly.

Cheops laughed at her own stupidity. "That makes sense," she agreed. "Willy knows this part of Egypt very well. She has lived here before. She can take care of herself," Cheops reassured the group. *Aaron Scott is going to be a difficult old coot*, Cheops thought. *The son, Bob, too*, she guessed, by the way he was leering at her.

"She doesn't look too well," observed the rather prim wife from Salt Lake, her husband nodding his agreement.

Jean and Bill Bartlett, Cheops' mind registered. "Here are the Laytons now!" said Cheops happily, changing the subject as quickly as she could.

Betty came bustling up with Abe trailing behind. "Have you seen Willy?" asked Aaron persistently.

"She's on the bus eating the banana I gave her," explained Betty. "She's English and she's been medically discharged from the R.A.F.

because she was held prisoner by terrorists and tortured!" revealed Betty proudly. The group looked at her in surprise.

Abe explained proudly, "That's my Betty. She shoulda been an interrogator. She could get information from a corpse."

Several of the group giggled at this and Cheops used the moment to lead her group back to the bus. She hid how upset she was behind a stream of facts about some of the exhibits the tourists had seen, wondering on another level why she should care that the woman who was going to try to kill her had been a prisoner of war.

Willy's long legs were stretched out along the back seat of the bus and she had leaned her head against the window, her eyes closed. She looked exhausted. Cheops knew, however, that she was probably aware of everything happening around her. She was like that, observant, alert, and always on guard.

The group piled back into the mini-bus with a good deal of noise and confusion and then settled down for the ride back to Giza. Cheops stood at the front and leaned against the safety rail as she used the mike to give her group a little bit of background information on the Great Pyramids of Giza.

"The pyramids at Giza were built as royal tombs between 2700 B.C. and 1000 B.C. The largest one is Khufu's, which stands some 480 feet tall. It is made of 2.3 million blocks of stone each weighing about 2.5 metric tonnes! It is still, today, the largest single structure ever built by man."

"Wow! That's fantastic!" encouraged Bob, who had taken the seat directly across from Cheops. "Do you ever know a lot about this stuff!"

Cheops laughed good-naturedly, "Well, I do have a doctorate in Egyptology. In fact, I grew up in Giza. My parents were both archaeologists. They worked on the remains of the City of the Dead that surrounds the great pyramids. They are the mastaba tombs of the pharaoh's family, officials and courtiers."

"What does mastaba mean?" asked Bob, hanging on to every word that Cheops was saying. Willy, sitting quietly at the back, could feel the hairs at the back of her neck starting to rise in irritation.

"Mastaba means literally mud-brick bench. The Egyptians thought that these ancient tombs looked a lot like the sun-dried mud benches you see in front of local homes," explained Cheops.

"So are you saying we gonna see a graveyard?" asked Betty loudly.

"Basically, yes," Cheops affirmed. "Traditionally, the living of Egypt lived on the east side of the Nile, the side of the rising sun, and the dead lived on the west side, the side of the setting sun. In Cairo, there is a huge City of the Dead. Families build houses there over where their dead are buried. There are streets with rich houses and poorer neighborhoods too. It looks from the hillside just like a sprawling suburb, only everyone there is dead."

"Wow! What a great place for a D. and D. game!" suggested Bob.

"I wouldn't recommend it. Moslems take their beliefs very seriously," responded Cheops and then went on to change the subject. "I was named after the pharaoh Khufu. Cheops is the Greek word for Khufu." Cheops clicked off her mike and handed it back to the driver before slipping back into her seat.

Willy's eyes narrowed as Bob leaned over and continued to ask questions of Cheops. After a few minutes he slipped in beside her on the same bench. When his arm wrapped around the seat back, Willy was on her feet and walking unsteadily towards the front of the bus. She tapped Bob forcefully on the shoulder. "I need to talk to the guide," she stated bluntly and Bob, after a moment's hesitation, moved sulkily back to his seat.

Willy sat down beside Cheops and stared out the front window. *What the hell did I do that for?* she wondered. "Willy?" Cheops asked softly, leaning close to the agitated warrior.

"Hmmm," responded Willy, looking down and catching the scent of desert flowers and sunlight that she remembered was the taste of the beautiful woman beside her.

Cheops reached out and covered Willy's hand. She felt the woman jump in revulsion but the hand did not move from where it lay beneath her own. "Thanks."

"It's okay," she muttered disinterestedly.

"Betty told us about... what happened to you," Cheops confessed. The hand stiffened and shook slightly. Cheops wrapped her own hand around it. The hand was pulled away sharply.

"What the hell are you doing?" hissed Willy.

"Caring," Cheops responded softly.

"Find someone else to mother!" Willy growled cruelly.

"There is a river of bad blood separating us, Willy, but I can answer honestly that after you there could never be another. You were my soulmate." Willy got up and walked back to the rear of the bus with out another word. Cheops sighed sadly and picked up her knapsack to place on the now empty seat to discourage Bob from returning. Then she looked moodily out the window.

In bed with the enemy, wasn't that the expression? She wasn't getting very far in breaking down Willy's wall of hate, but then she knew the odds were stacked in the warrior's favor in this contest of wills. Yet she had come to Cheops' rescue. There must be some fragment of what they once were deep inside. If she could only find it.

Chapter Two

They rode back to the hotel, and after a light lunch, walked through the gardens and up the hill to the pyramids. Arabs riding camels and wearing traditional dress offered to have their pictures taken with the tourists for a price and Abe insisted on Betty posing. The Bartletts too were anxious to get their picture taken. Bob and Aaron walked on, after being told to meet at the Sphinx in an hour's time. That left Cheops once again with Willy.

"I read you are still working on KV 5," Willy observed, kicking at the gravel with her sneaker.

"Yes, it's been... hard at times. I still can't make myself go near Hatshepsut's temple," confessed Cheops, a lump forming in her throat. She swallowed with difficulty. "Would you like to see one of the mastaba my parents worked on?" she asked, more to change the dangerous subject than for any other reason.

"Sure," came the quick response.

Cheops looked up quickly. "You won't get a chance to kill me, Willy. I'm not likely to take you anywhere where there are no witnesses."

Willy smiled coldly. "There have been plenty of opportunities so far to off you, Cheops. But I'm in no hurry. I paid for the tour."

Cheops' face drained of colour. Glacial-blue eyes seemed to reach in and freeze her soul. She forced herself to stand straighter and give Willy a dirty look. "I'll make sure you get your money's worth, Major, as far as the tour goes. This way," she instructed, carefully negotiating the loose hillside down into the City of the Dead that lies in the shadow of Khufu's pyramid.

Willy adjusted her pace and stayed close enough to grab Cheops if she should fall. There was definitely something wrong with her ankle. It didn't seem to bend.

They approached a Mastaba where several archaeologists and their assistants were surveying. A lean, dark haired woman with a row

309

of gold studs in one ear smiled and got up from where she was pounding in a survey stake. "Cheops! Great to see you!" she exclaimed, giving the petite woman a hug and leaving her arm over the woman's shoulder as she turned to face Willy.

"This is Dr. Sophia Polinski, Willy. Soph, this is Major Wilhelminia Kyrtsakis."

She seemed relaxed and comfortable under the other archaeologist's arm. Were they lovers? Willy could feel her anger fighting to break free. *This is stupid! Why should I care?* she wondered.

"Glad to meet a past friend of Cheops," the wiry woman said pointedly, grasping Willy's hand in a strong handshake.

Willy squeezed until she saw the flash of pain cross Sophia's face, then let go. "Doctor," Willy acknowledged. "Let's go, Cheops," she said impatiently.

Cheops turned to Sophia. "Is it okay if we check out tomb KP 326?" she asked.

"Sure, Hon, go ahead." Sophia smiled and stepped aside after giving Cheops' shoulder one last squeeze.

Cheops led the way down into the tomb with Willy moodily following behind. The tomb was cool and dark after the intense afternoon sun. For a minute, they stood close together, letting their eyes adjust.

"I thought I was your soulmate, and there could never be another," remarked Willy with bitter sarcasm.

"I'm not having an affair with Sophia," responded Cheops calmly.

"She'd like to," snarled Willy.

"Yes, she would."

"Do you find her appealing?"

"Physically, yes," Cheops admitted honestly.

Willy nodded and walked farther into the tomb. The walls were covered in rows of black hieroglyphics on orange plastered walls. The barrel roof was painted navy and covered in stylized stars in yellow.

"What does it mean?" asked Willy, looking around, hands on hips and a thunderous expression on her face.

"It's the text from the Egyptian Book of the Dead," explained Cheops, looking at the walls with interest.

Willy's laugh burst out. "You've got guts, Cheops! I'll give you that! You'd better read your prayers, while you have the time."

"Alright," the small archaeologist responded. "The eastern wall over here has the morning prayers on it. It reads, 'Worship the sun god when he rises on the eastern horizon of heaven.' Then here it says, 'Sun god, you rise and shine honoring your mother, Nut, who made all the gods.' Over here on the western side it says, 'Receive in the west our sun god, content and safe in the righteousness of your nations. May the sun god give us splendor and power.'"

"You'd be better to put your trust in yourself, instead of a stupid god," said Willy bitterly.

"I do. But more than that, I put my trust in you," replied Cheops, coming to stand in front of Willy, and looking up at her sincerely.

"Don't," Willy shot back and pushed past Cheops to climb out of the tomb.

"But I do. My life depends on it," whispered Cheops, and awkwardly made her way back out of the tomb. The sun blinded her for a minute, then, looking around, she saw Willy storming off in the distance. Sophia came up to stand beside her. "Listen, when you finally decide to let go, let me help kiss it better."

Cheops gave her a dirty look and limped off.

She found the group dutifully waiting for her by the Sphinx and pasted on a happy smile for them. "Legend has it that Oedipus was able to kill the Sphinx by knowing the answer to this riddle: 'First on four legs, then on two, lastly, on three legs.' Do you know the answer? No? It's the baby who crawls, the man who walks, the old man who uses a cane."

"I don't use a cane," grumbled Aaron.

Cheops gritted her teeth but laughed politely. "That's because you are young of heart and still handsome too," Cheops flattered him. The old man beamed and poked his son, Bob, in the ribs. The group laughed and Cheops went on, "The Sphinx is actually a lion with the face of the pharaoh. It was common to make sphinxes and we'll see lots of them. But this one is unique because of its gigantic size. Carved from a natural outcrop of rock, it is 66 feet high and 240 feet long!

"It's really hot out here now. I bet you are all ready to head back to the hotel and have a cool drink by the pool. I'll see you at dinner at 8:00 p.m. This way, we'll take the back door out," concluded Cheops, walking slowly around the far side of the Great Pyramid. She didn't want to over tax Aaron, although the old man seemed in remarkably good shape. Her keen sight had noticed, too, that Willy looked exhausted and her movements were again stiff and shaky.

Cheops spent the late afternoon seeing to the various needs of her clients. Aaron wanted his room changed so that he was next to his son. Betty needed to know if the ice was made from bottled water and the Bartlett's needed their return flight times verified. She had only enough time to slip home and change into her gallabeeya and return for dinner.

All eyes were on her when she entered the dining room in the navy blue, flowing robe decorated in intricate geometric patterns of gold braid. "Honey," said Betty, "you'd charm the devil himself in that get up!"

"It's beautiful!" admired Jean. "Bill, I must get one while I'm here. What is this Arab dress called again?"

"It's a gallabeeya," Cheops repeated patiently for the fifth time.

"Ain't it hot?" asked Aaron.

"Well, this one is for evening wear and it is pretty heavy. The desert, as I'm sure you have noticed, gets chilly at night. The daytime ones are usually light cotton so they are quite airy and cool. Having grown up in Egypt, I feel just as comfortable in Arab dress as I do in European."

The waiter arrived with their menus then and conversation turned to other subjects. Cheops was disappointed that Willy had not shown up. She had wanted the woman to see her in this outfit. There was a time... It was perhaps better not to think of those heady days of love before the incident. The floorshow started and Cheops forced her mind on to the here and now, clapping with the others during the folk dances and watching the belly dancer with approval.

When it was politely possible, Cheops took her leave and walked slowly back through the hotel gardens to catch the trail that would take her behind the City of the Dead and down to her own backyard. Her mind wandered again to happier times. Willy used to put on Arabic music and insist that Cheops belly dance for her. It always led to other activities together that lasted long into the night.

Lost in thought, Cheops did not hear the steps behind her until she was caught around the middle in a pair of lanky arms. "Bet you can belly dance real nice too," Bob whispered in her ear.

"Let go, Mr. Scott," Cheops said firmly, pushing at him. The arms tightened and Cheops realized that she was in trouble. "Back off!" she ordered. Bob's breath was heavy with whiskey, and he laughed softly as he spun her around for a kiss. Cheops lost her balance on her one good foot and fell, pulling Bob down with her. *Oh god!* she thought.

She struggled to push Bob off as he laughed with drunken delight. Then to her relief he was up and off of her, held by the scruff of his neck by a warrior who looked only a hair's breadth away from murder. "Get out of here! And don't ever come near her again!" Willy ordered, as she shook the terrified drunk until his teeth rattled. She gave him a good push in the right direction and he stumbled off into the darkness whining that it was all a mistake.

Willy reached down and pulled Cheops to her feet. She toppled forward and the warrior caught her in her arms. "You okay?"

Cheops did not miss the opportunity. She rested her head under Willy's chin and nodded, her head buried in the soft material of the taller woman's shirt. It smelt of freshly ironed cotton and the spicy scent that was uniquely Willy's.

Willy stepped back. "I'll walk you home."

Cheops laughed shakily. "Saved from an amorous drunk to be walked home by my killer. I'm not having a good night!"

Willy looked uncomfortable. "I told you, I want my money's worth. You're safe enough tonight."

Cheops looked deep into Willy's eyes. She could see the doubt. *I'm winning you back, Willy. You just don't know it yet*, she thought. Out loud she said, "Thanks."

The two of them walked side by side along the stony path back to Cheops' home. In the backyard Willy stopped and looked around, the pain and strain showing on her face. Cheops licked her lips nervously and took the chance. "Sometimes, I can still hear them playing out here," she said softly and Willy nodded, swallowing hard. "I never would have..."

"I know," cut in Willy quickly. "I don't want to talk about it."

Cheops nodded. "You didn't come to dinner," she observed.

Willy looked uncomfortable and shuffled the dry gravel around with a foot. "I don't do so well in those sort of settings. I don't like noise and crowds."

"Would you let me fix you a snack? It is the least I could do for you, after saving my honor."

"You could have handled him. He was just a stupid drunk. You're not too good on that foot now, huh?" Willy observed.

Cheops swallowed. She was going to have to tell Willy the truth and she had better do so now, even though she was very much afraid that it would end any chance they had of ever being together again. She had seen the look of revulsion on people's faces before, when they saw her foot was artificial. "My foot and ankle were amputated, Willy. I wear a prosthesis." The body next to hers started and then went very still.

"You've got an artificial foot?"

"Yes," responded Cheops, staring at the ground, afraid to look into Willy's eyes and see the revulsion.

She was taken completely by surprise when Willy wrapped her in a strong embrace. "I didn't know," she whispered into Cheops' hair.

"It's okay. Thanks for caring." Cheops looked up and met Willy's eyes. "Listen, seeing as we have a truce tonight, would you like to come in, and I'll make you something to eat?"

Willy drew back and let her arms fall to her sides. For a minute, they stood looking at each other in silence while Willy fought her demons. "No," Willy finally said and turned and disappeared into the night.

Cheops limped to her door and let herself in. Mechanically, she went through the process of packing and getting ready for bed. Tomorrow, they would visit Sakkara and then take the 300-mile flight up the Nile to Luxor. She was anxious to see the progress that had been made at KV 5 and talk to Inge, her field archaeologist.

Sleep was a long time coming. At Luxor, Willy was going to have to relive that awful day, as Cheops had many times, in working each season in the Valley of the Kings. If she could not reach Willy soon, she didn't think she had too much time left. Willy would have a plan, she was sure of that. She'd have a place and a time and a weapon and there was little Cheops could do but hope that there was a grain of the woman she loved still inside the tortured soul.

What had happened to Willy, anyway? Now that the passing years had healed some of the raw emotion, she could understand why Willy wanted nothing more to do with her. And if what Willy had said was true, that she had given her first aid and notified the hospital of where she had buried her daughter, then some of the resentment that she had held against the Major was not fair. Willy had not wanted to kill her then, why now? It was only in the blood red dawn that Cheops finally fell asleep.

*****

The dream was always the same. It recalled the nauseating feeling of drug-induced disorientation, as body and mind tried to function efficiently in a cotton wool existence. The dream brought back the memories of how the hot spots of pain became a positive, reminding her that she was still alive and part of a physical world. The pain was, on days when she was too weak and drugged to open her eyes, her only link with reality.

She woke with a start, the sweat dripping and her heart pounding. The dream faded and her mind shifted to those long days of recovery. When she was able to communicate rationally again, the doctor had asked her how she had survived the torture. How had she not broken? *It was so easy. All I did was focus on the one thing I had left undone,* she thought. *The only thing left to live for… revenge. I couldn't die, you see, not until I got revenge. Once I knew this, survival was easy. I would never talk because to do so would have resulted in immediate execution. I didn't break and I didn't die and now I've earned my revenge.*

But she didn't say this. The doctor would have said she was still medically unfit if she had. No, instead she had responded that she tried to do her duty and not betray her fellow soldiers. For this, they had given her a medal for valor. She never wore it on her regimentals. It would be a lie.

Her head shifted and she looked out the window. The sun was just starting to bring colour to the night sky. 'Worship the sun god when he rises on the eastern horizon of heaven.' Where the hell had that come from? *Cheops.* She had read it off the walls in that mastaba. *What had she said?* That it was verses from the Book of the Dead.

There it was again, the light knocking on her door. It was Cheops. Years ago, they had decided on a signal knock, two short, one long, so that Willy would know who was there and not over react. Willy rolled out of bed and walked over to the door, opening it without concern. Cheops stood there holding a breakfast tray.

"It is still dark so I'm safe under the banner of truce, right?"

Willy nodded, too weak and confused from her drug-induced dreams to think straight. Cheops slipped into the room, placing the tray on the vanity. Then she came back and took the doorknob out from under Willy's hand and closed the door. "Hey, are you sick? You have a fever. You're all sweaty. Come and lie down again, okay," she whispered, gently leading the warrior over to the bed, as a mother would lead a child.

Willy allowed herself to be pushed down on the bed. She felt like she was watching from far away as Cheops fluffed the pillow and helped her settle back. She disappeared into the bathroom and returned with a damp, cool cloth to wipe Willy's face. "There. Is that better? What is it, Willy? You know that you can trust me to keep your secret. What happened?"

The cool cloth felt so good. The smell of coffee, too, seemed wonderful. Willy's eyes drifted over to the tray. Cheops smiled and went and got the tray and placed it on the bedside table. She poured Willy a cup of black coffee and passed it to her. Their fingers touched as Cheops reached out to steady Willy's shaking hands that grasped the cup.

Connected suddenly with her lost soulmate, Willy blurted out what she had no intention of sharing with Cheops. "I was tortured, drugs and electrodes, for a long time. I get dreams sometimes." Cheops nodded and waited. "The drugs, they still sometimes cause a rush and I get kinda... sick."

Again Cheops nodded. "Here, I brought you some rolls and fruit for breakfast. Try and eat, okay." She took the cup from Willy's hands and offered her a basket of freshly baked, still warm, sweet rolls. Willy took one and tore off half, offering it to Cheops. The archaeologist looked surprised and then smiled softly, taking the bread. "Thanks."

"It won't work," Willy informed her.

Cheops looked up, startled. "What won't?"

"Trying to show me you're sorry."

Cheops felt the anger boil up like magma from deep inside her. Who the hell did Willy think she was, dumping the responsibility of fate on her! She'd lost a child too, and a foot. And Willy had walked out on her, left her to face her grief and pain alone in the hospital! It should be Willy who was sorry! She swallowed; anger was not going to make the situation better. Willy was not rational, that was clear.

"I love you, Willy."

"No, don't say it. Don't even think it."

Tears welled in Cheops' eyes. She got up and softly let herself out.

Chapter Three

They took the mini-bus to Sakkara right after breakfast. From long experience at running this tour, Cheops knew better than to start her lecture this early in the morning. She left her charges to digest their breakfasts in sleepy contemplation of the desert landscape.

It was Betty who broke the morning quiet by bouncing to the front of the bus to ask about the tall, conical structures that she had seen. "Hey, Cheops. What is that in people's backyards?" she asked, pointing to one of the unusual structures as they slipped past in the bus. They were about twenty feet tall and had holes in rows around the cone from the top to about half way down.

"Those are pigeon roosts. Pigeon meat is highly prized as a delicacy in Egypt," explained Cheops.

"They eat pigeons! Like ya find in Central Park!?"

Cheops nodded with a smile. "It is a tender, white meat. Really, it is very nice."

"Did ya hear that, Abe? When we get home, I'm getting you a net and we'll export frozen pigeon dinners to Egypt."

Everybody laughed.

"Oh yeah, I'm gonna sell New York pigeons to Egypt! They got so much pollution in them, they'd combust if you tried to cook 'em!" protested Abe.

"Hey, America could use them as a new secret weapon!" suggested Bob. "Do they eat pigeon in Iraq?"

Betty ignored him. "There is money and fame in this, I'm telling you, Abe," Betty teased. "The mayor will give you a medal for getting rid of the darn things!"

The bus laughed at the interplay between the New York couple, and now, more awake than before, they started to talk amongst themselves.

Bob leaned over and balanced himself with one arm on Cheops' seat. "Listen, I'm sorry about last night, Cheops," he said casually with a smile. "I got a little pie-eyed at dinner."

"Moslems do not drink, Mr. Scott. It is not advisable to over indulge; you would not want the people to think less of you," answered Cheops neutrally. A shadow fell over them and Willy pushed Bob's arm aside as she slipped into the seat beside Cheops.

Bob gave her a dirty look and then went back to reading his gaming magazine.

"Having trouble making up your mind if you are my protector or my executioner, aren't you?" remarked Cheops dryly.

"Shut up," came the soft growl. The rest of the trip was made in silence.

* * * * *

"This was the first of the great pyramids to be built," explained Cheops to her tour group, as they stood outside the entrance to Sakkara. "The Step pyramid of King Zoser was built around 2650 B.C. and really is a series of mastaba built one on top of the other, each level a little smaller than the last.

"As well as the age of this site, and the vision of creating such a structure, this site is significant because you can see here the outer structures around the pyramid. These structures, at most of the other sites, are no longer visible or have been destroyed. Here at Sakkara, however, you can see the walls and some of the out buildings quite clearly."

Willy, standing in the background, looked up at the rubble structure of the step pyramid and then off in the distance where the pyramids of Giza could still be seen towering on the horizon. It was impressive. Willy had never taken an interest in archaeology in the heady days of her affair with Cheops. She wished now that she had learned more. Cheops had never pried into her work, knowing that a lot of what Willy did was classified. In return, Willy had never expressed an interest in Cheops' work.

What had they talked about in those days of love? Not very much talking, really. A lot of time had been spent with the kids and their private time had mostly been devoted to love making. Willy had been very self-absorbed, focused on her own work and needs. Cheops had always been willing to understand and co-operate with the soldier's timetable. *I'd do it better now, Cheops. My priorities have changed a lot. Too bad you are not going to live long enough to know that.*

They walked down the long hall of columns that led to the inner courtyard, in the center of which stood the step pyramid of Sakkara. Cheops showed them the ritual pit around which the pharaoh had to run seven times to prove himself fit enough to continue to rule. She also showed them the private shrine where only the high priests and pharaoh could go to make the necessary sacrifices to the gods.

She walked them up the narrow, steep stairs of the parapet and showed them the deep pit that was a shaft leading to underground treasure rooms. She was very aware of Willy standing near by and made sure that she was always facing her. One push from here and Willy would have achieved the end she wanted and could easily say that Cheops had lost her balance because of her prosthesis.

She could feel the tautness of her muscles and her palms sweated with the strain. Outwardly, however, she was smiling and relaxed. This cat and mouse game that Willy was insisting on was nerve-wracking in the extreme. But that was what Willy wanted... revenge.

Cheops found her own heart hardening. She had experienced a greater loss than Willy and had to live with the guilt of having been the one who had taken the children to Deir El-Bahari.

It was clear now that Willy was not the person she had known. Willy had been a soldier, yes, but she had been so very honorable. It had been that old fashioned sense of duty and honor that had first attracted Cheops to the warrior. This woman had no sense of what was morally right. Somehow the torture and drugs had warped her mind and killed that beautiful soul that she had known.

She had to forget that this was the person she had once loved. There was only bad blood between them now. If it came to a decision of kill or be killed, Cheops knew that she had to be ready. She was not going to let Willy take her life. Like Willy, she too was a survivor, but she had survived intact; Willy hadn't. She must not forget that.

They moved on to look at some beautiful frescos in one of the back rooms of a small temple before Cheops gave them some free time to walk around and take photographs. For safety, she attached herself to the Brants and discussed health food recipes with them. Willy went off scowling in the other direction.

Willy wandered about aimlessly. She kind of wished that she had brought a camera. Funny, she had been in a lot of countries but had never really taken an interest before. It had always been the enemy that occupied her interests; understanding him, defeating him. Now she was a civilian, retired on a medical pension, and it was like she was seeing the world for the first time.

319

She sat down in a small patch of shade and rubbed her head. "Hey, I've got your banana," came the flat voice of Betty. Willy looked up to find the New Yorkers standing in front of her. *How had they got that close with out her awareness? Damn, I'm sicker than I thought!*

"Betty, maybe she don't like bananas!" protested Abe.

"You stay out of this, you are only a male, and don't know nothin' but how the Mets are doin. Here," insisted Betty, with rough kindness, pushing the banana at Willy.

Willy took it and smiled. "Thanks." She really had no idea how to handle Betty.

Betty took this acceptance speech on the part of Willy as an excuse to sit down. "Abe and I had two sons who fought in the Gulf War. Josh, our youngest, was a P.O.W. for three days but then he got lucky and escaped."

Willy smiled ruefully. "I didn't get lucky." Then she added, to try and change the subject, "You and Abe been married long?" She waited for an answer as she peeled the banana.

"Fifty years! Can you imagine that?" Abe beamed, patting Betty's shoulder affectionately.

Betty's round face lit up with love. "It hasn't been so bad. Of course, he promised me minks and diamonds and I'm still waitin' for them!" The two older lovers laughed. "You got someone special in your life?"

"No."

"That's a shame, because there is nothin' quite like the bond between two people that were meant to be together," observed Betty, giving Abe a poke. Abe rolled his eyes good-naturedly.

"She's told me this so often, I've started to believe it!" joked Abe and Willy laughed.

"Marriages don't seem to last nowadays," Willy observed, as she looked moodily after Cheops, who was walking some distance away with the Brants. Betty's sharp eyes noted the glance and she smiled softly.

"People think marriage is about sex and love. Well, it ain't about neither. You can have sex with anyone..."

"Betty!"

"Well, you can, Abe! And as for love, well you fall in and out of love all your life, one way or another."

"Listen to her," scoffed Abe.

Willy smiled. "So what is marriage then, if it isn't based on love and sex?"

"Friendship and forgiveness. Ya gotta know in your heart that your partner wants the best for you no matter how short they might fall from meeting that goal. Ya gotta forgive them for bein' human. 'Course rich people are humans too, I always used to remind my boys. No harm in looking for a partner at the full end of the trough!"

Willy laughed whole-heartedly and popped the last of her banana into her mouth. "Thanks, for the banana and the advice."

"Betty mothers everyone," observed Abe happily. "Our boys adore her. In fact, they paid for this anniversary trip!"

"Nice kids," observed Willy.

"They done good, both of them. Abe, he's always wanted to see the pyramids. I wasn't sure about coming to these foreign parts. Ya know, a lot of these foreigners don't like Americans. There were two terrible terrorist attacks in the last few years, right here!"

Willy paled and the banana peel slipped from her fingers. She bent to pick it up to cover her gut reaction. The older couple did not seem to notice. "I said to John, he's my oldest, if anything happens to us, sell the house and kill the cat."

"What?" exclaimed Willy, completely taken by surprise.

"Bootsy, my poor baby, would be miserable without us. We've had her for fifteen years. The boys are good, but they wouldn't spoil her like I do. No, I'd want her put down so I'd know her life had been good."

"Good," snorted Abe. "If the house was burning, she'd save the cat before she'd look for me!"

Betty batted him playfully. "So why would I run into a burning building to save someone that should be smart enough to get out themselves?"

The three of them laughed and then walked over to join the rest of the group in the courtyard. Then they all walked out together to meet their bus. Cheops saw Willy laughing with the Laytons, that amazing flash of white that transformed the hard lines of Willy's face into sparkling beauty.

She felt a pang of jealousy very deep in her gut and turned away. "This way, ladies and gentlemen; we will be going to a lovely cafe by the Nile where they bake the bread fresh for you in a village wood-burning oven. We'll have a nice break, then hurry to the airport to catch our flight. From here, we will be flying 300 miles up the Nile Valley to the city of Luxor."

Obediently, her small party trooped back to the bus. Willy turned to get a last glimpse of Sakkara and beyond it, across the miles of barren desert, the three tall pyramids of Giza on the horizon. "The ancient Egyptians called Sakkara the Stairway to the Sky," observed Cheops from behind her. Willy nodded and got on the bus without a word. Cheops' face hardened in anger as she limped up into the bus.

* * * * *

She had thought that it would be very unpleasant. The three pairs of tourists took their seats on the plane and that meant Cheops had to sit beside Willy. She knew that Willy had trained originally as a jet pilot with the R.A.F. "Do you still fly?" she asked to break the cold silence.

"No, I'm not even allowed to drive at the moment."

"What were you talking to the Laytons about?" she asked, surprising herself at her jealous need to know.

"Marriage."

Cheops sighed in frustration and gave her attention to the safety video. After it was over, it was Willy who made the effort to start a conversation, much to Cheops' surprise.

"I'd do it differently now," she said, looking out the window.

"W... What?"

"I'd be more caring. I just wanted you to know before..."

"Yeah, I know," cut in Cheops bitterly, "still tying up the loose ends."

"I wish I'd taken a greater interest in your work. The last couple of days, I've learned a lot," Willy stated, ignoring Cheops' tone. "It's interesting stuff. That Rameses was a great warrior, huh?"

"Yes, Rameses the Second, many of the pharaohs were."

Willy looked out the window at the ribbon of green that stretched along the Nile surrounded by the sand of the desert. "Militarily, a fairly good place to defend," Willy observed.

Cheops tried not to smile. "Yes, its isolation from surrounding empires allowed it to have long periods of great political stability. And the spring floods guaranteed re-fertilized farmlands. Life was good in the Nile Valley."

"You tell good stories. You make the history come alive."

"Thanks. You look better, are you feeling better?"

"Yes, more clear-headed. Betty keeps feeding me bananas," Willy laughed.

"You have a beautiful smile," Cheops found herself saying, despite her resolve to treat this woman as ruthlessly as she was being treated. "When you feel better, you don't want to kill me, do you?"

"Yes, I do!" came the snarl, as ice blue eyes snapped up and took aim.

"No, you don't," came the quick response, as green eyes fired back a challenge. "What if it is only the drugs, Willy? What if you really regret this course of action after the drugs have completely worked through your system?"

"I know what I'm doing!"

No, you don't, thought Cheops. *If you kill me Willy, it will kill what you are deep inside. I don't want to die and I don't want you to have to live with the guilt of the revenge you took against me while under the influence of drugs.*

Cheops decided to change tactics while she had the stoic woman talking. "Why did you bury the children together?"

"They would have been soulmates. He died protecting her. It is what he would have wanted."

"Yes, I agree."

"Plane's losing altitude," remarked Willy, turning to look out the window and abruptly ending their conversation.

There was doubt there, Cheops reasoned. *I just have to be patient and not lose my temper with her. There is still protectiveness and now there is doubt. I'm making headway but will it be in time to save my life... and hers?*

A new mini bus met them at Luxor and drove them to the three-story boat that would take them slowly up the Nile to the Aswan Dam. Cheops wondered how far she would get. When would Willy decide that she had got her money's worth and want her revenge? *Well, at least she is interested in the archaeology. If she had been bored, I might have been dead already!*

Chapter Four

They were settled into their teak and brass rooms on the second floor and left to familiarize themselves with the ship. Most by-passed the bar and dining room on the third floor and went to the open upper deck to read, watch the Nile boats or swim in the small pool. Bob left his father talking to the Laytons and Brants and went back down to the bar. Willy went down to the main floor where the crew quarters were and talked to some of the sailors who had served in the Egyptian armed forces and spoke some English. It was there that she met the children.

They were two pairs of huge, dark brown eyes looking out of tan faces, lean with hunger and exhaustion. They sat timidly on sacks of grain watching every move made by the adults around the table. The sailors were uncomfortable sitting and talking with a woman. Willy was at ease. As a woman in an area of the military that rarely accepted females, she was used to male company.

They talked of weaponry and the Gulf War, Willy carefully bringing the conversation around to transportation systems along the river and security procedure. After her mission, she would need to get out of the area quickly. She wasn't about to rot away in an Egyptian prison. One of the men turned and gruffly said something to the oldest child. Without a word, she slid from her place and scurried off.

"They are your children?" asked Willy.

"No. Parents die. Deir El-Bahari. Mother, she no good woman. Daddy, he European." The man frowned and pretended he was drinking from a bottle. "No good. He works as foreman on site. Mother, she bring lunch and very bad people they kill so many that day."

Willy looked out the porthole and tried to push the emotions back. She nodded her understanding. "Why are they here?"

The big, burly man frowned. "Mother, she cousin once of my aunt. She asks, I help. They hide here. Work for crew. They have place to sleep and food to eat. Better than street for them."

The little girl returned with a basket of oranges. The man gave her one and then offered the rest around. The little girl returned to her perch and peeled and shared the orange with her brother.

Willy watched them. Small figures in the shadows. Like spirits left wandering after death had passed by. "I want them."

* * * * *

Cheops went up to the bridge and made contact with the tour agency to let them know that they had arrived safely and that everything was going well.

It was later in the afternoon, after seeing to all the ship's paper work, that Cheops headed back to her room to shower and change before dinner. She had just unlocked her door when an arm slammed into her back and sent her sprawling into her room.

* * * * *

The girl sat on one bed and her brother on the other. She was afraid but was trying not to show it. Abutti had told her that the woman was going to care for them. The woman had paid Abutti money. Abutti had said the woman was kind and to be good and obedient. She was afraid though. She did not understand what the strange European wanted with them. Europeans, like her father, were infidels.

The woman had said her name was Willy. She had said other things too and Amand had smiled and nodded but she did not really understand. She watched the woman intently as she showed them the bathroom and gestured that they were each to have a bed. Then the woman pretended she was eating. Amand smiled and nodded but the woman did not seem pleased. She looked angry.

She pulled back when the tall, dark woman reached out her hand, but all the woman did was give her a sad smile and pat her hair. Then she went and got some clothes out and disappeared into the bathroom.

* * * * *

Willy freshened up and slipped into beige slacks and an R.A.F. T-shirt. She was just running a comb through her hair when she heard a thump against her wall. Then another. Loud voices, not quite discernable, came from the room beside hers. *Cheops' room!*

Willy took off at a dead run and barely stopped to open Cheops' door before she rushed in. Bob was on the floor looking rather ill and

Cheops was deathly white and panting hard as she leaned against the bulkhead. Willy took in the situation in one glance and advanced on the prone man with murder in her eyes.

"Willy!" Willy stopped and looked over at Cheops. "Don't hurt him. Just get him out of here!" she asked.

Willy nodded, picked Bob up by the collar and dragged him out of the room, kicking the door closed with her foot. From outside, Cheops heard a number of thumps. A short time later, a soft knock came at the door, two short, one long.

Shakily, Cheops made her way to the door and opened it. Willy stood there, looking worried. "You alright?"

Cheops nodded, tears in her eyes. "Can we have a truce for a bit?" Her nerves were now giving way to shock. Bob had been drunk and obnoxious and Cheops had gotten bounced off the wall several times before she had been able to get her balance by bracing herself in the corner and using one of the chokes Willy had taught her to end Bob's clumsy attentions. Willy stepped in and scooped her up in her arms, using her foot again to close the door. She carried Cheops over to the bed and carefully lowered her down.

"Hey, you did good. Told you, you didn't need my help," whispered Willy, kneeling beside the bed because Cheops had hold of her and wasn't letting go. They stayed that way for some time; then Willy pulled back. She could feel the drugs starting to surge through her system again and taste the chemical smell at the back of her mouth. *Time to get out of here.* Without a word she stood up and left.

* * * * *

Amand told her small brother not to cry as they listened to the fight next door, eyes wide with fright. Her brother wanted to run back to the hold. Amand explained that they didn't belong to Abutti anymore, but to this strange European woman.

After a while, the tall woman returned looking very angry. The two children sat very still and quiet. The woman seemed to have forgotten them. She sat down on the sofa and buried her head in her hands. Amand wondered if she had been hurt.

Pulling away from her brother, who was trying to stop her, she softly walked over to her new master and pulled gently on her sleeve. The dark head came up and Amand gasped as the full force of those blue eyes met hers. *She has the evil eye! And now I am cursed!* But the woman called Willy smiled and gave her a quick hug.

327

The woman talked to her in a soft, deep voice that was very nice. Again, she pretended to be eating. Amand nodded seriously, knowing not to smile this time. This seemed to please the woman, who smiled softly and hugged her. Then the woman left them. Amand explained to her brother that she thought the woman had said she was going to eat and then she would bring them scraps. Her brother moved over and sat close to her on the couch while they waited.

* * * * *

Cheops did not show up for dinner. Neither did Bob. After a beautifully served meal, the guests aboard the ship took their coffee up on deck to watch the sun set red over the Nile. Willy pulled Aaron aside. "You've got to talk to your son," she informed him seriously. "He's been drinking and he's hit on Cheops a few times."

The old man laughed. "Chip off the old block! I was pretty wild when I was young too!"

Willy's face hardened into marble lines of anger. "Let me be a little clearer. Bob stays away from Cheops or that chip of yours is going to be ground to dust beneath my heel."

"You threatening my boy?" the old man demanded. "Nothin' wrong with Bobby, I tell people. He's just got more wild oats to sow than most."

"No, I'm not threatening anyone. I'm making you a guaranteed promise," Willy hissed and Aaron drew back in fear. "Keep that idiot away from Cheops!"

Willy went down the stairs two at a time and entered the dining hall again. "Hey, can you make up a few plates of food for the children and I'll need to take a plate to Cheops too," she asked one of the waiters whom she had met on the lower deck earlier that day. He nodded and disappeared into the kitchen. A short time later, he returned with plates of lamb and vegetables, a coffee urn and honey cakes on a huge tray.

"Thanks, put it on my tab." Willy smiled and carefully carried the tray down a floor and along the hall to her room. She gave her new friends a smile, and left some of the plates of food for them. The rest she took to Cheops' room. She knocked softly, two short, one long, and waited. Cheops answered, wearing only a thin nighty of raw cotton. Willy's eyes traveled up and down. She liked what she saw. *Okay, admit it, you've still got a thing for Malone! It doesn't matter. It doesn't change anything.*

"I needed to talk to you," she stated abruptly.

328

"Truce?"

Willy sighed. "For God's sake, Malone, yes, truce! Damn it!"

"Malone; you haven't called me that since... since before you went away. You always called me by my surname, remember?"

Willy looked uncomfortable. "So what? I'm a soldier. That's how we usually address each other."

"I know. But you never called civilians by their last name, only your military buddies and me. It made me feel that you accepted me into your life. It was a cute term of endearment."

"It was not!"

Cheops smiled and took the tray of food. It was a large tray for the amount of food on it. "Come in. What do you need to talk about?"

Willy looked around the small, beautiful stateroom and, rejecting the couch, she went and sat in one of two green leather armchairs.

Cheops took the other, balancing the tray on the small end table. "Well?"

Willy looked at her hands, then out the window, then cleared her throat and went back looking at her hands.

Cheops waited patiently and quietly ate her meal. *Oh boy. What ever this is, Willy is really upset about it. She only gets this tongue tied when it is something really personal. I hope she didn't do anything to Bob.*

"Ahh, there are these kids. You know, street kids. Nubians. Mixed race actually. Their dad was a European. Their parents were killed at Deir El-Bahari. He was a foreman of a repair crew and she had gone to take him lunch. They got caught in the cross fire."

"Go on," encouraged Cheops.

"They're in my room."

"What!" exclaimed Cheops, pushing her meal away.

"They've been working on the ship for scraps. No one wants them. They're just kids, Cheops!"

"You are telling me that they are stowaways."

"Well, not exactly. I mean most of the crew knew that they were on board."

"Let me guess, the owners and the captain don't!"

Willy gave a sheepish smile.

Cheops smiled back. "Okay, Willy, what do you want?"

"I want you to talk to the captain so that I can buy passage for them. Then tomorrow, we'll buy them clothes and..."

Cheops took Willy's hands. "Willy, these are not our children. You can't just take them."

The face went hard, the voice soft and deadly. "Yes, I can." For a long time there were only the harbor sounds, dull and far away.

"Let's go see them," Cheops said and Willy smiled.

"Thanks, Malone."

"Give me a chance to change," Cheops said. She reached for the clothes that she had left draped over a chair then realized that Willy was not leaving. *Okay, I can handle this*, she thought, glad now that she had sent a message in the afternoon to a University colleague back in Leeds to contact her aboard the ship. He had, she knew, dealt with psychoses in military personnel returning from combat zones.

She was going to need all the help she could get. It wasn't just her life at stake but Willy's and now, two children. Willy did not seem to see anything unusual in planning murder and adoption at the same time. Willy wasn't fit to be any child's guardian in her present state of mind. The problem was, how to make Willy realize that without making her angry.

Cheops slipped out of her nighty and picked up a pair of lace panties to put on. She didn't look at Willy but she knew Willy was looking at her. How would Willy react to seeing her prosthesis for the first time? Willy, whose own body was so physically beautiful and fit, had always loved sports and outdoor activity. Could she still find her attractive, when the last 30 cm. of her right leg was artificial? She could sense Willy's eyes on her. She wondered insecurely if Willy was looking at her body or her prosthesis. Cheops straightened her shoulders; either way, this was who she was and she had to hope that she could rekindle in Willy memories of the deep attraction that had once existed between them.

She glanced over at Willy. She was definitely looking at her. What Cheops saw burning in those remarkable eyes made her throb with need. For the first time, Cheops began to feel real hope that she could find her old lover again. *Your soul isn't really dead, is it Willy? You just buried it really deep, so the pain wouldn't rip you apart.*

Cheops didn't bother with a bra. She slipped on an over sized T-shirt and a pair of slacks, then she turned to meet Willy's eyes.

Willy rose slowly, like a panther stretching out its long limbs. She moved over to stand right in front of Cheops. "This won't work either," she muttered in a voice rough with desire.

"Yes, it will, Willy," Cheops responded softly, as she wrapped her arms around her warrior's neck and kissed her with all the passion that had been building over the last two years. Willy lifted her and put her up against the bulkhead, their kisses becoming more hungry and searching. When they finally came up for breath, Willy was leaning into her and Cheops had wrapped her legs around the waist of her ex-lover. They looked into each other's eyes, each realizing that they had gone a lot farther than they had meant to.

Cheops untangled herself from her former lover and Willy, once she was sure that Cheops had her balance, pulled back. "We'd better go see the kids, Malone. I tried to talk to them, but I don't think we communicated very well."

Cheops nodded but the two of them didn't move. Willy bent her head and kissed Cheops once more. "I don't have a bed."

"Yes, you do," Cheops promised and they kissed again.

They went to Willy's room, where two small, wide-eyed children sat on the floor looking well fed but bewildered. Cheops smiled broadly, sat on the floor and started chatting away to the older girl and her younger brother. Willy waited, not too patiently, behind.

"They are orphans, Willy!"

"That's what I told you."

"They look half starved! They've been sleeping down in the storage compartments and helping out the crew for board and food."

"I told you that too!"

"The girl's name is Amand and the boy's Zahi."

"Hello, Amand, Zahi." Willy smiled.

"Okay, I'll talk to the captain. But Willy, you understand that I'll have to notify the police and they'll have to do a search for relatives to take them."

Willy nodded her head seriously. Cheops turned and explained things to the two children, who smiled broadly and hugged Cheops and Willy. Willy met Cheops' eyes with her own. For the first time, they were that soft sea blue that she loved. "Tell the children, it's time for bed," Willy ordered. Cheops complied. She thought she knew what her warrior wanted and she wanted it desperately too.

The children were coaxed to take turns showering and then they were given fresh R.A.F. T-shirts to sleep in. Willy combed their wet hair as Cheops explained to them that they would be in the next room and that tomorrow they would no longer be stowaways but paid guests. Willy's hand shook. She was drained and the drugs were once again causing her joints to ache and her thoughts to be sluggish.

It was the girl who responded. In broken English she said, "You are so kind. You are so kind. My brother also, we thank you!" The women wished the children good night and tucked them into their new beds.

"They are not very old, Willy," worried Cheops.

"No, Amand would be maybe eight or nine, Zahi, maybe five or six," responded Willy, holding the door open for Cheops to pass through into her room.

Willy closed the door and leaned against it. Cheops turned in surprise. "I appreciate your help on this, Cheops, but I need to tell you that it is not going to make any difference to your fate."

Cheops limped forward until she was right in front of Willy. She searched deep into those remarkable eyes, realizing that the pupils looked dilated again. "You still love me, even if it is buried under a layer of hate. I will reach you again," she said, reaching up to caress Willy's face.

Her hand was brushed away, sharply. "Give me the key. I'll be back later to sleep in the other twin bed," ordered Willy coldly.

Cheops nodded. Willy had changed again and this woman was not to be pushed. "Here," she said, pulling the key from her pocket and handing it over at arm's length. Willy took the key and left without another word.

She strode along the hall and up two flights of stairs to the open deck. There, in the dark, she paced, until, hours later, she was too tired to walk any longer. Then she headed back down to Cheops' cabin. She stripped down and lay on the bed, enjoying the quiet and darkness. Why had she protected Cheops from Bob? It made no sense to do so. Maybe it was because something was not quite right about Bob Scott. He gave her the creeps! Maybe that was why. Or maybe Cheops was right; she was having trouble deciding if she was her former lover's protector or executioner. Were the drugs still distorting her frame of reality? No, she was being rational. It was rational to save Cheops from being raped by Bob so that she could kill her later. Wasn't it?

It was also logical that she should find Malone still physically attractive. You could hate someone and still be turned on by them, couldn't you? That was rational anyway. She could hear Malone's gentle breathing. How many nights had she laid in bed with that woman, after they had made love, and let her soft breathing lead her to sleep?

She had wanted to die after she had left Egypt, but she hadn't. Instead, she had been captured by terrorists and tortured and humiliated for months. At first, she had closed her mind to the pain and abuse by imagining the summer of love she had shared with Cheops and their children. But the fantasies had always ended in a horrifying pool of blood. Later, she stopped trying to hold on to the memories of what had once been and fostered instead visions of what her life had become... one filled with hate. Hate for her torturers, hate for Cheops, hate for life itself. At her lowest point, she remembered the one single reason her hatred had to go on - revenge. After that it was easier.

Willy rolled on to her back and stared at the ceiling; the best thing was not to try and think, just react. If she started now to doubt her whole reason for surviving, she was not sure if she could hold it together. All that pain, humiliation, torture; what was the point of having survived if there was no revenge?

Chapter Five

Willy, groaning in her sleep, woke Cheops from her own troubled slumbers. She switched on her reading light and sat up. Willy was lying naked on the bed. Cheops' heart pounded as her eyes slowly drifted over the warrior's magnificent body. Then her gut twisted into a knot as she saw the deep scars from the electrodes. "Oh God!" she whispered softy and sat up, reaching for her prosthesis so that she could slip from her bed to go to the one she loved.

She checked herself just in time. If she touched Willy now or even woke her from her nightmare, God knows what she would do! Cheops bit her lip. How could she help Willy without endangering her own life? She leaned back against the bulkhead and tucked the stump of her amputated foot under her other knee. "A long time ago, a great king arose in the north. He brought prosperity and stability to the Upper Nile and then, in a series of brilliant military maneuvers, he overpowered the weaker kings of the Lower Nile and united Egypt for the first time. He was Narmer and this is his story..."

Slowly, the moans grew softer and Willy's stiff, jerky movements eased until she was in a deep, relaxed sleep. Her breathing became regular and her face softened into classically beautiful lines.

"And so, by using King Narmer's tablet, we were able to look deep into the past and know of the pharaoh's achievements. That simple scribe had made the mighty pharaoh immortal," Cheops concluded an hour later. Then she slipped back into her bed, turned off the light and slept deeply. When she woke, Willy had already gone.

Cheops dressed quickly and went immediately to the captain. After an hour's heated discussion and the exchange of money, Cheops had managed to change the children's designation from stowaways to first class passengers.

She found Willy and the two children playing ping-pong on the top deck. The Brants and the Laytons were also there, rooting for the children in their bid to defeat Willy. Willy caught the ball in her hand without so much as looking when she saw Cheops coming up the stairs with her uneven gait. Everyone turned and looked at her as she made her way over to the table.

"Well?" asked Willy, real worry in her voice.

"Everything is settled. The children are now booked into your cabin and you into mine," Cheops smiled.

"Yes!" cried Willy, wrapping Cheops in her arms and spinning her around.

"It is okay dokay?" asked Amand nervously.

Willy suddenly realized what she was doing and put Cheops back down again, taking a step away. "Thanks, Malone," she said formally. Cheops nodded coldly and saved her smile to give to the children as she explained to them that all was well.

"Well, that's fine news, isn't it, Jean?" beamed Betty.

"It's wonderful news!"

"Look, I'm a lawyer and if there is anything I can do to help with the paper work, well, just ask," Bill Brant offered.

"Thanks," said Willy, now grinning again with delight.

"Can the children come with us on the tour today?" asked Jean, patting down Zahi's thick crop of hair in a motherly way.

"Yes, of course, Willy has paid for their tour! If everyone is ready, we can tour Luxor this morning and Karnac this afternoon. I think that's our bus pulling up now." The group moved down the stairs, Cheops doing a little hop as she brought her artificial foot down each step. Willy carried two giggling children over each shoulder as she galloped down the stairs ahead of everyone else.

"You've made her very happy. I would have not have thought her the motherly type," Jean observed, walking along slowly with Cheops.

"Willy is a wonderful mother," defended Cheops automatically.

Jean looked surprised. "She has other children?"

There was no avoiding this issue. "Willy and I both lost children in the massacre at Deir El-Bahari," she said, her voice tight with the effort of controlling her emotions. "It's nothing we like talking about."

Jean looked truly distressed. "I'm so sorry," she said, and wrapped an arm around Cheops and gave her a quick hug. Downstairs, they found the Scotts had joined the group. Willy had a murderous look on her face.

Aaron Scott turned as Cheops dropped off the last step. "There was nothin' about kids on this trip!" he complained to Cheops.

"There was nothing in the tour description that said there couldn't be children either," observed Cheops happily. "The children's trip has been paid for and so far they have been very well behaved. But I understand your concern, Aaron. I'm sure you have had your fill of children over the years." Her eyes strayed to Bob. "I'll make sure Willy keeps them well away from you."

Willy smiled. Malone always could slit your throat verbally and you wouldn't notice until you turned around and your head fell off. The party, smiling and giving each other knowing looks behind the Scotts' backs, proceeded down the gangplank and up the stone stairs that lined the riverbank to get on the bus.

The bite to Cheops' seemingly friendly remark had not been lost on Bob. He was, too, smarting from the slapping he had got from Willy yesterday. He closed his eyes and felt the fire of desire growing in him. Desire and hate, side by side, became a burning need. He smiled. He was a man who had to have the last laugh.

The Temple of Luxor sat at the edge of the road back-dropped by the city of Luxor. At first sight, the tour group was not impressed. They got off the bus some distance away and Cheops limped over to get their tickets. Willy played tag with the two children a little distance away from the others. "Now she smiles," observed Betty as she stood beside Jean, watching the lone woman come alive as she played with the children.

"I don't know what happened, but both Cheops and Willy lost children at Deir El-Bahari," explained Jean.

"The day of the massacre?" Betty asked in shock.

"I think so."

"So that's what ended their... that explains why they both seem so sad at times," said Betty, censoring her remarks in case Jean and Bill were not accepting of gay couples. Salt Lake City was not known for its liberal views.

"Everyone ready?" called Cheops and then said something in Egyptian that brought the two children to her side. Willy scowled and followed at a distance. Betty shook her head. Watching the two women reminded her of her old Ford on a wintry day. It kept turning over but there just wasn't a big enough spark for ignition.

As always they had to line up for a security check. Each person went through a metal detector as the tourist police searched bags. Every effort was being made to make sure that there would not be another terrorist attack. Once they entered the site and took the stairs down into the outer court, the full impact of Luxor left them speechless. Cheops smiled; she had seen this reaction many times before. To their left was the Avenue of the Sphinxes. At one time, rows of sphinxes lined a ceremonial road that joined Karnac to Luxor. Sadly, the city had grown over most of it. In some homes, the sphinx were still there, used for tables and chairs. Only a half-mile remained of this impressive walkway now, but it still never failed to fill the visitor with awe at the majesty that was ancient Egypt.

To the right stood the main gates to the temple of Luxor, towering overhead, and on each side of the entrance stood the two colossal statues of Rameses II. The base alone, on which each figure stood, was taller than a man. "Ladies and gentlemen, meet Rameses the Second, the conqueror," announced Cheops dramatically, and then waited for her group to take pictures of the gate and walk down the Avenue.

She explained to Amand and Zahi, in Egyptian, the significance of the site and then led them over to one of the sphinxes. Carefully, she lifted Zahi up on the back of one of the mythical creatures and then offered Amand a leg up. Suddenly, strong arms swung Amand up and onto the sphinx.

"Thanks," said Cheops. "I wanted to get their photo. Why don't you get in the picture too? The police can use it for evidence at my inquest," suggested the archaeologist, cheekily.

An eyebrow went up. "Sure," agreed Willy ghoulishly. "You're in rare form today. First, you nail Aaron and then me."

"You might not have realized this, Willy, but I am a reluctant player in this little game of yours," came the response from behind the camera.

"Like I care, Malone," responded Willy, turning to lift the two children down again after the photo.

"You do care," observed Cheops. "You just won't let yourself believe it. You owe me a favor and since I might not have much time left, I'd like to claim it right now."

Willy went still. The intense, blue eyes locked on Cheops'. "What do you want?"

"The four of us to spend the day together as a family," dared Cheops.

Anger flowed from Willy like a storm surge hitting the shore. "Bitch!"

"Your debt. My terms," responded Cheops, holding her ground.

"It won't work, Malone," Willy growled.

"It is working," smiled Cheops. "Agreed?"

"Like you said, I owe you a debt that needs to be paid quickly. Just don't believe this illusion, Malone. There is only one thing left between us."

Willy swung Zahi up onto her shoulders so he could see above the crowds. He giggled happily down at his sister, who held onto Cheops' hand possessively. As a family, they walked back to the main gates and joined the others. Betty and Jean were beaming knowingly. Aaron, Abe and Bill were discussing the Republicans' chances in the upcoming elections and Bob was standing in the shadows watching quietly, a feverish light shining in his dark eyes.

Cheops showed them the white alabaster statue of the sitting pharaoh and his wife. She explained that it was probably some other poor pharaoh's statue but that Rameses was the world's worst graffiti artist. During his reign he had written his name over the top of many other pharaohs' names. She showed them the beautiful and graceful hieroglyphs of King Sety's rule and below it, in big messy symbols, the boasts of his son, Rameses the Second.

"Sety was the philosopher-artist and his son the warrior and propaganda master supreme," explained Cheops with a laugh. "I guess if you are going to be a warrior pharaoh you are likely to be very concerned about protecting your after life."

"How long ago did Sety live?" asked Bill, taking notes for his travel journal while his wife handled the family camera.

"In and around 1280 B.C.," Cheops replied and led her group on to see the standing wall of Rameses' statues and the inner sanctum where the sacrificial table sat. Here the high walls were still roofed in massive slabs of limestone and the walls were blackened by thousands of night fires. They followed Cheops through the rows of towering columns and she pointed out the Greek style and the Egyptian lotus leaf capitols.

It was a tired and hot group that headed back to the bus to return to the ship for lunch. "Lunch will be served in half an hour and then, at two, we'll head over to Karnac," Cheops explained.

"Not me," grumbled Aaron. "I've seen all I need to see of temples. I'm staying here this afternoon."

"Are you sure, Mr. Scott? Karnac is an amazing site," Cheops said encouragingly.

"Said I was staying here," repeated the stubborn man.

"I'll stay with my father," offered Bob, playing the dutiful son.

"Fine, as long as you don't mind missing the site," agreed Cheops, just as glad to get rid of them. With that, people disappeared to freshen up before lunch.

"We need to get the kids some better clothes," remarked Willy, rubbing her temple.

"Yes, that's my job," stated Cheops and when Willy looked up sharply, she added, "I'm the bargainer and I speak the lingo. I'll take the kids out right after lunch to the market down the street. Why don't you have a nap then?"

"I'm fine," snapped Willy defensively.

"It's going to be a long afternoon, Willy," Cheops responded softly. "Try and get some rest. The kids are going to need you. It will be a long day for them too."

Willy nodded moodily. She wasn't feeling well. The chemical taste was back in her mouth and her head ached, but she was not going to admit that to Malone. She would start that crap again about her not being rational because of the drugs."

"Willy?"

"What?"

"I said I'll see to the kids in their room and you can have the bathroom first, okay?"

"Yeah, okay," Willy agreed gruffly and patted the two dark heads before using her key to enter Cheops' room. The bathroom smelt of the two of them; spice and sweet, warm herbs. Images of them showering together came uninvited to her mind. She had loved Malone from the moment she first saw her. She had thought that love would have lasted forever. Memories came flooding back.

"My God, you are sexy!" Malone had gasped as she had entered their bedroom and seen Willy dressed in her regimentals for the first time. Willy laughed and sided stepped the grasping arms.

"Don't even think about touching me! My commanding officer would blow a gasket if I showed up with strawberry blond hair on my shoulder or lipstick on my collar. Hell, a crease in my jacket would probably get me court-martialed!"

"Hmmm, those medals. What are they for?" asked Cheops, looking at the three ribbons with their decorative metal discs.

"Actions beyond the call of duty," answered Willy vaguely. "You look beautiful. Just my luck to have to go to this damn evening on one of the rare nights when the kids are staying over at a friends."

"Hmmm. What are the little bars of colour?"

"Service ribbons. Places overseas where I served," Willy explained, her eyes following the curves of Malone's body. "Take your clothes off."

"What?"

"Please."

Cheops smiled in surprise but followed the instructions, slowly undoing her shirt and letting it trail to the floor. Then she unzipped her shorts, watching Willy's eyes following every move. The shorts dropped to a puddle around her feet and she stepped out of them. Then the bra went and she lifted her arms through her hair, letting Willy enjoy the view of her upturned breasts. Her hands slid down her body and under her lace panties. The underwear fell in a gentle cloud leaving her completely exposed to her warrior.

Willy's mouth curled softly in a knowing look and her eyes sparkled with devilment. One eyebrow went up. "There is some body oil warming in the bathroom. Would you mind getting it, please," requested Willy. Cheops trotted to the bathroom and returned with the sweet oil bottle that had been soaking in hot water in the sink. Clearly, her warrior had planned this love game well ahead of time.

"Now, lie on the bed and pour some of the oil right there," purred her lover stroking a line down between Cheops' breasts with the tip of her finger. Cheops had shivered with excitement at the touch and, giving Willy a challenging look, she had gone over and lain down.

Willy moved to the side of the bed and nodded and Cheops had poured a small pool of warm, fragrant oil where she had been instructed. "Now take your hands and rub the oil over your breasts. Play with yourself while I watch. Close your eyes and imagine me running my hands over your lines and planes. Feel my warmth and my need."

A small moan came from Cheops as she pleasured herself at the bidding of her lover. Lips dropped to whisper just above hers. "When I come home tonight, I am going to make love to you until the morning sunrise wraps the two of us in a pink blanket of love. Feel me in you, Malone. All evening the scent of you will be haunting my thoughts." Their lips had touched in the softest, whisper of a kiss before Willy had left.

Willy smiled at the memory. Her return that night had been everything that she had imagined and more. And as they had lain in the pink of the desert sunrise, Willy had slipped a simple gold band onto Cheops' finger. "I love you," she had said. "This ring is a pledge to you of my life, my soul and my love."

I wonder what happened to the ring? Willy pushed the thoughts out of her mind. She could feel her mind getting slow and sluggish. Maybe she would just lie down for a few minutes before lunch.

Chapter Six

The woman called Cheops Malone had taken her and her brother to the street market. At first, Amand was afraid that she would leave them as indentured labor with some merchant. To her surprise and delight, the blond woman bought them beautiful clothes instead. Each of them got four outfits, two Egyptian and two European. Amand had been very proud and impressed with Cheops Malone. She drove a hard bargain and got good prices for their clothes. She was known in the market place and people treated her with great respect and kindness. It made Amand and Zahi feel proud. No one had ever treated their parents with such honor.

Here too she had learned from a shopkeeper, while Cheops was busy picking out clothes for Zahi, that the woman limped because she had an artificial foot. Her real foot had been cut off, the shopkeeper had said, during the terrorist attack at Deir el-Bahari. Perhaps that was why the blond woman was helping them; maybe she had known their parents.

"Why are you being so kind?" Amand had asked at Zahi's insistence.

"Willy Kyrtsakis wishes that you have these things. We will see that you are found a good home and that you get the chance to go to school," explained Cheops.

"Willy Kyrtsakis and you are very kind. My brother and I pray for you and thank you a thousand times. Always we will be grateful."

Cheops smiled and gave the serious child a quick hug. "Don't you worry, sweetheart, everything will be fine. I'm going to see to that."

Back on the boat the two excited children waited impatiently for Willy to wake to thank her for her kindness and show off what Cheops had bought them. Amand explained at great length to the puzzled soldier the pride she had for Cheops. Willy turned to Cheops for an

343

explanation, realizing by the girl's gestures that she was talking about the archaeologist.

Cheops blushed. "She wants you to know that I drive a hard bargain and that many people know me in the market."

Willy's eyes traveled over the small, blond woman, dressed in the green gallabeeya. "Tell her that I have seen you bargain."

But before Cheops could translate, Amand responded. "She is good so much. But you send her. I thank you. My brother thanks you."

Willy smiled and stroked Zahi's hair as he stood close to the tall woman's leg. "You and your brother are very welcome, Amand."

Cheops supervised the two children changing into their new clothes. Then once again as a family, they left their cabins to meet the group for the afternoon tour. The others were delighted with the two clean and well-dressed children who now waited quietly behind Willy's tall legs. Cheops saw Willy reach down with pride and rub each dark head reassuringly and a lump formed in her throat. *Oh Willy, no, don't get attached to these children*, she prayed.

With a smile she didn't feel, Cheops led her small group down the gangplank and up the worn stone stairs of the embankment to the waiting bus. Much to Cheops' surprise, Willy came up beside her and took her elbow, steadying her as she laboriously lifted her artificial foot up each step. She hesitated and looked up at Willy. "You said as a family," the soldier explained coldly and Cheops nodded, not sure at all about what was going on in Willy's head.

The tour group followed Cheops through the courts and ruined temples of Karnac with their mouths open in wonder. Fields of pillars towered over their heads. The bases of the columns alone were as tall as Cheops. The cross lintels of these massive structures were mounted on smaller blocks at the top of the column, giving the feeling that the ceiling was floating. The underside of these huge, stone beams, protected from wind and sun, still had the remains of colorful, mysterious murals. They were ghostly images of the activities of this lost civilization.

The delicate hieroglyphics were like musical scores, as they flowed in rhythmic patterns across walls and columns. Cheops showed them the vast sacred pool, the inner temple with its sacrificial alter, and the hidden obelisks. Then she gave them some free time to wander.

Willy had followed with the children, keeping to the family role with grim determination. She listened intently to what Cheops said and amused the children with hide and seek games or pointed out interesting scenes of animals in the frescoes.

Cheops watched her group dissipate then turned to Willy. "You want to let the children run a bit behind the temple?"

Willy nodded her head. "Good idea, Malone. They've been good. Let them burn off some energy."

Cheops pulled a small rubber ball, which she had picked up at the market that day, from her knapsack and gave it to the delighted children. In Egyptian, she gave them instructions about where to play safely. Amand smiled happily, took her little brother's hand and led him over to the edge of the huge archaeological site to play.

Cheops took Willy by the arm and led her through the nearby rubble to show her the ruins of the harem. Willy found herself wrapping an arm around Cheops to help her along. On flat surfaces, Cheops' limp was barely noticeable, but on uneven terrain she had great difficulty. Willy wondered how she managed on archaeological sites.

"Do you see the beauty of these walls, Willy? Isn't it amazing?" enthused Cheops, her eyes dancing with delight.

Willy smiled despite herself. Cheops was beautiful. Her hair was golden firelight in the sun and her cute face was lit with animation. *The woman still has the power to excite me to the core of my being*, Willy acknowledged to herself. The smile faded. She'd have to be careful not to let Cheops use her desire to try to seduce her from her mission.

"You know what they found here, Willy? Hundreds of covers of poetry books. They had titles like, *to My True Love*, or *to My Absent Love*. But only one small phrase survived of the pages inside. One small glimpse of the beautiful souls of those ancient people."

"What was the fragment?" asked Willy softly, pulling Cheops into the shadows, well away from prying eyes.

Cheops ran her hands up Willy's chest, only stopping when her hands lay softly on the tall woman's shoulders. "For I have loved you as the strong river wind embraces the fragile reed," Cheops coached.

Willy leaned down, hesitated and then whispered, "For I have loved you, Malone, as the strong river wind embraces the fragile reed." They kissed, Willy pushing Cheops against the wall in her hunger. Cheops raised her chin and exposed her soft neck to Willy's kisses.

"You don't want to kill me, Willy. You still can love. Please try to find that warm spot inside your soul. Give up the hate before you do something that you, Willy, will regret for the rest of your life."

Willy stopped; her arms dropped away from Cheops' body. She stood looking down at the small archaeologist, who was half lost in shadows. There was confusion in Willy's eyes for a second, then they hardened in determination. "Desire is not love. You killed our children," she growled and then stormed off.

Cheops watched her go, anger ripping across her own face. Why should she bother trying to save Willy's soul? She owed this woman nothing! Tonight, she should have an e-mail waiting for her at her apartment in the city, and if she was advised to hand Willy over to the authorities, that was exactly what she was going to do, before she hurt either her or the children.

"Amand, Zahi, it is time to go," she called out in Egyptian. Then she waited for the children to run over so that they could help her keep her balance on the rough terrain.

Amand looked with worried eyes at the beautiful blond woman and then off in the distance to where the strange, dark woman stood in the shadows of a temple. They did not seem to like each other and yet they did everything together. It did not make sense. She and Zahi had talked, and they did not understand why the two women were helping them or what they wanted to do with them. Part of her was very grateful, but the other part was very afraid. Were they going to be made slaves? She looked at the blue and red ball with the band of white that Zahi held tightly in his hand. For a while, they could be happy. This was good. But she had learned in her short but hard life, that every kindness had a price.

The day had gone well and the group chatted happily over dinner. Even the Scotts were more sociable than usual. Cheops had arranged that evening that she would take them back to Karnac to see the Sound and Light show. As the show was a guided walk through the site, Cheops wasn't needed once she had got their tickets and had shown them where to meet the bus for the ride home. She had gotten her group organized, she had said her good nights and then she used the opportunity of a free evening to slip back to her apartment. These tours helped meet the expenses, but Cheops was an archaeologist first and she was anxious to learn about her dig, now tantalizingly close just on the other side of the river.

The encounter with Willy that afternoon had left her feeling bitter and short tempered. It was hard to have to live with the memories of Deir el-Bahari and with the losses. So many losses; her daughter, Willy's son, her lower leg and Willy's love. Too many loses for one person to absorb without very deep wounds, and Willy insisted on rubbing salt into them.

Now there was the extra worry of the children. Willy had to be using them. She knew Willy, knew how focused she was when she was on an assignment. The woman would have worked out her plot in detail; how, when, where, and she would have escape plans too. It was unlikely that the children were an impulse decision. They had to have a part in Willy's plans, but how?

Cheops walked up the dusty street, greeting those she knew along the way. She wore her gallabeeya, the long, hooded robe of the Arab nations. This was Cheops' eastern world; the other side of her existence. Cheops had been born in Egypt of British parents and enjoyed the privilege of dual citizenship. Having spent so much of her life in sites along the Nile, and at her parent's small home in Giza, she was just as Egyptian as she was English in her outlook. Willy too had been the child of two cultures.

That summer, they had rented a sailboat and taken the children fishing down the Nile. Willy had cleaned the fish they had caught, and Cheops had cooked them on a small charcoal brazier. In the afternoon, the two children had cooled off with a swim, while the adults watched.

"How did you come by your Greek name?" Cheops had asked, absently stroking Willy's hand, that rested near her own, with a fingertip.

"My father was a Greek resistance fighter and my mother was an English WAC stationed in liberated Greece at the end of the war. My father always said that Hitler he could resist, but mom, he couldn't! It was love at first sight, so they told me."

Cheops had gathered her courage and responded softly, "I know that feeling."

Those sky-blue eyes had turned to her. "Yes, so do I. I love you, Cheops," Willy had responded, giving Cheops far more than she had expected.

Cheops had smiled broadly, her green eyes sparkling like emeralds. "I love you too, Willy."

Cheops shook the memory from her thoughts as she entered the government owned apartment building and took the elevator up to the sixth floor. The apartment she entered was basic. It was, officially, the apartment given to the chief archaeologist working at site KV5. The walls were cinder block and there were only three rooms; a basic bathroom, a small bedroom, and the main room, which was used for storage and research. Three makeshift tables filled the space. Two were loaded down with the trappings of an archaeology lab; the other was Cheops' computer station.

Cheops didn't bother turning on a light. She walked over, and taking a seat, she clicked her computer on and waited for it to load. Then she went to her e-mail, clicking on the Leeds' response.

It read:

Cheops, get out of there! You are in grave danger! People suffering from deep drug induced psychosis and/or the effects of torture can be deeply psychopathic. You could well be dealing with a killer! Symptoms could include: joint pain, flashbacks, seizures, headaches,   disorientation,   slurred   speech,   lack   of   balance, confusion, acute paranoia, personality changes, violence and/or other anti-social behavior. I advise you to get away and call the authorities to deal with this individual.

Roger

Cheops face tightened into grim lines. To save her own life and to protect the children, she was going to have to betray Willy to the police. She didn't think it would help. The police would have little power or resources to deal with a crazed tourist. But the reality was she didn't have too many options left. Willy's behavior was becoming more and more irrational and unpredictable. Today had taught her not to believe in the gentle moments. They seemed always to be followed with emotional violence.

She sensed her more than heard her, the energy that ebbed and flowed in the air whenever Willy was near. Cheops turned in her chair. A figure in black stood silhouetted against the open balcony doors. Dangling from one hand was a garrote.

Realization swept over Cheops. Her murder would look like a break and entry. Willy would be back on the ship, babysitting her sleeping children. *The perfect alibi. Such a tragedy about Cheops!* She stood, squared her shoulders and looked death in the face.

The door rattled as a key was put in. Cheops twisted to look at the door. *Inge!* Her heart pounded in fear for her assistant, who was going to walk into a death trap unawares. Cheops looked back with pleading eyes to her killer. No one was there. The curtains blew gently on the night air.

"Cheops! You scared me! What are you doing in the lab in the dark? Cheops. Are you alright?" Cheops slumped into her chair and put her head on the desk.

On the stern of the ship was a wide, railess platform that the crew used when loading cargo. It was there that Willy went. She sat with her feet hanging over the edge, looking out into the darkness. Over the dark strip of the Nile, she could make out the old escarpment, silhouetted in front of the starry sky. The escarpment was eroded into two deep canyons, The Valley of the Kings and The Valley of the Queens. Deir el-Bahari lay there.

She had never been back. She wandered if Cheops had. It must be hard for the archaeologist to work just a narrow ridge away from the place where their children had died.

There had been lots of time to kill Cheops tonight. There had been time for her to slip from her spot in the shadows of the balcony and move to stand close enough that she could read the screen over Cheops' shoulder. She had the garrote taut between her two hands. It would have been so easy.

Instead, she had backed quietly away until the flap of the curtain on a sudden gust of wind had alerted Cheops to her presence. The knock at the door had given her the seconds she needed to escape and avoid a confrontation. It would have been the perfect murder! She'd planned it for months while she lay in agony. The bitch deserved to die! Why the hell had she not killed her?

An unsteady hand wiped over her face. Tonight, her joints were throbbing. The pain felt good. It was punishment for climbing up to Cheops' apartment and then not having the guts to do her in. Maybe, it was being in that apartment again after all this time that unnerved her.

"This is where you live?" she had asked looking into a packing case filled with Styrofoam chips. "The artifacts have a better place to sleep!"

Cheops had laughed and walked over to rub her hands up Willy's chest as she had done earlier that day. "Why would it concern you that my bed is a double mattress on the floor?"

"Maybe I thought I'd like to try it out," Willy had challenged, her eyes locking on Cheops like a missile seeking its target.

"Maybe, I like sleeping alone," she had teased.

"You can't ever be alone again," Willy had muttered sexily, nuzzling Cheops' ear and throat as she talked. "We are one. Our bond is forever!"

Tears rolled down Willy's face and she wiped them away with annoyance. It should have lasted forever. They should have watched their children grow and gotten old together. *Damn! Damn Cheops! Why did she have to lead our children to their deaths?*

She had read the e-mail. It had said she was dangerous. It used words like psychosis and psychopathic. Was she crazy? Had she broken under torture after all? A break so deep inside her soul that no one but Cheops could detect it? Would she regret it if she killed Cheops? If? When had that word crept into her plans? *If. Damn.*

* * * * *

Cheops slept on Inge's couch that night. Well, not slept; she had been too tense to sleep, although she had been exhausted after the police had left. "Yes, Madame," they had said. They understood the problem, they had assured her, but if she had not seen the face of the intruder, if no one could verify the threats, then there was little they could do. Willy was a British subject and not their problem. They would take her in for questioning tomorrow and see what they could do. And they would arrange for the children to be taken to an orphanage.

Cheops stared at the cracked plaster ceiling. *I've betrayed Willy again.* And once again, Willy's hate had betrayed their love. It was a vicious circle that could only lead to disaster.

Chapter Seven

The next day, Cheops gathered her group together after breakfast and they boarded the bus to take them to the Valley of the Kings on the other side of the river via the Luxor Bridge. Willy had gotten the children fed and dressed but left them with Cheops at the front of the bus. Looking pale and shaky, Willy went to the back and sat quietly, with her head leaning against the window.

The bus ride was fairly long as it involved going down river, crossing the bridge and then heading north again before turning inland to the Valley of the Kings. The group was quiet as they piled out. This was a place of legends and although there was little to see above ground, the power of this sacred place flooded their hearts with awe.

The terrain was rocky and dry; a silent wasteland filled only with the anguished whimper of the wind. Square, stone tunnels marked the entranceway of each famous tomb. Each had a wrought iron gate that would be closed and locked at night. Not that there was anything left to steal. Ancient grave robbers and collectors had long since drained Egypt of its heritage. Now tourists saw only the shadowy remains, painted in frescoes on the tomb walls.

Cheops led them through Rameses II's tomb and several of the other tombs near by, taking them down the long, sloping corridors to the deep shafts where the sarcophaguses lie. Along the way, she would point out the false passages and traps that the grave robbers overcame on their quest for treasure. She would stop at a scene painted on a wall and make the stiff figures come alive as she related their stories.

"Here are Rameses and his bride, in a boat, hunting water fowl along the Nile. You see, they are nestled in a patch of flowering lotus reeds, the symbol of eternal life. See his pride as he shows off for his sister and queen, shooting at the ducks with a jeweled and gold-leafed bow and arrow. His Queen reaches to him in love and adoration. It must have been a special day that he shared with her. He must have ordered that it be painted here amongst the history of his battles and achievements. I wonder if his immortal soul still wanders at night and stops to relive this day again. He must have loved her very deeply."

As the strong wind embraces the fragile reed, Malone, Willy thought while she followed along at the end of the group, watching Cheops' animated face and her sparkling eyes as she talked softly to the children, explaining to them about their proud heritage.

Lastly, she led them through the tomb of King Tutankhamen. Earlier that day she had pointed out to them the house of Howard Carter, which sat on top of a high mesa down from the Valley of the Kings. She related his remarkable story and laughed at the so-called curses that the popular press had created around his discovery.

"No, Carter did not die of a mysterious, poisonous bite. He died from a simple mosquito bite that got infected. Infected wounds were a common cause of death in those days. Remember this was well before antibiotics. Carter was already weak from malaria and dysentery, so his immune system could not fight off the infection. I'm sorry, I know people love mystery and curses, but I'm afraid archaeology is just hard, meticulous, and back-breaking work."

Cheops finished answering questions as she brought them back to the entrance of KV5. "This is where I am currently working. This is the famous KV5. It was only discovered in 1995. Actually, rediscovered. The explorer James Burton noted its existence way back in 1925. We know he had explored the tomb because he had made a map of it. In the pillared hall, he wrote his name on the ceiling with the smoke from his candle. It can still be quite clearly seen; Burton 1925.

"The tomb was lost for two reasons. First, because the early archaeologists working in this area thought that it was an unfinished tomb and not of any importance. Second, because you'll notice that Tut's tomb is conveniently close. We have a picture of Carter in 1922, toasting his guests as they ate lunch in an unfinished tomb near to the Tut site. We think this might have been the tomb. The American team that rediscovered this site and are overseeing the excavation found a wine glass buried in the rubble near the entrance. It might very well have been left over from one of Carter's famous luncheons!"

Cheops pointed back to the entrance of Tut's tomb. "We believe that Carter dumped the waste from his own dig into what he thought was a convenient empty pit! We now know that in reality this is an extensive tomb site associated with the sons of Rameses II. I'm sorry, I can't take you in. It is not open to the public yet because it is structurally unsafe. The roof is badly cracked because the heavy tourist buses used to come up this far and the chambers are full of rubble and years of eroded debris."

"Hello, Willy," came a voice from the tall woman's right. Willy pulled her attention away from what Cheops was saying to look down at a small, wiry woman.

"Hello, Inge. It has been a long time."

"Yes."

Willy looked back to where Cheops stood on the other side of the group. She found it hard, for some reason, to look Inge in the eyes. "Ah, I heard you were there for Cheops... after..." Willy looked down at her feet.

"Someone had to be," came the bitter response.

Willy nodded, her jaw muscles rippling with tension. "Thank you," she said, so low that Inge was not sure she heard her.

"Inge! Come up here!" called Cheops, catching sight of her feisty assistant and breaking out in a big smile. "Ladies and gentlemen, this is my chief assistant, Dr. Inge Gardener. She's going to lead you over the Agatha Christie's Walk to visit Deir El-Bahari and the temple of Hatshepsut. While you are doing that, I'm going to check out how the dig is going. If anything new has been discovered, I'll show you when you get back."

Cheops turned and spoke to the two children in Egyptian. "Our bus driver, Fekri Hawass, has to go back to Luxor to have the bus serviced. He said he would take you with him and buy you ice cream while I work. Would you like that?"

Zahi smiled broadly and looked at his big sister with pleading eyes. Amand wrapped a protective arm around him. "Thank you, Cheops Malone. We would like this very much. We do not wish to go to Deir El-Bahari and ice cream is very good." Cheops' heart went out to this poor, serious child, who had had to face so much in her short life. She gave each of them a hug and turned them over to the fatherly Fekri to guide them back to the bus.

Betty poked the long-suffering Abe. "You see what you can do to find me one of those hidden treasures along the way," she ordered with a smile.

Abe scoffed, "At my age, I'll need every ounce of energy I've got just to get up that path, woman! Find your own gold!"

"Come on, Betty," laughed Jean, hooking her arm around the New Yorker's. "We'll go ahead so the men don't slow us down!"

With much scoffing and teasing, the small group started off with Inge in the lead. Bob hung back. "I could stay behind and help if you want, Cheops," he oiled.

"No," Cheops answered firmly and turned away.

"Hey, you'd better treat me right or..."

"Or what?" came an icy growl from behind him. Bob turned to see Willy Kyrtsakis standing arms folded, looking at him with eyes as cold as a glacier.

"I'd better go," he muttered and trotted to catch up to the others.

Willy turned to meet Cheops' sad eyes. "I don't understand you anymore, Willy," she said.

Willy nodded and looked at her foot piling loose gravel into a ridge. "You ever go there?"

"Each year, to leave flowers. Many people do. I keep their grave nice, too."

"Where did you send Amand and Zahi?"

"I didn't think they needed to see Deir el-Bahari. Fekri is going to take them for ice cream in Luxor."

Willy nodded to the ground again. Then she squared her shoulders and without a word started to walk up the valley to where the dirt trail led over the ridge to the Valley of the Queens. Cheops watched her go. Part of her was relieved that Willy was leaving her alone and part of her was aching to go after her.

"Dr. Malone, we've finished the survey of the hall of the sixty chambers."

"Coming," called Cheops over her shoulder, then, turning, she joined her crew below ground. It was difficult for her to get about the cave with her prosthesis. Often, in low areas, she had to crawl propelling herself forward with her arms. On rough ground, with enough headroom, she would use a small spade for balance. As a last resort, if the exploration of the cave involved tight fits, she simply removed the leg altogether.

Willy walked to the base of the ridge and stopped. She turned and looked down the narrow canyon, now crowded with tourists eager to see the various gravesites. Cheops must have brought them on site before it was open to the public, Willy realized. She turned and started off again. Three steps, then she stopped. She wasn't afraid to go to the site of her son's death. In her career, she had come to terms with the loss of close comrades. The site couldn't hurt her, only the memories, and she carried them with her all the time.

Then why did something keep pulling her back? Some uneasiness deep in her gut. She found a patch of shade and sat down. She needed to think. From her waist pouch, she pulled a bottle of water and took a long swig, then slipped the plastic bottle back into place. She sat for a long time but no clear thoughts came. Sitting there, still and quiet, she felt like she was going through a metamorphosis. It tired her. She should move, make a decision, do something. Instead she just sat, not sure any longer who she was or who she might become.

There really was very little sound. Neither a roar nor a bang, more of a whoosh, like air released from a giant balloon. Willy looked up to see a dust cloud shooting from the mouth of KV5 and drifting out over the surprised tourists, who yelled and coughed, now ghostly figures in the small dust storm. Willy stood slowly and watched the scene as it unfolded like an action movie. Then she was in motion, hitting the wall of tourists like a football player and plowing through to the entrance. Gasping, coughing workers were staggering out and falling to the ground, eyes red and weeping. The outside workers grabbed water and rags and started to help those who were on the ground.

Willy grabbed an emergency knapsack from its peg on the wall, pulled out a gas mask and slipped it in place. Picking up a flashlight, she entered the collapsing tomb. Two blackened figures staggered past her. She let them go. They could make it on their own. Some of the electrical lighting was still functioning, casting yellow pools of light in the grey haze of dust. But visibility was almost nil.

Only the first room was cleared to any extent. After that, Willy had to crawl on her belly through room two and then on to the hall of the sixteen pillars. The tops of the pillars stood out like lonely sentinels guarding a lost frontier. Some of the roof blocks had fallen, huge squares of rock weighing tons each. Willy crawled around them like a slalom skier, trying not to think about the tons of rock just inches over her head.

Squeezing through into the next chamber, she skidded down the sharp limestone flakes to a room that was relatively clear of debris. Here, in the settling dust, she found Mohammed. He was breathing shallowly and coughing up mud and phlegm but he was conscious. Willy quickly squirted some water over his face and into his mouth, then wiped his face clean as best she good. She slipped a mask over his face and left him for the rescue team to find. She knew they would not be too far behind her.

She found Cheops partly buried by limestone chips at the far end of the chamber; her body was still and limp. Willy listened for a heart beat and was relieved to hear one, pounding still on its adrenalin rush. Gently, she washed the woman's face and cleaned the mud from her eyes and nose. Cheops moaned and Willy squirted some water on her lips. A hand came up and wiped her face as she coughed. "Water," Cheops choked. Willy squirted a little into her mouth and the archaeologist washed it around and spat it out. Then she took the bottle from Willy's hand and took a bigger swig, swallowing this time, only to throw it up again.

Willy pulled a mask out of the bag and slipped it into place. Then, she used her bloodied hands to scoop Cheops free. Cheops lay still, only lifting the mask now and again for a quick drink. She felt dazed and sick to her stomach and just wanted the pain in her chest to go away. Soon figures loomed out of the fog, and Cheops was carefully lifted and strapped to a stretcher, although she hoarsely protested that she was all right. Slowly, the group inched back out of the cave, Willy staying close to Cheops' side and only now wondering why she had come to the archaeologist's aid.

The light was dazzling when they emerged. Order had been restored and except for the nosy stares of passing tourists, on their way to see the tombs farther up the canyon, things were back to normal. No one had been seriously hurt, although those caught inside were cut and bruised and suffering from asthmatic conditions caused by the amount of dust in their lungs.

Cheops sat on a wood box and wheezed instructions. She had a nasty bruise and lump on her right temple but insisted that she was all right. Willy had stood back, quietly watching with worried eyes. She too was badly scraped and she had the chemical taste in her mouth that forewarned of another drug rush. Her joints throbbed and her head ached painfully. Slowly, she sat on the ground and lowered her head to her knees.

"Madame, you are Major Wilhelminia Kyrtsakis?"

Willy looked up with blurry eyes, feeling very disorientated. "Yes," she slurred at a pair of navy police pants.

"I have here a warrant for your arrest. I am to take you to police headquarters in Luxor for questioning. You will please stand and face the cliff wall."

Willy looked up in surprise, trying to focus on the police officer's face. "What did I do? What charge?" she managed to get out with difficulty.

"A complaint has been made by Dr. Cheops Malone that you threatened to kill her. You will stand please and face the cliff wall."

Willy nodded in shock and slowly pulled herself to her feet. She turned and leaned her hands against the wall, allowing the young police officer to pat her down. Her arms were pulled painfully behind her back and metal handcuffs snapped into place. Turning, her eyes made contact with Cheops' as she sat by the tomb entrance. The green eyes were hurt and filled with sorrow, the innocent face streaked with dirt and distorted with pent up emotion.

Cheops, with a jolt of guilt, had seen a young police officer ask a question of one of her workers and watched him walk over to where Willy sat on the ground. She stared in horror as Willy was searched for weapons and then handcuffed. The tall woman turned and her eyes locked onto Cheops. The blue was dull, lifeless, the face, an empty plain devoid of any emotion. The young officer pulled on Willy's arm and like an obedient child, Willy turned and followed the policeman down the road to his waiting car. *My God, what have I done?* Cheops moaned inside.

Chapter Eight

Inge had stopped at the stone wall two hundred yards back from the outer courtyards of Hatshepsut's temple. She had explained to Cheops' group about the architectural importance of this site and about the powerful female pharaoh, who had taken the crown at her husband's death and often portrayed herself in statues and paintings with a beard. "Her first minister's grave is just over there," Inge explained. "From paintings, we know that he was very close to Hatshepsut and her children. The close proximity of his grave reinforces speculation that their relationship might have involved more than the running of the State."

The group had then wandered off to see the site. Inge never went on site except when she went with Cheops. None of the guides did. Respect, superstition, emotional pain, there were a lot of reasons for why this practice had started after the shooting. It had never been discussed, just by some common, silent consent, the guides never went back.

The day after the shootings, the tourists had started to leave. The Egyptians had paraded with signs. 'The terrorists were not Egyptians!' 'Tourists, do not leave, we love you!' But the tourists had left. Deir el-Bahari had been opened to the public the very next day. Crews of workmen had scrubbed the blood from the stone, and plastered over the bullet holes. While a few brave tourists watched, they repainted the lost sections of ancient frescoes.

Security now was very tight. Tour buses were guarded, metal detectors were used at the gates of all the sites and armed escorts were sometimes assigned to tourist buses. It did no good. Tourism to Egypt had dropped by two million visitors. Thousands were out of work and poverty and sorrow filled the old streets. Egypt's population would double in the next ten years. It was a country now on the brink of disaster. All because of the teachings of religious fanatics. Inge sighed; she, like Cheops, had come to love this country, and it broke her heart to see the pain.

It had been a shock to see Willy again. She was so pale and thin. It was only when she had turned those blue eyes on Inge that she felt again the animal magnetism that made the woman both scary and fascinating at the same time. She had only been a young grad when Cheops and Willy had been lovers. She had been shocked by her boss's conduct at first, then warmed by their love. The two women and their children had been inseparable that season. After, she hadn't been sure that Cheops would ever recover. Those were the months of blackness that Inge tried not to dwell on, when she had found herself trying to help Cheops through the grief and pain.

Now Willy was back for revenge. Cheops had told her last night what had been going on. It was Inge who had encouraged Cheops to call the police as she had been advised. She had come to like Willy in the old days, but she had always been a little afraid of her. Willy had called herself a security officer attached to the British embassy, but you only had to be with the woman for a short time to know that she was a lot more than that. There was something not quite human about Willy, something wild, dangerous and beautiful. Only Cheops seemed to be able to control the turbulent personality. Cheops had no fear of Willy... until now.

Inge was glad to see the group reform. She was concerned that Willy had not joined them and was anxious to get back to Cheops. Surely, the soldier would not try anything in such a public place? She hoped the police had come as they promised. "Everyone ready for the climb back?" Inge said brightly. "Isn't it a beautiful site? Come on, this way. If you have any questions, I'll be glad to answer them on the walk."

The group surged forward with concern and questions when they saw Cheops standing filthy and bleeding outside the dig. Inge's first reaction was to look around for Willy. Cheops saw the angry look and explained in a voice husky with dust and emotion, "There was a small cave in. Fortunately, no one was badly hurt. Willy crawled in and helped Mohammed and me, until a rescue crew arrived.

"Where is that strange woman, anyway?" asked Aaron, looking around in annoyance.

Cheops looked uncomfortable. "Ah, she had some sudden business come up. I don't know if she will be able to get back to finish the rest of the tour."

"That's too bad," observed Bill in disappointment. "She sure knew a lot about international law. I enjoyed talking to her the few chances I got."

"She knew a lot about sports too," added Abe to the tribute.

Betty and Jean exchanged a knowing look. Something had definitely gone wrong while they were away.

"Good riddance to the stupid dyke," Bob muttered under his breath, looking angry and resentful.

The group headed back to the bus when it arrived shortly after. Amand and Zahi looked frightened when they saw Cheops and ran to hug her. Cheops quietly explained about the cave in and that Willy had been called away on business. She would wait to tell them her other plans until after she had dealt with her tour group.

On the bus, Cheops explained that they would have the afternoon to shop in the old market of Luxor. Betty and Jean clapped their hands with delight and Abe and Bill groaned in mock dismay. The Scotts were anxious to know where a good gold smith might be found. After answering all their questions, Cheops slumped into her seat. Amand slipped in beside her and held her hand as they made their way across the desert. Back at the boat, the group dispersed to wash and change for lunch and their afternoon excursion.

Cheops led the children to her cabin and gave them some paper and crayons to draw with while she showered and treated her many cuts. Then, dressed in a fresh pair of blue jeans and t-shirt, she sat down to talk to the two children about their future.

"Amand, Zahi, Willy and I want only the best for you. We will see to it that you are well cared for and educated properly. You must understand, however, that there are laws that must be followed. Willy cannot adopt you because she is not Egyptian. She is also... not very well at the moment."

"She has been sick, Cheops Malone?" Zahi asked.

"Yes, very sick but I hope... I hope she will get better soon. I have arranged that this afternoon, I will take you to an orphanage that I know. It is a very good one. I am having the authorities check to see if you have any family who might want to raise you. If that is not the case, then I will adopt you, and raise you as my own children, if you would like that."

Amand wrapped herself around Cheops in a tight hug and Zahi snuggled up to her arm. "Oh, please, Cheops Malone! Please!"

Cheops rubbed the small child's back, fighting back her own tears. "Whatever happens. I will always be there for you and... and so will Major Kyrtsakis."

* * * * *

Willy did not answer the older police officer's questions. To be truthful, she would have had trouble doing so. She had used a lot of energy up helping Cheops and now the drugs warred in her system. It had been a very long day and the room she sat in, on a hard wood chair, was stuffy and smelt of dry paper and dust.

The older officer, dressed in a well-used grey suit, went over to talk to the uniformed cop who had arrested her. "Dilated eyes, running nose; she's a crazy pot head. She's probably come to the Middle East to get drugs more easily. I imagine all she wants from Dr. Malone is money for her habit."

"We must be careful here. We do not want an incident with the British. See that the nurse cleans her wounds. We can't afford for her to die of infection at our hands or the European press will be writing about what savages we are," the officer sighed. "Release her this evening. This is not our problem. We have done all we can."

The young officer nodded and walked out of the room to see to arranging a temporary cell for Major Kyrtsakis. The older officer went back to the beautiful woman, who was slumped in the chair, her handcuffed hands behind the straight back stopping her from falling over. He reached down and lifted her chin so that they looked at each other.

"You are to leave Cheops Malone alone. If I get a complaint that you have been bothering her again, I will send you to the woman's prison and throw away the key. Do you understand?"

Willy nodded dully. The uniformed officer returned and helped Willy stand up. Then he led her to the detention block. He wondered if it was true, what the archaeologist had said, that this woman had been a soldier and tortured. Why would a country send its women to do a man's job?

* * * * *

It was a nice orphanage. Well run, caring and modern. Still, it broke Cheops' heart to leave the two wide-eyed children there and walk away. They had cried and Cheops once again had to reassure them that they were safe and that Willy and she would be looking after their interests. It was difficult to explain to children that life was governed by legal procedures that must be followed.

Once back on the ship, she checked to make sure her tour group had all gotten back safely and then hurried to her room to change for dinner. Fortunately, each of her guests had a story to tell of their shopping excursions and it wasn't until the end of the meal that Aaron brought attention to the missing people. "Where's Willy and them street kids?" he'd grumbled.

The table went quiet and looked at Cheops. She looked at her plate and then up at the group of expectant faces. "Willy has some business that she needs to attend to, as I told you. The children are now in the care of a government agency until such time that a suitable relative can be found to take them."

"But what if there is no one?" asked Jean in concern.

Cheops gave a shaky smile, feeling right at the end of her endurance. It had been a very hard and traumatic day, physically and emotionally. "I'm rather hoping that will be the case, because as an Egyptian, I can then legally adopt the children," she explained. "I've already signed the necessary papers to put the legal wheels in motion."

The table burst into applause and congratulated Cheops, except for the Scotts. Bob sat scowling and Aaron demanded, "What about Willy? She found them. They should be her responsibility, not yours!"

Cheops gritted her teeth to stop from snapping. Her head was pounding and all she wanted to do was lie down. "Willy is a British subject and cannot legally adopt an Egyptian. I was born here and have dual citizenship, so I can."

"Well, like I said before, Cheops, if you need any help with the paper work you just let me know," offered Bill Brant.

Cheops smiled. "Thanks, Bill. Thank you all for your well wishes and support. You are a great group to tour with. Now, if you don't mind, I think I'll retire early. It has been a long day."

To a chorus of good nights and well wishes, Cheops made her way down to her cabin and downed some painkillers. Too tired to even undress, she flopped down on the bed and looked in misery at the empty bed beside hers. "I loved you, Willy. I will always love you. I am so sorry. So terribly sorry," she whispered, the tears rolling down her face until exhaustion drove her into a fretful sleep.

* * * * *

Willy was released from jail in the evening and just made it back to the ship before it cast its moorings and set sail. For a long time, she sat on the platform at the back and watched the wake of their ship leave silver ribbons of moonlight down the dark waters of the Nile. *The moon is going to set early tonight*, she observed.

She had come here for two reasons. First, because she needed time to decide what to do next and second because she didn't want to be seen by Cheops. When they were farther down river, it would be too late for Cheops to have her thrown off. Her exhausted state had allowed the drugs that still remained in her system to run riot today. It was hard for her to think things through clearly. Still, she was getting better. The flashbacks were gone and she was finding it easier to follow a chain of thought.

Revenge, she realized, was not going to make the pain go away. She had stayed alive for the wrong reasons during all those months of captivity and torture. So why was she living? Maybe so she could help those little Egyptian kids. Give them the chances that she would have given her own son and Cheops' daughter. If her son was alive, sitting here beside her, that is what he would want. Somehow, it gave some meaning to his senseless murder if his death made some other child's life better.

The terrorist attack at Deir el-Bahari had not been Cheops' fault. She had lost just as much, more, than Willy had. It was just easier to hate than to mourn. Easier to seek revenge than to feel helpless. She had been so wrong. Now she needed to set things right. She'd rent a sailboat at the next port of call and she and the kids would disappear down the Nile. Willy was a good sailor; she would sail along the coast to Alexandria and there obtain, through her old secret service network, three passports to get them safely back to England.

She stretched her long frame and settled her head back against the bulkhead. A place in the Lake District would be nice. The kids could go to school. Maybe she could have a small farm, some sheep, horses, who knows. She could teach rock climbing on the nearby rock faces to tourists. Her eyes closed and she slept.

A few hours later, she woke cold and stiff and staggered to her feet. She had been allowed to clean up in the prison and a nurse had treated her cuts, but she was still wearing the clothes that she had crawled through the tomb in that morning. That seemed ages ago. What should she do next? She could hardly sleep in Cheops' room: it might lead to her being arrested again. She didn't need anymore police involvement if she wanted to slip quietly from the country with the children.

She'd better stay in the kids' room and slip into Cheops' room to get her things when Cheops went up to breakfast with the kids. She'd have to explain to the kids somehow that her presence aboard the ship had to be kept a secret. She opened the door and slipped down the hall.

She didn't want any trouble with Cheops. A lump formed in her throat and she swallowed it down. That was past history. She slipped into the children's room and went over to check on them before she went to sleep on the couch. The beds were empty. *NO!* a voice screamed in her head. *NOT AGAIN!*

A figure in the shadows of the stairwell saw Willy charge from one room and into the other.

Chapter Nine

Something had awakened Cheops and she got up, groggily surprised to find herself still in her street clothes. She looked out the window and saw that they were long on their way up river to Edfu.

She unlatched the frame and pushed the window down, allowing the swirl of the water and the cool night air of the desert to enter the cabin. Tears welled again in her eyes. *Willy, please be safe. Please get well*, she wished, looking at the dark heavens.

The door to Cheops' room slammed open and she turned in surprise. "Where are my kids?" demanded Willy, her eyes cold fire as she stood bristling with rage.

Cheops met the challenge with calm reason, hiding the fear that made her heart pound in her chest. "I placed them with a government agency who handle orphaned children. Once..."

"You bitch!" snarled Willy, rocketing forward. Cheops didn't see the blow coming, she simply doubled up with pain when it hit. Nor did she see the second that sent her senseless to the floor. Willy scooped her up and carried her down the hall and out to the open back deck. She held the unconscious woman out over the black water. Then she hesitated, and pulled the body back close to her.

A split second later, an elbow smashed into Willy's nose, blinding her with pain. Blood spurted out as she dropped Cheops to the deck and grabbed her face. "I hate you! I hate you!" Cheops cried in her own pain and fear, backing close to the edge. Willy grabbed for her, but another pair of hands was there first, pushing the smaller woman off the open platform and out into the darkness.

Instinctively, Cheops grabbed Willy's outstretched arm and the two of them fell into the muddy waters of the Nile. The ship continued on its way. The moon hung low over the west bank of the Nile. The side of the sunset. The side of the dead.

Cheops splashed about in panic. *Where is Willy?* "I can't swim!" she called out to the darkness as she went under again. Strong arms grabbed her from behind and pulled her to the surface.

Cheops clung desperately to the strong neck, sending them both under once more. Willy kicked her off and, grabbing her hair, pulled Cheops back to the surface. "Stop fighting!" she slurred out.

"I can't swim!" Willy got a hold around Cheops' neck and pulled her up against her chest. With strong strokes, she started to swim after the retreating lights of the ship.

"What are you doing?"

"Swimming to the boat," Willy explained in surprise, then stopped swimming to look at Cheops. *Why are we in the water?* she wondered. Her exhaustion and anger had left her confused and disorientated. They went under and Willy remembered to swim.

Cheops gasped for air and tried not to panic. "Keep swimming, Willy!" Willy started out again toward the distant lights of the ship.

"Willy! It's gone! Oh shit! Listen to me, you're not thinking straight. Listen to me, honey. Listen, okay?" Cheops coaxed as Willy trod water, holding the two of them barely above water level. "The boat has gone. We need to swim to shore. Go that way," Cheops ordered, pointing over Willy's shoulder towards the distant shore.

Willy started off swimming in a circle, not sure what she was supposed to do. "No! Not that way! Willy, listen, not in a circle! That way," Cheops sobbed in a panic. Willy followed the pointing arm. "Okay, that's good, towards the bank. Good, don't let go."

Willy set her jaw and ignored the pain in her cold joints. She fought back the confusion and the exhaustion and concentrated on Cheops' words. They had to forget their differences and work together or they were never going to get out of this. They had to get out of this and get back to the kids.

"Willy! Don't stop swimming!"

"Tired."

"No! Swim! Just a little farther. No, that way!" With relief, Cheops felt the muddy riverbank under her one good foot. Willy was still swimming, barely conscious of her actions. Cheops let her pull her close to shore and then she crawled up on the bank, reaching to pull the larger woman up beside her. For a while they lay panting for breath.

"Everyone knows how to swim, Malone," slurred Willy mockingly.

"I grew up in the desert, damn it!

"You gotta learn," came the sleepy response.

For a bit, the two women lay in exhaustion. Then Cheops spoke. "Willy, I didn't take your children away from you again. I've taken steps to adopt them if a suitable relative cannot be found to take care of them. They are well taken care of, Willy, and they understand that we will be there for them. You're not well enough at the moment to help them, Willy."

Silence. Then, "I shouldn't have hit you."

"I shouldn't have hit you either, or pulled you off the boat."

"Who pushed us?"

"Bob."

"Bastard."

"Yeah."

"Cheops?"

"Hmmm?"

"Are there Nile crocodiles or did they mummify them all?"

"It's okay. They don't think that there are any below the Aswan dam now."

Silence. Then, "How sure are they?"

Cheops laughed gently. "Well, I guess we are testing that theory right now!"

Willy rolled over on her side with effort and looked at Cheops in the fading moonlight. "You're shivering. We need to find shelter. The night is going to be cold and we'll need medical attention or that water is likely to kill us. Can you get up?"

Cheops looked at Willy and reached a hand out to touch her face. "Yes, but Willy, I don't think I can walk far with the prosthesis wet. It's going to rub."

Willy nodded. She had to find the energy within her to get them somewhere safe or they were likely to die of exposure and shock. "I'm going to try to carry you, okay? But my mind isn't too clear when I get tired."

"Really?" Cheops teased gently. "We can get out of this, Willy. If we help each other." Their two hands linked together in an unspoken bond.

* * * * *

Willy lay on the muddy bank and tried not to think too deeply about what she had just done. By going to Cheops' aid again, she had pulled out the last thread that held the patch she had so carefully applied over her raw emotions. She wasn't sure there was anything now to stop her anger and violence from hemorrhaging out.

She lay still for a while, trying to focus the energy that she still had left in her. Then she reeled to her feet and stood unsteadily on the steep bank of the Nile. Once her world stopped spinning, she bent to help a half conscious archaeologist to her feet. "Come on, Malone. We gotta go."

"Okay, I'm with you," groaned Cheops, leaning heavily on Willy for support. Together, they staggered up the bank and onto a farmer's trail that ran along the edge of the river. Beyond were small fields of grain.

"Why?" Cheops asked, looking up at the lean, hard face, etched into contrasting planes of dark and light relief by the moonlight.

"Why what?" asked Willy, disinterestedly, as she looked around for light that would indicate habitation. Some distance down the path, there was the flicker of firelight through bushes.

"Why didn't you let me drown?" Cheops held her breath, knowing this answer could mean all the difference to her future and Willy's. The answer that would tell her what was going on in Willy's mind.

"Okay, listen, we gotta get down there," said Willy, pointing to the light off in the distance. "I'll carry you piggy-back but you gotta kind of keep me on track because I might start to wander off a bit."

Temper, fed on days of tension, flared inside Cheops. "Damn it, Willy! Why!" she yelled, grabbing the arm of the exhausted soldier and spinning Willy around to face her.

"Because I couldn't! That's why!" Willy yelled in her face. And then, softly, "Because I couldn't. I... I... still love you." Cheops gave a moan of relief and wrapped herself in Willy's arms. Willy kissed the smaller woman's head softly.

After a few minutes, Willy pushed Cheops away gently. With effort, Willy bent her aching knees and allowed Cheops to wrap herself around her own body. Hooking her long arms around Cheops' legs, she then stood. "Hold on tight in case I let go," warned the soldier.

"Willy?"

"Hmmm?" came the grumpy reply.

"I still love you, too," Cheops confessed, crying softly into the dark wet hair she had buried her face in.

Willy started up the path, her jaw tensed in the effort. Cheops tried to be as still as she could, realizing that this walk was taking everything that the soldier had physically and mentally.

"Tell me some history," came the surprising command after a few minutes of silence.

"What?" exclaimed Cheops, looking up.

"You know, your stuff. Ah... I kinda like it. It will keep my mind off this walk... and things."

"You like it?" asked Cheops softly, leaning her head back down against Willy's wet hair.

"Yeah."

"Okay. Queen Cleopatra wanted to meet the Roman general Mark Anthony who had conquered Alexandria. She sent several invitations to him to meet but he always refused. She was a very intelligent and talented woman, and she knew that the only way to save Egypt was for her to make an alliance with Mark Anthony. She was an Egyptian by birth but not race. Her family actually was Macedonian."

"A fellow Greek! Cool."

"She wasn't a dark, exotic beauty either. She was short, plump and blond!"

"Hey, I thought she was supposed to look like Elizabeth Taylor!"

"I'm afraid not," responded Cheops with a laugh, pleased that an old, familiar banter was re-establishing itself in their conversation.

"Well, that's the pits!"

"Hey! You love short blonds!" growled Cheops in fun, giving Willy a poke.

Willy's instant reaction was anger. Then she checked herself. She hadn't killed Cheops because she loved her. Cheops seemed, by her teasing, to be giving Willy yet another chance to express that love. Did she dare take it? Did she want to try to rebuild a life with Cheops? Yes, she did. "Oh yeah, I remember now!"

"And don't you forget it, Kyrtsakis!" ordered Cheops with more confidence than she felt. For a second there, she thought Willy was going to drop her. "Where was I? Oh yeah, she decided to send him a valuable Persian rug as a gift. The rug was carried into his presence and unrolled and out popped Cleopatra!"

"Talk about your carpetbaggers," muttered Willy.

"Willy!" exclaimed Cheops in shock.

"Well?" justified the soldier weakly. *Okay Willy, clean up your mouth, Cheops doesn't like that sort of rough talk. Save it for the barracks.*

"Well?" repeated Cheops indignantly, and then laughed. "Well, she had had an affair with Caesar and had several children by him. That was before she literally threw herself at the feet of Mark Anthony. And before that, she had originally been wed to her brother, the King of Egypt, but he died."

"Hmmm, so did Mark Anthony take her up on her offer?"

"Oh yeah, it was one hot affair! She was charming, rich and powerful, not to mention very, very bright."

"Ah, a marriage of convenience!"

"Yep, but at the naval battle of Actium she saw Mark Anthony was going to lose, so she dumped him and took her ships and went home."

"Not nice!"

"All's fair in love and war," Cheops announced blithely.

"I'll remember that," observed Willy dryly, her insecurities revealing themselves again. Was Cheops just coming on to her to save her life, or did she really still feel something for her?

Cheops picked up the insecurity in Willy's tone and hastened to reassure her. "Don't. That was then, this is now. No games, just love."

Silence, then softly, "I'm glad... so did she kill herself in remorse?"

Cheops laughed. "Fat chance! She just realized she was too old, frumpy and tired to seduce yet another Roman. She knew she would lose her throne, so she opted out. She let an asp bite her."

"Hmmm, so Mark Anthony was heart broken when he found out and acted like Romeo."

"Willy, you are a babe in the woods! He was pissed that Cleo had deserted him and came after her, only to find out she had beaten him to the punch. Without Egypt for support, he knew he was defeated and that the Romans were going to do horrible things to him, so he fell on his sword."

"All politics," slurred Willy, staggering a bit.

"'Fraid so. Sweetheart, you're heading for the bushes, go right," directed Cheops, giving Willy affectionate hug. "Do you want me to walk? I can."

"No, I'm okay."

Willy is something amazing, Cheops thought, as they slowly made their way down the dirt road. All she had gone through emotionally, and the torture she had endured, and yet here she was, digging deep into that amazing reserve, and forgiving and aiding her. Yes, Cheops had lived through a lot too, but she had friends to support her and the ability to talk through the pain. Willy had to bottle it all up inside and somehow cope with all the raw emotion and anger alone.

"Okay. We're almost at the farm house," gasped Willy.

"Let me down now, Sweetheart."

"Right. What did you call me?"

"Sweetheart," Cheops responded feeling awkward and embarrassed.

"I tried to kill you."

"No, you didn't. Had you tried, you would have succeeded. You thought about it, but you changed your mind."

Cheops hesitated and then added guiltily, "I had you arrested."

Willy stood, swaying slightly. "You did the right thing. You should have done it sooner. Still," she added with a smile, "I'm never going to let you live it down, Malone!"

"Okay. What did you call me?"

"Malone. It's a term of endearment," Willy responded, looking out over the black Nile.

Cheops reached up and cupped her chin, bringing Willy's face around to look at her. "Good," she whispered softly.

Willy wrapped the dirty, wet woman in her arms, feeling the wave of relief and love flow through her. She struggled, trying to get her tired mind to express how she felt. "You smell."

"So do you. See, already we are finding things in common, again."

Willy laughed weakly and wrapped a supportive arm around Cheops. "Come on. Let's go and give a farmer a story to tell the neighbors."

They had indeed given a poor, local farmer material for many evening stories. Willy had fallen through the doorway when a timid woman opened it. The shocked woman screamed, no doubt imagining a tree was falling on her. Cheops' arrival was not much better, stumbling into the terrified woman, as she tried to maneuver around Willy's body on her water soaked prosthesis.

"We need help," Cheops explained in English, forgetting in her concern for Willy to speak in Egyptian. She awkwardly knelt beside Willy. "We need to get to a doctor. We fell off a tourist boat and my friend is very sick. Can you take us to a doctor?"

The woman looked wide-eyed at her husband, who nodded. "I will get my wagon. You are not to worry. I am Mohammed Hassan and I will take you to the clinic," came the response in stilted English.

"Thank you, Mohammed Hassan, we are truly grateful. May Allah bless your house," responded Cheops, continuing in English so as to show respect for the farmer's learning. She used, however, the correct Egyptian response to a kindness offered.

She gently stroked the damp hair from Willy's face. Dull blue eyes tried to focus on her. "I'm going to kill you," Willy slurred.

Cheops put her finger tips on Willy's lips. "No, you're not. Remember. You saved me from the cave and the river."

Anne Azel

The eyes closed for a second as she realized what she had just done. They reopened. "I'm sorry, Malone."

"It's okay."

"I'm not well. Be careful," Willy mumbled.

"I will," reassured Cheops, although her fear of Willy was gone. She knew now that the love had returned to Willy's soul and that she would never hurt her intentionally again. She cradled Willy's head in her lap and wrapped her small hand around Willy's big, warm palm. *I love you, Willy*, she thought.

The wagon ride was bumpy and the night cold. The farmer had put a few pitchforks of straw on the cart for warmth and comfort but it did little good. The ride, however, had been easy compared to the problem of getting Willy on the cart. The woman was becoming delirious. She had taken a few erratic swings at both Cheops and the farmer, and had connected a left hook to Hassan's rather prominent nose! They had finally managed to convince Willy that they would leave her alone and let her sleep, if she would just climb into the back of the wagon.

It was almost two hours before the wagon finally pulled up in front of the mud brick clinic. Already the sun was starting to filter light into the night sky. How long had they been in the water and on the riverbank? Cheops had no idea. Exhaustion muddied her mind and she was starting to feel very sick to her stomach. She had swallowed some of the Nile's water in her panic. After four thousand years of waste and garbage being dumped in the river, the bacteria levels were dangerously high.

The farmer brought the mule to a standstill and hopped down from his cart. He went to the door and pounded loudly, yelling out in his broken English to impress all those who would hear and understand, "Doctor, Doctor, you wake please! Tourists have fallen off the tourist boat tonight and are near drowned! Doctor come quickly, they are English tourists, whom Allah has placed in your hands. If they die, the government will be very angry with you!"

Had Cheops been able to muster any energy at all, she would have laughed at the farmer's dramatics. Lights up and down the small village came on and heads appeared at the windows. The farmer now appealed to the crowd. "They are English tourists, who fell from the big tourist boat. The one, I think, has died!" he announced, pointing to Willy's sleeping body.

"Hush! Mohammed Hassan," chastised the sleepy doctor, hurriedly buttoning his shirt as he padded out to look in the wagon. "You could raise the dead with your bellowing. Get some men. I will

374

need them to help carry this one in," ordered the doctor, as he evaluated the situation. "Can you walk?" he asked, turning to Cheops.

"Yes, but not well. I have a prosthesis on my lower leg and it has really rubbed. We've swallowed a lot of Nile water and are starting to feel the effects. My... my friend has other problems that I'll tell you about inside. Handle her carefully; she can be violent."

"Allah protect us, the big English woman thinks she is Lawrence of Arabia!" exclaimed Hassan, who had not forgotten the good clout he had gotten from Willy. By now the air was full of Egyptian voices. Strong, wiry arms helped Cheops out and into the clinic. Oaths and curses drifted in to Cheops as they then fought to get the delirious Willy on a stretcher and into the clinic.

"Allah has sent us an English devil woman to test our faith!" came Hassan's voice over the others and Cheops managed a weak laugh. *Boy, they've gotten that right!*

With much clamor and confusion, the now unconscious soldier was brought in and placed on the examination table. Then, the doctor shooed the crowd out with much thanks. Turning, he padded back to Cheops. "Can you explain what has happened?" he asked, reaching for his stethoscope and turning to examine Willy.

"Yes, we were pushed from the open back deck of the tourist ship. My friend saved my life and pulled me to shore, but she has been sick. She was infiltrating a terrorist cell, was captured and held prisoner for a long time. They used drugs and torture on her to try and get her to reveal the names of the other operatives. She never broke but she paid an awful price for her silence. She is okay when she is rested, but when she is tired or upset, she can be... violent."

The doctor nodded and turned to smile at Cheops. "This I have seen," he said with a smile. "I am Doctor Hamada Khaled. Your friend has a remarkably strong and steady heart beat. How do you feel?"

"Sick to my stomach," complained Cheops.

"I will give you both shots and stomach medication. Still, I think tomorrow you will be very sick, but by the next day, you will feel better. I think," continued the doctor, looking back at Willy's still form, "it might be the better part of valor to tie this woman down before she wakes again."

Cheops bit her lip. She wasn't sure how Willy would handle being tied. Then again, Willy had warned her to be careful. "Okay, but I have to stay with her so she knows everything's all right."

Chapter Ten

Cheops was so sick that she thought she would die. Then she got sicker and hoped that she would, just to be out of her misery. Through bouts of illness, she managed to contact her tour agency and Inge to let them know not to worry. She asked the agency to contact the boat when it made port at Edfu. Mostly, she stayed with Willy.

Willy had woken after a few hours and lost it when she found herself tied. Cheops tried her best to calm her, but the woman was raving. Finally, when the doctor slipped out of the room to get a sedative for Willy, Cheops grabbed Willy firmly on both sides of her head and kissed her soundly. Willy's eyes opened wide and for a second, awareness flickered into the blue.

"Listen to me, Willy. The drugs are very bad. I want you to remember that you love me and that I love you too, okay? Just hold on to that one thought, and it will lead you back to me. I love you and you love me."

"I love you," muttered Willy as she fell at last into a quiet sleep. It was a very surprised doctor who returned to find Cheops holding Willy's hand as the soldier slept.

* * * * *

The boat the next morning had been a hot bed of speculation. What had happened to Cheops during the night? Was there any connection between Cheops' disappearance and the disappearance of Willy? The tour group was very upset and could get little information from the crew because of the language barrier.

Aaron Scott looked moodily at his son, who was very elated that morning, and offering his own theories as to what might have happened. None of his suggestions were very believable. Most of the group tended to ignore him. But Aaron didn't. He noted with horror

377

the way Bob kept rubbing his thumb against his finger tips in a nervous manner, and Bob's ghoulish grin.

He knew the signs. He had seen them often before. When he got the chance, he pulled Bill aside. "Can I talk to you?" asked Aaron, uncharacteristically hesitant.

"Of course," responded Bill, picking up on Aaron's tone and switching automatically to a professional manner, a frown forming on his face.

Aaron looked out over the Nile. His throat worked but the words took awhile in forming. When he did speak, it was like he was thinking out loud to the river. "He always had to have his own way, even as a tyke. Always had to have what he couldn't have. And when he was frustrated in his efforts, well, he'd holler bloody murder. It was cute when he was a toddler.

"His mother and I tried. We got him counseling when things started to happen. He hurt things, for revenge, he said. I... I... It was scary. Cost me a lot of money too. You know, to pay for damages. I thought he'd been getting better. Since his mother died, last fall, there hasn't been an incident. I thought if I brought him on this trip... we could get to know each other, again."

Tears flowed freely down Aaron's face but he swallowed and went on. "That crazy woman, Willy, she said Bob had been bothering Cheops and he was to stay away. I didn't take her seriously. Christ! Bill, I think Bob's killed Cheops!" sobbed Aaron, burying his head in his hands.

Bill's hand shook as he patted Aaron's shoulder. "Steady, Aaron. You've done the right thing. I think what we need to do is notify the police that we have concerns, and then see what your son has to say to them. You know I'll do everything I can to help."

The old man took Bill's hand. "Thanks, thank you. I can't let him go on hurting things! My God, what if he's killed her! He's done something, I can tell by his mood and actions."

"Well, let's not think the worst yet. It might be quite a minor offence, if any. First, we need to find out from someone what has happened to Cheops, and talk to the police. You just take it easy. You have done the right thing. Hopefully, we can sort this out without anyone getting hurt," reassured Bill.

The inspector was not happy. First, he had got a call that two tourists had been pushed from a boat and were at a local clinic. Then, he got a call saying the well-known archaeologist, Cheops Malone, was missing from her tour. And next an American lawyer wished to talk to him about a delicate matter related to the disappearance. *It is not*, he thought, *going to be a good day.*

He slipped from the back seat of the buggy that had brought him to the dock at Edfu. Horse and buggy were still the preferred means of travel around town, in this city. The tourists loved the quaintness, the horsemen got to breed and train their fine Arabian horses, as they had for hundreds of years, and the locals got a cheap public taxi system. Most days, he would enjoy a ride along the Nile, but this whole issue was leaving a bad taste in his mouth.

The last thing Egypt needed was a negative incident involving tourists! He just knew before this day was over the Minister of Tourism would be breathing down his neck! At least, this time it did not appear to be a killing. Still, he had prayed to Allah that morning that this was not a botched terrorist attack.

* * * * *

The next day, a very weak and very pale soldier lay in the cool sand under an olive tree, beside an equally shaky archaeologist, who sat with her back against the trunk. The bindings of Cheops' artificial leg flapped on a clothesline and Cheops was busy with a rag, drying the plastic parts of her prosthesis. An uncomfortable silence hung between them.

Cheops had deliberately rolled up her pant legs so that the stump of her lower leg was visible. She needed Willy to know what to expect, in case she was not comfortable with trying to rebuild their relationship. It was one thing to have a lover with a slight limp, it was another to see a partial leg moving about like some strange and exotic life form. Cheops kept busy, not daring to look into Willy's eyes and see the revulsion there.

For her part, Willy watched Cheops with fascination. She wanted to reach out and pull Cheops on top of her. She knew she couldn't do this publicly, nor was she sure Cheops would welcome her touch. They had flirted, after they had made it to shore, talked of love, but they were both in shock and not themselves. Hell, they'd only nearly drowned because Willy had beat on her, and had almost thrown her unconscious body into the Nile!

Willy felt the red creeping up her face. She had been pretty messed up in her thinking. She still didn't feel good but somehow now that awful anger was no longer eating at her. It had been replaced by guilt. She had treated Cheops appallingly; used her as a target for her anger and feelings of uselessness. The head of counter-terrorist activities, and she couldn't even protect her own son. Willy closed her eyes and pushed back the pain.

"Ah, Malone, about us," Willy started, knowing that she owed Cheops this and was just going to have to swallow her own foolish pride and get on with it.

Cheops hand froze at her job. *Oh God! Here it comes! She's going to try to tell me nicely that I revolt her!*

"I just wanted you to know that I realize that I've treated you badly. Ah, I... I needed someone to blame because I couldn't deal with not protecting... Then the drugs and stuff... I was really messed up... still am, I guess. I... I... ah, never mind!"

Cheops looked out across the barren sand dunes, afraid still to look at Willy. "Never mind what?"

Silence.

"I wanted to say... I mean... last night I realized... I love you," Willy managed at last to get out.

"No, don't say anything," Willy hurried on when Cheops turned towards her. "I know I don't deserve your love. I understand you were just trying to make me see past my anger. I..."

"I love you."

"I won't... What?!" Willy exclaimed, turning to look into Cheops' eyes.

"You have made me very angry at times, Willy. And I think it will take time to rebuild the trust we once had, but I want to try, because I have never stopped loving you."

"Cheops..." Willy barely checked herself from wrapping the woman in her arms and kissing her soundly. She looked around sheepishly. "I'm really glad," she finished, smiling inanely.

Cheops laughed. "I was sitting here terrified that, well, you wouldn't want me... You know... you are very physically fit, active... I thought when you saw...."

"No! No, it doesn't change who you are, Cheops." Then, seeing Cheops glance to her partial leg, Willy realized that, for Cheops, it had changed everything. She reached over and stroked the damaged limb reassuringly. "If possible, my respect for you has gone up. You just faced it all and carried on. I didn't."

Cheops drew patterns in the sand with her finger. "Neither did I. After... well, I was very depressed for a very long time. Inge helped me through the dark nights, and covered for me on the site, or I would probably have lost my job."

Willy paled even more. "You and her... you... I mean..."

"No! Willy, there could only be you. Don't you know that?"

"I mean, I could understand... I... I... Oh God, I feel sick."

Cheops reached out her hand and covered Willy's. "No, Inge is only a good friend. Okay?"

Willy smiled shakily. "Okay."

"Could you do me a favor?"

"Sure."

"I think my bindings are dry. Could you get them for me, and then I can reassemble this thing. If you feel up to it, we should take a plane up to Edfu and catch up to the tour. I have a few words to say to Bob Scott!"

Willy stood and looked down at Cheops. "You do know, I want to kill him."

"Yes, but can you let me handle it my way? I don't want to visit you in jail for the next twenty-five years!"

"Sure, but I'm going to be right behind you waiting for a chance to beat his little brains in if you need me to!" agreed Willy, moving off to retrieve the bindings from the line. Cheops watched her go. Damn, but she loved that woman!

When Willy returned, she took the artificial limb from a surprised Cheops. It was a complex bit of engineering. The plastic ankle was actually a ball joint that allowed flexibility, while still providing support. The top had been molded specifically to Cheops' leg. Bending over she kissed the partial leg softly. "Okay, you explain to me how I put this together."

Cheops looked uncomfortable and embarrassed. "I can do it, Willy," she protested.

"No!" Willy responded sharply. "I... If we are going to try to rebuild something between us, then you have to let me deal with your disability. Okay?"

Cheops nodded, as she blinked back tears. "This padding lines the top, to stop my leg from rubbing." Willy pushed the pad into place and carefully smoothed it. Then she looked up at Cheops for more instructions. "Now these padded leather straps go through the slots on the two flat arms that extend up on each side. They reduce any side movement of my leg in the socket and also provide the support for buckling the prosthesis to my leg."

Willy manipulated the straps into place and when she was finished, Cheops reached for the assembled prosthesis. "No," stated Willy firmly. Cheops licked her lips nervously but leaned back, allowing Willy to place the artificial lower leg over her stump and fasten it into place. When she was finished, she ran her fingers over the plastic and then up the inside of Cheops' leg past her knee. Willy was rewarded by a soft moan of pleasure.

Sitting back, she looked at Cheops. "You turn me on because of what you are and what you do to me in here," whispered Willy, patting her heart. She smiled, "I would show you just how much I mean that, if I could, right here and now!"

"Thank you, Willy," Cheops responded, her chin quivering with emotion. "I'll take a rain check on that promise, okay."

Willy rolled down Cheops' pant leg. "Count on it," she said confidently, looking up to meet Cheops' beautiful eyes.

Cheops and Willy arrived in Edfu in the late afternoon. A horse and buggy took them from the small airstrip down to the landing dock. Both women had been tired by the time they had landed, having used up any reserve of energy they had. But the buggy ride through the old streets, as they secretly held hands, had rejuvenated them and filled their senses with the majestic beauty that is Egypt.

Once at the dock, Willy hopped out and reached up to swing Cheops to the ground. Cheops used the excuse of the uneven stone stairs leading down the riverbank to the boat ramp to continue to hold onto Willy. They were barely inside the ship, when they found themselves being embraced by the Laytons and Brants.

"Cheops! Honest to God, woman, you gave us all a scare! Honey, don't ever do that again," ordered Betty, hugging the stuffing out of Cheops after Jean had let her go.

Willy found herself being hugged by Abe and patted on the back by Bill at the same time. "Damn good to see you, Major! Knew you'd be back!" Bill pounded happily.

"This calls for a happy hour!" suggested Jean. "I move that we head up to the lounge and insist on hearing the parts of the story we don't already know!"

"I second that motion!" sang out Bill.

Cheops looked at Willy and then said quietly, "Actually, we need to talk to the Scotts first."

The group went quiet and looked at Bill Brant, who had handled the rather nasty situation. "There have been some rather surprising developments here, while you were gone, ladies. I think, if you will accept our invitation, you'll find we have quite a story to relate too."

* * * * *

The group sat in comfortable chairs around a coffee table loaded down with bar snacks and glasses. The quaint sailboats of the Nile slipped by outside the window as they talked. Cheops had related their story to a spellbound audience, embarrassing Willy to no end. Then, it had been Bill's turn. The police inspector was firm but fair with Bob, Bill related. "Truthfully, it didn't take much to get the boy to confess. He was pretty proud of himself for having gotten even with both of you for giving him grief. It was hardest on Aaron. But I think, in the end, he had, at last, accepted how disturbed his son really was, and was prepared to take steps to have him hospitalized for treatment."

"The next step is up to you, ladies. The inspector will be here tomorrow to see if you want to press charges. If you do, Bob will go to trial and be jailed here. If you don't, Aaron will take him home and have him committed."

Cheops looked up into eyes the colour of ice. "Willy, I don't want to hurt Aaron anymore than he already has been. Bob is not responsible for his actions."

Willy nodded. "I agree."

The group relaxed then, and after a few more drinks, Cheops began telling stories of close encounters with mummies that had them all in stitches. Willy, who couldn't drink, sipped her coffee and reveled in being home at last.

Chapter Eleven

The blond woman stood in the shadows cast by the tangled foliage and looked at the old, cracked grave. She wasn't sure how she had ended up here, but she knew she was in the right spot. Turkey was a long way away from Tallahassee, Florida, and yet, she felt as if she had come home.

"Can I help you?" asked a deep, melodic voice with a faint and lyrical accent. Robin gasped in surprise, then almost fainted in seeing in front of her someone who looked so very much like Joanne.

The woman stepped forward and grasped Robin by the forearm. "Are you all right?"

Robin's mouth moved but no words came out for a few seconds. The tall, exotic woman waited patiently. "I... I'm sorry. You surprised me! You look like someone I once knew, only Joanne's black," rambled Robin, trying to pull her wits about her.

An eyebrow went up, just the way Joanne's used to do. "Would that be Joanne Tsakiris?"

"You know, Joanne? Are you related?" Robin asked in complete surprise.

"No, I do not know Joanne Tsakiris, and yes, I believe in the distant past, we might have shared an ancestor. She is, I know, an American of black ancestry. You have an American accent and you said your friend was black, so I assumed that it must be the Joanne to whom you were referring. I have often been told we look alike. Having won the Nobel Prize for Peace, she is a very famous person, and I have seen her picture in the papers."

"Oh."

"This is my property. I am General Gunnul Dedemann. You have come because the grave has called you, no?"

Robin looked surprised, "Yes. Yes, that's it! It calls to me. I... I just sort of ended up here. It is hard to explain."

"There is no reason to, you are not the first to come. Those who share a part of this story seem to be called to this place. There has been a crisis," explained Gunnul, touching the cracked grave sadly. "But, I think, the worst is over now. The grave no longer is cracking. Please, you will come to our house and meet my partner, Jamie. There is much we must share with you."

Robin nodded dumbly and followed the tall Turk through the underbrush and out into beautiful, manicured gardens. Together, they walked side by side up to a magnificent house that was framed by the Mediterranean Sea and the Taurus Mountains.

Jamie sat on the huge stone patio, typing on the laptop that Gunnul had bought her for her birthday. Gunnul spoiled her terribly! Even after all this time, there was in Gunnul this fear that her dark side might scare Jamie away. Jamie needed always to reassure her lover that she was not afraid of her strange strength and abilities. It was, in fact, the contrast between Gunnul's violent soul and her caring disposition that Jamie found so fascinating.

Jamie gave a start, as long arms wrapped around her and Gunnul bent to kiss the top of her head. "Jamie, I have found another one," she said seriously. Jamie looked up to see someone remarkably like herself looking back at her. "This is Robin Bradley, of Tallahassee, Florida. She knows Joanne Tsakiris," Gunnul explained.

Jamie stood and placed the crutch under her arm. "Welcome, Robin! I bet we are a bit of a surprise to you! Please sit down, and I will see to welcoming you properly."

Gunnul talked quietly to Robin about Turkey until Jamie returned with a crystal bottle of lemon cologne. "When I first came to Turkey, Gunnul greeted me in the traditional manner of her people. Cup your hands. This is a delicate lemon alcohol. You rub it on your hands and face to refresh yourself after your travels."

Gunnul sat with pride and watched, a lump in her throat. Jamie had, over the last two years, become her partner in every sense of the word. They shared a daughter, a bed, and together ran a vast business empire. But in the past, Jamie had never taken the lead in entertaining. Whenever they entertained guests, she would stay quietly in the background.

This had worried Gunnul. Did Jamie not see their homes as hers too? If she did not see herself as the hostess of their homes, might she not leave some day? It was a small thing, but it had quietly rubbed on Gunnul's insecurities. Those fears had been renewed lately, with the crisis of the grave. Today, for the first time, Jamie was playing the hostess and doing so, Gunnul thought, with beautiful grace and charm.

A servant had wheeled out a trolley, and from it Jamie had offered Robin Turkish Delights to sweeten her palate. Now, she limped to her lover's side and offered her one of the sweet, jelly treats too. She looked up into blue eyes that danced with joy and pride and knew instantly what Gunnul was feeling.

Oh, Gunnul! This was important to you, wasn't it, and I didn't realize! You needed me to welcome guests to our home. Jamie reached out and squeezed Gunnul's arm before turning away to the trolley, to light the burner on the small brass stove to make the Turkish coffee. She promised herself that when they were alone tonight, she would lie in Gunnul's arms and they would talk.

For now, she had to concentrate on what she was doing. The thick, boiled coffee had to be made just right, with lots of froth on the top and a rich, sweet texture. As was tradition, she made each cup separately, serving Robin first. She made Gunnul's extra sweet as a symbol of her love. The gesture was not lost on her lover, who took a sip and then smiled with delight.

The three women sat on lounges and looked out over the aqua sea. "You and Joanne are soulmates?" asked Gunnul in her straightforward manner.

Robin's hands shook, as she held the small cup. "No. I was a street kid she took in. I was fifteen. Joanna was only twenty-two then, and was just finishing her doctorate. She is something else, you know."

Gunnul's eyes met her partner's in question. "She means that Joanne Tsakiris is an amazing person," Jamie explained. Gunnul tended to take all statements literally. Although her English was excellent, she did not always understand English expressions.

Gunnul nodded in understanding and continued her probing. "You are not together?"

Robin snorted and put the cup on the table before her trembling hands dropped it. "I haven't seen her in years. I was a very confused kid. I... I... was doing drugs and making anyone who would buy them for me... Joanne... It was winter... We were living in Chicago, then. Joanne told me later that..."

The windshield wipers were only just keeping the heavy snow off the window. Twice, Joanne had had to stop and get out into the swirling wind to remove the ridge of snow that was building up at the sides of the windscreen, and reducing her area of visibility. It was a hell of a night, and she cursed herself for working so late at the university library.

She was anxious to get home, not so much for herself but because of the kid who had been sleeping in the back of her parents' garage. She had been there several weeks now, ever since the weather had turned cold and nasty. She came after dark and left in the early morning, sleeping curled up under some cardboard that Joanne had forgotten to put out in the garbage.

Had Joanne's parents been there, they would have called the police and had the vagrant removed. But her parents were away on a cruise, so Joanne had ignored the intruder and left the sheets of cardboard in the garage. Over the last few weeks, she had left a few old blankets on a shelf for the small girl to use, and a bushel of apples in a back corner. The blond waif looked half starved.

Tonight was cruelly cold, and Joanne was worried about her garage stowaway. Luckily, the garden service had been out and plowed the driveway, although it was drifting over again quickly. She pulled into the long lane and circled behind the Tsakiris home to the garage. It was actually a large carriage house that had been modified to suit modern times. It was only when she pulled up that she realized the garden service had conscientiously locked the garage before leaving.

Joanne had taken a flashlight and looked around but no windows were broken and the street kid was not around. Joanne checked for footprints but saw none. If the child had come, her footprints had long been covered in. It was only later, when she stood inside at the kitchen window watching her Golden Retriever, Nugget, running in circles through the new snow, that she finally found her. Nugget suddenly stopped, sniffed under the low, thick branches of a blue spruce, then backed off and started to bark.

Joanne was out the door immediately. The sudden tightness in her heart had told her that it was the teen. She was unconscious and curled in a small ball, like a wild animal's cub. Joanne had lifted her carefully into her arms and carried her into the house.

"So she cared for me. Bought me clothes, gave me a room and food. She even took me to movies and things. She... she was a real friend," finished Robin, tears painting patterns down her cheeks.

"What happened?" asked Jamie, reaching over to touch her counterpart's arm.

Robin's head dropped in shame. "Some drugs were hidden in Joanne's car without her knowing. She got pulled over and busted. Her parents had to fly home. You know, they were big society people. It was an awful scandal. I went to the police and confessed how I'd been using the carriage house to... make money for drugs."

"You were a prostitute?" asked Gunnul bluntly.

Robin blushed deeply and stared at her hands. "I'd been sleeping with the man who supplied me whenever he wanted it. Joanne, she was there in the room when I made my statement. It was awful."

For a few minutes they sat in silence, giving Robin time to pull herself together. Gunnul's jaw worked angrily and Jamie made eye contact, sending a silent plea to her soul mate not to lose her temper. Gunnul was faithful to her Moslem faith and expected people to live by high moral standards. For Gunnul, it was also harder because naturally she identified with Joanne, her look-a-like.

The ice blue of Gunnul's eyes melted a bit. "Then what happened?" she asked softly.

"I was jailed for six months and I never saw Joanne again. It would be ten years ago this winter... I've never forgotten her. Never forgiven myself."

"You still take drugs?"

"No! I never touched them again. I owed Joanne that at least. I went back to school and after got a job down in Florida as a journalist for a small newspaper. I just had a novel published and it is doing well. It gave me enough money to come here."

"What is the title of your novel?" asked Jamie with interest, trying to draw Robin away from her pain.

"*The Roundabout.*"

"You are R. R. Bradley? We've read your excellent novel. It's on the best seller list this week!"

Robin nodded and looked out across the sea. "I went to a travel agent and when I saw the brochures on Turkey, I just knew that I'd find answers here. So I came, and I've been searching ever since, until I ended up here this morning. Tell me what is going on. Why can't I let Joanne go from my heart?" begged Robin, looking up at the two women whose life so reflected the special bond she had glimpsed briefly with Joanne.

"We have been trying desperately to find the answer to that question," explained Gunnul. "We have made discreet inquires, run ads, talked to, as one woman called them, the Others, and researched the local history closely."

"The grave belongs to a warrior and a bard," said Jamie, taking up the story. "They traveled together and fought for justice during the time when this land was part of ancient Greece. There appear to be descendants of that remarkable pair who share the same distinct characteristics. My Gunnul and your Joanne take after the warrior.

You and I have the qualities of the Bard. So far, we are aware of six couples and two single individuals, who seem to be part of this genetic web."

"But what does it mean?" asked Robin.

"We are not sure. One of the women we talked to seemed convinced that the original pair were, well, not quite human, that they were somehow related to the Greek gods!" laughed Jamie and they all smiled. "What we do know is that the original pair faced a crisis in their relationship. At that time, the grave started to crack and more and more people were drawn to it."

"We believe," Gunnul said, "that the grave is drawing the energy from our loves to somehow help those in the past. That could be very important to all of us. Can we exist today if the original pair's strange relationship did not survive? We seem to be part of a loop in the space/ time continuum."

Jamie nodded and took over the story again. "Two significant things have happened in the last twenty-four hours; the grave has stopped disintegrating and you have shown up."

"I'm significant?"

"Yes, you are not lame and you have no contact with drugs now. That makes you unique. I think you might be the link to a time after the crisis. When the Host pair stopped crippling each other and the confusion, lies and misunderstandings that existed between them started to clear.

"All the other couples who have made contact with us have had a lame bard character and a warrior involved with drugs in some manner. Somehow, whatever the events are in the past involving the Bard, they seem to cripple the present day character. I think the Bard must have experienced great pain."

It was Gunnul who continued the explanation. "The warrior, we think, must have been very confused, and made decisions that were not wise. That is why so many of the warrior Others have been involved in things..." Jamie's hand came out and took Gunnul's, knowing the pain she felt because of the many lives she had taken in defense of her country, "they regret."

"But your story is different. We think it is very important that you make contact with Joanne," said Jamie, taking up the conversation again. "The grave called you, so you must be part of the process to help the Hosts. Do you know where to find Joanne?"

Robin nodded; her jade green eyes filled with hope and worry, as she looked out over the sea. "Yes, she is the American Ambassador to Peru."

Chapter Twelve

Willy paced back and forth while Cheops talked in Egyptian on the phone. Cheops looked very serious and the conversation had been going on for some time. Cheops was talking to the agency which was looking after Amand and Zahi. Willy paced some more. Finally, Cheops hung up and looked at Willy. "So, would you like to stick around and help me raise two children?" she asked.

"Yes!" Willy cheered, throwing her head back and closing her eyes. Then she looked at the small, brave woman standing across the room and went to her, wrapping her gently in her arms.

"You are wonderful. I don't know what I did to be allowed to have this second chance at life, but I am so very blessed."

The two women kissed tenderly and stood in each other's arms for a very long time. Then they went to find the tour group. In the late afternoon they had continued the tour, Cheops taking them to see the imposing Temple of Horus with its brooding, black, stone statue of the falcon god. The building still had its immense stone ceiling intact and within its walls, the cool, shaded interior housed massive murals and capitols of carved stone. It was when they got back to the boat that they found a message waiting for Cheops to call the orphanage about Amand and Zahi.

Bill and Abe sat at the bar having a beer and talking baseball. The two women had moved to the far end of the ship to watch the sun set over the Nile, while they waited to hear Cheops' news about the children.

"Ah, Betty, in Salt Lake City we tend to be pretty conservative and well, I might sound rather stupid here, but Bill said he thought Cheops and Willy were, well, ah... gay," Jean stumbled out.

Betty laughed out loud. "I think they're two women very much in love! You see a lot of that in New York."

Jean blushed and looked awkward. "I've never met any before. They are both really nice. I was raised to think this sort of thing was a sin and perverted but well, I don't think it's for me to judge. They seem happy and I would be proud to have them visit me anytime. Although, God knows what the neighbors would say!"

Betty chuckled happily and patted the confused woman's hand. "Live and let live, I always say. I always think it's a shame that gays are labeled by their bedroom practices. I mean, no one ever asks me what Abe and I are doing in our bedroom."

"Betty!"

"Well, it's true! Jean, my advice is don't speculate on their sex life, just enjoy their company like you do any other couple. They are a pair of remarkable women."

"But Betty, what about the children?"

"They would be better off half starved in the hold of a ship? What kid ever believes their parents are having sex, anyway?"

Jean laughed and buried her red face in her hands before looking up at Betty. "Betty, you sure put things in perspective! I'm sure my parents never had sex!"

"Mine neither, our entire generation must have been adopted!" The two women shared another laugh and then saw Cheops and Willy. They met them over where the men stood at the bar.

"I'm going to be able to adopt the children," Cheops announced happily.

Jean stepped forward and hugged Cheops and then Willy, with the others following in turn. "That is wonderful news!" Jean exclaimed. "You two will be wonderful parents for Amand and Zahi."

Bill looked over Willy's shoulder at his conservative wife in surprise. Willy looked down at Cheops, her face showing all her love openly now, as she slipped a protective arm around the archaeologist. Bill saw the red creeping up his wife's neck and smiled; new, liberated thought is one thing, but old attitudes die hard!

After a loud and merry celebration, Cheops and Willy said their goodnights and walked hand in hand back to their cabin. It was funny, Cheops thought, as she tried to look busy tidying up things. They had been lovers and yet now she felt as embarrassed and awkward as a girl on her first date. Long arms wrapped around her and Willy whispered softly into her ear, "I want to be your soulmate, Malone. I can be a better partner, I know. Can you be patient with me, until these drugs get out of my system?"

Cheops turned, trusting Willy to support her if she went off balance. For a second, she looked deep into those powerful eyes and then gently pulled Willy's head down to kiss her passionately. Some minutes later, she released Willy long enough to lift a chain from around her neck. Willy's eyes brimmed with emotion as she realized that the ring she had given Cheops, that wonderful season two years ago, was attached. Cheops slipped it off and placed it in Willy's palm, then held out her hand for the warrior to place it back on her finger.

Gently, Willy took Cheops' hand and slipped the simple gold band into place. "I love you, as the strong river wind embraces the fragile reed. Please, do me the honor of being my soulmate in life," Willy whispered, lifting Cheops' hand to place it on her lips.

"You are the river that runs through my lands and my heart, my warrior," responded Cheops, tears running down her face. Their night was spent in each other's arms, rediscovering the magic of their bond. Only in the small hours of the morning did they fall into an exhausted sleep. To the east, the sun slowly rose from the under world, filling the desert sky with light. The eastern side of the Nile. The side of life.

A thousand miles away, the cracks in an old grave slowly knit together. A soft breeze blew through the foliage and on it was the sweet scent of spice and sun drenched herbs.

Peruvian

Encounter

Chapter One

Robin Bradley was squished into the centre seat of the centre row of an overcrowded 747. *At least a sardine has the advantage of being dead,* she thought, trying to remove the cellophane from her dinner without elbowing the lady next to her in the face. *I don't understand why planes are not high jacked for the purpose of throwing every other person off to make some legroom! And the toilets! Why don't they put up signs for the men telling them that you can't aim straight in turbulence and to sit down! That or issue wading boots at the door!*

A steward came around and took away Robin's dinner tray. With relief, she folded up her table into the back of some else's seat. *Wow! Six more inches of space all to myself!* Now fortified with dinner, Robin pressed the button to lower her seat back and closed her eyes, hoping to sleep through the next six hours.

Her mind, however, was too excited to rest. So this was it! She was really headed for Peru! It had taken six months of hard work to sell her idea to the network and then to finally get permission from the State Department. Three times, she had been refused and then, suddenly, everything had been approved and she was on her way. She mentally went through the list of things she needed to do, her mind gradually drifting, and finally returning to that night over ten years ago.

Robin had found the perfect spot! Let the others sleep close to the exhaust fans behind the Chicago main library or huddled in doorways until they froze, she had a better plan. Each evening during the rush hour, she would take the subway to the end of the line. Rush hour was the best time to sneak through the turnstiles without paying. Robin was an expert at it. Even when she was suspected, she had that innocent sort of decent face that made the operators doubt their suspicions.

At the end of the subway line, she would pick up the jogging trail and head up past the beautiful homes with their manicured gardens that sloped down to Lake Michigan. It took about forty-five minutes, on a good day, to get from the downtown area to the old, gracious house on the hill. Up there the air was cleaner and the beauty of the gardens made her feel happy. Also, there was a heated garage converted from the original stables.

Robin had come to think of the garage as her home and the people who lived in the big house as distant cousins. She had a family, of course. Her parents had owed a rundown tavern in a working class neighborhood. People liked her parents. They would often sit and drink with their customers. Sometimes, they would drink too much and on those nights, Robin could never figure out which of her parents was abusing the other.

She had grown up unwanted, unloved and spoilt with material goods. At fourteen, she had run away with her eighteen year old boyfriend whom she had been seeing secretly. Six months later, he had left her on a street corner, ending a relationship that was going nowhere. She was fifteen now and street wise. To her knowledge, her parents had never looked for her. She did okay. Stole for what she needed and found good places like the garage to call home. When life became unbearable, which it did more and more frequently now, she would go with Roger. He would give her drugs in return for a roll in the hay. He liked kids and Robin looked younger than her age.

She never went near the house until she was sure the servants had left for the day. She knew the owner, well, knew of him. Tsakiris was his name. He was a Greek, a self-made man who was now a multi-millionaire. He'd married a black American who had been a dancer with the Detroit African Dance Company.

Robin had seen her too, on Roger's T.V. set. She had her own talk show now. The only person Robin had seen in person was their daughter though. She was tall, graceful, and stunningly beautiful. Her skin was the colour of coffee with cream and her eyes were an amazing winter blue. She drove a B.M.W. with a parking sticker on it that said Chicago State University. Robin liked to know about the family. They were her family. She had tried to explain this to Roger one day after they had sex. But Roger had laughed and told her that she was just white trash and that no respectable family would have anything to do with her. Roger was right.

It was snowing hard that night, and the winds were howling, as they are famous for doing in Chicago. Roger had given her a hit that morning, telling her that it was really good stuff, but now she felt really sick. It took all her strength to get to the garage and when she did, she found it locked. Her numb mind and her exhausted body could not think what to do. In the end, she had curled up under the boughs of a blue spruce. It smelt good under there, and she was warm and tired and could finally sleep.

Joey had found her, and saved her life. She'd carried her into the big house and cared for her. Joey was wonderful. Joey knew and could do anything. She would take her places and would bring Robin small gifts that made the tears spill from her eyes. She loved Joey. She still loved and needed the drugs too. Secretly, she would go with Roger. Joey didn't know. Joey was too nice.

When the drugs were found in Joey's car, Joey had no idea how they had gotten there. She was arrested and her parents had to fly home from their world cruise. Roger had planted them there, of course, and then tipped the police. Roger was a pimp and he hadn't wanted to lose a girl he was training up for the business.

When Robin had found out, she had gone to the police station. She couldn't tell them about Roger. He would kill her. Instead, she told them that Joey was a sucker. That she had planned to put the touch on her for money and then clean out everything in the house she could sell and skip town. She told them she was the addict and that she hid her supply in Joey's car. Joey was there, sitting at the table, when Robin confessed, her hands still in the metal cuffs. Robin would never forget the look of betrayal and hurt in those blue eyes.

Robin started awake. They were not far out now. Why the hell was she doing this? Joey must hate her! Her mind drifted back six months, to when she had met Gunnul and Jamie in Turkey. They had told her about the Others, all the couples who seemed to be descendants of the original Host pair. Gunnul and Jamie believed that they were all somehow caught in some sort of a loop in the space/time continuum. Somehow, the love that the Others were able to find for one another, despite the obstacles, was being used to help the Hosts through their own crisis. They had asked Robin to play her part. In order to maintain the equilibrium of events, somehow she had to resolve the rift that existed between her and Joey.

The seatbelt signs flashed on and the pilot's voice came over the intercom to let them know that they were fifteen minutes out of Lima, Peru. This was it. There was no turning back! Her hands clenched into tight fists as she steeled her nerve to face the most important challenge of her life.

She had worked hard, finishing up her last year of high school while in prison, and then applying to a local college to study journalism. She'd worked as a proofreader at a big daily to help finance her studies. After graduation, she'd been hired by a small newspaper in Tallahassee, Florida and had later made a switch to TV reporting. It had been a hard climb back, but she had owed Joey that.

* * * * *

Ambassador Joanne Tsakiris sat at her carved mahogany and gilt desk and wrote with a graceful hand across the page with a fountain pen. The room was designed to impress. The two end walls were lined with books. Across the large room from her, a sitting area formed a U around a crackling fire framed by a mantelpiece of marble. Behind her, a wall of French doors opened out into a walled garden.

They would start with onion and truffle tarts. This would allow her to serve the new Gewurztraminer that the American Wine Growers were anxious to promote. Then, a salad of mixed greens with New England strawberry dressing over pine nuts. An orange sorbet served in small, delicate cones would then be offered to clean the palette in preparation for the fish course. They would have Washington State rainbow trout accompanied by a prize winning California Chardonnay. The main course would be Texas beef served with fiddle heads and Idaho baked potatoes. A red wine, for this course, the Lagrein from that small winery in Maine. Then they would finish with a selection of American cheeses and fruit and serve the Cabernet from Rhode Island.

Joey sighed; she needed a degree in home economics not a doctorate in international affairs! She pressed a button on her desk and a few minutes later, Captain Perkins walked in, barely making a sound on the thick carpets. "Perkins, this is the dinner menu for the third. Please, remind the Sergeant that it's regimental dress. Let the cook know that we'll be sitting forty."

"Yes, Ambassador Tsakiris," responded her attaché. "Here are the applications for immigration. I don't feel you will be comfortable recommending any of them. This stack is the requests for visas waiting your signature. I remind you, Ambassador, that the Senate Committee reviewing the progress of the Organization of American States will be meeting in October. Your report on Peru's readiness for a free trade partnership needs to be submitted by the end of this month."

Joey listened as she scanned her mail box, clicking on messages that she felt needed priority. "Already done, Perkins. I just want to have one more meeting with the Association of South American Bankers, to make sure my figures are current, before submitting. Is there anything else?"

"No, Ambassador."

"Thank you, Perkins."

Joey answered those messages that needed immediate attention. Then she stood and looked out the French doors to the garden beyond. It was a scaled down replica of Thomas Jefferson's walled garden.

Always, there were walls. There were walls inside walls; brick walls, security walls, fire walls, walls of protocol. It never ended. It was like being a prisoner. Is this what she wanted to do for the rest of her life?

She was proud of her success. Proud to represent the United States of America. Her father told her that she was ear marked for greater things in the diplomatic service. Her mother asked her if she was happy. Was she happy?

She frowned and wandered over to the grand piano that sat in front of one wall of books. Sitting, she did a few scales to warm her fingers up. Her mother would have liked her to become a concert pianist. The soft, sorrowful sound of an old Spiritual drifted through the room. Gradually, the rhythm picked up and the melody transformed into familiar Minstrel numbers, then fragmented and reformed into the fast, rhythmic beat of Swing. The patterns became more integrated and varied, the style now clearly Jazz. Slowly, the notes mellowed out into Blues. Once again, the haunting melody of the old spiritual reappeared then ended abruptly in a sour chord.

Joey stood and walked back to the windows. It was Robin Bradley who was responsible for her melancholy mood. Why had she overruled security to allow Robin to come and do her documentary? She wasn't sure. Partly curiosity, she supposed, to see how Robin had turned out, and partly to promote the work of American Embassies throughout the world.

Who was she trying to kid? She just wanted to see Robin. She had loved the way Robin's face used to light up with devilment. She loved the way she laughed so easily, and got such joy out of simple things. Robin had made Joey happy. It was the only time in her life when she had felt free. She just did things with Robin spontaneously, and didn't worry about the consequences. She should have worried, she supposed. Then she wouldn't have been arrested.

There was a discreet knock at the door, and Perkins entered. "Ambassador, Ms. Bradley to see you."

"Please send her in," responded Joey, going to stand behind her desk.

Chapter Two

Robin had arrived at the designated entrance, at the designated time, with her letter of approval, customs tourist card, and passport. All of these were taken from her. Then, she'd gone through a metal detector and had been hand frisked. "Do all embassy guests have to go through this?" she asked the young marine who was making up plastic ID tags for her.

He didn't answer. Instead, he threaded two cards onto a metal chain and told her to put it around her neck. Then he led her to a side door off the parking lot and escorted her down a functional hallway to a room. "Wait in here," he ordered and left, closing the door firmly behind him. Robin tried the door. It was locked. *What is this place? Fort Knox?*

Robin sat down on a grey metal folding chair by a plywood topped table. After a few minutes, a mountain of a man walked in. He wore a business suit pressed to perfection, but his military bearing and brush cut hair cut left little doubt as to his occupation.

"Ms. Robin Bradley?"

"Yes."

"I'm Major Sak, Embassy Security," the man said, coming to stand by the table. "I wanted to meet you before you were escorted to the Ambassador. You will note that you are wearing two tags. One indicates that you do not have security clearance and the other indicates that the Ambassador has approved your visit."

Robin's eyes widened in surprise. So it had been Joey who had made it possible for her to come here to do her documentary!

"I have read the background report on you and frankly, I have concerns. Why were you in Turkey this spring?"

"I was on holiday."

"Turkey is a place where it is easy to obtain drugs, as are certain parts of South America," Major Sak observed. Robin felt her insides crunch, but she said nothing.

"You have served time for drug possession, have you not, Ms. Bradley?"

This time Robin reacted, the blood rushing to her face. "I don't do drugs, Major Sak! Nor do I associate with those who do!"

"That's good to hear," the large man responded conversationally. "You will please follow me."

Robin dutifully trotted behind the human wall down to the end of the hall where an elevator stood ready. Sak stepped aside and indicated Robin should get in. "Please make sure your tags are visible at all times, Ms. Bradley. The security staff will shoot anyone without proper ID, whether they recognize you or not." He reached in a big, beefy arm and pressed a button. "Captain Perkins will meet you upstairs."

Nothing the Major had said had been threatening, and yet Robin had gotten the clear impression that Sak was just looking for an opportunity to shoot her dead. She nervously rearranged her tags so that they could be better seen.

The door opened, and a man about her own age stood there waiting. He wore an immaculate grey suit. *Don't these guys ever sit down and get creased?* "This way, Ms. Bradley. Please wait here, while I see if the Ambassador is free to see you." Fear suddenly slashed at her insides. If she hadn't been equally afraid of being shot dead by Sak, she'd have made a run for it!

The door opened and a smiling Perkins indicated that she should step into the room. "Ambassador Tsakiris, Ms. Robin Bradley of the United Television Network."

"Thank you, Perkins," came a cool, calm voice and Captain Perkins left, closing the door softly behind him. The woman standing behind her desk, bathed in the afternoon sunlight, radiated confidence and power. "It has been a long time, Robin," the beautiful woman said. "Please, have a seat," she continued, a long, graceful arm indicating the visitor's chair at the other side of her desk.

Robin realized that she had been staring at Ambassador Tsakiris in awe. Then suddenly, a wide smile lit up her face. This was her Joey! She walked across the room, circled the desk and wrapped her arms around the startled Ambassador. "Oh Joey! Look at you, an Ambassador and the winner of the Nobel Peace Prize! I'm so proud of you! I've missed you so much. I keep a scrap book of all the articles about you."

Joey found herself hugging the petite figure to her, lowering her head to touch the soft, golden hair. It still smelt like the sun soaked herbs that used to hang in her parents' greenhouse. "This is really not the proper protocol for greeting a senior representative of the United States of America," Joey pointed out with a nervous laugh.

"Screw protocol," responded Robin happily, but she did let go of Joey to sit in the chair that the Ambassador had indicated earlier.

Joey sat down, feeling weak kneed and flustered. The familiar solidity of her desk helped her ground her emotions. "So, suppose you tell me why you are here?"

Robin looked up into those remarkably blue eyes. Joey was as beautiful as ever, perhaps more so, with the maturity of years. Her face was cut in classic lines, like a fine wood carving of some ancient African Queen. Robin told as much of the truth as she dared. "I pulled out every stop to sell my idea of a documentary to the network and the State Department. It is, I think, a good concept, but it was just a means to get to you. I... I need to resolve what happened to us all those years ago. It's important to me. The time I spent in prison, and the years after, trying to get my life together, I never forgot you."

Tears brimmed in Robin's eyes and her chin quivered with the effort of holding back the emotion. "I used to say to myself, you are doing this for Joey, because she believed in you."

Joey forced her face to remain expressionless. Inside, she was fighting the urge to wrap Robin in her arms until Robin's pain went away. "What happened back then is a closed issue," Joey said calmly. "I am more concerned with the here and now. I am not just a person now, Robin, I'm an officer of the United States of America. I'm taking a hell of a risk in allowing you in to do this documentary. I have no guarantee that..."

"That I won't betray you again," cut in Robin, shaking with emotion.

"That you are up to the assignment. You've never made a film documentary before, have you?"

"No," Robin responded quietly. She could feel her chin starting to quiver with the pain she felt at Joey's emotional distance.

"You have to understand that I'm hesitant to except your word without some guarantees," Joey went on, looking at the surface of her desk with eyes that were reliving the past.

The tears came now, rolling down Robin's face unchecked. "I lied that day, Joey. I'm sorry! I had too." Joey's head snapped up. Robin tried desperately to explain. "Roger would have killed me! It was Roger who planted the drugs and tipped off the police. I'd been still... going with him, to get the drugs... he was a pimp and he didn't want you taking away a kid he was training up for his business." Robin buried her face in her hands and sobbed uncontrollably.

Joey found herself on her knees beside Robin's chair. Robin threw her arms around Joey's neck and buried her face into the older woman's broad shoulder. "Shh, it's okay, Robin. Shh, I'm here," soothed Joey, holding the small, shaking frame close.

Joey was filled with uncertainty and confusion. Was Robin lying her way out of her betrayal all those years ago? Or was she a decent adult trying to resolve the poor decisions of a child? She just didn't know. What she did know was she couldn't stand to see Robin in emotional pain.

After the tears had slowed, Joey whispered into Robin's hair. "Hey, how about we go sit by the fire and you tell me about what it is you want me to do, okay?"

Robin nodded, wiping away her tears. She followed Joey and they sat on opposite ends of the couch. The heat of the fire felt good on Robin's cold flesh. Joey waited. "I read your novel. It was wonderful," she said hesitantly, after a little while.

"Thanks." The younger woman blushed and went silent again, trying to find words that would help bridge some of the hurt between them. Finally she swallowed hard and pulled herself together enough to answer Joey's question. "This is a small budget, pilot program. If it does well, and I think it will, then a series will be made highlighting some of the outstanding American women of this decade.

"If that happens, I would research a woman's career and achievements and then write a script for her to read, while a crew films. Then I'd edit it down for T.V., but on this pilot, I'm it: director, producer, sound and film crew. I know you, Joey, and I'm betting you know this country inside out."

"I've tried to get a feel for the land, yes."

Robin smiled and nodded. "So, I thought, I'd just let you take me places that you think are important. I'll have you talk about them, and your insights and views. Then we'll discuss what should go onto film, and I'll have you say it again, while I record it, okay?"

Joey's face didn't show the confidence that Robin's did. "Well, we can give it a try. I'm not really used to speaking on camera except in a press scrum, and believe me, they are no fun!"

They talked about plans for the filming for almost an hour. Then Perkins arrived to remind Joey that she had a meeting. Joey rose and so did Robin. "Perkins will show you the way out," she smiled. "My office will be in touch."

That was it. Robin was taken back down through the functional halls of the working section of the embassy and out the car park door. Her tags were taken from her and her documentation returned to her inside a plastic bag labeled with a yellow sticker: Bradley, Robin, American and the date. Robin went back to the El Pardo hotel in Lima where she was staying and waited impatiently for a few days.

She filled in her time doing some background research. She visited the outstanding anthropology museum, and went to the university to interview a number of experts there. One day, she went to the small and well protected gold museum where the remainder of the fine Indian gold items, those that had not been taken and melted down by the Spanish Conquistadors, were on display.

It was while she was returning from this outing, and crossing the lobby to step in the elevator, that the bomb went off. It was a small bomb placed inside a paper bag and left tucked down between the cushions of a couch in the foyer. Robin had just stepped into the elevator when the explosion occurred. The shock wave sent her flying backward and crashing into the wall before she slipped dazed to the floor. The elevator doors closed, leaving her in complete darkness.

Groggily, she staggered to her feet, only to be knocked down again as the elevator suddenly dropped a few inches and then stopped with a jerk. Robin tried to decide, in her shocked state, whether she should stay in the elevator and run the risk of falling to her death or force the doors open and take her chances with whatever was going on in the lobby. She could clearly hear shouts, crying and sirens.

The smell of smoke seeping through to her sent her in a panic to the doors. With a desperate effort, she managed to push the automatic doors apart and step out into the chaos of the lobby. Over in the corner, several people were comforting a seriously hurt news stand girl, whose life had been saved by the heavy metal counter. Bits of smoldering magazines and newspapers littered the floor. The two employees at the shattered hotel desk seemed to have fared a little better, although they were cut and bruised. Smoke drained out the shattered front window in a blue-grey curl.

There was little Robin could do to help, medical and fire personnel were already arriving to give aid. She wished she had her camera with her, but no filming was allowed at the gold museum, and so she had left the heavy camera behind that morning. For a minute, Robin considered going upstairs to get it and then rejected the idea. By the time she got back here the authorities would have the situation in hand, and she might run the risk of having her video camera confiscated. Instead, she moved to a quiet corner and tried to take in as much as she could. This story would make a good introduction to the explosive nature of the South American political scene and the courage that Joey had in representing America here.

407

Some time later, a medic stepped over to her. "You have been hurt, lady. Can I bandage your head? I think you should come to the hospital. You might have a concussion." Dumbly, Robin reached up and touched the sore spot on the back of her head. Her hand came away covered in blood. Looking down she was surprised to see her shirt splashed with red.

"That's okay, the lady will be coming with me," said a voice, tight with stress.

Robin looked up with confused eyes to meet a pair of stormy blue. "Joey, a bomb went off," she said stupidly.

A strong hand took her arm and led her out of the corner, "It's okay, Robin. Give your room key to Perkins here, and he will bring your luggage over to the embassy. Okay now, you come with me," Joey instructed gently.

Joey led Robin through the wrecked lobby and across the street, where Sak waited by the car watching the street with worried eyes. He helped the two women in and then slipped behind the wheel, glad to be getting the Ambassador the hell out of there.

Chapter Three

"Here, lean forward and let me have a look," ordered Joey, reaching for the extensive first aid kit that was standard equipment in all embassy vehicles. She took a wad of dressing and carefully dabbed at the blood and matted hair. There was an oozing cut about four inches long along the base of Robin's skull. Joey supported the half conscious woman in her lap with one arm and held the dressing over the wound with the other, unaware of the blood that dripped down on her. She worried that Robin might have a serious head injury.

Sak had phoned ahead and staff medical personnel were standing by. Joey watched as they wrapped a neck brace into place and then carefully lifted Robin off her to lay her on the stretcher.

Robin was unconscious now and looked fragile and deathly pale. Joey followed the stretcher into the embassy.

Sak took Joey's arm gently. "Ambassador, you need to clean up," he said. "I'll hang around down here and report back to you as soon as the doctor has made an assessment." Joey looked down and was shocked to see that her camel skirt was saturated with Robin's blood. With effort, she stopped herself from being sick. She nodded and walked down the hall to the elevator.

Robin woke up with a throbbing headache. She reached her hand up but it was intercepted gently by another. "Hey, leave that alone," whispered a deep, melodic voice. Robin blinked, focusing her eyes, and then moved her head sideways to see Joey sitting on a chair by her bed. Joey was wearing an Independence Day T-shirt and blue jeans.

"Hi, aren't you working?" Robin asked.

"I took the day off," Joey smiled.

"You look cute," Robin mumbled in her sleepy state.

Joey blushed. "Ah, you've got ten stitches in your head, so be careful. Fortunately, there was not any more serious damage."

"The bomb went off just as I stepped into the elevator. I think I hit my head on the hand rail."

"You were lucky you weren't out in the open. You might have been killed," observed Joey objectively, although inside she was an emotional wreck.

"Was it the Shining Path, Joey?"

"They have phoned a radio station and taken credit for the bombing, yes," responded the Ambassador, still holding on to Robin's hand.

Suddenly, Robin's eyes sparkled with devilment. This was going to be a really powerful introduction to the dangerous situations that American Embassies often found themselves in. "Neat, huh?" she smiled.

Joey laughed in relief and at the sheer resilience and positiveness of Robin's personality. "Yeah, neat," she agreed, giving the small hand a squeeze.

Joey left Robin to sleep and went back up to her office to clear some of the paper work. However, her mind kept going back to why she had charged like some white knight to Robin's side when she had learned of the explosion. Why had she been so upset to see Robin hurt and vulnerable? Seeing Robin again had brought back very deep feelings, ones she had thought she had learned to suppress. She was attracted to Robin.

That evening, a much recovered journalist met Joey in the morning room for dinner. "The dining room is a barn of a place that sits fifty comfortably. So, I usually eat down here," Joey explained. They ate quietly together, talking of general things, re-establishing a data bank of shared information.

Robin had brought her research notes for the documentary series down for Joey to see. The woman sat flipping through the pages while Robin, beside her, stole the remaining French fries off Joey's plate. Joey had a beautifully shaped head, Robin thought, as she observed the Ambassador while her intelligent eyes moved back and forth across the page. She had nice ears too. She liked the way her dark hair curled around her ear.

Joey suddenly looked up and their eyes met. "This is great stuff, Robin! I'm impressed." Joey smiled and Robin felt warmed down to the core of her being.

"Thanks," she said, and blushed.

"Ah, why don't we head over to my study, and sit by the fire, okay?" asked Joey, getting up. She was reluctant to end the evening. They had just fallen back into the easy way they used to have with each other, as if nothing had happened to separate them. Being with Robin again was... neat. The explosion at the hotel had brought home to Joey in a big way that what she felt about Robin went pretty deep.

"Sure," responded Robin, glad that the evening in Joey's company was going to go on a bit longer. She needed to talk to Joey. But it was hard to find the right words, when they were both carrying so much emotional baggage from the past.

Robin sat down on the sofa and Joey bent to light the firewood that was already stacked and ready. "I usually have a night cap," Joey explained. "Can I get you something?"

A sadness passed across Robin's eyes, but she smiled. "No thanks. I don't drink. I never have. My parents owned a tavern and they both drank hard. It just never appealed to me. But you go ahead!"

Joey nodded and splashed Scotch into a glass. It was Cardhu, a single malt whiskey from Morayshire. A good Scotch was one of the few vices that Joey allowed herself. "I didn't know you had a family."

"Oh, yeah, I had a family," Robin answered, in a tone that indicated that she didn't want to discuss them. Joey took the hint, and for a while they sat in silence, watching the fire. The fire made Joey feel hot and bothered. She had loved the little street kid like a big sister, but Robin wasn't a kid anymore and what Joey was feeling was a very different sort of attraction.

Finally, Robin took a deep breath and, looking at the fire, she said, "Joey, I need to tell you something and I need you to hear me out without freaking out on me or anything, okay?"

Joey's stomach tied in a knot. She got up and placed her glass on the mantel and braced herself mentally, her face expressionless. Had she been set up by Robin again? "Okay."

Robin licked her lips nervously and swallowed several times. Finally, she stood up and faced Joey. "I'm gay and I'm in love with you. I always have been," she announced. Joey was silent, looking at the smaller woman in shock.

Robin turned away and looked at the darkening embers in the fire. She went on miserably, "When we were young, I tried everything to get you to make a pass at me. I was afraid to come on to you in case you were horrified and threw me out. I know, I'm not in your league, Joey. I won't ever embarrass you by coming on to you. I just needed to be honest about how I feel. It's important. I... I've never slept with anyone since. I don't ever want to have just sex again. I want it to be with the person I love. Whom I've always loved."

Joey felt like she had been hit by a truck! Robin was gay? But she'd been sleeping... Robin loved her? She wanted Robin, she knew she did. Over the years, it was her fantasies about Robin that had made her slowly realize that she was gay. But she had never planned to... Finally, her mind just stopped trying to find logic in the situation, and her raging emotions forced her into action.

Robin stood looking at the fire. The room had remained silent for a long time. Had she horrified Joey? Should she leave? Suddenly, strong arms took her by the shoulders and turned her around. Blue eyes filled with hope and confusion looked down at her. Then, very slowly, Joey lowered her head and brushed the lightest of kisses across her lips. Robin's insides melted and she groaned in need, reaching up to pull Joey back to her.

This time the kiss was hard and needy. Open lips allowed Robin to thrust her tongue into Joey's mouth, sweetened by the Scotch. Joey started at the intimate invasion, then wrapped Robin closer to her and let their tongues dance to a rhythmic need.

The passion built. Robin stood on tip toes to draw patterns with the tip of her tongue around Joey's cute ear. The woman gasped with pleasure and lowered her head to kiss and nibble at Robin's throat.

Robin thought she was going to come right there. "I need you, Joey!" she gasped.

The taller woman went still and pulled back.

"What?" asked Robin in confusion. "Did I do something to offend you? Joey, I'm sorry, I..."

"No! It's not that!" reassured Joey, sitting down weakly.

"What is it?" asked Robin, slowly sinking to the couch next to her.

Joey gave a quick look at Robin and laughed nervously. "We're going kind of fast here. We haven't seen each other in years. Ah, I've never... you know," she confessed.

"Oh," Robin said. "Look, if you don't want to have a gay relationship, I'll understand." Robin tried to say this lightly, although her heart contracted in pain with the effort. "Or if you want to go slower..."

"No, I mean, I haven't... at all!" confessed Joey, looking anywhere but at Robin.

It was Robin's turn for shocked silence. Then she blurted out, "How old are you?"

Joey got up and paced the hearth rug in agitated embarrassment. "Thirty-two, damn it!" She rubbed her hand over her head. "It's hard to explain. I was always pushing myself. There was a lot of pressure. Two really successful parents to live up to and a public image to maintain. It wasn't just me; I represented a way of life, coming from a mixed marriage. Failure was not an option for me. After the trouble..."

"You mean after I betrayed you and humiliated you and your family by getting you arrested on a drug charge," stated Robin bluntly.

Joey went on, "After, I just had to try harder not to make any mistakes. Not to disappoint anyone again. Then, when I joined the diplomatic service, well, everything has to seem to be proper, anyway. You can't afford to get a black mark on your record and still move up. There were opportunities, but I just wasn't interested... I... I wanted you. I loved you," she finished, blushing deeply in surprise at what she had just said.

Robin gasped and jumped up, wrapping her arms around Joey tightly and burying her head into the woman's chest. She could hear Joey's heart pounding with emotion and smell the spicy, warm scent that she had never forgotten. "Joanne Tsakiris, I think that was the most wonderful thing that any human being could say to another!"

"You do?" Joe laughed nervously, rubbing her head alongside Robin's. *Tsakiris, are you crazy? What the hell have you just done?* screamed her logical mind. *I don't care! I do love her! I do!* Her emotions warred. *I don't care about the consequences!*

"Yes," whispered Robin, kissing Joey softly. "We'll just go slowly, okay? Just learn about this love thing together."

Joey nodded and Robin kissed her softly, and then said good night. Joey did something that she never did. She poured herself another Scotch and sat down to try to think through the tidal wave of feelings that had burst through tonight. A few days ago, she had been looking forward, with some apprehension, to meeting a child that she had once befriended. Okay, whom she had fantasized about over the years. Now she had to accept that over the years her feelings had changed. She was in love. How had that happened?

In her room, Robin was trying to come to terms with her own emotions. It was hard enough having to deal with what had happened years ago but now she was facing a new set of problems. She had thought the worst case scenarios would have been Joey hating her or not wanting to be involved in a gay relationship. She had imagined that Joey, being beautiful, charismatic, and a woman of the world, well, would have had plenty of experience. It had never occurred to her that she'd be a virgin!

For the first time in a very long time, Robin felt cheap. Joey knew her past and, although she hadn't been sexually active since, she had sold her body to Roger for drugs and there was no getting around that. She just didn't know where to go from here.

Chapter Four

The next morning, Captain Perkins delivered the message that the Ambassador would be tied up for the day. However, she had instructed him to invite Robin to the formal dinner that she was giving for the President of Peru that night.

Robin was warmed by Joey's confidence in her. "Please, thank the Ambassador very much, but tell her I can't go. I don't have a formal dress."

Perkins, with a smile, produced an envelope. Robin took it in surprise, and opened it up to find a note written in Joey's flowing hand. It read:

I know you don't! I've instructed Perkins to take you to a store where you'll be able to find just the thing. It is a chance for you to be part of my world. Please.

Love J.

Robin smiled softly. "I understand, Captain Perkins, that you know where the best ladies' formals can be found in Lima."

Perkins smiled broadly. "Sure do! I'll meet you at the parking lot at ten."

"Okay," laughed Robin brightly.

Perkins hummed all the way down the hall. This was his chance to get to know the beautiful Ms. Bradley better. He couldn't think why Sak didn't like her. But then, Sak was very protective of Tsakiris. He was your typical tight-assed Marine.

* * * * *

"So what do you think of this number, Al?" Robin laughed, stepping out of the changing area to model a formal with a plunging neck line and low back.

Captain Allan Perkins' eyes got big. "I'll tell you that would give a few old Ambassadors heart attacks!"

Robin laughed again, her eyes sparkling with mischief. "Well, we wouldn't want that, would we?" she said, over her shoulder, as she disappeared back into the change rooms.

Within an hour, a flattering but conservative dress had been found and Robin, with a grimace, had handed over her credit card. She was going to have to talk to Joey about expenses. She was just now starting to get a reasonable salary, but she still had a student loan to pay off. This dress was going to max her card.

Perkins took Robin to the President's Square next. They wandered around looking at the beauty of the old Spanish colonial architecture. The cathedral was made from intricately carved limestone in a high baroque style that was truly breathtaking. Then they went to the Spanish Quarter for lunch and sat in the walled courtyard under a sprawling tree to eat a tasty meal that was a blend of Spanish and Indian cooking. They laughed a good deal and discovered that they had a love for football and thought along the same lines on social issues. Altogether, Robin had a really fun day and she thanked Captain Perkins profusely for being such a good host.

Joey's day had not been as successful. She had words with Major Sak and she hated getting into arguments with her staff. He had objected to Robin attending the dinner. "Ambassador, I realize that you feel Ms. Bradley should be allowed a second chance, and that is very commendable, but she is an untried element. We have no idea how she may behave."

Joey felt her temper rising. "What does that mean?"

Sak wisely did not clarify. "I just have reservations," he responded, standing stiffly.

"Noted," snapped Joey angrily. "Now, about the security for the documentary tour, I can't accept this report. The security would be way out of proportion to the need. Your people would just get in the way. I think it would be better if Robin and I just went off in an unmarked car and acted like any other tourists."

"Out of the question, Ambassador! The Shining Path are very active at this time. To assassinate the Ambassador of the U.S. would provide exactly the sort of world wide coverage that this terrorist group needs!" growled the security officer with feeling.

"Well, this will not do!" barked Joey, tossing the report across the table.

Major Sak picked it up and, fighting for control, said as calmly as he could, "Anything else, Ambassador?"

"No, Major, that's all," Joey responded with the same controlled anger. Sak had turned and left without another word.

That night, Robin stood beside Joey in the reception line, and was introduced as the guests arrived. She wore a formal gown in brushed cotton that was both flattering to her figure and proper in its cut. The cost of it was all made worthwhile when Joey leaned close and whispered that she looked lovely.

Joey, of course, looked spectacular. She wore a formal gown in deep red silk, enhanced with diamond earrings and necklace. It took all Robin's control not to stare. After the guests arrived, Joey excused herself and went to buttonhole the Ambassador from Brazil. Robin found herself surrounded by a group of Peruvian generals. She found them both charming and arrogant in their manner, like the Spanish Conquistadors of old. They made her laugh, and she found herself relaxing and having a good time. Every once in a while she would look up and catch Joey's eye wherever she was in the room.

When dinner was announced, Joey led the guests into the banquet hall on the arm of the President of Peru. Robin found herself at the far end of the table beside the Under Secretary to Agriculture from Ecuador. The table was beautiful. It was lit with shining brass candelabras that cast the room in a soft, mellow glow. Three cut crystal glasses, of different shapes, marked each place and sparkled in the candle light. Every place setting was gold rimmed and bore the crest of the United States of America. The cutlery was silver and there were four forks and three knives and a small spoon.

Robin recognized the fish fork but after that things got a bit dicey. Fortunately, everyone was eating the same meal, so she just picked up whatever the man across from her did. She looked down the long table to where Joey sat at the other end, talking and laughing. The President of Peru sat to her right and the Ambassador of Great Britain to her left. It was a different world than Robin had ever experienced before.

Okay, Robin, don't make a fool of yourself here. You've worked hard to escape your past, don't let yourself get overwhelmed. You can do this! She steeled herself to carry on but it didn't stop the butterflies from invading her stomach.

The meal was unbelievable and Robin tucked into everything that was served by the quiet and efficient Marines in regimental kit. The small spoon turned out to be used with the fish fork to de-bone and eat the trout. She declined the wines and drank ice water from each of the three wine glasses instead. She found the Under Secretary of Agriculture to be a big soccer fan and he was delighted to find that the beautiful, young, American woman could hold her own in a discussion on this year's contenders for the World Cup.

The seating arrangement had been made with care to stimulate conversation and people lingered over the cheese and fruit trays. It was late when Robin returned to her room and stripped off her dress, glad to see that she had not gotten any stains on it. She fell back onto the bed in her undies and stared at the ceiling. It had been a magical evening, and Robin had been completely out of her element. How could she have a relationship with Joey without embarrassing her?

As a gay lover from the other side of the tracks, she would have to be a shadowy figure in the background of Joey's life. Could she live like that? Would Joey want to take that risk? Robin felt a deep depression settle on her like a blanket. She loved Joey so much, and yet she could only see herself as a liability to her.

A soft knock came at the door. "Robin, are you still awake?" asked the voice that she loved.

"Yes," she answered quickly, sitting up.

"Would you like to join me in the study for a night-cap?"

"I'll be right there," answered Robin happily, her depression thrown back as she slid from the bed. She slipped on a Seminoles baseball shirt that almost came to her knees. Then, bare foot, she trotted up the hall to the study.

The Ambassador was, of course, prepared this time. She poured a chilled glass of watermelon juice for Robin and a Lagavulin for herself. It was a single Islay malt whiskey, sixteen years in the making. It had been a very successful night and that called for a special whiskey. The glass, however, stopped half way to her mouth when she saw Robin standing there. Robin looked down insecurely at her sweatshirt with its logo of a smiling cartoon Seminole wearing a baseball cap. "Ah, should I change?" she asked shyly, not sure what the protocol for late night wear while having a night-cap with the Ambassador was. She was sure, however, that Captain Perkins would be able to look it up in the regulations for her.

Joey smiled wolfishly and carried the drinks over, offering Robin the watermelon juice that she had poured for her. "No, I think you look cute as a button. It's just chilled juice. I think you'll like it." She leaned forward and kissed Robin tenderly. "I missed you, today."

Robin kissed back. "I missed you!"

"I was jealous," confessed Joey moodily, sipping her drink.

"Jealous?"

"Mmm, of all those military types who cornered you before dinner. I had to force myself not to walk over there and knock their blocks off!"

Robin giggled and a pretty blush coloured her cheeks. "Don't be jealous. I love you," she stated simply, reaching up to kiss soft, warm lips. "Come on, let's sit by the fire and I'll tell you everything I learned about your world tonight!" They moved over and sat close, Robin curled up under Joey's arm. What Joey learned was that Robin was indeed a very smart woman and that she had a way about her that made people talk. Joey gathered some very interesting tidbits from Robin.

* * * * *

"Thank you, Major Sak. The changes you made in your plans for security during the filming of the documentary are much appreciated. I can assure you that we will cooperate with you fully." Sak relaxed a bit. That was one of the things that he liked about Ambassador Tsakiris; she'd always meet you half way if she could. He was glad now that he'd swallowed his anger and pride and reworked the report.

"I think you made some valid points, yesterday, Ambassador." There, they had buried the hatchet.

Joey smiled and then went on, "I need you to check a few things that came to light last night. General Garcia indicated that the armed forces are not happy with this year's military budget. He felt, and rightfully too, that they had shown great patience and efficiency in breaking into the Japanese Embassy when it was held by the Shining Path terrorists and safely freeing all but one of the hostages. The military felt there should have been some reward forthcoming for a job well done.

"General Garcia is a powerful and ambitious man. The American government would not wish Peru to return to a military government, especially with the O.A.S. negotiations going on. Keep me closely posted on Garcia's moves.

"Secondly, a Mr. Perez, who is the Under Secretary of Agriculture to the Ecuadorian government, indicated that he could arrange a meeting with the Shining Path. He might have been just bragging, or maybe he has a relative involved in one of the cells, but I think we need to look into it. The border dispute between Ecuador and Peru has never been resolved and certain individuals might feel that supporting a terrorist organization that undermines the economic and political stability of Peru is a very good idea. Have someone befriend Mr. Perez and find out what he knows."

"Yes, Ambassador," Sak smiled. "You seem to have picked up a lot of information last night."

"Actually, I learned nothing until I talked to Robin. She seems to have a unique ability to make people relax and talk."

"That's great," observed Sak, although privately he worried what the Ambassador might have let slip.

"I might have been overly concerned about Ms. Bradley. The information I've just received back on my inquiries would indicate that she has lived a very conservative lifestyle since her release from prison. She did well at school, has no debts except a five thousand dollar student loan, has received some attention in her field for a series of articles she wrote about life on the streets, and has even had a novel published."

"I'm glad to hear that," commented Joey evenly, although she was uncomfortable knowing that Sak's people had been digging deeper into Robin's life.

"Perkins has taken quite a shine to her. I understand that they had a great day yesterday. He helped pick out her dress and then they toured the city and had lunch in the Spanish Quarter at that restaurant with the walled courtyard where you sometimes entertain guests. They're about the same age and have, I understand, a mutual love for the Big Ten Football League."

Joey's guts tied in a knot. Her face retained a smile. "I'm glad they had a good time."

Sak nodded in agreement, feeling he had bonded a little closer with his boss with this friendly chat. "Anything else, Ambassador Tsakiris?"

"No, that's all, Major." Sak left the study feeling things had gone very well. Joey swiveled her chair to stare moodily out the window. Was Robin playing her for a fool? Was she going to be lied to and betrayed again? She was seven years older than Robin and, she had to admit, a bit stodgy. Could she compete against the young and charming Captain Perkins? He'd taken her touring and to lunch. Robin had modeled her outfits for him. Joey had her stand with a boring group of old soldiers and then had stuck her at the end of the table with a bunch of clerks! She felt a cold dread spreading through her being.

Chapter Five

Robin met Joey in the morning room for lunch. "Hi, love," Robin said with a smile, kissing Joey after she had checked to make sure no one was around.

"Hi," responded Joey, with a lightness she didn't feel and giving Robin a quick hug. They sat down at the table and rang for lunch.

"So, what have you being doing today?" Joey asked, folding and unfolding her napkin on her lap.

"Reading up on embassy protocol," Robin revealed with a giggle. "Al lent me some books."

"Al?"

"Captain Perkins." Their meal arrived and Robin's eyes lit up with pleasure at the sight of the crisp green salad and Spanish omelet. Following proper protocol, however, she waited for Joey to start.

"Why are you staring at me?" the preoccupied Ambassador asked in annoyance.

"You have to start before I can, section twenty-seven, subsection three. 'When a grace is not given, junior members sitting at table will not begin dining until such time as the most senior member at the table picks up his or her utensils'."

Joey picked up her knife and fork and Robin smiled and dug into her food. "I am not senior," Joey muttered.

"What?"

"Nothing. I understand that you and Perkins had a good time yesterday," remarked Joey, pushing a piece of omelet around her plate with her fork.

"Oh yeah, we had a great time! He's a lot of fun. He took me to the President's Square to see the beautiful architecture and then we had lunch, sitting under this big tree at this really nice restaurant. It was lovely. Al's a Big Ten fan, too." Absorbed in her lunch, and babbling away happily about her day, Robin didn't even see it coming. She jumped when Joey's fork hit the plate with a rattle and the Ambassador got up and walked to the window, standing there bristling with rage.

Realization exploded into Robin's surprised mind. She got up and walked over to Joey. "You're jealous!"

Joey turned on her. "I thought you told me you loved me," she hissed. "Just how many of us are you playing for fools?"

Robin's face drained of colour and her eyes flashed with green fire. "I had a nice day with Al. He is a friend. Nothing more. I was a pretty messed up teenager, but I'm not the whore you seem to think I am. I've fought damn hard to escape that fate!" she responded, her voice tight with rage. Spinning on her heel, she stormed off.

Sometime later, the phone by Robin's bed rang. It was Perkins. "Hi, Robin, Ambassador Tsakiris would like you to join her in her study if you are free."

Robin toyed with the idea of telling Tsakiris where she could shove it. *No, that would just make matters worse*, she thought. "Please let the Ambassador know that I will be right down," Robin replied, evenly.

Robin washed her face and applied some make up to her pale skin. After a moment's hesitation, she took two photographs out of her hand bag and slipped them into her pocket. Then, she headed down to the study.

She entered quietly and found Joey pacing nervously. When Joey looked up, Robin saw the pain and stress that was eating at the person she loved. Quietly, she walked across the room and wrapped her arms around the stiff form, letting her head tuck under the taller woman's chin.

"I'm so sorry," Joey managed to get out emotionally. "I never meant... I was so upset... I just got so jealous, I wasn't thinking straight. Do you think I'm a senior?"

Robin giggled at Joey's feeble attempts at explaining her feelings. "You, Joanne Tsakiris, are not a senior! But you are an idiot! Come on, let's sit down and sort this out."

Joey allowed herself to be led by the hand to the couch and pushed down into the sofa corner. Then Robin trotted over to the study door and stuck her head out. "Captain Perkins, the Ambassador has a headache; she has requested no phone calls or visitors until further notice."

"Yes, Ms. Bradley," Perkins replied. He had noticed that the Ambassador had cut her lunch short and had come back looking pale. *Probably her monthly*, he concluded.

Robin locked the door and walked back over to a surprised Ambassador. "That was bad," Joey scolded.

"Mmm, I need to tell you why I really came here, Joey. It is a pretty wild story and I'm not sure you are going to believe me, but I think it is really important that you know, so we both understand how I feel about you." Joey felt the dread returning to her soul. She thought she did know why Robin had come. She had said she loved her.

Robin climbed into a surprised Ambassador's lap and wrapped her arms around Joey's neck. "I want to do this every time you sit down," she murmured against Joey's lips and then kissed her with all the love that she felt. Sometime later, Robin, snuggled deep into Joey's arms, began her story. She took a picture out of her pocket and showed it to Joey. In it were two women who looked remarkably like them, close enough that they could be related. They were standing on a stone terrace overlooking an ocean. The taller of the two stood behind, her arms wrapped protectively around a lame woman wearing a leg brace, who leaned for support on her partner.

"This one's Gunnul. She's Turkish. She is so like you, Joey! You could be sisters. This one's Jamie; she and I are alike. It's hard to explain, Joey, but I was called to Turkey. I just knew that was where I needed to go to get answers. I met Gunnul by the grave and for a second I thought it was you."

"Grave?" asked Joey, suddenly alert.

"Does it call you too?" Robin asked. She showed Joey the second picture of an old, worn grave sitting in a dense tangle of trees.

Joey took the picture and looked at it for a very long time. "I have this dream. I've had it for as long as I can recall. I'm looking down at this stone grave that is all carved with intricate patterns. I'm dead and the grave is mine, and yet I'm holding the hand of someone. We are going away together, and I am very happy and so... so at peace."

"Jamie and Gunnul have met a number of couples like us. They have all found their way to the grave, one way or another, over the last few years. Jamie and Gunnul are the Keepers of the Grave. They believe that the grave belongs to a warrior and a bard who local legend says traveled together in ancient times, fighting for good. They think that we are the descendants of the original pair, and that we are caught in some sort of loop in the space/time continuum. The host pair seem to be going through a crisis and they are drawing on our love to help them find their way.

"Jamie and Gunnul have heard many stories. Some of the Others have had dreams, some have trace memories and others, like me, are simply called. All the couples they have met have gone through a crisis and have managed to hold their love together and come out stronger. You are like the warrior and I am like the bard. All the other bards are lame but I'm not. Jamie feels that's significant. The grave is no longer falling apart like it was. It is actually mending. They think that we are an important link in resolving the crisis that the hosts are facing."

Joey lifted Robin off her lap and stood to pace back and forth, trying to make sense of what Robin was telling her. To her logical and practical mind, the whole thing sounded silly, and yet... she knew that grave!

"One visitor told them that the warrior and bard were not really human," giggled Robin, "that they had the blood of the ancient Greek Gods in their veins!"

"Ares," Joey muttered, looking at the black ashes in the fire.

"What?"

Joey turned and looked at Robin. "I love you. I always have. Do you really love me?"

"With all my heart, Joey," Robin answered confidently, looking up with sincere eyes.

Joey nodded, "But love is not the same as trust."

"No, it's not. And I think that is our challenge," Robin said sadly.

Chapter Six

They left the next morning on the first of their days filming, in three unmarked Ford Escorts. Captain Perkins drove in front with the equipment and supplies. Joey drove the next car with Robin as a passenger and in the rear of the small convoy were Sak and a sharp shooter by the name of Private David Luc.

They drove through the capital city of Lima, passing the new, functional high rises with lines of laundry hanging from the balconies. Progress, explained Joey, was one small step at a time. The standard of living in Peru was low due to a high population, years of mismanagement, and a poor education base. The beautiful old architecture of the colonial age stood now neglected and dog-eared. A city of crowded, poor buildings had grown up around. On busy corners, people stood on the roads selling items to make a living; newspapers, fruit, crafts, cigarettes, anything.

They stopped by the roadside, where a river separated functional, neat homes from one room, dirty squatter shacks built along the edge of a railway line. Robin listened to Joey talk with passion about the need to equalize, to some extent, the gap between the have and have-not nations. But when she tried to film the sequence, Joey stood stiffly and talked woodenly.

Oh boy! Camera fright! She lowered the camera from her shoulder and walked over to the Ambassador. "Joey, that was awful." Joey's face crumpled into worry. "I want you to forget about the camera on my shoulder, okay. Forget about maintaining the dignity of the office, and just talk from the heart. I give you my word that I will edit out anything you don't like." *Trust me, Joey, just this little bit.*

She moved closer and whispered in Joey's ear. "I love you. Talk to me. Tell me what you need me to understand." Their eyes met, and unspoken messages passed from one soul to the other. Robin smiled, encouragingly, and Joey nodded, some of the fear in her eyes replaced by determination.

Robin's camera started filming again. "It is hard to believe that people can live in such poverty and with so little opportunity," started Joey, looking down at the railway squatter homes. "We live in a world were twenty per cent of the nations control eighty per cent of all the world's wealth. Countries like Peru must fight to get part of that remaining twenty per cent in order to develop their nation. The United States is committed to the principles of the Organization of American States, which will be implemented in the year 2005. It will allow for free trade throughout the Americas. A larger, stronger, trading block is good for us on the international market as we compete with such mega-organizations as the EU, and allows developing nations the opportunity to close the gap between the have and have-not nations. Economic strength goes hand and hand with political stability and improved human rights."

Joey pointed out across the dry sands to a ghost town of partly built homes of mud and straw brick. "These are the homes of the future. The Peruvians stake out a piece of land at the outskirts of the city and build one room. As they get money, they add onto it, sometimes taking a lifetime to make their home a reality. On a weekend, you will see family groups all working together on a house. These are a proud, hard working people, who want a better life for their families and their nation."

Robin lowered the camera and ran over and gave Joey a quick hug. "That was great! I had tears in my eyes." Joey relaxed and began to enjoy the day. They traveled on down the highway out into the desert where high sand dunes skirted the Pacific Ocean.

"A lot of the early desert movies were actually made in Peru or Chile and not in the Sahara. The Humboldt Current, from Antarctica, runs up the west coast of South America and keeps the warm, moist air of the ocean from reaching shore. South of here, where the famous Nazca Lines are, it hasn't rained in over forty years! That's why people can build their homes over such a long period of time. The climate is so dry and stable that there is very little erosion due to weathering."

Robin watched the long, graceful, brown hand as it lay lightly on the gear shift. Impulsively, she placed her hand on top. Joey gave her a quick look, and then wrapped her hand around Robin's. After that, whenever they could, they held hands while driving. It was a small step towards a greater bond.

Joey pulled up in front of a jumble of ruined mud brick buildings that stretched out in all directions. "This is Pachacamac. Pacha means 'earth' in Indian. This site was called Earth-oracle. Come on, we'll look round," encouraged Joey excitedly. Robin saw a rare opportunity to film Joey at her best, with her eyes fired with interest and her body radiating energy. She hefted the camera to her shoulder and just filmed.

Joey talked to Robin, forgetting the camera and the security personnel who quietly trailed them in her enthusiasm. "There have been three cultural centres here. Each invasion built and added to the former, respecting and absorbing their culture into their own. Because the city was never leveled in war, the site is a jumble of styles and cultures. The oldest culture was the Maranga, that lived here between 100 B.C. and 700 A.D. They built that pyramid over there." Joey pointed towards it.

Robin handed her camera to a startled Perkins. "Race you to the top!" Robin challenged Joey, and took off at a dead run along the path that led up the side of the crumbling step pyramid. Joey gave her a head start and then took off, much to Sak's surprise. He knew, of course, that Joey was physically fit, but he had no idea how athletic she was. He and his men followed at a much slower pace.

Joey overtook Robin near the top and pulled her behind some earthworks. Panting and laughing, they stood in each other's arms. Joey lowered her head and kissed Robin, feeling the warmth and softness of her caresses sending shoots of passion through her being. The heat of the day burned down on them.

"I love you," Joey whispered. "You make me feel alive."

"I love you too. You open up the world to me," responded Robin. Then they prudently separated and walked to where they could see the view from the top.

"Wow! Look at the size of this site!" exclaimed Robin, looking inland. She ran to the other side of the pyramid, passing the men with a smile as they panted to the top. The view from the other side looked down on the coastal lands and the Pacific Ocean beyond. "This is going to make a great shot. Captain Perkins, give me my camera, please. Just stand on the edge, Ambassador, and talk to me," teased Robin.

Joey walked to the very edge of the last platform, scaring her security personnel out of a number of years of life. "This pyramid was not built as a tomb, but a sacrificial altar to the Rain God. It was built in a series of twelve levels, each one a little smaller than the last. The construction is very different from that of the pyramids in Egypt. Here, a thick wall of mud bricks was built with an outside layer of cut stone. The entire inside of the pyramid was just rubble. That's why, as the outside walls collapsed, the pyramid took on the appearance of a mountain of loose rock."

"What's that large, circular area down there in the plain?" asked Robin, when they had finished the taping.

"A local ring for bull fighting or cock fighting," explained Joey. "They are both very popular in Peru." Robin pulled a face and shuddered and they climbed back down to the base. Joey was off like a shot, pointing out other things of interest on the site, talking only to Robin, while she kept the film rolling.

"This is a cobbled road of cut limestone. Notice that there is a wall down each side and behind it a wide, flat bed. They think this lower, central road was for foot travel and the high roads on either side were for carts, one going into the city and one leaving. This was the first freeway! It was built by the second culture, the Wari, between 700 and 1,000 A.D."

Joey took the camera from Robin and then offered her a hand to pull her up onto the wall to see the ruined buildings on the other side. Their eyes met, and a squeeze of each other's hand before letting go reassured both of their love. Joey gave the camera back and waited for the red light to flash on again. "These people put very high walls around their cities with terraces and lookout platforms. Their homes were one to three stories high because the city was, at this time, very densely populated. The archaeologists have found all sorts of pottery, sculpture, jewelry and even textile fragments from these people."

Joey dropped off the wall and then reached up and swung Robin down. The urge to pull the smaller woman close was overpowering, so she let go quickly and put some distance between them. She just wanted this day over so that she could be alone with Robin again.

"See this square, stone tunnel running out of the sand bank here? This is Inca. It is the end of an underground water system that starts in the high Andes eight hundred miles that way," Joey pointed to a blue ridge of mountains in the distance. "It brought water to the city. Amazing, huh? There are Inca waterways and canals that are still in use today."

Joey led them back to the cars and they picked up the lunch baskets that the embassy kitchen staff had prepared. "Come over here and look down into the valley. This site has been reconstructed so you can see clearly the Inca style of construction. They usually built long buildings in the form of a large U. Then a wall was added on the last side to make a courtyard. The buildings were often up to three stories high, each story set back from the one below to make a balcony walk way. The facades were a mathematically precise set of doorways evenly spaced. The overall impression is of rows of natural colonnades growing out of the landscape."

They stood on the edge of a high ridge and looked down on a huge palace complex. The men gave the beautiful architecture a brief glance. They were more interested in scanning the many hills and ruins. This was ideal terrain for a terrorist attack. Robin filmed, while Joey stood at her side, explaining the significance of the palace.

"This is the Temple of the Chosen Women of the Inca. His harem, I suppose. The women spent most of their spare time weaving because the Inca could only wear his clothes once. The women that were chosen came here when they were eighteen and at thirty-five they could leave. Many chose to stay and teach the new women, but if they returned to their village they were greatly revered.

"The Incas were the last culture to settle at Pachacamac. They took over this land around 1400 A.D., so they were here only for a short time. The Spanish arrived in 1532. The Oracle of Pacha had warned that the Inca Ataphualpa would never rule. It was proven to be true. Even though he won the civil war and killed his brother, the Spanish used it as an excuse to execute him for murder."

They ate lunch in the shade of the Temple of the Chosen Women. Perkins made a valiant effort to get to sit by Robin, but Joey managed to herd her from the group, and so keep Robin to herself. After lunch, they wandered through the cool of the restored buildings. An old woman, proclaiming herself to be the descendant of the Oracle, offered to tell each their future by looking at the pattern of the stones they cast.

The men each paid their ten-thousand Soles de Oro, which was equivalent to an American dollar, and went first. "Your future is filled with red," she told Luc. "You will father many children," she laughed at Perkins, clapping her hands with everyone else. Perkins blushed deeply. "You should enjoy today," she told Sak, who rubbed his nose, but said nothing.

Then it was the women's turn. She looked at Robin's arrangement for a very long time. "You must have courage," she finally said, patting Robin on her shoulder in respect and smiling toothlessly. She did not ask Joey to toss the stones. She turned to her and took her hands. "There is little time," she warned and then picked up her magic stones, and sat back down by the wall to wait for her next customers.

It was a strangely solemn group that made their way back to the cars and headed back to Lima. It wasn't that the old woman had said anything meaningful or that any of them really believed in an Indian oracle; it was a presence of evil that had suddenly sent goose bumps up their skin. No one acknowledged the feeling but they all reacted to it. The men casually surrounded the two women as they all called it a day and moved off.

Old, black eyes watched them go from the cool shadow of the wall. Knurled, brown fingers played absently with the worn stones. The black eyes shifted, and watched as a figure moved silently away.

Chapter Seven

"It was just an old woman trying to make a living. You know that," responded Joey later that evening, as she sat propped up on the sofa, whiskey in one hand and Robin under the other arm.

"I know!" protested Robin, "but you have to admit we all felt something! Al did, he told me!"

Joey let the pang of jealousy pass with an annoyed lifting of an eyebrow. "Okay, I admit, the lady freaked us out. Hey, that's her job!" She gave Robin a reassuring squeeze and a peck on her head.

"I guess so," admitted Robin. "What do you suppose she meant?"

Joey laughed. "Oracles are understood only after the fact!"

For a minute, Robin was silent, gently stroking Joey's arm as she watched the flames of the fire. "Joey, can I ask you a favour?"

"Sure, pet, anything."

"Can I sleep with you tonight?" She felt Joey stiffen with tension. "I just want to be close to you."

"Okay, I guess we should, huh? I mean we love each other, right?" Joey stammered.

Robin sat up and looked at Joey, her head to one side as she thought. "Why don't you want to have sex?"

Joey flipped her legs around and sat up. "I do want to have sex. I'm desperate to have sex. I'm just not sure I want it with you!"

Robin looked like she had been hit and Joey rushed on, realizing she had made a real mess out of explaining. "No! That's not what I mean! I mean I haven't, and you have, and I feel inadequate. I've never been in a situation where I wanted to impress and didn't have the skills to do so! The more I want to, the more stressed I get!"

Robin laughed.

"What's so funny?" Joey snapped, red in the face with humiliation.

"You are, Joanne Tsakiris, the biggest tight-assed, over-achieving idiot I have ever met!"

Joey swallowed the rest of her drink and sat scowling at the fire. Robin reached over and took the empty glass from her hands. Then she kissed the back of Joey's neck, feeling her arch her back as the goose bumps formed.

"You listen to me, Joey. I don't want to have sex with you either. I could have gotten that easily over the last ten years. I want you to love me. I want you to trust me enough that you can feel my orgasm and know that only you can give me that completion."

Joey played absently with her watchband. "I don't know if I can," she admitted.

"Can we start by sleeping in the same bed?" asked Robin again.

Joey stood and offered her hand to Robin. She led her through to her private chambers.

The room was large and had been designed for a married couple with double walk-in closets and two baths. Robin broke lose and looked around impishly, bouncing on the bed and checking in closets and drawers. "Your underwear drawer is neat! No one has a neat underwear drawer. My God, you fold your undies!" joked Robin in mock shock.

Joey stood in the centre of her room, arms crossed and the corner of her mouth quirked in a half smile. "Tight-asses can only wear panties with straight creases," she observed.

Robin grinned over her shoulder at the jest, as she moved to Joey's walk-in closet. She turned, wiggled her eyebrows like Groucho Marx and closed the doors. Joey waited. The doors opened again, and Robin stepped out dressed only in one of Joey's silk shirts.

Joey looked her up and down with a mixture of sheer wonderment and open desire. "That is a three hundred dollar silk shirt!" she growled, moving closer like a lioness.

"Make it worthwhile," Robin challenged. She saw the look in Joey's eyes and pushed on. *Let it happen, so she has no time to fret about her inexperience*, Robin decided. She slid up Joey's body, kissing her hungrily. Joey forgot all her inhibitions and, picking Robin up, carried her to the bed.

Much later, Robin stirred and looked up dreamily into Joey's blue eyes. "You, okay, pet?" Joey asked.

Robin leaned down and played with a soft nipple with her tongue. Her lover moaned with pleasure. "I would just like to go on record as saying that the diplomatic service is excellent." She felt more than heard Joey's laugh.

"Oh yeah! I'd really like that recommendation on my file!"

Robin looked up with sheer devilment in her eyes. "What?" demanded Joey with a grin.

Robin smiled with the sheer joy of life. "Hey, I'm sleeping with the Tsakiris who had her face on the cover of *Newsweek* and *Time Magazine!* Neat!"

Joey laughed at Robin's delight, and then rolled her lover under her to show her again just how much she loved her.

The next day, they flew to Arequipa, a town farther down the coast. Perkins sat beside Joey, going through the last minute paper work of a working embassy, while Sak and Luc discussed security matters. Robin settled back in her first class seat and enjoyed the after glow of a night spent in her soulmate's arms.

It had been wonderful; the excitement of having all her fantasies about Joey come true, and the sense of protectiveness and joy she took at being Joey's first lover. She had done her best to make it special for Joey, to give back to Joey just a little bit of the happiness and joy that Robin found with her. She didn't know how to tell Joey that she was her hero. Every success that Robin had was because she had been trying to live up to Joey's faith in her. Last night, she had tried to tell her with her actions that what she felt for her was only a small part lust and a whole universe of love.

Things were going much better than she had hoped. Not that Joey trusted her completely yet, she didn't, but they had at least recognized their love for one another. It was an important step in rebuilding the trust that she had destroyed. She had to look at the positive. When she looked on the negative, and saw how out of place she was in Joey's world, or considered the risk Joey was taking in her career and reputation in associating with her, it scared Robin. Robin didn't belong in Joey's world and she knew it.

Joey and Robin stood against the wall of the small, shabby Arequipa airport terminal waiting for Perkins to get the luggage and sign for the hired cars. Sak and Luc nonchalantly formed a human wall in front of them, both men dressed casually in jeans and T-shirts.

Robin smiled; their attempt at blending in failed miserably! Their military hair cuts and the way they alertly scanned the crowd identified them immediately as security personnel. Not to mention the fact that their clothes were pressed perfectly. They might as well have flashing signs over their heads!

"Joey, are you really in danger?" Robin asked, realizing suddenly that the security being provided for them was overly tight. Robin moved to stand closer to her lover, unconsciously shielding her.

Blue eyes that had been far away in thought suddenly focused on the journalist. "American Embassies have certainly been targeted for terrorist attacks in the past. My work to resolve the ten year war in Central Africa made me very high profile. As a Nobel Prize winner, my face is very well known. That makes me a priority target."

Robin's eyes clouded with worry. "Does that bother you?"

Joey thought about that question. "I've been scared sometimes, in tense situations. You'd be foolish not to be! But one can't give in to terror. As soon as leaders do that, then the principles of democracy are lost. Change has to come from the will of the people, not the narrow ideology of fanatics... I'm sorry. I didn't mean to preach."

Robin smiled and risked giving her lover a little bump. "You didn't. You were just being you, and I love you for it. In fact, I'd like you to say it again on film. It really sums up what you are all about." Joey's eyes softened and she reached up to give Robin's shoulder a reassuring squeeze.

Once organized into the cars, they headed through the city of Arequipa. Robin filmed, while Joey talked as she drove. "Arequipa is over four hundred and fifty years old. It's known as the White City because so much of it is made of white volcanic rock." Joey pointed out the windows. "That's them, the three volcanic mountains that surround the city; Arequipa, El Misti and Pishu Pichu. They are dormant but the area still gets lots of earthquakes."

They drove around the city, while Joey pointed out the significant sites. At the city square, they got out and toured the old cathedral and the beautiful Jesuit Monastery that had been converted into stores. Robin loved the colonnade of white volcanic stone columns, each one beautifully carved with panels of intertwined roses.

Then Joey took them to the famous Convent of Santa Catalina. They walked through the walled religious town now surrounded by the city. Most of it was deserted. The Order had moved to a section of the grounds where the housing and accommodations were more modern. "These were cloistered nuns," Joey explained, as they walked through the narrow cobbled streets of Spanish architecture. The men, following at a discreet distance, so as not to be picked up on Robin's camera, looked curious but vaguely uncomfortable at being in a world where only nuns walked before.

"Usually, the first daughter was married off and the second was given to the church to be a nun. It wasn't a cheap act of faith, believe me! The family had to either buy or build a home for her within the grounds of Santa Catalina and put up one hundred pieces of gold for her training. Once her schooling was completed, the family had to give another two hundred gold coins before she was allowed to take her vows and become a nun."

Robin pulled a face from behind the camera and Joey laughed, walking over to her. "Are you a second daughter?" she asked, trying to find out more about Robin's family.

Robin, fishing in her battery belt to change over from a low battery to a new one, snorted bitterly. "I was the only one, unplanned and unwanted."

"I'm sorry," Joey said simply.

Robin looked up to see stormy eyes genuinely upset that Robin had not been loved. Robin shrugged. "It happens a lot." Then, she quickly changed the topic. "So only daughters of families that could afford to buy their way to heaven got sent here?"

"Oh no, a daughter of a poor family could come here to work as a servant to the nuns. Come on, down here," Joey indicated, letting the original topic drop. "I don't know if you can film in here, it's pretty dark."

"I can get it, if you move closer to that beam of light coming through the door on the other side of the wood screen."

Joey obligingly went to stand where she had been asked. "Yup, that will do it," Robin confirmed, "It will make for a nice dramatic shot with the contrast between light and dark on your face."

Joey nodded and waited for the red light to come on the camera. "Once a girl entered the monastery of Santa Catalina, she was never allowed to leave. But on a religious holiday, they were allowed to stand at this wood screen behind a black curtain and talk to family and friends who came to visit. They were allowed five to ten minutes depending on their seniority and their conversations had to be monitored by another nun!"

"It's beautiful and serene, but I bet most girls had to be brought here kicking and screaming!" commented Robin, as they checked out the laundry, which was a series of halved ceramic wine kegs fed by a central channel of water.

"Well, I guess there were a lot who would have chosen a more conventional life, but it was a time of great faith, and for many women life would be a lot easier in here than toiling from sun up to sun down for a family. Imagine bearing ten children; you would have been pregnant for seven and a half years!"

Robin whizzed on poor Perkins. "And you're going to have lots of children! Brute!" Everyone laughed and Perkins blushed a deep red.

"This is the last stop," observed Joey, leading them down two steps into a whitewashed room. The walls and ceiling had been painted with elaborate jungle vines, wild flowers and colourful birds. Robin filmed the room, taking a few close up shots of the detailed work. "This is an example of the faith I was talking about. All the nuns here came from the Arequipa area except the one who lived in this room and painted these designs. She was a poor Bolivian girl who had a dream that called her to become a nun. She walked alone, carrying a fifteen pound cross as her only protection, through the jungles from Bolivia to here. They refused her entry at first, but after hearing her story they decided that God must have protected and guided her here. Her trip had taken her two years!"

"This room is lovely! I could live here." Robin nodded with approval.

"No, you couldn't. The nuns took a vow of silence and only talked when it was necessary. You'd explode!" Everyone laughed and they headed back to the main gate.

When they left Santa Catalina, Joey gave instructions for them to drive out to the countryside to have lunch at an Inn that was still a working grist mill. They sat on a shady, old patio overlooking the cool, clear river. Farther downstream from them, the worn, wood wheel turned slowly, moving the gears within the stone mill.

Perkins and Luc had managed to get themselves on either side of Robin and Joey was forced to sit across the table with Sak. She tried not to glower while she thought of horrible fates that she could arrange for her pleasant and efficient assistant. Robin saw the look and smiled. She understood. Wouldn't it be nice if they could just date openly? It wasn't fair to be denied even the simple pleasure of holding hands while waiting for lunch to arrive.

After lunch, the two women headed for the toilets behind the mill. Once around the corner, Joey grabbed Robin's hand and ran down the dusty farm lane and around the corner. Laughing and out of breath, they crossed a stone bridge and stopped behind a big, old oak. Robin felt the rough bark against her back as Joey pinned her with her body and kissed her passionately. "I can't get enough of you," Joey groaned. "I'm going to have to kill Perkins!"

Robin laughed, doing a fair bit of fondling of the Ambassador's body too. "He's harmless," she gasped, as Joey sent a shiver of need down to the warm centre of her being.

"He's going to have lots of kids! They don't come in Cracker Jack boxes!" growled Joey, half in jest and half in jealousy.

"Well, he's not having them by me!" protested Robin. "You are the only lover I will ever need or want."

When a worried Sak came looking for them, they were laughing and joking as they came out of the ladies. *Women! What do they do in washrooms?* he wondered.

The small convoy of cars headed back to their hotel. It was a magnificent old colonial building at the edge of a tree lined square. Joey had craftily suggested that, for security reasons, it might be best for her not to be alone in a room. Robin was moved in and Sak was on one side with Luc and Perkins in the room on the other. "You are devious and ever-so marvelous," Robin had praised her in a whisper as they hugged in the relative privacy of their room. Joey had smiled happily at the praise.

Chapter Eight

Dinner was tender beef cooked over a hardwood fire and served with a hot pepper salad and roast potatoes. Sak relaxed enough to tell some funny stories about his earlier days as a recruit stationed in Hawaii. Luc, to everyone's surprise and delight, took the stage for a set and played haunting Spanish melodies on a twelve string guitar he had borrowed from the local band. The evening ended with them all giving Perkins a rough time again about his future litter of children, just to watch the poor man blush and splutter denials.

Back in their room, Joey handed Robin a box of chocolates. "I seem to remember that you could home in on chocolate within a fifty miles radius like a heat seeking missile," teased Joey. Robin's eyes lit up as she reached for the box hungrily.

Then she paused. "Have one?" Robin politely asked Joey. Joey pulled a face and declined, not being fond of sweet things.

"They say that the best chocolate in the world is made here in Arequipa, Peru. Because it is made with all fresh, natural ingredients, it does not keep, so it is not sold anywhere else but right here. I am told that true chocolate lovers have been known to come to Peru for the sole purpose of eating Arequipa chocolate. So, what do you think?"

Robin chose a solid piece of chocolate so that she could judge fairly. It had a creamy, rich smell that was a delight in itself. With reverence, the sweet disappeared through Robin's lips. The chocolate melted slowly into a soft mousse. Vapors with a hint of bitter chocolate blended with the sweet taste of milk chocolate. The treat lasted a long time and when, with regret, Robin swallowed the last traces, a finish of fresh ground cocoa remained to tease her.

"Well?" asked Joey again, laughing at her lover sitting there with her eyes closed and a dreamy look on her face.

"You remember when I said that you were the only lover I would ever need or want?" asked Robin.

Joey looked surprised and a little insecure. "Yeah," she answered, a nervous knot already forming in her gut.

"Well, forget it! This stuff is MUCH better than sex!"

Joey snatched the box back.

They lay naked in each other's arms, Joey enjoying the aftertaste of chocolate that still haunted Robin's mouth. She slipped forward, half covering Robin with her long, graceful lines. Her hand followed a now familiar path, running long, dark fingers across blond, silky hairs. Robin groaned with need and her world shook. Then it shook again!

Joey rolled from bed and threw Robin her jeans and t-shirt. "Quick, we've got to get out of here. It's a quake!" Plaster dust snowed down as Joey took Robin by the hand and they wobbled to the shaking door. Opening it, they met Sak in the hall. He grabbed Joey, covering her head with his arm. "This way, Ambassador!"

"No, Robin!" shouted Joey, as the second wave hit. Sak grabbed his charge around the waist and half carried her and half pushed her through the courtyard and entrance hall out to the safety of the open plaza. The earth buckled and rolled with a grating sound and chunks of mortar, stone and roofing tile rained down out of the dust clouds. Luc and Perkins came running over.

"Where's Robin? Where is she? Robin!!" Joey cried frantically, trying to run back into the building. Sak, with difficulty and help from Luc, managed to restrain her.

Only after the worst of the after shocks were over would he agree to let Luc and Perkins go back in to check. Joey watched quietly as the two men stepped over debris and disappeared through the entrance. Then, with a sudden jerk, she was free and running towards the building with the much bigger, but slower, security officer in pursuit.

The wall of the courtyard had collapsed, although structurally everything else seemed, superficially, okay. Robin wasn't in the hall or the room. If she hadn't made it out, it meant the wall must have collapsed on her. The four remaining Americans started to dig with their hands frantically.

"Robin! Robin!" they called.

Finally, there was a muffled reply. "Joey! Are you okay?"

Relief almost made Joey pass out. "Where are you?"

"In the decorative well in the corner of the courtyard, but something fell on top of us."

"Us? What's on you? Are you hurt? Keep talking, Robin!" Joey called frantically, as they tried to locate the well in the debris of the collapsed wall.

"I was right behind you when I saw this little girl. The wall behind her was just cracking up like a shattered windscreen. So I ran and grabbed her and the only place I could see for cover was the fake well. It's really dark in here. I think something's covering the top."

By now the frantic searchers had located the well and were struggling to push a large piece of wall off the crushed well top. Joey yelled down, "Don't worry, Robin. We'll get you out soon!"

"Hey, take your time," came the cheery voice. "We've got the chocolates."

The four desperate diggers froze in their actions and looked at one another and then laughed in relief. "I'm for leaving her in there!" grumbled Joey. "She scared me half to death!"

"Yeah," sighed Sak. "At least until after breakfast tomorrow, anyway." A small tremor, however, got them all heaving on the masonry again.

Two men with a distraught maid showed up, searching for the woman's child. With the extra hands, they were able to shove the debris back enough that Sak could reach in and pull first the child out, then the box of chocolates and finally Robin, cut and bruised.

Joey was right there, wrapping Robin in her arms and holding on to her tightly, tears of relief rolling down her face. Robin clung to her lover. She had been far more afraid than she had been willing to let on in front of the little girl. When the small after shakes had hit, her heart had pounded, fearing they would be buried alive.

"That was an incredibly brave thing you did," Joey choked. "Don't ever do anything like that again! You scared the hell out of me!"

The three men looked at each other. Luc scowled in disgust, Perkins looked hurt and disappointed and Sak scratched his ear in embarrassed amusement. "Ah, Ambassador? We probably should go out to the main square." Joey nodded, still too emotional to speak. With her arm around Robin, they led the way through the rubble.

Perkins was dispatched to get the first aid kit from the car to treat Robin's abrasions and Luc was assigned to collecting wood debris for a fire to keep off the night chill. Sak stood guard at a discreet distance. Joey sat on the ground of the plaza her back propped up against an overturned park bench. Her legs were out straight and she held Robin curled in her lap.

Around them, shaken people collected loved ones together or dug through the rubble. Emergency personnel and the army started to arrive to provide assistance. Already people worked to restore order. Sak had wanted to notify the army of the Ambassador's presence. Joey had vetoed the suggestion, saying they were safe enough and many others needed help.

"This doesn't look good," Robin muttered. "I'd better get off you."

"No. Our relationship is out in the open now. Stay where you are," responded Joey, holding the woman she loved close.

"But Joey! Your career!" protested Robin.

"Shh."

Perkins came back with the first aid kit and several bottles of drinking water. Joey used one sparingly to clean the worst of Robin's abrasions and put antibiotic cream over the top. Then, the five of them sat around the fire Luc had built and prepared to wait out the night. Robin leaned up against her lover, the shock of the evening finally beating out the adrenalin rush that had kept her going.

Around the large square, fires burnt and shadowy figures huddled. Now that the worst was over, people talked and laughed shakily. There had been many injuries but no deaths that anyone knew about and the damage to homes was nothing that couldn't be fixed over time. The people were used to quakes. Tomorrow, in the light, when the worst of the after shocks were over and people could assess the damage, they would return to their homes and life would go on.

Joey looked down at Robin, who now slept peacefully against her. A soft smile hovered at the edge of the older woman's mouth, and she reached to push a truant strand of hair off Robin's face. Sak watched with embarrassed fascination. "Ms. Bradley's got the right stuff. She showed a lot of guts back there," he observed, preferring talk to the awkwardness of silently watching the two women in so loving a situation.

"Yeah, she has," Joey admitted with pride, meeting Sak's eyes with frankness.

Perkins had been sitting moodily looking at the fire. "Ambassador," he finally said, after swallowing his nervousness several times, "Robin is a very gentle, caring person..." He closed his mouth, not knowing how to continue without offending and yet feeling a need to defend and protect a person that he really liked.

Joey smiled, admiring Perkins for risking his career by trying to protect Robin. "It's okay, Perkins. We both understand the consequences of our actions. We love each other." Perkins nodded sadly and went back to looking at the fire. Luc got up suddenly and walked off, muttering something about looking for more wood.

For breakfast, they ate some of Robin's chocolates and washed them down with the bottles of water. Robin filmed some of the devastation and had Joey talk on tape about what they had experienced the night before. Luc went to rescue their luggage and Perkins got the cars to the safety of the road by running a slalom course through a rubble covered parking lot. Fortunately, the airport to the north had experienced little damage, the epicenter of the quake having been the downtown section of Arequipa.

They piled into their vehicles and made their way slowly to the airport. This time Sak insisted on driving Joey's car and the two women sat in the back, Robin under Joey's protective arm. The flight to Juliaca, in the Andes highlands, was uneventful. From the plane window during take off, they could see that the majority of the quake damage was centered within just a few square blocks.

Robin spent her time checking and cleaning her camera. She would rewind and play sections of video over and over again, her eyes watching intently. Occasionally, she would freeze frame and stare at an image for the longest time. After she had packed everything away carefully, Joey talked.

"Please, Robin, I need you to be very careful once we land. We'll be at an altitude of ten thousand feet. The air is very thin. Walk slowly and don't try to talk and walk at the same time until you adjust. We'll take a taxi over the pass and at one point we'll hit fifteen thousand feet. On the other side is Puna by Lake Titicaca. It is the highest town and lake in the world, at fourteen thousand feet above sea level."

Robin nodded, preoccupied, and sat quietly holding on to Joey's hand. Joey was surprised by her lover's lack of enthusiasm. Maybe she was hurt more than she had let on. She had lived through an explosion, fallen in love and been buried in an earthquake. Perhaps even Robin's zest for life had been worn down.

At Juliaca, they hired a taxi van to take them to Puna. At this altitude, it would have been foolish to drive the narrow, hairpin, dirt road over the pass, even if they could have hired cars in this remote area.

Robin found herself light headed and queasy by the time they reached the top of the pass and started to drop down into the wide plain that held the great lake of Titicaca. Half of the huge, shallow lake was in Peru and the other half in Bolivia.

The hotel was a modern building and afforded a spectacular view of the lake. It was on a small island called Isla Esteues that was joined to the mainland by a single lane causeway. The exhausted group booked in the spacious lobby and then went to their rooms to sleep, agreeing to meet in the lobby lounge sometime later in the afternoon.

Robin and Joey showered together, taking turns washing the dust from each other's hair and bodies, too tired from lack of sleep and oxygen to do more than kiss softly before curling up naked together under the crisp, clean sheets. For a while Joey lay there, enjoying the feel of being close and intimate with Robin. She closed her sore eyes for a while longer and dozed. Then, waking half an hour later, she crawled quietly from the bed, dressed and went down to the lobby.

At the main counter, she asked to see the manager and, showing him her diplomatic service card, she was escorted immediately to his office, so that she could use his Internet system. She typed several messages, read each over carefully, and then clicked to let it go. For a minute she sat and looked at the screen, coming to terms with what she had just done. Then she smiled and went into the control panel to wipe out the history of her e-mail.

Robin woke in the afternoon feeling slightly light headed but much recovered. Beside her, Joey still slept peacefully. *You are so beautiful, all the way through, and I love you so very much.* She leaned over and kissed Joey, softly. "Joey, love? I'm going downstairs. I'll see you there."

"Hmmm," came the sleepy response.

Robin busied herself taking some filler film of the lake and the hotel. Then, back in the lobby, she met Perkins and they ordered the local tea while they waited for the others. "What the hell are you doing?" came Joey's angry voice from behind Robin. The journalist jumped, spilling the tea that she was pouring into Al's cup.

"Having tea with Al," Robin responded with an annoyed tone, as she put down the tea pot and hurried to wipe up the spill on the coffee table with her napkin.

Perkins stood. "Ambassador Tsakiris, I assure you that..."

"You're dismissed, Perkins!" Joey snapped.

Perkins came to attention. "Yes, Ambassador," he said stiffly, then turned on his heel and left.

Robin stared at Joey. "What are you doing! That was really rude!"

"Not here. Upstairs, where it's private. Come," ordered Joey, her lips tight with suppressed rage.

They took the elevator up to their floor and walked down the hall to their room in a silence bristling with tension. As soon as they were inside the room, Robin wheeled on Joey. "What was that about?"

"You're out of my sight for a few minutes and I find you drinking coco tea with Perkins! What are you on? Come on, tell me! I don't want anymore ugly surprises!"

"What are you taking about? I don't do drugs!" snapped Robin in anger.

"Yeah, I've heard that one before," Joey responded bitterly. Robin backed up, looking like she had been hit. "Coco tea is made from the leaves of the cocaine plant. Do you think I'm stupid?"

Robin looked at her in stunned shock. "W... What?"

"It's not addictive in that form, so I don't think it will give you the kick you're looking for. It is used as a bronchial dilator to allow you to take in more oxygen at this altitude," spat out Joey, her lips pale from the lack of oxygen and emotion.

There was a long moment of silence. Then Robin straightened herself with dignity. "I don't do drugs. Perkins and I were told it was the local tea. I think I want to be alone for awhile, Joey."

Joey looked at her closely. Had she over reacted? Was Robin telling the truth? A greater dread replaced the one that had filled her when she saw Robin happily pouring the yellow coco tea. *Oh God, what have I done?*

"Look, Robin if I..."

"I want to be alone," repeated Robin with an edge to her voice. Joey nodded and left the room. Down in the lobby she found Sak talking to a badly shaken Perkins. He turned when he saw Joey.

"Ambassador Tsakiris, I understand that there has been an incident," he stated.

Joey shook her head and sat down, indicating the others should do the same. "Perkins, did Robin ask for the tea?"

"No, Ambassador. We were waiting for the rest of you, and a waiter asked if we would like to have some of the local tea. I am sorry if I gave the wrong impression. I assure you..."

Joey held up her hand. "I'm sorry. I overreacted. Coco tea is made with the leaves of the cocaine plant. I... It would make Ms. Bradley... sick. Ah, a reaction with other things, you understand."

Perkins looked genuinely distressed. "Oh, I am sorry! **We** thought it was a herbal tea! I wouldn't expose Ro... Ms. Bradley to any danger!"

"That's okay, Perkins. My fault for over reacting. You can go now."

Perkins stood and withdrew, leaving Sak sitting with Joey. "She doesn't have anything on her. I've checked a few times," her security officer said.

Joey looked up sharply, eyes blazing with anger, then realized she was not in a position to criticize someone else's suspicions.

"When I saw her with the tea, I just lost it."

Sak nodded but said nothing at first. Then he said, "When I first went into the military, I had a good friend. We'd joined up together. I loved him like a brother. We still keep in touch, but he was a lousy soldier. He'd panic under pressure. I just couldn't trust him. To be close to someone, you've got to be able to trust them."

Joey looked up and met honest brown eyes. "You don't trust her."

Sak thought about that. "Not at first. The prison record put me off, and her visit to Turkey. But I can't find anything in her recent background that would indicate any problems and believe me, I've looked! It was clear to me that Ms. Bradley had got to you, and that could have been a big security concern." Joey blushed at Sak's blunt honesty. She thought that until last night they had been pretty discreet.

"I like her, but I'll go on monitoring the situation pretty closely because that's my job. It's yours too. Remember that, okay? And watch what you say." Joey looked down at her hands, worry and chagrin written all over her face. He was right. Her office had to come first.

"On the other hand, I'd be surprised to find that Robin Bradley isn't what she seems; pretty, intelligent, deeply in love and a damn spunky lady." Joey looked up in surprise. "With due respect, Ambassador, it wouldn't hurt to go up there and tell that young lady that you made a real jackass of yourself!" He smiled, in a fatherly way.

Joey's eyes opened in surprise. Then she laughed and stood, placing a hand on his shoulder and looking down at him with that face that could turn a man's guts to molten lava. "Thanks, Sak. I owe you one," she said and headed for the elevators.

Sak watched her go with thoughtful and worried eyes.

Joey entered the room quietly to find Robin sitting in a chair by the huge picture window, a panoramic view of Lake Titicaca before her. Walking over, Joey placed her hands on Robin's shoulders. When the journalist didn't pull away, Joey risked bending down and kissing her on the head. "I'm sorry. I acted... like a jackass. When I saw you with the tea, I... I just lost it. It was stupid and completely uncalled for. Can you forgive me?"

Robin's hand came up and covered one of Joey's cold ones. "I was sitting here thinking about the night of the banquet. I love you so much, Joey," Robin said, her voice heavy with emotion. "But what chance do we have? I don't fit into your world. I can't live with who you are. And you will never be able to trust me again. Maybe, we are the end. Maybe our love was never meant to be, and our ways go in separate directions."

Joey's heart crunched in fear. "I don't think I could go on if I accepted that," Joey responded, coming around to kneel in front of Robin. She took Robin's shaking hands and held them between her own, that were cold with fear. "Okay, I failed this test of our love miserably. But I don't want to give up on us. I can't. Please, Robin, forgive me!"

Robin wrapped her arms around Joey. "Oh Joey, of course I do," she whispered into her lover's ear. "I'm just so worried about taking someone so special to this world and dragging her down! You have no idea what a hero you are to me!"

"I know you make me happy. You bring to my life... something very special. There is nothing I wouldn't give up to keep you," responded Joey, holding on to the woman she loved as tightly as she dared. "As for being special, the rest of us ran from that hotel last night. You stayed behind and risked your life to save a child. I think that makes you pretty special."

For a long time they stayed that way, until Joey pulled back and looked at Robin. "I bet you're starved. All you've had to eat today were chocolates this morning!"

Robin giggled and nodded. Then she got that look of sheer devilment in her eyes. "So what do they put in the coffee, opium?"

Joey laughed. "Nope, sorry, just regular or decaffeinated," she responded, pulling Robin to her feet as she got up herself.

Robin reached up and kissed Joey tenderly. "You are the only opium I would ever need in my life."

Chapter Nine

They had dinner on an open terrace on the top floor of the hotel and watched the sun set over the lake, fire and water blending in liquid reds and blues. It was a slow, relaxed meal, Joey having warned Robin to take breaks to replenish her blood with oxygen so that she didn't pass out. They sat and watched the stars come out while Robin had her coffee and Joey her night-cap. Robin found the way they made coffee fun. The waiter would pour a thick, hot, syrupy coffee from a silver carafe into the cup until it was half full and then dilute it with boiling water. The resultant beverage was rich and full bodied and very much to Robin's taste after she had added a heaping spoonful of sugar. The hotel Scotch was Pinch, a dubious blended endeavor that normally would leave Joey scowling. But she was having it with Robin and that made all the difference.

Robin sat quietly now, chewing on her lower lip. She looked over at Joey. Joey hadn't trusted her this afternoon. Should she risk telling Joey about her suspicions? Would Joey laugh at her and tell her that her imagination was running away with her? There was only one way to find out. "Joey?"

"Hmmm?"

"I think you are being followed."

Joey sat up and put her glass down. Blue eyes focused seriously on Robin's face. "I'm listening," she said, and Robin felt her insides relax.

"I saw this man in the plaza square last night. There was just something about the way he moved, more like an animal. I was sure that I had seen him before. Then I remembered seeing him, or someone who moves like him, off in the distance at Pachacamac, in some of the video I took. And I filmed him, again, I think, when we were at the Jesuit monastery that had been converted to stores in Arequipa.

"I went over the film this morning, and you are going to have a hard time believing me, but I'm sure it's him. And if I'm right, he has been at most of the sites we have!"

"We need to talk to Sak and his merry men. Come on," Joey said without hesitation. She signed the bill and took Robin's elbow, leading her to the elevator. They went to their room and Joey called Sak to tell him they were having a conference in her room in five minutes. The men were there in less time than that.

Robin played the video while they formed a tight group looking over her shoulder at the small viewing screen. On the first tape, a shadowy figure backlit by the sun moved along the top of a desert ridge for a second, and then disappeared from sight. Robin rewound and played it again. The man did move strangely, his arms swinging in time to his steps like a monkey's would do.

On the second tape, a figure in the shadows of the colonnade walked between two pillars and was gone. Again Robin rewound and they watched. Again there was nothing to see but shadow. The dark figure moved with the same strange motion.

"What do you think?" Joey asked Sak.

Sak grimaced and shook his head. "I'd say Ms. Bradley has the sharpest eyes and best recall that I've ever seen!"

"I'm always looking for things like that. This is rejected footage because that movement would distract from the visual presentation. So when I saw it a second time and then a third, I became suspicious," she explained.

Sak rubbed his chin and looked at the others. "It could be a tourist following the same route, thousands do every year. But he seems to be very elusive and I don't like the way Robin keeps picking him up on the tape, as if he is staying close to us. I think we need to take this seriously. Robin can you describe him?"

The journalist nodded. "He's between 5'6" and 5'8". I'd say around thirty-five years old. His skin is fairly light and his features more European than Indian, but he has the thick, cropped hair of a Peruvian with Indian blood. He has a large straight nose, dark hair and dark eyes, most likely brown, although it was hard to be sure by firelight. He was wearing old, grey dress pants that had been cut and hemmed at the bottom and on his right leg there was a grease mark about the size of a fist. His shirt was short sleeved and basically white with a fine pattern going vertically through it. He cuts his own hair or an amateur does. He is very under weight and he had a heavy five o'clock shadow... I'm sorry that's all I noticed," she finished, looking from one to the other.

There was a moment of silence and then Sak shook his head. "Bradley, anytime you wanna join my team you're welcome!"

"You did good, girl!" beamed Joey. Perkins smiled delightedly and Luc stayed in the background. He'd do his duty, but he didn't think much of mixed couples or gays. Neither was the way God intended, as far as he could figure.

They discussed heading back to Lima. Perkins and Robin felt it was a good idea. Luc gave no opinion. Sak and Joey felt that it was wrong to give into the fear generated by terrorism. He hadn't approved the documentary, but now that they were committed, he felt it would send the wrong message if they quit. "Americans aren't cowards and they're not quitters, right, Tsakiris?" he growled.

Joey smiled. She had really come to like her chief security officer on this trip. She had seen him in a different light, and she knew him to be trustworthy and fair, if a bit over zealous in his job. "That's how I see it," Joey said quietly, and that had ended the discussion. The men trooped out and Joey made sure the door was locked and bolted.

She turned to see a worried Robin fighting for control. "I've put you in great danger with this stupid documentary!"

Joey went over to her. "No, my job puts me in some danger. This could just as easily be some weird tourist who is completely unaware that we exist. Still, it is best to be on the safe side and be forewarned and more cautious."

A knock came at their door and both women started. Joey frowned, and was about to reach for the phone to contact Sak, when she heard his deep, gruff voice on the other side of her bedroom door.

"It's okay, Ambassador, it's room service with the oxygen. I'm right here with him."

Joey smiled and wiggled her eyebrow at Robin, then went over and opened the door. A hotel employee stood there with a canister of oxygen on wheels. Joey waved him in. "Robin, it is hard to sleep deeply in a thin atmosphere. This is air enriched with oxygen. Breathe it in until you feel your toes start to tingle, then your blood will be saturated with oxygen and you'll sleep better."

Robin smiled with that twinkle she got in her eye at any new experience, and sat down on the edge of the bed while Joey fitted the mask on. After a few minutes, Robin nodded and Joey slipped it off to put it on herself. When she felt the pins and needles in her toes, she removed the mask and handed it back to the operator. Sak led him over to where the men were roomed and once again Joey locked and bolted the door.

Robin laughed. "Now that has got to be the most unique room service in the world!"

Joey smiled at Robin's joy in the simplest experiences, and came over and hugged her. "You're terrific, you know that?"

"Oh, yeah, I'm terrific, Ms. Nobel Prize winner before I'm thirty!" Robin snorted, rolling her eyes.

Joey took her face in her hands and looked deep into her eyes. "Yes, you are. I am very proud to be your lover and friend." She leaned down and kissed Robin hungrily and Robin responded to every need her woman had.

Chapter Ten

The next morning, a sleepy Robin woke to the smell of fresh coffee and oven baked bread. Rolling over, she blinked the last of her dreams from her mind and sat up to see Joey reading her e-mail, at the desk, with the cute frown of concentration she got when absorbed in a task. Blue eyes looked up and scanned greedily over Robin's naked form. Joey got up and came over to the bed, and let her lover wrap around her while Robin fought off the last of her morning drowsiness. Joey helped by nibbling and caressing her ear and neck.

"Mmm, I've created a monster!" Robin grumbled playfully. "Don't you ever get enough!"

"No."

"Then get out of those clothes and get in here, Tsakiris. No decent person should be up at this hour of the morning!"

Joey sighed. "As much as I want to, my love, we have boats hired for nine and that's in less than one hour's time. Come on, sleepyhead, up you get," laughed Joey, pulling her lover up on her lap so that she could lower her head and kiss Robin in a very private place, enjoying the knowledge that the privilege of doing so was hers alone. Robin groaned and bucked with pleasure, then wiggled out of Joey's brown arms.

"Damn it, Joey," she complained with a smile, "now I'm going to spend all day waiting to get you back here tonight!" Joey laughed, feeling delightedly pleased with herself that she could excite Robin to a hungry need. Robin had a quick shower, and then, wrapped in a towel, she joined Joey for coffee and hunks of warm bread covered in fresh butter and peach preserves.

They met the men in the lobby, and were escorted closely out to two aluminum outboards. Robin was put alone in the bow seat with Joey on the bench, flanked, on the right, by Sak. The second boat came alongside. This allowed Luc to cover Joey's left, while Perkins, in the bow, kept watch. With the local drivers in the back, Joey was effectively surrounded. She sighed in annoyance. Robin reached out with a foot and gently tapped Joey's foot. "Hey, for me, okay?" she asked.

Joey smiled, "Okay."

From the shore, a brown eye watched through the sights of a telescopic lens. There was no need to follow. They would be going to the reed islands and maybe on to the Sillustani site, then they would be back. The man scratched at his beard and smiled. The photos he had taken of the woman had at last been identified as Tsakiris by the freedom fighter leaders.

This would mean he would move up in the ranks of the People's Army of the Shining Path. He was a very ambitious man. The group leaders had said he had done well. They wanted him to continue monitoring Tsakiris' movements. They were weighing what action to take. *The leaders were too cautious now*, he thought. Since the capture of their founder and the killing of their brothers at the Japanese Embassy, they had acted like scared children.

He knew what needed to be done; kill Tsakiris and get world wide attention for the cause, and in doing so make the present Peruvian government look like they could not control the situation. For now, he could wait. He lacked the power and the inner knowledge of the organization to do otherwise. But soon he would have that power and then he would take over the leadership and lead the Shining Path to glory.

* * * * *

They motored some distance off shore until they came to a series of reed islands. Robin filmed Joey talking as they approached the island while Sak leaned away as much as possible to be out of the picture.

"These reed islands we are heading to at the moment are artificial. They were made and are maintained by the Uros Indians," Joey yelled above the outboard motor. On the island, while Robin filmed a family homestead, Joey went on, "The legend is that the Uros lived on the mainland at one time and warring tribes pushed them out. They had nowhere to go, so they cut the reeds and made rafts and sailed safely away. Over the years, layer after layer of reeds have been laid down on top of those rotting underneath until these large floating islands formed that the people live on permanently."

Joey picked up a small girl dressed in the long, colourful full skirt, blouse and sweater that were typical dress for the Andes women.

On her head, she wore a round brimmed felt hat. "They keep their heads and bodies covered partly out of modesty, partly because it can be very cold at night here, and partly to protect themselves from the sun. The atmosphere is so thin here, that the sun's ultra violet rays can burn your skin very easily," Robin smiled behind the camera. Joey had insisted on buying her a baseball cap from the souvenir store before they had left.

They wandered around the little homestead while Robin filmed sheaves of reeds drying in the sun, and the small, pointed roof homes made from woven reeds. Then they came to the famous boats of the Uros people. They too were made from reeds. The reeds were dried and tied into bundles and then in turn these bundlwere tied to form a small canoe with pointed, curved ends. Joey faced the camera, concern on her face. "Tourism is the only way these people have to better their lives. They live at a subsistence level, the lake providing all their needs," Joey looked out over the lake and then back at the camera. "These people are not the exception. Three quarters of the world's children live in poverty. I was born into a wealthy family. I guess one of the reasons I am here is to give back a little to this world.

"When the Ra Expedition tried to prove that Egyptians had sailed across the Atlantic on reed boats to influence the cultures of South America, the boat was built here. It was all nonsense of course. There is no connection between the pyramids of Egypt and those of South America, nor those found in the Far East. But the Uros were able to build a reed boat that was sea-worthy enough to sail almost across the Atlantic. It started to become water logged and sink only a short distance off the coast. These are not a primitive people. They are disadvantaged."

Joey arranged for them to take a few of the reed boats out, and they poled in a convoy through the reeds. The Ambassador explained that the reed boats were poled, rowed with a single oar or sailed. They stopped to film a woman cutting and collecting the reeds that grew in abundance in the shallow lake. "When there is a storm, sometimes the islands will break in two or float off somewhere else, so the Uros are always a people on the move!"

The smiling Indian woman offered Joey some reeds. Joey thanked her in her fluent Spanish, stripped the reeds down to their pith and handed them out to the others. "Go ahead, try eating some," she suggested, "The Uros eat it as a green, either raw or boiled."

Robin bit into hers bravely and chewed and swallowed. "It tastes like a mild corn," she commented. Sak sniffed his cautiously, and then threw it overboard. Luc and Perkins tried theirs reluctantly.

"Where do they bury their dead and go to the toilet?" asked Sak, and watched three of his companions turn green and start coughing. Joey laughed with glee.

"Actually, the dead are buried on one of the few natural islands. It's about twenty miles from here. Some of the dead are now buried on the mainland too. As for the toilet, well, it's a big lake," she grinned. The guinea pigs threw the remainder of their reeds at her.

Back on the reed island, Joey showed them how a thick sand and clay base was used to build a fire on so that the reeds would not be burnt. The Indian women even had small bake ovens on the islands. They thanked the Uros for their hospitality, Joey paying them for the use of the boats and for allowing the filming. They got back into their motorboats and headed down the lake a bit before making for the mainland again.

Here the land rose in a steep hill and on top stood curious-looking, vase-shaped, stone structures about thirty feet high. "Okay, we've got to be careful here," warned Joey. "At the top, we'll be at fourteen thousand two hundred feet above sea level. We'll go up real slow. Try not to talk. You'll probably feel some mountain sickness; headache, dizziness, queasiness," she listed, squinting in the bright sun before she put her sunglasses back on to protect her eyes from the rays that could so easily penetrate the thin atmosphere.

They moved off, walking slowly. It took them almost half an hour to walk up the steep cliff path, that couldn't have been more than five hundred feet long. Sweat beaded on their foreheads and they had to stop now and again to get their breath. "You adjust fairly quickly to the thin air," Joey explained at one such stop, "but it does take a few days."

At last, at the top, they could stand and look over Lake Titicaca. The huge stone urns now towered overhead. "These are the graves of the Sillustani. They were a contemporary culture to the Incas. You see you get into these things through this little crawl space in the bottom. The inside walls had large niches in them and that is where the male dead of the Sillustani were buried, in a fetal position. At one time, of course, the tombs were capped with stone, but erosion and earthquakes have caused considerable damage over the years."

Joey walked over to the other side of the mesa edge. "These little square boxes of stone are the graves of the women and children. What is amazing about this site is that this is volcanic stone brought all the way from Arequipa! We are not sure how they managed it, because some of these blocks weight tonnes. Most likely they were floated up rivers during the rainy season and then brought down the lake. Five hundred years ago the water was much higher than it is today."

Robin quietly kept pace with her fit lover, although her head swam and pounded with the extra exertion of carrying the camera equipment and the heavy battery belt. She smiled despite how rotten she felt. It was wonderful to have the opportunity to see these things and she loved how animated Joey became when she started talking about cultures and people.

"Robin! Come over here! I've got to show you these, they are really neat!" called Joey, unconsciously using her lover's expression. Robin walked over slowly, feeling a bit wobbly. "Hey, are you okay?" asked Joey, taking the camera from her hands.

Robin sank onto a shaded boulder. Joey sat beside her while the others discreetly scanned the countryside. They sat for a few minutes in comfortable silence until Robin started to feel a little better. "Can I have some water, please, Joey?" she asked.

Joey unclipped her water bottle from her belt. "Drink very slowly and only a little bit. The digestion process uses up oxygen," Robin nodded and did as she was told. Now feeling cooler, and her head more clear, she stood slowly, knowing not to make any sudden moves.

"Okay, let me have my camera and show me what is so neat!" grinned Robin and Joey's eyes sparkled with happiness.

"See here, the Sillustani carved a snake on one of the grave stones. That's a symbol of intelligence and medicine. Over here is a lizard, that symbolizes goodwill and prosperity. Okay, come around this side," ordered Joey, grabbing Robin by the arm in her excitement and pulling her around the grave urn.

"See this? Four rings carved around a small circle? And here, beside them, a deep cut hole with a flared tail?" she smiled, eyes sparkling, as she waited for Robin to work it out herself.

Robin looked closer. "This symbol out here looks like a comet! And those rings could be the four orbits of the planets that can be seen by the naked eye around the sun!" exclaimed Robin excitedly.

"Right! Way to go, girl! Some shaman stood here and made one of the first news pictures of Haley's Comet passing by."

"Wow! That's amazing!"

"Yeah, it could be seen clearly here the last time it passed, in 1986, but this carving is much older, most likely five or six hundred years ago. To me, old ruins like these are a testament to the human spirit! The media so often only report on the actions of the ancestral animal that lives in our genes, instead of the humanity that dwells in our souls."

"That is so neat, Joey! Here stand beside it while I film, and tell me all about it again." Joey rolled her eyes, but good-naturedly explained the significance of each of the carvings again and her viewpoint on them. Before they left the area, Joey walked them along a sheep trail to look down on a large circle made of thin, upright slabs of stone about two feet to three feet high. To one end of the circle was a large, round boulder and beside it a smaller one with a channel carved in it that led to a natural depression in the rock.

"It looks like a miniature Stonehenge," observed Perkins with interest.

Joey nodded. "That's what it is. Both the Sillustani and the Incas were superior astronomers. They used these rings and also sighting stones to predict the changing of the seasons, eclipses, and the movement of the planets. You find them all over. That channel and depression in the rock were used to drain off the blood in sacrifices." After Robin had taped her film sequence, Joey took them on a little farther and showed them a sighting stone.

It was at the top of the ridge, on the very edge of the mesa, overlooking the lake below. A rock had been carved so that it formed a rectangular base about one foot by two. At each end was a knob of stone, and in an arch in between were small hatch lines. Joey showed them with a stick how the design was really a sort of protractor marking off the degrees across the sky. "We are not sure how it was used, but it might have been sort of like a sextant for plotting the movement of the constellations.

"We don't know very much about the Sillustani, but we do know that the Inca knew tremendous amounts about astronomy, did trigonometry and were amazing engineers," Joey explained, as they made their way back to the boats. They motored back to the hotel for a late lunch and then, against Sak's wishes, Joey insisted they take a local taxi to Puno so that Robin could film a local highland market.

They were all tense and stayed in a close group as they walked through the stalls of alpaca and llama blankets, colourfully striped in red, blue and green patterns. Robin bought a warm, soft alpaca blanket for only twelve dollars and gave it to Perkins to carry while she filmed the women using back looms to make the blankets.

Farther in the market, farm wives in their bright full skirts and round brimmed felt hats sat on the ground and sold skinned sides of lamb, piles of eggs, cakes of goats' cheese, vegetables and fruits and just about anything else that one could imagine. The market was colourful and exotic and Robin was anxious to capture it on film. Yet she found it hard to concentrate, worrying about Joey being so vulnerable to attack in such a place. She taped as quickly as she could, and then they headed back towards the edge of the market square where they could get a taxi back to Isla Esteues.

Joey had them stop at a gaudy cross that stood outside a Catholic Church. "This is a good example of how people take a foreign faith and change it to make it more compatible with their own view of reality. See, the church door is blue and has diamond shaped mirrors on it for decoration. Both blue and mirrors were used traditionally to ward off evil spirits.

"The cross is painted green because, to the Indians, green symbolizes good fortune to come. But note the symbols of the crucifixion that have been added to the cross; Roman spears, a knife, a crown of thorns, a ladder, a skull and bones at the foot of the cross and so on. On one level, they tell the story of the crucifixion. On another, however, they are the sort of symbols of death and violence that you find associated with the old pagan Indian sites.

"You see, in the Indian traditional world view, it is not the resurrection that is important, but the blood letting to please the Gods." Robin filmed, fascinated not only by Joey's knowledge of Indian culture, but also by her deeper understanding and acceptance of their traditional reality.

A worried Sak then insisted that they find a taxi and head back to the hotel before the sun set. All the way back, Robin continued to scan the crowds for any sign of the mysterious man while Sak and Joey argued.

Joey had planned to take the eleven hour train trip over the Andes to Cuzco, so that Robin could film the scenery and see the volcanic hot springs that were located there. Sak vetoed the plan, saying the train was too open for attack as it moved slowly through the isolated mountain passes. The Shining Path were known to be very active in the highland area. They had attacked several communities and had killed villagers who would not support their movement.

Joey gave in. They would fly to Cuzco in the morning, instead. However, she was not above sulking about it. Sak smiled at Robin and winked. The journalist rolled her eyes. Her lover had given into the wisdom of Sak's argument but hated having to change the plans she had so carefully worked out.

Robin lay in Joey's arms, the two women relaxed and satiated. "Joey, doesn't it bother you to be under guard all the time?"

Joey drew patterns on Robin's back with her finger tips. "Yes, some embassy assignments are safer than others. Security is a concern at the moment in Peru because of what happened at the Japanese embassy and the activities of the Shining Path. The bombings of the American embassies in Africa made everyone a little more cautious."

"I don't like living like this, always searching the background for someone who might want to harm you," revealed Robin, honestly.

Joey kissed Robin's head. "It is who I am, Robin. Even if I leave the diplomatic service, whatever job I took would involve working for peace and a fairer, more just world. That's who I am. I'm always going to be a warrior for peace, and that makes me a target at times."

"I'm not sure that's my way," Robin said quietly.

Joey felt her guts tie in a knot. She held Robin close, but said nothing.

Chapter Eleven

The next morning, they took the local flight from Juliaca to Cuzco. While Robin was off buying bottles of water, Luc getting the bags and Perkins arranging for some jeeps, Joey took the opportunity to have a word with Sak. "I need you to be less obvious about the security."

Sak looked up sharply. "You know I can't do that. Avoiding an international incident is essential. Nor do I particularly want to see your brains splattered across the country side."

Joey frowned. "It's scaring Robin."

Sak sighed and turned to face the Ambassador. "Look, I understand. I had a wife that left me because she couldn't take the stress." Joey looked away, swallowing hard. "I also know that if we are being watched, it is for a moment's lapse when they can make a move."

Sak hesitated, and then plunged ahead; better to say it all. "I've talked it over with Luc too. We'd be foolish not to be aware of the fact that the best way to get information is to plant someone inside." Blue eyes flashed back and burned into his. Sak went on, "And the best way for that person to guard their true identity would be to pretend they were trying to protect you by seeing gun men that were never there. It could have been luck, but it's strange that Robin's camera twice picked up the so-called stalker, yet none of us have noticed him."

"Robin is not a terrorist!" Joey growled.

"No, I don't think so either, but I'd be a fool not to consider the possibility. You sent her to jail, Ambassador. You don't think she doesn't have some hard feelings about doing time?"

"Hi, guys! What are you two looking so glum about?" Robin asked, her mood changing from cheery to insecure in an instant.

Sak grinned. "Your star is still chewing me out about insisting that we fly here," lied Sak, easily.

Robin looked up at Joey in surprise. "Joey! Leave the poor man alone. Whatever he needs to do to protect you is okay by me!"

Joey's eyes met Sak's in some secret communication. "Okay," she agreed. "I'll be good," she told them in frustration.

They piled into the usual three cars and headed off on a day's adventure. Along the road, they stopped to buy bread, fruit and cheese at a small farmers' market. Robin took the opportunity to film the mountainsides, which to one side were a crazy patchwork quilt of irregular farm fields in a kaleidoscope of colours. To the other, the Incas had leveled the steep mountainside hundreds of years ago into beautiful farm terraces.

They headed to Sacsayhuaman, a once huge religious site of the Incas not far out of their capitol city, Cuzco. The Spanish had torn this enormous Temple of the Sun down, Joey explained as they drove along, so that they could use the stone for their colonial city. "The majority of the first story is still there," Joey said, "and some of the archways and windows. It will give a good idea of the superb engineering that went into their work and the incredible size of their structures. Some of the foundation level blocks weigh five tons!

"The Incas never invented the wheel, so all these massive stones were pushed here. We believe that they did use stone balls to move things along on. You find them all over. They cut the rock with steam and water pressure though! They could do some amazing things!"

Joey wasn't wrong, the site was impressive. Robin got some excellent shots, made more picturesque by a small boy dressed in the bright striped poncho and woolly hat that was the traditional dress in this area. He was tending a small flock of woolly lambs among the ghostly remains of his ancestors' temple.

Joey stood by the massive cut stones of the ruined temple while Robin filmed. "Note the fine craftsmanship of this stone work. These blocks are huge and each one has been shaped like a piece of a jigsaw puzzle so that it fits tightly into the next. There are no gaps. The edges meet in perfectly straight lines without any mortar, so well that you couldn't slip a piece of paper in. The Incas realized that if you built buildings in even blocks, you would have long, straight joins like in a brick and mortar house. When an earthquake struck, the energy of the shock wave would travel down the line and the wall would fall over. So the Inca built jigsaw pieces instead. That spread the energy equally all through the building so that it stayed standing. California could learn a lot from these guys!"

Joey jumped up the massive stone blocks like a mountain goat. Robin smiled as she and the others followed more carefully. Joey had focused on the task, and was completely unaware of anything else. *She is so cute when she gets excited about something*, Robin thought

Joey stopped by an arch way and waited impatiently for Robin to get ready. When the red light came on, she started again. "If you look at this Inca post and lintel doorway, you can see how the stones got smaller and narrower as they built up. This meant the walls were wide at the bottom and narrower at the top." Joey demonstrated with her hands. "The extra weight at the bottom created stability in a quake. All the doors and windows were trapezoidal too, wide at the bottom and narrower at the top. The Inca buildings have remained intact through many massive earthquakes.

"If the Spanish hadn't scavenged this site for building blocks, what you would have seen here was a huge, pyramid style structure, with a Temple to the Sun God on the top. These rows of niches in the walls would have had fires burning in them. It must have been an amazing sight."

Robin's camera scanned the rows of niches, as Joey went on. "Now if you... oomph!" Robin hurled herself at Joey, knocking them both off the ledge. They would have taken a nastier fall still, if Luc, guarding their rear a level down, had not grabbed them and stopped them rolling off.

Sak and Perkins jumped down. Joey lay still on the rock ledge, winded from the fall. Robin, unhurt, staggered to her feet, only to be grabbed by Luc and spun around to be smashed up against the wall. Her arms were pulled painfully behind her back. "Damn queer! I knew you were up to no good!"

Sak bent over Joey. "Ambassador, don't move. Let us ascertain the amount of damage."

"I'm fine," Joey protested, sitting up. "I just got my bell rung when I hit. Hey! Let her go!" Joey was on her feet in a second, and pulling Luc away from Robin.

"Ambassador, she pushed you off!" Luc yelled in frustration at the furious woman who stood between him and his prisoner.

"She did not!" Joey yelled back, although she wasn't really sure what had happened.

"Actually, yes, I did," came a small, sheepish voice from behind her. Joey turned and looked at Robin in disbelief. "I saw that man again, up there," she explained, pointing to another ruin near by. "I thought he had a gun so I just tackled you. I didn't realize we'd go over the edge. Are you all right?" Robin asked, reaching out an arm and then checking the motion uncertainly.

Joey smiled. "Yeah, I'm fine, love," she said openly, pulling Robin close and giving her a reassuring hug.

Luc looked disgusted. "I'm just going to check over there," he said, in a tone that indicated that he thought it was a waste of time.

Sak checked Joey's head and decided that she was all right after all, while Perkins climbed up to get the camera Robin had dropped. "Looks like the lens is cracked," he stated, bringing it down.

Robin looked dismayed, and then relief flooded her features. "Oh, thank God, it is just the filter I had on top. The light is so bright, I've been using a polarizing filter to reduce glare and deep shadows," she explained. They climbed back down slowly, Perkins and Sak staying very close to Joey. At the bottom they met Luc, who handed them a battered telescopic lens off a rifle.

"He must have been using it as telescope," Luc stated. "He dropped it down a crevice in his hurry to get the hell out of there. I could see a truck off in the distance, moving pretty fast down the road," Luc turned and faced Robin, who had her arm wrapped around Joey. "I owe you an apology, Ms. Bradley," he said stiffly. "I hope I didn't hurt you."

"It's okay, you were just doing your duty."

"Don't ever touch her again!" snarled Joey. Luc took a startled step back, and the others looked at Joey in shock. The normally conciliatory woman was vibrating with anger, and her eyes were as cold as glacial ice.

"Yes, Ambassador," Luc said quickly.

"Joey, it's okay. Come on, love," whispered Robin, pulling Joey away and back to the jeep. They sat waiting in silence, while the others talked and then got in their vehicles. Joey's eyes radiated anger as she watched Luc.

"Sweetheart, I've never seen you like this before. It's okay, really," soothed Robin.

Joey turned and looked at Robin with eyes filled with passion. "I've never had anything that I have wanted to cherish so deeply before," she responded, honestly. "When I saw him manhandling you, I just wanted to tear him apart."

"He doesn't like gays, he doesn't trust me, and he is trying his best to protect you despite the fact that you are mixed race. I don't like his bigotry and narrow mindedness, but I do believe that he would give his life to protect you, and that's just fine with me."

Joey looked surprised. Robin never failed to impress her with her insights into human nature, and her willingness to roll with the punches and go on without complaining. She herself had not picked up on Luc's biases.

"Stupid bastard!" Joey muttered angrily.

"Joey!"

"Okay, okay, but he'd better keep his views to himself, and his hands off you, or else!" grumbled Joey, slipping the car into gear to follow behind Perkins.

"He will. His reality might be frighteningly fundamentalist to us, but his word is good."

* * * * *

The man felt the sweat trickling down his back as he drove the old, battered truck down the dirt road. He had made a terrible mistake in being seen by the blond woman. Now, they would be on their guard and waiting for an attack.

Should he tell the leaders of his blunder? No, they would use that as an excuse not to promote him, even though anyone could make a mistake. Worse still, they might call off whatever plans they were working on. That would never do. He needed this recognition. No, he would stay quiet about the incident and just tell the leaders that Tsakiris' security was tighter now.

* * * * *

They made their way along the highland road until they came to Kenko. This time, Sak stood at Joey's door, not letting her out until Perkins and Luc had checked the area. Joey sulked and Robin pulled faces at her until she had to laugh. Some of the tension broke, and they headed out as a tightly knit group to the circle of stones next to a hillside.

Joey sat in one of a series of stone seats that had been carved out of the rocky hill itself and waited for Robin's camera to start rolling. "I am sitting on a throne, overlooking an Earth Temple of great importance. Perhaps at one time the Inca himself sat in this very chair. It is carved out of the mountainside where the commoners would sit to take part in the ceremonies and sacrifices. They happened over there, in the centre of this sacred ring of stones, where that huge outcrop of rock sticks out."

Robin turned the camera to film the object that Joey had been pointing at. *We work so well together, as if we had known each other forever.* "That was great, Joey! Okay, go over there, and explain."

Joey trotted over and leaned on a misshapen boulder in front of the outcrop. She waited again for the red light. "We know from diaries that this rock was once carved in the shape of a puma but was destroyed by the Spanish because it was a pagan god." She frowned. "If I could give anything to this earth, it would be tolerance of other people's beliefs. We'd then be a richer and wiser world."

Joey turned and pointed. "Up there, on top of the rock, is a sighting stone that was used to find magnetic north, and at the base is the entrance to a very special cave. Come on, we'll have a look," Joey told the camera.

Luc stood guard above while the rest filed down the curved stairs that had been carved into the rock. Below was a small room with a deep niche in the wall that contained a large altar stone. Light from a chimney above highlighted the sacrificial table. "Here the Inca priests made sacrifices to the god of the afterlife that lives deep within the earth." Joey looked at Robin. For a second, both women experienced a feeling of being on the verge of remembering something very important.

"What was that channel for?" asked Sak, taking an interest and shattering the moment.

"For a stream of water, and these niches here would have had bronze bowls of hot coals glowing in them. All Inca sites have the three elements: fire, water and earth. Down here, too, the bodies of dead royalty were mummified."

They headed back to the surface and ate a picnic lunch of the items they had bought at the market, sitting on the thrones of the Inca kings. Once they had packed everything away, they headed off again to the last site Joey wanted to show them that day, Tamhomachay.

Joey stood on the second level of a three tiered temple built against a cliff face. "For the Incas there were three holy symbols: fire, which was represented by the Sun Temple at Sacsayhuaman; earth, the sacrificial site at Kenko; and water, which is represented by this site at Tamhomachay. Water was brought to the top of this temple by an underground channel that runs for five miles. The water cascaded in a single waterfall to the second level, where it was divided and fell again to the third level in two waterfalls, and then to the ground level in three waterfalls. In the Inca culture, everything is in multiples of three. The three holy elements.

"See how there are nine deep niches evenly spaced along the top. Some held statues of the mummies of the Incas. The real mummies were kept in Cuzco. The other niches would have held fire and over there, behind the temple, is a small, deep cave." Joey jumped down to the first level and sat down. "The three elements were controlled by three gods: the Sun, the Moon and the stars, represented by the planet Saturn."

Robin lifted the camera off her shoulder with relief and smiled at Joey. "Hey, you're a natural! That was just a great bit of filming today!" Joey smiled from ear to ear. Making Robin happy was just about the most important thing she could think of. Her mounting work and responsibilities back in Lima seemed very remote and unimportant at the moment. Despite the possible danger she was in, she couldn't recall feeling so relaxed and carefree in years.

They all trooped back to their jeeps and headed back to Cuzco, the legendary capital of the Inca empire. They booked into the Picoaga Hotel, which had been the home of a local Spanish general. Once settled, they had an early dinner and Perkins brought Joey the dispatches that had been forwarded to Cuzco by her embassy staff. She worked quietly at the hotel desk, a glass of Glenlivet whiskey at her side. It was a twelve year old, single malt of satisfactory quality, and Joey was feeling just a little more than contented with life. Her mail had brought the responses to her e-mails that she hoped.

Robin sat cross-legged on the bed, sorting through the film and making notes on content and time. Sadly, a lot of the cultural material would have to be edited out, but the video had caught the power and humanity of the woman Joey was. The documentary was going to be very strong, she could see that. Robin smiled; it was hard to miss, really, when you had a host as famous, beautiful, and intelligent as Joanne Tsakiris! She looked over at the woman, who was working with complete concentration on what she was doing. That was Joey, she gave a hundred per cent all the time.

What does she see in me? I'm not as bright, or as good looking. I don't have her sophistication or education. What does she see in me? As if Joey could hear her thoughts, she looked up and made eye contact. "Have you any idea how happy and carefree you make my life?" she asked the journalist with a smile.

Robin looked surprised. "I do? Don't you live like this all the time?"

Joey laughed and walked over to sit by her lover on the bed. "No, I find it hard to be spontaneous and devil-may-care, but you bring a little of that out in me. Life with you is... just fun," she finished lamely, not finding the right words to explain the deep happiness that she experienced when Robin was near.

Robin leaned over and kissed the serious woman. "I'm glad. It's pretty intimidating at times, walking in that big shadow you cast." Joey blushed. "I love you," Robin reinforced.

Joey smiled and took Robin's hands in her own, playing with them nervously. "I love you," she told them, too insecure to look up.

"Ah, I've had a few job offers. One is to work for the World Bank; the other is to work with the Save the Children program. What do you think?"

Robin was floored. She had no idea that Joey had been planning a career change. "It's really not for me to say," she floundered.

Joey looked up. "It is if you are planning to spend the rest of your life with me," she asked more than stated. Robin searched those marvelous blue eyes for doubt and saw none. With a gasp of joy, she hugged Joey close to her.

"Does that mean, okay?" Joey asked, needing the security of hearing the words. "Because you weren't too comfortable with my life style."

"I'm not always, Joey. I worry about you. But I do know that we need to be together. Where you go, I go," she said, and they both felt a jolt of familiarity.

"So what should it be, World Bank or Save the Children? With the bank, we'll be very wealthy and move among the movers and shakers of the financial world. With Save the Children, we'll be on the road a lot and not always in countries where conditions are very pleasant."

Robin looked at Joey, her eyes dancing with glee. "Now which life would my lover seek? One of a rich, financial fat-cat or one of a warrior fighting for the rights of the children of the world?" she asked innocently.

Joey blushed. "It doesn't matter what I want. Both jobs are good and meaningful work. I want you to feel that whatever career I follow, you feel it is your way too."

"Then you are going to fight for a more just world, and I'll be at your side, recording the need for better rights for the world's children, okay?"

Joey grinned broadly and pulled Robin down on the bed, to show her just how much she loved her, over and over and over again.

Chapter Twelve

The next morning, they headed out to see the Temple of the Sun at Cuzco, which was the major religious centre of the Inca people. Joey explained that no one had known where the site was until the devastating earthquake of 1950. The Spanish stucco exterior of the building collapsed and underneath, in perfect condition, was the Inca temple. She also pointed out the ornaments perched on the red tile roofs of all the homes. Some were crosses with miniature ladders attached, others were ceramic bulls with hollowed backs filled with water and on poorer homes were recycled glass bottles of water. "They are offerings to appease the sky god," Joey explained. "The sacred element of water is for the sky god, and the ladder on the cross is so good fortune can descend from the sky. Again, it is a blending of ancient belief with the newer Christian elements."

"How do you know all this stuff?" Sak had asked, as they walked from the cars to the temple.

"In the diplomatic service, misunderstanding and nasty surprises often occur when dealing with another race and culture. I've learned that traditional culture never really dies; it just goes underground or takes on the trappings of modern society. To really understand and get along with a people, you need to know their traditional beliefs and ways."

"Well, I'm glad I've got a European education, and don't believe in gifts to the rain god!" snorted Luc, contemptuously.

"Oh, we are just as much prisoners of our savage heritage as everyone else. Eggs are associated with the Christian Easter ceremony, but really they are the remains of a fertility cult that goes back to early Celtic times.

"So is the making of buns in the spring to use up the winter flour as a symbol to the gods that humans trusted them to bring the warm weather and spring rains. The practice was so ingrained in European people that the early Christian Church couldn't stop the pagan practice. Instead they passed a law saying that each bun had to have a cross on it."

"Hot cross buns!" giggled Robin.

"Got it in one, girl!" praised Joey. "Scratch the surface, and we are all tribal pagans underneath."

They entered the massive stone structure of the Temple of the Sun and stood in awe. The gigantic jigsaw pieces of stone fit together as if they had been custom made by high-tech machinery. The surface of the blue-grey stone was evenly pebbled to add texture to the walls. The trapezoidal doorways and windows all lined up perfectly in mathematical precision. The building was an engineering marvel!

Joey stood by a double-framed doorway and waited for Robin to start filming, while the three men faced out in a semicircle, always watching and on alert. "When you see the double-framed door it indicates an important room. This one was the Room of the Sun. The wall niches would have held sacred religious items made in green jade, and the walls were covered in a fine-thread mesh of solid gold! The room next to this one was the Room of the Moon. It was done in silver mesh."

Joey walked them out to stand looking over a balcony. "Down there, at one time, was the Garden of the Earth. It had life size plants and trees all made in silver and gold. Here in this huge niche was a life-sized gold statue of the Inca and in front of it a disc of solid gold!"

"Wow! The Spanish did all right," observed Perkins.

"We know all this because the Spanish leaders kept detailed records of where things were found and what they looked like. For example, we know that it took them five months to melt down all the silver and gold that was found here."

"The Inca must have been heartbroken!" Robin said, looking sadly about.

"Well, they were upset about losing their capital, but they were puzzled about why the Spanish wasted their time with the decorative silver and gold. It was to them, pretty, but worthless. They had hidden away the really valuable items and couldn't understand why they were not tortured to give away the hiding places."

"Diamonds?" asked Luc, who despite himself was becoming interested in what Joey was saying.

"Nope, green jade." Joey smiled at the disbelief on the others' faces. "Honest! Green jade is very rare here and therefore had great value. It was also green, the colour of the earth god and good fortune to come."

"Oh brother!" snorted Luc.

"That is so neat!" laughed Robin excitedly.

They finished touring the site and then had lunch in the courtyard of a local inn. After, they toured the city in their jeeps, and stopped at the Roman Catholic cathedral to see its three story, silver altar screen and the holy statues that were also covered in gold and silver. They were created from donations made by the Spanish soldiers who had sacked Inca Cuzco.

"Must be nice, to be so rich you can afford to put silver ingots on the collection tray," observed Sak.

Joey laughed. "There is a story about the soldier who found the gold plated disk. It was four feet across in size, and he rolled it down the street to the nearest tavern. The story goes that he lost it in a poker game that night!"

They headed back to the hotel. Joey went off with Sak on some embassy business, and Robin reviewed the day's videoing. Joey seemed pleased when she returned, explaining to Robin that they had hired a helicopter to take them to Machu Picchu, the day after tomorrow. Normally, the only way to the famous archaeological site was by small train or by walking and camping along the old Inca trail for a week. Sak wouldn't consider either possibility. The helicopter had been the compromise.

Joey settled back to her paper work, the responsibilities of her job filtering back. Robin worked quietly, cleaning her camera lenses, knowing not to disturb her lover when she had work to do. It was quite late in the night when the Ambassador crawled into bed and curled around her lover. Robin took Joey's long, capable hand in her own and sighed, feeling complete again.

* * * * *

The leader put the phone down quietly. He had just been informed by the man who was tailing Tsakiris that security around the ambassador had been tightened. The man had said he did not know why. The leader knew, however; the idiot had let himself be seen! There was no room in the organization for people who made careless mistakes.

Still, he smiled. It was only fair to let the man redeem himself. If he was successful, any suspicion of an assassination plan by the freedom fighters would be avoided. Yes, it was a good plan. This man deserved to be a captain in the great cause.

* * * * *

The next day, Joey had planned a busy schedule for in and around the Cuzco area. First, they drove out to Ollantaytambo in the sacred Valley of the Inca Kings. It was, in the time of the Incas, a training school for priests. On its towering rows of terraces, an amazing variety of crops were grown and cross bred as a show case of Inca superiority. Fifty different types of maize alone had been identified by the Inca and genetically improved by cross breeding to bring out specific qualities. Sadly, many of these species and the knowledge associated with them were lost when the Inca society was wiped out by the Spanish.

Joey took them next to the quaint village of Pisac. Here the Incas had rallied behind a new leader in one last attempt at defeating the Spanish. The attempt failed and now a sleepy, Spanish market town stood on the battlefield. They walked around the square and Joey bartered for what they would need for a picnic lunch while the others stood near by.

* * * * *

The man moved slowly through the crowds. He was feeling very proud. Today, the leader himself had come to him and offered him the honor of killing the American woman. He had been made a captain and would now sit on the council with the other leaders! The leader had given him his own gun in order to carry out the kill. This was going to be a glorious day for him and the cause!

He moved as close as he dared. Then he took the gun out, holding it under the poncho he was wearing to keep the morning chill off. He waited for his opening, darted forward, put the gun to Tsakiris' head and pulled the trigger. He heard the crack of a discharge.

* * * * *

People screamed and ran about in confusion. A police whistle sounded. Sak and Robin knelt beside Joey, Perkins and Luc stood over the man who Luc had just killed. "Stay down, Ambassador, damn it!" Sak snapped, his knee firmly in Joey's back. "Perkins, get a car over here!"

Joey and Robin were shoved roughly into the back of one of the cars that Perkins had driven carefully through the milling crowds. Sak took the wheel and left Luc and Perkins to handle the police. He honked the horn and made his way steadily out of the village, while Robin fought to keep her lover on the floor and covered.

"Okay, we're clear," Sak said, looking in the rear view mirror. Two disheveled faces appeared in the back. "You okay, Ambassador?" he asked.

"Yeah, fine," Joey answered calmly. "I can't believe he missed!" She became aware of Robin clinging to her and wrapped her arm around the terrified woman.

"He wouldn't have. The gun misfired or something. Luc killed him."

Joey grimaced. "This is going to be diplomatically messy," she sighed. Robin squeezed her hand.

They headed back to the hotel, where Joey and Robin were basically locked in their room while Sak stood guard until the others could report in.

"It happened so quickly!" shivered Robin. "He was just there! Joey, no one can protect you from that sort of thing!" she observed for the tenth time in one form or another that evening.

Joey lay on the bed, while her lover paced with nervous energy. Joey's head ached from being tackled to the ground for the second day in a row. "No, no one can. Terrorism is meaningless and random, whether you are in Lima, Beirut, or Oklahoma City. That's what makes it terrifying," she observed philosophically.

Robin's retort was interrupted by a soft knock on the door that Joey recognized. "It's Sak. Let him in, will you, Robin." Robin opened the door on its chain and verified that it was indeed Sak. Then she closed the door again to remove the chain before opening it cautiously. Sak stepped in with Perkins behind him.

"Everything looks good, Ambassador. The Shining Path have not taken credit for the attack and you can be sure they would have by now. That means that this guy was probably some sort of nutter working alone. He hasn't been identified. The police were being difficult with Luc over him killing the guy. Your call to the Peruvian government worked. A government representative showed up, and things are now getting straightened out. Luc will be back here as soon as he fills in and signs the ten thousand forms for the release of his firearm."

Joey nodded. "Good, I'm glad this hide-and-seek game is all over."

Sak grimaced. "Ambassador, I think we should continue to proceed with caution. I think it is likely that the man was working alone, but it is very strange that he would be using a gun that had an empty clip. There is only one day left before we return to Lima, let's continue to proceed with all due caution."

Joey nodded. "Thank you, Sak, and please thank the others. You handled the situation very well. I will see that a commendation goes in your files."

"Thank you, Ambassador. Good night." Sak left the room and Robin locked the door, put on the chain and pushed the dead bolt into place.

Joey watched with an amused grin on her face. "Hey, you going to pace about all night? Come to bed."

"I can't sleep, I'm too worked up," protested Robin.

"Good," responded Joey with a lazy, sexy grin.

* * * * *

The ride by helicopter over the pinnacle peaks of the Andes was breathtaking. Slowly, they dropped down into the valley where the Vicanota railway station stood beside the Urybamba river. The 'copter touched down on the graveled area used for the buses that taxied the tourists up the series of hairpin bends to Machu Picchu, fifteen hundred feet above their heads.

Robin was virtually dancing with excitement, much to Joey's delight. They piled onto an empty bus, the tourist train not being due in for another three hours. Joey was immediately surrounded by the others, despite the fact that she pointed out that the stalker had been killed. "We are not taking any chances," Sak had said firmly, and the others had nodded grimly.

Joey sighed, "You are a great bunch, and boy, do you get on my nerves!" They all laughed.

* * * * *

The leader smiled. The plan had gone well. Of course, either way it would have. Had the man been captured, his story would have seemed so ridiculous that he would not have been believed. The Americans had continued with their trip, confident that they had removed a lone assassin. The man had died a hero of the people. He had died just as he had lived, nameless. It was sad that yet another captain had died for the cause. It was amazing how many new captains did! The leader chuckled; everything was back on track and going well.

* * * * *

The view from the top was mystically beautiful. Around them lush, green, pinnacle mountains rose up from the narrow valley far below. Those farther in the distance were tinted blue and veiled in swirls of mist The Urybamba river, almost a half mile below, was just a strip of silver in the sunlight. Around them, clinging to the steep mountainside, were the stone ruins of Machu Picchu, the last frontier post of the mighty Inca empire. The five of them just stood for a while and looked in awe. Machu Picchu is one of those rare places in the world where nature and man lived in aesthetic harmony.

Joey broke the silence, quietly. "Machu Picchu was never conquered by the Spanish. It was eventually abandoned but we don't know why; perhaps because the empire ceased to exist. It is one of the many mysteries that remain unraveled about this site. Another is the makeup of its graveyard. We believe that a community of some five hundred people lived and worked here. Yet the graveyard contains mostly the bones of women between the ages of eighteen and thirty-five and a few old men.

"Some believe that this was once just a small outpost that was established as part of the Inca's plan to conquer the Upper Amazon, which is just to the other side of this range. It might have been enlarged if the Inca had decided to send his Chosen Women here when the Spanish arrived. We might never know."

Joey led them along a three-foot ledge, one of the many that terraced the side of the steep mountain to provide gardens for the people. A cool breeze whispered around them and glancing down, the five hundred feet of terracing looked like a steep stairway that suddenly ended at a cliff face that dropped to the valley way below. Robin decided not to look down. Sak and Luc moved closer to Joey, realizing that a quick push could mean a drop to her death.

Joey showed them the nobles' houses, or perhaps where the Chosen Women lived. Here the buildings still were finely finished block, but the houses were very small with once peaked and thatched roofs. The other homes on the site were just crude dry-stone construction.

They carefully walked down steep, broken stone steps to the priests' round house and Joey showed them the marks in the natural rock floor that were used for astronomy sightings, the windows having been placed so that the sun would rise directly down the valley and shine through the window. To the one side of the priests' dwelling was the terraced water fountain; one stream, then two, then three. To the other side, between the priests' house and that of the chief, or perhaps the Inca, was a natural cave that had been enlarged by carving out stone steps and a sacrificial altar.

They moved back up the stairs and over to a second peak. Joey looked at Sak and Sak sighed and nodded. "Leave your camera equipment with the men. They are staying here," Joey told Robin. "I want to show you the view from the observatory up there."

A little surprised, Robin did what she was asked, seeing in Joey's eyes a sparkle of excitement. Together, they made their way up very steep and broken stone steps with a vertical drop to either side. Joey held onto Robin's hand and helped her along. At the top were the walls of a stone observatory room with three windows to let in the sun and moon's rays. They would shine directly on the three altar stones that stood in the centre of the room side by side.

Robin looked from each window with delight at the panoramic view of the mountain valley framed by the ruins of Machu Picchu in the foreground. Joey saw a wild, pink orchid growing on one of the ledges, reached out and picked it. Gathering her courage, she went over and took Robin's hand, leading her over to the altars.

Robin looked up into the bluest of eyes, as Joey gently settled the orchid between Robin's breasts. "I love you with all my heart, and here at the top of the world, in this ancient, holy place, I want to ask you to be my partner and remain with me forever."

"Oh yes, Joey, yes," whispered Robin in joy as Joey slipped on to her lover's finger a plain, gold band of the purest Peruvian gold that she had bought the day before. They kissed. The flame, their passion; the water, their tears of joy; the earth, the rocky embrace of the Inca world. They were at last one.

Chapter Thirteen

Sometime later, they joined the men at the base on the observatory stairs. Sak noted that the two women were beaming and Robin now wore a gold band on the third finger of her left hand. Joey led them across the flat ceremonial grounds and over to the workers' and artisans' homes. She pointed out to them the various clever methods that the Incas had used to secure the thatched roofs to the stone gables.

On one house, stone rings carved along the top of each peak allowed poles to be run from end to end. On another, round knobs of stone stuck out, so that roofing poles could be tied to them. "We know from the size of the gardens that about five hundred people lived here. There were gardeners, artisans, religious leaders, affluent and poor, leaders and laborers, but where are their bodies? Did the Incas work at these outposts for only short periods of time and then return to the bigger settlements?"

"That would explain the small graveyard but not who was found there," observed Robin, as she switched tapes.

"Right."

"Maybe it was only at the end, when the Inca sent his women here, that it became a permanent community," suggested Sak.

"Or they haven't found the warriors' graveyard yet," put in Luc, "Maybe it slid into the river valley."

"What's that place up there?" asked Perkins, pointing to more Inca ruins high on the next peak.

"That's Huayna Picchu. It was probably a look-out fort, although some scholars think it might have been a religious retreat for the priests," explained Joey.

"This isn't isolated enough!" scoffed Luc, and the others laughed.

"So are you guys game for a hike up to Huayna Picchu?" asked Joey.

"I could do with some exercise," commented Sak and they headed off.

It was a steep and high climb that took them well over an hour. Joey used the opportunity to hold onto her lover's hand. The view from the top was worth it. They looked down on the peak of Machu Picchu, patterned with the ruins of the famous Inca site. Beyond was the Urybamba River valley, surrounded by green velvet pinnacles rooted in mist.

Joey stood behind Robin, her hands on the smaller woman's shoulders, both of them memorizing the place where they had become one. Later, Robin filmed as Joey explained, "This is the Urybamba river valley. That way, the pass runs down to tributaries that lead to the Amazon River. This way the river winds across the high Andes and broadens out into the Sacred Valley of the Kings near Ollantaytambo. The Ollantaytambo valley was a huge, fertile flood plain that provided much of the food supply to Cuzco."

"Here comes the train up the pass." Sak pointed. "I think, Ambassador, for security reasons, it would be a good idea for us to make our way back before the tourists start arriving up here."

Joey nodded and carefully they side-stepped and slid down the near vertical path back to Machu Picchu and picked up a taxi bus to take them down the corkscrew, single lane path to Vilcanota. Sitting side by side, Joey held Robin's hand as their plane lifted off and flew above the peaks back to Cuzco.

That night, they had a quiet dinner together by candlelight on the roof top patio. The rusty red tiled roofs of the city spread out below them and Robin and Joey counted how many roof offerings for the sky god they could find.

"Joey, do you believe in God?" Robin asked, suddenly aware that there was so much about her partner that she was yet to discover.

"Yes, although not fanatically so. It seems to me that religion is a guide book for living a decent and moral life. I don't think a God would really split hairs about religious law and ceremonies. When you remove all the trappings, all faiths have basically the same message. My father was raised Roman Catholic, although he does not practice his faith. My mother is a Baptist and she goes faithfully to church each week. When I was young, the two of us used to sing in the church choir together. I still go with mom when I'm home. What about you?"

Robin shook her head. "My parents never practiced a religion, and I was never taught anything about the Bible. I know Jesus was supposed to have been born at Christmas, but that's about it. I guess I believe there is some sort of Being watching over the universe. I don't know. I liked that you took me somewhere special to ask me to be your partner. It felt right."

For a minute they sat in silence, watching the sun set behind the hills and the stars slowly come out. "I play the piano. Do you play anything?" Robin asked.

Joey laughed. "Am I getting the third degree?"

Robin blushed. "Come on, old closed mouth. I'm your partner now. It comes under The Right To Know Act."

Joey smiled. "Okay, I can play a flute, pretty well. I learned in school. And I play the piano very well. Good enough to have been a concert pianist."

"Oh, YOU would!" moaned Robin, in mock frustration.

"Well, YOU asked!" defended Joey, with a laugh. "How well do you play?"

"Hey, I played professionally!" bragged Robin.

Joey's eyes opened wide. "Yeah?"

Robin giggled. "Well, in my parents' tavern. I only play by ear, mostly jazz and blues."

"Hey, I love jazz!"

"Me too!"

Joey looked at her lover. "Tell me about your family, Robin."

Robin frowned. "There's not much to tell. I'm an only child. I grew up in the back three rooms of a run-down, working class tavern. My parents saw to my material needs. I always got fed, and there was always money for clothes and treats and things. I went to the local public and high schools. In my spare time, right from when I was a little girl, I worked in the tavern: washing glasses, sweeping up, playing the piano and so on. I think my parents saw me as live-in help, if they saw me at all.

"I can't blame them for the mess I made of my life. I started dating a senior. All the girls thought it was wonderful because I was just a junior dating this older man. We ran away together. I guess I was looking for someone to love me. He dumped me on a street corner after about six months. I learned to survive," she finished, unwilling to talk about those years when she had hit rock bottom. "I begged and stole. I'd probably have ended up as a prostitute and a drug addict if I hadn't met you," she added honestly.

"I can blame them!" snarled Joey, protectively. "You were looking for the love and emotional security that every child should have from a parent!" Robin reached out and rubbed Joey's hand, thankful that she now had Joey to provide those needs in her life. "Didn't your family look for you?" Joey asked gently, capturing Robin's hand in her own for a second.

"Not that I know of," Robin looked up at the darkening sky. "Joey, what will happen with your parents? You seem to have such a good relationship with them. I don't want to mess that up."

Joey looked sad. "It might just do that, Robin. I won't lie to them, and I don't know how they will handle it. My mother is pretty broadminded but she is a practicing Christian and might see our relationship as sinful. I don't ever remember her expressing an opinion one way or the other. My dad is easy going, but he is very conservative and he can get his back up about things. I just don't know. I do know, though, that you come first. I hope they don't put me in a position to have to make a decision."

Joey reached over and took Robin's hand. "I love you. I don't care about your past or your family. I have always believed in you. That is all that matters."

"I don't ever want to embarrass you, Joey," fretted Robin.

"You couldn't, love," Joey smiled.

Joey woke to the sight of their two naked bodies wrapped together in a tangle of sheets. They were so completely different in every way, and yet they fit together as well as the stones of the Inca buildings. For a long time, she just lay there and let her eyes drift over the beautiful lines of her lover, memorizing every freckle and curve. *I want to come to know her so well that I can love her in the dark of night and see in my mind each part I caress as clearly as if there was light. How did I get so lucky as to find her again? You are my soulmate, the other half of me.*

Joey bent down and gently nuzzled Robin's soft ear. "Mmm," came the sleepy response.

"Time to wake up, my love."

Robin rolled over and looked up at the lean, hard muscles in the face of the woman she loved. She smiled and her eyes danced with joy.

"What?" asked Joey, smiling in response.

"You're my partner, forever! Oh, Joey! I'm so happy!" exclaimed Robin, hugging her lover closely.

"Mmm, me too!" responded Joey, pulling the smaller woman up on top of her and kissing her neck.

Robin pulled back and sat up so she straddled her lover. Joey could feel Robin's desire, warm and moist against her abdomen. She reached up and caressed Robin's breasts, feeling the nipples harden at her touch. Robin groaned and bucked against Joey's hard body. Then she bent down and sucked one of Joey's nipples into her mouth. Need flooded like a storm surge through Joey's being. She hoped the men didn't mind waiting.

"So what was that about, yesterday?" asked Luc, as the three men enjoyed a big breakfast.

"What was what about?" evaded Sak, helping himself to another piece of toast to sop up his egg.

"What were they up to up in the observatory yesterday, while we stood guard like a bunch of idiots," clarified Luc, pouring himself some more coffee and adding the hot water. *Stupid way to make coffee. They could do with some American know how around here.*

"I guess the Ambassador just needed some private time to talk to Robin. They'd had a bit of a scare the day before. I'm sure she wouldn't want anything in that documentary that would embarrass the United States," he responded. He wasn't going to tell Luc that the Ambassador had bought a ring when he was out with her the other day. He figured Tsakiris had made some sort of proposal up there yesterday, or whatever gays do. Robin was wearing the ring, anyway, when they came back down.

"Hell, they sleep together, how much time do they need to talk," snarled Luc with disgust.

Sak looked up sharply. "You're out of line, Luc. We don't discuss the private lives of those we are assigned to protect. It's none of our damn business!" Which wasn't quite true, and they all knew it, but he liked both girls. He found their attraction to each other kind of embarrassing and just plain weird, but it was their life, and he couldn't see why they shouldn't be allowed to be happy.

Luc's face went white with anger and he would have responded if Perkins had not cut in. "There is no use us getting all in a twist about it. Face it, guys, we're just all a little frustrated that two beautiful women whom we have spent a holiday with prefer each other's company to ours."

Sak snorted and laughed and Luc, realizing he had almost said things that he would have regretted when the report came down, laughed along weakly too.

"You ever think about the two of them together? Makes me horny, I gotta tell you," Perkins confessed.

"I think I could handle the two of them, and make them see a better way," smirked Luc.

Sak sighed, feeling his age. "I think that Tsakiris would eat me alive, and spit me out as dog food. That's one hell of a woman. Can't figure how that little blond handles her, but she seems to." He looked at his watch. "They seem to be late. We might as well use the opportunity to check the vehicles over. I'll stay here, you two go see to it."

"Yes, sir," responded Perkins and he and Luc drained their coffees and left. *Stupid young bucks*, Sak thought, shaking his head.

They drove to the Cuzco airport and boarded a DC 10 heading back to Lima. Once they were settled and in the air, Robin turned to Joey. "I'll have to go back to the States and put this documentary together. That could take quite a while," she announced sadly.

Joey nodded. "Yeah, I realized that. It will take me some time here to hand over my position to a new Ambassador. It's going to be really hard."

"Yeah. No regrets, Joey?" Robin asked softly, needing to know that she wasn't pulling Joey from a life she loved.

"No. None," Joey said without hesitation. Then a worried frown crossed her face. "What about you?"

Robin smiled. "Well, one small regret," she confessed.

Joey's face hardened into an expressionless mask, and she went very still. "What?" she managed to get out between tight lips.

"That all the Arequipa chocolate is gone," giggled Robin, and the Ambassador threw her flight pillow at her.

They moved quickly through the airport, leaving Perkins behind to see to the luggage. In a single car, they drove back through Lima and swung up to the concrete and iron double gates of the embassy. Clearing security and getting their tags, Sak drove them through the concrete security pillars and pulled up in the main courtyard. He was damn glad that all had gone well, and he had the Ambassador back safely.

He and Luc got out of the car and opened the back doors for the ladies to get out. Robin and Luc came around and the four of them moved as a group to the door.

* * * * *

The leader watched through a window. Fear was generated by killing the enemy when an opportunity arose. Terror, the kind that grabs at the souls of rulers and brings governments down, was having the power to kill the enemy in the safety of their own homes.

The leader smiled and dropped his arm. Three gunmen with high powered rifles opened fire. The first bullet hit Joey in the arm. Robin was hit by her second as she dove to protect her lover. Two bullets passed through Robin's chest and into Joey before they hit the ground, lying in a spreading pool of their own blood.

Sak and Luc fired back, forming a wall in front of the two women. They both fell in the crossfire. The courtyard went strangely quiet and still. Four bodies were picked up by the security cameras lying motionless accept for the flapping of a green airplane tag on Robin's camera case.

Off in the distance, there was still firing as marines closed in on a nearby house, taking out the terrorists. A siren wailed. People from the embassy rushed out to do what they could. The camera high on the security fence objectively filmed it all. The tape would be used later during the official enquiry.

Chapter Fourteen

Gunnul and Jamie sat together in the garden. "This is where we sat the first day you brought me here to meet Chrissy," Jamie observed.

"It was very hard," admitted Gunnul, smiling at Jamie as her capable, strong hands worked on massaging the muscles in Jamie's badly damaged leg. Jamie never complained, but Gunnul had learned to tell when her partner was in pain. She had carefully made massaging Jamie's leg part of their quiet time, when they would talk and laugh over the day's activities. Jamie relaxed then, and forgot the pain of her lameness.

"Yes, it was very hard, but you made it work. I love you so much, Gunnul!" Jamie reached out and covered one of the strong, warm hands of her partner. Gunnul leaned forward and would have kissed those inviting lips if a scream had not come from the house.

"Allah save us! Allah we are in your hands!"

Gunnul looked at Jamie. "Go ahead! I'll catch up," Jamie said and Gunnul took off at a dead run for the house. Jamie strapped her brace on and swung her leg off the bench. Then she placed her crutch around her arm and hurried as quickly as she could to the house, trying not to let the frustration of her slow progress get to her.

Following the wailing to the kitchen, she found Gunnul on the floor giving Chrissy CPR. "My God! Chrissy!" she gasped, her hand going to her mouth to stifle a scream. Her heart gave a painful spasm and beat wildly as the world faded and then cleared.

"Has an ambulance been called?" she demanded, as she awkwardly dropped down beside her daughter.

"Yes, Mrs. Dedemann, I have called. Oh Allah save us!"

"What happened?" Jamie managed to choke out, as she felt for a pulse on the small, limp wrist.

"The evil eye, Misses! She was standing there laughing, then she grabbed her chest and fell over. Someone has been jealous of her beauty and has placed a curse on her! Allah protect our Chrissy!"

It had been a hellish ride, bathed in flashing red light and pulsating with the scream of the ambulance siren. Descending into the

485

emergency bay, the doors had opened into a chaos of doctors, admission forms, and busy nurses. Once they had filled out all the forms, they had been ignored, unwanted spectators in a life and death struggle.

Now, almost a day later, they sat in stunned silence by Chrissy's bed. They had saved her... and just for a time. She clung to life with the help of a mechanical cat's cradle of wire and tubing that threaded its way from Chrissy to the life support systems and back. The doctors could find no reason. Chrissy was simply dying.

"General Dedemann?" Gunnul turned to see the doctor standing at the door. She squeezed Jamie's shoulder and walked out into the hall. "It is in Allah's hands, General. We have done all we can. The choice is yours. We can keep her here indefinitely... but you might want to take her home..." Gunnul nodded. The words just wouldn't come from her tight, sore throat.

The doctor looked uncomfortable. "I'll see to the arrangements for you," he stated and hurried away.

Gunnul turned and looked in at her family through eyes grey with sorrow. Swallowing down her tears, she walked back in to place her hand on Jamie's shoulder. "We are going to take Chrissy home now," she choked out. Jamie nodded and then fell into Gunnul's arms, sobbing.

* * * * *

Nick Tsakiris picked up the two day old newspaper that sat on a scruffy metal table in a dingy waiting room. **WARRIOR OF PEACE GUNNED DOWN** was the headline. There was a fuzzy grey picture of his daughter taken two years ago in Stockholm. He read:
"Ambassador Joanne Tsakiris of the American Embassy in Lima was gunned down this morning, outside the embassy, by three gunmen stationed in a nearby building. Ambassador Tsakiris is in critical condition at a private hospital in the city. A hospital spokesperson listed Tsakiris' condition as grave and worsening.

"Two security officers were killed in the attack and a woman filming a documentary for the American Television Network was also critically wounded and is now listed as being in a serious but stable condition.

"Ambassador Tsakiris won world wide acclaim two years ago when she won the Nobel Peace Prize for her efforts in bringing a lasting peace to the bloody fighting in Central Africa. Tsakiris walked into the rebel camp alone and unarmed..."

Nick threw the paper back on the table. He knew what his daughter had done. He blinked back tears. They had traveled all night to be with their daughter, perhaps in her last few hours. They had come straight to the hospital from the airport only to find that JoJo had been taken back down to surgery to try and locate and stop some internal bleeding.

He got up and stared out the window to the street below. His daughter had always been that special child who seemed perfect in every way. Bright, caring, athletic, beautiful, she could have been anything she wanted! He would have liked her to take over his business interests, but what she wanted was to make the world a better place. Well, she had, and it might have cost her life.

He sighed. His wife, Beedee, had chosen to wait by that woman's bed. She had been the cause of JoJo's one mistake, and now she was the cause of his daughter's shooting. If she hadn't been making that stupid documentary... He sighed. No, that wasn't fair. She could have been shot at any function. Still, he didn't see why his wife was concerned about her. It was JoJo they were here for.

Beatrice Tsakiris sat by Robin's bed watching the small figure labour to breathe. Captain Perkins, who had brought them to the hospital, had said that Robin had shielded her daughter with her body. Two bullets had ripped through her right lung and a third had grazed along her left arm, breaking it. Perkins had been drawn and deeply upset by what had happened. He had told Beedee, in a breaking voice, that both women were very special people.

The shock of her daughter's shooting was a knife in her own heart, but she took some comfort in knowing that Robin had been with JoJo. She knew that with Robin there, her daughter would have been happy at last. She had known that JoJo loved the street child. That was obvious by the anguish she had gone through after Robin had been sent to jail. JoJo had been caught between her own love and her knowledge that Robin hadn't cared for her in return, but had used and betrayed her.

JoJo had dated all through university and in the early years of her career, but there had never been anyone special. As soon as a relationship turned serious, JoJo would end it. Beedee didn't understand what her daughter saw in this little blond, but she knew the attraction was strong. She loved Nick Tsakiris, and they'd had a wonderful life together, but she had always had a vague feeling that there should be more. She felt in her heart that whatever bond existed between JoJo and Robin, it was that very special something that was so very rare.

The nurse had told her that both women had been very agitated, Robin calling out in her sleep for Joey. The doctor had finally ordered that they be put in the same room together, and then both women had seemed to relax. By the time she and her husband had arrived, however, JoJo had been taken back down to surgery.

Oh, JoJo, you fight with everything you've got, you hear! And know, if you can't hold on, that Robin will be my daughter too. There is enough love in my heart for you both. Tears ran down Beedee's face. Why would anyone want to kill such a beautiful soul as her daughter's?

"Joey?" asked a voice, gasping with effort.

Beedee looked up into deep green eyes. A jolt ran through her. Those eyes! They stirred some powerful memory in her! Had she noticed the girl's eyes before? She didn't think so, but she was sure that she knew and loved those eyes. "No, it's Beedee, Robin. JoJo's mother."

"JoJo?" smiled the weak woman, fighting to keep her eyes open. Then fear flashed across them. "Where is Joey?" she gasped, getting agitated.

"Shh, girl," Beedee soothed, getting up and tucking Robin's sheets around her. "Joey's in surgery. She'll be back up here soon. You rest. Nick and I are going to take good care of you both." Robin nodded and closed her eyes, drifting back to sleep.

Nick picked up the paper again, reading the headline for the thousandth time. "No use reading it again. It's not going to change none," Beedee stated, gently taking the newspaper out of her husband's hands and kissing him tenderly on the head. "The nurse said JoJo's back in recovery now. They'll be bringing her up here in another hour or so."

Nick nodded, taking his wife's hands. "I just can't believe it," he choked.

Beedee slipped in beside her husband on the couch. "I know, Hon, I know." Then she approached the subject that she knew they had to discuss. "JoJo is in love with that woman, you know, Nick."

Tsakiris bristled. "No, she isn't!"

Beedee gave him a hug. "How well do you know our daughter?" she asked with a smile of disbelief.

"I don't want her to be gay."

"Well, Hon, she is, and she seems to have found that little Robin of hers again. She's gotta know that we can come to accept Robin as part of our family, Nick, because if it comes to a choice she'll choose Robin, just like I chose you over daddy's objections."

Nick looked at his hands, the same way his daughter did when she was upset. "I don't know if I can do that."

"I promised God and JoJo that if anything happened... that Robin would be our daughter," Beedee said, as if that settled it.

Nick looked into his wife's eyes and took strength there as he always did. After a while, he nodded. "Let's go see how the little one is doing," he got out, swallowing hard. Beedee smiled and hugged him close. That's why she loved this man. Together, they went back to the room to sit by Robin.

Sometime later, they wheeled Joanne Tsakiris back into the room. Nick barely recognized the pale, hollow cheeked face as his daughter's. Tubes and machinery were connected to her from all sides and she barely seemed to breathe under the green plastic oxygen mask.

"Joey?" called a voice from behind them, as if JoJo's presence had reached into Robin's subconscious as she slept restlessly.

"Shhh, Honey. Don't you worry, your Joey is here beside you now." She had barely got the words out when the beep of the heart monitor became a steady wail and the screen showed a straight line. Medical personnel came from all sides, pushing the Tsakirises out of the way. They stood against the wall by Robin's bed and watched in horror as the doctor used electric paddles to shock JoJo's heart back into use. Nothing. Another doctor did C.P.R. while the machine recharged.

"Oh baby, please, come on," cried Beedee, holding onto Nick tightly. Joanne's body jumped again with the shock. The line didn't change. The doctor gave her a shot of adrenalin and continued C.P.R. For the third time, they used the paddles. Nothing. He straightened up and turned off the machine.

Robin, who had been tossing in her sleep, moaned one long, desperate note that faded to nothing.

* * * * *

Joey stood by a stone sarcophagus. The top was carved with beautiful interlocking patterns of tree leaves and feathers. It was her grave, she knew, and now she was going to go away with the person she loved. She felt very happy and at peace.

Her eyes lifted from the grave and turning, Joey smiled at her partner. A stranger smiled back. Joey frowned. The beautiful blond woman dressed in archaic clothes shook her head and smiled again. In confusion, Joey looked back at the grave.

* * * * *

Joey's parents stood in shocked silence, watching the nurse gently remove the I.V. from the still body that had once been their daughter. Robin thrashed around in her sleep, fighting to regain consciousness. Silent words formed on her lips, as she struggled through her own exhaustion to open her eyes.

"Joey! No! Come back to me!" Robin finally managed to cry out, turning blue around the lips with the strain as she struggled to sit up and reach for the woman she loved.

Nick Tsakiris gently wrapped her in his arms and lowered her to her bed. "Robin, we understand. We are here for you," he choked, the tears rolling down his face.

Joey's eyelids flickered as the nurse removed the mask. "Robin?" came a whisper of a voice.

"Doctor!" called the nurse, quickly placing the mask back in place, and switching the monitor on again. A small, steady beat, pulsed across the screen.

"You stay with me, you promised," Robin whispered, barely conscious.

"Okay," came the answer.

* * * * *

Joey sat up in bed, a frown of concentration on her face as she went through some of the embassy dispatches slowly. In the bed next to hers, Robin tried to open the wood puzzle that Nick had bought her in the market. "Your father only does this because he knows it bugs the hell out of me until I can do it!"

Joey laughed without looking up. "My father does it because you hug and kiss him every time he brings you a new toy. The man has got it bad!"

"He's nice," Robin said. "So is your mom. I... I didn't think they'd understand. I mean they must have hated what I did to you and then..."

Joey looked over. "I don't think it was easy for them, Robin. But they love me, and they were wonderful enough parents to see if they could accept you too. You won them over, of course," Joey shrugged as if that had been a given.

"I love you, over there," smiled Robin.

"I love you, over there," responded Joey with a smile and then turned back to her work. She was anxious to get everything in order so

490

that she could return to the States with Robin. She still only had the strength to work a few hours each day. Suddenly, there was Robin beside her. "Hey, what are you doing? You are supposed to be in bed!"

"I needed a real kiss," argued Robin breathlessly.

"Mmm, me too," sighed Joey, as they kissed for the first time in their new life together.

Chapter Fifteen

Gunnul and Jamie had struggled through a living hell for over a week, expecting at any time that Chrissy's heart would simply stop forever. Gradually, there had been improvement. The two tired mothers dared to hope that their vibrant daughter might somehow give them a miracle. The doctors came and went. No one seemed to have any answers.

Gunnul paced her office in angry frustration. "There must be some other test you can give! Our daughter is trying to live! We must help her!" she snapped at the doctor who stood by Jamie's chair, a comforting hand on her shoulder.

"So far the tests have not picked up anything. Her symptoms are very strange, more consistent with someone who has gone into shock from loss of blood."

Gunnul stopped her pacing in surprise, and Jamie looked up startled. "Well, is she bleeding inside?" Gunnul asked, her voice shaky with fear. Jamie struggled to her feet and limped heavily over to her lover, who hugged her close.

"No, we can find no trace of such trauma. It is, as I told you, nothing that we have seen before. It might be a new strain of virus that attacks the blood system. We have sent blood samples to London and to the States for analysis. We will just have to wait for the results. The crisis seems to be over at this time. Christine is very weak but stable. We will just have to see."

"Thank you, doctor, we do appreciate all you are doing," Jamie responded for them both, in her increasingly fluent Turkish.

The doctor smiled. "We will trust Allah to protect her until we can find an answer." He went out, leaving the two women to hold each other tight.

* * * * *

A tall, painfully thin child, with dark hair and deep green eyes, pushed her way weakly to where the tomb stood. Touching it, she once again felt its warmth. The cracks had almost disappeared now and the

493

pattern of interlaced leaves and feathers could be seen much clearer than it ever had in the past.

She looked up to see a boy standing on the other side of the grave. He was barely visible and glowed with a pale golden light. "Is everything all right now in your world?" she asked, and the figure smiled and nodded. "I'm glad. I think it is okay, here too."

They stood there for the longest time looking at the grave. "Will I be as happy?" the young girl asked, looking back at the figure that now wavered in and out of focus. Blue eyes met green. He nodded.

She smiled and nodded back. "Your spirit is already in someone, isn't it?" The boy nodded and grinned happily.

"Then I will wait for him," she stated confidently, knowing that someday she would meet someone very special and the loop would be completed. "I wish I could tell them," she said as she touched the grave, "that if you die before your time, you will live again."

She looked up into eyes as blue and as old as the sky itself. "But we all know that, don't we? Because we are all part of the same love."

The boy smiled and nodded and slowly faded from sight. The young girl looked down at the grave. The names carved there now were Robin Bradley and Joanne Tsakiris. Then they changed, and changed again. A thousand different names, but the same two souls. The last two names to appear and fade away, the little girl buried deep in her heart.

"*Always,*" said the wind.

"*Always,*" responded the earth's song.

"Gunnul!" came a scream of anguish, "She's gone!"

Gunnul dropped the medical report she was reading and charged out of her room and down the hall, fear filling her soul. Jamie wobbled to the door holding on to the frame for support. "She's not here!" Gunnul ran into the room, relieved at first that Jamie hadn't meant that their daughter was dead. Then fear returned. She checked the bathroom, closet, balcony; Chrissy was too weak to be up.

"She's gone to the grave," Gunnul said in panic. "Meet me there," she instructed as she shot past Jamie and leapt down the stairs. Jamie found her crutch and followed as quickly as she could.

Her daughter was lying on top of the grave in the warmth of a golden beam of sunlight that broke through the foliage. Gunnul moved forward, her hands shaking with fear. "Chrissy, Chrissy? Are you all right?"

Chrissy Dedemann woke from her dream and smiled. "Hi, mom. Everything is all right now. We don't have to worry!" Gunnul wrapped her special daughter in her arms, and carried her out of the garden.

Half way down the path she met a frantic Jamie, who hugged her daughter as she lay in Gunnul's arms.

"It's okay, mommy. The ladies that were shot are going to be fine. The boy told me," explained Chrissy, in the same matter of fact way that Gunnul had.

Jamie stroked her daughter's hair. "What boy, Chrissy?" she asked.

"The one who guards the grave and called us all to help," explained the child. "He's gone now. I can walk," she said, looking up at Gunnul.

Gunnul carefully put her daughter down. She did look stronger and less pale. The three of them walked slowly back to the patio. "Will we get to meet this boy?" Jamie asked gently. She and Gunnul had come to realize that the daughter they shared had a bond and awareness with the Host and Others that no one else seemed to possess.

Chrissy laughed. "Yes, someday I'll bring him home and introduce him to you," she said, a sparkle returning to her eyes. Gunnul looked at Jamie with confused and worried eyes. Jamie looked back, her eyes sparkling with happiness. Tonight in bed, Jamie would explain to Gunnul that she was going to have a very special son-in-law one day.

A golden leaf drifted and fell to rest on the grave. It was followed by another in dark brown. On the air there was a gentle scent of spice mixed with summer herbs. Love is eternal.

English

Encounter:

The Final Story

Chapter One

Gunnul finished her prayers in the dawn's light and rolled up her prayer rug. She had let her daughter and Jamie sleep in. Normally, the two joined her in prayer but Chrissy had been dangerously ill only a few months before and Gunnul felt she should rest and rebuild her strength, even though the puzzled doctors could not now find a thing wrong with her.

As for Jamie, she wasn't sure really why she had not called her partner to morning prayer. Although Jamie was not Moslem, she always joined Gunnul in prayer if they were together. Jamie could say all the prayers in perfect Turkish, much to Gunnul's pride. But somehow calling Jamie to prayer now that they were in England didn't seem right. They were in the European world, not in Turkey, and although Jamie was American, not English, Gunnul felt that maybe Jamie would like to practice the customs of her own heritage while she was here.

Gunnul slipped silently across the small bedroom and crawled under the warm sheets once more.

Jamie groaned and rolled over to wrap Gunnul close to her. "You're cold," she muttered. "Were you up doing morning prayers?"

"Yes," Gunnul responded, kissing her partner's forehead tenderly.

"Mmm, why didn't you call me?" Jamie muttered from where she had nestled in Gunnul's arms.

"Jamie, do you miss your culture?" Gunnul asked. "Do you get homesick?"

Jamie's head came up and thoughtful green eyes looked into worried blue. "Sometimes I miss specific things and sometimes I get a little frustrated with the attitude of some Turkish males towards women, but my home and my family are in Turkey, so how could I possibly feel home sick?" Jamie reassured her lover.

"I did not wake you this morning because I did not know if you wished to honour Turkish and Moslem ways when you were amongst your own people," Gunnul confessed, looking down at the bed sheet with a worried frown. "Besides, it is very cold."

Jamie smiled and kissed her thoughtful lover's bowed head. "My soulmate is Turkish and for the most part so is our daughter. I wish to be part of that culture. I am proud to be an American but that doesn't mean I can't appreciate and enjoy my family's culture. I don't pray in a Moslem manner when you are away on business but when we're together I like to do so because it's part of who we are."

Gunnul looked up with serious eyes but the slight curl to her mouth let Jamie know that her answer had pleased the Turk. "Tomorrow I will wake you then," Gunnul promised.

"Hmm, well, it was nice to sleep in a bit. I was tired after the late flight into Heathrow last night and sitting for so long always makes my bad leg sore. You are always so thoughtful, my love, but just one thing..."

"What is that, Jamie?"

"The British are not my people. Do I lump the Turkish people together with all the Arab nations? I am not British, although some of my ancestors were. I am American."

"Genetically, we Turks are only a small part Arabic. We have more Greek and Bulgarian blood than Arabic," observed Gunnul, with her usual logical precision.

Jamie smiled and kissed the end of Gunnul's nose. "I love you," she stated.

"I love you too, Jamie," Gunnul smiled. The smile flashed across her features changing her classic, stern beauty into radiant delight. Jamie hugged her lover close and thanked God for bringing this amazing woman into her life.

It hadn't been an easy relationship to foster. Jamie had been married to Gunnul's brother and had Chrissy by him. But where Gunnul had inherited all the fine and noble traits of her family, her brother Moe had inherited all the weak ones. His substance abuse had made him unpredictable, unreliable and violent. It had been Moe who had left Jamie lamed for life after a violent beating and it had been Moe who had taken their daughter back to Turkey to be raised by his sister, Gunnul. It had been ten years later, when Jamie had accepted Gunnul's invitation to visit Chrissy, that they had met in open confrontation. Gunnul had believed Moe's lies that Jamie was a prostitute and Jamie had believed that Gunnul was a drug lord and kidnapper.

Jamie giggled. "What is so funny?" Gunnul asked.

"I was remembering the first time we met," Jamie confessed.

Gunnul felt the heat rising up her neck. She had not acted very nobly that first day. "I am sorry, Jamie. I did not behave myself."

"No, you didn't, did you?" teased Jamie, looking up at her lover with eyes sparkling. Gunnul smiled and raised an eyebrow. There was time yet before they needed to get ready to go to the museum.

It was some time later that Gunnul once again slipped from their bed and padded back with coffee, rolls, white cheese and olives. It had taken Jamie a while to acquire a taste for this traditional Turkish breakfast but now she quite enjoyed it. "You spoil me, Gunnul!" protested Jamie, pulling herself up in bed and trying to hide the pain that her cripple leg inflicted.

"I could tell, when we made love, that today your leg hurts far more than you have admitted," answered Gunnul, kissing Jamie's temple gently.

"Hmm, a little, but it will be better once I move around a bit." She leaned over to slip a black olive into Gunnul's mouth and then followed the treat with a kiss. Jamie thought, sometimes, that her twisted leg hurt Gunnul far more than it did her. Knowing that it was her own brother that had caused the injury made her lover feel responsible. "I am head of the family, Jamie. That means I am ultimately responsible for every family member's actions," Gunnul had explained once.

So whenever Jamie saw that Gunnul was upset, she made a special effort to show her love. Gunnul was so strong and capable in many ways and yet insecure and fragile in her need to feel loved. "What do you have planned for us today?" Jamie asked.

"I had planned to take you and Chrissy to the British Museum," Gunnul stated. "Now I am not sure. It is a huge complex, Jamie. Four hundred feet long and three stories high and yet they can only display ten per cent of all the treasures that the British stole from other nations. It is a pilgrimage to go to the museum because it has some of the best examples of other nations' heritage."

Jamie smiled at Gunnul's biased explanation, filled with both bitterness and awe. "I thought it was Germany that took most of the treasures from Turkey," Jamie reminded quietly.

"That is true. Schliemann, he took so much from Troy! And some say, Jamie, that he was not even an honourable academic!"

Jamie's eyes twinkled at her serious lover's discussion. She loved it when Gunnul got all worked up about an issue and let her guard down to show the passionate woman behind the often cold exterior. It was time to swallow her own determined pride to give her Gunnul some comfort. "I don't think that on even a good day, Gunnul, I could manage a museum of that size. Would you mind terribly if I asked you to take me around in a wheelchair?"

Intelligent blue eyes, the colour of a summer sky, searched her lover's face. Then Gunnul took the breakfast plate from Jamie's hand and placed it on the bedside table so that she could carefully pull her lover into her arms. Gunnul buried her face into Jamie's soft hair. It always carried a scent of herbs drying on a warm summer's day. The scent was familiar, like some trace memory from her past that brought her comfort. "You have never asked this before, Jamie. When we have visited sites in Turkey you have walked."

"I've never had to do so much walking as I will while we're in England. And I've learned to trust our love and know that my lameness does not make you feel that I am a burden in your life."

"Jamie! I would never feel that!" Gunnul protested.

"You are beautiful, rich, powerful, you could have anyone you want for a partner. That you chose a lame, working widow from a foreign country shocked and surprised nearly everyone who knew you. It took me a little while to believe that it wasn't just a dream and that I was going to be part of my daughter's life and your partner."

"You are so much more than that to me, Jamie. You are my soulmate!" responded the earnest Turk.

"Yes, we are soulmates," reassured Jamie. "Will you wheel me about?"

"Of course, this is no problem. This way we can stay longer and we can instruct Chrissy in many things that will broaden her learning and knowledge."

Jamie smiled and snuggled tighter into Gunnul's arms. Gunnul was such a sweetie and so impossibly focused!

By the time they had gotten Chrissy awake and the three of them had showered and dressed, Teefo and his wife Peeti had arrived at the small flat that Gunnul owned in London. Teefu was General Gunnul Dedemann's administrative assistant and general man of all trades. He was very loyal to the Turkish war hero and was one of the few people that Gunnul trusted completely.

That he was here with his wife as a chaperone for Chrissy had caused some tension between Jamie and Gunnul. "I will not have our daughter treated as an object that must be protected as if she is marketable goods in some prearranged marriage!" Jamie had snapped. "We have argued about this before, Gunnul. Chrissy will be free to have equal opportunities and to chose her own partner!"

"I have agreed that I would never force Chrissy to marry anyone she did not wish to marry. I see no harm, however, in introducing her to the man and family that I think are the most suitable match for her.

A decision as important as one's life partner should not be left to chance! It is important that no doubt falls on Chrissy's reputation."

"I found you by chance," argued Jamie. "I don't want Chrissy feeling like she is under guard!"

"I am very lucky that you came into my life, but for many, their relationships are not as lucky. Chrissy must be guarded. She is the sole heir of the Dedemann empire and the daughter of a woman who lives in a man's world in defiance of my traditional culture. The growing power of the Moslem traditionalists makes that position open to attack."

"You single-handedly saved the nation from invasion! You are a hero to your people! They are very grateful for your sacrifice on their behalf!"

"Fanatics are grateful to no one. We must be careful. England is a foreign land and Chrissy must be protected!" stated Gunnul firmly. Jamie had sighed and nodded her consent. Gunnul was right, of course. Chrissy was not just another child. She had been born into a family of fame, wealth and power. Still, Jamie harboured some resentment because she suspected that one of the concerns that Gunnul had diplomatically not expressed was that they were going to a land that Gunnul saw as decadent and infidel. There was, below Gunnul's veneer of international lifestyle, a very traditional Turkish mind.

Right on opening time, the Dedemanns and their entourage arrived at the British Museum. The 1852 colonnaded facade in a Greek architectural tradition towered over them as they entered through the doorway into the marble floored lobby. Ahead of them was the famous Reading Room, crowned by its 110 foot dome. Floor to ceiling glass fronted doors protected some of the eighteen million books which formed the largest collection in the world. The circular room had concentric rings of oak desks and straight wood chairs with cushioned seats of green leather. The air held the faint, sweet scent of leather bindings and rag paper.

"Many famous scholars have worked and studied in these rooms, Chrissy," Gunnul explained in a whisper as they stood looking in. "In fact, it was in the Reading Room of the British Museum that Karl Marx wrote the Communist Manifesto."

"It has a wonderful atmosphere, Mommy," Chrissy sighed. She liked books very much. It was the one thing that her natural and adopted mothers never put a restriction on. Chrissy was allowed as many books as she wanted.

"I'm glad we got to see it before it's moved. This space is to become an educational area for the museum and the books are all being transferred to a new facility on Euston Road by St. Pancras. That's good, Chrissy, because there will be more room for the books and the environmental controls will help to preserve them longer, but it's always a shame to see the end of a bit of history," Jamie commented. Chrissy nodded. She was a sensitive girl and the moving of the books seemed sad to her.

"It is that things do not last forever that make them precious to us," observed the ever practical Gunnul. "I do not approve of rebuilding ruins or repairing them with cement. They should be allowed to die with dignity and we should appreciate not only their history but also their aging."

Chrissy smiled up at her taller mother, with respect and love. Gunnul petted Chrissy's hair and then took Jamie's arm that was not supported in her metal walking stick. "We need to go up these stairs to get to the area that displays the manuscripts and books. I will leave you there to look around as I need to see to a small matter and also, Jamie, I will get you a wheelchair," Gunnul organized, as she helped her soulmate up the stairs to the manuscript gallery.

Here a collection of works by some of the most famous authors in the English language could be found. There were also Egyptian papyri, Greek and Roman texts and letters from famous writers and musicians along with many amazing selections from other cultures' written history. In the Grenville Gallery, Jamie and Chrissy found the oldest known Bible written in Greek, the Codex Sinaiticus and Alexandrinus, and in another case the original Magna Carta! Jamie carefully answered Chrissy's questions as they walked around in wonder.

A respectful distance behind, Teefo and Peeti walked, also enjoying the many wonders of the famous museum. Jamie had found this arrangement awkward at first when they were out in public. She felt that she was slighting Teefo by ignoring him. But Teefo had explained that it made it easier for him to do his job in protecting them when he was following behind and could observe better who was around. Still, Jamie included Teefo and Peeti when she could.

Jamie left Chrissy showing Teefo and Peeti illustrations from famous children's books and limped over to look into a case that contained early Greek manuscripts. The case seemed to draw her to it and she needed to know what it contained. The Greek manuscripts within were old and beautifully written and illustrated.

One caught her eye and held her gaze. It was a small illustration of flames rising from a stone alter. As Jamie stared, the flames lifted from the page and curled like fingers around her. Even as her conscious mind denied what she saw, her heart pounded in fear and her senses felt scaly, red hot talons curling around her arms. She could feel herself being dragged back into the illustration. A gasp escaped her parched lips and far away she could hear Gunnul calling her name in fear.

Gunnul had entered the gallery pushing the wheelchair to see Jamie leaning over a display case, her face white and distorted with terror. Calling her lover's name, she rushed to Jamie's side and wrapped her in her arms. "I've got you, Jamie. It is okay. I've got you!" Gunnul whispered.

Teefo, Peeti and Chrissy now crowded around in worry. "What happened?" Gunnul demanded of her assistant, her eyes burning with anger.

"I do not know, General Dedemann. She only just left our side while Chrissy showed us some Beatrix Potter illustrations. No one else has entered this gallery. I was watching," Teefo reported.

Gunnul nodded, satisfied that Jamie had not been attacked. Then what had happened? "Jamie? Jamie, are you all right?" the Turkish woman asked, gently supporting her lover as Jamie clung to her in fright.

"I... I'm fine now. I... I'm sorry. I don't know what came over me! I... I felt... it's hard... I'm okay really!" Jamie finished in a confused rush, as Gunnul carefully lowered her into the wheelchair that Chrissy had run to bring over. "I just fainted. Silly. I'm fine now. It was probably just a reaction to the time change... a little jet lag," Jamie tried to rationalize, looking at the circle of worried faces around her.

"Are you sure?" Gunnul demanded. "Nothing happened?"

"No! No, nothing. I'm fine now, really. I'm sorry to have upset you all."

"It's okay, Mommy. I fainted once when I was out in the heat too long. Do you feel sick to your stomach? I did," said Chrissy reassuringly, holding her mother's hand.

Jamie smiled up at Chrissy and gave her daughter's hand an affectionate squeeze. "No, I feel fine now. It was just one of those passing things. I wonder where Gunnul has been and what she's been preparing for us?" Jamie asked, trying to change the subject.

"Perhaps it would be better if we go back to the flat," Gunnul stated, feeling Jamie's cold and clammy forehead with worry.

"No! I am fine. Please, Gunnul, I have my wheelchair now and you can push me around so I can relax and still see all there is to see!" argued Jamie, embarrassment colouring her face.

505

Gunnul nodded, realizing that Jamie was determined. "Very well. But you must tell me immediately, Jamie, if you start to feel ill again."

"I will, Gunnul," Jamie promised, as she was wheeled from the room at the head of their little possession. She stubbornly refused to look back at the case that contained the terrifying illustration, even though she could feel it calling to her.

They went on to explore the halls of armour and weaponry and Gunnul remarked on how impractical the knights' heavy armour was. The knights would have to be lifted by cranes onto their mounts and when they fell off in battle they couldn't get up again. Chrissy and Jamie started to laugh, imagining helpless knights, arms and legs flailing like turtles stranded on their backs.

Jamie's fainting spell forgotten, they continued by investigating three million year old stone age tools from Africa, priceless porcelain and sculptures from the Far East, hand woven rugs from ancient Persia, stone and gold figurines from the Middle East and countless other treasures, including the famous Rosetta Stone.

They sat in a small courtyard and ate a picnic lunch that Peeti had prepared and quietly said their noon prayers. Then they followed a scholar to the room that contained the Elgin Marbles as well as a full size and complete Greek temple that Lord Elgin had simply packed up and brought back to England! The speaker stood on a box and told the small crowd that formed about the Elgin marbles having been the sculptures on the frieze of the Parthenon in Athens. The temple, he explained, had been complete until the 1600s when invading Turks had used the Parthenon to store gun powder. Lightning had hit the temple during a storm and the roof had been blown off.

Jamie and Chrissy looked at Gunnul in mock annoyance and the Turkish general shrugged and grinned sheepishly. But when the lecturer finished by laughingly remarking that the Greek government kept asking for the Marbles and temple back but the museum was pretending not to hear, Jamie had to grab Gunnul's arm to prevent her from lecturing the man about the robbery of antiquities from other nations by the Europeans, particularly the English, French and Germans.

At the end of their tour of the museum, Teefo and Peeti took the rented wheelchair back while Gunnul led her family to a small room not normally open to the public. There they put on white gloves and sat at a table covered with green felt and waited for her friend, a Turkish-born curator, to bring out a special treasure for them to see. It was the great book of the Lindisfarne Gospels!

With care the curator laid the book on the table and used a flat wand to turn the pages while Gunnul explained, "We must be very careful not to touch the pages or breathe too close to them. The oils in our hands could damage the colours and stain the parchment. I wanted you to have this experience because it explains why I feel bringing you here is like a pilgrimage. Being this close to an ancient work of art and sacred book is a spiritual experience."

The curator's eyes shone with understanding and pride at Gunnul's words. He turned to the first illustration and explained to the three women: "The Gospels were done in the Hiberno-Saxon style by Irish monks in Saxon England. Their monasteries were isolated specks of Christianity clinging to the edges of a pagan dark age. Their devotion to their faith gave them the strength to stubbornly hold on to the ancient knowledge of Greece and Rome against a savage world.

"Those that study these manuscripts will tell you that there are complex rules of order in the illustrations that are superimposed one on top of the other. For example, organic and geometric forms are never put together. In the areas where there are animals, all the interweaving lines go out so that they become part of the animals' body. On top of these basic rules, there are rules for patterns of symmetry, flipped images, knots, colour and even texture."

The curator turned to the most famous illustration, that of "The Cross". Jamie had found a dread creeping over her again as she had looked at the gold images of pagan monsters and serpents interwoven into the borders. The last illustration seemed to chase the fear from her heart and replace it with a feeling of warmth and contentment. She stared at the complexity of patterns that seemed almost musical in their harmony of line and colour. The miniature patterns were worthy of a Tiffany jeweler. Geometric animals and plants interwove in complex patterns as faith brought order to chaotic and pagan images.

Gunnul took her daughter's and partner's hands in her own. "Many of the scribes couldn't read or write, but for thirty or forty years, they would get up at dawn and sit on hard wooden benches in damp stone monasteries and copy the sacred symbols faithfully; a lifetime given to copy out by hand one Bible that they would never read. They loved their God so much that they decorated each page with the most incredible art work to glorify his name.

"To me this book represents all that is truly great about humanity. It is a work of art, of devotion, duty and love. I'm sure the scribes who wrote this Bible must have wondered what their humble lives meant to this world. They were illiterate nobodies who would die and be buried without family in nameless graves. And yet a thousand years later, what they did is treasured as a moment of human genius. Every life has meaning, Chrissy, and every life impacts. We just rarely get the opportunity to see how. This museum is filled with such treasures. When you are a leader, you must remember always that every individual has worth."

Chrissy nodded seriously, taking in everything that Gunnul said as she watched the curator carry the magnificent book away. Jamie smiled softly at her lover with eyes filled with love and pride. Gunnul saw the look and blushed.

"But Mommy, in our faith we are taught that it is vain and arrogant for man to try to create images of Allah's creations. That is why all our art work is geometric designs. Yet in this Bible and others I have seen man and animals are represented."

"That is true, Chrissy, but each person must worship God as they feel they ought. In the past, the Christians and Moslems have had terrible wars trying to prove their faiths were better. It was wrong to do so; only God can judge our soul's worth. We share the same holy books, a common history of belief and even the same God. We should never have been enemies."

The three thanked the curator for letting them see the holy book and walked out to join Teefo and Peeti. Jamie gave her crutch to Chrissy to carry and leaned on Gunnul for support instead as she limped along. "That was beautiful, what you said to Chrissy, Gunnul. You are a marvelous mother. I'm so lucky you were there to raise my daughter after Moe kidnapped her from me."

"I try to train her as my father trained me. I want her to grow up to be a wise and kind leader but I also want her to be confident and happy. I am glad that you came into our lives. I do not always agree with your American attitudes but I think you bring that confidence and happiness into Chrissy's life that I could not. I know you have made me happy. I was not whole until I met you," Gunnul answered, in her honest and straight forward way.

Jamie smiled up at Gunnul and squeezed her lover's arm. She knew she too had not been complete until she had met Gunnul. Now the three of them were a family and they shared a very special love.

Chapter Two

The same day that the Dedemanns had arrived in London, Robbie Williams was also at the airport. Robbie bounced on her heels the way she did when trying to be patient. The film producer and actor was not by nature a patient person. Her genius and her temper were legendary in the film business. It was not business, however, that had brought Robbie to Heathrow Airport near London this day. She was here instead to meet her family; her partner and wife Janet Williams and their two daughters, Ryan and Rebecca.

Robbie had been in England for three weeks, checking and approving the sites that the scouts had chosen for consideration for her new film. Now her family was joining her and she could hardly wait. She had missed them terribly. That feeling always surprised and scared her a little. It made her feel very vulnerable; all her life she had remained aloof, taking what pleasure she could from casual relationships and maintaining high walls between her heart and soul and the rest of the world. Then Janet, her brother's widow, had shown up, and her walls crumbled one after another. Robbie smiled from under the sloppy hat that she had pulled down to help hide her identity from fans. *Who would have thought it! Me, an old married woman with a family!* That thought filled her with a warmth that spread all the way to her toes.

Her amazing blue eyes, hidden behind thick framed glasses, flicked up to check the overhead arrival screens. The plane was on time and due in about five minutes. Robbie had spent a lot of time at airports over the years and hated it. Her restless, active personality did not handle down time well. Still, she had to admit that if there was an airport to love, it would be Heathrow. It was nothing special to look at really, just an airport like any other. A bit worn and dirty, due to the thousands of people who passed through the doors every day, and filled with over-tired, over-stressed humanity.

Yet, Heathrow had a personality that was unique. It reminded Robbie of the line in the original Star Wars movie where the Jedi Knight, Obi Wan, tells Luke Skywalker that all the best pilots of the galaxy could be found at some time at the Mos Eisley Spaceport. That was Heathrow. All international flights to and from the Americas to Europe and the Far East had to funnel through this one single place.

Being here was as close as a human could get to feeling like a time traveler.

Your attention, please. This is the last call for flight 329 to Nairobi, Kenya.

Robbie wondered how many Heads of State had walked through these gates, how many spies, soldiers, tourists, billionaire Sheiks, refugees, terrorists... Her mind saw their stories as promos for films. Her intelligent eyes recorded details that would become part of her director's arsenal of ideas.

Passenger Mr. Rada Singh, on route to New Delhi, India, please report to the information desk.

Robbie watched a haggard looking man stepping up to place his order at a fast food stand. His wife and children stood off to the side, leaving the male of the house to bring back the fatted mastodon on a bun. Robbie's mouth took on a sneer; she had no patience for those who maintained traditional roles. Not that she supported any woman's liberation organizations either. Freedom to live her life as she wanted was something that the confident, rich and powerful woman took for granted.

Flight 976 to Bangkok, Thailand will be delayed...

Even the MacDonald's counter had been infected by the spirit of internationalism, Robbie noted, as her eyes traveled down the posted menu. They offered such treats as MacCurries and MacLamb burgers! The smile returned to Robbie's lips and she moved closer to the gate where she knew her family would be appearing at any minute.

* * * * *

The 747 touched down and the roar of the braking systems filled the cabin. Janet sighed. Thank God they were here. It wasn't that she minded flying. She didn't, but flying with a three year old and a bored teenager was right up there with suicide missions! Not that Ryan wasn't a pretty special kid. She had really been wonderful in the way she had worked to be part of their family unit. It must have been very hard for her, having been raised by a series of nannies or in boarding schools. She didn't have a very good idea about what family life was like, anymore than her famous mother, Robbie Williams, did. Yet she had taken on the challenge with a focused and determined attitude so typical of the Williams family.

Janet instinctively reached over and brushed Ryan's bangs into place. Ryan smiled back, relief that the long flight was over written on her face. "It won't be long now, Ryan. Your mom will be there waiting," reassured Janet. "We just need to get wiggle bum here through customs and pick up our bags." Janet grabbed the hand of her fearless baby daughter and held on tight to prevent the three year old from running to the open hatch, while Ryan got their hand luggage down from the over-head compartments.

Janet frowned and gave herself a mental shake. That feeling of foreboding had suddenly swept over her again. It was silly. There was no reason to feel any anxiety. Here she was, visiting a country that she had always wanted to see and meeting up with Robbie, whom she had missed so much! It was silly to feel any apprehension. *Maybe I'm just over-tired*, she thought, as they now stood in line waiting for their customs clearance. As always, Robbie had dreamed the impossible and then made it happen just by the force of her personality and will alone. With Janet working at her side, they had put into motion the construction of a state of the art school and studio in film and animation. It was a tremendous achievement but one that had really stretched their endurance.

Janet smiled as they now waited for their bags to be dropped down onto the baggage carousel. Well, it had taxed Janet's endurance. Robbie, as always, had any number of irons in the fire. She had planted the seeds for her school and then left Janet and Gwen in charge while she worked with Brian on the planning sessions for the new motion picture that they hoped to start filming this fall. For the last three weeks, Robbie had been in England seeing to the final details.

"No! Reb!" Janet screamed, snapping out of her thoughts as she saw her daughter crawl up onto the metal baggage carousel while her big sister was busy lifting one of their bags off. Reb, giggling with delight, sat down between the bags and spun away past the row of startled passengers patiently waiting for their luggage to appear. "Reb!" called Janet in fear, as she envisioned a heavy piece of luggage dropping down on her adventurous daughter. Two long, strong arms reached out and lifted the child out of harm's way and as Janet battled her way through the crowd she heard Reb squeal, "Obby!"

Obby was Reb's pet name for her adopted mother and aunt, Robbie Williams. What was Robbie doing down here? Janet pushed through the crowds to see a tall, beautiful woman holding a rather startled looking Reb. The woman did look a lot like her Obby, the same build and graceful cat like movement and the same dark hair and brilliant blue eyes. The features were stronger, however, and the skin had the golden tan of the Arabic people.

"Oh, I'm sorry, she got away from me! Thank you for saving her," Janet said, reaching up to take the confused child from the stranger's arms.

"I thought it was my Obby, mommy," the small child explained.

"I know, sweetie," Janet reassured Reb. She and Robbie had needed to give Reb a talk about not going with strangers a few months ago. Reb had grown up in a town where everyone knew her and was a friend. As a result, she was a little too trusting and friendly. Since the talk, Reb felt the need to justify her actions every time she went ahead and talked to strangers anyway!

"That is all right. I remember when my Chrissy was that age, she too was such a handful," responded the exotic woman with a twinkle in her eye.

Janet smiled back, liking the woman instantly. "Well, thank you again. Reb, say thank you and goodbye to the lady who helped you."

"Thank you, and goodbye."

The tall woman smiled and responded formally, "You are very welcome, Little One." Then Janet hurried to join Ryan with the cart loaded with their bags and they headed for the exit.

Robbie was there and wrapped Ryan in her arms for a big hug before scooping Reb up, kissing her and depositing the child in Ryan's arms so that she could wrap Janet in a bear hug. "I have missed you so much!" she whispered into the small blonde's ear.

"Mmm, I missed you too," Janet confessed, as she satisfied herself for the time being by dropping a tender kiss on the tall woman's temple. Robbie smiled down at her, her eyes soft with love and pride.

"Come on then, let's get back to the hotel and settle in," suggested Robbie happily, as she took command of the baggage and led her family towards the exit that would lead to where she had parked their car.

* * * * *

After Robbie had gotten her family settled in the hotel and they'd had a decent meal and rest, she gave into Reb's demands.

It seemed that Ryan had alleviated her boredom on the plane by convincing Reb that the one thing that she had to see in England was the Bloody Tower. The bulk of Reb's conversation since she had arrived had been, "Obby, take me to the Bloody Tower!" *What is it with my daughters and swear words anyway!* Robbie wondered good-naturedly, as she swung the small child into the cab beside Ryan, who was trying her best to look innocent.

Robbie, who had been to England on many occasions, found that being a tour guide for her family was fun. They walked along the Victoria Embankment beside the river Thames while Robbie lectured. "The Tower of London..."

"Bloody Tower!" protested Reb loudly.

Robbie knelt down beside her younger daughter having given her older daughter a stern look first. Ryan smiled wickedly and Janet rolled her eyes. "Reb," explained Robbie, "the right name for the place is the Tower of London, okay? We don't use the other name."

"Ryan does!"

"Ryan isn't going to anymore!" stated Robbie firmly, looking up at her teenage daughter with a raised eyebrow. Ryan smiled and shrugged.

Robbie got up and took Reb's hand again. They started walking once more towards the main gate of the Tower of London. "The Tower was originally built by William the Conqueror in 1066 as a fortress but over time it has served as a royal residence and a garrison. The Captain of the Tower was the commander of London's defense forces. But it has gone down in history as one of the most infamous prisons in the world! The guards here are called Beef Eaters. No one is sure why. Their jobs have been passed down through their families for generations. One of their jobs is looking after the huge black ravens that are always around the Tower." Robbie squatted down and pointed for Reb to see. "There is one over there on the grassy bank. Legend has it that if the ravens ever leave, England will fall."

"I like that," muttered Janet. "I must make a note of it." Robbie smiled at her wife. She was well aware of Janet's love of mythology. Janet knew lots of the myths of the Eastern Woodland Indians and she had been doing a lot of reading on Celtic myths since she knew she would be visiting England.

They paid the entrance fee and had their bags checked by security. Afterwards they wandered into the courtyard. "The Tower has had many famous prisoners. Some survived to tell the tale such as Elizabeth I, who went on to rule Britain. Others, such as Charles I, Sir Thomas Moore, Anne Boleyn, Katherine Howard, Lady Jane Grey, and William Penn died here," Robbie explained ghoulishly. "Most of them were beheaded over there on that little patch of stone. If you were a commoner they used an axe but if you were royalty they used a sword."

"Nice touch!" smirked Ryan.

Robbie raised a warning eyebrow in fun and Janet and Ryan laughed. "Don't encourage her!" Robbie ordered Janet with a smile.

"As I was saying, the last prisoner to stay here was Rudolf Hess, one of the Nazi leaders."

They looked around the various towers and rooms checking for ghosts. Then Robbie took them to view the Crown Jewels. As they stood on the moving walkway, Robbie explained, "Queen Elizabeth II is the third richest woman in the world but these jewels are owned by the Crown." She pointed into a case. "That's the Star of Africa. It's the largest diamond ever cut in the world. It weighs 530 carats! See the Imperial Crown? It's the one you see the monarch wear at the coronation. It has three thousand diamonds alone in the setting! And the Crown of India over here has a thirty-four carat emerald in the centre and six thousand diamonds around it! Not a bad jewelry collection, huh?!"

The Williams played tourist, looking into the cases that protected and illuminated the spectacular collection. "Boy! I bet they have an army protecting that stuff!" Ryan commented.

Robbie shrugged. "I asked once and they said no. That when the Queen needs one of the crowns they just stick it in a cardboard box and run it over to the palace in a truck. They said a large guard and armored vehicle would just be a sign that the jewels were being moved. Delivery trucks come and go from here all the time, so no one would be the wiser!"

"British understatement, at its best!" laughed Janet.

* * * * *

The Williams hailed a cab and headed back to the hotel. Janet and Robbie worked together to get Reb fed, washed, changed and into bed for a bedtime story. When Janet went back to the connecting room she was sharing with Robbie to shower, the actor started negotiations with Ryan, who had been lying on the other bed reading a book.

"How much?" asked Robbie, leaning against the wall with her arms crossed and one eyebrow up.

Ryan smiled evilly as she bookmarked her spot and tossed the novel on the table between the two beds. "Fifty dollars an hour plus the use of your laptop. I want to e-mail some friends back home."

"Fifty dollars! That's robbery!" growled Robbie.

"Nope, that's supply and demand and the free enterprise system. You haven't seen Mom in three weeks and are desperate for some time alone with her and I'm the only available babysitter. Besides, I'm saving for a car," responded Ryan, getting up and unconsciously folding her arms like her mother.

"What ever happened to love and family support," grumbled Robbie, pushing off from the wall to shake Ryan's hand and seal the deal.

"Tomorrow, we can be a loving, caring family. Tonight, you are paying through the nose for a little private time with my other Mom," smiled Ryan, with a grin. "And I won't even charge you extra for reassuring Aunt Janet that I'm perfectly happy to babysit Reb while I e-mail my friends," responded Ryan, shaking her Mom's hand.

"You are a shark!"

"Takes one to know one!" laughed Ryan. "You and Aunt Janet have a good time!"

Robbie gave her daughter a hug. "Sure you don't mind?"

"Not at all," Ryan reassured her.

* * * * *

Janet fought to escape the flames. They surrounded her and held her tight in a burning grasp. She opened her mouth to scream for help but nothing came out as she gagged on smoke and flame. With superhuman effort she forced herself up and woke with a start to see that she had fallen asleep in the tub and slipped down until she had taken in a mouthful of water. The bathroom was steamy and hot.

She struggled out and wrapped a towel around her as she fumbled at the door handle to get out. Back in the bedroom, the air felt chilled and fresh. Janet closed the door to the bathroom and leaned against it, her heart pounding still in fear. That had to be the worst nightmare that she'd had in a long time! Maybe *the* worst! Slowly, the fear dissipated and was replaced again with a heavy feeling of dread. Janet shivered and then pushed the feeling away. It must be some chemical imbalance her body was experiencing. It was nothing more than a stupid mood swing. She must be over-tired. A few weeks visiting Robbie here in England and she would be feeling like herself again.

"Are you alright?" asked Robbie, coming back into the hotel room she was sharing with her soulmate. Janet stood wrapped in a bath towel, leaning against the bathroom door, white and shaky.

"I'm... yes, I'm fine," responded Janet, leaning into Robbie's outstretched arms. "I fell asleep in the bathtub and had the worst nightmare! It's probably jet lag. I'm fine. Hmm, it is so nice to be back with you!"

Robbie bent and picked Janet up in her arms and carried her over to the bed. It never ceased to amaze Janet just how strong Robbie was.

Her lover laid her down on the bed and bent over her to nuzzle at the soft, warm skin below her jaw line.

"Hmm, no, ooh that's nice, but the kids," Janet managed to articulate with difficulty.

"S'okay, I've bribed Ryan to babysit for the evening," muttered Robbie, as she lowered her lean form over Janet's now naked body.

"Oh, you're good, very, very good," moaned Janet, as she arched into the touch of her soulmate's lips on her nipple. Robbie's hands drifted along the lines and curves of her lover's body as the two of them felt the rhythmic need building with each touch. Janet's hands slid down her lover's form and unfastened the actor's shirt and bra. Robbie groaned and arched her back, allowing Janet to lean up and suck on the actor's waiting breasts. Need rose to passion and all else was forgotten.

Some time later, Janet and Robbie dressed and called for one of the quaint London cabs. "I'm taking you to visit my girlfriend," Robbie had teased her love sated partner. Janet had looked up at Robbie with wide eyes and arched eyebrows but Robbie had just laughed and tucked her soulmate into the cab. In the late afternoon light, they drove down towards the Thames and got out near Westminster, asking the driver to wait.

Robbie grinned with excitement. "This way, Janet, down here. This gold statue of a chariot pulled by two horses and driven by a woman with bare breasts is to honour Queen Boadicea of the Icenii. In 61 A.D., she and her two daughters led an attack that defeated the Romans. She burnt the Roman town of London to the ground!

"They say she was six feet tall, when most men of the time were much shorter, and she had flaming red hair. For almost two thousand years, her name has remained a legend. Bold, strong of character and loyal, she represents to me what all women should strive to be. Whenever, I am in London, I come and visit her and pay my respects."

Janet laughed and looked from Robbie's animated face to the monument of the daring and brave woman. "I can see why you would want her as your girlfriend, Robbie. She is definitely your type! Maybe in another life you knew her!"

Robbie laughed and took Janet's arm to lead her back to the cab. "If I did, I'm sure we were on opposite sides. I'd probably be supporting Rome in the conquest of the known world!"

Janet looked up at her lover thoughtfully. "No, you'd get bored with that quickly and be out there fighting for the under dog. That's why you identify with Queen Boadicea. She stood up to the might of Rome and won."

"Maybe," Robbie conceded, but she wasn't so sure she was as honourable a character as Janet liked to believe. She slipped into the cab beside Janet and looked back at Boadicea, the bronze charioteer charging forever into battle. For a second, she could smell the dust and leather, hear the flags cracking in the wind and the scraping of swords as they were drawn from their scabbards. She smiled, winked at the statue and ordered the driver to take them to St. Catherine's Gate.

There they walked, arms linked, past Tower Bridge and the Tower of London. Janet caught Robbie up on all the news from home and Robbie shared with Janet some of her plans for the filming of Harold: King of England.

Later, they returned to have dinner at the Charles Dickens Pub by a window that overlooked the Pool of London. They looked out at the many sailboats that were moored there and through their rigging watched the sun set, turning the harbour water into a golden strip. They shared a bottle of Mouton Cadet de Rothchild over a meal of venison and wild truffles, then sauntered around the dock to look more closely at the working and recreational boats that were moored there before taking a cab back to their hotel room. Their love making this time was tender, familiar and long.

Chapter Three

After Teefo and Peeti had left, Gunnul had insisted on going out with Chrissy to bring back curry from the corner shop for dinner rather than having Jamie cook. Jamie was instructed to rest while they were out, but instead, she sat in the window that looked over Russell Square and the Bloomsbury area which had once been the home of Virginia Woolf and her artistic friends.

Gunnul's London flat was small, yet because she worked so closely with Gunnul on her accounts Jamie was aware that the one bedroom, third story walk up with its roof patio was worth over a million and a half dollars. London property was some of the most expensive in the world. Of course, the apartment had been designed and decorated professionally and the kitchen was by Smallbones! Jamie hoped she got a chance to use the kitchen before they left London. Gunnul was clearly worried about what had happened at the museum today. Knowing how close they had come to losing Chrissy to some mysterious illness, Gunnul was feeling more than her usual over-protectiveness.

Jamie frowned. She would have to explain to Gunnul what happened this morning when she looked at that illustration and the strange feelings of dread that she had been experiencing. She wasn't sure that the ever practical and logical Turk was going to understand. Jamie sighed and picked up her latest book on Celtic religion that she had been studying. She had developed quite an interest in the ancient beliefs and was looking forward to visiting some of the sites on Salisbury Plain, including Stonehenge.

She read quietly until she smelt the hot tangy scent of curry and heard the laughter of her family as they raced up the stairs. They ate informally on the living-room rug watching a video that Gunnul had deemed appropriate for Chrissy to watch. Then they played scrabble until Jamie said it was time for Chrissy to go to bed. Gunnul and Jamie sat quietly, working on the last of the business contracts that had brought Gunnul to London. Then, when Chrissy was asleep on the sofa bed, Gunnul helped Jamie up the steep stairs that led to the roof garden.

There, softened by the evening light, was London. Below them to the right was the British Museum and Jamie knew that farther along

Oxford Street was Baker Street, where the legendary Holmes was supposed to have lived. To the south of Bloomsbury were the Soho area and Covent Garden. Big Ben chimed the hour over the Thames. The dirt of the city was mellowed by the yellow street lights, slipping London back into its nineteenth century elegance. It was a Mary Poppins world up there, of Romanesque chimney pots, push bikes leaning against dust bins in back alleys, London cabs bustling down tree lined streets and singing drifting up from a local pub. Samuel Johnson once wrote that to be tired of London was to be tired of life.

Gunnul stood behind Jamie, who was nestled deep in her arms, and let her lover soak up the magic of the city before she spoke. "What happened today, Jamie? Were you ill?"

Jamie stiffened a little in Gunnul's arms, then relaxed, knowing that she couldn't be in a more secure place. "No, I wasn't sick, Gunnul. I was terrified. I saw this illustration in a manuscript of a fire rising from a stone altar and suddenly I had this vision."

"Vision, Jamie?"

"Yes, the flames reached out to me with hot talons that wrapped around my arms and pulled me towards them. I could feel it, smell it..."

"Shh, do not talk of it if it upsets you," soothed Gunnul, holding Jamie close in her arms.

"Since we arrived, I've been getting these moments of foreboding, dread... I put it down to jet lag and being tired, but today really scared me. Do you believe me, Gunnul?"

For a moment there was silence as Gunnul pondered the question in her logical way. "I do not believe that a picture can pull you into its flames but I do accept that you had a vision that seemed very real to you. There was a time when I would have told you it was silliness, but I have felt the power of the grave and I have seen how the visions from the grave visit our daughter and give her sight. I do not understand but I know it has happened."

"I thought all the trouble with the grave was over, that our ancestors had found their way back to loving each other. Do you think the vision was a warning?"

"Maybe, maybe not. At the airport, Jamie, while I waited for our bags with Teefo, I saw one of the Others. One of your lineage, Jamie, with a child that carried the same traits as myself. It was not one we have met before."

"Then it is not over! Oh Gunnul, I'm worried!"

"Don't be, Jamie. Everything will be fine. The past can not hurt us," Gunnul reassured, kissing the top of Jamie's head. They stood there for a long time watching the lights of London. Less than a mile away, Robbie walked with Janet along the waterfront and Boadicea stood frozen on the edge of battle.

* * * * *

Evil is a seed that lies within all of us. Like a desert plant, it can lie dormant for years or even a life time until such time as its genetic code is activated and then it grows quickly, madly and completely out of proportion. We all sense it within us, that minute kernel of evil. It is what compels us to set down laws of social behaviour and dire consequences for those who break them. It sends us seeking a god that will protect us from our wrong doings. Yet in the end, we execute the murderer, kill in our god's name and evil laughs in triumph.

Even the power of the wind let loose on the plain howled around the massive ancient stones in terror. They stood like sentries guarding a lost secret. Neither good nor bad, they were the silent Watchers though time. The price of neutrality is indifference. The Watchers were cold stone without feeling.

The ring of massive stones capped by lintels weighing tonnes cast shadows that could be read by believers as clearly as a scientific instrument. Summer solstice was not far off. The setting sun's rays knifed through the arches and cut a jagged line across the wind tossed grass, barely missing the heel stone.

The darkness nearby shifted and shadow became a well of blackness far denser than the night. A scaly hand reached up from out of the ground and talons dug into Mother Earth. The figure heaved his massive bulk up out of the timeless void in which he had disappeared so long ago and stood before the cold, stone Watchers.

A voice, harsh and forced with lack of use, rumbled a promise to the ring of stones. "I will revenge!"

Chapter Four

Robbie sat in a hard hotel chair staring out at the dark room. After a super evening, they had returned to their room to make love long into the night. After Janet had fallen asleep, Robbie had tossed and turned and had finally gotten up so as not to disturb her soulmate.

She felt very depressed, almost fearful. She had no idea why; maybe one of those chemical imbalance things, although she had never really had much trouble that way. The plans for the movie were going well and it was super having her family back with her. Robbie had missed them terribly! No, it wasn't any of those things.

It was a creepy sort of dread, as if there was something ready to pounce. It was like the fear she had carried all those years believing that she had killed her father and would eventually be caught and jailed. Yes, that sort of fear. A fear that came from inside because you knew that within, you had a streak of evil that allowed you to kill with your bare hands.

Robbie lifted her hands and looked at the long, artist's fingers in the eerie light from the window. They were elegant hands, yet strong. It might have been Alexandria who had killed Phillip Williams, but Robbie knew she could have. She was angry enough when she saw what he had been doing to her sister and brother. She had hit him hard enough to break his jaw.

Yes, that was the dread. It was knowing that she was a murderer at least in spirit if not in action. How could she justify being a loving wife, a good mother to two wonderful daughters, when there was a spot in her soul that was so black. No, more than just a darkness, it was a patch of true evil. It scared the hell out of her! What if she lost her temper that quickly and explosively again? What if she hurt someone, Janet or the kids... she forced that thought away. It made her feel sick to her stomach.

It was Janet moaning and thrashing about suddenly in the bed that snapped Robbie from her depths of despair. She went over and sat on the edge of the bed and softly stroked Janet's hair.

"Shh Love, I've got you. Everything's okay," Robbie whispered. Gradually, Janet's nightmare passed and the petite woman again slept peacefully, her right hand clutched tightly around Robbie's.

Janet had been dreaming of sitting in the coffee shop waiting for Billy Williams, the race-car driver. She had met him the night before at a party and had made a deal. They were meeting today to formalize the details before going to a lawyer. The deal was simple. Billy would pay Janet a lot of money to marry him and have his child.

Her cold hands bent stiffly around the warm mug of coffee. She needed the money desperately to pay off some large gambling debts that her grandfather had accumulated in her name. She had tried to get a bank loan but had been refused because she already had a mortgage and a student loan. If she didn't get the money she was going to jail.

So she was here, waiting to coldly talk out the terms for selling her body. *I can't do this! I'd like to have a child someday but not as a business deal! What kind of mother would I be if this is what I am prepared to do to get money? What kind of a person am I? I always thought I was a good person, but now that I'm desperate, I'm willing to do anything to survive! There is something deep inside me that is really bad.*

The bitter taste of bile rose in her throat and she swallowed it back down as she looked up into the ice blue eyes of the man who had slipped into the chair opposite her. This was it. The dread spread through her like a flood. There was no going back.

In her sleep, she cried out in panic, fighting against the inevitability of her dream. Then a low, soft voice reached her and she felt herself move back from the edge of despair. "Shh, I've got you."

* * * * *

Across the city, Gunnul lay in bed beside Jamie with her eyes open. The eyes were unaware of the soft city lights that danced rhythmically across the ceiling of their bedroom. Her mind had taken her back to that last day on the frontier of Turkey so many years ago. She and her traveling companions had bravely defended a narrow pass against an invading force.

From where she hid, she could see those she and the others had killed lying out on the barren ground. Flies danced in and out of their nostrils and open mouths or walked across staring, frozen eyes. Some of the dead were so young, no longer children but not yet men. Their skin had drained of colour then gradually turned patchy green as their bodies bloated with the gasses of decay. Eventually, the skin burst open, exposing rotting meat and white maggots. Gunnul could tell by the stage each corpse had reached on what day each boy-man had been killed.

When the dry, hot wind blew from that direction the bitter-sweet smell of decay was horrifying. It was better, however, than when the wind came from behind. Back there, they had hurriedly buried their own dead, kicking a thin layer of pebbles and dirt over their blood soaked bodies. One of the dead was the man she had been engaged to marry. Yesterday, she had watched in horror as the maggots had wormed their way out of his shallow grave.

There were only two of them left now. Her companion hadn't opened his eyes in hours. He still breathed though, in irregular, raspy gasps. His chest was covered with blood. Gunnul wasn't sure anymore from which wound he was dying. The diary he had kept so faithfully until yesterday lay in the dirt beside him. The pages turned one after the other in the wind.

Gunnul had taken command from the men. She had shown them how to close the pass with dynamite and defend the narrow opening. From where had that blood lust come? What had given her the strength to plan coldly and kill without mercy? What kind of person was she to be able to butcher? She looked down at her bloody hands. One hand, fingers spread, held her guts in from a ragged wound across her abdomen. She was too weak now to brush away the flies. It was not necessary really. The maggots would eat the rotting flesh and prevent gangrene from setting in early.

Not that it really mattered; there would be no more defense. She waited now for the enemy to over run their position and finish them off. *There is but one God and Allah is his name. Allah protect my soul!* In the distance, she could hear tanks advancing. It would be weeks later that she would wake in a hospital bed and learn that the tanks had been those of her own country's army.

Gunnul, lost in her horrific thoughts, was startled when her lover woke suddenly, stifling a scream of fear. Gunnul caught her and held her close. "Jamie, I have got you. Shh, my special one," Gunnul reassured her. Jamie buried her face deep into Gunnul's shoulder and held on tight. She had been dreaming of those days when she had been married to Gunnul's twin brother, Moe. Gunnul had got all the strength and decency of her family, Moe had inherited all the weakness. He was a substance abuser and when he mixed drugs and alcohol he became violent. Jamie could hear his voice whining from the past. "It is the drugs, it is not me!"

"Then get help again! You kicked the habit once, you can do it again!"

"I can't as long as you keep nagging me! It's your fault! Make that baby stop crying or I will! You couldn't even give me a son!"

"You stay away from my daughter, you fucking bastard. Get out, do you hear! Get out of my life and never come back!" she had yelled. It was then that she had watched in horror as he had picked up the baseball bat and come after her. He had almost killed her; smashed her leg so that she would be crippled for the rest of her life and kidnapped her daughter. Thank God, he had turned Chrissy over to Gunnul to be raised! Thank God.

Had she been the problem? Had she been so bitchy with him that he had slipped back into substance abuse? Was there something really mean living inside her? A dread exploded in her gut and she woke with a stifled scream, relieved to find Gunnul there beside her to hold on to until her heart stopped pounding.

"Are you okay, Jamie?" Gunnul asked with concern.

Jamie nodded her head. "Yes, I... I... do you think, Gunnul, if I'd been less critical... more understanding of Moe's problems, that he would have been a better person?"

Gunnul felt like she had been hit. She forced her face to remain expressionless. "My brother was not a good man, Jamie. He was a nasty, sneaky little boy who grew into a violent, weak man. That had nothing to do with you. You are a good person."

Silence hung heavily. Gunnul had to ask, although she wasn't sure she could deal with the answer. "Do you regret that things did not work out between you and my brother?"

Jamie looked up with surprised, startled eyes. "No, if my marriage had not failed, I would never have met you. I can't imagine going through life and never having known the happiness and love that you have given me! I love you so much, Gunnul!"

The knot inside Gunnul lessened once again. It never went completely away. Gunnul felt the ghosts of those she had killed weigh heavily on her soul. She was sure that someday Jamie and Chrissy would find out how much blood was on her hands and be revolted by the knowledge.

One of the few times they had fought in their marriage had been over the lumpy scar that slashed across Gunnul's abdomen. Whenever possible, Gunnul would keep that part of her body covered by the way she laid or by the draping of an arm or sheet. One night, after Jamie had made love to her, Jamie had laid her head on the scar and Gunnul had reacted instantly, rolling her off and covering herself up.

"I do not wish ever to be touched there!" she had commanded, to her startled lover.

Large eyes turned worried. "Does it still hurt you?"

"No."

"Does the scar embarrass you? It doesn't bother me, Gunnul, anymore than you say my twisted leg bothers you."

"It is not that."

"Then what is it?" probed Jamie.

"It is... you will let it drop and never mention it again!" Gunnul had snapped, getting up from their bed and storming off. She had come back hours later and had found Jamie sitting in a chair by the window. Stiffly, she had apologized. Jamie had nodded her acceptance sadly.

The incident had never been mentioned again. Jamie was very careful not to look at or touch the ugly scar. It bothered Jamie that it was a small barrier between them. She hoped that some day Gunnul would be able to trust her love enough to tell her.

She lay in Gunnul's arms, letting the Turk's warmth invade her being and settle the fears that the nightmare had unleashed. Gunnul was her hero; was everyone's hero. She knew the modest woman would not tell her of her heroism, so she had read everything she could find, including a translation of the journal kept by the last man to die.

"Sometimes, when I am in your arms like this or when I see you laughing and playing with Chrissy, I have to sort of shake myself and remember that the woman I love is General Gunnul Dedemann. The person who led six heroes against the invading force and held them off for three days until reinforcements could arrive. Five of you died and over two hundred of... Gunnul? What's the matter?!"

The woman beneath her had jumped in shock and gone cold and rigid with fear. "Don't leave me, Jamie. I... I won't hurt you or Chrissy, please, I am not like my brother... I know I have killed but..."

"Gunnul, Sweetheart! Stop, where did this come from? Darling, do you really think I'd think less of you for sacrificing everything to save your people? Do you think I'd believe for a minute that you would kill in cold blood?! Gunnul, how could you think that?!"

It was now. It had to be said. She could not live with the awful truth any longer and not tell Jamie.

"I came alive. It was exhilarating, the fear, the challenge. I didn't think about it beyond making a devastating hit on the enemy. And then later, I lay there for hours waiting for the next attack, looking over this field of dead..."

Jamie saw Gunnul's eyes drifting back into the past. She turned the sad face with her fingertips and kissed Gunnul softly. "You listen to me. You have a natural ability to be a military leader. It is not surprising. I have read your family history. There were many military leaders in your family. That does not mean you are a killer, Gunnul. Oh Gunnul, you are one of the softest, most caring people I know!"

"There is so much blood on my hands, Jamie," Gunnul admitted sadly. "I wished to protect you and Chrissy from that."

"Gunnul, Chrissy and I are both well aware of what you did. It is not we that need protecting. We did not live it or carry the memories of that awful time. It is you that needs protecting. You are not a killer, Gunnul. You are a born soldier. A natural leader. There is no shame in that. There is nothing to fear in having those talents!"

Gunnul wrapped Jamie close, shaking with emotional release. "I must have done something good in my life for Allah to have blessed me with you!"

Jamie decided to take a chance. "Here," she said gently, "let me see the scar." She ran her finger tips over the ragged, rough wound. "You have bled enough, Gunnul; physically, emotionally, spiritually. Allah sent you there that day because he knew the traits that he had given you would help save Turkey. Don't feel this scar marks you as violent. It doesn't. It is a symbol of how kind you are that you would willingly give your life for others."

"It made me barren," Gunnul choked out.

"You are not barren, Gunnul. You have a daughter by me. You might not have given me your seed but you raised and molded our daughter into a very special human being. She is just as much a child of your body as she is mine."

"Do you think this is true, Jamie?" asked Gunnul, not daring yet to let go of a pain she had held for a long time.

"I know it to be true!" Jamie responded firmly. They lay wrapped in each other's arms until it was time for the dawn prayers.

In the next room, Chrissy lay awake too. She had followed him in her mind as he spread his evil first on one side of the city and now here. He had kept to the shadowy places, his bulk moving with surprising agility and silence. He was close now, waiting for her.

Quietly, she slipped from the couch bed and went to the window. There, in the darkness, beneath an old, twisted tree, stood the distorted, massive figure. *You have come after all these centuries.*

It is time. Come to me!

Soon. When I am ready. The young child smiled knowingly. She knew the time would be soon.

Chapter Five

Robbie signed for the room service and brought the coffee and toast over to the bed. It was still too early to wake their daughters in the next room. "What are you reading?" Robbie asked as she handed Janet a coffee.

"Another book on Celtic mythology. Do you know that some people believe that there are lines of power running through the ancient landscape. They believe the Celts actually shaped sighting points and aligned pathways along these lines."

"Do you believe that?" Robbie asked in surprise.

Janet laughed. "Having gotten kicked out of my church for marrying you, I'm not sure what I believe anymore. I guess I'm searching for answers."

"You think too much!" Robbie complained good-naturedly. "You had a bad dream last night."

Janet looked uneasy. "I had a dream about meeting Billy and working out the terms for having Reb... it embarrasses and shames me what I did then."

Robbie shrugged. "It shouldn't. You found a way to survive. You didn't sleep with a stranger; it was done at a clinic. You love Reb with all your heart, care for her, and are raising her well, where is the problem? Hell, I got knocked up having sex with my teacher and deserted my kid! If anyone should feel they are evil it should be me!"

Janet leaned forward and kissed Robbie's temple. "Well, you are not. You supported and protected Ryan as best you could. We are both lucky to have two such wonderful kids!"

"Yeah, we are," smiled Robbie softly. "I'd better go get the two of them up. We got a busy day ahead of us!"

When Robbie knocked gently and entered the connecting room, she found Ryan standing at the window, already dressed. Her daughter's jaw was set and her eyes looked off into the distance.

"Hey, you okay?" asked Robbie, coming forward to place her hand on Ryan's shoulder.

Ryan started as she became aware of her mother's presence. "Oh yeah, fine. The rugrat got me up at four to go to the bathroom and then went back to sleep again! I've been reading and thinking about things. Mom, do you believe in fate?"

Robbie leaned on the wall and looked at her daughter. She was getting past that gawky stage and it was clear she was going to be gorgeous. The dark golden hair, deep green eyes and the tall athletic figure made Ryan really stand out in a crowd. She was bright too and a really good kid. Someone was going to be lucky to get her daughter as a partner. That thought sent a jolt of fear and sadness through Robbie. *Shit! I hope she picks someone as nice as Janet! Not some loser. And I hope it is not too soon because I'm not ready to give up my kid!*

"I think I make my own fate. No one and no thing controls me!" stated Robbie firmly with a half smile and raised eyebrow.

"Aunt Janet controls you!" Ryan laughed, and poked her Mom as she saw the colour rise in her mother's face.

"Yeah, well that's different. She has legal permission to do so!"

Ryan looked back out the window thoughtfully. "I think I'm destined to be part of something very important. I can feel it."

"Yeah, I think it's breakfast!" joked Robbie, pulling her kid in for a kiss to the head. "Whatever your future, Ryan, I want you to always remember to live up to your beliefs and follow your heart."

The Williams' day started with a trip to the Tate Gallery. After, Janet firmly believed that the famous modern art institution would never be quite the same again. Robbie was in high spirits and Ryan simply egged her on. Janet had stopped to bend down to Reb's stroller and point out to her a wood sculpture of a horse, letting the others move on. Entering the next room, she found her lover doing a Barbara Walters impersonation as she interviewed a Henry Moore sculpture. From behind the bronze rotund shape, Ryan fed her the gag lines.

Robbie spoke into a closed cell phone, using it as her mike. "I see by the identification tag that Moore named you *The Kneeling Mother*. Any reaction to that?" she asked, holding up the fake microphone to the huge metal sculpture for an answer.

"Well, at two and a half tonnes and with a brassy attitude, I don't have too much problem keeping the kids in line."

"Good point, *Kneeling Mother!* Just how many children do you have?"

"I'm not sure actually... art is a very creative endeavour!"

"Oh yes, that's MOORE isn't it!"

"He does say that a lot."

A small crowd was forming. "Okay you two, fall in before you get us thrown out of here!" ordered Janet with a laugh, leading them into the next gallery to the clapping and cheers of those who had stopped to listen. "You two are so bad!"

Robbie smiled happily. She wore baggy clothes to hide her figure and with her trade-mark hair tucked up under a floppy hat and big horn-rimmed glasses on, she looked about as different as she could be from her media image. It was the "at home" Robbie that so few people saw.

They entered a small room off to one side and Robbie came to a complete halt. Her blues eyes were mirrored in a pair just as blue in the picture that hung directly opposite them. It was Vincent Van Gogh's *Portrait of an Artist*. Looking around the room, they realized that the entire room was a showing of Van Gogh's work!

Robbie walked forward and stood in the centre of the room, slowly turning around to look at each picture. There were the sunflowers, brilliant in their colour. One similar had sold for one of the highest prices ever paid for a painting. There were the muted browns of *The Sower*, a poor peasant sowing seeds by hand in roughly turned soil. Van Gogh understood the peasant. Their plight showed up clearly in his artistry, yet also there was the quiet dignity of their hard work and simple lives.

Janet came over, wheeling Reb. "You like his stuff, huh?"

"Oh yeah!" Robbie lifted Reb from the stroller and herded her family over to stand in front of *Starry Night*, a piece on loan from the States. The image was the view from the window of the mental institution where Van Gogh had once stayed. A wind-tossed evergreen framed a picture of the village asleep in the valley below. The sky dominated the picture, swirling ribbons of darkness and stars. "Reb, Ryan, I want you to remember this picture," Robbie said quietly. "To me, it is all about being an artist. The night sky becomes the emotional tempest of his soul and the huge stars the flash of his genius."

"Van makes the stars move, Obby," Reb observed seriously.

Robbie smiled with pride, looking first at Janet and then at the three year old she held in her arms.

"Yes, he does, Reb. Van Gogh makes the stars move." She placed the small child back in the stroller and went to stand by Ryan, who had moved on to a picture of a corn field.

"He painted this field many times," Robbie told her. "In the end, it was there he went to shoot himself. He didn't die, instead he managed to get back to his rooms. The doctor, his friend, was called to tend to him. The doctor packed and took away Van Gogh's paintings to sell, while the artist lay dying."

"That's sad and so unfair," observed Ryan.

"Artists are always one step ahead of the trends and beliefs of a society. They reflect what will be, not what is. They can pay a high price for that."

Ryan looked up into her mother's serious eyes. She nodded and they moved on to join Janet and Reb. Together they walked through galleries containing Gainsboroughs, Hogarths, Constables, Cezannes, Gauguins, Manets, Rousseaus, Picassos, Chagalls, Matisses, Robins and many other modern artists. The Tate was huge and yet at any time only one sixth of its collection was on display.

"Look Mom, Turners!" smiled Ryan, as they moved into the next gallery.

"Cool, steal one for me will ya?" Robbie challenged.

"Robbie!" Janet warned, an eyebrow rising.

Robbie smiled innocently but dropped into her tour guide mode. "The collection of Turners was the foundation of this gallery. Look at them, Ryan. They are so vibrant, even though the water colour has faded over the years. No one has come close to matching his genius for light in water colour."

"This place is really great, Mom," Ryan observed.

"What do you think?" Robbie asked Janet, while Ryan wheeled Reb over to see a picture of a dog that looked something like Rufus.

"I think to walk through the Tate is to breathe the colours of God's universe. I can't describe to you how this art moves me!" Janet confessed. Robbie smiled, pride and understanding shining from her eyes. She knew her soulmate would feel as she did.

Checking to see that Ryan and Reb were still busy, Robbie pulled Janet into a room that held one of Monet's huge murals of the waterlily garden. "When I first saw this work, I made a promise to myself that I would bring some very special person here to stand by this romantic Parisian painting. Look, Janet, how the paint seems to shimmer across the canvas like the reflected light off water. There is only one thing missing."

"What's that?" asked Janet, her eyes sparkling at Robbie's excitement.

"The soft kiss of two lovers," Robbie whispered, bending her head to capture Janet's lips and make the scene perfect.

Chapter Six

Gunnul had planned their day very carefully so as to not tire Jamie out. They would have to do some walking but she had hired a cab and driver for the day to keep the walking to a minimum. She had toyed with the idea of renting a car as they would need one later in the week when they left London. But finding a parking spot was almost impossible in the city and so a driver was a much better idea.

Teefo and his wife joined them and Gunnul led them downstairs to the waiting cab. She had lifted a surprised Jamie into her arms and trotted down the stairs with an eager Chrissy at her side. Teefo and Peeti had followed at a much more sedate pace. Their first stop was St. Paul's.

"Whenever I think of this building, I remember a news picture I saw in a history book of the dome of St. Paul's visible above the smoke of the fires and bombings of the war," Jamie observed.

Gunnul smiled down at the woman she loved. Jamie knew what to say to reach her heart. Gunnul turned to explain to Chrissy, "St. Paul's Cathedral was rebuilt to Christopher Wren's design after the Great Fire of London in 1666. He is buried inside, as is Horatio Nelson. There are many famous military and state leaders buried here. People come and leave flowers on the graves of these people, who have been dead hundreds of years. I find it very touching. Fame and power does have its form of immortality, I guess, but leave a bit of art behind and you can touch people's souls forever."

"Then I will become an artist, Mommy. I would like to touch people's souls," observed Chrissy, as the Dedemann party walked through the Gothic doorways into the vast interior space of St. Paul's.

For awhile, they sat in a back pew and absorbed the beauty and spirituality around them, despite the tourists that came and went in flocks. Gunnul was pleased that she had taken part of her education in London. Her father had wanted her to have a good command of the English language and a knowledge of the European world. Gunnul was happy now that she could use some of that knowledge to show her family the marvelous history of the last great empire. "There are actually two domes on St. Paul's, one inside the other," Gunnul explained in a respectful whisper. "The inside one has a hole in the centre to let the light through. St. Paul's is designed in a high Gothic style with the classical Greek forms that were very popular in the Italian Renaissance."

"Gunnul, I'll sit here with Teefo and Peeti while you take Chrissy up to the Whispering Gallery at the base of the dome. I think she'd like that!" Jamie organized.

Gunnul gave her wife's hand a squeeze. "Come on, Chrissy! This is really wonderful!" Jamie watched as the two people she loved the most disappeared up the worn stone stairs to the walkway around the dome above. While they were climbing, the others took the opportunity to walk around the huge cathedral and look at some of the architectural details. Modern functionalism had its place, but these ancient halls continued to attract huge crowds because they weren't just art, they had an atmosphere and presence that modern construction lacked, Jamie observed. These old buildings had soul, the new ones were cold and impersonal.

"There has been a church on this site since the 7th century," Jamie noted, as she read the guidebook Gunnul had bought her. "That was when St. Augustine brought back Roman style Christianity to England."

"It is indeed a holy place," observed Teefo, who found Christianity a hard faith to understand. *Why do they use a symbol of torture like the cross to represent their faith?* he wondered. Sometime, when they were back in Turkey and had more time, he would ask Jamie Dedemann if she would mind explaining to him. Teefo was fiercely loyal to General Dedemann but Jamie had won his heart even if she was an infidel. Where the General was a lion with the heart of a lamb, Jamie was a lamb with a heart of a lion.

High over head, Gunnul said, "I will stand here, Chrissy and you go around the walkway to the other side of the dome. I will whisper to the wall and because the acoustics are so good, you will hear what I say to you." She watched as Chrissy took her place, then turned and whispered, "I love you, Little One." Across the open spans of the dome, Chrissy smiled, turned and blew a kiss at her mother.

Gunnul joined her daughter and they leaned over to wave to Jamie so far below, and then headed back down, to join the others.

They walked slowly down the Strand, Jamie letting Chrissy carry her crutch while she enjoyed walking, arms linked, with Gunnul. To their left were the offices of the lawyers of the Inns of Court and to the right the Royal Court of Justice sat. Gunnul entertained them with funny stories of trials that had occurred there. She had studied business law while a student in London years ago.

"Central London is only one square mile in size, but there is a lot to see in a very small area. We'll stop at Convent Garden to do a little shopping for lunch. For three hundred years, this was the market for veggies and flowers, but now it has become very trendy, with up market gourmet shops, boutiques and art galleries," Gunnul explained in her serious manner. Then she bent and whispered in Jamie's ear, "They have taken the Cockney out of the place if you ask me!" Jamie laughed softly, knowing that her lover would have identified with the colourful Cockney street vendors of her student years. The atmosphere then would have been more like a Turkish market.

Gunnul continued to her group, "This is where Eliza got her flowers in *My Fair Lady*. Jamie, would you and Chrissy pick up something for us to eat while I run an errand?"

Jamie agreed without question. She could tell by the sparkle in Gunnul's eye that the errand would be some sort of surprise for her. Her lover was like that. She and Peeti checked out some of the galleries and shopped for cheese and fruit. Teefo was sent off with Chrissy to buy bread and some lemonade for them.

Once they had all gathered again, Gunnul walked them down the rest of the Strand and out into Trafalgar Square. There was Lord Nelson on his column. The column stood 160 feet tall and was put up in 1843 to commemorate the British defeat of the combined Spanish and French naval forces in 1805.

They sat on a bench so Jamie could rest her crippled leg a bit while Teefo, Gunnul and Chrissy fed the pigeons with bags of seed that Gunnul had secretly bought. Pretty soon the pigeons had them surrounded in a grey-white cloud of flapping wings and noise. Peeti and Jamie laughed with delight as the three retreated from the onslaught, having left their bags of seed to the conquerors. Jamie limped over to her soulmate and used a tissue to wipe bird droppings from Gunnul's arm. "You are worse than a kid, do you know that, Gunnul Dedemann?" she laughed.

"It was fun, Jamie!" Gunnul protested, like a small child, and Teefo and Chrissy laughed as Peeti helped them remove the direct hits and fallen feathers of the battle.

They moved on, detouring down Whitehall to see Downing Street. "When I was here as a student, you could walk right up to number ten," Gunnul observed, "but now, because of the fear of terrorism, that is no longer possible." They continued on, cutting left until St. James park was on their right and ahead of them Buckingham

Palace. Gunnul could see that Jamie was tiring. They found a comfortable place to sit amid the crowd of tourists and waited for the Changing of the Guard that happened at 11:30.

Gunnul sat down beside her partner on the edge of the Victoria fountain. "You are okay, Jamie?"

"Yes, Gunnul, I am having a wonderful time. Don't worry, I can manage," Jamie reassured her with a smile.

Serious blue eyes scanned Jamie's soul for the truth and then relaxed. "When I was here as a student, there was an old man who spent all day at the main gate of the palace. He had a twig brush and he would broom the entrance clean all day long. It is like the flowers that people leave on the ancient graves in St. Paul's, poetically beautiful in spirit and so sad in reality."

Jamie nodded and squeezed Gunnul's hand, knowing immediately what her lover was feeling. Gunnul was an excellent leader because she balanced efficiency with an understanding of and empathy for the common people.

Gunnul watched the performance with the keen eye of a soldier. She took in the precision, the tradition of the uniforms and the smartness of the drill and evaluated it in terms of military standards. She was quick to note that the rifles the soldiers carried were modern and that some of the soldiers wore ear receivers. Heritage was clearly tempered by the need for modern security. Chrissy and Jamie sat side by side and simply enjoyed the show. Teefo and Peeti sat quietly, watching with interested eyes. The European world to them was a mixture of old traditions seeping through a veneer of modernism. They were not sure just what was important to the English and what was just show.

Gunnul felt the hairs on the back of her neck stand out. Carefully, she surveyed the crowd around. They had not picked a good spot to stand. Yes, they had a great view of the parade but they were also out in the open and vulnerable to attack. Logically, she could not think of a reason for such an attack but in her gut she sensed danger. It was simply a feeling of dread.

She made eye contact with Teefo, who immediately stood and moved closer, scanning the crowd too with interest. He wasn't sure why his boss was on the alert but he knew better than to not take the look of concern seriously.

Jamie shivered and instinctively wrapped an arm around Chrissy. It was that feeling again. As if there was a great evil nearby that was ready to pounce on them. She felt feverish and an image of flames invaded her mind. She forced a smile onto her face and looked up at

Gunnul. Her lover was right beside her, looking about with ice-cold eyes. *She senses something too! It is not just me!*

Chrissy watched the parade with delighted eyes. She was not afraid. It was not time yet and so they were all safe for now. He was just stalking them, needing to be close, as a cat makes a game out of killing the mouse. If she felt anything it was anticipation. The Others were close by too. Soon she would meet the one that would help give her triumph.

Chapter Seven

Ryan was standing on Speaker's Corner, talking about why there should be no censorship for art. Her family stood around listening and a few other curious souls had also been drawn to the speaker. The corner, next to Hyde Park, was a symbol of the right of free speech in Britain. Anyone who wanted could come here and set up a soap box to talk on what they thought was an important issue. Tourists and passing Londoners would stop to listen and often get involved in lively debates with the speakers. It was a place for the fringe viewpoint, the strange and also the brilliantly insightful.

On the way there, Robbie had told them about stopping years ago to hear a man who looked much like Lenin speak on the need for more than an economic union between all the European nations. At the time, Robbie had laughed, feeling that the national pride and years of rivalry and strife between European nations would prevent any such union from taking place. But today, the existence of the European Union had proven her narrow view of reality wrong. She wondered if the man was still alive and had seen his vision come true.

Ryan had presence, Robbie realized with a start. Real star quality. That both filled her with pride and worried her. She had to admit that it fed her sizeable ego to see that her daughter had inherited some of her own talents and traits. However, she did not want Ryan following along the same path that she had taken. She knew better than most how ugly and cut throat the business could be. She didn't want some bastard using her daughter's hopes for his own gains.

Janet grinned and held on to her smaller daughter's hand. Ryan was a superb speaker and her ability to ad-lib and talk comfortably in front of a crowd was a marvelous skill. She could see Ryan, in fifteen years time, lecturing students or running the school that her mothers had started.

"That's Ryan! She my big sister!" Reb told anybody that would listen. Rebecca felt that Ryan and her dog, Rufus, could do no wrong. Her loyalty to both her pet and her big sister was steadfast.

They had passed Marble Arch on the way to Speakers' Corner. Robbie had wisely pulled Ryan aside while Janet and Reb continued on to share with her older daughter that this was the site of public executions for hundreds of years. At Marble Arch, the guilty and perhaps less than guilty would meet a grisly end either by hanging or by drawing and quartering after they had been paraded down Oxford Street for all to see.

The Williams family circled around Hyde Park at a leisurely place, stopping to play tag with Reb, who needed to burn off some energy. Then they headed over to see Kensington Palace and the gardens around. Kensington today was really a series of apartments for the lesser members of the Royal family when they were in London. Janet told the children that it was here that the bulk of the flowers had been left when Lady Diana had died. She'd had an apartment at Kensington Palace.

Janet explained to Ryan that Kensington Palace was built in a Romanesque style and pointed out the ornate chimney designs. Robbie in the meantime had struck up a conversation with an English nanny who was wheeling a big, navy blue pram around the garden. Janet looked over and smiled softly as she saw Robbie proudly showing off Reb, who sat in her stroller playing with a small teddy bear dressed as a London Bobby that Robbie had bought for her.

Janet thought back to the night in the car, well over a year ago, when she had asked Robbie to be Reb's guardian should anything happen to her. Robbie had almost put them in a ditch in surprise! She was glad she had gone with her gut feeling. It had brought Robbie and Ryan into her life and forged a very special love.

After a leisurely lunch at a nearby restaurant, the Williams rented rowboats and stroked out onto The Serpentine, the large lake that dominates Hyde Park. Janet and Ryan were in one boat and Robbie and Reb in the other. Janet was enjoying watching the equestrians exercising their mounts along Rotten Row, the horse trail in the centre of the ancient city. For hundreds of years, the aristocracy of London had met here informally, bonded by their common love of riding.

A sharp bump brought Janet out of her daydream. Armed with oars and two rowboats, her olives had immediately created a game of naval attack! "Go Obby! We get Mommy and Ryan!" Reb squealed with delight. Janet reached over the side and splashed water at her lover.

"Hey, no fair! My Able Seaman can't reach the water!" protested Robbie, with a laugh as she brought her boat along side.

"All's fair in love and war, sailor!" Janet growled, reaching over to Robbie's boat to tickle Reb, who sat on the bench barely able to move in her lifejacket.

They floated side by side then, enjoying the heat of the afternoon sun and talking about the pictures they had seen at the Tate that morning. Janet listened while Robbie and Ryan discussed whether animation was a technical skill or a true art form. Robbie argued that only the backdrops were art because they were the work of individual artists where the animated figures were a team effort. Ryan argued that many of the masters in the past had used students to do much of the painting based on their sketches and then the master would just finish the canvas off. This was to her the same sort of team effort. Reb had slipped into an afternoon nap, warmed by the sun and propped up in her red lifejacket.

Janet watched the sun reflecting like diamonds on the water. Her eyelids drooped. The afternoon sun was hot on her flesh. The sparkle of light on the water became flames waving, curling around her, drowning her in their heat. The bands of flashing flame grew tighter and she felt herself being lifted from the boat and pulled into a rhythmic tide. She felt the dread course through her and she gripped the gunnels, holding on with white knuckles. A stifled scream burnt away in her throat as she felt herself slipping.

Suddenly cool, strong arms were holding her. "I've gotcha, easy! Janet, shh, what happened, Baby?" Janet snuggled into Robbie's chest and the image that had made her body quiver with fear slowly dissipated.

Ryan had been focused on her mother's discussion when she had felt the boat heave to one side. Quickly, she lurched the other way, using her weight to stabilize the rowboat. Looking back, she saw her Aunt Janet, clinging to the gunnels with a look of complete terror on her face. "Aunt Janet, are you all right?!"

Robbie had seen the fear and acted immediately. She grabbed the gunnels of Ryan's craft and held it tight against her own. "Quick, Ryan, switch boats!" Robbie had ordered. Ryan had hopped lightly from one craft to the other and Robbie, equally agile, had slipped over and taken her place. She leaned out and grabbed Janet, pulling her forward into her arms. "I've gotcha, easy! Janet, shh, what happened, Baby?" she whispered softly, holding her lover close.

"Oh, Robbie! It seemed so real! It was like that dream I had, I... I... I just panicked!"

"It's okay, sweetheart. You probably drifted off to sleep and the dream returned because you were thinking about it. It's gone now," reassured Robbie. Yet inside, she felt this oppressive dread, as if something, something horrible, was going to happen. As soon as Janet calmed, she picked up her oars, and with a terse nod to Ryan, the mother and daughter rowed for shore.

* * * * *

Gunnul let Teefo and Chrissy gallop on ahead while she and Jamie walked their horses along Rotten Row. A ride, using horses borrowed from a friend, seemed like a romantic way to end the day. Peeti did not ride and chose instead to wait in a small café by The Serpentine for their return.

"I have been reading a lot about ancient cultures and beliefs, Gunnul," Jamie said. "I find it strangely fascinating."

"It is good to know and respect all beliefs, Jamie, but you will remember that there is but one God and Allah is his name," cautioned the literal Turk.

Jamie smiled and reached over to touch Gunnul's thigh. "We have different religions but our God is the same, Gunnul. I am not searching to replace God with some pagan belief. I am just extending my knowledge. I suppose being the partner of a Moslem has made me look past the Christian teachings of my childhood and want to know more about what religion and belief really are."

Gunnul looked perplexed as she tried to understand what Jamie was saying. Her belief was part of her culture, part of who she was. She wasn't sure why Jamie needed to explore farther. "You mean you need to understand the human need behind faith?" she questioned.

"Yes, that's it. Did you know, Gunnul, that there has never been a culture found, no matter how small or isolated, that does not have rituals for glorifying God. Even Neolithic man buried his dead with flowers and drew spirit symbols on the walls. Why? And if there is only one God, Gunnul, why do we fight wars over doctrine? Look at how close our faiths and beliefs are, and yet we have fought for hundreds of years over how we worship that God."

"Does it matter, Jamie? Religion is an act of faith. You must trust in God and his mercy, not question his ways."

"I just need to know more. We will be going to some really interesting religious sites while we are here and I want to get the most out of that experience. I know you have traveled a lot but I haven't and I'm really excited about the things we are going to see. Particularly Stonehenge! It has always fascinated me! It calls to me, Gunnul!"

Gunnul laughed at Jamie's excitement, pleased that the trip to England was giving Jamie so much delight after all. She had wondered, after Jamie's panic attack in the museum and bad dream, whether she should call the trip off and return to Turkey. Perhaps it was the strain that they had gone through when Chrissy had been so very, very sick catching up to Jamie. She had been so strong then.

Her head turned to observe two rowboats out on The Serpentine. They seemed in trouble. She wandered if she could help. Then the two boats parted and the rowers headed for shore at a steady pace. Whatever the problem was, it seemed okay now.

Her mind focused fully on what Jamie was saying again. It was wonderful to be here with her family, with Jamie, riding under the mottled patterns of shadow cast by the old trees along the bridle path. Life was good.

* * * * *

Robbie took off her glasses and put them on the bedside table along with the report that had been faxed to her by Brian. She looked over to see Janet engrossed in yet another book on Celtic lore.

She smiled; Janet was a true academic. She studied everything that was new to her.

Robbie rolled on her side and used the tip of her tongue to tease the soft pink of Janet's ear. "I love you," she whispered, feeling the responsive shiver run through her lover. Janet stifled a moan and kept reading. Robbie smiled. *Oh, playing hard to get, huh!?*

Robbie moved closer letting her long length lean against the small form beside her. She tilted her head and nuzzled the soft, vulnerable flesh under Janet's jaw. She felt Janet's pulse quicken on her exploring lips. The tips of her dark, thick hair, she knew, trickled across the top of Janet's breast. Robbie felt Janet lower her book as a shudder ran through her body. Robbie smirked, her head buried in Janet's shoulder. She reached and took the book from Janet's limp fingers.

"What are you doing?" Janet managed to moan.

"I'm going to show you what trust and faith are all about," Robbie promised, her voice rough with desire. "I'm going to worship you until you reach that very special ecstasy that only two people joined as one very deeply can reach."

Robbie rolled over, her hips slipping between Janet's legs. She could feel her lover's excitement hot and wet against her belly and felt herself skyrocketing to that special plane of awareness. She dipped her

543

tongue into the hollow on Janet's shoulder. *Some worship should be a slow, beautiful exploration of spiritual strength until need demands decisive action,* Robbie concluded, as she felt her lover's passion grow beneath her.

* * * * *

Ryan lay in bed staring up at the ceiling. The Venetian blinds on the hotel window divided the city light into strips and projected the bars of light over her head. In the bed across from her, Reb slept soundly. Ryan knew the time was near that she would have to prove herself. She wasn't sure how or when, but she knew that her strength and courage would help to make all the difference.

It was funny, she never had believed in second sight or predestination, yet she was sure about this. She had tried to tell her mom the other day but couldn't think how without sounding like some New Age wannabe. So she'd let her mother make a joke of it and allowed the subject to drop. She should warn her though, but how and when?

Whatever was going to happen, it involved a girl around her own age. She was sure of this, just as she was convinced that the girl was near. In fact, when she was out in the rowboat today, she had scanned the shoreline feeling the girl's presence almost like a force against her chest. Was the girl a good influence or bad? Ryan wasn't sure. She knew only that they were destined to be part of something very important. *Now how could I explain that to my mother!? Mom would just think that all those blows to my head had finally done some damage! Maybe it has!* Ryan sighed, rolled over and drifted off to sleep.

Chapter Eight

The massive figure hunched in the darkness. He knew it was dangerous to be about but the little one drew him like a magnet. Once again, he waited in the shadows of the trees looking up with blood red eyes at the small pane of light glowing from the top floor of the building. The shape smiled, revealing sharp fangs. It had been dangerous, yes, but satisfying to feel the fear within these weak descendants of the original pair. Still, he would have to be careful. There could be no mistakes this time. Even gods can fail if no one believes in their power. The shadowy form smiled, teeth exposed in a snarl; she knew he was near. He could sense it.

Turning, he moved away. It was time to prepare. It would not be too many days now. Only a blink of time in the thousands of years he had lain waiting. He covered the miles in long, loping steps, traveling fast and sure through the night. Finally, near dawn, he arrived again at the place close to the centre of the universe. Here, on this wind swept field, space and time looped back on itself. Here history did not have to repeat but could change in a blinding, terrifying flash.

The ring of Watchers observed with silent, stone cold hearts as the blackness opened to receive its monstrous father once more. The circle of stones remained silent as they always did, not judging, not warning, simply recording objectively the vast flow of space and time through the cosmic heavens.

* * * * *

The next few days in London went quickly for both families. The Williams visited the Science Museum and wandered around in awe at the size and depth of the collection. There was even a piece of grey moon rock sitting in a case that Robbie and Ryan plotted to steal. Janet led them away with a good humoured shake of her head before the two allowed creative thought to become a competitive dare. *God help me when Reb is old enough to join in these Williams' highjinks! I'm beginning to suspect that Reb will be the worst of the bunch!*

They had moved on down the street to the Natural History Museum, where Ryan and Reb had to be bodily dragged from the earthquake room! "Reb, if you start to feel sick you just throw up on Ryan, okay, partner?" Robbie teased.

"Okay, partner," Reb responded happily.

"Thanks, Mom!" Ryan protested in disgust.

"Did I tell you to take her three times into the earthquake room?!"

"She thought it was fun, didn't you, Reb?" argued Ryan, with a grin down at her little sister who was holding onto Ryan's hand with pride.

"The floor giggled like jello, Ryan," the three year old observed.

"Jiggled, Reb. Yes, it sure did," Ryan laughed.

* * * * *

The Dedemanns had started their last day in London at the Madame Tussaud's Wax Museum on Marylebone Road. Madame Tussaud had been a Swiss caught up in the events of the French Revolution. The sad faces of those who had seen their concept of an orderly world chopped short by the blade of the guillotine were the basis of the oldest collection of wax effigies in the world. The first Tussaud museum had been founded in 1776. The Dedemanns wandered from display to display, picking out the famous people whose likenesses were captured in wax. Gunnul, however, refused to take her family into the Chamber of Horrors even though Jamie and Chrissy begged her to. "You two are very bad," Gunnul had smiled with a shake of her head, leading them firmly towards the exit.

"Jamie, did you really want to go?" Gunnul asked, though, before they reached the door.

"No, and I agree it is not suitable for Chrissy," Jamie admitted. "I just wanted to get a rise out of you!"

Gunnul raised an eyebrow and looked down at her feisty wife with amusement. Had Jamie said yes, she would have left Chrissy with Teefo and Peeti and taken Jamie through the chamber. She was glad Jamie had said no. Gunnul did not like to be reminded of the violence of humans, especially her own. Her thoughts must have shown on her face, for Jamie quietly handed her cane to Chrissy and leaned on Gunnul's arm instead for balance. Her fingers intertwined with her lover's in silent understanding and support.

After lunch, they took a cab to catch an afternoon children's performance of the London Symphony Orchestra at The Royal Albert

Hall across the street form the Science and Natural History Museums. Then the Dedemanns finished the day off with a tour of the Victoria and Albert Museum. It was not a place where Gunnul wished to go but she had refused to take Jamie through the Chambers of Horrors so she thought she owed her partner this one. The museum housed one of the finest collections of Victoriana, including some outstanding paper maché pieces and lots of ornate china. There was also decorative art from around the world and exhibitions of modern artists too.

Gunnul pasted a smile on her face and endured. In the morning, she thought, before they left the city, they would go to London Zoo! Now that would be fun! As a student, she used to like to walk through Regent's Park and on to the Zoo. It was one of the oldest zoos in the world and although it was primarily involved in research and preservation it did have a collection of over twelve thousand animals! Then in the afternoon, they could drive over to Greenwich and on towards Canterbury.

The sun set. Time moved forward as events moved closer. Fate raised its hand to draw the innocent into a tidal stream of events.

Chapter Nine

"Okay, that is it! Stop the car!" snapped Janet.

"I can't stop the damn car, I'm on this friggin' roundabout!" Robbie growled back. In the back seat, Reb looked startled by the loudness of the exchange and Ryan looked upset. Ryan didn't like anything that threatened her family stability. She still had real fears about being rejected. She never told her Moms, but sometimes she had nightmares about being sent back to boarding school because she wasn't good. She chewed on her lip nervously.

Robbie pulled the car to the side of the road and got out, muttering to herself. Janet sighed and slipped over into the driver's seat and waited for Robbie to take her place as a passenger. Robbie thumped down and slammed the car door, folding her arms across her chest. "I don't know what you can do that I can't!" she complained. "There are too many damn cars and not enough road signs! I hate driving in the city!"

"Well, for starters, I thought I'd pull into that petrol station over there and ask directions. Then I thought I'd follow the directions without snarling, swearing and flashing my lights at the car in front of me," suggested Janet, giving Robbie a meaningful look.

"You have to flash your lights!" Robbie protested, humour starting to return to her voice as she felt the stress lessening. "They don't lay on the horn and flash the finger here!"

Janet laughed and shook her head, reaching over to squeeze her lover's hand. "How did you ever manage in Toronto?"

"I knew the way to work. On all other occasions I used a limo. That's why God made me rich, so I wouldn't have to abuse people out here on the road!"

Janet made a disgusted noise. "You are impossible, Olive Oil!" she concluded, putting the car in gear, signaling and pulling out into the traffic cautiously. "Let's make a deal. I'll do the city driving and you can do the country stuff."

"This is good. I can do country driving!" Robbie agreed happily.

"Just as long as you don't fight," said a quiet voice from the back seat. The adults' startled eyes met each other's in surprise. A red wash spread up Robbie's face. She tossed the map over the seat at Ryan. "Here, you read the map. I think you'll do a better job than me. You know Janet and I were not really angry at each other, don't you, Ryan?"

"You sounded angry," muttered Ryan, resentfully.

"Obby mad!" agreed Reb, supporting her sister faithfully.

Robbie squirmed uncomfortably. This parenting thing was such a bitch! "Yeah, I guess I did. I'm sorry, guys, for upsetting you and, Janet, I'm sorry I lost my temper."

Janet kept her eyes on the road in the heavy traffic but she reached down and took Robbie's hand in her own, holding on as she gently stroked her thumb over her partner's skin. It was hard to know at times who hurt more, Robbie or Ryan. "It's okay, Love, I knew you weren't angry at me. I'm feeling quite stressed driving in this traffic too. I guess leaving London during morning rush hour was not the best decision."

The Williams had spent two more days in Central London and then had gotten the car that morning to head over to Greenwich, which was only five miles away, if one stopped to ask for directions. Janet, feeling that they all needed to unwind a bit first, went down to the waterfront, knowing that her family loved boats of any sort. There, at the docks, was the *Cutty Sark*, one of the last of the fast and beautiful East India Clippers. These tall ships had once been the backbone of British trade.

"Isn't she gorgeous, Mom!" Ryan whispered.

"Oh, yes! Now this is a woman I could love!" Robbie teased and got a poke from Janet. "I bet she had a hull speed of fifteen, maybe seventeen knots!"

They went aboard and looked around. Below deck there were two interesting displays. One was a history of the spice trade with artifacts and pictures from that era and the other was a collection of figure-heads that had once graced the prows of the old sailing ships. The family had walked around discussing and laughing about the things they saw. Janet enjoyed the section on the history of the spice trade but the figure-heads upset her, bringing back that all too familiar feeling of dread. Looming out of the darkness, the stiff, lifeless figures seemed macabre and sinister. She disguised her discomfort behind a happy smile, wanting her family to have a pleasant day and get over the tension of the drive that morning. *What the hell is the matter with me?! Why do I keep getting these panic attacks?!*

With relief, Janet climbed back up on deck with the family. Looking over the stern, Ryan laughed with delight. "Look, Aunt Janet, that's the *Gipsy Moth IV* down there!" Janet passed the squirming Reb over to Robbie and looked over the side. A tiny little sailboat bobbed at the side of the dock. "It's Sir Francis Chichester's boat. I read about him! He single-handed it in a circumnavigation back in 1966. It is still the smallest boat ever to sail around the world. Isn't that cool?! I'm going to sail around the world when I'm older," stated the teen.

"I go too, Ryan!" demanded the three year old of her big sister.

Ryan turned and ruffled her little sister's hair. "Sure kid, that way if we get shipwrecked or something I'll have something to eat!"

"Okay, Ryan," Reb beamed, not understanding what Ryan meant.

"Ryan!" Robbie growled.

The teen shrugged and looked at her Mom with her eyes sparkling with mischief. Robbie smiled back and whispered into Reb's ears. "Tell you what, Reb. When you and Ryan get this boat of yours, I'll show you how to get Captain Ryan here to walk the plank!"

"Like Captain Hook, Obby," Reb giggled.

"Yup, just like in the Peter Pan movie, Sweetie," agreed Robbie with a smile, pleased at how quickly Reb caught on to things.

The rest of the day went pleasantly. They walked down the quiet streets past the famous naval academy and had morning tea at a baker's shop. Then they walked up to the old observatory, just as Sir Isaac Newton had done hundreds of years before, while Janet explained about the formation of time zones by the Canadian Sir Standford Flemming and how the world's time was set from the observatory of this small community.

* * * * *

The Dedemann family had left a day earlier and had headed across country to the city of Canterbury. The countryside was beautiful! Small, irregular shaped fields looked like patch work quilts, each outlined by a hedge row or occasionally an old stone wall. Nestled in their midst, sometimes, were whitewashed cottages, some still with shale or thatched roofs. Pretty little villages could still be found amongst the urban sprawl and once, they saw horses tethered outside an old village pub.

At the last minute, Gunnul had changed the plans and there had been words between her and Teefo about it. "Peeti is here to help chaperone Chrissy and I am here to help protect you and Mrs. Dedemann," he argued stubbornly.

"I can take care of my family!" Gunnul had snapped. Teefo's words had hit a raw spot. Gunnul still felt embarrassed that Jamie and her daughter had been kidnapped and Jamie shot because Gunnul had left in a temper several years before. And only a few months ago, Gunnul had sat helpless by Chrissy's bed while a mysterious illness threatened to claim her daughter's life.

"As you say, General Dedemann," Teefo had said formally, realizing he had over stepped a boundary with his complex and moody boss.

Gunnul sighed. "I am sorry, Teefo. You are right but I need some time with Jamie. These dreams... I just want to create a safe, special place for her for a little while. Do you understand?" Gunnul explained awkwardly. She was not used to having to reveal her feelings, even to someone as close and trusted as her assistant Teefo.

Teefo nodded respectfully, realizing he had been shown a side of his employer that few rarely saw. "Yes, I understand and respect your wishes, General."

"Thank you. I... I will be careful, Teefo," Gunnul reassured with difficulty. Teefo nodded again and tried to look less worried. He was well aware of how intelligent and strong the General was but he also knew that her one weakness was her family.

It was near sunset when the two cars approached Canterbury and the towers of the old Cathedral in the distance were silhouetted against the evening sky. "Imagine being a pilgrim in the Middle Ages, walking or riding here to pray at the shrine of Thomas Becket," Jamie commented with a sigh. "Have you read Chaucer's *Canterbury Tales*, Gunnul?" she asked her partner.

Gunnul blushed and admitted that in her student days she had studied the sometimes spicy tales from that epic mediaeval manuscript about a group of pilgrims entertaining each other with stories as they walked along. Gunnul, trying to change the subject, went on to tell them some stories of her years as a student and the three of them were laughing so hard that Jamie did not realize at first that Teefo's car had gone on towards Canterbury while they had turned off onto a side road.

"Gunnul, where are we going?" Jamie finally asked.

"I have a special treat planned for you and Chrissy," Gunnul revealed with a smug smile. "Canterbury straddles the River Stour and it is to the river that I now go. I have rented a houseboat for the night and tomorrow we will go down the river to Canterbury."

"Mommy! That is so nice! Will it be one of those long, narrow barges that are painted so prettily? Will it be motorized or pulled by a horse?"

Gunnul laughed. "It is a very old and pretty houseboat, Chrissy. You will like it, I think. It is run for tourists so, yes, it will be pulled alongside one of the old tow-paths. I am glad you are pleased."

Jamie had said nothing but had reached across and captured Gunnul's hand in her own. She saw the flush rise in her lover's face and knew that Gunnul was aware of how much the surprise had meant to her.

The barge was a pretty affair. Within the cabin there was an efficient galley, a saloon that also acted as a dining room, a head with a shower, and two sleeping cabins. In the saloon there was a small fireplace to keep the night chill off and Gunnul made a fire, while Chrissy brought their bags aboard and Jamie saw to getting them a light meal from the groceries they had bought earlier in the day.

Later that night, Gunnul slipped into bed beside Jamie and felt the small, warm body immediately roll over to pull her long, strong frame into a close embrace. "You are wonderful!" Jamie said, her voice muffled by Gunnul's breasts. "I am so lucky you came into my life!"

Further talk was not possible as Jamie used her mouth to suck and nip at Gunnul's nipples until the tall woman squirmed with need. Jamie slipped her body over that of her lover and the sensual feel of the Turk's well-toned flesh beneath her own made her body respond dramatically to its own needs. She started moving rhythmically against Gunnul's leg, mirroring what she was doing to her lover.

The water lapped softly at the hull of their houseboat. Their temporary home bobbed gently. The night was young and the lovers had many paths yet to explore.

* * * * *

Very early the next morning, Gunnul left the comfort and warmth of their bed to meet the horseman who was to pull their barge down into the town. At 5:30 a.m. the mist hung heavily over the fields of hops and grain. The only sound was the clip clop of the draught horse as it plodded along and the tinkle of the rills of water past the hull of their houseboat.

Gunnul brought Jamie hot cider and warm home-made bread for breakfast, bought at a local farm that they passed along the way. The two women sat on deck in each other's arms and watched the sun rise over England as they enjoyed the natural music of river and trail.

A sleepy Chrissy climbed up on deck and snuggled between her mothers, eating the bread and drinking the apple juice her parents had gotten for her as they drifted into Canterbury past the old Roman walls. They docked and the three Dedemanns disembarked and walked to the outer gates of Canterbury Cathedral. They stepped through the Romanesque arch and then, suddenly, there it was, towering overhead, the seat of the Church of England and the cathedral of the Primate, The Archbishop of Canterbury. The cathedral sat bathed in the pinks of morning mist, a pastel jewel wrapped in clouds.

They followed the tourist signs that led to the crypt. Down there, many famous historical figures of Britain were buried. Stone arches in the English perpendicular Gothic style stretched out into darkness beyond the reach of light. Off in the distance, they could hear the approach of singers; male voices harmonizing beautifully the ancient Gregorian chants.

The Dedemanns waited quietly by a stone pillar. Soon they could see flickering candle light. Down ancient passages came a procession of young, hooded men dressed in grey. Each carried a candle as they sang to the glory of God on their way to Prime prayers. The music was mediaeval, a whisper from the past that reached to the very origins of the soul. Chrissy curled into Jamie's side and the woman wrapped her arm around her daughter as she in turn leaned back against the tall form of her partner, who stood in silent awe.

It was only when the last flicker of candle light had disappeared through the ancient arches and the sound of the male voices had echoed away that any of the Dedemanns spoke. "That was a very beautiful moment. One I will remember always," Jamie stated and Gunnul nodded. She too had been touched by the quiet strength and beauty of faith. Chrissy said nothing. A chill ran down her back and she looked out into the darkness with knowing eyes. The time was near and the growing violence without beckoned.

They walked back up the worn stone stairs. Gunnul stopped to look over at the crypt, where the Huguenots had taken refuge after their escape from France. A gasp of fear brought her out of her thoughts just in time to catch Jamie as she tumbled. "Are you alright?" Gunnul asked in worry, holding Jamie close.

"Yes, I must have lost my balance. It felt like I was grabbed from behind. Oh, that was scary! I'm okay now. Thanks, Gunnul. You are always there for me. You have the most remarkable reflexes," Jamie pattered on with nervous energy.

Gunnul's eyes were fixed on her daughter's several steps farther down. "Did you see anyone, Chrissy?"

"No, Mom, no one," her daughter answered.

Gunnul frowned. Just before she had heard Jamie's gasp of fear, Gunnul thought she had seen a huge, dark bulk out the corner of her eye. Her blue gaze scanned the darkness and a feeling of dread forced her to hurry her family out of the crypt and back into the light. They wandered around some more, stopping to see the plaque that marks the spot where Thomas of Becket was killed by order of Henry II and also the graves of Edward, The Black Prince and Henry III.

Jamie, feeling herself again, explained to Chrissy that Henry II was very upset that Beckett had been killed. He always maintained that he had never actually given an order for the Archbishop to be murdered. In fact, the King was said to have crawled from London to Canterbury on his knees as penitence to God for Beckett's death.

"This story is famous and was made into a verse play by T.S. Eliot called *Murder in the Cathedral*," Gunnul noted, as they walked on into the town of Canterbury. "We will see to going to the play next time it is being produced."

They strolled through the narrow Tudor streets. Some of the houses were actually much older. Saint Augustine founded the abbey at Canterbury in 597 A.D. and in the sixth century King Ethelbert of Kent reigned from the city. The Cathedral itself had been first built in 1067 and then rebuilt after a fire in 1374. Although Canterbury was still a very beautiful old city, some of the history had been lost when Canterbury's town centre had taken a few direct hits during World War II.

The Dedemanns spent their day visiting the other tourist sites and shopping around the stores. Then they met Teefo and Peeti, who had picked up their car outside of town that morning and their bags from the boat and were waiting for them. In the late afternoon, the two cars headed off once again to work their way down to Dover.

Chapter Ten

Civilization, the arts and social justice are all walls we put up to separate ourselves from the rest of the animals. It is, however, only that tissue-paper thin cerebral cortex, the outer layer of the brain, that gives us a veil of awareness beyond that of the other beasts. We are animals. The hairs on the back of our neck stand on end still when we feel fear. Our palms sweat and our eyes dilate. The heart races as our primeval instincts override our civilized circuitry and we revert to the flight or fight reaction of our reptilian brain deep within us.

We still feel the heat come on us and seek mates to satisfy our needs, love often growing after a far more basic want has sent us out to prowl. Fear, anger, passion are catalysts that tap into our mammalian awareness and make us by far the most violent animal ever to evolve. Blood is the path of our history and the fear of our future. We are animals.

The presence lurked in the darkness, eyes watching. He had prepared for the coming and then a need deep inside had driven him out once again. Red eyes glowed from within, as they watched the frail humans with interest. They were strange creatures, small and weak looking. But the creature now knew not to underestimate the soft, fragile forms. Humans could, in a split second, cast off their belief and revert to cold, unfeeling violence. The canines of the creature showed as a cruel smile spread across the distorted features. These humans might have noble souls but their hearts were as savage as his own.

* * * * *

The wind blew around the figures of the Watchers as they stood silently in a circle. Their cold stone was etched through hundreds of years with marks of history that no one could read. If anyone could, like the mythical Faust, their brittle souls would be lost in the horror of awareness. The Watchers waited, as they always had, for history to repeat itself. They were the neutral seat of power. They were the Guardians of the centre of the universe where time and place met and the spirit world could reach out and touch the living. They were the holders of the scales; balanced equally with goodness and evil. How often had they witnessed that scale tip?

* * * * *

"Damn fog!" muttered Robbie. "What is it with the English Channel and fog?! Every time I come down to see the white cliffs of Dover, they are fog bound! I'm getting a complex!"

Ryan laughed and Janet snorted as she unbuckled Reb from her car seat.

"Never mind, Obby. We can still see the castle. I've always wanted to see castles!" reassured Janet kindly, as she raced to grab Reb before the three year old could run across the parking lot.

Robbie did not look convinced. "Okay, let's walk up there. Maybe this stuff will burn off by noon." She leaned over and whispered into Janet's ear playfully, "You'd better wrap your arm around me, you know, so you don't get lost."

Janet rolled her eyes and gave her mischievous wife a bump with her hip. "I think I'd better hold on to our younger daughter instead."

Ryan giggled. "Cool, Mom, what a loser!"

"Hey, I got her to marry me!" Robbie protested. They all laughed as they followed the signs towards the gate of Dover Castle.

They paid their admission, got their tour pamphlets and entered into the grounds. "Well, here you are in the castle," observed Robbie dryly. "They are disappointing places really, just walled Keeps."

"Robbie, you can FEEL the history here!" Janet protested. "The brochure says that the tower over there to our right is really an old Roman lighthouse. The Pharos, it is called. Dover was named Dubris by Rome. According to this guide there is a Roman house farther up the cliffs that is dated 200 A.D. It is called the Painted House because of the wall frescoes they found. Most of them were scenes of Bacchus, the God of wine," read Janet as she followed the others up on the parapet.

"If I had to live in this fog I'd make my god the bottle too!" Robbie muttered to Ryan, who snorted. Janet gave them her teacher look and then laughed too.

At the top, they stood looking out into the fog. "Wow! What a view!" exclaimed Robbie, throwing her arms wide.

Reb scrunched up her little face in thought and looked out through the parapet and then up at her tall Mom. "It's white, Obby," she observed.

Robbie laughed and boosted her smaller daughter up for a better look at the white mist. "Yeah, well, so are the white cliffs of Dover, Reb, so we'll just pretend."

"We act!" Reb giggled.

"That's right, Reb!" smiled Robbie, giving her adopted daughter a hug. Reb liked to play act. They would romp around the lodge back home pretending to be African animals. Robbie showed Reb how to act like a pirate and the two of them were looking out for Captain Hook when they heard Janet cry out and a thump.

Robbie picked Reb up and hurried along the length of the walkway. There she found Ryan helping Janet to her feet. Janet had fallen down a small flight of stairs and had scraped her knees.

"Are you okay?" Robbie asked, as she lowered Reb to the ground. "What happened?"

"I don't know really. Ryan and I were walking along talking about British history when I felt this push and over I went," Janet responded shakily. She had not been seriously hurt but the fall had given her a shock. Her knees stung and her shoulder felt bruised.

Robbie looked at Ryan. "You were here. Who did it?" she snapped.

"I didn't see anyone," Ryan stated honestly, a little bewildered. Was Janet saying she had pushed her?

"Ryan, damn it!" Robbie barked angrily. "Janet said she was pushed!" Robbie could feel herself losing her temper. She knew she was acting all out of proportion to what had happened but she couldn't seem to stop herself. Anger had flared up in her like a flash fire. She was back in the den of her parents' house and she was witnessing her father abusing her sister. She raised her fist to strike out at the bastard.

Ryan took a step back and looked really frightened. "Robbie?" Janet asked quietly, stepping quickly between Ryan and her mother. "Are you alright?!"

For a second Robbie stood there, quivering in anger, before she turned and disappeared in a few bounds down to the castle courtyard. The three remaining Williams stood in stunned silence. Then Ryan choked out, "She was going to kill me! She thought I pushed you down the stairs!"

Janet pulled the shaking child into her arms. "No, Ryan. Robbie would never think that and neither would I! No, there is something else going on. Robbie took off because she knew she had upset us and your Mom has a really soft heart that she tries to hide."

"She sure has been quick tempered lately," Ryan muttered in annoyance.

"Yes, she has sometimes," agreed Janet. "Maybe the pressure of the film and all that has happened this year has caught up to her, Ryan. She has been really strong for us all."

"Mommy?" Reb asked with a little voice. She was not sure what had happened but she knew something had.

"It's okay, Reb. Mommy just fell and scraped her knees," responded Janet, stroking her daughter's thick, dark hair. She was going to be so much like Robbie! "Ryan, could you hold Reb's hand going down the stairs. I'll follow. I need to go slow. My knees are a bit stiff."

They found Robbie waiting by their car, looking absolutely miserable. When she saw her family she walked over and lifted the limping Janet up into her arms and carried her back to the car. Carefully, she lowered her wife into the seat and then kneeled to clean her scraped knees with a tissue and water from a water bottle. "I need to apologize to you for leaving, Janet. I... I had this flashback... to the night at my father's house... I... I haven't had that happen in years."

"You okay, now?" Janet asked, reaching out to brush Robbie's bangs into place.

"Yeah, you okay? The knees don't seem to be swelling."

"I'm fine. It was more of a shock than a fall. I'll buckle Reb into place if you want," Janet offered, looking into Robbie's eyes. Robbie swallowed hard and nodded.

She stood and turned to face her older daughter, who was standing some distance off looking really scared. Robbie walked over slowly. "Did you hear what I said?" she asked her daughter sadly.

Ryan nodded, her eyes filled with tears like her Mom's, but said nothing.

"Ryan." Robbie's voice cracked. "I'm so sorry you had to witness that! I... It had nothing to do with you. I wasn't angry at you! I was back in that room and..."

"It's okay, Mom," Ryan cut in, feeling awkward and too wounded to carry on the conversation.

Robbie nodded sadly, realizing that she had managed yet again to build a barrier between herself and her daughter and to undermine Ryan's sense of security. "I guess we should be going now," Robbie stated.

"Okay." Ryan walked past Robbie, keeping at a safe distance, and got in the back seat of the car. Robbie came around and got in the driver's seat. Silently they made their way down into the town of Dover.

Chapter Eleven

The Dedemanns too had arrived in Dover and had spent the morning wandering around the many interesting sites in the fog. By late morning, the sun was starting to peek through. Gunnul had stopped on the 140 foot long stairway cut in the white cliffs to look down at Jamie, whom she had been helping down the stairs. At the bottom Chrissy, Teefo and Peeti waited. "Why are you laughing, Jamie?" asked the serious Turk.

Jamie looked at her partner with love. Gunnul's English was excellent but she didn't always understand the varied colloquial use of a word. Gunnul smiled simply because Jamie was laughing. "What is so funny? It is true that The Shaft was made so the sailors could get up quicker."

Jamie started to laugh again and leaned against her bewildered partner. Composing herself she explained, "Gunnul, in English a shaft can mean..." She reached up and whispered into her lover's ear.

The red climbed up the Turk's neck. "This is not what I meant, Jamie!" the conservative woman protested in embarrassment. "It is what the stairway is called! It was built in the time of Napoleon so that the sailors could get up into the town easier from the harbour below."

Jamie bit her lip and looked at her serious lover with eyes dancing with merriment. Gunnul blushed very red this time and raised an eyebrow. "Jamie! This is what I get for taking a partner who is an infidel!" she teased.

Looking up, she pointed along the coast where the fog had now burnt off in the noon sun. "Look, Jamie, there are the white cliffs of Dover! You can see them for miles out to sea, a white ribbon against a blue sky. They are made of chalk."

Standing behind her partner, with her hands on her shoulder to balance Jamie on the steep chalk stairs, Gunnul pointed again. "This is a very good spot to stand. Do you see way off in the distance there, to those mounds on the horizon? They are bronze age chieftains' graves.

Then there is the Roman lighthouse, the Norman fort and some of the remaining fortification from the Battle of Britain. From here you can see almost three thousand years of history. Is that not amazing?"

Jamie agreed, using the opportunity to lean against the tall, strong body of the woman she loved so much. She was always surprised at what Gunnul knew and didn't know. She had an amazing knowledge of European and Middle East history and was a power house in business matters and yet she would not understand the sexual connotations of a word. She could head a vast business empire, lead men into battle and yet be embarrassed by an off-colour joke. The more she learned about the woman she loved the more she realized just how wonderful a person she was. Together they walked down the remaining steps and joined the others on the shore line.

After a pleasant lunch in town, the Dedemanns picked up the A28 and headed along the south coast. There were some lovely marine towns along the way but they kept on the road until they reached Folkestone, where they stopped for afternoon tea. Here they took some time to visit Spade House where H.G. Wells once lived and worked. They also walked along The Leas, a pretty grass path that followed the cliff edge along the coast.

Refreshed they went on and finally found a nice seaside hotel some miles east of Hastings. Over dinner, it was Chrissy who played the tour guide. On the way to the hotel, they had passed through the town of New Romney and the small village of Rye. "I read a story about this area. New Romney was a major sea port until 1287 when a terrible storm built up a huge sand spit and changed the path of the River Rother. The sea-going vessels had to be moved farther down the coast to find a safe harbour at Rye."

The adults looked at Chrissy, not sure why this should be significant. "Rye," Chrissy repeated as if they had not heard her the first time. "You know, Dr. Syn!"

"I think I've heard of him," Jamie responded, wrinkling her nose in thought in a way that Gunnul found absolutely adorable. "Wasn't he a pirate?"

"One of the worst!" smiled Chrissy. "They called him Scarecrow! He was born in England in 1768. His adopted parents died of plague when he was fifteen so he joined the merchant navy. While the ship he was on was trading in the Caribbean, they were captured by pirates. The crew was taken to the island of indoctrination, which was a nice way of saying become a pirate or we'll torture you to death!"

"I do not think this is good reading, Chrissy," protested Gunnul, who was surprised by her daughter's blood thirstiness. Jamie smiled, realizing that twelve year olds loved these sort of tales, as do many adults.

"All the crew died of the torture accept for Scarecrow and his friend Meriweather. They turned against their fellow crewmen and became pirates themselves! By 1772, Scarecrow had mutinied against his pirate captain and taken over the pirate ship. Meriweather was his first mate. Together they terrorized the trade routes to the Caribbean. Soon he was wanted dead or alive, so Scarecrow turned over his command to Meriweather and retired rich to Rye."

"Ah, the town we came through. That is where the pirate retired," Gunnul laughed, starting to see the point of the story.

"Not likely!" Chrissy went on with relish. "He forged some papers calling himself Dr. Syn and the local Squire hired him on as the rector at the local Anglican church."

"That was very bad!" exclaimed Gunnul, who was very devoted in her faith.

"That's only the half of it! He acted as a respectable rector during the day but at night he was smuggling goods in and out of England! Wasn't he amazing!" laughed Chrissy.

Jamie laughed but Gunnul looked seriously at her daughter. "Chrissy, this is not the sort of person I would have you admire."

Chrissy looked at her adopted mother with eyes that revealed nothing. "It is just a story. A bit of local history," she said.

"Well, I rather enjoyed the tale!" responded Jamie, giving her serious partner a poke. The evening wore on and after Chrissy had said her prayers with her family, she was tucked into bed and soon fast asleep.

Gunnul took the opportunity to work on business at her laptop and Jamie read a book quietly by the window. Neither woman was really focused on what they were doing. Gunnul was being visited by her private demons. When Jamie had nearly fallen down the stairs, Gunnul had come very close to accusing Chrissy of having pushed her mother.

Chrissy would never do a thing like that, Gunnul knew. Yet, Gunnul's first reaction was to turn on her daughter. What would make her doubt Chrissy? At dinner tonight, this sudden interest Chrissy had in undesirables like Scarecrow heightened her fears over Jamie's near fall. It was a completely illogical connection. Gunnul knew that there was violence within her own soul and that there certainly had also been in that of her brother, a weak and nasty man. Had Chrissy inherited that spot of darkness too?

Gunnul often wondered where her sudden anger came from that blocked out all logical reason. She had killed. And although the ghosts of those she had slaughtered on the battlefield haunted her, she had to admit that the challenge and danger of war had thrilled her. Even now, knowing the sacrifice she and the others had made, she would take command again and make the same decisions. What did that say about her? Unconsciously, she put her hand over her abdomen where the scar that had left her barren was.

Deep in her subconscious she heard Jamie's angry voice from two years ago: "At least I had a child. I didn't have to steal someone else's!" The pain of those words shot through Gunnul and she placed her head on the cool desktop and closed her eyes. Jamie had apologized. Explained that she hadn't meant those cruel words, but the fact of the matter was they were true. Gunnul couldn't have children of her own. She had willingly adopted her brother's child as her own even though she knew that Chrissy's birth mother was searching for her daughter.

Jamie stared moodily out at the darkening seascape. Her leg hurt badly tonight. She had not wanted to slow her family's sight-seeing down. The stairs had really tired her out and Gunnul, so strong and fit, had patiently helped her slowly down them. Gunnul was a beautiful, rich, and active woman. Jamie knew that Gunnul loved her but did the Turk ever feel restricted by having made a commitment to someone who was lame? Did she stay with Jamie out of guilt because it had been Gunnul's brother who had damaged her leg beyond repair?

The now familiar dread that had started as a depression tonight spread throughout her being. She turned to see Gunnul bent over, her head on the desk and her eyes closed. She looked so tired and sad. "Gunnul, I wouldn't want you to stay with me if you weren't happy. We could go our separate ways. I'm sure we could make some arrangement about sharing Chrissy."

Gunnul's eyes opened and her head slowly lifted and turned to look at Jamie with an expression of shocked horror. For a minute there was only the sound of the sea washing on the shore and the tick of the clock on the wall. Finally, Gunnul managed to clear her throat. "You want to leave me, Jamie?"

"No! I just... I don't want to restrict your life. There are so many things that you could see and do that I wouldn't be able to handle..."

Gunnul swallowed, then swallowed again. Her head felt light and her heart refused to beat regularly. Tears welled in her eyes. "I do not think I could live if I lost you or Chrissy. You are all I have. I am barren."

"What?"

Gunnul got up, suddenly angry that she might be losing one of the only things that meant anything to her. She wasn't going to let it happen! She couldn't! "If you wish to leave I will not stop you, but you will not take my daughter! Never!"

Jamie looked like she had been hit. Awkwardly, she got to her feet and wrapped her cane in place. She limped across the room past Gunnul, who stood shaking with emotion. Stopping at the door, she turned to face her partner. "I love you, Gunnul, I love you and I love Chrissy. Please don't make our separation something that will fill us all with bitterness and hate," she choked out.

Gunnul saw the tears rolling down her lover's face. She sank to her knees. "Don't leave me, Jamie. Please."

Jamie limped over to Gunnul and threw herself into the Turk's arms. "How did we end up in this discussion?! I don't ever want to leave you, Gunnul! I just suddenly felt this dread that you might only be staying with me because you felt sorry for me. I thought I might be restricting your life," Jamie sobbed into Gunnul's shoulder.

Gunnul held Jamie so tight the smaller woman could barely breathe. "Oh God! Thank you, Allah! Jamie, I can't be rational when it comes to you and Chrissy! I love you both so much. No, you don't restrict my life, sweet one. You give it meaning."

Gunnul shifted around on the floor so that she held Jamie in her arms and they could look into each other's eyes. "In my culture, even though in many ways we are very westernized, the role and goal of a woman is to bear children. If you can not it is a very great shame. People feel so sorry for you..."

Gunnul stopped, her lip trembling with emotion. Then she collected herself and went on. "I was left a huge business empire to run because my brother could not. I was a woman who fought and killed as a man would in battle. My injuries were in the newspapers when I lay so close to death. Everyone knew that I would be barren if I lived. After... my family, business associates, they started to treat me as a man. It didn't bother me. It made it easier not to have to face being a woman in a man's world.

"But always I felt incomplete. I wasn't a man. I didn't want to be a man. I knew that if I could I would want to have a child. But I could not physically and by then I had also accepted the fact that it was not men I was attracted to. Then you and Chrissy came into my life. I can not tell you how much that has meant to me."

"I love you so much, Gunnul. I did not realize... I thought your family and associates had always treated you that way."

"No."

"I find you a very beautiful woman, Gunnul, not a substitute for a man. And you are a wonderful mother and partner."

"Tonight, I felt this terrible depression come over me. I was afraid again that the violence that my brother and I had might be inherited by Chrissy," Gunnul admitted with embarrassment.

"Gunnul! How could you think such a thing? Chrissy is a wonderful person. She doesn't have a mean bone in her body and neither do you! There is a difference, Gunnul, between fighting for your people and killing for fun. Gunnul, I thought we had talked through this. You are not a bad person because you had to kill to save your nation and Allah did not punish you by making you barren. Allah rewarded your courage by giving you back your life and bringing Chrissy and me to you."

"Do you believe that, Jamie?" Gunnul asked.

"Yes," Jamie answered firmly, meeting Gunnul's eyes with a steady stare. Gunnul wrapped her close. "I love you."

"I love you too."

* * * * *

Robbie paced up and down their hotel room. Janet read her book in bed, knowing that her lover needed time to calm down before she would be able to talk. The pacing was slowing a bit.

"Do you want to talk about it?" she asked softly.

"What is there to talk about? I lost my temper. Scared my kid half to death and ruined my relationship with her because I'm such a stupid shithead!" muttered Robbie, kicking the rattan wastepaper basket and sending it flying.

Janet slipped out of bed and came and wrapped her arms around the stiff body of her wife. She held on tight until Robbie started to relax despite herself. "That's better. Now we can talk," Janet sighed, standing on her tiptoes to kiss Robbie softly. "Come over here and sit."

Janet took Robbie's hand and led her over to a chair, pushing her down into it. Then she knelt in front of her problematic partner and folded her arms across Robbie's knees. With a significant look at Robbie, she reached out and lifted the wastepaper basket up and placed it under the table, out of the way. Then she placed her arm back on her lover's knee. "Okay, today was a botch up. No argument there, but it is NOT the end of the world, Robbie! You and Ryan are doing really well. You have a great friendship and it is clear that you love and respect each other very much. But Ryan is a teen and they are very difficult people! She is also a teen who is struggling with her childhood feelings of rejection and with trying to define her role in a ready-made family.

"You, on the other hand, have gone from playing the role of debauched playgirl to being a mother and wife. You didn't even have a concept of true family to model your actions after. You are doing really well, but you have to accept the fact that there will be failures. Ryan will get over this, Robbie."

"What if she doesn't? I mean, teens run away or... or worse when their parents can't communicate with them."

Janet laughed and shook her head at her fretting lover. "Ryan is very happy with us. She is not going to do anything drastic. She is really a remarkably stable child considering her background. She just gets hurt and defensive really, really easily. Do you know anyone like that?"

Robbie blushed. "Should I talk to her again?"

"Yes, but not for a bit. Give her the luxury of having a bit of a snit and then I'll give her a gentle dose of reality and send her in your direction."

"What if I say something to send her off again?"

"You won't. You are a natural mother. A rather unorthodox one, but a good one never the less," reassured Janet.

Robbie nodded, feeling much better. The terrible sense of dread that had been hanging over her lifted. "Thanks."

"My pleasure. Now come to bed. I need a foot warmer," teased Janet.

Robbie picked her wife up with a laugh and carried her back to bed. Stripping, she crawled in beside Janet and sighed as her partner immediately curled up to her. She knew that Ryan was going to be difficult tomorrow and that would probably make her feel awful again, but with Janet on her team she felt that she could get through this crisis after all.

* * * * *

Outside the white cliffs dropped to the English Channel below. An endless ocean, dark, deep and cold. Until the sun rose again tomorrow, the world belonged to those who dwelled in the darkness. Light, dark, good, evil, opposites of the same element. The key was balance: without it chaos ruled. The figure loped awkwardly across the countryside, returning to his home once again before the first rays of light. He had caused all the emotional turmoil he could among the humans; soon they would be his. The circle of stones noted his arrival, their dark faces refracting the first pink rays in the eastern sky. The time of reckoning was near.

Chapter Twelve

The day was overcast and still. The air was heavy with moisture that sent a chill deep into bones. Robbie had wandered off from her family feeling moody and restless. Her on-again-off-again relationship with her daughter had deteriorated once more into monosyllables and stiff routine. She hated it. Worse still, she hated dealing with the guilt of knowing the fault was hers. The dread washed through her again. Why couldn't she control her temper? She had thought married life had mellowed her a bit. Lately, however, she had found the rising anger within her hard to control. Nor did it have a source anymore, it was simply a violence within her needing to get out.

She wandered down the road, moodiness and restlessness going hand in hand. Then with a sudden spurt of energy she sprinted up the hill to look down on the patchwork quilt countryside of England. The modern world vanished before her eyes. It was October thirteenth, 1066. For the last three nights a great comet had filled the sky. They called it the Hairy One because it had a tail like a horse. It was, in fact, one of the first recorded sightings of Halley's Comet.

To the people then it was simply an omen. In her imagination, Robbie stood on the hill with the men of Harold Godwinson. She could smell their sweat and feel the pinch of her own armor and the reassuring weight of the sword sheathed at her side. They were holding the hill for King Harold of England, who had taken the throne of the land after the death of Edward the Confessor. Harold Godwinson was a true Englishman and his men, Robbie knew, loved him. So much so that they had fought off the Danes with him and then force marched the length of England to be here to meet the army of William the Bastard, Duke of Normandy.

In the director's eyes, the ghosts of a thousand years ago lined up, drew their swords and waited for the battle to start that would change the face of history. Robbie felt the fear and exhilaration course through her veins. She loved being here. Maybe she had been a warrior once in another life and had tested her skills and strength against the best of the enemy. The price of victory, an entire country; the cost of defeat; death. A cruel smile curled her lip, as she imagined waiting to give her battle cry and charge forward into battle.

* * * * *

Some distance away, Janet sat with her two daughters on a sunny bank. The Williams had left Dover that morning and traveled west along the coastline, past Folkestone and New Romney and on to Hastings. Janet played with Reb, helping her to make a necklace of dandelions. Her eyes were on her older daughter though, who lay moodily on the grass, shredding the yellow dandelion heads that Reb had rejected.

"You want to talk about it?" Janet probed quietly.

"About what?" responded Ryan defiantly.

"About what happened between you and your Mom back in Dover."

"Where is she any way?" Ryan snapped in frustration, evading the topic.

"She needed some space. Her demons are bothering her. She feels awful about yesterday," Janet answered honestly, knowing how restless and distracted Robbie had been last night.

"She was going to kill me! If you hadn't stopped her, Tyrannosaurus Robbie would have torn me apart because you got hurt," Ryan muttered bitterly.

"No!" Janet protested in shock. "It never occurred to me for a minute that Robbie would hurt you physically! She would never touch any of us. She loves us so much that it hurts her when we hurt. I stepped between you to stop Robbie from saying something she might regret. She had been terrified that something had happened to me and upset that she could do nothing to protect me. All that frustration bubbled to the surface and you were the nearest scapegoat. Robbie can be like that, impetuous, and then regret it dearly later."

"Maybe," sighed the unconvinced teen. "I just think that we are getting on okay and then something happens that makes me really feel unwanted around here. I mean, you've got Reb and all. And I've been trouble for you and in the way."

Janet reached over and brushed Ryan's truant locks back behind her ear. "Not so, Ryan. Yes, we have Reb, but she is not you. She is never going to be. You are something else, kid, and Robbie and I are very proud of you. More than that, we love you. Your Mom doesn't always show you that love in an appropriate manner. She is well out of her depth here. She comes from a really dysfunctional family and she has been a bachelor for over thirty years. She has gone from a loner living life wildly because of her fear of being incarcerated to the head of a family in just one year. It hasn't been easy for her. She has the heart but not always the coping skills."

"Seems like we are always having to forgive each other," Ryan whined.

"Of course, that is what love and friendship are all about. Welcome to life with all different perspectives, needs and wants. No matter how much you care for someone, you are going to jostle their reality sometimes. If the loyalty and love go really deep, however, you work through that."

"You sound just like a guidance teacher," complained Ryan.

Janet laughed. "That is because I am one!" She turned to pass Reb another flower and her heart jumped into her throat. Her three year old was gone!

* * * * *

Robbie stood scanning the battlefield below. She wanted to film, if possible, on location. The terrain was right but the setting lacked the wild nature of Senlac hill at the time of Harold. She sighed, wondering if it was worth the effort to create the illusion. They could just find another place that had the elements she needed. Normally, that is what she would do, but something drew her to this place. Something called her to do battle.

Her eyes scanned right to where the road to the site cut through the green slope of grass. Her eyes widened in horror as she saw her small daughter running down the road with a yellow chain of dandelions in her hand. A car, hidden from Reb by a curve around the hill, was going to be right on top of her in just a few seconds.

Robbie dived down the hill, knowing as she did so that she had no chance of saving her daughter, but willing to shatter her heart in trying.

* * * * *

Gunnul smiled happily while she drove along. She had been looking forward to visiting this site. As a student of military history, she knew that this battleground stood with battles such as Marathon and Agincourt in deciding the European world's history. Hastings was a moment of destiny.

Beside her Jamie looked out the window with interest, her thoughts on the latest book she was reading, *Stonehenge Decoded*.

Gunnul knew Jamie was equally excited because she was looking forward to seeing Stonehenge later today. Gunnul did not really understand this obsession Jamie had developed for Celtic culture and particularly for Stonehenge. It was after all just a pagan monument. It wasn't like Hastings, where one of the greatest battles in European history had taken place.

Gunnul's eyes widened in horror and her mind snapped into the present as she saw someone dashing down the hill directly into the path of their car once they came around the next bend. "Hold on!" Gunnul warned her family, turning the wheel hard to the right as she hit the brakes. Right in front of them now, they could see a small child happily trotting down the centre of the road.

Gunnul brought the car out of a skid and onto the shoulder of the road. The car's wheel hit an object, caught and spun the vehicle around and up onto the bank. "Are you two all right?" Gunnul asked her family, her voice shaky with fear.

"Yes," came the shocked responses. Gunnul was immediately out of the car and heading over to where the tall, dark woman now knelt, holding a little child in her arms.

"Is she all right?" the Turk asked with concern.

"Yes," responded the woman, a bit breathless after her panic stricken charge down the hill. "Thanks, for that amazing reaction. I don't know how you managed to miss her."

"I wasn't sure we had," responded Gunnul honestly, sinking to the ground, her legs not able to support her anymore. "We felt a bump. It must have been when we hit the kerb. Are you sure she is all right?"

"Yes, she's fine," Robbie stated, holding her younger daughter close to her wildly beating heart for reassurance. "I'm sorry. That must have scared you as much as it did me."

"Am I in tubble, Obby?" asked the frightened little child in Robbie's arms.

"Yes, you are," Robbie stated honestly, but in a voice soft and caring. "You know you are not to go off by yourself. You almost caused an accident here." Robbie looked up at the approaching women. One was a small blond who was strikingly similar to Janet in appearance. The woman leaned heavily on a metal crutch that wrapped around her forearm. The other was a preteen, dark and clearly related to the woman who sat beside her on the grass verge of the road.

"Is she all right?" asked the woman earnestly as she limped over.

"Yes, she is fine," Gunnul reassured her own shaken family. She turned to the beautiful woman who sat holding the pretty child so lovingly. "I am Gunnul Dedemann. This is my family, Jamie Dedemann and our daughter Chrissy."

Robbie stood, using the time to decide how she should respond, and then decided that she owed this woman the truth. "I am Roberta Williams. This is my younger daughter, Rebecca the Escape Artist."

"Aahh, Rebecca! I think we have met before, at the airport last week. You had escaped then too and were going around the baggage carousel!" laughed Gunnul, reaching out to brush the soft hair of the small child. Except for the big blue eyes, Reb looked a lot like her daughter Chrissy had at that age. Chrissy had been such a beautiful baby. Gunnul wished that Jamie had not had those years of Chrissy's childhood stolen from her.

Robbie raised an eyebrow and looked down at her truant child. "Yes, I heard about that! Reb, we gotta talk, Sweetheart, about this need you have to bolt like a young horse."

Reb's lip formed into a pout. "Ryan and Mommy talk. I bring you my daddylion necklace. I make it," Reb explained, holding up the mushed chain and trying to reach it over Robbie's neck. Robbie lowered her head so the small child could slip the necklace in place. *Hell! I'm wearing dandelions and in front of people!* Robbie thought, laughing at herself in surprise.

"Reb!" came a relieved exclamation, as Janet and Ryan crested the hill and came running down the other side. "Oh thank God! We've been looking all over for her. I should have realized that she would have made a bee line for you! Reb that was very naughty of you!" scolded Janet, lifting her daughter from Robbie's arms and giving the child a hug.

"I sorry, Mommy," whispered Reb, holding on to her Mom tightly.

"May I present my family, my wife Janet and our daughters Ryan and Rebecca," Robbie said formally. "This is Gunnul and Jamie Dedemann and their daughter Chrissy."

Janet looked up in surprise, noting the others for the first time. "You are the lady who scooped my daughter off the baggage carousel at Heathrow."

"She is also the woman who put her car off the road to avoid hitting our daughter," cut in Robbie, looking at her youngest meaningfully.

Janet paled, knowing she would have felt responsible if anything had happened. "Oh! I'm sorry! Reb, do you see what happens when you don't do as you are told? You are lucky that Ms. Dedemann was able to avoid hitting you. I think you owe the Dedemanns an apology for not being good and a promise that you won't run off again."

Tears welled in Reb's eyes but her Mom steeled her heart and looked at her daughter firmly. "I sorry," said Reb. "I no be naughty again."

Ryan stood stiffly and silently, waiting for her Mom to blame her for distracting her Aunt Janet from watching Reb. Instead, Robbie pulled Ryan aside in a hug while the others talked. "Thanks for charging after Reb. Did she scare you as much as she scared me?"

"Yeah, pretty much," Ryan admitted, liking the feel of her mother's warmth.

"You mean the world to me," Robbie whispered, as she gave her older daughter a final hug and pulled away to look into the serious green eyes. "I don't always show you that."

Ryan smiled to let her Mom know that everything was okay again. "Neither do I," she admitted.

They turned back to the conversation of the others. Jamie and Janet were into a mutual discussion on the history of Stonehenge and Gunnul was checking Chrissy's bruised arm where she had hit heavily against the car door as they span around.

"Dedemann is a very famous name. Are you related to General Dedemann of the Dazgir Pass fame?" Robbie asked. She saw a flash of pain cross the tall Turk's face and wondered if she had said something inappropriate.

It was Gunnul's daughter who answered proudly, "My Mom is General Dedemann."

Robbie beamed with delight. "General, this is an honour! I bet you are here to see Hastings. I am making a movie this year about the battle. If you have a few minutes to spare I would appreciate your insights into the battle."

Jamie looked between Robbie and Gunnul. It was pretty obvious to her that they had once again run into some of the "Others". The likeness between the two tall women could make them sisters. "Are you the director? One of the amazing Williams?" she asked.

"Yes," responded Robbie, looking embarrassed.

Janet found Robbie's funny blend of arrogance and humility charming. Among her colleagues, her capacity to soak up praise knew no limits, but among strangers she was always slightly embarrassed that she was an actor and not a scientist like her sister. Janet came to her lover's aid. "Yes she is, and we are very proud of her. Although, in the little northern Canadian town we call home, Robbie is more famous for having decked Jim Ableton during a hockey game than she is for her career!"

"Janet!" protested Robbie, going very red.

"She was protecting me because Ableton had tripped me from behind," Ryan defended proudly.

"Were you hurt?" asked Chrissy, entering the conversation for the first time. Ryan's blue eyes turned to look into the softest pair of moss green.

"Yeah, I got knocked out," Ryan bragged.

"Oh dear!" gasped Chrissy, looking truly upset.

"Robbie, why don't you and Gunnul see about getting the car out of the ditch and Jamie and I will walk the kids up to the coffee shop for lunch. You can meet us there."

Robbie looked at Gunnul and the Turk nodded and smiled. "This I think is a good idea. My assistant and his wife should already be there. They will be worried about what has delayed us. You are okay to walk this far, Jamie?"

Jamie nodded. "Yes, the road is flat. I'll be fine."

Robbie pulled her older daughter aside as Ryan moved alongside Chrissy. "You remember that conversation we had about dating?"

"Yeah."

"Well, don't start experimenting with the daughter of a famous Turkish general, okay!"

Ryan snorted. "Coward!"

"No, just not suicidal," responded Robbie, raising an eyebrow and giving her daughter a significant look.

Ryan looked wide-eyed and innocent but the cheeky smile gave her away. "I'll be good, Mom."

Robbie rolled her eyes. "I hear that a lot from my family, usually just before all hell breaks loose!"

Teefo was standing at the door of the tea house waiting when the combined Dedemann and Williams families walked up. His worried face changed to one of astonishment as he looked from Jamie to Janet and back again. Then his face collapsed into worried lines again as he looked over Jamie's shoulder to where his employer should be.

"It is okay, Teefo, Gunnul is with Ms. Williams and they should be along any minute now. Janet, Ryan, this is Teefo, our friend and personal assistant. Ah, here comes our car now. Come in and meet Peeti. She is Teefo's better half!" Jamie joked.

They all filed in and soon the remaining members joined the group to make for quite a rowdy luncheon party. Later, they walked outside to see the spot where Harold was reported to have died from an arrow through the eye, although this legend was probably not true. The families trooped around as Robbie and Gunnul became more involved in the legendary battle by the minute. The others quickly grew bored.

"Robbie, Gunnul, Jamie and I have been talking. Why don't we leave you two here to review military history and we'll take the family on to Stonehenge. You can join us there later in the afternoon," Janet suggested.

The two tall women looked at the others in surprise and then had the good grace to blush. "This is a good idea. If it is acceptable to Robbie," answered the Turk.

Robbie shrugged. "Suits me."

"Teefo, you will go with my family please," Gunnul ordered. Teefo looked sharply at Robbie, decided she could be trusted with his boss and nodded.

"There won't be room for us all in the car, Gunnul. How about instead, Teefo and Peeti find some place to relax here, while you and Robbie look around. Then the four of you can drive over in the other car. We'll be fine. Don't worry," smiled Jamie, a little embarrassed by Gunnul's insistence on providing her and Chrissy with a babysitter. Gunnul saw the flash of annoyance in her partner's eye and wisely decided not to insist, although she would have liked to.

"I stay with Obby?" Reb asked.

"Sure you can, Monkey," Robbie agreed, rubbing the head of the small child who was wrapped around one of her long legs.

The families broke up and reformed, allowing Robbie and Gunnul to continue in their reconstruction of the battle of 1066. As the day wore on, Reb became sleepy, still needing her afternoon nap. Peeti and Teefo were happy to sit under a shady chestnut tree not far off while Reb slept peacefully in Peeti's lap. Gunnul and Robbie had gradually been pulled away from their families by their love of battle. Far away now, Jamie, Janet, Chrissy and Ryan made their way to Stonehenge, and to an appointment with destiny.

The dark figure hunched moodily in a shadow. It growled angrily. They were to kill the child! The monster had planned it that way. Once again these humans had changed their fate by their bold and unpredictable actions. There must be a blood letting! Still, there was time, and now the group had broken up and reformed it would be much easier. Once again the warrior's heart had been drawn away from the one she should protect by her lust for battle.

A strong black tongue ran across jagged teeth, licking up saliva. The time was very close now. Once again the seed of true evil would be planted in this world and this time it would triumph!

Chapter Thirteen

Gunnul stood beside Robbie on the hillside at Hastings. She had found an easy bond of respect with the actor that she had not anticipated. Acting, in her culture, was not considered an honourable profession. Yet Gunnul sensed in this woman the true heart of a warrior. "The battle started in the early morning," Gunnul related. "On October 14th, 1066. Harold Godwinson had his men form up where we now stand, on Senlac Hill. All day the battle raged and Harold was able to keep pushing back the enemy. By late afternoon the forces of England could taste victory.

"William of Normandy was desperate. He knew the only way to defeat Harold was to find some way to break their line. He ordered his men to fall back in disarray. The poorly trained and inexperienced forces of King Harold thought the enemy was retreating. They broke their lines and gave chase down the hillside. Harold rode forward to call them back to regroup, but they wouldn't listen. It was at this point that Harold might have been killed by an archer. William now had the English where he wanted them. He signaled to his cavalry to charge in from the flanks. The English were slaughtered. Ironically, they might still have won over the lightly armed Norman cavalry, but the English were not able to pull the riders from their horses. The Normans were using the latest weapon in battle, the stirrup."

Robbie listened intently, as Gunnul explained and pointed out the points of attack on the terrain. "You mean the English lost one of the greatest battles of history because the Normans had put stirrups on their saddles?" she exclaimed in disbelief.

Gunnul shrugged. "Who can tell. War is not like chess where you can play again and try a different approach. Many historians believe that it was the stirrup that made all the difference. War is often won not on military might but on simple, unforeseen factors. They say the battle of Marathon was won because the Greeks were prepared to die to the last man before giving up their right to democracy to an invading force. Agincourt was won because of the superiority of the English long bow. War is full of random circumstance and irony."

"Like you being on the Turkish border to command a small group of defenders against a huge army," Robbie smiled.

Gunnul shrugged and looked off in the distance. "Fate is often placed in our own hands to choose. Our decisions we must live with for the rest of our lives."

The sun slipped behind a cloud and a sudden chill filled the air around them. A dread as heavy as a weight descended on them. They looked at each other, both afraid to utter their sudden fear. Gunnul's words, "Fate is often placed in our own hands", echoed ominously in Robbie's mind. "We've made a mistake," Robbie finally got out between lips stiff with fear.

"We must hurry," ordered Gunnul, turning to run towards the car. Robbie was right with her, leaving a startled Teefo and Peeti and a sleeping Reb behind.

* * * * *

Jamie and Janet drove happily from Hastings over to Stonehenge. Along the way they chatted about some of the books they had both read pertaining to Stone Age henges as well as some New Age literature.

In the back seat, Chrissy studied Ryan's face. "So you like what you see?" Ryan asked, one eyebrow up.

"I am sorry. I didn't mean to stare, but you see, I knew I would see you here today and I am fascinated to at last meet you."

"What?" Ryan asked, rather taken a back by the calm confidence of the younger girl beside her.

"Shh, not now. Later," Chrissy warned. The two children fell silent once again. Ryan stared out the window feeling suddenly chilled. A sense of dread seeped through her. Something was going on, that was for sure, and she didn't have the slightest idea what it was. She needed to be on the alert.

Chrissy settled back in her seat, confident that this time things would work out. She smiled softly. Ryan would be no problem at all.

They motored on to Salisbury plain, the lands of old Sarum. Janet sighed. "Jamie, our partners might feel they have found the heart of England at Hastings, but I think right here we have found England's soul. This area simply vibrates with the history and spirit of this island's roots!"

"I've wanted to come here ever since I was a small child and saw a picture of Stonehenge. This place calls to me!" Jamie agreed with an excited smile.

"Yes, indeed!" Janet responded wholeheartedly, as she turned off the highway to enter New Sarum. *New is a relative term in England*, Janet thought. In actual fact, the foundations for New Sarum were laid back in 1220 A.D. when old Sarum, some three miles down the road, was abandoned. The ancient cathedral they stopped to inspect was not too structurally sound these days but it seemed a mystical piece of history to the women who looked at it. It had been built in the shape of a double cross and its bell tower was over four hundred feet high, each stone cut and placed by devoted hands.

They traveled on, passing by Old Sarum on their way to Stonehenge. Old Sarum was on a windswept hill, built on the ruins of iron age tribal settlements, Roman forts, Saxon and Danish encampments and lastly Norman lands. It was now a mound rising from the plain, only the bare backbone of the old cathedral foundations, grass covered, giving any indication of the rich layers of history that lay beneath.

History is a study of the irony of fate, Jamie mused silently as she looked at the silent mound while they drove past. One historian she had read said that each generation got the Stonehenge they deserved. To the Victorians, still maintaining some of the world view of the age of Romanticism, it was a Druid temple to worship Mother Nature. To the early twentieth century, caught in the Great Wars, it was a calendar marking the passing of time. The micro chip age saw it as an astronomical computer, a Stone Age monument to calculate planetary motion. Today's materialistic generation had reduced the mysterious stone circle to no more than a prop for movies.

Jamie knew that it was, in reality, none of these things. Henges and circles were common and their remains are still found all through Europe. It was as if those ancient people kept building them until they found the perfect spot here on Salisbury plain. Such circles were not unique to European cultures either. The Inca made them, as did many other cultures throughout the world in one form or another. The sky dominated the world of our ancestors and many cultures knew a lot about astronomy and plotted the movement of the stars and planets and recorded the passing of the seasons. Still, Stonehenge was something special. It was as if this one monument really had been constructed on the centre of the universe.

The car came to a stop in the parking lot outside the Visitors' Centre across the road from Stonehenge. For a moment the four of them sat there, quietly looking at the massive forms that silently waited in a circle. Then Janet open her door and stepped out.

At the same instant, some distance away, Reb stirred in her sleep. Her bare arm, hanging from Peeti's lap, brushed against a sharp thorn of a thistle. The tender baby skin tore and a single drop of crimson blood ran like a tear down the soft white skin and fell to the earth. Black clouds rolled across the sun once more and the world turned colder. A huge dark presence groaned with relief as the smell of blood once again filled his lungs. The darkness had been summoned, the door opened. All that was left was for evil to once again enter the world.

* * * * *

There are only two types of people in this world: those who have experienced evil and those who have not. The latter group know of evil. It is a concept that has been taught to them from an early age. They protect themselves from unknown horrors by locking their doors at night, not talking to strangers, carrying travelers cheques when they go away. They are cautious people but live in the comfortable knowledge that bad things happen only to the bad or those who are not cautious.

The former group, through rape and abuse or both, know that evil strikes randomly, violently and without warning. They too take precautions but in their hearts they do not worry about whether evil will strike, only when it will happen again. Their physical and emotional scars are the true mark of Lucifer.

Janet was really excited. She had read a lot about this site and somehow it had come to represent in her mind a turning point in her life. Marrying Robbie and being "outed" by the press, losing her job, being asked to leave her church, her battle with cancer, all of those things and more had left her wondering about who she was and what was the meaning of life. Her values and beliefs had been tested and where once she had felt secure in her concept of self, now she was again trying to redefine who she was. Stonehenge had called her for a long time and although she knew there was little to be learned here, she felt that somehow the place was tied to her destiny with Robbie.

Jamie slipped from the car and wrapped her crutch around her forearm. She felt as if she was on the threshold of a new segment in her life. The last few years had been like a dream. She had gone from being a single working woman to being a mother and lover, as well as an equal partner of the owner of a powerful, wealthy estate. She'd had to learn a new language and become part of a new culture and religion. It had been wonderful and yet the culture shock had left her emotionally drained and questioning just what she did believe in. Perhaps that was why she had recently taken a real interest in comparative religious studies and in researching the origins of European belief. Coming here was sort of like a pilgrimage to her ethnic roots: a starting point in redefining herself.

Ryan stood looking across the road at the circle of stones. She felt grumpy and moody. She had read in one of her Mom's books that each of the stones in the ancient ring weighed about twenty-five tons. She had thought they would tower over them. Instead, the famous ring of stones looked rather small and insignificant. So what was the big deal? It was primarily a religious centre used to predict the winter and summer solstices, she knew. Its axis was aligned for these events so that the sun rose between the arches and cut in a shaft to the heel stone. So? You could find similar structures all over the world. Tribal people knew a lot about the sky; they lived under it continually.

Chrissy stood several steps behind Ryan. She could feel the strength seeping from the depths back into her being. *It has been too long. At last the day of reckoning is here!* She too had felt the surge of energy as the single drop of innocent blood had dripped from Reb's arm. Fate had set a path for them all to follow. There was no going back. The fabric of the universe stretched and prepared to be ripped in two by the forces of good and evil.

The four bought their tickets and then took the underground passage beneath the roadway to the fenced-in site. Janet and Jamie had walked ahead, talking about various books they had read on religion. They were about halfway down the tunnel when Janet stopped, suddenly overcome by a feeling of unbelievable dread.

"Ryan?" she called to her teenage daughter who walked along a few steps behind. "I need you to go back to the Visitors' Centre and wait for your Mom and Ms. Dedemann."

Ryan was about to protest but then saw something in her adopted Mom's eyes that made the protest die on her lips. Fear. The same fear Ryan had seen in Aunt Janet's eyes when she had sat beside Robbie's bed at the hospital after the firestorm. If Aunt Janet was sending her back to wait, she must be concerned about her natural mother! "Okay," she answered, their eyes meeting and a clear message of concern being shared. Janet smiled weakly. Somehow she knew the danger lay ahead of them not behind. Just as she now knew that the dread she had been feeling since she had arrived in England would have a name once she stepped out the end of the tunnel.

Jamie leaned against the wall, feeling weak and afraid. She too had suddenly felt the dread. Whatever it was, she sensed it lay ahead of them and it called to her in a way that she could not resist. There was no going back. For a minute she closed her eyes. When she opened them Chrissy was standing silently in front of her. "Ryan has been sent to safety. I need you to go too," she managed to get out, her throat dry with fear and her voice shaking with emotion.

Chrissy did not seem to notice. She smiled softly and gave her Mom a hug, then turned and retraced her steps back along the path that Ryan had taken only moments before. Jamie looked over to meet Janet's eyes. "What is it?"

"I don't know."

"Are you scared?"

"Yes, but I need to go anyway. Whatever is there is calling me and my destiny lies within that ring of stone. If I walk away now, I'd just have to come back another time."

Jamie nodded. She felt the same. She pushed off the wall and took that first terrifying step into the unknown. Janet was right at her side.

Back at the entrance, Ryan stood in a spot where she could see down the road and over at Stonehenge. For some reason the stones seemed much bigger now. Maybe it was because clouds had rolled in bringing the sky lower and the wind had gotten damp and chilly.

As she watched, the world seemed to go out of focus and then reform. The Visitor Centre with its many tourists were gone and the land around was wild and windswept. Stonehenge dominated the plain.

"Ryan?" said a soft voice behind her.

Ryan turned in shock to see a different Chrissy, older, standing there. "Yes?"

"I've come for you."

Chapter Fourteen

The two women walked the remaining distance not through space alone but also through time. They entered as iron age women into a stone temple. "This is not good," Janet whispered.

"No, this has got to relate to the tomb. We are back in that time and whatever trouble started here we are here to fix," murmured Jamie, as she looked around carefully.

"You seem to know a lot more than I do. I think I need an explanation."

Jamie turned to look at the woman who looked so much like herself that they could be sisters. "There is an ancient Greek grave on our estate. It contains the bodies, we believe, of two women. Local legends say they fought for good in those troubled times.

"Over the last few years, the grave has been giving off a strange energy and the stone has been cracking. Gunnul and I became aware that the original two, the Host pair as we call them, have left descendants who seem to have very similar character traits. We called them the Others and they kept showing up! Somehow the grave was calling them and each time their love proved to be strong, the cracks in the grave healed some more. It was like the past was using the energy of the future to bring about change... You don't believe me, do you?"

Janet frowned. "I'm an educator. I believe in things that have some logical and proven credence to them. This..." Janet shrugged in frustration. "I don't know. It seems like madness but I am here and this all seems very real."

Jamie nodded. "At first, Gunnul and I had a very hard time accepting what was happening. We still don't know for sure what is going on. Until now, I thought it was all over, but now I wonder if all the energy was focused by the grave to bring us here."

Janet looked around in concern. "Since I've been in England, I keep getting this feeling of dread. It just washes over me as if I have suddenly sensed the presence of evil waiting to bring harm to those I care about."

"Yes! I have felt that too! Gunnul is not herself either. She's more moody and quick tempered."

Janet turned to look into Jamie's eyes. "Robbie has been the same."

"Where do you think we are?" Jamie asked nervously, looking around at the domed temple that they stood in. The massive rocks of Stonehenge had become supports that held up the stone dome over their heads. Ahead of them was a large circular platform with a hole in the centre. She fought to stay calm, sensing that her fate depended on her actions.

"Where and when more likely, unless this is one very big elaborate trick," responded Janet, her eyes thoughtful and filled with real concern. She swallowed her fear. Whatever was happening to them, they had to get through. She wasn't about to give up her life with Robbie and the girls.

"Is that possible? Is this a nasty trick?" Jamie asked, feeling the anger build within her.

"I don't see how it could be anything else. This is unbelievable! Impossible! And yet I don't know anyone who would do such a thing or have the time and money to pull off such a hoax!"

"Robbie would have the knowledge and the money, I should think," Jamie said quietly. "Gunnul would have the money but not the knowledge. She is not one to be involved in practical jokes."

Janet wavered between anger and doubt. "No, Robbie can be very funny but this is definitely not her style! Something like this would make her really angry."

The two women walked forward towards the platform that was the focal point of the room. Through holes in the clerestory, high above, light shone in palely. The door they had entered by had disappeared.

"Welcome," said a voice from behind them and they turned in unison to see a huge, misshapen figure standing in deep shadow between two massive standing stones.

"What's going on here?" demanded Janet, her voice surprisingly strong and confident although she was feeling anything but.

There was no answer from the figure. Instead, a roar of flame burst from behind them and they found themselves the next instant caught between long, swirling tongues of fire. With a cry, Jamie fell and a long tentacle of fire curled around her body. Janet ran to her, shocked to find, as she reached to help Jamie, that the hot flame did not seem to burn her skin. It was as if the fire was contained within a membrane and functioned like the limbs of some hideous being!

"Get out of here! Go, Janet. I'll get out as best I can!" Jamie yelled over the deep roar of fire. "Ahhh!" she ended in terror as the tentacle started to drag her across the stones back towards the dark hole from which the flames grew.

"Like hell I'm going to leave you," responded Janet determinedly, as she dug her heels in and wrapped her arms around Jamie, pulling against the force of the monstrous arms of flame. A new tongue of orange lashed out and wrapped around Janet and she felt suddenly dirty and violated. Jamie beside her lashed out at the coil of flame that was attacking her with her metal cane. The vice-like grip around Janet lessened for a split second and she rolled clear. Turning, she grabbed the cane from Jamie's hand and started pounding at the fire-creature. The tentacle of flame pulled back and Janet grabbed Jamie by the arms and dragged her into one of the alcoves formed by the huge standing stones.

"Sorry about the rough ride," Janet said, as she deposited Jamie and turned to hit an approaching glowing arm with a baseball swing.

"I don't think I'm in a position to complain. That thing had me in a death-grip until you started hitting it," responded Jamie, grabbing a candle stand to use it as yet another weapon.

"I was tied up pretty tightly myself until you had the sense to stab at it with your cane. Look out over there!" yelled Janet, as she swatted at the flames reaching for them.

Jamie hit at the one that was curling around the standing stone with the stand. "It doesn't seem to like the touch of metal but we won't be able to hold this thing off forever!"

"Yeah well, right at the moment I don't have a better idea," gasped Janet, cracking the cane down on a finger of flame reaching for her ankle.

Before they had a chance to think of anything else, the massive figure loomed out of the flames in front of them.

* * * * *

The distance between Hastings and Salisbury Plain was only a few hours drive but it seemed like it was taking days to Robbie and Gunnul. They did not speak to each other but occasionally Robbie swore under her breath as she drove and Gunnul fingered her prayer beads as her lips moved silently.

Robbie alternated between a feeling of incredible dread and blinding anger. If anything had happened to her family she would go mad! They were all that mattered to her. How could she have gotten all caught up in a battle that happened a thousand years ago and just let her family go off by themselves?

Gunnul seemed to shake herself from her meditations. "I need to give you some background information as you drive. It might be relevant to what we are feeling although I am not sure. On our estate in Turkey there is this old grave..."

Sometime later, they arrived at their destination. The car the women had used sat in the parking lot, rain splattered but untouched. Gunnul sighed in relief. At least her family had gotten this far safely. Other tourist cars crowded the lot and their owners could be seen inside the Visitors' Centre, gathering information, buying tickets and shopping. Gunnul looked over at Stonehenge.

Everything looked normal. A few tourists were following the walkways around the massive stones. None of them were her family. Had she made a fool of herself, telling Robbie about the grave and the Others? She looked over at her new friend, who stood rigid, looking around with angry intensity. "You think I speak only fantasies?" she asked, her English deteriorating as it tended to do when she was stressed.

Robbie looked at her sharply. "It was crap, but my family IS in trouble. Where the hell are they? Come on!" The two headed into the building and checked for their family. Yes, they had bought tickets, the clerk remembered them. Weren't they still on site? Robbie and Gunnul bought tickets and headed down into the underground passage and there the world changed. The smell of fire and the screams for help from their partners assailed them almost immediately. They ran forward into an inferno of swirling flame and sulphurous smoke.

Janet and Jamie were trapped against a wall, exhausted and traumatized by their battle to protect themselves from the invading tongues of flame. Just as the horrible demon had stepped out of the flames in front of them and grabbed Janet by the throat, he was attacked by a second massive creature. Janet had been dropped and managed to crawl away. Before Jamie and Janet's horror-filled eyes the two monsters fought in vicious battle. Black blood ran with red and claws and teeth flashed like lightning within the firestorm.

Gunnul and Robbie entered the dome and, skirting the two monsters that fought amongst the flames, they ran to where Janet and Jamie were fighting back the arms of fire. Gunnul and Robbie were surprised as they passed through that the red hot flames did not burn their flesh but instead stung like bee stings. They took the makeshift weapons from the failing hands of their partners and turned to form a single wall of protection against the fiery tentacles that had grown in their power and intensity.

Stone blackened and cracked, walls shook and silhouetted forms struggled against a backdrop of hellish light. The battle of the monsters raged on, neither side giving and no gains being made. Through the fury, the four women would get hideous glimpses of two vile creatures lashing at each other in vicious battle as the women fought their own war to keep the groping flames back.

The threads of space and time curled and bent within the infinite blackness of the universe. The tiny source of life, the only awareness in the great reaches of space, flickered and wavered between the forces of good and the blackness of evil. All that was, is, and would be hung in balance upon a single entity.

Chapter Fifteen

Sometime before, Ryan too had been pulled into another time and place. She heard Chrissy call her and when she turned everything was different. She realized that she was no longer a teen but a grown woman and the child she had expected to see was a beautiful adult.

"Don't be afraid, Ryan. Look into your soul. You know we were meant to be here! I need you. I need your strength and your goodness to fight off an evil that has hung over me since my father gave me life," Chrissy begged earnestly.

"What is going on? This is crazy!" Ryan said, looking around wide-eyed.

"We are caught in a rip in time," Chrissy explained, coming over to wrap her arms around Ryan. Ryan held the grown Chrissy close. "We need to make love, Ryan. We need to join as one to help them."

* * * * *

This was not how Ryan had expected her first time would be. The smaller body thrusting with hers was powerful, demanding and invading. She felt her barrier break with a sudden searing pain and who she was, her essence, dripped like a single drop of crimson blood from her body.

The entity entered her, pushing Ryan screaming over some high, emotionally intense wall. Beyond, she was no longer who she had been. There was within her a new awareness, a new hunger. Her own body was no more; now she moved with the power and confidence of a wild creature. She was no longer a single entity but part of another; two halves of the same force of life now together again for a single deadly purpose.

Her life forces loomed within a massive form acutely aware of the other soul that made up her being. She stood, muscles rippling and

589

deep red eyes focused on her goal. With a lumbering stride the creature that she had become entered the fires of hell.

Through the orange, searing world, the new creature saw its opposite grabbing one of the humans by the throat and lifting her off the ground like a rag doll. The other bravely hit out from where she lay among the flames on the ground. With a roar the beast attacked.

The captured woman was dropped and the surprised monster turned to see the cold eyes of the other. With a scream of rage he threw himself at his opposite and tore at its flesh. Locked in vicious battle, the two monstrous forms screamed their rage above the flames that engulfed them.

So engrossed were they in their violent struggle that they did not even note the arrival of Gunnul and Robbie sometime later.

At last strong, sharp teeth bit into a sinewy neck and shook, snapping the vertebra of the other. Massive, rope-like muscles strained to pick up the dead weight. Staggering through the flames, the remaining monster heaved its enemy up on the flaming alter and dropped the stinking flesh down into the abyss from which the fiery tentacles emerged.

For a second, the victor felt the heady power of true evil soaking through its being. It could have all this. Having killed its rival, it could take its rightful place as His divine ruler on earth. Its future lay in the use of its power. Might was right! Then the other soul within reached out. No. No, true victory is not a single success but the dreams and aspirations of those who say, "I can". The creature pulled back from the edge of oblivion, straightened and smiled. "Good riddance, monster. Your dreams are as hollow as the wish for power. My dreams are filled with the richness of love."

The walls cracked and crumbled around. The flames shot high in the sky and dissipated in black clouds of smoke. The temple was no more; instead a ring of silent stones stood in its place.

* * * * *

At last the fire seemed in retreat. Robbie turned and sank down beside her exhausted wife, who only minutes before had been held in the death grip of the monster. "Janet. Janet, Love, are you all right?" she whispered, through lips cracked and dry.

Janet stirred and rolled over, looking into the eyes she loved. "I'm okay, I think. Quick, Robbie! Get back in the corner!" the teacher ordered, as dust and rock chips started to rain from the cracks opening in the dome. The four women huddled together under a massive arch. In front of them, the flames reared back and pulsated in intensity as they slowly pulled back. Again they could see the shadow forms of two massive creatures. Then the roof in front of them gave way and they were lost in a shower of debris.

* * * * *

When Gunnul became aware of anything again, it was to find that she sat on the grass, her back to the towering standing stones. She blinked in the sunlight that shone down from a blue sky. In her arms Jamie rested, still trembling from the ordeal. "Gunnul? Is it over?"

"I think, yes." She looked around for the others. By the next stone stood Robbie, her arms curved to protect Janet from any falling debris. There wasn't any. There wasn't a thing that left evidence of what they had experienced. They were just two couples at the outer edges of a ring of stone.

Some distance away, Ryan woke with a terrible sense of loss. She rolled over to see the child, Chrissy, sitting close beside her. "We are no longer one."

Chrissy nodded sadly. "As I promised you. Thank you, Ryan. I couldn't have resisted without your help."

Ryan scrambled to her feet. "Are they all right? Where are they?"

"They are fine. They're on the other side. Give them a few minutes. They have been through a lot and need some quiet time with each other."

"They have been through a lot!" Ryan snorted. "How about suddenly finding yourself all grown up and having to share a monster's body with another female after she'd..."

"You must never tell, Ryan. What happened is not part of this time. It never happened here. You know what we agreed."

Ryan looked down at the dark, exotic girl at her feet. She offered her hand and Chrissy put her own in it, allowing Ryan to pull her to her feet. "I know you said that, but I can still feel a part of you in here," Ryan said, tapping her chest.

Chrissy smiled and touched her own chest. "I feel you here too, Ryan. Our destinies are very different but we are now linked. We are part of the same fabric."

Ryan smiled. "Like blood sisters."

"Yes," Chrissy agreed, hugging Ryan. "We will always have a bond that is as close as family."

"What's he like, this guy you are waiting for?" Ryan asked.

Chrissy's eyes lit up with happiness. "He loves life and everything in it!"

Ryan smiled back. "I'm glad. He's going to be a lucky guy!"

"I think not! He will have to face my mothers and they are both so protective in their own ways!" Chrissy laughed.

"Hey! It can't be any worse than my mom! She gave the poor guy who picked me up to go to the local dance the third degree. Honest, I thought he was going to pee himself!"

"Ryan, you are so bad! We should go now." Chrissy hesitated, then reached up and kissed Ryan's lips softly. "I hope my true love is as wonderful as you."

Ryan smiled smugly and raised an eyebrow. "We Williams' aim to please." Side by side they went to find their parents.

* * * * *

Robbie's worried eyes saw Ryan walking around the fencing that protected the circle from tourists. Chrissy was beside her. "Ryan," she called, running over to her daughter and giving her a big hug. "Are you all right?"

"Yeah, we were worried about you. We could see everything but we weren't able to help you," Ryan explained, leaving out large sections of what had really happened. It made her feel uncomfortable. She didn't like to have secrets from her Moms but she also realized there were some things that parents weren't mature enough to handle. Some day, perhaps, she would be able to share the whole story with her Moms. Janet joined them and insisted on a long hug from Ryan too.

Chrissy had run over to her parents and hugged each mother in turn. "We saw you but you were separated from us by the fire! It was so scary! I am so glad to see you."

Jamie looked hard at her daughter. She was such a complex blend of innocence and wisdom. She knew deep inside that Chrissy's relationship to the powers within the grave was far stronger than anything she and Gunnul had experienced. "Is it over now, Chrissy?" she asked.

Chrissy looked at her in surprise and then stepped close for another hug. "It's over. All is well now, then and in the future," she reassured.

Then, looking at her Moms, she worked to change the subject. "I like Ryan very much. We are going to keep in touch. She and Reb are going to be my adopted sisters! Now I have sisters and my cousins will not be able to tease me about being an only child!"

592

Across the ring, Janet's eyes were dancing with fire. "You left Reb?"

"We knew you were in trouble!"

"With strangers!"

"Gunnul said I could trust them!" Robbie protested. "I asked!"

"On the way over here?"

"Well... yeah... but it was an emergency!"

"Don't ever do that again. Reb is going to be really upset when she wakes up and finds herself with strangers!"

Robbie looked just as upset and worried as Janet now. "I didn't think. I was worried," she muttered. "Gunnul called Teefo on her phone. He should be here soon in a rented car," she cajoled.

"Never again," reinforced Janet.

Robbie nodded and Ryan smirked at her but when Janet turned at the sound of her name to see a smiling Reb in Teefo's arms, Ryan put an arm around her Mom. "It's okay, Mom. You did the right thing. If you hadn't stopped the tongues of fire from dragging them up on the altar... well, things would have been a lot worse, I think!"

Robbie smiled at her daughter. Ryan was such a complex mixture of child and adult. "Thanks kid, I needed you on my side," Robbie smiled. They walked over and joined the others where they had all gathered outside the ring, two families tied by a bond of love as old as the stones that stood behind them. The drama had come full circle.

The ring of stones stood silent. They were The Watchers, seeing all, knowing all and telling nothing.

Miles away in a secret garden in Turkey, the sun warmed the stone of an ancient grave. For a second it seemed to glow from within and the world seemed warmer and filled with love.

Anne Azel is the author of four popular book series: Seasons, The Murder Mysteries, Encounters and Journeys. As well as writing, she has a number of degrees, her main interest being forensic anthropology.

Anne enjoys her work and the opportunity to travel the world. Many of her adventures have been the basis for her stories. Anne lives in the Toronto area of Canada and, when not working or travelling, likes to spend time canoeing in the north.

Says Anne, "I enjoy writing about the courage and strength of women. I like to think my characters face life straight on with boldness, humour and passion."

I

Order More Great Books Directly From Limitless, Dare 2 Dream Publishing

Book	Price	Note
Daughters of Artemis by L M Townsend	16.00	
Connecting Hearts by Val Brown and MJ Walker	16.00	
Mysti: Mistress of Dreams by Sam Ruskin	16.00	HOT
Family Connections by Val Brown & MJ Walker	16.00	Sequel to Connecting Hearts
Under the Fig Tree by Emily Reed	16.00	
The Amazon Nation by C. Osborne	15.00	Great for research
Poetry from the Featherbed by pinfeather	16.00	If you think you hate poetry, you haven't read this.
None So Blind, 3rd Edition by LJ Maas	16.00	NEW
A Saving Solace by DS Bauden	17.00	NEW
Return of the Warrior by Katherine E. Standell	16.00	Sequel to Desert Hawk
Journey's End by LJ Maas	16.00	NEW
	Total	

South Carolina residents add 5% sales tax.
Domestic shipping is $3.50 per book
Please mail orders with credit card info, check or money order to:

Limitless, Dare 2 Dream Publishing
100 Pin Oak Ct.
Lexington, SC 29073-7911

Please make checks or money orders payable to **Limitless**.

Order More Great Books Directly From Limitless, Dare 2 Dream Publishing

Shattering Rainbows by L. Ocean	15.00	
Black's Magic by Val Brown and MJ Walker	17.00	
Spitfire by g. glass	16.00	NEW
Undeniable by K M	17.00	NEW
A Thousand Shades of Feeling by Carolyn McBride	15.00	
Omega's Folly by C. Osborne	12.00	
Considerable Appeal by K M	17.00	sequel to Undeniable-NEW
Nurturing Souls by DS Bauden	16.00	NEW
Superstition Shadows by KC West and Victoria Welsh	17.00	NEW
Encounters, Revised by Anne Azel	21.95	OneHuge Volume - NEW
For the Love of a Woman by S. Anne Gardner	16.00	NEW
	Total	

South Carolina residents add 5% sales tax.
Domestic shipping is $3.50 per book
Please mail orders with credit card info, check or money order to:

Limitless, Dare 2 Dream Publishing
100 Pin Oak Ct.
Lexington, SC 29073-7911

Please make checks or money orders payable to **Limitless**.